IN DEATH

D1005352

IN DEATH
THE FIRST CASES

J. D. ROBB

BERKLEY BOOKS, NEW YORK

THE BERKLEY PUBLISHING GROUP
Published by the Penguin Group
Penguin Group (USA) Inc.
375 Hudson Street, New York, New York 10014, USA
Penguin Group (Canada), 90 Eglinton Avenue East, Suite 700, Toronto, Ontario M4P 2Y3, Canada
(a division of Pearson Penguin Canada Inc.)
Penguin Books Ltd., 80 Strand, London WC2R 0RL, England
Penguin Group Ireland, 25 St. Stephen's Green, Dublin 2, Ireland (a division of Penguin Books Ltd.)
Penguin Group (Australia), 250 Camberwell Road, Camberwell, Victoria 3124, Australia
(a division of Pearson Australia Group Pty. Ltd.)
Penguin Books India Pvt. Ltd., 11 Community Centre, Panchsheel Park, New Delhi—110 017, India
Penguin Group (NZ), 67 Apollo Drive, Rosedale, North Shore 0632, New Zealand
(a division of Pearson New Zealand Ltd.)
Penguin Books (South Africa) (Pty.) Ltd., 24 Sturdee Avenue, Rosebank, Johannesburg 2196,
South Africa

Penguin Books Ltd., Registered Offices: 80 Strand, London WC2R 0RL, England

PRINTING HISTORY
Berkley trade paperback edition / February 2009

Library of Congress Cataloging-in-Publication Data

Robb, J. D., 1950–
  [Naked in death]
  In death : the first cases / J. D. Robb.—Berkley trade pbk. ed.
    p. cm.
  ISBN 978-0-425-22853-1
  1. Dallas, Eve (Fictitious character)—Fiction. 2. Policewomen—New York (State)—New
York—Fiction. 3. New York (N. Y.)—Fiction. I. Robb, J. D., 1950– Glory in death. II. Title.

PS3568.O243N35 2009
813'.54—dc22   2008048547

PRINTED IN THE UNITED STATES OF AMERICA

10 9 8 7 6 5 4 3 2 1

CONTENTS

NAKED IN DEATH

GLORY IN DEATH

NAKED IN DEATH

What's past is prologue.
—WILLIAM SHAKESPEARE

Violence is as American as cherry pie.
—RAP (HUBERT GEROLD) BROWN

CHAPTER

ONE

She woke in the dark. Through the slats on the window shades, the first murky hint of dawn slipped, slanting shadowy bars over the bed. It was like waking in a cell.

For a moment she simply lay there, shuddering, imprisoned, while the dream faded. After ten years on the force, Eve still had dreams.

Six hours before, she'd killed a man, had watched death creep into his eyes. It wasn't the first time she'd exercised maximum force, or dreamed. She'd learned to accept the action and the consequences.

But it was the child who haunted her. The child she hadn't been in time to save. The child whose screams had echoed in the dreams with her own.

All the blood, Eve thought, scrubbing sweat from her face with her hands. Such a small little girl to have had so much blood in her. And she knew it was vital that she push it aside.

Standard departmental procedure meant that she would spend the morning in Testing. Any officer whose discharge of weapon resulted in termination of life was required to undergo emotional and psychiatric clearance before resuming duty. Eve considered the tests a mild pain in the ass.

She would beat them, as she'd beaten them before.

When she rose, the overheads went automatically to low setting, lighting her way into the bath. She winced once at her reflection. Her eyes were swollen from lack of sleep, her skin nearly as pale as the corpses she'd delegated to the ME.

Rather than dwell on it, she stepped into the shower, yawning.

"Give me one oh one degrees, full force," she said and shifted so that the shower spray hit her straight in the face.

She let it steam, lathered listlessly while she played through the events of the night before. She wasn't due in Testing until nine, and would use the next three hours to settle and let the dream fade away completely.

Small doubts and little regrets were often detected and could mean a second and more intense round with the machines and the owl-eyed technicians who ran them.

Eve didn't intend to be off the streets longer than twenty-four hours.

After pulling on a robe, she walked into the kitchen and programmed her AutoChef for coffee, black; toast, light. Through her window she could hear the heavy hum of air traffic carrying early commuters to offices, late ones home. She'd chosen the apartment years before because it was in a heavy ground and air pattern, and she liked the noise and crowds. On another yawn, she glanced out the window, followed the rattling journey of an aging airbus hauling laborers not fortunate enough to work in the city or by home-links.

She brought the *New York Times* up on her monitor and scanned the headlines while the faux caffeine bolstered her system. The Auto-Chef had burned her toast again, but she ate it anyway, with a vague thought of springing for a replacement unit.

She was frowning over an article on a mass recall of droid cocker spaniels when her tele-link blipped. Eve shifted to communications and watched her commanding officer flash onto the screen.

"Commander."

"Lieutenant." He gave her a brisk nod, noted the still wet hair and sleepy eyes. "Incident at Twenty-seven West Broadway, eighteenth floor. You're primary."

Eve lifted a brow. "I'm on Testing. Subject terminated at twenty-two thirty-five."

"We have override," he said, without inflection. "Pick up your shield and weapon on the way to the incident. Code Five, Lieutenant."

"Yes, sir." His face flashed off even as she pushed back from the screen. Code Five meant she would report directly to her commander, and there would be no unsealed interdepartmental reports and no co-operation with the press.

In essence, it meant she was on her own.

Broadway was noisy and crowded, a party where rowdy guests never left. Street, pedestrian, and sky traffic were miserable, choking the air with bodies and vehicles. In her old days in uniform she remembered it as a hot spot for wrecks and crushed tourists who were too busy gaping at the show to get out of the way.

Even at this hour there was steam rising from the stationary and portable food stands that offered everything from rice noodles to soy dogs for the teeming crowds. She had to swerve to avoid an eager merchant on his smoking Glida-Grill, and took his flipped middle finger as a matter of course.

Eve double-parked and, skirting a man who smelled worse than his bottle of brew, stepped onto the sidewalk. She scanned the building first, fifty floors of gleaming metal that knifed into the sky from a hilt of concrete. She was propositioned twice before she reached the door.

Since this five-block area of Broadway was affectionately termed Prostitute's Walk, she wasn't surprised. She flashed her badge for the uniform guarding the entrance.

"Lieutenant Dallas."

"Yes, sir." He skimmed his official compu-seal over the door to keep out the curious, then led the way to the bank of elevators. "Eighteenth floor," he said when the doors swished shut behind them.

"Fill me in, Officer." Eve switched on her recorder and waited.

"I wasn't first on the scene, Lieutenant. Whatever happened up-stairs is being kept upstairs. There's a badge inside waiting for you. We have a Homicide, and a Code Five in number Eighteen-oh-three."

"Who called it in?"

"I don't have that information."

He stayed where he was when the elevator opened. Eve stepped out and was alone in a narrow hallway. Security cameras tilted down at her and her feet were almost soundless on the worn nap of the car-pet as she approached 1803. Ignoring the handplate, she announced herself, holding her badge up to eye level for the peep cam until the door opened.

"Dallas."

"Feeney." She smiled, pleased to see a familiar face. Ryan Feeney was an old friend and former partner who'd traded the street for a desk and a top-level position in the Electronics Detection Division. "So, they're sending computer pluckers these days."

"They wanted brass, and the best." His lips curved in his wide, rumpled face, but his eyes remained sober. He was a small, stubby man with small, stubby hands and rust-colored hair. "You look beat."

"Rough night."

"So I heard." He offered her one of the sugared nuts from the bag he habitually carried, studying her, and measuring if she was up to what was waiting in the bedroom beyond.

She was young for her rank, barely thirty, with wide brown eyes that had never had a chance to be naive. Her doe-brown hair was cropped short, for convenience rather than style, but suited her trian-gular face with its razor-edge cheekbones and slight dent in the chin.

She was tall, rangy, with a tendency to look thin, but Feeney knew there were solid muscles beneath the leather jacket. More, there was a brain, and a heart.

"This one's going to be touchy, Dallas."

"I picked that up already. Who's the victim?"

"Sharon DeBlass, granddaughter of Senator DeBlass."

Neither meant anything to her. "Politics isn't my forte, Feeney."

"The gentleman from Virginia, extreme right, old money. The

granddaughter took a sharp left a few years back, moved to New York, and became a licensed companion."

"She was a hooker." Dallas glanced around the apartment. It was furnished in obsessive modern—glass and thin chrome, signed holograms on the walls, recessed bar in bold red. The wide mood screen behind the bar bled with mixing and merging shapes and colors in cool pastels.

Neat as a virgin, Eve mused, and cold as a whore. "No surprise, given her choice of real estate."

"Politics makes it delicate. Victim was twenty-four, Caucasian female. She bought it in bed."

Eve only lifted a brow. "Seems poetic, since she'd been bought there. How'd she die?"

"That's the next problem. I want you to see for yourself."

As they crossed the room, each took out a slim container, sprayed their hands front and back to seal in oils and fingerprints. At the doorway, Eve sprayed the bottom of her boots to slicken them so that she would pick up no fibers, stray hairs, or skin.

Eve was already wary. Under normal circumstances there would have been two other investigators on a homicide scene, with recorders for sound and pictures. Forensics would have been waiting with their usual snarly impatience to sweep the scene.

The fact that only Feeney had been assigned with her meant that there were a lot of eggshells to be walked over.

"Security cameras in the lobby, elevator, and hallways," Eve commented.

"I've already tagged the discs." Feeney opened the bedroom door and let her enter first.

It wasn't pretty. Death rarely was a peaceful, religious experience to Eve's mind. It was the nasty end, indifferent to saint and sinner. But this was shocking, like a stage deliberately set to offend.

The bed was huge, slicked with what appeared to be genuine satin sheets the color of ripe peaches. Small, soft focused spotlights were trained on its center where the naked woman was cupped in the gentle dip of the floating mattress.

The mattress moved with obscenely graceful undulations to the rhythm of programmed music slipping through the headboard.

She was beautiful still, a cameo face with a tumbling waterfall of flaming red hair, emerald eyes that stared glassily at the mirrored ceiling, long, milk white limbs that called to mind visions of *Swan Lake* as the motion of the bed gently rocked them.

They weren't artistically arranged now, but spread lewdly so that the dead woman formed a final X dead center of the bed.

There was a hole in her forehead, one in her chest, another horribly gaping between the open thighs. Blood had splattered on the glossy sheets, pooled, dripped, and stained.

There were splashes of it on the lacquered walls, like lethal paintings scrawled by an evil child.

So much blood was a rare thing, and she had seen much too much of it the night before to take the scene as calmly as she would have preferred.

She had to swallow once, hard, and force herself to block out the image of a small child.

"You got the scene on record?"

"Yep."

"Then turn that damn thing off." She let out a breath after Feeney located the controls that silenced the music. The bed flowed to stillness. "The wounds," Eve murmured, stepping closer to examine them. "Too neat for a knife. Too messy for a laser." A flash came to her—old training films, old videos, old viciousness.

"Christ, Feeney, these look like bullet wounds."

Feeney reached into his pocket and drew out a sealed bag. "Whoever did it left a souvenir." He passed the bag to Eve. "An antique like this has to go for eight, ten thousand for a legal collection, twice that on the black market."

Fascinated, Eve turned the sealed revolver over in her hand. "It's heavy," she said half to herself. "Bulky."

"Thirty-eight caliber," he told her. "First one I've seen outside of a museum. This one's a Smith & Wesson, Model Ten, blue steel." He looked at it with some affection. "Real classic piece, used to be standard police issue up until the latter part of the twentieth. They stopped making them in about twenty-two, twenty-three, when the gun ban was passed."

"You're the history buff." Which explained why he was with her. "Looks new." She sniffed through the bag, caught the scent of oil and burning. "Somebody took good care of this. Steel fired into flesh," she mused as she passed the bag back to Feeney. "Ugly way to die, and the first I've seen it in my ten years with the department."

"Second for me. About fifteen years ago, Lower East Side, party got out of hand. Guy shot five people with a twenty-two before he realized it wasn't a toy. Hell of a mess."

"Fun and games," Eve murmured. "We'll scan the collectors, see how many we can locate who own one like this. Somebody might have reported a robbery."

"Might have."

"It's more likely it came through the black market." Eve glanced back at the body. "If she's been in the business for a few years, she'd have discs, records of her clients, her trick books." She frowned. "With Code Five, I'll have to do the door-to-door myself. Not a simple sex crime," she said with a sigh. "Whoever did it set it up. The antique weapon, the wounds themselves, almost ruler straight down the body, the lights, the pose. Who called it in, Feeney?"

"The killer." He waited until her eyes came back to him. "From right here. Called the station. See how the bedside unit's aimed at her face? That's what came in. Video, no audio."

"He's into showmanship." Eve let out a breath. "Clever bastard, arrogant, cocky. He had sex with her first. I'd bet my badge on it. Then he gets up and does it." She lifted her arm, aiming, lowering it as she counted off. "One, two, three."

"That's cold," murmured Feaney.

"He's cold. He smooths down the sheets after. See how neat they are? He arranges her, spreads her open so nobody can have any doubts as to how she made her living. He does it carefully, practically measuring, so that she's perfectly aligned. Center of the bed, arms and legs equally apart. Doesn't turn off the bed 'cause it's part of the show. He leaves the gun because he wants us to know right away he's no ordinary man. He's got an ego. He doesn't want to waste time letting the body be discovered eventually. He wants it now. That instant gratification."

"She was licensed for men and women," Feeney pointed out, but Eve shook her head.

"It's not a woman. A woman wouldn't have left her looking both beautiful and obscene. No, I don't think it's a woman. Let's see what we can find. Have you gone into her computer yet?"

"No. It's your case, Dallas. I'm only authorized to assist."

"See if you can access her client files." Eve went to the dresser and began to carefully search drawers.

Expensive taste, Eve reflected. There were several items of real silk, the kind no simulation could match. The bottle of scent on the dresser was exclusive, and smelled, after a quick sniff, like expensive sex.

The contents of the drawers were meticulously ordered, lingerie folded precisely, sweaters arranged according to color and material. The closet was the same.

Obviously the victim had a love affair with clothes and a taste for the best and took scrupulous care of what she owned.

And she'd died naked.

"Kept good records," Feeney called out. "It's all here. Her client list, appointments—including her required monthly health exam and her weekly trip to the beauty salon. She used the Trident Clinic for the first and Paradise for the second."

"Both top of the line. I've got a friend who saved for a year so she could have one day for the works at Paradise. Takes all kinds."

"My wife's sister went for it for her twenty-fifth anniversary. Cost damn near as much as my kid's wedding. Hello, we've got her personal address book."

"Good. Copy all of it, will you, Feeney?" At his low whistle, she looked over her shoulder, glimpsed the small gold-edged palm computer in his hand. "What?"

"We've got a lot of high-powered names in here. Politics, entertainment, money, money, money. Interesting, our girl has Roarke's private number."

"Roarke who?"

"Just Roarke, as far as I know. Big money there. Kind of guy that touches shit and turns it into gold bricks. You've got to start reading more than the sports page, Dallas."

"Hey, I read the headlines. Did you hear about the cocker spaniel recall?"

"Roarke's always big news," Feeney said patiently. "He's got one of the finest art collections in the world. Arts and antiques," he continued, noting when Eve clicked in and turned to him. "He's a licensed gun collector. Rumor is he knows how to use them."

"I'll pay him a visit."

"You'll be lucky to get within a mile of him."

"I'm feeling lucky." Eve crossed over to the body to slip her hands under the sheets.

"The man's got powerful friends, Dallas. You can't afford to so much as whisper he's linked to this until you've got something solid."

"Feeney, you know it's a mistake to tell me that." But even as she started to smile, her fingers brushed something between cold flesh and bloody sheets. "There's something under her." Carefully, Eve lifted the shoulder, eased her fingers over.

"Paper," she murmured. "Sealed." With her protected thumb, she wiped at a smear of blood until she could read the protected sheet.

ONE OF SIX

"It looks hand printed," she said to Feeney and held it out. "Our boy's more than clever, more than arrogant. And he isn't finished."

Eve spent the rest of the day doing what would normally have been assigned to drones. She interviewed the victim's neighbors personally, recording statements, impressions.

She managed to grab a quick sandwich from the same Glida-Grill she'd nearly smashed before, driving across town. After the night and the morning she'd put in, she could hardly blame the receptionist at Paradise for looking at her as though she'd recently scraped herself off the sidewalk.

Waterfalls played musically among the flora in the reception area of the city's most exclusive salon. Tiny cups of real coffee and slim glasses of fizzling water or champagne were served to those lounging on the cushy chairs and settees. Headphones and discs of fashion magazines were complimentary.

The receptionist was magnificently breasted, a testament to the salon's figure sculpting techniques. She wore a snug, short outfit in the salon's trademark red, and an incredible coif of ebony hair coiled like snakes.

Eve couldn't have been more delighted.

"I'm sorry," the woman said in a carefully modulated voice as empty of expression as a computer. "We serve by appointment only."

"That's okay." Eve smiled and was almost sorry to puncture the disdain. Almost. "This ought to get me one." She offered her badge. "Who works on Sharon DeBlass?"

The receptionist's horrified eyes darted toward the waiting area. "Our clients' needs are strictly confidential."

"I bet." Enjoying herself, Eve leaned companionably on the U-shaped counter. "I can talk nice and quiet, like this, so we understand each other—Denise?" She flicked her gaze down to the discreet studded badge on the woman's breast. "Or I can talk louder, so everyone understands. If you like the first idea better, you can take me to a nice quiet room where we won't disturb any of your clients, and you can send in Sharon DeBlass's operator. Or whatever term you use."

"Consultant," Denise said faintly. "If you'll follow me."

"My pleasure."

And it was.

Outside of movies or videos, Eve had never seen anything so lush. The carpet was a red cushion your feet could sink blissfully into. Crystal drops hung from the ceiling and spun light. The air smelled of flowers and pampered flesh.

She might not have been able to imagine herself there, spending hours having herself creamed, oiled, pummeled, and sculpted, but if she were going to waste such time on vanity, it would certainly have been interesting to do so under such civilized conditions.

The receptionist showed her into a small room with a hologram of a summer meadow dominating one wall. The quiet sound of birdsong and breezes sweetened the air.

"If you'd just wait here."

"No problem." Eve waited for the door to close then, with an indulgent sigh, she lowered herself into a deeply cushioned chair. The moment she was seated, the monitor beside her blipped on, and a friendly, indulgent face that could only be a droid's beamed smiles.

"Good afternoon. Welcome to Paradise. Your beauty needs and your comfort are our only priorities. Would you like some refreshment while you wait for your personal consultant?"

"Sure. Coffee, black, coffee."

"Of course. What sort would you prefer? Press *C* on your keyboard for the list of choices."

Smothering a chuckle, Eve followed instructions. She spent the next two minutes pondering over her options, then narrowed it down to French Riviera or Caribbean Cream.

The door opened again before she could decide. Resigned, she rose and faced an elaborately dressed scarecrow.

Over his fuchsia shirt and plum-colored slacks, he wore an open, trailing smock of Paradise red. His hair, flowing back from a painfully thin face echoed the hue of his slacks. He offered Eve a hand, squeezed gently, and stared at her out of soft doe eyes.

"I'm terribly sorry, Officer. I'm baffled."

"I want information on Sharon DeBlass." Again, Eve took out her badge and offered it for inspection.

"Yes, ah, Lieutenant Dallas. That was my understanding. You must know, of course, our client data is strictly confidential. Paradise has a reputation for discretion as well as excellence."

"And you must know, of course, that I can get a warrant, Mr.—?"

"Oh, Sebastian. Simply Sebastian." He waved a thin hand, sparkling with rings. "I'm not questioning your authority, Lieutenant. But if you could assist me, your motives for the inquiry?"

"I'm inquiring into the motives for the murder of DeBlass." She waited a beat, judged the shock that shot into his eyes and drained his face of color. "Other than that, my data is strictly confidential."

"Murder. My dear God, our lovely Sharon is dead? There must be a mistake." He all but slid into a chair, letting his head fall back and his eyes close. When the monitor offered him refreshment, he waved a hand again. Light shot from his jeweled fingers. "God, yes. I need a brandy, darling. A snifter of Trevalli."

Eve sat beside him, took out her recorder. "Tell me about Sharon."

"A marvelous creature. Physically stunning, of course, but it went deeper." His brandy came into the room on a silent automated cart. Sebastian plucked the snifter and took one deep swallow. "She had flawless taste, a generous heart, rapier wit."

He turned the doe eyes on Eve again. "I saw her only two days ago."

"Professionally?"

"She had a standing weekly appointment, half day. Every other week was a full day." He whipped out a butter yellow scarf and dabbed at his eyes. "Sharon took care of herself, believed strongly in the presentation of self."

"It would be an asset in her line of work."

"Naturally. She only worked to amuse herself. Money wasn't a particular need, with her family background. She enjoyed sex."

"With you?"

His artistic face winced, the rosy lips pursing in what could have been a pout or pain. "I was her consultant, her confidant, and her friend," Sebastian said stiffly and draped the scarf with casual flare over his left shoulder. "It would have been indiscreet and unprofessional for us to become sexual partners."

"So you weren't attracted to her, sexually?"

"It was impossible for anyone not to be attracted to her sexually. She . . ." He gestured grandly. "Exuded sex as others might exude an expensive perfume. My God." He took another shaky sip of brandy. "It's all past tense. I can't believe it. Dead. Murdered." His gaze shot back to Eve. "You said murdered."

"That's right."

"That neighborhood she lived in," he said grimly. "No one could talk to her about moving to a more acceptable location. She enjoyed living on the edge and flaunting it all under her family's aristocratic noses."

"She and her family were at odds?"

"Oh definitely. She enjoyed shocking them. She was such a free spirit, and they so . . . ordinary." He said it in a tone that indicated ordinary was more mortal a sin than murder itself. "Her grandfather continues to introduce bills that would make prostitution illegal. As if the past century hasn't proven that such matters need to be regulated for health and crime security. He also stands against procreation regulation, gender adjustment, chemical balancing, and the gun ban."

Eve's ears pricked. "The senator opposes the gun ban?"

"It's one of his pets. Sharon told me he owns a number of nasty antiques and spouts off regularly about that outdated right to bear arms business. If he had his way, we'd all be back in the twentieth century, murdering each other right and left."

"Murder still happens," Eve murmured. "Did she ever mention friends or clients who might have been dissatisfied or overly aggressive?"

"Sharon had dozens of friends. She drew people to her, like . . ." He searched for a suitable metaphor, used the corner of the scarf again. "Like an exotic and fragrant flower. And her clients, as far as I know, were all delighted with her. She screened them carefully. All of her sexual partners had to meet certain standards. Appearance, intellect, breeding, and proficiency. As I said, she enjoyed sex, in all of its many forms. She was . . . adventurous."

That fit with the toys Eve had unearthed in the apartment. The velvet handcuffs and whips, the scented oils and hallucinogens. The offerings on the two sets of colinked virtual reality headphones had been a shock even to Eve's jaded system.

"Was she involved with anyone on a personal level?"

"There were men occasionally, but she lost interest quickly. Recently she'd spoken about Roarke. She'd met him at a party and was attracted. In fact, she was seeing him for dinner the very night she came in for her consultation. She'd wanted something exotic because they were dining in Mexico."

"In Mexico. That would have been the night before last."

"Yes. She was just bubbling over about him. We did her hair in a gypsy look, gave her a bit more gold to the skin—full body work. Rascal Red on the nails, and a charming little temp tattoo of a red-winged butterfly on the left buttock. Twenty-four-hour facial cosmetics so that she wouldn't smudge. She looked spectacular," he said, tearing up. "And she kissed me and told me she just might be in love this time. 'Wish me luck, Sebastian.' She said that as she left. It was the last thing she ever said to me."

CHAPTER

TWO

No sperm. Eve swore over the autopsy report. **If she'd had sex with** her killer, the victim's choice of birth control had killed the little soldiers on contact, eliminating all trace of them within thirty minutes after ejaculation.

The extent of her injuries made the tests for sexual activity inconclusive. He'd blown her apart either for symbolism or for his own protection.

No sperm, no blood but for the victim's. No DNA.

The forensic sweep of the murder site turned up no fingerprints—none: not the victim's, not her weekly cleaning specialist's, certainly not the murderer's.

Every surface had been meticulously wiped, including the murder weapon.

Most telling of all, in Eve's judgment, were the security discs. Once again, she slipped the elevator surveillance into her desk monitor.

The discs were initialed.

Gorham Complex. Elevator A. 2-12-2058. 06:00.

Eve zipped through, watching the hours fly by. The elevator doors opened for the first time at noon. She slowed the speed, giving her unit a quick smack with the heel of her hand when the image hobbled, then studied the nervous little man who entered and asked for the fifth floor.

A jumpy John, she decided, amused when he tugged at his collar and slipped a breath mint between his lips. Probably had a wife and two kids and a steady white-collar job that allowed him to slip away for an hour once a week for his nooner.

He got off the elevator at five.

Activity was light for several hours, the occasional prostitute riding down to the lobby, some returning with shopping bags and bored expressions. A few clients came and went. The action picked up about eight. Some residents went out, snazzily dressed for dinner, others came in to keep their appointments.

At ten, an elegant-looking couple entered the car together. The woman allowed the man to open her fur coat, under which she wore nothing but stiletto heels and a tattoo of a rosebud with the stem starting at the crotch and the flower artistically teasing the left nipple. He fondled her, a technically illegal act in a secured area. When the elevator stopped on eighteen, the woman drew her coat together, and they exited, chatting about the play they'd just seen.

Eve made a note to interview the man the following day. It was he who was the victim's neighbor and associate.

The glitch happened at precisely 12:05. The image shifted almost seamlessly, with only the faintest blip, and returned to surveillance at 02:46.

Two hours and forty-one minutes lost.

The hallway disc of the eighteenth floor was the same. Nearly three hours wiped. Eve picked up her cooling coffee as she thought it through. The man understood security, she mused, was familiar enough with the building to know where and how to doctor the discs. And he'd taken his time, she thought. The autopsy put the victim's death at two A.M.

He'd spent nearly two hours with her before he'd killed her, and nearly an hour more after she'd been dead. Yet he hadn't left a trace.

Clever boy.

If Sharon DeBlass had recorded an appointment, personal or professional, for midnight, that, too, had been wiped.

So he'd known her intimately enough to be sure where she kept her files and how to access them.

On a hunch, Eve leaned forward again. "Gorham Complex, Broadway, New York. Owner."

Her eyes narrowed as the date flashed onto her screen.

Gorham Complex, owned by Roarke Industries, headquarters 500 Fifth Avenue. Roarke, president and CEO. New York residence, 222 Central Park West.

"Roarke," Eve murmured. "You just keep turning up, don't you. Roarke?" she repeated. "All data, view and print."

Ignoring the incoming call on the 'link beside her, Eve sipped her coffee and read.

Roarke—no known given name—born 10-06-2023, Dublin, Ireland. ID number 33492-ABR-50. Parents unknown. Marital status, single. President and CEO of Roarke Industries, established 2042. Main branches New York, Chicago, New Los Angeles, Dublin, London, Bonn, Paris, Frankfurt, Tokyo, Milan, Sydney. Off-planet branches, Station 45, Bridgestone Colony, Vegas II, Free-Star One. Interests in real estate, import-export, shipping, entertainment, manufacturing, pharmaceuticals, transportation. Estimated gross worth, three billion, eight hundred million.

Busy boy, Eve thought, lifting a brow as a list of his companies clicked on-screen.

"Education," she demanded.

Unknown.

"Criminal record?"

No data.

"Access Roarke, Dublin."

No additional data.

"Well, shit. Mr. Mystery. Description and visual."

Roarke. Black hair, blue eyes, 6 feet, 2 inches, 173 pounds.

Eve grunted as the computer listed the description. She had to agree that in Roarke's case, a picture was worth a couple hundred words.

His image stared back at her from the screen. He was almost ridiculously handsome: the narrow, aesthetic face; the slash of cheekbones; and sculpted mouth. Yes, his hair was black, but the computer didn't say it was thick and full and swept back from a strong forehead to fall inches above broad shoulders. His eyes were blue, but the word was much too simple for the intensity of color or the power in them.

Even on an image, Eve could see this was a man who hunted down what or who he wanted, bagged it, used it, and didn't bother with frivolities such as trophies.

And yes, she thought, this was a man who could kill if and when it suited him. He would do so coolly, methodically, and without breaking a sweat.

Gathering up the hard data, she decided she'd have a talk with Roarke. Very soon.

By the time Eve left the station to head home, the sky was miserably spitting snow. She checked her pockets without hope and found she had indeed left her gloves in her apartment. Hatless, gloveless, with only her leather jacket as protection against the biting wind, she drove across town.

She'd meant to get her vehicle into repair. There just hadn't been time. But there was plenty of time to regret it now as she fought traffic and shivered, thanks to a faulty heating system.

She swore if she got home without turning into a block of ice, she'd make the appointment with the mechanic.

But when she did arrive home, her primary thought was food. Even as she unlocked her door, she was dreaming about a hot bowl of soup, maybe a mound of chips, if she had any left, and coffee that didn't taste like someone had spilled sewage into the water system.

She saw the package immediately, the slim square just inside the door. Her weapon was out and in her hand before she drew the next breath. Sweeping with weapon and eyes, she kicked the door shut behind her. She left the package where it was and moved from room to room until she was satisfied she was alone.

After bolstering her weapon, she peeled out of her jacket and tossed it aside. Bending, she picked up the sealed disc by the edges. There was no label, no message.

Eve took it into the kitchen, tapping it carefully out of its seal, and slipped it into her computer.

And forgot all about food.

The video was top quality, as was the sound. She sat down slowly as the scene played on her monitor.

Naked, Sharon DeBlass lounged on the lake-sized bed, rustling satin sheets. She lifted a hand, skimming it through that glorious tumbled mane of russet hair as the bed's floating motion rocked her.

"Want me to do anything special, darling?" She chuckled, rose up on her knees, cupped her own breasts. "Why don't you come back over here . . ." Her tongue flicked out to wet her lips. "We'll do it all again." Her gaze lowered, and a little cat smile curved her lips. "Looks like you're more than ready." She laughed again, shook back her hair. "Oh, we want to play a game." Still smiling, Sharon put her hands up. "Don't hurt me." She whimpered, shivering even as her eyes glinted with excitement. "I'll do anything you want. Anything. Come on over here and force me. I want you to." Lowering her hands, she began to stroke herself. "Hold that big bad gun on me while you rape me. I want you to. I want you to—"

The explosion had Eve jolting. Her stomach twisted as she saw the woman fly backward like a broken doll, the blood spurting out of her forehead. The second shot wasn't such a shock, but Eve had to force herself to keep her eyes on the screen. After the final report there was silence, but for the quiet music, the fractured breathing. The killer's breathing.

The camera moved in, panned the body in grisly detail. Then, through the magic of video, DeBlass was as Eve had first seen her, spread-eagled in a perfect **X** over bloody sheets. The image ended with a graphic overlay.

ONE OF SIX

It was easier to watch it through the second time. Or so Eve told herself. This time she noticed a slight bobble of the camera after the first shot, a quick, quiet gasp. She ran it back again, listening to each word, studying each movement, hoping for some clue. But he was too clever for that. And they both knew it.

He'd wanted her to see just how good he was. Just how cold.

And he wanted her to know that he knew just where to find her. Whenever he chose.

Furious that her hands weren't quite steady, she rose. Rather than the coffee she'd intended, Eve took out a bottle of wine from the small cold cell, poured half a glass.

She drank it down quickly, promised herself the other half shortly, then punched in the code for her commander.

It was the commander's wife who answered, and from the glittering drops at her ears and the perfect coiffure, Eve calculated that she'd interrupted one of the woman's famous dinner parties.

"Lieutenant Dallas, Mrs. Whitney. I'm sorry to interrupt your evening, but I need to speak to the commander."

"We're entertaining, Lieutenant."

"Yes, ma'am. I apologize." Fucking politics, Eve thought as she forced a smile. "It's urgent."

"Isn't it always?"

The machine hummed on hold, mercifully without hideous background music or updated news reports, for a full three minutes before the commander came on.

"Dallas."

"Commander, I need to send you something over a coded line."

"It better be urgent, Dallas. My wife's going to make me pay for this."

"Yes, sir." Cops, she thought as she prepared to send the image to his monitor, should stay single.

She waited, folding her restless hands on the table. As the images played again, she watched again, ignoring the clenching in her gut. When it was over, Whitney came back on-screen. His eyes were grim.

"Where did you get this?"

"He sent it to me. A disc was here, in my apartment, when I got back from the station." Her voice was flat and careful. "He knows who I am, where I am, and what I'm doing."

Whitney was silent for a moment. "My office, oh seven hundred. Bring the disc, Lieutenant."

"Yes, sir."

When the transmission ended, she did the two things her instincts dictated. She made herself a copy of the disc, and she poured another glass of wine.

She woke at three, shuddering, clammy, fighting for the breath to scream. Whimpers sounded in her throat as she croaked out an order for lights. Dreams were always more frightening in the dark.

Trembling, she lay back. This one had been worse, much worse, than any she'd experienced before.

She'd killed the man. What choice had she had? He'd been too buzzed on chemicals to be stunned. Christ, she'd tried, but he'd just keep coming, and coming, and coming, with that wild look in his eyes and the already bloodied knife in his hand.

The little girl had already been dead. There was nothing Eve could have done to stop it. Please God, don't let there have been anything that could have been done.

The little body hacked to pieces, the frenzied man with the dripping knife. Then the look in his eyes when she'd fired on full, and the life had slipped out of them.

But that hadn't been all. Not this time. This time he'd kept coming. And she'd been naked, kneeling in a pool of satin. The knife had become a gun, held by the man whose face she'd studied hours before. The man called Roarke.

He'd smiled, and she'd wanted him. Her body had tingled with terror and sexual desperation even as he'd shot her. Head, heart, and loins.

And somewhere through it all, the little girl, the poor little girl, had been screaming for help.

Too tired to fight it, Eve simply rolled over, pressed her face into her pillow and wept.

"Lieutenant." At precisely seven A.M., Commander Whitney gestured Eve toward a chair in his office. Despite the fact, or perhaps due to the fact that he'd been riding a desk for twelve years, he had sharp eyes.

He could see that she'd slept badly and had worked to disguise the signs of a disturbed night. In silence, he held out a hand.

She'd put the disc and its cover into an evidence bag. Whitney glanced at it, then laid it in the center of his desk.

"According to protocol, I'm obliged to ask you if you want to be relieved from this case." He waited a beat. "We'll pretend I did."

"Yes, sir."

"Is your residence secure, Dallas?"

"I thought so." She took hard copy out of her briefcase. "I reviewed the security discs after I contacted you. There's a ten-minute time lapse. As you'll see in my report, he has the capability of undermining security, a knowledge of videos, editing, and, of course, antique weapons."

Whitney took her report, set it aside. "That doesn't narrow the field overmuch."

"No, sir. I have several more people I need to interview. With this perpetrator, electronic investigation isn't primary, though Captain Feeney's help is invaluable. This guy covers his tracks. We have no physical evidence other than the weapon he chose to leave at the scene. Feeney hadn't been able to trace it through normal channels. We have to assume it was black market. I've started on her trick books and her personal appointments, but she wasn't the retiring kind. It's going to take time."

"Time's part of the problem. One of six, Lieutenant. What does that say to you?"

"That he has five more in mind, and wants us to know it. He enjoys his work and wants to be the focus of our attention." She took a careful breath. "There's not enough for a full psychiatric profile. We can't say how long he'll be satisfied by the thrill of this murder, when he'll need his next fix. It could be today. It could be a year from now. We can't bank on him being careless."

Whitney merely nodded. "Are you having problems with the rightful termination?"

The knife slicked with blood. The small ruined body at her feet. "Nothing I can't handle."

"Be sure of it, Dallas. I don't need an officer on a sensitive case like this who's worried whether she should or shouldn't use her weapon."

"I'm sure of it."

She was the best he had, and he couldn't afford to doubt her. "Are you up to playing politics?" His lips curved thinly. "Senator DeBlass is on his way over. He flew into New York last night."

"Diplomacy isn't my strong suit."

"I'm aware of that. But you're going to work on it. He wants to talk to the investigating officer, and he went over my head to arrange it. Orders came down from the chief. You're to give the senator your full cooperation."

"This is a Code Five investigation," Eve said stiffly. "I don't care if orders came down from God Almighty, I'm not giving confidential data to a civilian."

Whitney's smile widened. He had a good, ordinary face, probably the one he was born with. But when he smiled and meant it, the flash of white teeth against the cocoa-colored skin turned the plain features into the special.

"I didn't hear that. And you didn't hear me tell you to give him no more than the obvious facts. What you do hear me tell you, Lieutenant Dallas, is that the gentleman from Virginia is a pompous, arrogant asshole. Unfortunately, the asshole has power. So watch your step."

"Yes, sir."

He glanced at his watch, then slipped the file and disc into his safe drawer. "You've got time for a cup of coffee . . . and, Lieutenant," he added as she rose. "If you're having trouble sleeping, take your authorized sedative. I want my officers sharp."

"I'm sharp enough."

Senator Gerald DeBlass was undoubtedly pompous. He was unquestionably arrogant. After one full minute in his company, Eve agreed that he was undeniably an asshole.

He was a compact, bull of a man, perhaps six feet, two hundred and twenty. His crop of white hair was cut sharp and thin as a razor so that his head seemed huge and bullet sleek. His eyes were nearly black, as were the heavy brows over them. They were large, like his nose, his mouth.

His hands were enormous, and when he clasped Eve's briefly on introduction, she noted they were smooth and soft as a baby's.

He brought his adjutant with him. Derrick Rockman was a whip-like man in his early forties. Though he was nearly six-five, Eve gave DeBlass twenty pounds on him. Neat, tidy, his pin-striped suit and slate blue tie showed not a crease. His face was solemn, attractively even featured, his movements restrained and controlled as he assisted the more flamboyant senator out of his cashmere overcoat.

"What the hell have you done to find the monster who killed my granddaughter?" DeBlass demanded.

"Everything possible, Senator." Commander Whitney remained standing. Though he offered DeBlass a seat, the man prowled the room, as he was given to prowl the New Senate Gallery in East Washington.

"You've had twenty-four hours and more," DeBlass shot back, his voice deep and booming. "It's my understanding you've assigned only two officers to the investigation."

"For security purposes, yes. Two of my best officers," the commander added. "Lieutenant Dallas heads the investigation and reports solely to me."

DeBlass turned those hard black eyes on Eve. "What progress have you made?"

"We identified the weapon, ascertained the time of death. We're gathering evidence and interviewing residents of Ms. DeBlass's building, and tracking the names in her personal and business logs. I'm working to reconstruct the last twenty-four hours of her life."

"It should be obvious, even to the slowest mind, that she was murdered by one of her clients." He said the word in a hiss.

"There was no appointment listed for several hours prior to her death. Her last client has an alibi for the critical hour."

"Break it," DeBlass demanded. "A man who would pay for sexual favors would have no compunction about murder."

Though Eve failed to see the correlation, she remembered her job and nodded. "I'm working on it, Senator."

"I want copies of her appointment books."

"That's not possible, Senator," Whitney said mildly. "All evidence of a capital crime is confidential."

DeBlass merely snorted and gestured toward Rockman.

"Commander." Rockman reached in his left breast pocket and drew out a sheet of paper affixed with a holographic seal. "This document from your chief of police authorizes the senator access to any and all evidence and investigative data on Ms. DeBlass's murder."

Whitney barely glanced at the document before setting it aside. He'd always considered politics a coward's game, and hated that he was forced to play it. "I'll speak to the chief personally. If the authorization holds, we'll have copies to you by this afternoon." Dismissing Rockman, he looked back at DeBlass. "The confidentiality of evidence is a major tool in the investigative process. If you insist on this, you risk undermining the case."

"The case, as you put it, Commander, was my flesh and blood."

"And as such, I'd hope your first priority would be assisting us to bring her killer to justice."

"I've served justice for more than fifty years. I want that information by noon." He picked up his coat, tossed it over one beefy arm. "If I'm not satisfied that you're doing everything in your power to find this maniac, I'll see that you're removed from this office." He turned toward Eve. "And that the next thing you investigate, Lieutenant, will be sticky-fingered teenagers at a shop-com."

After he stormed out, Rockman used his quiet, solemn eyes to apologize. "You must forgive the senator. He's overwrought. However much strain there was between him and his granddaughter, she was family. Nothing is more vital to the senator than his family. Her death, this kind of violent, senseless death, is devastating to him."

"Right," Eve muttered. "He looked all choked up."

Rockman smiled; he managed to look amused and sorrowful at once. "Proud men often disguise their grief behind aggression. We have every confidence in your abilities and your tenacity, Lieutenant. Commander." He nodded. "We'll expect the data this afternoon. Thank you for your time."

"He's a smooth one," Eve muttered when Rockman shut the door quietly behind him. "You're not going to cave, Commander."

"I'll give them what I have to." His voice was sharp and edged with suppressed fury. "Now, go get me more."

Police work was too often drudgery. After five hours of staring at her monitor as she ran makes on the names in DeBlass's books, Eve was more exhausted than she would have been after a marathon race.

Even with Feeney taking a portion of the names with his skill and superior equipment, there were too many for such a small investigative unit to handle quickly.

Sharon had been a very popular girl.

Feeling discretion would gain her more than aggression, Eve contacted the clients by 'link and explained herself. Those who balked at the idea of an interview were cheerfully invited to come into Cop Central, charged with obstruction of justice.

By midafternoon she had spoken personally with the first dozen on the client list, and took a detour back to the Gorham.

DeBlass's neighbor, the elegant man from the elevator, was Charles Monroe. Eve found him in, and entertaining a client.

Slickly handsome in a black silk robe, and smelling seductively of sex, Charles smiled engagingly.

"I'm terribly sorry, Lieutenant. My three o'clock appointment has another fifteen minutes."

"I'll wait." Without invitation, Eve stepped inside. Unlike De-Blass's apartment, this one ran to deep, cushy chairs in leather and thick carpets.

"Ah . . ." Obviously amused, Charles glanced behind him, where a door was discreetly closed at the end of a short hallway. "Privacy and confidentiality are, you understand, vital to my profession. My client is apt to be disconcerted if she discovers the police on my doorstep."

"No problem. Got a kitchen?"

He let out a weighty sigh. "Sure. Right through that doorway. Make yourself at home. I won't be long."

"Take your time." Eve strolled off to the kitchen. In contrast to the elaborate living area, this was spartan. It seemed Charles spent little time eating in. Still, he had a full-size friggie unit rather than a cold cell, and she found the treasure of a Pepsi chilling. Satisfied for the moment, she sat down to enjoy it while Charles finished off his three o'clock.

Soon enough, she heard the murmur of voices, a man's, a woman's, a light laugh. Moments later, he came in, the same easy smile on his face.

"Sorry to keep you waiting."

"No problem. Are you expecting anyone else?"

"Not until later this evening." He took out a Pepsi for himself, broke the freshness seal from the tube, and poured it into a tall glass. He rolled the tube into a ball and popped it into the recycler. "Dinner, the opera, and a romantic rendezvous."

"You like that stuff? Opera?" she asked when he flashed a grin.

"Hate it. Can you think of anything more tedious than some big-chested woman screaming in German half the night?"

Eve thought it over. "Nope."

"But there you are. Tastes vary." His smile faded as he joined her at the little nook under the kitchen window. "I heard about Sharon on the news this morning. I've been expecting someone to come by. It's horrible. I can't believe she's dead."

"You knew her well?"

"We've been neighbors more than three years—and occasionally we worked together. Now and again, one of our clients would request a trio, and we'd share the business."

"And when it wasn't business, did you still share?"

"She was a beautiful woman, and she found me attractive." He moved his silk-clad shoulders, his eyes shifting to the tinted glass of the window as a tourist tram streamed by. "If one of us was in the mood for a busman's holiday, the other usually obliged." He smiled again. "That was rare. Like working in a candy store, after a while you lose your taste for chocolate. She was a friend, Lieutenant. And I was very fond of her."

"Can you tell me where you were the night of her death between midnight and three A.M.?"

His brows shot up. If it hadn't just occurred to him that he could be considered a suspect, he was an excellent actor. Then again, Eve thought, people in his line of work had to be.

"I was with a client, here. She stayed overnight."

"Is that usual?"

"This client prefers that arrangement. Lieutenant, I'll give you her name if absolutely necessary, but I'd prefer not to. At least until I've explained the circumstances to her."

"It's murder, Mr. Monroe, so it's necessary. What time did you bring your client here?"

"About ten. We had dinner at Miranda's, the sky café above Sixth."

"Ten." Eve nodded, and saw the moment he remembered.

"The security camera in the elevator." His smile was all charm again. "It's an antiquated law. I suppose you could bust me, but it's hardly worth your time."

"Any sexual act in a secured area is a misdemeanor, Mr. Monroe."

"Charles, please."

"It's a nitpick, Charles, but they could suspend your license for six months. Give me her name, and we'll clear it up as quietly as possible."

"You're going to lose me one of my best clients," he muttered. "Darleen Howe. I'll get you the address." He rose to get his electronic datebook, then read off the information.

"Thanks. Did Sharon talk about her clients with you?"

"We were friends," he said wearily. "Yeah, we talked shop, though it's not strictly ethical. She had some funny stories. I'm more conventional in style. Sharon was . . . open to the unusual. Sometimes we'd get together for a drink, and she'd talk. No names. She had her own little terms for them. The emperor, the weasel, the milkmaid, that kind of thing."

"Was there anyone she mentioned who worried her, made her uneasy? Someone who might have been violent?"

"She didn't mind violence, and no, nobody worried her. One thing about Sharon, she always felt in control. That's the way she wanted it because she said she'd been under someone else's control most of her life. She had a lot of bitterness toward her family. She told me once she'd never planned on making a career out of professional sex. She'd only gotten into it to make her family crazy. But then, after she got into it, she decided she liked it."

He moved his shoulders again, sipped from his glass. "So she stayed in the life, and killed two birds with one fuck. Her phrase."

He lifted his eyes again. "Looks like one of the fucks killed her."

"Yeah." Eve rose, tucked her recorder away. "Don't take any out-of-town trips, Charles. I'll be in touch."

"That's it?"

"For the moment."

He stood as well, smiled again. "You're easy to talk to for a cop . . . Eve." Experimentally, he skimmed a fingertip down her arm. When her brows lifted, he took the fingertip over her jawline. "In a hurry?"

"Why?"

"Well, I've got a couple of hours, and you're very attractive. Big golden eyes," he murmured. "This little dip right in your chin. Why don't we both go off the clock for a while?"

She waited while he lowered his head, while his lips hovered just above hers. "Is this a bribe, Charles? Because if it is, and you're half as good as I think you are . . ."

"I'm better." He nibbled at her bottom lip, let his hand slide down to toy with her breast. "I'm much better."

"In that case . . . I'd have to charge you with a felony." She smiled as he jerked back. "And that would make both of us really sad." Amused, she patted his cheek. "But, thanks for the thought."

He scratched his chin as he followed her to the door. "Eve?"

She paused, hand on the knob, and glanced back at him. "Yes?"

"Bribes aside, if you change your mind, I'd be interested in seeing more of you."

"I'll let you know." She closed the door and headed for the elevator.

It wouldn't have been difficult, she mused, for Charles Monroe to slip out of his apartment, leaving his client sleeping, and slip into Sharon's. A little sex, a little murder . . .

Thoughtful, she stepped into the elevator.

Doctor the discs. As a resident of the building, it would have been simple for him to gain access to security. Then he could have popped back into bed with his client.

It was too bad that the scenario was plausible, Eve thought as she reached the lobby. She liked him. But until she checked his alibi thoroughly, Charles Monroe was now at the top of her short list.

CHAPTER

THREE

Eve hated funerals. She detested the rite human beings insisted on giving death. The flowers, the music, the endless words and weeping.

There might be a God. She hadn't completely ruled such things out. And if there were, she thought, It must have enjoyed a good laugh over Its creations' useless rituals and passages.

Still, she had made the trip to Virginia to attend Sharon DeBlass's funeral. She wanted to see the dead's family and friends gathered together, to observe, and analyze, and judge.

The senator stood grim-faced and dry-eyed, with Rockman, his shadow, one pew behind. Beside DeBlass were his son and daughter-in-law.

Sharon's parents were young, attractive, successful attorneys who headed their own law firm.

Richard DeBlass stood with his head bowed and his eyes hooded, a trimmer and somehow less dynamic version of his father. Was it coincidence, Eve wondered, or design that he stood at equal distance between his father and wife?

Elizabeth Barrister was sleek and chic in her dark suit, her waving mahogany hair glossy, her posture rigid. And, Eve, noted, her eyes red-rimmed and swimming with constant tears.

What did a mother feel, Eve wondered, as she had wondered all of her life, when she lost a child?

Senator DeBlass had a daughter as well, and she flanked his right side. Congresswoman Catherine DeBlass had followed in her father's political footsteps. Painfully thin, she stood militarily straight, her arms looking like brittle twigs in her black dress. Beside her, her husband Justin Summit stared at the glossy coffin draped with roses at the front of the church. At his side, their son Franklin, still trapped in the gangly stage of adolescence, shifted restlessly.

At the end of the pew, somehow separate from the rest of the family, was DeBlass's wife, Anna.

She neither shifted nor wept. Not once did Eve see her so much as glance at the flower-strewn box that held what was left of her only granddaughter.

There were others, of course. Elizabeth's parents stood together, hands linked, and cried openly. Cousins, acquaintances, and friends dabbed at their eyes or simply looked around in fascination or horror. The president had sent an envoy, and the church was packed with more politicians than the Senate lunchroom.

Though there were more than a hundred faces, Eve had no trouble picking Roarke out of the crowd. He was alone. There were others lined in the pew with him, but Eve recognized the solitary quality that surrounded him. There could have been ten thousand in the building, and he would have remained aloof from them.

His striking face gave away nothing: no guilt, no grief, no interest. He might have been watching a mildly inferior play. Eve could think of no better description for a funeral.

More than one head turned in his direction for a quick study or, in the case of a shapely brunette, a not so subtle flirtation. Roarke responded to both the same way: he ignored them.

At first study, she would have judged him as cold, an icy fortress of a man who guarded himself against any and all. But there must have been heat. It took more than discipline and intelligence to rise so high so young. It took ambition, and to Eve's mind, ambition was a flammable fuel.

He looked straight ahead as the dirge swelled, then without warning, he turned his head, looked five pews back across the aisle and directly into Eve's eyes.

It was surprise that had her fighting not to jolt at that sudden and unexpected punch of power. It was will that kept her from blinking or shifting her gaze. For one humming minute they stared at each other. Then there was movement, and mourners came between them as they left the church.

When Eve stepped into the aisle to search him out again, he was gone.

She joined the long line of cars and limos on the journey to the cemetery. Above, the hearse and the family vehicles flew solemnly. Only the very rich could afford body internment. Only the obsessively traditional still put their dead into the ground.

Frowning, her fingers tapping the wheel, she relayed her observations into her recorder. When she got to Roarke, she hesitated and her frown deepened.

"Why would he trouble himself to attend the funeral of such a casual acquaintance?" she murmured into the recorder in her pocket. "According to data, they had met only recently and had a single date. Behavior seems inconsistent and questionable."

She shivered once, glad she was alone as she drove through the arching gates of the cemetery. As far as Eve was concerned, there should be a law against putting someone in a hole.

More words and weeping, more flowers. The sun was bright as a sword but the air had the snapping bite of a petulant child. Near the gravesite, she slipped her hands into her pockets. She'd forgotten her gloves again. The long, dark coat she wore was borrowed. Beneath it, the single gray suit she owned had a loose button that seemed to beg her to tug at it. Inside her thin leather boots, her toes were tiny blocks of ice.

The discomfort helped distract her from the misery of headstones and the smell of cold, fresh earth. She bided her time, waiting until the last mournful word about everlasting life echoed away, then approached the senator.

"My sympathies, Senator DeBlass, to you and your family."

His eyes were hard; sharp and black, like the hewed edge of a stone. "Save your sympathies, Lieutenant. I want justice."

"So do I. Mrs. DeBlass." Eve held out a hand to the senator's wife and found her fingers clutching a bundle of brittle twigs.

"Thank you for coming."

Eve nodded. One close look had shown her Anna DeBlass was skimming under the edge of emotion on a buffering layer of chemicals. Her eyes passed over Eve's face and settled just above her shoulder as she withdrew her hand.

"Thank you for coming," she said in exactly the same flat tone to the next offer of condolence.

Before Eve could speak again, her arm was taken in a firm grip. Rockman smiled solemnly down at her. "Lieutenant Dallas, the senator and his family appreciate the compassion and interest you've shown in attending the service." In his quiet manner, he edged her away. "I'm sure you'll understand that, under the circumstances, it would be difficult for Sharon's parents to meet the officer in charge of their daughter's investigation over her grave."

Eve allowed him to lead her five feet away before she jerked her arm free. "You're in the right business, Rockman. That's a very delicate and diplomatic way of telling me to get my ass out."

"Not at all." He continued to smile, smoothly polite. "There's simply a time and place. You have our complete cooperation, Lieutenant. If you wish to interview the senator's family, I'd be more than happy to arrange it."

"I'll arrange my own interviews, at my own time and place." Because his placid smile irked her, she decided to see if she could wipe it off his face. "What about you, Rockman? Got an alibi for the night in question?"

The smile did falter—that was some satisfaction. He recovered quickly, however. "I dislike the word *alibi*."

"Me, too," she returned with a smile of her own. "That's why I like nothing better than to break them. You didn't answer the question, Rockman."

"I was in East Washington on the night Sharon was murdered. The senator and I worked quite late refining a bill he intends to present next month."

"It's a quick trip from EW to New York," she commented.

"It is. However, I didn't make it on that particular night. We worked until nearly midnight, then I retired to the senator's guest room. We had breakfast together at seven the next morning. As Sharon, according to your own reports, was killed at two, it gives me a very narrow window of opportunity."

"Narrow windows still provide access." But she said it only to irritate him as she turned away. She'd held back the information on the doctored security discs from the file she'd given DeBlass. The murderer had been in the Gorham by midnight. Rockman would hardly use the victim's grandfather for an alibi unless it was solid. Rockman's working in East Washington at midnight slammed even that narrow window closed.

She saw Roarke again, and watched with interest as Elizabeth Barrister clung to him, as he bent his head and murmured to her. Not the usual offer and acceptance of sympathy from strangers, Eve mused.

Her brow lifted as Roarke laid a hand on Elizabeth's right cheek, kissed her left before stepping back to speak quietly to Richard DeBlass.

He crossed to the senator, but there was no contact between them, and the conversation was brief. Alone, as Eve had suspected, Roarke began to walk across the winter grass, between the cold monuments the living raised for the dead.

"Roarke."

He stopped, and as he had at the service, turned and met her eyes. She thought she caught a flash of something in them: anger, sorrow, impatience. Then it was gone and they were simply cool, blue, and unfathomable.

She didn't hurry as she walked to him. Something told her he was a man too used to people—women certainly—rushing toward him. So she took her time, her long, slow strides flapping her borrowed coat around her chilly legs.

"I'd like to speak with you," she said when she faced him. She took out her badge, watched him give it a brief glance before lifting his eyes back to hers. "I'm investigating Sharon DeBlass's murder."

"Do you make a habit of attending the funerals of murder victims, Lieutenant Dallas?"

His voice was smooth, with a whisper of the charm of Ireland over it, like rich cream over warmed whiskey. "Do you make a habit of attending the funerals of women you barely know, Roarke?"

"I'm a friend of the family," he said simply. "You're freezing, Lieutenant."

She plunged her icy fingers into the pockets of the coat. "How well do you know the victim's family?"

"Well enough." He tilted his head. In a minute, he thought, her teeth would chatter. The nasty little wind was blowing her poorly cut hair around a very interesting face. Intelligent, stubborn, sexy. Three very good reasons in his mind to take a second look at a woman. "Wouldn't it be more convenient to talk someplace warmer?"

"I've been unable to reach you," she began.

"I've been traveling. You've reached me now. I assume you're returning to New York. Today?"

"Yes. I have a few minutes before I have to leave for the shuttle. So . . ."

"So we'll go back together. That should give you time enough to grill me."

"Question you," she said between her teeth, annoyed that he turned and walked away from her. She lengthened her stride to catch up. "A few simple answers now, Roarke, and we can arrange a more formal interview in New York."

"I hate to waste time," he said easily. "You strike me as someone who feels the same. Did you rent a car?"

"Yes."

"I'll arrange to have it returned." He held out a hand, waiting for the key card.

"That isn't necessary."

"It's simpler. I appreciate complications, Lieutenant, and I appreciate simplicity. You and I are going to the same destination at the same

approximate time. You want to talk to me, and I'm willing to oblige."
He stopped by a black limo where a uniformed driver waited, holding
the rear door open. "My transport's routed for New York. You can, of
course, follow me to the airport, take public transportation, then call
my office for an appointment. Or you can drive with me, enjoy the
privacy of my jet, and have my full attention during the trip."

She hesitated only a moment, then took the key card for the rental
from her pocket and dropped it into his hand. Smiling, he gestured
her into the limo where she settled as he instructed his driver to deal
with the rental car.

"Now then." Roarke slid in beside her, reached for a decanter.
"Would you like a brandy to fight off the chill?"

"No." She felt the warmth of the car sweep up from her feet and
was afraid she'd begin to shiver in reaction.

"Ah. On duty. Coffee perhaps."

"Great."

Gold winked at his wrist as he pressed his choice for two coffees on
the AutoChef built into the side panel. "Cream?"

"Black."

"A woman after my own heart." Moments later, he opened the
protective door and offered her a china cup in a delicate saucer. "We
have more of a selection on the plane," he said, then settled back with
his coffee.

"I bet." The steam rising from her cup smelled like heaven. Eve
took a tentative sip—and nearly moaned.

It was real. No simulation made from vegetable concentrate so
usual since the depletion of the rain forests in the late twentieth. This
was the real thing, ground from rich Columbian beans, singing with
caffeine.

She sipped again, and could have wept.

"Problem?" He enjoyed her reaction immensely, the flutter of the
lashes, the faint flush, the darkening of the eyes—a similar response,
he noted, to a woman purring under a man's hands.

"Do you know how long it's been since I had real coffee?"

He smiled. "No."

"Neither do I." Unashamed, she closed her eyes as she lifted the cup again. "You'll have to excuse me, this is a private moment. We'll talk on the plane."

"As you like."

He gave himself the pleasure of watching her as the car traveled smoothly over the road.

Odd, he thought, he hadn't pegged her for a cop. His instincts were usually keen about such matters. At the funeral, he'd been thinking only what a terrible waste it was for someone as young, foolish, and full of life as Sharon to be dead.

Then he'd sensed something, something that had coiled his muscles, tightened his gut. He'd felt her gaze, as physical as a blow. When he'd turned, when he'd seen her, another blow. A slow-motion one-two punch he hadn't been able to evade.

It was fascinating.

But the warning blip hadn't gone off. Not the warning blip that should have relayed *cop*. He'd seen a tall, willowy brunette with short, tumbled hair, eyes the color of honeycombs and a mouth made for sex.

If she hadn't sought him out, he'd intended to seek her.

Too damn bad she was a cop.

She didn't speak again until they were at the airport, stepping into the cabin of his JetStar 6000.

She hated being impressed, again. Coffee was one thing, and a small weakness was permitted, but she didn't care for her goggle-eyed reaction to the lush cabin with its deep chairs, sofas, the antique carpet, and crystal vases filled with flowers.

There was a viewing screen recessed in the forward wall and a uniformed flight attendant who showed no surprise at seeing Roarke board with a strange woman.

"Brandy, sir?"

"My companion prefers coffee, Diana, black." He lifted a brow until Eve nodded. "I'll have brandy."

"I've heard about the JetStar." Eve shrugged out of her coat, and it was whisked away along with Roarke's by the attendant. "It's a nice form of transportation."

"Thanks. We spent two years designing it."

"Roarke Industries?" she said as she took a chair.

"That's right. I prefer using my own whenever possible. You'll need to strap in for takeoff," he told her, then leaned forward to flip on an intercom. "Ready."

"We've been cleared," they were told. "Thirty seconds."

Almost before Eve could blink, they were airborne, in so smooth a transition she barely felt the g's. It beat the hell, she thought, out of the commercial flights that slapped you back in your seat for the first five minutes of air time.

They were served drinks and a little plate of fruit and cheese that had Eve's mouth watering. It was time, she decided, to get to work.

"How long did you know Sharon DeBlass?"

"I met her recently, at the home of a mutual acquaintance."

"You said you were a friend of the family."

"Of her parents," Roarke said easily. "I've known Beth and Richard for several years. First on a business level, then on a personal one. Sharon was in school, then in Europe, and our paths didn't cross. I met her for the first time a few days ago, took her to dinner. Then she was dead."

He took a flat gold case from his inside pocket. Eve's eyes narrowed as she watched him light a cigarette. "Tobacco's illegal, Roarke."

"Not in free air space, international waters, or on private property." He smiled at her through a haze of smoke. "Don't you think, Lieutenant, that the police have enough to do without trying to legislate our morality and personal lifestyles?"

She hated to admit even to herself that the tobacco smelled enticing. "Is that why you collect guns? As part of your personal lifestyle?"

"I find them fascinating. Your grandfather and mine considered owning one a constitutional right. We've toyed quite a bit with constitutional rights as we've civilized ourselves."

"And murder and injury by that particular type of weapon is now an aberration rather than the norm."

"You like rules, Lieutenant?"

The question was mild, as was the insult under it. Her shoulders stiffened. "Without rules, chaos."

"With chaos, life."

Screw philosophy, she thought, annoyed. "Do you own a thirty-eight caliber Smith & Wesson, Model Ten, circa 1990?"

He took another slow, considering drag. The tobacco burned expensively between his long, elegant fingers. "I believe I own one of that model. Is that what killed her?"

"Would you be willing to show it to me?"

"Of course, at your convenience."

Too easy, she thought. She suspected anything that came easily. "You had dinner with the deceased the night before her death. In Mexico."

"That's right." Roarke crushed out his cigarette and settled back with his brandy. "I have a small villa on the west coast. I thought she'd enjoy it. She did."

"Did you have a physical relationship with Sharon DeBlass?"

His eyes glittered for a moment, but whether with amusement or with anger, she couldn't be sure. "By that, I take you to mean did I have sex with her. No, Lieutenant, though it hardly seems relevant. We had dinner."

"You took a beautiful woman, a professional companion, to your villa in Mexico, and all you shared with her was dinner."

He took his time choosing a glossy green grape. "I appreciate beautiful women for a variety of reasons, and enjoy spending time with them. I don't employ professionals for two reasons. First, I don't find it necessary to pay for sex." He sipped his brandy, watching her over the rim. "And second, I don't choose to share." He paused, very briefly. "Do you?"

Her stomach fluttered, was ignored. "We're not talking about me."

"I was. You're a beautiful woman, and we're quite alone, at least for the next fifteen minutes. Yet all we've shared has been coffee and brandy." He smiled at the temper smoldering in her eyes. "Heroic, isn't it, what restraint I have?"

"I'd say your relationship with Sharon DeBlass had a different flavor."

"Oh, I certainly agree." He chose another grape, offered it.

Appetite was a weakness, Eve reminded herself even as she accepted the grape and bit through its thin, tart skin. "Did you see her after your dinner in Mexico?"

"No, I dropped her off about three A.M. and went home. Alone."

"Can you tell me your whereabouts for the forty-eight hours after you went home—alone?"

"I was in bed for the first five of them. I took a conference call over breakfast. About eight-fifteen. You can check the records."

"I will."

This time he grinned, a quick flash of undiluted charm that had her pulse skipping. "I have no doubt of it. You fascinate me, Lieutenant Dallas."

"After the conference call?"

"It ended about nine. I worked out until ten, spent the next several hours in my midtown office with various appointments." He took out a small, slim card that she recognized as a daybook. "Shall I list them for you?"

"I'd prefer you to arrange to have a hard copy sent to my office."

"I'll see to it. I was back home by seven. I had a dinner meeting with several members of my Japanese manufacturing firm—in my home. We dined at eight. Shall I send you the menu?"

"Don't be snide, Roarke."

"Merely thorough, Lieutenant. It was an early evening. By eleven I was alone, with a book and a brandy, until about seven A.M., when I had my first cup of coffee. Would you like another?"

She'd have killed for another cup of coffee, but she shook her head. "Alone for eight hours, Roarke. Did you speak with anyone, see anyone during that time?"

"No. No one. I had to be in Paris the next day and wanted a quiet evening. Poor timing on my part. Then again, if I were going to murder someone, it would have been ill advised not to protect myself with an alibi."

"Or arrogant not to bother," she returned. "Do you just collect antique weapons, Roarke, or do you use them?"

"I'm an excellent shot." He set his empty snifter aside. "I'll be happy to demonstrate for you when you come to see my collection. Does tomorrow suit you?"

"Fine."

"Seven o'clock? I assume you have the address." When he leaned over, she stiffened and nearly hissed as his hand brushed her arm. He only smiled, his face close, his eyes level. "You need to strap in," he said quietly. "We'll be landing in a moment."

He fastened her harness himself, wondering if he made her nervous as a man, or a murder suspect, or a combination of both. Just then, any choice had its own interest—and its own possibilities.

"Eve," he murmured. "Such a simple and feminine name. I wonder if it suits you."

She said nothing while the flight attendant came in to remove the dishes. "Have you ever been in Sharon DeBlass's apartment?"

A tough shell, he mused, but he was certain there would be something soft and hot beneath. He wondered if—no, when—he'd have the opportunity to uncover it.

"Not while she was a tenant," Roarke said as he sat back again. "And not at all that I recall, though it's certainly possible." He smiled again and fastened his own harness. "I own the Gorham Complex, as I'm sure you already know."

Idly, he glanced out the window as earth hurtled toward them. "Do you have transportation at the airport, Lieutenant, or can I give you a lift?"

CHAPTER

FOUR

Eve was more than tired by the time she filed her report for Whitney and returned home. She was pissed. She'd wanted, badly, to zing Roarke with the fact that she knew he owned the Gorham. His telling her in the same carelessly polite tone he used to offer her coffee had ended their first interview with him one point up.

She didn't like the score.

It was time to even things up. Alone in her living room, and technically off the clock, she sat down in front of her computer.

"Engage, Dallas, Code Five access. ID 53478Q. Open file DeBlass.

Voiceprint and ID recognized, Dallas. Proceed.

"Open subfile Roarke. Suspect Roarke—known to victim. According to Source C, Sebastian, victim desired suspect. Suspect met her requirements for sexual partner. Possibility of emotional involvement high.

"Opportunity to commit crime. Suspect owns victim's apartment building, equaling easy access and probably knowledge of security of murder scene. Suspect has no alibi for eight-hour period on the night of the murder, which includes the time span erased from security discs. Suspect owns large collection of antique weapons, including the type used on victim. Suspect admits to being expert marksman.

"Factor in personality of suspect. Aloof, confident, self-indulgent, highly intelligent. Interesting balance between aggressive and charming.

"Motive."

And there, she ran into trouble. Calculating, she rose, did a pass through the room while the computer waited for more data. Why would a man like Roarke kill? For gain, in passion? She didn't think so. Wealth and status he would, and could gain by other means. Women—for sex and otherwise—certainly he could win without breaking a sweat. She suspected he was capable of violence, and that he would execute it coldly.

Sharon DeBlass's murder had been charged with sex. There had been a crudeness overlaying it. Eve couldn't quite reconcile that with the elegant man she'd shared coffee with.

Perhaps that was the point.

"Suspect considers morality a personal rather than legislative area," she continued, pacing still. "Sex, weapon restriction, drug, tobacco, and alcohol restrictions, and murder deal with morality that has been outlawed or regulated. The murder of a licensed companion, the only daughter of friends, the only granddaughter of one of the country's most outspoken and conservative legislators, by a banned weapon. Was this an illustration of the flaws the suspect considers are inherent in the legal system?

"Motive," she concluded, settling again. "Self-indulgence." She took a deep, satisfied breath. "Compute probability."

Her system whined, reminded her it was one more piece of hardware that needed replacement, then settled into a jerky hum.

Probability Roarke perpetrator given current data and supposition, eighty-two point six percent.

Oh, it was possible, Eve thought, leaning back in her chair. There was a time, in the not so distant past, when a child could be gunned down by another child for the shoes on his feet.

What was that if not obscene self-indulgence?

He had the opportunity. He had the means. And if his own arrogance could be taken into account, he had the motive.

So why, Eve thought as she watched her own words blink on the monitor, as she studied her computer's impersonal analysis, couldn't she make it play in her own head?

She just couldn't see it, she admitted. She just couldn't visualize Roarke standing behind the camera, aiming the gun at the defenseless, naked, smiling woman, and pumping steel into her perhaps only moments after he'd pumped his seed into her.

Still, certain facts couldn't be overlooked. If she could gather enough of them, she could issue a warrant for a psychiatric evaluation.

Wouldn't that be interesting? she thought with a half smile. Traveling into Roarke's head would be a fascinating journey.

She'd take the next step at seven the following evening.

The buzz at her door brought a frown of annoyance to her eyes. "Save and lock on voiceprint, Dallas. Code Five. Disengage."

The monitor blipped off as she rose to see who was interrupting her. A glance at her security screen wiped the frown away.

"Hey, Mavis."

"You forgot, didn't you?" Mavis Freestone whirled in, a jangle of bracelets, a puff of scent. Her hair was a glittery silver tonight, a shade that would change with her next mood. She flipped it back where it sparkled like stars down to her impossibly tiny waist.

"No, I didn't." Eve shut the door, reengaged the locks. "Forgot what?"

"Dinner, dancing, debauchery." With a heavy sigh, Mavis dropped her slinkily attired nighty-eight pounds onto the sofa where she could eye Eve's simple gray suit with disdain. "You can't be going out in that."

Feeling drab, as she often did within twenty feet of Mavis's outrageous color, Eve looked down at her suit. "No, I guess not."

"So." Mavis gestured with one emerald-tipped finger. "You forgot."

She had, but she was remembering now. They had made plans to check out the new club Mavis had discovered at the space docks in Jersey. According to Mavis, the space jocks were perennially horny. Something to do with extended weightlessness.

"Sorry. You look great."

It was true, inevitably. Eight years before, when Eve had busted Mavis for petty theft, she'd looked great. A silk swirling street urchin with quick fingers and a brilliant smile.

In the intervening years, they'd somehow become friends. For Eve, who could count on one hand the number of friends she had who weren't cops, the relationship was precious.

"You look tired," Mavis said, more in accusation than sympathy. "And you're missing a button."

Eve's fingers went automatically to her jacket, felt the loose threads. "Shit. I knew it." In disgust she shrugged out of the jacket, tossed it aside. "Look, I'm sorry. I did forget. I had a lot on my mind today."

"Including the reason you needed my black coat?"

"Yeah, thanks. It came in handy."

Mavis sat a minute, tapping those emerald-tipped nails on the arm of the couch. "Police business. Here I was hoping you had a date. You really need to start seeing men who aren't criminals, Dallas."

"I saw that image consultant you fixed me up with. He wasn't a criminal. He was just an idiot."

"You're too picky—and that was six months ago."

Since he'd tried to get her in the sack by offering a free lip tattoo, Eve thought it was not nearly long enough, but kept the opinion to herself. "I'll go change."

"You don't want to go out and bump butts with the space boys." Mavis sprang up again, the shoulder-length crystals at her ears sparkling. "But go ahead and get out of that ugly skirt. I'll order Chinese."

Relief had Eve's shoulders sagging. For Mavis, she would have tolerated an evening at a loud, crowded, obnoxious club, peeling randy pilots and sex-starved sky station techs off her chest. The idea of eating Chinese with her feet up was like heaven.

"You don't mind?"

Mavis waved the words away as she tapped in the restaurant she wanted on the computer. "I spend every night in a club."

"That's work," Eve called out as she went into the bedroom.

"You're telling me." Tongue between her teeth, Mavis perused the menu on-screen. "A few years ago I'd have said singing for my supper was the world's biggest scam, the best grift I could run. Turns out I'm working harder than I ever did bilking tourists. You want egg rolls?"

"Sure. You're not thinking of quitting, are you?"

Mavis was silent a moment as she made her choices. "No. I'm hooked on applause." Feeling generous, she charged dinner to her World Card. "And since we renegotiated my contract so I get ten percent of the gate, I'm a regular businesswoman."

"There's nothing regular about you," Eve disagreed. She came back in, comfortable in jeans and a NYPSD sweatshirt.

"True. Got any of that wine I brought over last time?"

"Most of the second bottle." Because it sounded like the best idea she'd had all day, Eve detoured into the kitchen to pour it. "So, are you still seeing the dentist?"

"Nope." Idly, Mavis wandered to the entertainment unit and programmed in music. "It was getting too intense. I didn't mind him falling in love with my teeth, but he decided to go for the whole package. He wanted to get married."

"The bastard."

"You can't trust anybody," Mavis agreed. "How's the law and order business?"

"It's a little intense right now." She glanced up from the wine she was pouring when the buzzer sounded. "That can't be dinner already." Even as she said it, she heard Mavis clipping cheerfully toward the door in her five-inch spikes. "Check the security screen," she said quickly and was halfway to the door herself when Mavis pulled it open.

She had one moment to curse, another to reach for the weapon she wasn't wearing. Then Mavis's quick, flirtatious laugh had her adrenaline draining again.

Eve recognized the uniform of the delivery company, saw nothing but embarrassed pleasure in the young, fresh face of the boy who handed the package to Mavis.

"I just love presents," Mavis said with a flutter of her silver-tipped lashes as the boy backed away, blushing. "Don't you come with it?"

"Leave the kid alone." With a shake of her head, Eve took the package from Mavis and closed the door again.

"They're so cute at that age." She blew a kiss at the security screen before turning to Eve. "What are you so nervous about, Dallas?"

"The case I'm working on has me jumpy, I guess." She eyed the gold foil and elaborate bow on the package she held with more suspicion than pleasure. "I don't know who'd be sending me anything."

"There's a card," Mavis pointed out dryly. "You could always read it. There might be a clue."

"Now look who's cute." Eve tugged the card out of its gold envelope.

Roarke

As she read over Eve's shoulder, Mavis let out a low whistle. "Not *the* Roarke! The incredibly wealthy, fabulous to look at, sexily mysterious Roarke who owns approximately twenty-eight percent of the world, and its satellites?"

All Eve felt was irritation. "He's the only one I know."

"You know him." Mavis rolled her green shadowed eyes. "Dallas, I've underestimated you unforgivably. Tell me everything. How, when, why? Did you sleep with him? Tell me you slept with him, then give me every tiny detail."

"We've had a secret, passionate affair for the last three years, during which time I bore him a son who's being raised on the far side of the moon by Buddhist monks." Brows knit, Eve shook the box. "Get a grip, Mavis. It has to do with a case, and," she added before Mavis could open her mouth, "it's confidential."

Mavis didn't bother to roll her eyes again. When Eve said *confidential,* no amount of cajoling, pleading or whining could budge her an inch. "Okay, but you can tell me if he looks as good in person as he does in pictures."

"Better," Eve muttered.

"Jesus, really?" Mavis moaned and let herself fall onto the sofa. "I think I just had an orgasm."

"You ought to know." Eve set the package down, scowled at it. "And how did he know where I live? You can't pluck a cop's address out of the directory file. How did he know?" she repeated quietly. "And what's he up to?"

"For God's sake, Dallas, open it. He probably took a shine to you. Some men find the cool, disinterested, and understated attractive. Makes them think you're deep. I bet it's diamonds," Mavis said, pouncing on the box as her patience snapped. "A necklace. A diamond necklace. Maybe rubies. You'd look sensational in rubies."

She ripped ruthlessly through the pricey paper, tossed aside the lid of the box, and plunged her hand through the gold-edged tissue. "What the hell is this?"

But Eve had already scented it, already—despite herself—begun to smile. "It's coffee," she murmured, unaware of the way her voice softened as she reached for the simple brown bag Mavis held.

"Coffee." Illusions shattered, Mavis stared. "The man's got more money than God, and he sends you a bag of coffee?"

"Real coffee."

"Oh, well then." In disgust, Mavis waved a hand. "I don't care what the damn stuff costs a pound, Dallas. A woman wants glitter."

Eve brought the bag to her face and sniffed deep. "Not this woman. The son of a bitch knew just how to get to me." She sighed. "In more ways than one."

Eve treated herself to one precious cup the next morning. Even her temperamental AutoChef hadn't been able to spoil the dark, rich flavor. She drove to the station, with her faulty heater, under sleeting skies, in a wild chill that came in just under five degrees, with a smile on her face.

It was still there when she walked into her office and found Feeney waiting for her.

"Well, well." He studied her. "What'd you have for breakfast, ace?"

"Nothing but coffee. Just coffee. Got anything for me?"

"Ran a full check on Richard DeBlass, Elizabeth Barrister, and the rest of the clan." He handed her a disc marked Code Five in bold red. "No real surprises. Nothing much out of the ordinary on Rockman, either. In his twenties, he belonged to a paramilitary group known as SafeNet."

"SafeNet," Eve repeated, brow wrinkling.

"You'd have been about eight when it was disbanded, kid," Feeney told her with a smirk. "Should have heard of it in your history lessons."

"Rings a distant bell. Was that one of the groups that got worked up when we had that skirmish with China?"

"It was, and if they'd had their way, it would have been a lot more than a skirmish. A disagreement over international space could have gotten ugly. But the diplomats managed to fight that war before they could. Few years later, they were disbanded, though there are rumors on and off about a faction of SafeNet going underground."

"I've heard of them. Still hear about them. You think Rockman's involved with a fanatic splinter group like that?"

It only took Feeney a moment to shake his head. "I think he watches his step. Power reflects power, and DeBlass has plenty. If he ever gets into the White House, Rockman would be right beside him."

"Please." Eve pressed a hand to her stomach. "You'll give me nightmares."

"It's a long shot, but he's got some backing for the next election." Feeney moved his shoulders.

"Rockman's alibied, anyway. By DeBlass. They were in East Washington." She sat. "Anything else?"

"Charles Monroe. He's had an interesting life, nothing shady that shows. I'm working on the victim's logs. You know, sometimes if you're careless in altering files, you leave shadows floating. Seems to me somebody just kills a woman could get careless."

"You find a shadow, Feeney, clear away the gray, and I'll buy you a case of that lousy whiskey you like."

"Deal. I'm still working on Roarke," he added. "There's a guy who isn't careless. Every time I think I've gotten over one wall of security, I hit another. Whatever data there is on him is well guarded."

"Keep scaling those walls. I'll try digging under them."

When Feeney left, Eve shifted to her terminal. She hadn't wanted to check in front of Mavis, and preferred, in this case, using her office unit. The question was simple.

Eve entered the name and address of her apartment complex. Asked: Owner?

And so the answer was simple: Roarke.

Lola Starr's license for sex was only three months old. She'd applied for it on her eighteenth birthday, the earliest possible date. She liked to tell her friends she'd been an amateur until then.

It was the same day she'd left her home in Toledo, the same day she'd changed her name from Alice Williams. Both home and name had been far too boring for Lola.

She had a cute, pixie face. She'd nagged and begged and wept until her parents had agreed to buy her a more pointed chin and a tip-tilted nose for her sixteenth birthday.

Lola had wanted to look like a sexy elf and thought she'd succeeded. Her hair was coal black, cut in short, sassy spikes. Her skin was milk white and firm. She was saving for enough money to have her eyes changed from brown to emerald green, which she thought would suit her image better. But she'd been lucky enough to have been born with a lush little body that needed no more than basic maintenance.

She'd wanted to be a licensed companion all of her life. Other girls might have dreamed of careers in law or finance, studied their way into medicine or industry. But Lola had always known she was born for sex.

And why not make a living from what you did best?

She wanted to be rich and desired and pampered. The desire part she found easy. Men, particularly older men, were willing to pay well for someone with Lola's attributes. But the expenses of her profession were more stringent than she'd anticipated when she'd dreamed away in her pretty room in Toledo.

The licensing fees, the mandatory health exams, the rent, and sin tax all ate into profits. Once she'd finished paying for her training, she'd only had enough left to afford a small, one-room apartment at the ragged edges of Prostitute Walk.

Still, it was better than working the streets as many still did. And Lola had plans for bigger and better things.

One day she'd live in a penthouse and take only the cream of clients. She'd be wined and dined in the best restaurants, jetted to exotic places to entertain royalty and wealth.

She was good enough, and she didn't intend to stay at the bottom of the ladder for long.

The tips helped. A professional wasn't supposed to accept cash or credit bonuses. Not technically. But everyone did. She was still girl enough to prefer the pretty little gifts some of her clients offered. But she banked the money religiously and dreamed of her penthouse.

Tonight, she was going to entertain a new client, one who had requested she call him Daddy. She'd agreed, and had waited until the arrangements were made before she allowed herself a smirk. The guy probably thought he was the first one to want her to be his little girl. The fact was, after only a few short months on the job, pedophilia was rapidly becoming her specialty.

So, she'd sit on his lap, let him spank her, while telling her solemnly that she needed to be punished. Really, it was like playing a game, and most of the men were kind of sweet.

With that in mind, she chose a flirty skirted dress with a scalloped white collar. Beneath she wore nothing but white stockings. She'd removed her pubic hair, and was as bare and smooth as a ten-year-old.

After studying the reflection, she added a bit more color to her cheeks and clear gloss on her pouty lips.

At the knock on the door she grinned, and her young and still guileless face grinned back in the mirror.

She couldn't yet afford video security, and used the Judas hole to check her visitor.

He was handsome, which pleased her. And, she assumed, old enough to be her father, which would please him.

She opened the door, aimed a shy, coy smile. "Hi, Daddy."

He didn't want to waste time. It was the one asset he had little of at the moment. He smiled at her. For a whore, she was a pretty little thing. When the door was shut at his back, he reached under her skirt and was pleased to find her naked. It would speed matters along if he could become aroused quickly.

"Daddy!" Playing her part, Lola let out a shrieking giggle. "That's naughty."

"I've heard you've been naughty." He removed his coat and set it neatly aside while she pouted at him. Though he'd taken the precaution of clear sealing his hands, he would touch nothing in the room but her.

"I've been good, Daddy. Very good."

"You've been naughty, little girl." From his pocket he took a small video camera, which he set up, aimed toward the narrow bed she'd piled with pillows and stuffed animals.

"Are you going to take pictures?"

"That's right."

She'd have to tell him that would cost him extra, but decided to wait until the deed was done. Clients didn't care to have their fantasies broken with reality. She'd learned that in training.

"Go lie down on the bed."

"Yes, Daddy." She lay among the pillows and grinning animals.

"I've heard you've been touching yourself."

"No, Daddy."

"It isn't good to tell lies to your daddy. I have to punish you, but then I'll kiss it and make it better." When she smiled, he walked to the bed. "Lift your skirt, little girl, and show me how you touched yourself."

Lola didn't care for this part. She liked being touched, but the feel of her own hands brought her little excitement. Still, she lifted her skirt, stroked herself, keeping her movements shy and hesitant as she expected he wanted.

It excited him, the glide of her small fingers. After all, that was what a woman was made for. To use herself, to use the men who wanted her.

"How does it feel?"

"Soft," she murmured. "You touch, Daddy. Feel how soft."

He laid a hand over hers, felt himself harden satisfactorily as he slipped a finger inside her. It would be quick, for both of them.

"Unbutton your dress," he ordered, and continued to manipulate her as she opened it from its prim collar down. "Turn over."

When she did, he brought his hand down on her pert bottom in smart slaps that reddened the creamy flesh while she whimpered in programmed response.

It didn't matter if he hurt her or not. She'd sold herself to him.

"That's a good girl." He was fully erect now, beginning to throb. Still, his movements were careful and precise as he undressed. Naked, he straddled her, slipped his hands beneath her so that he could squeeze her breasts. So young, he thought, and let himself shudder from the pleasure of flesh that had yet to need refining.

"Daddy's going to show you how he rewards good girls."

He wanted her to take him into her mouth, but couldn't risk it. The birth control her file listed she used would eradicate his sperm vaginally, but not orally.

Instead, he vaulted up her hips, taking the time to stroke his hands over that firm, young flesh as he drove himself into her.

He was rougher than either of them expected. After that first violent thrust, he held himself back. He had no wish to hurt her to the point where she would cry out. Though in a place such as this, he doubted anyone would notice or care.

Still, she was rather charmingly unskilled and naive. He settled on a slower, more gentle rhythm, which he discovered drew out his own pleasure.

She moved well, meeting him, matching him. Unless he was very mistaken, not all her groans and cries were simulated. He felt her tense, shudder, and he smiled, pleased that he'd been able to bring a whore to a genuine climax.

He closed his eyes and let himself come.

She sighed and cuddled into one of the pillows. It had been good, much, much better than she'd expected. And she hoped she'd found another regular.

"Was I a good girl, Daddy?"

"A very, very good girl. But we're not done. Roll over."

As she shifted, he rose and moved out of camera range. "Are we going to watch the video, Daddy?"

He only shook his head.

Remembering her role, she pouted. "I like videos. We can watch, and then you can show me how to be a good girl again." She smiled at him, hoping for a bonus. "I could touch you this time. I'd like to touch you."

He smiled and took the SIG 210 with silencer out of his coat pocket. He watched her blink in curiosity as he aimed the gun.

"What's that? Is it a toy for me to play with?"

He shot her in the head first, the weapon barely making more than a pop as she jerked back. Coolly, he shot again, between those young, firm breasts, and last, as the silencer eroded, into her smooth, bare pubis.

Switching the camera off, he arranged her carefully among blood-soaked pillows and soiled, smiling animals while she stared up at him in wide-eyed surprise.

"It was no life for a young girl," he told her gently, then went back to the camera to record the last scene.

FIVE

All Eve wanted was a candy bar. She'd spent most of the day testify- ing in court, and her lunch break had been eaten up by a call from a snitch that had cost her fifty dollars and gained her a slim lead on a smuggling case that had resulted in two homicides, which she'd been beating her head against for two months.

All she wanted was a quick hit of sugar substitute before she headed home to prep for her seven o'clock meeting with Roarke.

She could have zipped through any number of drive-through InstaStores, but she preferred the little deli on the corner of West Seventy-eighth—despite, or perhaps because of the fact that it was owned and ran by Francois, a rude, snake-eyed refugee who'd fled to America after the Social Reform Army had overthrown the French government some forty years before.

He hated America and Americans, and the SRA had been dispatched within six months of the coup, but Francois remained, bitching and complaining behind the counter of the Seventy-eighth Street deli where he enjoyed dispensing insults and political absurdities.

Eve called him Frank to annoy him, and dropped in at least once a week to see what scheme he'd devised to try to short credit her.

Her mind on the candy bar, she stepped through the automatic door. It had no more than begun to whisper shut behind her when instinct kicked in.

The man standing at the counter had his back to her, his heavy, hooded jacket masking all but his size, and that was impressive.

Six-five, she estimated, easily two-fifty. She didn't need to see Francois's thin, terrified face to know there was trouble. She could smell it, as ripe and sour as the vegetable hash that was today's special.

In the seconds it took the door to clink shut, she'd considered and rejected the idea of drawing her weapon.

"Over here, bitch. Now."

The man turned. Eve saw he had the pale gold complexion of a multiracial heritage and the eyes of a very desperate man. Even as she filed the description, she looked at the small round object he held in his hand.

The homemade explosive device was worry enough. The fact that it shook as the hand that held it trembled with nerves was a great deal worse.

Homemade boomers were notoriously unstable. The idiot was likely to kill all of them by sweating too freely.

She shot Francois a quick, warning look. If he called her lieutenant, they were all going to be meat very quickly. Keeping her hands in plain sight, she crossed to the counter.

"I don't want any trouble," she said, letting her voice tremble as nervously as the thief's hand. "Please, I got kids at home."

"Shut up. Just shut up. Down on the floor. Down on the fucking floor."

Eve knelt, slipping a hand under her jacket where the weapon waited.

"All of it," the man ordered, gesturing with the deadly little ball. "I want all of it. Cash, credit tokens. Make it fast."

"It's been a slow day," Francois whined. "You must understand business is not what it was. You Americans—"

"You want to eat this?" the man invited, shoving the explosive in Francois's face.

"No, no." Panicked, Francois punched in the security code with his shaking fingers. As the till opened, Eve saw the thief glance at the money inside, then up at the camera that was busily recording the entire transaction.

She saw it in his face. He knew his image was locked there, and that all the money in New York wouldn't erase it. The explosive would, tossed carelessly over his shoulder as he raced out to the street to be swallowed in traffic.

She sucked in a breath, like a diver going under. She came up hard, under his arm. The solid jolt had the device flying free. Screams, curses, prayers. She caught it in her fingertips, a high fly, shagged with two men out and the bases loaded. Even as she closed her hand around it, the thief swung out.

It was the back of his hand rather than a fist, and Eve considered herself lucky. She saw stars as she hit a stand of soy chips, but she held on to the homemade boomer.

Wrong hand, goddamn it, wrong hand, she had time to think as the stand collapsed under her. She tried to use her left to free her weapon, but the two hundred and fifty pounds of fury and desperation fell on her.

"Hit the alarm, you asshole," she shouted as Francois stood like a statue with his mouth opening and closing. "Hit the fucking alarm." Then she grunted as the blow to her ribs stole her breath. This time he'd used his fist.

He was weeping now, scratching and clawing up her arm in an attempt to reach the explosive. "I need the money. I got to have it. I'll kill you. I'll kill you all."

She managed to bring her knee up. The age-old defense bought her a few seconds, but lacked the power to debilitate.

She saw stars again as her head smacked sharply into the side of a counter. Dozens of the candy bars she'd craved rained down on her.

"You son of a bitch. You son of a bitch." She heard herself saying it, over and over as she landed three hard short arm blows to his face. Blood spurting from his nose, he grabbed her arm.

And she knew it was going to break. Knew she would feel that sharp, sweet pain, hear the thin crack as bone fractured.

But just as she drew in breath to scream, as her vision began to gray with agony, his weight was off her.

The ball still cupped in her hand, she rolled over onto her haunches, struggling to breathe and fighting the need to retch. From that position she saw the shiny black shoes that always said beat cop.

"Book him." She coughed once, painfully. "Attempted robbery, armed, carrying an explosive, assault." She'd have liked to have added assaulting an officer and resisting arrest, but as she hadn't identified herself, she'd be skirting the line.

"You all right, ma'am? Want the MTs?"

She didn't want the medi-techs. She wanted a fucking candy bar. "Lieutenant," she corrected, pushing herself up and reaching for her ID. She noted that the perp was in restraints and that one of the two cops had been wise enough to use his stunner to take the fight out of him.

"We need a safe box—quick." She watched both cops pale as they saw what she held in her hand. "This little boomer's had quite a ride. Let's get it neutralized."

"Sir." The first cop was out of the store in a flash. In the ninety seconds it took him to return with the black box used for transporting and deactivating explosives, no one spoke.

They hardly breathed.

"Book him," Eve repeated. The moment the explosive was contained, her stomach muscles began to tremble. "I'll transmit my report. You guys with the Hundred and twenty-third?"

"You bet, Lieutenant."

"Good job." She reached down, favoring her injured arm and chose a Galaxy bar that hadn't been flattened by the wrestling match. "I'm going home."

"You didn't pay for that," Francois shouted after her.

"Fuck you, Frank," she shouted back and kept going.

The incident put her behind schedule. By the time she reached Roarke's mansion, it was 7:10. She'd used over-the-counter medication to ease the pain in her arm and shoulder. If it wasn't better in a couple of days, she knew she'd have to go in for an exam. She hated doctors.

She parked the car and spent a moment studying Roarke's house. Fortress, more like, she thought. Its four stories towered over the frosted trees of Central Park. It was one of the old buildings, close to two hundred years old, built of actual stone, if her eyes didn't deceive her.

There was lots of glass, and lights burning gold behind the windows. There was also a security gate, behind which evergreen shrubs and elegant trees were artistically arranged.

Even more impressive than the magnificence of architecture and landscaping was the quiet. She heard no city noises here. No traffic snarls, no pedestrian chaos. Even the sky overhead was subtly different than the one she was accustomed to farther downtown. Here, you could actually see stars rather than the glint and gleam of transports.

Nice life if you can get it, she mused, and started her car again. She approached the gate, prepared to identify herself. She saw the tiny red eye of a scanner blink, then hold steady. The gates opened soundlessly.

So, he'd programmed her in, she thought, unsure if she was amused or uneasy. She went through the gate, up the short drive, and left her car at the base of granite steps.

A butler opened the door for her. She'd never actually seen a butler outside of old videos, but this one didn't disappoint the fantasy. He was silver haired, implacably eyed and dressed in a dark suit and ruthlessly knotted old-fashioned tie.

"Lieutenant Dallas."

There was an accent, a faint one that sounded British and Slavic at once. "I have an appointment with Roarke."

"He's expecting you." He ushered her into a wide, towering hallway that looked more like the entrance to a museum than a home.

There was a chandelier of star-shaped glass dripping light onto a glossy wood floor that was graced by a boldly patterned rug in shades of red and teal. A stairway curved away to the left with a carved griffin for its newel post.

There were paintings on the walls—the kind she had once seen on a school field trip to the Met. French Impressionists from what century she couldn't quite recall. The Revisited Period that had come into being in the early twenty-first century complemented them with their pastoral scenes and gloriously muted colors.

No holograms or living sculpture. Just paint and canvas.

"May I take your coat?"

She brought herself back and thought she caught a flicker of smug condescension in those inscrutable eyes. Eve shrugged out of her jacket, watched him take the leather somewhat gingerly between his manicured fingers.

Hell, she'd gotten most of the blood off it.

"This way, Lieutenant Dallas. If you wouldn't mind waiting in the parlor, Roarke is detained on a transpacific call."

"No problem."

The museum quality continued there. A fire was burning sedately. A fire out of genuine logs in a hearth carved from lapis and malachite. Two lamps burned with light like colored gems. The twin sofas had curved backs and lush upholstery that echoed the jewel tones of the room in sapphire. The furniture was wood, polished to an almost painful gloss. Here and there objets d'art were arranged. Sculptures, bowls, faceted glass.

Her boots clicked over wood, then muffled over carpet.

"Would you like a refreshment, Lieutenant?"

She glanced back, saw with amusement that he continued to hold her jacket between his fingers like a soiled rag. "Sure. What have you got, Mr.—?"

"Summerset, Lieutenant. Simply Summerset, and I'm sure we can provide you with whatever suits your taste."

"She's fond of coffee," Roarke said from the doorway, "but I think she'd like to try the Montcart forty-nine."

Summerset's eyes flickered again, with horror, Eve thought. "The forty-nine, sir?"

"That's right. Thank you, Summerset."

"Yes, sir." Dangling the jacket, he exited, stiff-spined.

"Sorry I kept you waiting," Roarke began, then his eyes narrowed, darkened.

"No problem," Eve said as he crossed to her. "I was just . . . Hey—"

She jerked her chin as his hand cupped it, but his fingers held firm, turning her left cheek to the light. "Your face is bruised." His voice was cool on the statement, icily so. His eyes as they flicked over the injury betrayed nothing.

But his fingers were warm, tensed, and jolted something in her gut. "A scuffle over a candy bar," she said with a shrug.

His eyes met hers, held just an instant longer than comfortable. "Who won?"

"I did. It's a mistake to come between me and food."

"I'll keep that in mind." He released her, dipped the hand that had touched her into his pocket. Because he wanted to touch her again. It worried him that he wanted, very much, to stroke away the bruise that marred her cheek. "I think you'll approve of tonight's menu."

"Menu? I didn't come here to eat, Roarke. I came here to look over your collection."

"You'll do both." He turned when Summerset brought in a tray that held an uncorked bottle of wine the color of ripened wheat and two crystal glasses.

"The forty-nine, sir."

"Thank you. I'll pour out." He spoke to Eve as he did so. "I thought this vintage would suit you. What it lacks in subtlety . . ." He turned back, offering her a glass. "It makes up for in sensuality." He tapped his glass against hers so the crystal sang, then watched as she sipped.

God, what a face, he thought. All those angles and expressions, all that emotion and control. Just now she was fighting off showing both surprise and pleasure as the taste of the wine settled on her tongue. He was looking forward to the moment when the taste of her settled on his.

"You approve?" he asked.

"It's good." It was the equivalent of sipping gold.

"I'm glad. The Montcart was my first venture into wineries. Shall we sit and enjoy the fire?"

It was tempting. She could almost see herself sitting there, legs angled toward the fragrant heat, sipping wine as the jeweled light danced.

"This isn't a social call, Roarke. It's a murder investigation."

"Then you can investigate me over dinner." He took her arm, lifting a brow as she stiffened. "I'd think a woman who'd fight for a candy bar would appreciate a two-inch fillet, medium rare."

"Steak?" She struggled not to drool. "Real steak, from a cow?"

A smile curved his lips. "Just flown in from Montana. The steak, not the cow." When she continued to hesitate, he tilted his head. "Come now, Lieutenant, I doubt if a little red meat will clog your considerable investigative skills."

"Someone tried to bribe me the other day," she muttered, thinking of Charles Monroe and his black silk robe.

"With?"

"Nothing as interesting as steak." She aimed one long, level look. "If the evidence points in your direction, Roarke, I'm still bringing you down."

"I'd expect nothing less. Let's eat."

He led her into the dining room. More crystal, more gleaming wood, yet another shimmering fire, this time cupped in rose-veined marble. A woman in a black suit served them appetizers of shrimp swimming in creamy sauce. The wine was brought in, their glasses topped off.

Eve, who rarely gave a thought to her appearance, wished she'd worn something more suitable to the occasion than jeans and a sweater.

"So, how'd you get rich?" she asked him.

"Various ways." He liked to watch her eat, he discovered. There was a single-mindedness to it.

"Name one."

"Desire," he said, and let the word hum between them.

"Not good enough." She picked up her wine again, meeting his eyes straight on. "Most people want to be rich."

"They don't want it enough. To fight for it. Take risks for it."

"But you did."

"I did. Being poor is . . . uncomfortable. I like comfort." He offered her a roll from a silver bowl as their salads were served—crisp greens tossed with delicate herbs. "We're not so different, Eve."

"Yeah, right."

"You wanted to be a cop enough to fight for it. To take risks for it. You find the breaking of laws uncomfortable. I make money, you make justice. Neither is a simple matter." He waited a moment. "Do you know what Sharon DeBlass wanted?"

Her fork hesitated, then pierced a tender shoot of endive that had been plucked only an hour before. "What do you think she wanted?"

"Power. Sex is often a way to gain it. She had enough money to be comfortable, but she wanted more. Because money is also power. She wanted power over her clients, over herself, and most of all, she wanted power over her family."

Eve set her fork down. In the firelight, the dancing glow of candle and crystal, he looked dangerous. Not because a woman would fear him, she thought, but because she would desire him. Shadows played in his eyes, making them unreadable.

"That's quite an analysis of a woman you claim you hardly knew."

"It doesn't take long to form an opinion, particularly if that person is obvious. She didn't have your depth, Eve, your control, or your rather enviable focus."

"We're not talking about me." No, she didn't want him to talk about her—or to look at her in quite that way. "Your opinion is that she was hungry for power. Hungry enough to be killed before she could take too big a bite?"

"An interesting theory. The question would be, too big a bite of what? Or whom?"

The same silent servant cleared the salads, brought in oversized china plates heavy with sizzling meat and thin, golden slices of grilled potatoes.

Eve waited until they were alone again, then cut into her steak. "When a man accumulates a great deal of money, possessions, and status, he then has a great deal to lose."

"Now we're speaking of me—another interesting theory." He sat there, his eyes interested, yet still amused. "She threatened me with some sort of blackmail and, rather than pay or dismiss her as ridiculous, I killed her. Did I sleep with her first?"

"You tell me," Eve said evenly.

"It would fit the scenario, considering her choice of profession. There may be a blackout on the press on this particular case, but it takes little deductive power to conclude sex reared its head. I had her, then I shot her . . . if one subscribes to the theory." He took a bite of steak, chewed, swallowed. "There's a problem, however."

"Which is?"

"I have what you might consider an old-fashioned quirk. I dislike brutalizing women, in any form."

"It's old-fashioned in that it would be more apt to say you dislike brutalizing people, in any form."

He moved those elegant shoulders. "As I say, it's a quirk. I find it distasteful to look at you and watch the candlelight shift over a bruise on your face."

He surprised her by reaching out, running a finger down the mark, very gently.

"I believe I would have found it even more distasteful to kill Sharon DeBlass." He dropped his hand and went back to his meal. "Though I have, occasionally, been known to do what is distasteful to me. When necessary. How is your dinner?"

"It's fine." The room, the light, the food, was all more than fine. It was like sitting in another world, in another time. "Who the hell are you, Roarke?"

He smiled and topped off their glasses. "You're the cop. Figure it out."

She would, she promised herself. By God she would, before it was done. "What other theories do you have about Sharon DeBlass?"

"None to speak of. She liked excitement and risk and didn't flinch from causing those who loved her embarrassment. Yet she was . . ."

Intrigued, Eve leaned closer. "What? Go ahead, finish."

"Pitiable," he said, in a tone that made Eve believe he meant no more and no less that just that. "There was something sad about her under all that bright, bright gloss. Her body was the only thing about herself she respected. So she used it to give pleasure and to cause pain."

"And did she offer it to you?"

"Naturally, and assumed I'd accept the invitation."

"Why didn't you?"

"I've already explained that. I can elaborate and add that I prefer a different type of bedmate, and that I prefer to make my own moves."

There was more, but he chose to keep it to himself.

"Would you like more steak, Lieutenant?"

She glanced down, saw that she'd all but eaten the pattern off the plate. "No. Thanks."

"Dessert?"

She hated to turn it down, but she'd already indulged herself enough. "No. I want to look at your collection."

"Then we'll save the coffee and dessert for later." He rose, offered a hand.

Eve merely frowned at it and pushed back from the table. Amused, Roarke gestured toward the doorway and led her back into the hall, up the curving stairs.

"It's a lot of house for one guy."

"Do you think so? I'm more of the opinion that your apartment is small for one woman." When she stopped dead at the top of the stairs, he grinned. "Eve, you know I own the building. You'd have checked after I sent my little token."

"You ought to have someone out to look at the plumbing," she told him. "I can't keep the water hot in the shower for more than ten minutes."

"I'll make a note of it. Next flight up."

"I'm surprised you don't have elevators," she commented as they climbed again.

"I do. Just because I prefer the stairs doesn't mean the staff shouldn't have a choice."

"And staff," she continued. "I haven't seen one remote domestic in the place."

"I have a few. But I prefer people to machines, most of the time. Here."

He used a palm scanner, coded in a key, then opened carved double doors. The sensor switched on the lights as they crossed the threshold. Whatever she'd been expecting, it hadn't been this.

It was a museum of weapons: guns, knives, swords, crossbows.

Armor was displayed, from medieval ages to the thin, impenetrable vests that were current military issue. Chrome and steel and jeweled handles winked behind glass, shimmered on the walls.

If the rest of the house seemed another world, perhaps a more civilized one than what she knew, this veered jarringly in the other direction. A celebration of violence.

"Why?" was all she could say.

"It interests me, what humans have used to damage humans through history." He crossed over, touching a wickedly toothed ball that hung from a chain. "Knights farther back than Arthur carried these into jousts and battles. A thousand years . . ." He pressed a series of buttons on a display cabinet and took out a sleek, palm-sized weapon, the preferred killing tool of twenty-first century street gangs during the Urban Revolt. "And we have something less cumbersome and equally lethal. Progression without progress."

He put the weapon back, closed and secured the case. "But you're interested in something newer than the first, and older than the second. You said a thirty-eight, Smith & Wesson. Model Ten."

It was a terrible room, she thought. Terrible and fascinating. She stared at him across it, realizing that the elegant violence suited him perfectly.

"It must have taken years to collect all of this."

"Fifteen," he said as he walked across the uncarpeted floor to another section. "Nearly sixteen now. I acquired my first handgun when I was nineteen—from the man who was aiming it at my head."

He frowned. He hadn't meant to tell her that.

"I guess he missed," Eve commented as she joined him.

"Fortunately, he was distracted by my foot in his crotch. It was a nine-millimeter Baretta semiautomatic he'd smuggled out of Germany. He thought to use it to relieve me of the cargo I was delivering to him and save the transportation fee. In the end, I had the fee, the cargo, and the Baretta. And so, Roarke Industries was born out of his poor judgment. The one you're interested in," he added, pointing as the wall display opened. "You'll want to take it, I imagine, to see if it's been fired recently, check for prints, and so forth."

She nodded slowly while her mind worked. Only four people knew the murder weapon had been left at the scene. Herself, Feeney, the commander, and the killer. Roarke was either innocent or very, very clever.

She wondered if he could be both.

"I appreciate your cooperation." She took an evidence seal out of her shoulder bag and reached for the weapon that matched the one already in police possession. It took her only a heartbeat to realize it wasn't the one Roarke had pointed to.

Her eyes slid to his, held. Oh, he was watching her all right, carefully. Though she let her hand hesitate now over her selection, she thought they understood each other. "Which?"

"This." He tapped the display just under the .38. Once she'd sealed it and slipped it into her bag, he closed the glass. "It's not loaded, of course, but I do have ammo, if you'd like to take a sample."

"Thanks. Your cooperation will be noted in my report."

"Will it?" He smiled, took a box out of a drawer, and offered it. "What else will be noted, Lieutenant?"

"Whatever is applicable." She added the box of ammo to her bag, took out a notebook, and punched in her ID number, the date, and a description of everything she'd taken. "Your receipt." She offered him the slip after the notebook spit it out. "These will be returned to you as quickly as possible unless they're called into evidence. You'll be notified one way or the other."

He tucked the paper into his pocket, fingered what else he'd tucked there. "The music room's in the next wing. We can have coffee and brandy there."

"I doubt we'd share the same taste in music, Roarke."

"You might be surprised," he murmured, "at what we share." He touched her cheek again, this time sliding his hand around until it cupped the back of her neck. "At what we will share."

She went rigid and lifted a hand to shove his arm away. He simply closed his fingers over her wrist. She could have had him flat on his back in a heartbeat—so she told herself. Still, she only stood there, the breath backing up in her lungs and her pulse throbbing hard and thick.

He wasn't smiling now.

"You're not a coward, Eve." He said it softly when his lips were an inch from hers. The kiss hovered there, a breath away until the hand she'd levered against his arm changed its grip. And she moved into him.

She didn't think. If she had, even for an instant, she would have known she was breaking all the rules. But she'd wanted to see, wanted to know. Wanted to feel.

His mouth was soft, more persuasive than possessive. His lips nibbled hers open so that he could slide his tongue over them, between them, to cloud her senses with flavor.

Heat gathered like a fireball in her lungs even before he touched her, those clever hands molding over the snug denim over her hips, slipping seductively under her sweater to flesh.

With a kind of edgy delight, she felt herself go damp.

It was the mouth, just that generous and tempting mouth he'd thought he'd wanted. But the moment he'd tasted it, he'd wanted all of her.

She was pressed against him; that tough, angular body beginning to vibrate. Her small, firm breast weighed gloriously in his palm. He could hear the hum of passion that sounded in her throat, all but taste it as her mouth moved eagerly on his.

He wanted to forget the patience and control he'd taught himself to live by, and just ravage.

Here. The violence of the need all but erupted inside him. Here and now.

He would have dragged her to the floor if she hadn't struggled back, pale and panting.

"This isn't going to happen."

"The hell it isn't," he shot back.

The danger was shimmering around him now. She saw it as clearly as she saw the tools of violence and death surrounding them.

There were men who negotiated when they wanted something. There were men who just took.

"Some of us aren't allowed to indulge ourselves."

"Fuck the rules, Eve."

He stepped toward her. If she had stepped back, he would have pursued, like any hunter after the prize. But she faced him squarely, and shook her head.

"I can't compromise a murder investigation because I'm physically attracted to a suspect."

"Goddamn it, I didn't kill her."

It was a shock to see his control snap. To hear the fury and frustration in his voice, to witness it wash vividly across his face. And it was terrifying to realize she believed him, and not be sure, not be absolutely certain if she believed because she needed to.

"It's not as simple as taking your word for it. I have a job to do, a responsibility to the victim, to the system. I have to stay objective, and I—"

Can't, she realized. Can't.

They stared at each other as the communicator in her bag began to beep.

Her hands weren't quite steady as she turned away, took the unit out. She recognized the code for the station on the display and entered her ID. After a deep breath, she answered the request for voiceprint verification.

"Dallas, Lieutenant Eve. No audio please, display only."

Roarke could just see her profile as she read the transmission. It was enough to measure the change in her eyes, the way they darkened, then went flat and cool.

She put the communicator away, and when she turned back to him, there was very little of the woman who'd vibrated in his arms in the woman who faced him now.

"I have to go. We'll be in touch about your property."

"You do that very well," Roarke murmured. "Slide right into the cop's skin. And it fits you perfectly."

"It better. Don't bother seeing me out. I can find my way."

"Eve."

She stopped at the doorway, looked back. There he was, a figure in black surrounded by eons of violence. Inside the cop's skin, the woman's heart stuttered.

"We'll see each other again."

She nodded. "Count on it."

He let her go, knowing Summerset would slip out of some shadow to give her the leather jacket, bid her good night.

Alone, Roarke took the gray fabric button from his pocket, the one he'd found on the floor of his limo. The one that had fallen from the jacket of that drab gray suit she'd worn the first time he'd seen her.

Studying it, knowing he had no intention of giving it back to her, he felt like a fool.

CHAPTER

SIX

A rookie was guarding the door to Lola Starr's apartment. Eve pegged him as such because he barely looked old enough to order a beer, his uniform looked as if it had just been lifted from the supply rack, and from the faint green cast of his skin.

A few months of working this neighborhood, and a cop stopped needing to puke at the sight of a corpse. Chemi-heads, the street LCs, and just plain bad asses liked to wale on each other along these nasty blocks as much for entertainment as for business profits. From the smell that had greeted her outside, someone had died out there recently, or the recycle trucks hadn't been through in the last week.

"Officer." She paused, flashed her badge. He'd gone on alert the moment she'd stepped out of the pitiful excuse for an elevator. Instinct warned her, rightly enough, that without the quick ID, she'd have been treated to a stun from the weapon his shaky hand was gripping.

"Sir." His eyes were spooked and unwilling to settle on one spot.

"Give me the status."

"Sir," he said again, and took a long unsteady breath. "The landlord flagged down my unit, said there was a dead woman in the apartment."

"And is there . . ." Her gaze flicked down to the name pinned over his breast pocket. "Officer Prosky?"

"Yes, sir, she's . . ." He swallowed, hard, and Eve could see the horror flit over his face again.

"And how did you determine the subject is terminated, Prosky? You take her pulse?"

A flush, no healthier than the green hue, tinted his cheeks. "No, sir. I followed procedure, preserved crime scene, notified headquarters. Visual confirmation of termination, the scene is uncorrupted."

"The landlord went in?" All of this she could learn later, but she could see that he was steadying as she forced him to go over the steps.

"No, sir, he says not. After a complaint by one of the victim's clients who had an appointment for nine P.M., the landlord checked the apartment. He unlocked the door and saw her. It's only one room, Lieutenant Dallas, and she's— You see her as soon as you open the door. Following the discovery, the landlord, in a state of panic, went down to the street and flagged down my patrol unit. I immediately accompanied him back to the scene, made visual confirmation of suspicious death, and reported in."

"Have you left your post, Officer? However briefly?"

His eyes settled finally, met hers. "No, sir, Lieutenant. I thought I'd have to, for a minute. It's my first, and I had some trouble maintaining."

"Looks like you maintained fine to me, Prosky." Out of the crime bag she'd brought up with her, she took out the protective spray, used it. "Make the calls to forensics and the ME. The room needs to be swept, and she'll need to be bagged and tagged."

"Yes, sir. Should I remain on post?"

"Until the first team gets here. Then you can report in." She finished coating her boots, glanced up at him. "You married, Prosky?" she asked as she snapped her recorder to her shirt.

"No, sir. Sort of engaged though."

"After you report in, go find your lady. The ones who go for the liquor don't last as long as the ones who have a nice warm body to lose it in. Where do I find the landlord?" she asked and turned the knob on the unsecured door.

"He's down in one-A."

"Then tell him to stay put. I'll take his statement when I'm done here."

She stepped inside, closed the door. Eve, no longer a rookie, didn't feel her stomach revolt at the sight of the body, the torn flesh, or the blood-splattered child's toys.

But her heart ached.

Then came the anger, a sharp red spear of it when she spotted the antique weapon cradled in the arms of a teddy bear.

"She was just a kid."

It was seven A.M. Eve hadn't been home. She'd caught one hour's rough and restless sleep at her office desk between computer searches and reports. Without a Code Five attached to Lola Starr, Eve was free to access the data banks of the International Resource Center on Criminal Activity. So far, IRCCA had come up empty on matches.

Now, pale with fatigue, jittery with the false energy of false caffeine, she faced Feeney.

"She was a pro, Dallas."

"Her fucking license was barely three months old. There were dolls on her bed. There was Kool-Aid in her kitchen."

She couldn't get past it—all those silly, girlish things she'd had to paw through while the victim's pitiful body lay on the cheap, fussy pillows and dolls. Enraged, Eve slapped one of the official photos onto her desk.

"She looks like she should have been leading cheers at the high school. Instead, she's running tricks and collecting pictures of fancy apartments and fancier clothes. You figure she knew what she was getting into?"

"I don't figure she thought she'd end up dead," Feeney said evenly. "You want to debate the sex codes, Dallas?"

"No." Wearily, she looked down at her hard copy again. "No, but it bums me, Feeney. A kid like this."

"You know better than that, Dallas."

"Yeah, I know better." She forced herself to snap back. "Autopsy should be in this morning, but my prelim puts her dead for twenty-four hours minimum at discovery. You've identified the weapon?"

"SIG two-ten—a real Rolls-Royce of handguns, about 1980, Swiss import. Silenced. Those old timey silencers were only good for a couple, three shots. He'd have needed it because the victim's place wasn't soundproofed like DeBlass's."

"And he didn't phone it in, which tells me he didn't want her found as quickly. Had to get himself someplace else," she mused. Thoughtful, she picked up a small square of paper, officially sealed.

TWO OF SIX

"One a week," she said softly. "Jesus Christ, Feeney, he isn't giving us much time."

"I'm running her logs, trick book. She had a new client scheduled, 8:00 P.M., night before last. If your prelim checks, he's our guy." Feeney smiled thinly. "John Smith."

"That's older than the murder weapon." She rubbed her hands hard over her face. "IRCCA's bound to spit our boy out from that tag."

"They're still running data," Feeney muttered. He was protective, even sentimental about the IRCCA.

"They're not going to find squat. We got us a time traveler, Feeney."

He snorted. "Yeah, a real Jules Verne."

"We've got a twentieth-century crime," she said through her hands. "The weapons, the excessive violence, the hand-printed note left on scene. So maybe our killer is some sort of historian, or buff anyway. Somebody who wishes things were what they used to be."

"Lots of people think things would be better some other way. That's why the world's lousy with theme parks."

Thinking, she dropped her hands. "IRCCA isn't going to help us get into this guy's head. It still takes a human mind to play that game. What's he doing, Feeney? Why's he doing it?"

"He's killing LCs."

"Hookers have always been easy targets, back to Jack the Ripper, right? It's a vulnerable job, even now with all the screening, we still get clients knocking LCs around, killing them."

"Doesn't happen much," Feeney mused. "Sometimes with the S and M trade you get a party that gets too enthusiastic. Most LCs are safer than teachers."

"They still run a risk, the oldest profession with the oldest crime. But things have changed, some things. People don't kill with guns as a rule anymore. Too expensive, too hard to come by. Sex isn't the strong motivator it used to be, too cheap, too easy to come by. We have different methods of investigation, and a whole new batch of motives. When you brush all that away, the one fact is that people still terminate people. Keep digging, Feeney. I've got people to talk to."

"What you need's some sleep, kid."

"Let him sleep," Eve muttered. "Let that bastard sleep." Steeling herself, she turned to her tele-link. It was time to contact the victim's parents.

By the time Eve walked into the sumptuous foyer of Roarke's mid-town office, she'd been up for more than thirty-two hours. She'd gotten through the misery of having to tell two shocked, weeping parents that their only daughter was dead. She'd stared at her monitor until the data swam in front of her eyes.

Her follow-up interview with Lola's landlord had been its own adventure. Since the man had had time to recover, he'd spent thirty minutes whining about the unpleasant publicity and the possibility of a drop-off in rentals.

So much, Eve thought, for human empathy.

Roarke Industries, New York, was very much what she'd expected. Slick, shiny, sleek, the building itself spread one hundred fifty stories into the Manhattan sky. It was an ebony lance, glossy as wet stone, ringed by transport tubes and diamond-bright skyways.

No tacky Glida-Grills on this corner, she mused. No street hawkers with their hot pocket PCs dodging security on their colorful air boards. Out-of-doors vending was off limits on this bite of Fifth. The zoning made things quieter, if a little less adventuresome.

Inside, the main lobby took up a full city block, boasting three tony restaurants, a high-priced boutique, a handful of specialty shops, and a small theater that played art films.

The white floor tiles were a full yard square and gleamed like the moon. Clear glass elevators zipped busily up and down, people glides zigzagged left and right, while disembodied voices guided visitors to various points of interest or, if there was business to be conducted, the proper office.

For those who wanted to wander about on their own, there were more than a dozen moving maps.

Eve marched to a monitor and was politely offered assistance.

"Roarke," she said, annoyed that his name hadn't been listed on the main directory.

"I'm sorry." The computer's voice was that overly mannered tone that was meant to be soothing, and instead grated on Eve's already raw nerves. "I'm not at liberty to access that information."

"Roarke," Eve repeated, holding up her badge for the computer to scan. She waited impatiently as the computer hummed, undoubtedly checking and verifying her ID, notifying the man himself.

"Please proceed to the east wing, Lieutenant Dallas. You will be met."

"Right."

Eve turned down a corridor, passed a marble run that held a forest of snowy white impatiens.

"Lieutenant." A woman in a killer red suit and hair as white as the impatiens smiled coolly. "Come with me, please."

The woman slipped a thin security card into a slot, laid her palm against a sheet of black glass for a handprint. The wall slid open, revealing a private elevator.

Eve stepped inside with her, and was unsurprised when her escort requested the top floor.

Eve had been certain Roarke would be satisfied with nothing but the top.

Her guide was silent on the ride up and exuded a discreet whiff of sensible scent that matched her sensible shoes and neat, sleek coif. Eve secretly admired women who put themselves together, top to toe, with such seeming effortlessness.

Faced with such quiet magnificence, she tugged self-consciously at her worn leather jacket and wondered if it was time she actually spent money on a haircut rather than hacking away at it herself.

Before she could decide on such earth-shattering matters, the doors whooshed open into a silent, white carpeted foyer the size of a small home. There were lush green plants—real plants: ficus, palm, what appeared to be a dogwood flowering off season. There was a sharp spicy scent from a bank of dianthus, blooming in shades of rose and vivid purple.

The garden surrounded a comfortable waiting area of mauve sofas and glossy wood tables, lamps that were surely solid brass with jewel-colored shades.

In the center of this was a circular workstation, equipped as efficiently as a cockpit with monitors and keyboards, gauges and tele-links. Two men and a woman worked at it busily, with a seamless ballet of competence in motion.

She was led past them into a glass-sided breezeway. A peek down, and she could see Manhattan. There was music piped in she didn't recognize as Mozart. For Eve, music began sometime after her tenth birthday.

The woman in the killer suit paused again, flashed her cool, perfect smile, then spoke into a hidden speaker. "Lieutenant Dallas, sir."

"Send her in, Caro. Thank you."

Again Caro pressed her palm to a slick black glass. "Go right in, Lieutenant," she invited as a panel slid open.

"Thanks." Out of curiosity, Eve watched her walk away, wondering how anyone could stride so gracefully on three-inch heels. She walked into Roarke's office.

It was, as she expected, as impressive as the rest of his New York headquarters. Despite the soaring, three-sided view of New York, the lofty ceiling with its pinprick lights, the vibrant tones of topaz and emerald in the thickly cushioned furnishings, it was the man behind the ebony slab desk that dominated.

What in hell was it about him? Eve thought again as Roarke rose and slanted a smile at her.

"Lieutenant Dallas," he said in that faint and fascinating Irish lilt, "a pleasure, as always."

"You might not think so when I'm finished."

He lifted a brow. "Why don't you come the rest of the way in and get started? Then we'll see. Coffee?"

"Don't try to distract me, Roarke." She walked closer. Then, to satisfy her curiosity, she took a brief turn around the room. It was as big as a heliport, with all the amenities of a first-class hotel: automated service bar, a padded relaxation chair complete with VR and mood settings, an oversized wall screen, currently blank. To the left, there was a full bath including whirl tub and drying tube. All the standard office equipment, of the highest high-tech, was built in.

Roarke watched her with a bland expression. He admired the way she moved, the way those cool, quick eyes took in everything.

"Would you like a tour, Eve?"

"No. How do you work with all this . . ." Using both hands, she gestured widely at the treated glass walls. "Open."

"I don't like being closed in. Are you going to sit, or prowl?"

"I'm going to stand. I have some questions to ask you, Roarke. You're entitled to have counsel present."

"Am I under arrest?"

"Not at the moment."

"Then we'll save the lawyers until I am. Ask."

Though she kept her eyes level on his, she knew where his hands were, tucked casually in the pockets of his slacks. Hands revealed emotions.

"Night before last," she said, "between the hours of eight and ten P.M. Can you verify your whereabouts?"

"I believe I was here until shortly after eight." With a steady hand he touched his desk log. "I shut down my monitor at eight-seventeen. I left the building, drove home."

"Drove," she interrupted, "or were driven?"

"Drove. I keep a car here. I don't believe in keeping my employees waiting on my whims."

"Damned democratic of you." And, she thought, damned inconvenient. She'd wanted him to have an alibi. "And then?"

"I poured myself a brandy, had a shower, changed. I had a late supper with a friend."

"How late, and what friend?"

"I believe I arrived at about ten. I like to be prompt. At Madeline Montmart's townhouse."

Eve had a quick vision of a curvy blonde with a sultry mouth and almond eyes. "Madeline Montmart, the actress?"

"Yes. I believe we had squab, if that's helpful."

She ignored the sarcasm. "No one can verify your movements between eight-seventeen and ten P.M.?"

"One of the staff might have noticed, but then, I pay them well and they're likely to say what I tell them to say." His voice took on an edge. "There's been another murder."

"Lola Starr, licensed companion. Certain details will be released to the media within the hour."

"And certain details will not."

"Do you own a silencer, Roarke?"

His expression didn't change. "Several. You look exhausted, Eve. Have you been up all night?"

"Goes with the job. Do you own a Swiss handgun, SIG two-ten, circa 1980?"

"I acquired one about six weeks ago. Sit down."

"Were you acquainted with Lola Starr?" Reaching into her briefcase, she pulled out a photo she'd found in Lola's apartment. The pretty, elfin girl beamed out, full of sassy fun.

Roarke lowered his gaze to it as it landed on his desk. His eyes flickered. This time his voice was tinged with something Eve thought sounded like pity.

"She isn't old enough to be licensed."

"She turned eighteen four months ago. Applied on her birthday."

"She didn't have time to change her mind, did she?" His eyes lifted to Eve's. And yes, it was pity. "I didn't know her. I don't use prostitutes—or children." He picked up the photo, skirted the desk, and offered it back to Eve. "Sit down."

"Have you ever—"

"Goddamn it, sit down." In sudden fury, he took her shoulders, pushed her into a chair. Her case tipped, spilling out photos of Lola that had nothing to do with sassy fun.

She might have reached them first—her reflexes were as good as his. Perhaps she wanted him to see them. Perhaps she needed him to.

Crouching, Roarke picked up a photo taken at the scene. He stared at it. "Christ Jesus," he said softly. "You believe I'm capable of this?"

"My beliefs aren't the issue. Investigating—" She broke off when his eyes whipped to hers.

"You believe I'm capable of this?" he repeated in an undertone that cut like a blade.

"No, but I have a job to do."

"Your job sucks."

She took the photos back, stored them. "From time to time."

"How do you sleep at night, after looking at something like this?"

She flinched. Though she recovered in a snap, he'd seen it. As intrigued as he was by her instinctive and emotional reaction, he was sorry he'd caused it.

"By knowing I'll take down the bastard who did it. Get out of my way."

He stayed where he was, laid a hand on her rigid arm. "A man in my position has to read people quickly and accurately, Eve. I'm reading you as someone close to the edge."

"I said, get out of my way."

He rose, but shifting his grip on her arm, pulled her to her feet. He was still in her way. "He'll do it again," Roarke said quietly. "And it's eating at you wondering when and where and who."

"Don't analyze me. We've got a whole department of shrinks on the payroll for that."

"Why haven't you been to see one? You've been slipping through loopholes to avoid Testing."

Her eyes narrowed.

He smiled, but there was no amusement in it.

"I have connections, Lieutenant. You were due in Testing several days ago, standard department procedure after a justifiable termination, one you executed the night Sharon was killed."

"Keep out of my business," she said furiously. "And fuck your connections."

"What are you afraid of? What are you afraid they'll find if they get a look inside of that head of yours? That heart of yours?"

"I'm not afraid of anything." She jerked her arm free, but he merely laid his hand on her cheek. A gesture so unexpected, so gentle, her stomach quivered.

"Let me help you."

"I—" Something nearly spilled out, as the photos had. But this time her reflexes kept it tucked away. "I'm handling it." She turned away. "You can pick up your property anytime after nine A.M. tomorrow."

"Eve."

She kept her eyes focused on the doorway, kept walking. "What?"

"I want to see you tonight."

"No."

He was tempted—very tempted—to lunge after her. Instead, he stayed where he was. "I can help you with the case."

Cautious, she stopped, turned back. If he hadn't been experiencing an uncomfortable twist of sexual frustration, he might have laughed aloud at the combination of suspicion and derision in her eyes.

"How?"

"I know people Sharon knew." As he spoke, he saw the derision alter to interest. But the suspicion remained. "It doesn't take a long mental leap to realize you'll be looking for a connection between Sharon and the girl whose photos you're carrying. I'll see if I can find one."

"Information from a suspect doesn't carry much weight in an investigation. But," she added before he could speak, "you can let me know."

He smiled after all. "Is it any wonder I want you naked, and in bed? I'll let you know, Lieutenant." And walked back behind his desk. "In the meantime, get some sleep."

When the door closed behind her, the smile went out of his eyes. For a long moment he sat in silence. Fingering the button he carried in his pocket, he engaged his private, secure line.

He didn't want this call on his log.

CHAPTER

SEVEN

Eve stepped up to the peep screen at Charles Monroe's door and started to announce herself when it slid open. He was in black tie, a cashmere cape swung negligently over his shoulders, offset by the cream of a silk scarf. His smile was every bit as well turned out as his wardrobe.

"Lieutenant Dallas. How lovely to see you again." His eyes, full of compliments she knew she didn't deserve, skimmed over her. "And how unfortunate I'm just on my way out."

"I won't keep you long." She stepped forward, he stepped back. "A couple of questions, Mr. Monroe, here, informally, or formally, at the station with your representative or counsel."

His well-shaped brows shot up. "I see. I thought we'd progressed beyond that. Very well, Lieutenant, ask away." He let the door slide shut again. "We'll keep it informal."

"Your whereabouts night before last, between the hours of eight and eleven?"

"Night before last?" He slipped a diary out of his pocket, keyed it in. "Ah, yes. I picked up a client at seven-thirty for an eight o'clock curtain at the Grande Theater. They're doing a reprise of Ibsen—depressing stuff. We sat third row, center. It ended just before eleven, and we had a late supper, catered. Here. I was engaged with her until three A.M."

His smile flashed as he tucked the diary away again. "Does that clear me?"

"If your client will corroborate."

The smile faded into a look of pain. "Lieutenant, you're killing me."

"Someone's killing people in your profession," she snapped back. "Name and number, Mr. Monroe." She waited until he'd mournfully given the data. "Are you acquainted with a Lola Starr?"

"Lola, Lola Starr . . . doesn't sound familiar." He took out the diary again, scanning through his address section. "Apparently not. Why?"

"You'll hear about it on the news by morning," was all Eve told him as she opened the door again. "So far, it's only been women, Mr. Monroe, but if I were you, I'd be very careful about taking on new clients."

With a headache drumming at her, she strode to the elevator. Unable to resist, she glanced toward the door of Sharon DeBlass's apartment, where the red police security light blinked.

She needed to sleep, she told herself. She needed to go home and empty her mind for an hour. But she was keying in her ID to disengage the seal, and walking into the home of a dead woman.

It was silent. And it was empty. She'd expected nothing else. Somehow she hoped there would be some flash of intuition, but there was only the steady pounding in her temples. Ignoring it, she went into the bedroom.

The windows had been sealed as well with concealing spray to prevent the media or the morbidly curious from doing fly-bys and checking out the scene. She ordered lights, and the shadows bounced back to reveal the bed.

The sheets had been stripped off and taken into forensics. Body fluids, hair, and skin had already been analyzed and logged. There was a stain on the floating mattress where blood had seeped through those satin sheets.

The pillowed headboard was splattered with it. She wondered if anyone would care enough to have it cleaned.

She glanced toward the table. Feeney had taken the small desktop PC so that he could search through the hard drive as well as the discs. The room had been searched and swept. There was nothing left to do.

Yet Eve went to the dresser, going methodically through the drawers again. Who would claim all these clothes? she wondered. The silks and lace, the cashmeres and satins of a woman who had preferred the textures of the rich against her skin.

The mother, she imagined. Why hadn't she sent in a request for the return of her daughter's things?

Something to think about.

She went through the closet, again going through skirts, dresses, trousers, the trendy capes and caftans, jackets and blouses, checking pockets, linings. She moved on to shoes, all kept neatly in acrylic boxes.

The woman had only had two feet, she thought with some annoyance. No one needed sixty pairs of shoes. With a little snort, she reached into toes, deep inside the tunnel of boots, into the springy softness of inflatable platforms.

Lola hadn't had so much, she thought now. Two pairs of ridiculously high heels, a pair of girlish vinyl straps, and a simple pair of air pump sneakers, all jumbled in her narrow closet.

But Sharon had been an organized as well as a vain soul. Her shoes were carefully stacked in rows of—

Wrong. Skin prickling, Eve stepped back. It was wrong. The closet was as big as a room, and every inch of space had been ruthlessly utilized. Now, there was a full foot empty on the shelves. Because the shoes were stacked six high in a row of eight.

It wasn't the way Eve had found them or the way she'd left them. They'd been organized according to color and style. In stacks, she remembered perfectly, of four, a row of twelve.

Such a little mistake, she thought with a small smile. But a man who made one was bound to make another.

*   *   *

"Would you repeat that, Lieutenant?"

"He restacked the shoe boxes wrong, Commander." Negotiating traffic, shivering as her car heater offered a tepid puff of air around her toes, Eve checked in. A tourist blimp crept by at low altitude, the guide's voice booming out tips on sky walk shopping as they crossed toward Fifth. Some idiotic road crew with a special daylight license power drilled a tunnel access on the corner of Sixth and Seventy-eighth. Eve pitched her voice above the din.

"You can review the discs of the scene. I know how the closet was arranged. It made an impression on me that any one person should have so many clothes, and keep them so organized. He went back."

"Returned to the scene of the crime?" Whitney's voice was dry as dust.

"Clichés have a basis in fact." Hoping for relative quiet, she jogged west down a cross street and ended up fuming behind a clicking mi-crobus. Didn't anyone stay home in New York? "Or they wouldn't be clichés," she finished and switched to automatic drive so that she could warm her hands in her pockets. "There were other things. She kept her costume jewelry in a partitioned drawer. Rings in one section, bracelets in another, and so on. Some of the chains were tangled when I looked again."

"The sweepers—"

"Sir, I went through the place again after the sweepers. I know he's been there." Eve bit back on frustration and reminded her-self that Whitney was a cautious man. Administrators had to be. "He got through the security, and he went in. He was looking for something—something he forgot. Something she had. Something we missed."

"You want the place swept again?"

"I do. And I want Feeney to go back over Sharon's files. Some-thing's there, somewhere. And it concerns him enough to risk going back for it."

"I'll signature the authorization. The chief isn't going to like it." The commander was silent for a moment. Then, as if he'd just re-membered it was a fully secured line, he snorted. "Fuck the chief. Good eye, Dallas."

"Thank you—" But he'd cut her off before she could finish being grateful.

Two of six, she thought, and in the privacy of her car, she shuddered from more than the cold. There were four more people out there whose lives were in her hands.

After pulling into her garage, she swore she'd call the damn mechanic the next day. If history ran true, it meant he'd have her vehicle in for a week, diddling with some idiotic chip in the heater control. The idea of the paperwork in accessing a replacement vehicle through the department was too daunting to consider.

Besides, she was used to the one she had, with all its little quirks. Everyone knew the uniforms copped the best air-to-land vehicles. Detectives had to make do with clinkers.

She'd have to rely on public transportation or just hook a car from the police garage and pay the bureaucratic price later.

Still frowning over the hassle to come and reminding herself to contact Feeney personally to have him go through a week's worth of security discs on the Gorham, she rode the elevator to her floor. Eve had no more than unkeyed her locks when her hand was on her weapon, drawing it.

The silence of her apartment was wrong. She knew instantly she wasn't alone. The prickle along her skin had her doing a quick sweep, arms and eyes, shifting fluidly left then right.

In the dim light of the room, the shadows hung and the silence remained. Then she caught a movement that had her tensed muscles rippling, her trigger finger poised.

"Excellent reflexes, Lieutenant." Roarke rose from the chair where he'd been lounging. Where he'd been watching her. "So excellent," he continued in that same mild tone as he touched on a lamp, "that I have every faith you won't use that on me."

She might have. She very well might have given him one good jolt. That would have wiped that complacent smile off his face. But any discharge of a weapon meant paperwork she wasn't prepared to face for simple revenge.

"What the fuck are you doing here?"

"Waiting for you." His eyes remained on hers as he lifted his hands.

"I'm unarmed. You're welcome to check for yourself if you won't take my word for it."

Very slowly, and with some reluctance, she holstered her weapon. "I imagine you have a whole fleet of very expensive and very clever lawyers, Roarke, who would have you out before I finished booking you on a B and E. But why don't you tell me why I shouldn't put myself to the trouble, and the city to the expense of throwing you in a cage for a couple of hours?"

Roarke wondered if he'd become perverse that he could so enjoy the way she slashed at him. "It wouldn't be productive. And you're tired, Eve. Why don't you sit down?"

"I won't bother to ask you how you got in here." She could feel herself vibrating with temper, and wondered just how much satisfaction she'd gain from clamping his elegant wrists in restraints. "You own the building, so that question answers itself."

"One of the things I admire about you is that you don't waste time on the obvious."

"My question is why."

"I found myself thinking about you, on professional and personal levels, after you'd left my office." He smiled, quick and charming. "Have you eaten?"

"Why?" she repeated.

He stepped toward her so that the slant of light from the lamp played behind him. "Professionally, I made a couple of calls that might be of interest to you. Personally . . ." He lifted a hand to her face, fingers just brushing her chin, his thumb skimming the slight dip. "I found myself concerned by that fatigue in your eyes. For some reason I feel compelled to feed you."

Though she knew it was the gesture of a cranky child, she jerked her chin free. "What calls?"

He merely smiled again, moved to her tele-link. "May I?" he said even as he keyed in the number he wanted. "This is Roarke. You can send the meal up now." He disengaged, smiled at her again. "You don't object to pasta, do you?"

"Not on principle. But I object to being handled."

"That's something else I like about you." Because she wouldn't, he sat and, ignoring her frown, took out his cigarette case. "But I find it easier to relax over a hot meal. You don't relax enough, Eve."

"You don't know me well enough to judge what I do or don't do. And I didn't say you could smoke in here."

He lighted the cigarette, eyeing her through the faint, fragrant haze. "You didn't arrest me for breaking and entering, you're not going to arrest me for smoking. I brought a bottle of wine. I left it to breathe on the counter in the kitchen. Would you like some?"

"What I'd like—" She had a sudden flash, and the fury came so quickly she could barely see through it. In one leap, she was at her computer, demanding access.

That annoyed him—enough to have his voice tighten. "If I'd come in to poke through your files, I'd hardly have waited around for you."

"The hell you wouldn't. That kind of arrogance is just like you." But her security was intact. She wasn't sure if she was relieved or disappointed. Until she saw the small package beside her monitor. "What's this?"

"I have no idea." He blew out another stream of smoke. "It was on the floor inside the door. I picked it up."

Eve knew what it was—the size, the shape, the weight. And she knew when she viewed the disc she would see Lola Starr's murder.

Something about the way her eyes changed had him rising again, had his voice gentling. "What is it, Eve?"

"Official business. Excuse me."

She walked directly to the bedroom, closed and secured the door.

It was Roarke's turn to frown. He went into the kitchen, located glasses, and poured the burgundy. She lived simply, he thought. Very little clutter, very little that spoke of background or family. No mementos. He'd been tempted to wander into her bedroom while he'd had the apartment to himself and see what he might have discovered about her there, but he'd resisted.

It was not so much respect for her privacy as it was the challenge she presented that provoked him to discover her from the woman alone rather than her surroundings.

Still, he found the plain colors and lack of fuss illuminating. She didn't live here, as far as he could see, so much as she existed here. She lived, he deduced, in her work.

He sipped the wine, approved it. After dousing his cigarette, he carried both glasses back into the living room. It was going to be more than interesting to solve the puzzle of Eve Dallas.

When she came back in, nearly twenty minutes later, a white-coated waiter was just finishing setting up dishes on a small table by the window. However glorious the scents, they failed to stir her appetite. Her head was pounding again, and she'd forgotten to take medication.

With a murmur, Roarke dismissed the waiter. He said nothing until the door closed and he was alone with Eve again. "I'm sorry."

"For what?"

"For whatever's upset you." Except for that one flush of temper, she'd been pale when she'd come into the apartment. But her cheeks were colorless now, her eyes too dark. When he started toward her, she shook her head once, fiercely.

"Go away, Roarke."

"Going away's easy. Too easy." Very deliberately, he put his arms around her, felt her stiffen. "Give yourself a minute." His voice was smooth, persuasive. "Would it matter, really matter to anyone but you, if you took one minute to let go?"

She shook her head again, but this time there was weariness in the gesture. He heard the sigh escape, and taking advantage, he drew her closer. "You can't tell me?"

"No."

He nodded, but his eyes flashed with impatience. He knew better; it shouldn't matter to him. She shouldn't. But too much about her mattered.

"Someone else then," he murmured.

"There's no one else." Then realizing how that might be construed, she pulled back. "I didn't mean—"

"I know you didn't." His smile was wry and not terribly amused. "But there isn't going to be anyone else, for either of us, not for some time."

Her step back wasn't a retreat, but a statement of distance. "You're taking too much for granted, Roarke."

"Not at all. Nothing for granted. You're work, Lieutenant. A great deal of work. Your dinner's getting cold."

She was too tired to make a stand, too tired to argue. She sat down, picked up her fork. "Have you been to Sharon DeBlass's apartment during the last week?"

"No, why would I?"

She studied him carefully. "Why would anyone?"

He paused a moment, then realized the question wasn't academic. "To relive the event," he suggested. "To be certain nothing was left behind that would be incriminating."

"And as owner of the building, you could get in as easily as you got in here."

His mouth tightened briefly. Annoyance, she judged, the annoyance of a man who was weary of answering the same questions. It was a small thing, but a very good sign of his innocence. "Yes. I don't believe I'd have a problem. My master code would get me in."

No, she thought, his master code wouldn't have broken the police security. That would require a different level, or an expert on security.

"I assume that you believe someone not in your department has been in that apartment since the murder."

"You can assume that," she agreed. "Who handles your security, Roarke?"

"I use Lorimar for both my business and my home." He lifted his glass. "It's simpler that way, as I own the company."

"Of course you do. I suppose you know quite a bit about security yourself."

"You could say I have a long-standing interest in security matters. That's why I bought the company." He scooped up the herbed pasta, held the fork to her lips, and was satisfied when she took the offered bite. "Eve, I'm tempted to confess all, just to wipe that unhappy look off your face and see you eat with the enthusiasm I'd enjoyed last time. But whatever my crimes, and they are undoubtedly legion, they don't include murder."

She looked down at her plate and began to eat. It frazzled her that he could see she was unhappy. "What did you mean when you said I was work?"

"You think things through very carefully, and you weigh the odds, the options. You're not a creature of impulse, and though I believe you could be seduced, with the right timing, and the right touch, it wouldn't be an ordinary occurrence."

She lifted her gaze again. "That's what you want to do, Roarke? Seduce me?"

"I will seduce you," he returned. "Unfortunately, not tonight. Beyond that, I want to find out what it is that makes you what you are. And I want to help you get what you need. Right now, what you need is a murderer. You blame yourself," he added. "That's foolish and annoying."

"I don't blame myself."

"Look in the mirror," Roarke said quietly.

"There was nothing I could do," Eve exploded. "Nothing I could do to stop it. Any of it."

"Are you supposed to be able to stop it, any of it? All of it?"

"That's exactly what I'm supposed to do."

He tilted his head. "How?"

She pushed away from the table. "By being smart. By being in time. By doing my job."

Something more here, he mused. Something deeper. He folded his hands on the table. "Isn't that what you're doing now?"

The images flooded back into her brain. All the death. All the blood. All the waste. "Now they're dead." And the taste of it was bitter in her mouth. "There should have been something I could have done to stop it."

"To stop a murder before it happens, you'd have to be inside the head of a killer," he said quietly. "Who could live with that?"

"I can live with that." She hurled it back at him. And it was pure truth. She could live with anything but failure. "Serve and protect—it's not just a phrase, it's a promise. If I can't keep my word, I'm nothing. And I didn't protect them, any of them. I can only serve them after they're dead. Goddamn it, she was hardly more than a baby. Just a baby, and he cut her into pieces. I wasn't in time. I wasn't in time, and I should have been."

Her breath caught on a sob, shocking her. Pressing a hand to her mouth, she lowered herself onto the sofa. "God," was all she could say. "God. God."

He came to her. Instinct had him taking her arms firmly rather than gathering her close. "If you can't or won't talk to me, you have to talk to someone. You know that."

"I can handle it. I—" But the rest of the words slid down her throat when he shook her.

"What's it costing you?" he demanded. "And how much would it matter to anyone if you let it go? For one minute just let it go."

"I don't know." And maybe that was the fear, she realized. She wasn't sure if she could pick up her badge, or her weapon, or her life, if she let herself think too deeply, or feel too much. "I see her," Eve said on a deep breath. "I see her whenever I close my eyes or stop concentrating on what needs to be done."

"Tell me."

She rose, retrieved her wine and his, and then returned to the sofa. The long drink eased her dry throat and settled the worst of the nerves. It was fatigue, she warned herself, that weakened her enough that she couldn't hold it in.

"The call came through when I was a half block away. I'd just closed another case, finished the data load. Dispatch called for the closest unit. Domestic violence—it's always messy, but I was practically on the doorstep. So I took it. Some of the neighbors were outside, they were all talking at once."

The scene came back to her, perfectly, like a video exactly cued. "A woman was in her nightgown, and she was crying. Her face was battered, and one of the neighbors was trying to bind up a gash on her arm. She was bleeding badly, so I told them to call the MTs. She kept saying, 'He's got her. He's got my baby.'"

Eve took another drink. "She grabbed me, bleeding on me, screaming and crying and telling me I had to stop him, I had to save her baby. I should have called for backup, but I didn't think I could wait. I took the stairs, and I could hear him before I got to the third floor where he was locked in. He was raging. I think I heard the little girl screaming, but I'm not sure."

She closed her eyes then, praying she'd been wrong. She wanted to believe that the child had already been dead, already beyond pain. To have been that close, only steps away . . . No, she couldn't live with that.

"When I got to the door, I used the standard. I'd gotten his name from one of the neighbors. I used his name, and the child's name. It's supposed to make it more personal, more real if you use names. I identified myself and said I was coming in. But he just kept raging. I could hear things breaking. I couldn't hear the child now. I think I knew. Before I broke down the door, I knew. He'd used the kitchen knife to slice her to pieces."

Her hand shook as she raised the glass again. "There was so much blood. She was so small, but there was so much blood. On the floor, on the wall, all over him. I could see it was still dripping off the knife. Her face was turned toward me. Her little face, with big blue eyes. Like a doll's."

She was silent for a moment, then set her glass aside. "He was too wired up to be stunned. He kept coming. There was blood dripping off the knife, and splattered all over him, and he kept coming. So I looked in his eyes, right in his eyes. And I killed him."

"And the next day," Roarke said quietly, "you dived straight into a murder investigation."

"Testing's postponed. I'll get to it in another day or two." She moved her shoulders. "The shrinks, they'll think it's the termination. I can make them think that if I have to. But it's not. I had to kill him. I can accept that." She looked straight into Roarke's eyes and knew she could tell him what she hadn't been able to say to herself. "I wanted to kill him. Maybe even needed to. When I watched him die, I thought, He'll never do that to another child. And I was glad that I'd been the one to stop him."

"You think that's wrong."

"I know it's wrong. I know anytime a cop gets pleasure of any sort out of termination, she's crossed a line."

He leaned forward so that their faces were close. "What was the child's name?"

"Mandy." Her breath hitched once before she controlled it. "She was three."

"Would you be torn up this way if you'd killed him before he'd gotten to her?"

She opened her mouth, closed it again. "I guess I'll never know, will I?"

"Yes, you do." He laid a hand over hers, watched her frown and look down at the contact. "You know, I've spent most of my life with a basic dislike of police—for one reason or another. I find it very odd that I've met, under such extraordinary circumstances, one I can respect and be attracted to at the same time."

She lifted her gaze again, and though the frown remained, she didn't draw her hand free of his. "That's a strange compliment."

"Apparently we have a strange relationship." He rose, drawing her to her feet. "Now you need to sleep." He glanced toward the dinner she'd barely touched. "You can heat that up when you've gotten your appetite back."

"Thanks. Next time I'd appreciate you waiting until I'm home before you come in."

"Progress," he murmured when they'd reached the door. "You accept there'll be a next time." With a hint of a smile, he brought the hand he still held to his lips. He caught bafflement, discomfort and, he thought, a trace of embarrassment in her eyes as he brushed a light kiss over her knuckles. "Until next time," he said, and left.

Frowning, Eve rubbed her knuckles over her jeans as she headed to the bedroom. She stripped, letting her clothes lay wherever they dropped. She climbed into bed, shut her eyes, and willed herself to sleep.

She was just dozing off when she remembered Roarke had never told her who he'd called and what he'd discovered.

CHAPTER
EIGHT

In her office, with the door locked, Eve reviewed the disc of Lola Starr's murder with Feeney. She didn't flinch at the little popping sound of the silenced weapon. Her system no longer recoiled at the insult the bullet caused in flesh.

The screen held steady on the ending caption: Two of Six. Then it went blank. Without a word, Eve cued up the first murder, and they watched Sharon DeBlass die again.

"What can you tell me?" Eve asked when it was finished.

"Discs were made on a Trident MicroCam, the five thousand model. It's only been available about six months, very pricey. Big seller last Christmas, though. More than ten thousand moved in Manhattan alone during the traditional shopping season, not to mention how many went through the gray market. Not as much of a flood like less expensive models, but still too many to trace."

He looked over at Eve with his drooping camel eyes. "Guess who owns Trident?"

"Roarke Industries."

"Give the lady a bouquet. I'd say the odds were pretty good the boss man owns one himself."

"He'd certainly have access." She made a note of it and resisted the memory of how his lips had felt brushing over her knuckles. "The killer uses a fairly exclusive piece of equipment he manufactures himself. Arrogance or stupidity?"

"Stupidity doesn't fly with this boy."

"No, it doesn't. The weapon?"

"We've got a couple thousand out there in private collections," Feeney began, nibbling on a cashew. "Three in the boroughs. Those are the ones that've been registered," he added with a thin smile. "The silencer doesn't have to be registered, as it doesn't qualify as deadly on its own. No way of tracing it."

He leaned back, tapped the monitor. "As far as the first disc, I've been running it. I came up with a couple of shadows. Makes me certain he recorded more than the murder. But I haven't been able to enhance anything. Whoever edited that disc knew all the tricks or had access to equipment that knew them for him."

"What about the sweepers?"

"Commander ordered them for this morning, per your request." Feeney glanced at his watch. "Should be there now. I picked up the security discs on my way in, ran them. We've got a twenty-minute time lapse starting at three-ten, night before last."

"Bastard waltzed right in," she muttered. "It's a shitty neighborhood, Feeney, but an upscale building. Nobody noticed him either time, which means he blends."

"Or they're used to seeing him."

"Because he was one of Sharon's regulars. Tell me why a man who was a regular client or an expensive, sophisticated, experienced prostitute, chose a green, low-scale what do you call it, ingenue like Lola Starr for his second hit?"

Feeney pursed his lips. "He likes variety?"

Eve shook her head. "Maybe he liked it so much the first time, he's not going to be choosy now. Four more to go, Feeney. He told us right off the bat we had a serial killer. He announced it, letting us know Sharon wasn't particularly important. Just one of six."

She blew out a breath, unsatisfied. "So why'd he go back?" she said to herself. "What was he looking for?"

"Maybe the sweepers'll tell us."

"Maybe." She picked up a list from her desk. "I'm going to check out Sharon's client list again, then hit Lola's."

Feeney cleared his throat, chose another cashew from his little bag. "I hate to be the one to tell you, Dallas. The senator's demanding an update."

"I have nothing to tell him."

"You're going to have to tell him this afternoon. In East Washington."

She stopped a pace in front of the door. "Bullshit."

"Commander gave me the news. We're on the two o'clock shuttle." Feeney thought resignedly of how his stomach reacted to air travel. "I hate politics."

Eve was still gritting her teeth over her briefing with Whitney when she ran headlong into DeBlass's security outside his office in the New Senate Office Building, East Washington.

Their identification aside, both she and Feeney were scanned, and according to the revised Federal Property Act of 2022, were obliged to hand over their weapons.

"Like we're going to zap the guy while he's sitting at his desk," Feeney muttered as they were escorted over red, white, and blue carpet.

"I wouldn't mind giving several of these guys a quick buzz." Flanked by suits and shined shoes, Eve slouched in front of the glossy door of the senator's office, waiting for the internal camera to clear them.

"If you ask me, East Washington's been paranoid since the terrorist hit." Feeney sneered into the camera. "Couple dozen legislators get whacked, and they never forget it."

The door opened, and Rockman, pristine in needle-thin pin stripes, nodded. "Long memories are an advantage in politics, Captain Feeney. Lieutenant Dallas," he added with another nod. "We appreciate your promptness."

"I had no idea the senator and my chief were so close," Eve said as she stepped inside. "Or that both of them would be so anxious to waste the taxpayers' money."

"Perhaps they both consider justice priceless." Rockman gestured them toward the gleaming desk of cherrywood—certainly priceless—where DeBlass waited.

He had, as far as Eve could see, benefited from the change of temperature in the country—too lukewarm in her opinion—and the repeal of the Two Term Bill. Under current law, a politician could now retain his seat for life. All he had to do was buffalo his constituents into electing him.

DeBlass certainly looked at home. His paneled office was as hushed as a cathedral and every bit as reverent with its altarlike desk, the visitor chairs as subservient as pews.

"Sit," DeBlass barked, and folded his large-knuckled hands on the desk. "My latest information is that you are no closer to finding the monster who murdered my granddaughter than you were a week ago." His dark brows beetled over his eyes. "I find this difficult to understand, considering the resources of the New York Police Department."

"Senator." Eve let Commander Whitney's terse instructions play in her head: Be tactful, respectful, and tell him nothing he doesn't already know. "We're using those resources to investigate and gather evidence. While the department is not now prepared to make an arrest, every possible effort is being made to bring your granddaughter's murderer to justice. Her case is my first priority, and you have my word it will continue to be until it can be satisfactorily closed."

The senator listened to the little speech with all apparent interest. Then he leaned forward. "I've been in the business of bullshit for more than twice your life, Lieutenant. So don't pull out your tap dance with me. You have nothing."

Fuck tact, Eve decided instantly. "What we have, Senator DeBlass, is a complicated and delicate investigation. Complicated, given the nature of the crime; delicate, due to the victim's family tree. It's my commander's opinion that I'm the best choice to conduct the investigation. It's your right to disagree. But pulling me off my job to come here to defend my work is a waste of time. My time." She rose. "I have nothing new to tell you."

With the vision of both their butts hanging in a sling, Feeney rose as well, all respect. "I'm sure you understand, Senator, that the delicacy of an investigation of this nature often means progress is slow. It's difficult to ask you to be objective when we're talking of your granddaughter, but Lieutenant Dallas and I have no choice but to be objective."

With an impatient gesture, DeBlass waved them to sit again. "Obviously my emotions are involved. Sharon was an important part of my life. Whatever she became, and however I was disappointed in her choices, she was blood." He drew a deep breath, let it loose. "I cannot and will not be placated with bits and pieces of information."

"There's nothing else I can tell you," Eve repeated.

"You can tell me about the prostitute who was murdered two nights ago." His eyes flicked up to Rockman.

"Lola Starr," he supplied.

"I imagine your sources of information on Lola Starr are as thorough as ours." Eve chose to speak directly to Rockman. "Yes, we believe that there is a connection between the two murders."

"My granddaughter might have been misguided," DeBlass broke in, "but she did not socialize with people like Lola Starr."

So, prostitutes had class systems, Eve thought wearily. What else was new? "We haven't determined whether they knew each other. But there's little doubt that they both knew the same man. And that man killed them. Each murder followed a specific pattern. We'll use that pattern to find him. Before, we hope, he kills again."

"You believe he will," Rockman put in.

"I'm sure he will."

"The murder weapon," DeBlass demanded. "Was it the same type?"

"It's part of the pattern," Eve told him. She'd commit no more than that. "There are basic and undeniable similarities between the two homicides. There's no doubt the same man is responsible."

Calmer now, Eve stood again. "Senator, I never knew your granddaughter and have no personal tie to her, but I'm personally offended by murder. I'm going after him. That's all I can tell you."

He studied her for a moment, saw more than he'd expected to see. "Very well, Lieutenant. Thank you for coming."

Dismissed, Eve walked with Feeney to the door. In the mirror she saw DeBlass signal to Rockman, Rockman acknowledged. She waited until she was outside before she spoke.

"The son of a bitch is going to tail us."

"Huh?"

"DeBlass's guard dog. He's going to shadow us."

"What the hell for?"

"To see what we do, where we go. Why do you tail anyone? We're going to lose him at the transport center," she told Feeney as she flagged down a cab. "Keep your eyes out and see if he follows you to New York."

"Follows me? Where are you going?"

"I'm going to follow my nose."

It wasn't a difficult maneuver. The west wing boarding terminal at National Transport was always bedlam. It was even worse at rush hour when all northbound passengers were jammed into the security line and herded along by computerized voices. Shuttles and runabouts were going to be jammed.

Eve simply lost herself in the crowd, crammed herself into a cross terminal transport to the south wing, and caught an underground to Virginia.

After settling in her tube, ignoring the four o'clocks who were heading to the suburban havens, she took out her pocket directory. She requested Elizabeth Barrister's address, then asked for directions.

So far her nose was just fine. She was on the right tube and would have to make only one change in Richmond. If her luck held, she could finish the trip and be back in her apartment in time for dinner.

With her chin on her fist, she toyed with the controls of her video screen. She would have bypassed the news—something she made a habit of doing—but when an all-too-familiar face flashed on-screen, she stopped scanning.

Roarke, she thought, narrowing her eyes. The guy sure kept

popping up. Lips pursed, she tuned in the audio, plugged in her ear receiver.

". . . in this international, multibillion dollar project, Roarke Industries, Tokayamo, and Europa will join hands," the announcer stated. "It's taken three years, but it appears that the much debated, much anticipated Olympus Resort will begin construction."

Olympus Resort, Eve mused, flipping through her mental files. Some high-class, high-dollar vacation paradise, she recalled. A proposed space station built for pleasure and entertainment.

She snorted. Wasn't it just like him to spend his time and money on fripperies?

If he didn't lose his tailored silk shirt, she imagined he'd make another fortune.

"Roarke—one question, sir."

She watched Roarke pause on his way down a long flight of marble steps and lift a brow—exactly as she remembered he did—at the reporter's interruption.

"Could you tell me why you've spent so much time and effort, and a considerable amount of your own capital, on this project—one detractors say will never fly?"

"Fly is precisely what it will do," Roarke replied, "in a manner of speaking. As to why, the Olympus Resort will be a haven for pleasure. I can't think of anything more worthwhile on which to spend time, effort, and capital."

You wouldn't, Eve decided, and glanced up just in time to realize she was about to miss her stop. She dashed to the doors of the tube, cursed the computer voice for scolding her for running, and made the change to Fort Royal.

When she came above ground again, it was snowing. Soft, lazy flakes drifted over her hair and shoulders. Pedestrians were stomping it to mush on the sidewalks, but when she found a cab and gave her destination, she found the swirl of white more picturesque.

There was still countryside to be had, if you possessed the money or the prestige. Elizabeth Barrister and Richard DeBlass possessed both, and their home was a striking two stories of rosy brick set on a sloping hill and flanked by trees.

Snow was pristine on the expansive lawn, ermine draped on the bare branches of what Eve thought might be cherry trees. The security gate was an artful symphony of curling iron. However decorative it might have been, Eve was certain it was as practical as a vault.

She leaned out the cab window, flashed her badge at the scanner. "Lieutenant Dallas, NYPSD."

"You are not listed in the appointment directory, Lieutenant Dallas."

"I'm the officer in charge of the DeBlass case. I have some questions for Ms. Barrister or Richard DeBlass."

There was a pause, during which time Eve began to shiver in the cold.

"Please step out of the cab, Lieutenant Dallas, and up to the scanner for further identification."

"Tough joint," the cabbie muttered, but Eve merely shrugged and complied.

"Identification verified. Dismiss your transport, Lieutenant Dallas. You will be met at the gate."

"Heard the daughter got whacked up in New York," the cabbie said as Eve paid the fare. "Guess they're not taking any chances. Want I should pull back a ways and wait for you?"

"No, thanks. But I'll ask for your number when I'm ready to go."

With a half salute, the cabbie backed up, swung away. Eve's nose was beginning to numb when she saw the little electric cart slide through the gate. The curved iron opened.

"Please go inside, step into the cart," the computer invited. "You will be taken to the house. Ms. Barrister will see you."

"Terrific." Eve climbed into the cart and let it take her noiselessly to the front steps of the brick house. Even as she started up them, the door opened.

Either the servants were required to wear boring black suits, or the house was still in mourning. Eve was shown politely into a room off the entrance hall.

Where Roarke's home had simply whispered money, this one said old money. The carpets were thick, the walls papered in silk. The wide windows offered a stunning view of rolling hills and falling snow. And solitude, Eve thought. The architect must have understood that those who lived here preferred to consider themselves alone.

"Lieutenant Dallas." Elizabeth rose. There was nervousness in the deliberate movement, in the rigid stance and, Eve saw, in the shadowed eyes that held grief.

"Thank you for seeing me, Ms. Barrister."

"My husband's in a meeting. I can interrupt him if necessary."

"I don't think it will be."

"You've come about Sharon."

"Yes."

"Please sit down." Elizabeth gestured toward a chair upholstered in ivory. "Can I offer you anything?"

"No, thanks. I'll try not to keep you very long. I don't know how much of my report you've seen—"

"All of it," Elizabeth interrupted. "I believe. It seems quite thorough. As an attorney, I have every confidence that when you find the person who killed my daughter, you'll have built a strong case."

"That's the plan." Running on nerves, Eve decided, watching the way Elizabeth's long, graceful fingers clenched, unclenched. "This is a difficult time for you."

"She was my only child," Elizabeth said simply. "My husband and I were—are—proponents of the population adjustment theory. Two parents," she said with a thin smile. "One offspring. Do you have any further information to give me?"

"Not at this time. Your daughter's profession, Ms. Barrister. Did this cause friction in the family?"

In another of her slow, deliberate gestures, Elizabeth smoothed down the ankle-skimming skirt of her suit. "It was not a profession I dreamed of my daughter embracing. Naturally, it was her choice."

"Your father-in-law would have been opposed. Certainly politically opposed."

"The senator's views on sexual legislation are well known. As a leader of the Conservative Party, he is, of course, working to change many of the current laws regarding what is popularly called the Morality Issue."

"Do you share his views?"

"No, I don't, though I fail to see how that applies."

Eve cocked her head. Oh, there was friction there, all right. Eve wondered if the streamlined attorney agreed with her outspoken father-in-law on anything. "Your daughter was killed—possibly by a client, possibly by a personal friend. If you and your daughter were at odds over her lifestyle, it would be unlikely she would have confided in you about professional or personal acquaintances."

"I see." Elizabeth folded her hands and forced herself to think like a lawyer. "You're assuming that, as her mother, as a woman who might have shared some of the same viewpoints, Sharon would talk to me, perhaps share with me some of the more intimate details of her life." Despite her efforts, Elizabeth's eyes clouded. "I'm sorry, Lieutenant, that's not the case. Sharon rarely shared anything with me. Certainly not about her business. She was . . . aloof, from both her father and me. Really, from her entire family."

"You wouldn't know if she had a particular lover—someone she was more personally involved with? One who might have been jealous?"

"No. I can tell you I don't believe she did. Sharon had . . ." Elizabeth took a steadying breath. "A disdain for men. An attraction to them, yes, but an underlying disdain. She knew she could attract them. From a very early age, she knew. And she found them foolish."

"Professional companions are rigidly screened. A dislike—or disdain, as you put it—is a usual reason for denial of licensing."

"She was also clever. There was nothing in her life she wanted she didn't find a way to have. Except happiness. She was not a happy woman," Elizabeth went on, and swallowed the lump that always seemed to hover in her throat. "I spoiled her, it's true. I have no one to blame but myself for it. I wanted more children." She pressed a hand to her mouth until she thought her lips had stopped trembling. "I was philosophically opposed to having more, and my husband was very clear in his position. But that didn't stop the emotion of wanting children to love. I loved Sharon, too much. The senator will tell you I smothered her, babied her, indulged her. And he would be right."

"I would say that mothering was your privilege, not his."

This brought a ghost of a smile to Elizabeth's eyes. "So were the mistakes, and I made them. Richard, too, though he loved her no less than I. When Sharon moved to New York, we fought with her over it. Richard pleaded with her. I threatened her. And I pushed her away, Lieutenant. She told me I didn't understand her—never had, never would—and that I saw only what I wanted to see, unless it was in court; but what went on in my own home was invisible."

"What did she mean?"

"That I was a better lawyer than a mother, I suppose. After she left, I was hurt, angry. I pulled back, quite certain she would come to me. She didn't, of course."

She stopped speaking for a moment, hoarding her regrets. "Richard went to see her once or twice, but that didn't work, and only upset him. We let it alone, let her alone. Until recently, when I felt we had to make a new attempt."

"Why recently?"

"The years pass," Elizabeth murmured. "I'd hoped she would be growing tired of the lifestyle, perhaps have begun to regret the rift with family. I went to see her myself about a year ago. But she only became angry, defensive, then insulting when I tried to persuade her to come home. Richard, though he'd resigned himself, offered to go up and talk to her. But she refused to see him. Even Catherine tried," she murmured and rubbed absently at a pain between her eyes. "She went to see Sharon only a few weeks ago."

"Congresswoman DeBlass went to New York to see Sharon?"

"Not specifically. Catherine was there for a fund-raiser and made a point to see and try to speak with Sharon." Elizabeth pressed her lips together. "I asked her to. You see, when I tried to open communications again, Sharon wasn't interested. I'd lost her," Elizabeth said quietly, "and moved too late to get her back. I didn't know how to get her back. I'd hoped that Catherine could help, being family, but not Sharon's mother."

She looked over at Eve again. "You're thinking that I should have gone again myself. It was my place to go."

"Ms. Barrister—"

But Elizabeth shook her head. "You're right, of course. But she refused to confide in me. I thought I should respect her privacy, as I always had. I was never one of those mothers who peeked into her daughter's diary."

"Diary?" Eve's antenna vibrated. "Did she keep one?"

"She always kept a diary, even as a child. She changed the password in it regularly."

"And as an adult?"

"Yes. She'd refer to it now and again—joke about the secrets she had and the people she knew who would be appalled at what she'd written about them."

There'd been no personal diary in the inventory, Eve remembered. Such things could be as small as a woman's thumb. If the sweepers missed it the first time . . .

"Do you have any of them?"

"No." Abruptly alert, Elizabeth looked up. "She kept them in a deposit box, I think. She kept them all."

"Did she use a bank here in Virginia?"

"Not that I'm aware of. I'll check and see what I can find out for you. I can go through the things she left here."

"I'd appreciate that. If you think of anything—anything at all—a name, a comment, no matter how casual, please contact me."

"I will. She never spoke of friends, Lieutenant. I worried about that, even as I used it to hope that the lack of them would draw her back home. Out of the life she'd chosen. I even used one of my own, my own friends, thinking he would be more persuasive than I."

"Who was that?"

"Roarke." Elizabeth teared up again, fought them back. "Only days before she was murdered, I called him. We've known each other for years. I asked him if he would arrange for her to be invited to a certain party I knew he'd be attending. If he'd seek her out. He was reluctant. Roarke isn't one to meddle in family business. But I used our friendship. If he would just find a way to befriend her, to show her that an attractive woman doesn't have to use her looks to feel worthwhile. He did that for me, and for my husband."

"You asked him to develop a relationship with her?" Eve said carefully.

"I asked him to be her friend," Elizabeth corrected. "To be there for her. I asked him because there's no one I trust more. She'd cut herself off from all of us, and I needed someone I could trust.

He would never hurt her, you see. He would never hurt anyone I loved."

"Because he loves you?"

"Cares." Richard DeBlass spoke from the doorway. "Roarka cares very much for Beth and for me, and a few select others. But loves? I'm not sure he'd let himself risk quite that unstable an emotion."

"Richard." Elizabeth's control wobbled as she got to her feet. "I wasn't expecting you quite yet."

"We finished early." He came to her, closed his hands over hers. "You should have called me, Beth."

"I didn't—" She broke off, looked at him helplessly. "I'd hoped to handle it alone."

"You don't have to handle anything alone." He kept his hand closed over his wife's as he turned to Eve. "You'd be Lieutenant Dallas?"

"Yes, Mr. DeBlass. I had a few questions and hoped it would be easier if I asked them in person."

"My wife and I are willing to cooperate in any way we can." He remained standing, a position Eve judged as one of power and of distance.

There was none of Elizabeth's nerves or fragility in the man who stood beside her. He was taking charge, Eve decided, protecting his wife and guarding his own emotions with equal care.

"You were asking about Roarke," he continued. "May I ask why?"

"I told the lieutenant that I'd asked Roarke to see Sharon. To try to . . ."

"Oh, Beth." In a gesture that was both weary and resigned, he shook his head. "What could he do? Why would you bring him into it?"

She stepped away from him, her face so filled with despair, Eve's heart broke. "I know you told me to let it alone, that we had to let her go. But I had to try again. She might have connected with him, Richard. He has a way." She began to speak quickly now, her words tumbling out, tripping over each other. "He might have helped her if I'd asked him sooner. With enough time, there's very little he can't do. But he didn't have enough time. Neither did my child."

"All right," Richard murmured, and laid a hand on her arm. "All right."

She controlled herself again, drew back, drew in. "What can I do now, Lieutenant, but pray for justice?"

"I'll get you justice, Ms. Barrister."

She closed her eyes and clung to that. "I think you will. I wasn't sure of that, even after Roarke called me about you."

"He called you—to discuss the case?"

"He called to see how we were—and to tell me he thought you'd be coming to see me personally before long." She nearly smiled. "He's rarely wrong. He told me I'd find you competent, organized, and involved. You are. I'm grateful I've had the opportunity to see that for myself and to know that you're in charge of my daughter's murder investigation."

"Ms. Barrister," Eve hesitated only a moment before deciding to take the risk. "What if I told you Roarke is a suspect?"

Elizabeth's eyes went wide, then calmed again almost immediately. "I'd say you were taking an extraordinarily big wrong step."

"Because Roarke is incapable of murder?"

"No, I wouldn't say that." It was a relief to think of it, if only for a moment, in objective terms. "Incapable of a senseless act, yes. He might kill cold-bloodedly, but never the defenseless. He might kill, I wouldn't be surprised if he had. But would he do to anyone what was done to Sharon—before, during, after? No. Not Roarke."

"No," Richard echoed, and his hand searched for his wife's again. "Not Roarke."

Not Roarke, Eve thought again when she was back in her cab and headed for the underground. Why the hell hadn't he told her he'd met Sharon DeBlass as a favor to her mother? What else hadn't he told her?

Blackmail. Somehow she didn't see him as a victim of blackmail. He wouldn't give a damn what was said or broadcast about him. But the diary changed things and made blackmail a new and intriguing motive.

Just what had Sharon recorded about whom, and where were the goddamn diaries?

NINE

"No problem reversing the tail," Feeney said as he shoveled in what passed for breakfast at the eatery at Cop Central. "I see him cue in on me. He's looking around for you, but there's plenty of bodies. So I get on the frigging plane."

Feeney washed down irradiated eggs with black bean coffee without a wince. "He gets on, too, but he sits up in First Class. When we get off, he's waiting, and that's when he knows you're not there." He jabbed at Eve with his fork. "He was pissed, makes a quick call. So I get behind him, trail him to the Regent Hotel. They don't like to tell you anything at the Regent. Flash your badge and they get all offended."

"And you explained, tactfully, about civic duty."

"Right." Feeney pushed his empty plate into the recycler slot, crushed his empty cup with his hand, and sent it to follow. "He made a couple of calls—one to East Washington, one to Virginia. Then he makes a local—to the chief."

"Shit."

"Yeah. Chief Simpson's pushing buttons for DeBlass, no question. Makes you wonder what buttons."

Before Eve could comment, her communicator beeped. She pulled it out and answered the call from her commander.

"Dallas, be in Testing. Twenty minutes."

"Sir, I'm meeting a snitch on the Colby matter at oh nine hundred."

"Reschedule." His voice was flat. "Twenty minutes."

Slowly, Dallas replaced her communicator. "I guess we know one of the buttons."

"Seems like DeBlass is taking a personal interest in you." Feeney studied her face. There wasn't a cop on the force who didn't despise Testing. "You going to handle it okay?"

"Yeah, sure. This is going to tie me up most of the day, Feeney. Do me a favor. Do a run on the banks in Manhattan. I need to know if Sharon DeBlass kept a safe deposit box. If you don't find anything there, spread out to the other boroughs."

"You got it."

The Testing section was riddled with long corridors, some glassed, some done in pale green walls that were supposed to be calming. Doctors and technicians wore white. The color of innocence and, of course, power. When she entered the first set of reinforced glass doors, the computer politely ordered her to surrender her weapon. Eve took it out of her holster, set it on the tray, and watched it slide away.

It made her feel naked even before she was directed into Testing Room 1-C and told to strip.

She laid her clothes on the bench provided and tried not to think about the techs watching her on their monitors or the machines with the nastily silent glide and their impersonal blinking lights.

The physical exam was easy. All she had to do was stand on the center mark in the tubelike room and watch the lights blip and flash as her internal organs and bones were checked for flaws.

Then she was permitted to don a blue jumpsuit and sit while a machine angled over to examine her eyes and ears. Another, snicking out from one of the wall slots, did a standard reflex test. For the personal touch, a technician entered to take a blood sample.

Please exit door marked Testing 2-C. Phase one is complete, Dallas,
Lieutenant Eve.

In the adjoining room, Eve was instructed to lie on a padded table
for the brain scan. Wouldn't want any cops out there with a brain
tumor urging them to blast civilians, she thought wearily.

Eve watched the techs through the glass wall as the helmet was
lowered onto her head.

Then the games began.

The bench adjusted to a sitting position and she was treated to
virtual reality. The VR put her in a vehicle during a high-speed chase.
Sounds exploded in her ears: the scream of sirens, the shouts of con-
flicting orders from the communicator on the dash. She could see that
it was a standard police unit, fully charged. The control of the vehicle
was hers, and she had to swerve and maneuver to avoid flattening a
variety of pedestrians the VR hurled in her path.

In one part of her brain she was aware her vitals were being monitored: blood pressure, pulse, even the amount of sweat that crawled
on her skin, the saliva that pooled and dried in her mouth. It was
hot, almost unbearably hot. She narrowly missed a food transport that
lumbered into her path.

She recognized her location. The old ports on the east side. She could
smell them: water, bad fish, and old sweat. Transients wearing their uniform of blue coveralls were looking for a handout or a day's labor. She flew
by a group of them jostling for position in front of a placement center.

Subject armed. Rifle torch, hand explosive. Wanted for robbery
homicide.

Great, Eve thought as she careened after him. Fucking great. She
punched the accelerator, whipped the wheel, and kissed off the fender
of the target vehicle in a shower of sparks. A spurt of flame whooshed
by her ear as he fired at her. The proprietor of a port side roach coach
dived for cover, along with several of his customers. Rice noodles flew
along with curses.

She rammed the target again, ordering her backup to maneuver into a pincer position.

This time her quarry's vehicle shuddered, tipped. As he fought for control, she used hers to batter his to a stop. She shouted the standard identification and warning as she bolted from the vehicle. He came out blasting, and she brought him down.

The shock from her weapon jolted his nervous system. She watched him jitter, wet himself, then collapse.

She'd hardly taken a breath to readjust when the bastard techs tossed her into a new scene. The screams, the little girl's screams; the raging roar of the man who was her father.

They had reconstructed it almost too perfectly, using her own report, visuals of the site, and the mirror of her memory they'd lifted in the scan.

Eve didn't bother to curse them, but held back her hate, her grief, and sent herself racing up the stairs and back into her nightmare.

No more screams from the little girl. She beat on the door, calling out her name and rank. Warning the man on the other side of the door, trying to calm him.

"Cunts. You're all cunts. Come on in, cunt bitch. I'll kill you."

The door folded like cardboard under her ramming shoulder. She went in, weapon drawn.

"She was just like her mother—just like her fucking mother. Thought they'd get away from me. Thought they could. I fixed it. I fixed them. I'm going to fix you, cunt cop."

The little girl was staring at her with big, dead eyes. Doll's eyes. Her tiny, helpless body mutilated, blood spreading like a pool. And dripping from the knife.

She told him to freeze: "*You son of a bitch*, drop the weapon. *Drop the fucking knife!*" But he kept coming. Stunned him. But he kept coming.

The room smelled of blood, of urine, of burned food. The lights were too bright, unshaded and blinding so that everything, everything stood out in jarring relief. A doll with a missing arm on the ripped sofa, a crooked window shield that let in a hard red glow from the neon across the street, the overturned table of cheap molded plastic, the cracked screen of a broken 'link.

The little girl with dead eyes. The spreading pool of blood. And the sharp, sticky gleam of the blade.

"I'm going to ram this right up your cunt. Just like I did to her."

Stunned again. His eyes were wild, jagged on homemade Zeus, that wonderful chemical that made gods out of men, with all the power and insanity that went with delusions of immortality.

The knife, with the scarlet drenched blade hacked down, whistled.

And she dropped him.

The jolt zipped through his nervous system. His brain died first, so that his body convulsed and shuddered as his eyes turned to glass. Strapping down on the need to scream, she kicked the knife away from his still twitching hand and looked at the child.

The big doll's eyes stared at her, and told her—again—that she'd been too late.

Forcing her body to relax, she let nothing into her mind but her report.

The VR section was complete. Her vitals were checked again before she was taken to the final testing phase. The one-on-one with the psychiatrist.

Eve didn't have anything against Dr. Mira. The woman was dedicated to her calling. In private practice, she could have earned triple the salary she pulled in under the Police and Security Department.

She had a quiet voice with the faintest hint of upper-class New England. Her pale blue eyes were kind—and sharp. At sixty, she was comfortable with middle age, but far from matronly.

Her hair was a warm honey brown and scooped up in the back in a neat yet complicated twist. She wore a tidy, rose toned suit with a sedate gold circle on the lapel.

No, Eve had nothing against her personally. She just hated shrinks.

"Lieutenant Dallas." Mira rose from a soft blue scoop chair when Eve entered.

There was no desk, no computer in sight. One of the tricks, Eve knew, to make the subjects relax and forget they were under intense observation.

"Doctor." Eve sat in the chair Mira indicated.

"I was just about to have some tea. You'll join me?"

"Sure."

Mira moved gracefully to the server, ordered two teas, then brought the cups to the sitting area. "It's unfortunate that your testing was postponed, Lieutenant." With a smile, she sat, sipped. "The process is more conclusive and certainly more beneficial when run within twenty-four hours of an incident."

"It couldn't be helped."

"So I'm told. Your preliminary results are satisfactory."

"Fine."

"You still refuse autohypnosis?"

"It's optional." Hating the defensive sound of her voice.

"Yes, it is." Mira crossed her legs. "You've been through a difficult experience, Lieutenant. There are signs of physical and emotional fatigue."

"I'm on another case, a demanding one. It's taking a lot of my time."

"Yes, I have that information. Are you taking the standard sleep inducers?"

Eve tested the tea. It was, as she'd suspected, floral in scent and flavor. "No. We've been through that before. Night pills are optional, and I opt no."

"Because they limit your control."

Eve met her eyes. "That's right. I don't like being put to sleep, and I don't like being here. I don't like brain rape."

"You consider Testing a kind of rape?"

There wasn't a cop with a brain who didn't. "It's not a choice, is it?"

Mira kept her sigh to herself. "The termination of a subject, no matter the circumstances, is a traumatic experience for a police officer. If the trauma effects the emotions, the reactions, the attitude, the officer's performance will suffer. If the use of full force was caused by a physical defect, that defect must be located and repaired."

"I know the company line, Doctor. I'm cooperating fully. But I don't have to like it."

"No, you don't." Mira neatly balanced the cup on her knee. "Lieutenant, this is your second termination. Though that is not an unusual amount for an officer with your length of duty, there are many who never need to make that decision. I'd like to know how you feel about the choice you made, and the results."

I wish I'd been quicker, Eve thought. I wish that child was playing with her toys right now instead of being cremated.

"As my only choice was to let him carve me into pieces, or stop him, I feel just fine about the decision. My warning was issued and ignored. Stunning was ineffective. The evidence that he would, indeed, kill was lying on the floor between us in a puddle of blood. Therefore, I have no problem with the results."

"You were disturbed by the death of the child?"

"I believe anyone would be disturbed by the death of a child. Certainly that kind of vicious murder of the defenseless."

"And do you see the parallel between the child and yourself?" Mira asked quietly. She could see Eve draw in and close off. "Lieutenant, we both know I'm fully aware of your background. You were abused, physically, sexually, and emotionally. You were abandoned when you were eight."

"That has nothing to do with—"

"I think it may have a great deal to do with your mental and emotional state," Mira interrupted. "For two years between the ages of eight and ten, you lived in a communal home while your parents were searched for. You have no memory of the first eight years of your life, your name, your circumstances, your birthplace."

However mild they were, Mira's eyes were sharp and searching. "You were given the name Eve Dallas and eventually placed in foster care. You had no control over any of this. You were a battered child, dependent on the system, which in many ways failed you."

It took every ounce of will for Eve to keep her eyes and her voice level. "As I, part of the system, failed to protect the child. You want to know how I feel about that, Dr. Mira?"

Wretched. Sick. Sorry.

"I feel that I did everything I could do. I went through your VR and did it again. Because there was no changing it. If I could have saved the child, I would have saved her. If I could have arrested the subject, I would have."

"But these matters were not in your control."

Sneaky bitch, Eve thought. "It was in my control to terminate. After employing all standard options, I exercised my control. You've reviewed the report. It was a clean, justifiable termination."

Mira said nothing for a moment. Her skills, she knew, had never been able to more than scrape at Eve's outer wall of defense. "Very well, Lieutenant. You're cleared to resume duty without restriction." Mira held up a hand before Eve could rise. "Off the record."

"Is anything?"

Mira only smiled. "It's true that very often the mind protects itself. Yours refuses to acknowledge the first eight years of your life. But those years are a part of you. I can get them back for you when you're ready. And Eve," she added in that quiet voice, "I can help you deal with them."

"I've made myself what I am, and I can live with it. Maybe I don't want to risk living with the rest." She got up and walked to the door. When she turned back, Mira was sitting just as she had been, legs crossed, one hand holding the pretty little cup. The scent of brewed flowers lingered in the air.

"A hypothetical case," Eve began and waited for Mira's nod.

"A woman, with considerable social and financial advantages, chooses to become a whore." At Mira's lifted brow, Eve swore impatiently. "We don't have to pretty up the terminology here, Doctor. She chose to make her living from sex. Flaunted it in front of her well-positioned family, including her arch-conservative grandfather. Why?"

"It's difficult to come up with one specific motive from such general and sketchy information. The most obvious would be the subject could find her self-worth only in sexual skill. She either enjoyed or detested the act."

Intrigued, Eve stepped away from the door. "If she detested it, why would she become a pro?"

"To punish."

"Herself?"

"Certainly, and those close to her."

To punish, Eve mused. The diary. Blackmail.

"A man kills," she continued. "Viciously, brutally. The killing is tied to sex, and is executed in a unique and distinctive fashion. He records it, has bypassed a sophisticated security system. A recording of the murder is delivered to the investigating officer. A message is left at the scene, a boastful message. What is he?"

"You don't give me much," Mira complained, but Eve could see her attention was caught. "Inventive," she began. "A planner, and a voyeur. Confident, perhaps smug. You said distinctive, so he wishes to leave his mark, and he wants to show off his skill, his brain. Using your observation and deductive talents, Lieutenant, did he enjoy the act of murder?"

"Yes. I think he reveled in it."

Mira nodded. 'Then he will certainly enjoy it again."

"He already has. Two murders, barely a week apart. He won't wait long before the next, will he?"

"It's doubtful." Mira sipped her tea as if they were discussing the latest spring fashions. "Are the two murders connected in any way other than the perpetrator and the method?"

"Sex," Eve said shortly.

"Ah." Mira tilted her head. "With all our technology, with the amazing advances that have been made in genetics, we are still unable to control human virtues and flaws. Perhaps we are too human to permit the tampering. Passions are necessary to the human spirit. We learned that early this century when genetic engineering nearly slipped out of control. It's unfortunate that some passions twist. Sex and violence. For some it's still a natural marriage."

She stood then to take the cups and place them beside the server. "I'd be interested in knowing more about this man, Lieutenant. If and when you decide you want a profile, I hope you'll come to me."

"It's Code Five."

Mira glanced back. "I see."

"If we don't tie this up before he hits again, I may be able to swing it."

"I'll make myself available."

"Thanks."

"Eve, even strong, self-made women have weak spots. Don't be afraid of them."

Eve held Mira's gaze for another moment. "I've got work to do."

Testing left her shaky. Eve compensated by being surly and antago-nistic with her snitch and nearly losing a lead on a case involving boot-legged chemicals. Her mood was far from cheerful when she checked back in to Cop Central. There was no message from Feeney.

Others in her department knew just where she'd spent the day and did their best to stay out of her way. As a result, she worked in solitude and annoyance for an hour.

Her last effort was to put through a call to Roarke. She was neither surprised nor particularly disappointed when he wasn't available. She left a message on his e-mail requesting an appointment, then logged out for the day.

She intended to drown her mood in cheap liquor and mediocre music at Mavis's latest gig at the Blue Squirrel.

It was a joint, which put it one slippery step up from a dive. The light was dim, the clientele edgy, and the service pitiful. It was exactly what Eve was looking for.

The music struck her in one clashing wave when she walked in. Mavis was managing to lift her appealing screech of a voice over the band, which consisted of one multitattooed kid on a melody master.

Eve snarled off the offer from a guy in a hooded jacket to buy her a drink in one of the private smoking booths. She jockeyed her way to a table, pressed in an order for a screamer, and settled back to watch Mavis perform.

She wasn't half bad, Eve decided. Not half good either, but the customers weren't choosy. Mavis was wearing paint tonight, her busty little body a canvas for splatters and streaks of orange and violet, with strategically brushed splotches of emerald. Bracelets and chains jan-gled as she jittered around the small, raised stage. One step below, a mass of humanity gyrated in sympathy.

Eve watched a small, sealed package pass from hand to hand on the edge of the dance floor. Drugs, of course. They'd tried a war on them, legalizing them, ignoring them, and regulating them. Nothing seemed to work.

She couldn't raise the interest to make a bust and lifted a hand in a wave to Mavis instead.

The vocal part of the song ended—such as it was. Mavis leaped offstage, wiggled through the crowd, and plopped a painted hip on the edge of Eve's table.

"Hey, stranger."

"Looking good, Mavis. Who's the artist?"

"Oh, this guy I know." She shifted, tapped an inch-long fingernail on the left cheek of her butt. "Caruso. See, he signed me. Got the job free for passing his name around." Her eyes rounded when the waitress set the long, slim glass filled with frothy blue liquid in front of Eve. "A screamer? Wouldn't you rather I find a hammer and just knock you unconscious?"

"It's been a shitty day," Eve muttered and took the first shocking sip. "Jesus. These never get any better."

Worried, Mavis leaned closer. "I can cut out for a little while."

"No, I'm okay." Eve risked her life with another sip. "I just wanted to check out your gig, let off some steam. Mavis, you're not using, are you?"

"Hey, come on." More concerned than insulted, Mavis shook Eve's shoulder. "I'm clean, you know that. Some shit gets passed around in here, but it's all minor league. Some happy pills, some calmers, a few mood patches." She pokered up. "If you're looking to make a bust, you could at least do it on my night off."

"Sorry." Annoyed with herself, Eve rubbed her hands over her face. "I'm not fit for human consumption at the moment. Go back and sing. I like hearing you."

"Sure. But if you want company when you split, just give me a sign. I can fix it."

"Thanks." Eve sat back, closed her eyes. It was a surprise when the music slowed, even mellowed. If you didn't look around, it wasn't so bad.

For twenty credits she could have hooked on mood enhancer goggles, treated herself to lights and shapes that fit the music. At the moment, she preferred the dark behind her eyes.

"This doesn't seem quite your den of iniquity, Lieutenant."

Eve opened her eyes and stared up at Roarke. "Every time I turn around."

He sat across from her. The table was small enough that their knees bumped. His way of adjusting was to slide his thighs against hers. "You called me, remember, and you'd left this address when you logged out."

"I wanted an appointment, not a drinking buddy."

He glanced at the drink on the table, leaned over to take a sniff. "You're not going to get one with that poison.'"

"This joint doesn't run to fine wine and aged scotch."

He laid a hand over hers for the simple purpose of watching her scowl and jerk away. "Why don't we go somewhere that does?"

"I'm in a pisser of a mood. Roarke. Give me an appointment, at your convenience, then take off."

"An appointment for what?" The singer caught his attention. He cocked a brow, watching her roll her eyes and gesture. "Unless she's having some sort of seizure, I believe the vocalist is signaling you."

Resigned, Eve glanced over, shook her head. "She's a friend of mine." She shook her head more emphatically when Mavis grinned and turned both thumbs up. "She thinks I got lucky."

"You did." Roarke picked the drink up and set it on an adjoining table where greedy hands fought over it. "I just saved your life."

"Goddamn it—"

"If you want to get drunk, Eve, at least do it with something that will leave you most of your stomach lining." He scanned the menu, winced. "Which means nothing that can be purchased here." He took her hand as he rose. "Come on."

"I'm fine right here."

All patience, he bent down until his face was close to hers. "What you are is hoping to get drunk enough so that you can take a few punches at someone without worrying about the consequences. With me, you don't have to get drunk, you don't have to worry. You can take all the punches you want."

"Why?"

"Because you have something sad in your eyes. And it gets to me."
While she was dealing with the surprise of that statement, he hauled
her to her feet and toward the door.

"I'm going home," she decided.

"No, you're not."

"Listen, pal—"

That was as far as she got before her back was shoved against the
wall and his mouth crushed hard on hers. She didn't fight. The wind
had been knocked out of her by the suddenness, and the rage under it,
and the shock of need that slammed into her like a fist.

It was quick, seconds only, before her mouth was free. "Stop it,"
she demanded, and hated that her voice was only a shaky whisper.

"Whatever you think," he began, struggling for his own composure, "there are times when you need someone. Right now, it's me."
Impatience shimmering around him, he pulled her outside. "Where's
your car?"

She gestured down the block and let him propel her down the
sidewalk. "I don't know what your problem is."

"It seems to be you. Do you know how you looked?" he demanded
as he yanked open the car door. "Sitting in that place with your eyes
closed, shadows under them?" Picturing it again only fired his anger.
He shoved her into the passenger seat and rounded the car to take the
driver's position himself. "What's your fucking code?"

Fascinated with the whiplash temper, she shifted to key it in herself. With the lock released, he pressed the starter and pulled away
from the curb.

"I was trying to relax," Eve said carefully.

"You don't know how," he shot back. "You've packed it in, but you
haven't gotten rid of it. You're walking a real straight line, Eve, but it's
a damn thin one."

"That's what I'm trained to do."

"You don't know what you're up against this time."

Her fingers curled into a fist at her side. "And you do."

He was silent for a moment, banking his own emotions. "We'll talk
about it later."

"I like now better. I went to see Elizabeth Barrister yesterday."

"I know." Calmer, he adjusted to the jerky rhythm of her car. "You're cold. Turn up the heater."

"It's busted. Why didn't you tell me that she'd asked you to meet Sharon, to talk to her?"

"Because Beth asked me in confidence."

"What's your relationship with Elizabeth Barrister?"

"We're friends." Roarke slanted her a look. "I have a few. She and Richard are among them."

"And the senator?"

"I hate his fucking, pompous, hypocritical guts," Roarke said calmly. "If he gets his party's nomination for president, I'll put everything I've got into his opponent's campaign. If it's the devil himself."

"You should learn to speak your mind, Roarke," she said with a ghost of a smile. "Did you know that Sharon kept a diary?"

"It's a natural assumption. She was a businesswoman."

"I'm not talking about a log, business records. A diary, a personal diary. Secrets, Roarke. Blackmail."

He said nothing as he turned the idea over. "Well, well. You found your motive."

"That remains to be seen. You have a lot of secrets, Roarke."

He let out a half laugh as he stopped at the gates of his estate. "Do you really think I'd be a victim of blackmail, Eve? That some lost, pitiful woman like Sharon could unearth information you can't and use it against me?"

"No." That was simple. She put a hand on his arm. "I'm not going inside with you." That was not.

"If I were bringing you here for sex, we'd have sex. We both know it. You wanted to see me. You want to shoot the kind of weapon that was used to kill Sharon and the other, don't you?"

She let out a short breath. "Yes."

"Now's your chance."

The gates opened. He drove through.

CHAPTER

TEN

The same stone-faced butler stood guard at the door. He took Eve's coat with the same faint disapproval.

"Send coffee down to the target room, please," Roarke ordered as he led Eve up the stairs.

He was holding her hand again, but Eve decided it was less a sentimental gesture than one to make sure she didn't balk. She could have told him she was much too intrigued to go anywhere, but found she enjoyed that ripple of annoyance under his smooth manner.

When they'd reached the third floor, he went through his collection briskly, choosing weapons without fuss or hesitation. He handled the antiques with the competence of experience and, she thought, habitual use.

Not a man who simply bought to own, but one who made use of his possessions. She wondered if he knew that counted against him. Or if he cared.

Once his choices were secured in a leather case, he moved to a wall.

Both the security console and the door itself were so cleverly hidden in a painting of a forest, she would never have found it. The trompe l'oeil slid open to an elevator.

"This car only opens to a select number of rooms," he explained as Eve stepped into the elevator with him. "I rarely take guests down to the target area."

"Why?"

"My collection, and the use of it, are reserved for those who can appreciate it."

"How much do you buy through the black market?"

"Always a cop." He flashed that grin at her, and she was sure, tucked his tongue in his cheek. "I buy only through legal sources, naturally." His eyes skimmed down to her shoulder bag. "As long as you've got your recorder on."

She couldn't help but smile back. Of course she had her recorder on. And of course he knew it. It was a measure of her interest that she opened the bag, took out her recorder, and manually disengaged.

"And your backup?" he said smoothly.

"You're too smart for your own good." Willing to take the chance, she slipped a hand into her pocket. The backup unit was nearly paper thin. She used a thumbnail to deactivate it. "What about yours?" She glanced around the elevator as the doors opened. "You'd have video and audio security in every corner of this place."

"Of course." He took her hand again and drew her out of the car.

The room was high ceilinged, surprisingly spartan given Roarke's love of comfort. The lights switched on the moment they stepped in, illuminating plain, sand-colored walls, a bank of simple high-backed chairs, and tables where a tray holding a silver coffeepot and china cups had already been set.

Ignoring them, Eve walked over to a long, glossy black console. "What does it do?"

"A number of things." Roarke set the case he carried down on a flat area. He pressed his palm to an identiscreen. There was a soft green glow beneath it as his print was read and accepted, then lights and dials glowed on.

"I keep a supply of ammunition here." He pressed a series of buttons. A cabinet in the base of the console slid open. "You'll want these." From a second cabinet, he took earplugs and safety glasses.

"This is, what, like a hobby?" Eve asked as she adjusted the glasses. The small, clear lenses cupped her eyes, the attached earplugs fit snugly.

"Yes. Like a hobby."

His voice came with a faint echo through her ear protectors, linking them, closing out the rest. He chose the .38, loaded it.

"This was standard police issue in the mid-twentieth century. Toward the second millennium, nine millimeters were preferred."

"The RS-fifties were the official weapon of choice during the Urban Revolt and into the third decade of the twenty-first century."

He lifted a brow, pleased. "You've been doing your homework."

"Damn right." She glanced at the weapon in his hand. "Into the mind of a killer."

"Then you'd be aware that the hand laser you have strapped to your side didn't gain popular acceptance until about twenty-five years ago."

She watched with a slight frown as he slapped the cylinder shut. "The NS laser, with modifications, has been standard police issue since 2023. I didn't notice any lasers in your collection."

His eyes met hers, and there was a laugh in them. "Cop toys only. They're illegal, Lieutenant, even for collectors." He pressed a button. Against the far wall a hologram flashed, so lifelike that Eve blinked and braced before she caught herself.

"Excellent image," she murmured, studying the big, bull-shouldered man holding a weapon she couldn't quite identify.

"He's a replica of a typical twentieth-century thug. That's an AK-forty-seven he's holding."

"Right." She narrowed her eyes at it. It was more dramatic than in the photos and videos she'd studied. "Very popular with urban gangs and drug dealers of the era."

"An assault weapon," Roarke murmured. "Fashioned to kill. Once I activate, if he hits target, you'd feel a slight jolt. Low level electrical shock, rather than the much more dramatic insult of a bullet. Want to try it?"

"You go first."

"Fine." Roarke activated. The hologram lunged forward, swinging up his weapon. The sound effects kicked in instantly.

The thunder of noise had Eve jerking back a step. Snarled obscenities, street sounds, the terrifyingly rapid explosion of gunfire.

She watched, slack jawed, as the image spurted what looked entirely too much like blood. The wide chest seemed to erupt with it as the man flew back. The weapon spiraled out of his hand. Then both vanished.

"Jesus."

A little surprised that he'd been showing off, like a kid at an arcade, Roarke lowered his weapon. "It hardly makes the point of what something like this can do to flesh and bone if the image isn't realistic."

"Guess not." She had to swallow. "Did he hit you?"

"Not that time. Of course, one on one, and when you can fully anticipate your opponent, doesn't make it very difficult to win your round."

Roarke pushed more buttons, and the dead gunman was back, whole and ready to rock. Roarke took his stance with the ease and automation, Eve thought, of a veteran cop. Or, to borrow his word, a thug.

Abruptly, the image lunged, and as Roarke fired, other holograms appeared in rapid succession. A man with some sort of wicked looking handgun, a snarling woman aiming a long barreled weapon—a .44 Magnum, Eve decided—a small, terrified child carrying a ball.

They flashed and fired, cursed, screamed, bled. When it was over, the child was sitting on the ground weeping, all alone.

"A random choice like that's more difficult," Roarke told her. "Caught my shoulder."

"What?" Eve blinked, focused on him again. "Your shoulder."

He grinned at her. "Don't worry, darling. It's just a flesh wound."

Her heart was thudding in her ears, no matter how ridiculous she told herself was her reaction. "Hell of a toy, Roarke. Real, fun and games time. Do you play often?"

"Now and again. Ready to try it?"

If she could handle a session with VR, Eve decided, she could handle this. "Yeah, run another random pattern."

"That's what I admire about you, Lieutenant." Roarke selected ammo, loaded fresh. "You jump right in. Let's try a dry run first."

He brought up a simple target, circles and a bull's-eye. He stepped behind her, putting the .38 in her hands, his over them. He pressed his cheek to hers. "You have to sight it, as it doesn't sense heat and movement as your weapon does." He adjusted her arms until he was satisfied. "When you're ready to fire, you want to squeeze the trigger, not pump it. It's going to jerk a bit. It's not as smooth or as silent as your laser."

"I've got that," she muttered. It was foolish to be susceptible to his hands over hers, the press of his body, the smell of him. "You're crowding me."

He turned his head, just enough to have his lips brushing up to her earlobe. It was innocently unpierced, rather sweet, like a child's.

"I know. You need to brace yourself more than you're used to. Your reaction will be to flinch. Don't."

"I don't flinch." To prove it, she squeezed the trigger. Her arms jerked, annoying her. She shot again, and a third time, missing the heart of the target by less than an inch. "Christ, you feel it, don't you?" She rolled her shoulders, fascinated by the way they sang in response to the weapon in her hands.

"It makes it more personal. You've got a good eye." He was impressed, but his tone was mild. "Of course, it's one thing to shoot at a circle, another to shoot at a body. Even a reproduction."

A challenge? she noted. Well, she was up for it. "How many more shots in this?"

"We'll reload it full." He programmed in a series. Curiosity and, he had to admit, ego had him choosing a tough one. "Ready?"

She flicked a glance at him, adjusted her stance. "Yeah."

The first image was an elderly woman clutching a shopping bag with both hands. Eve nearly took the bystander's head off before her finger froze. A movement flickered to the left, and she shot a mugger before he could bring an iron pipe down on the old woman. A slight sting in her left hip had her shifting again, and taking out a bald man with a weapon similar to her own.

They came fast and hard after that.

Roarke watched her, mesmerized. No, she didn't flinch, he mused. Her eyes stayed flat and cool. Cop's eyes. He knew her adrenaline was up, her pulse hammering. Her movements were quick but as smooth and studied as a dance. Her jaw was set, her hands steady.

And he wanted her, he realized as his gut churned. Quite desperately he wanted her.

"Caught me twice," she said almost to herself. She opened the chamber herself, reloaded as she'd seen Roarke do. "Once in the hip, once in the abdomen. That makes me dead or in dire straits. Run another."

He obliged her, then tucked his hands in his pockets and watched her work.

When she was done, she asked to try the Swiss model. She found she preferred the weight and the response of it. Definitely an advantage over a revolver, she reflected. Quicker, more responsive, better fire power, and a reload took seconds.

Neither weapon fit as comfortably in her hand as her laser, yet she found both primitively and horribly efficient.

And the damage they caused, the torn flesh, the flying blood, turned death into a gruesome affair.

"Any hits?" Roarke asked.

Though the images were gone, she stared at the wall, and the afterimages that played in her mind. "No. I'm clean. What they do to a body," she said softly, and put the weapon down. "To have used these—to have faced having to use them day after day, and know going in they could be used against you. Who could face that," she wondered, "without going a little insane?"

"You could." He removed his eye and ear protectors. "Conscience and dedication to duty don't have to equal any kind of weakness. You got through Testing. It cost you, but you got through it."

Carefully, she set her protectors beside his. "How do you know?"

"How do I know you were in Testing today? I have contacts. How do I know it cost you?" He cupped her chin. "I can see it," he said softly. "Your heart wars with your head. I don't think you realize that's what makes you so good at your job. Or so fascinating to me."

"I'm not trying to fascinate you. I'm trying to find a man who used those weapons I just fired; not for defense, but for pleasure." She looked straight into his eyes. "It isn't you."

"No, it isn't me."

"But you know something."

He brushed the pad of his thumb over, into the dip in her chin before dropping his hand. "I'm not at all sure that I do." He crossed over to the table, poured coffee. 'Twentieth-century weapons, twentieth-century crimes, with twentieth-century motives?" He flicked a glance at her. "That would be my take."

"It's a simple enough deduction."

"But tell me, Lieutenant, can you play deductive games in history, or are you too firmly entrenched in the now?"

She'd wondered the same herself, and she was learning. "I'm flexible."

"No, but you're smart. Whoever killed Sharon had a knowledge, even an affection, perhaps an obsession with the past." His brow lifted mockingly. "I do have a knowledge of certain pieces of the past, and undoubtedly an affection for them. Obsession?" He lifted a careless shoulder. "You'd have to judge for yourself."

"I'm working on it."

"I'm sure you are. Let's take a page out of old-fashioned deductive reasoning, no computers, no technical analysis. Study the victim first. You believe Sharon was a blackmailer. And it fits. She was an angry woman, a defiant one who needed power. And wanted to be loved."

"You figured all that out after seeing her twice?"

"From that." He offered the coffee to her. "And from talking to people who knew her. Friends and associates found her a stunning, energetic woman, yet a secretive one. A woman who dismissed her family, yet thought of them often. One who loved to live, yet one who brooded regularly. I imagine we've covered much of the same ground."

Irritation jumped in. "I wasn't aware you were covering any ground, Roarke, in a police investigation."

"Beth and Richard are my friends. I take my friendships seriously. They're grieving, Eve. And I don't like knowing Beth is blaming herself."

She remembered the haunted eyes and nerves. She sighed. "All right, I can accept that. Who have you talked to?"

"Friends, as I said, acquaintances, business associates." He set his coffee aside as Eve sipped hers and paced. "Odd, isn't it, how many different opinions and perceptions you find on one woman. Ask this one, and you'll hear Sharon was loyal, generous. Ask another and she was vindictive, calculating. Still another saw her as a party addict who could never find enough excitement, while the next tells you she enjoyed quiet evenings on her own. Quite a role player, our Sharon."

"She wore different faces for different people. It's common enough."

"Which face, or which role, killed her?" Roarke took out a cigarette, lighted it. "Blackmail." Thoughtfully he blew out a fragrant stream of smoke. "She would have been good at it. She liked to dig into people and could dispense considerable charm while doing it."

"And she dispensed it on you."

"Lavishly." That careless smile flashed again. "I wasn't prepared to exchange information for sex. Even if she hadn't been my friend's daughter and a professional, she wouldn't have appealed to me in that way. I prefer a different type." His eyes rested on Eve's again, broodingly. "Or thought I did. I haven't yet figured out why the intense, driven, and prickly type appeals to me so unexpectedly."

She poured more coffee, looked at him over the rim. "That isn't flattering."

"It wasn't meant to be. Though for someone who must have a very poor-sighted hairdresser and doesn't choose the standard enhancements, you are surprisingly easy to look at."

"I don't have a hairdresser, or time for enhancements." Or, she decided, the inclination to discuss them. "To continue the deduction. If Sharon DeBlass was murdered by one of her blackmail victims, where does Lola Starr come in?"

"A problem, isn't it?" Roarke took a contemplative drag. "They don't appear to have anything in common other than their choice of profession. It's doubtful they knew each other or shared the same taste in clients. Yet there was one who, at least briefly, knew them both."

"One who chose them both."

Roarke lifted a brow, nodded. "You put it better."

"What did you mean when you said I didn't know what I was getting into?"

His hesitation was so brief, so smoothly covered, it was barely noticeable. "I'm not sure if you understand the power DeBlass has or can use. The scandal of his granddaughter's murder could add to it. He wants the presidency, and he wants to dictate the mood and moral choices of the country and beyond."

"You're saying he could use Sharon's death politically? How?"

Roarke stubbed his cigarette out. "He could paint his granddaughter as a victim of society, with sex for profit as the murder weapon. How can a world that allows legalized prostitution, full conception control, sexual adjustment, and so forth not take responsibility for the results?"

Eve could appreciate the debate, but shook her head. "DeBlass also wants to eliminate the gun ban. She was shot by a weapon not really available under current law."

"Which makes it more insidious. Would she have been able to defend herself if she, too, had been armed?" When Eve started to disagree, he shook his head. "It hardly matters what the answer is, only the question itself. Have we forgotten our founders and the basic tenets of their blueprint for the country? Our right to bear arms. A woman murdered in her own home, her own bed, a victim of sexual freedom and defenselessness. More, yes, much more, of moral decline."

He strolled over to disengage the console. "Oh, you'll argue that murder by handgun was the rule rather than the exception when anyone with the desire and the finances could purchase one, but he'll drown that out. The Conservative Party is gaining ground, and he's the spearhead."

He watched her assimilate as she poured yet more coffee. "Has it occurred to you that he might not want the murderer caught?"

Off guard, she looked up. "Why wouldn't he? Over and above the personal, wouldn't that give him even more ammunition? 'Here's the low-life, immoral scum that murdered my poor, misguided granddaughter.'"

"That's a risk, isn't it? Perhaps the murderer is a fine, upstanding pillar of his community who was equally misguided. But a scapegoat is certainly required."

He waited a moment, watching her think it through. "Who do you think made certain you went to Testing in the middle of this case? Who's watching every step you take, monitoring every stage of your investigation? Who'd digging into your background, your personal life as well as your professional one?"

Shaken, she set her cup down. "I suspect DeBlass put the pressure on about Testing. He doesn't trust me, or he hasn't decided I'm competent to head the investigation. And he had Feeney and me followed from East Washington." She let cut a long breath. "How do you know he's digging on me? Because you are?"

He didn't mind the anger in her eyes, or the accusation. He preferred it to the worry another might have shown. "No, because I'm watching him while he's watching you. I decided I'd find it more satisfying to learn about you from the source, over time, than by reading reports."

He stepped closer, skimmed his fingers over her choppy hair. "I respect the privacy of the people I care about. And I care about you, Eve. I don't know why, precisely, but you pull something from me."

When she started to step back, he tightened his fingers. "I'm tired of every time I have a moment with you, you put murder between us."

"There is murder between us."

"No. If anything, that's what brought us here. Is that the problem? You can't shed Lieutenant Dallas long enough to feel?"

"That's who I am."

"Then that's who I want." His eyes had darkened with impatient desire. The frustration he felt was only with himself, for being so impossibly driven he might, at any moment, beg. "Lieutenant Dallas wouldn't be afraid of me, even if Eve might."

The coffee had wired her. That's what had her system so jittery with nerves. "I'm not afraid of you, Roarke."

"Aren't you?" He moved closer, curling his hands on the lapels of her shirt. "What do you think will happen if you step over the line?"

"Too much," she murmured. "Not enough. Sex isn't high on my priority list. It's distracting."

The temper in his eyes lighted to a laugh. "Damn right it is. When it's done well. Isn't it time you let me show you?"

She gripped his arms, not sure if she intended to move in or away. "It's a mistake."

"So we'll have to make it count," he muttered before his mouth captured hers.

She moved in.

Her arms went around him, fingers diving into his hair. Her body slammed into his, vibrating as the kiss grew rough, then nearly brutal. His mouth was hot, almost vicious. The shock of it sent flares of reaction straight to her center.

Already, his fast, impatient hands were tugging her shirt from her jeans, finding her skin. In response, she dragged at his, desperate to get through silk and to flesh.

He had a vision of himself dragging her to the floor, pounding himself into her until her screams echoed like gunshots, and his release erupted like blood. It would be quick, and fierce. And over.

With the breath shuddering in his lungs, he jerked back. Her face was flushed, her mouth already swollen. He'd torn her shirt at the shoulder.

A room filled with violence, the smell of gunsmoke still stinking the air, and weapons still within reach.

"Not here." He half carried, half dragged her to the elevator. By the time the doors opened, he'd ripped aside the torn sleeve. He shoved her against the back wall as the doors closed them in, and fumbled with her holster. "Take this damn thing off. Take it off."

She hit the release and let the holster dangle from one hand as she fought open his buttons with the other. "Why do you wear so many clothes?"

"I won't next time." He ripped the tattered shirt aside. Beneath she wore a thin, nearly transparent undershirt that revealed small, firm breasts and hardened nipples. He closed his hands over them, watched her eyes glaze. "Where do you like to be touched?"

"You're doing fine." She had to brace a hand on the side wall to keep from buckling.

When the doors opened again, they were fused together. They

circled out with his teeth nipping and scraping along her throat. She
let her bag and her holster drop.

She got a glimpse of the room: wide windows, mirrors, muted colors. She could smell flowers and felt the give of carpet under her feet.
As she struggled to release his slacks, she caught sight of the bed.

"Holy God."

It was huge, a lake of midnight blue cupped between high carved
wood. It stood on a platform beneath a domed sky window. Across from
it was a fireplace of pale green stone where fragrant wood sizzled.

"You sleep here?"

"I don't intend to sleep tonight."

He interrupted her gawking by pulling her up the two stairs to the
platform and tumbling her onto the bed.

"I have to check in by oh seven hundred."

"Shut up, Lieutenant."

"Okay."

With a half laugh, she rolled on top of him and fastened her mouth
to his. Wild, reckless energy was bursting inside her. She couldn't
move quickly enough, her hands weren't fast enough to satisfy the
craving.

She fought off her boots, let him peel the jeans over her hips. A
wave of pleasure rippled through her when she heard him groan. It
had been a long time since she'd felt the tension and heat of a man's
body—a very long time since she'd wanted to.

The need for release was driving and fierce. The moment they
were naked, she would have straddled him and satisfied it. But he
flipped their positions, muffled her edgy protests with a long, rough
kiss.

"What's your hurry?" he murmured, sliding a hand down to take
her breast and watching her face while his thumb quietly tortured her
nipple. "I haven't even looked at you."

"I want you."

"I know." He levered back, running a hand from her shoulder
to her thigh while his gaze followed the movement. The blood was
pounding in his loins. "Long, slim . . ." His hand squeezed lightly on
her breast. "Small. Very nearly delicate. Who would have guessed?"

"I want you inside me."

"You only want one aspect inside you," he murmured.

"Goddamn it," she began, then groaned when he dipped his head and took her breast into his mouth.

She writhed against him, against herself as he suckled, so gently at first it was torture, then harder, faster until she had to bite back a scream. His hands continued to skim over her, kindling exotic little fires of need.

It wasn't what she was used to. Sex, when she chose to have it, was quick, simple, and satisfied a basic need. But this was tangling emotions, a war on the system, a battering of the senses.

She struggled to get a hand between them, to reach him where he lay hard and heavy against her. Pure panic set in when he braceleted her wrists and levered her hands over her head.

"Don't."

He'd nearly released her in reflex before he saw her eyes. Panic yes, even fear, but desire, too. "You can't always be in control, Eve." As he spoke he ran his free hand over her thigh. She trembled, and her eyes unfocused when his fingers brushed the back of her knee.

"Don't," she said again, fighting for air.

"Don't what? Find a weakness, exploit it?" Experimentally, he caressed that sensitive skin, tracing his fingers up toward the heat, then back again. Her breath was coming in pants now as she fought to roll away from him.

"Too late, it seems," he murmured. "You want the kick without the intimacy?" He began a trail of slow, open-mouthed kisses at the base of her throat, working his way down while her body shivered like a plucked wire beneath his. "You don't need a partner for that. And you have one tonight. I intend to give as much pleasure as I get."

"I can't." She strained against him, bucked, but each frantic movement brought only a new and devastating sensation.

"Let go." He was mad to have her. But her struggle to hold back both challenged and infuriated.

"I can't."

"I'm going to make you let go, and I'm going to watch it happen." He slid back up her, feeling every tremble and quake, until his face was close to hers again. He pressed his palm firmly on the mound between her thighs.

Her breath hissed out. "You bastard. I can't."

"Liar," he said quietly, then slid a finger down, over her, into her. His groan melded with hers as he found her tight, hot, wet. Clinging to control, he focused on her face, the change from panic to shock, from shock to glazed helplessness.

She felt herself slipping, battled back, but the pull was too strong. Someone screamed as she fell, then her body imploded. One moment the tension was vicious, then the spear of pleasure arrowed into her, so sharp, so hot. Dazed, disoriented, she went limp.

He went mad.

He dragged her up so that she was kneeling, her head heavy on his shoulder. "Again," he demanded, dragging her head back by the hair and plundering her mouth. "Again, goddamn it."

"Yes." It was building so quickly. The need like teeth grinding inside her. Free, her hands raced over him, and her body arched fluidly back so that his lips could taste where and how they liked.

Her next climax ripped through him like claws. With something like a snarl, he shoved her onto her back, levered her hips high, and drove himself inside her. She closed around him, a hot, greedy fist.

Her nails scraped at his back, her hips pistoned as he plunged. When her hands slid weakly from his sweat-slicked shoulders, he emptied himself into her.

CHAPTER
ELEVEN

She didn't speak for a long time. There really wasn't anything to say. She had taken an inappropriate step with her eyes wide open. If there were consequences, she would pay them.

Now, she needed to gather whatever dignity she could scrape together and get out.

"I have to go." With her face averted, she sat up and wondered how she was going to find her clothes.

"I don't think so." Roarke's voice was lazy, confident, and infuriating. Even as she started to get off the bed, he snagged her arm, overbalanced her, and had her on her back again.

"Look, fun's fun."

"It certainly is. I don't know as I'd qualify what just happened here as fun. I say it was too intense for that. I haven't finished with you, Lieutenant." When her eyes narrowed, he grinned. "Good, that's what I wanted to—"

He lost his breath and with it the words when her elbow shot into his stomach. In the blink of an eye, she'd reversed their positions. That well-aimed elbow was now pressing dangerously on his windpipe.

"Listen, pal, I come and go as I please, so check your ego."

Like a white flag, he lifted his palms out for peace. Her elbow lifted a half inch before he shifted and sprang.

She was tough, strong, and smart. That was only one more reason why, after a sweaty struggle, she was infuriated to find herself under him again.

"Assaulting an officer will earn you one to five, Roarke. That's in a cage, not cushy home detention."

"You're not wearing your badge. Or anything else, for that matter." He gave her a friendly nip on the chin. "Be sure to put that in your report."

So much for dignity, she decided. "I don't want to fight with you." It pleased her that her voice was calm, even reasonable. "I just have to go."

He shifted, watched as her eyes widened, then fluttered half closed when he slipped inside her again. "No, don't shut your eyes." His voice was whisper rough.

So she watched him, incapable of resisting the fresh onslaught of pleasure. He kept the rhythm slow now, with long, deep strokes that stirred the soul.

Her breath quickened, thickened. All she could see was his face, all she could feel was that lovely, fluid slide of his body in hers, the tireless friction of it that had an orgasm shivering through her like gold.

His fingers linked with hers, and his lips curved on hers. She felt his body tighten an instant before he buried his face in her hair. They lay quiet, bodies meshed but still. He turned his head, pressed a kiss to her temple.

"Stay," he murmured. "Please."

"Yes." She closed her eyes now. "All right, yes."

They didn't sleep. It wasn't fatigue so much as bafflement that as-saulted Eve when she stepped into Roarke's shower in the early hours of the morning.

She didn't spend nights with men. Always she'd been careful to keep sex simple, straightforward and, yes, impersonal. Yet here she was, the morning after, letting herself be pummeled by the hot pulse of his shower sprays. For hours, she'd let herself be pummeled by him. He'd assaulted then invaded parts of her she'd thought impregnable.

She was trying to regret it. It seemed important that she realize and recognize her mistake, and move on. But it was difficult to regret anything that made her body feel so alive and kept the dreams at bay.

"You look good wet, Lieutenant."

Eve turned her head as Roarke stepped through the crisscrossing sprays. "I'm going to need to borrow a shirt."

"We'll find you one." He pressed a knob on the tiled walls, cupped his hand under a fount to catch a puddle of clear, creamy liquid.

"What are you doing?"

"Washing your hair," he murmured and proceeded to stroke and massage the shampoo into her short, sopping cap of hair. "I'm going to enjoy smelling my soap on you." His lips curved. "You're a fascinating woman, Eve. Here we are, wet, naked, both of us half dead from a very memorable night, and still you watch me with very cool, very suspicious eyes."

"You're a suspicious character, Roarke."

"I think that's a compliment." He bent his head to bite her lip, as the steam rose and the spray began to pulse like a heartbeat. "Tell me what you meant, the first time I made love to you, when you said, 'I can't.'"

He angled her head back, and Eve closed her eyes in defense as water chased the shampoo away. "I don't remember everything I said."

"You remember." From another fount, he drew pale green soap that smelled of wild forests. Watching her, he slicked it over her shoulders, down her back, then around and up to her breasts. "Hadn't you had an orgasm before?"

"Of course I have." True, she'd always equated them with the subtle pop of a cork from a bottle of stress, not the violent explosion that destroyed a lifetime of restraint. "You're flattering yourself, Roarke."

"Am I?" Didn't she know that those cool eyes, that wall of resistance she was scrambling to rebuild was an irresistible challenge? Obviously not, he mused. He tugged lightly at her soap-slicked nipples, smiling when she sucked in a breath. "I'm about to flatter myself again."

"I haven't got time for this," she said quickly, and found her back pressed against the tile wall. "It was a mistake in the first place. I have to go."

"It won't take long." He felt a hard slap of lust when he cupped her hips, lifted her. "It wasn't a mistake then, or now. And I have to have you."

His breath was coming faster. It stunned him how much he could want her still, baffled him that she could be blind to how helpless he was under the clawing need for her. It infuriated him that she could, simply by existing, be his weakness.

"Hold on to me," he demanded, his voice harsh, edgy. "Goddamn it, hold on to me."

She already was. He pierced her, pinned her to the wall with an erection that filled her to bursting. Her frantic, helpless mewing echoed off the walls. She wanted to hate him for that, for making her a victim of her own rampant passions. But she held on to him, and let herself spin dizzily out of control.

He climaxed violently, slapped a hand on the wall, his arm rigid to maintain balance as her legs slid slowly off his hips. Suddenly he was angry, furious that she could strip away his finesse until he was no more than a beast rutting.

"I'll get you a shirt," he said briskly, then stepped out, flicking a towel from a rack, and leaving her alone in the billowing steam.

By the time she was dressed, frowning over the feel of raw silk against her skin, there was a tray of coffee waiting in the sitting area of the bedroom.

The morning news chattered quietly on the view screen, the curiosity corner at the lower left running fields of figures. The stock exchange. The monitor on a console was open to a newspaper. Not the *Times* or one of the New York tabs, Eve noted. It looked like Japanese.

"Do you have time for breakfast?" Roarke sat, sipping his coffee. He wasn't able to give his full attention to the morning data. He'd enjoyed watching her dress: the way her hands had hesitated over his shirt before she'd shrugged into it, how her fingers had run quickly up the buttons, the quick wriggle of hip as she'd tugged on jeans.

"No, thanks." She wasn't sure of her moves now. He'd fucked her blind in the shower, then had withdrawn to play well-mannered host. She strapped into her holster before crossing to accept the coffee he'd already poured her.

"You know, Lieutenant, you wear your weapon the way other women wear pearls."

"It's not a fashion accessory."

"You misunderstand. To some, jewelry is as vital as limbs." He tilted his head, studying her. "The shirt's a bit large, but it suits you."

Eve thought anything she could wear on her back that cost close to a week's pay couldn't suit her. "I'll get it back to you."

"I have several others." He rose, unnerving her again by tracing a fingertip over her jaw. "I was rough before. I'm sorry."

The apology, so quiet and unexpected, embarrassed her. "Forget it." She shifted away, drained her cup, set it aside.

"I won't forget it; neither will you." He took her hand, lifted it to his lips. Nothing could have pleased him more than the quick suspicion on her face. "You won't forget me, Eve. You'll think of me, perhaps not fondly, but you'll think of me."

"I'm in the middle of a murder investigation. You're part of it. Sure, I'll think of you."

"Darling," he began, and watched with amusement as his use of the endearment knitted her brow. "You'll be thinking of what I can do *to* you. Unfortunately, I won't be able to do more than imagine it myself for a few days."

She tugged her hand free and reached, casually she hoped, for her bag. "Going somewhere?"

"The preliminary work on the resort requires my attention, and my presence on FreeStar One for a number of meetings with the directorship. I'll be tied up, a few hundred thousand miles away, for a day or two."

An emotion moved through her she wasn't ready to admit was disappointment. "Yeah, I heard you wrapped the deal on that major indulgence for the bored rich."

He only smiled. "When the resort's complete, I'll take you there. You may form another opinion. In the meantime, I have to ask you for your discretion. The meetings are confidential. There's still a loose end or two to tie up, and it wouldn't do for my competitors to know we're getting under way so quickly. Only a few key people will know I'm not here in New York."

She finger combed her hair. "Why did you tell me?"

"Apparently, I've decided you're a key." As disconcerted by that as she, Roarke led the way to the door. "If you need to contact me, tell Summerset. He'll put you through."

"The butler?"

Roarke smiled as they descended the stairs. "He'll see to it," was all he said. "I should be gone about five days, a week at the most. I want to see you again." He stopped, took her face in his hands. "I need to see you again."

Her pulse jumped, as if it had nothing to do with the rest of her. "Roarke, what's going on here?"

"Lieutenant." He leaned forward, touched his lips to hers. "Indications are we're having a romance." Then he laughed, kissed her again, hard and quick. "I believe I could have held a gun to your head and you wouldn't have looked as terrified. Well, you'll have several days to think it through, won't you?"

She had a feeling several years wouldn't be enough.

There, at the base of the stairs, was Summerset, stone-faced, stiff-necked, holding her jacket. She took it and glanced back at Roarke as she shrugged it on.

"Have a good trip."

"Thanks." Roarke laid a hand on her shoulder before she could walk out the door. "Eve, be careful." Annoyed with himself, he dropped his hands. "I'll be in touch."

"Sure." She hurried out, and when she glanced back, the door was closed. When she opened her car door, she noticed the electronic memo on the driver's seat. Scooping it up, she got behind the wheel.

As she headed toward the gate, she flicked on the memo. Roarke's voice drawled out.

"I don't like the idea of you shivering unless I cause it. Stay warm."

Frowning, she tucked the memo in her pocket before experimentally touching the temperature gauge. The blast of heat had her yelping in shock.

She grinned all the way to Cop Central.

Eve closed herself in her office. She had two hours before her official shift began, and she wanted to use every minute of it on the DeBlass-Starr homicides. When her shift kicked in, her duties would spread to a number of cases in varying degrees of progress. This time was her own.

As a matter of routine, she cued IRCCA to transmit any and all current data and ordered it in hard copy to review later. The transmission was depressingly brief and added nothing solid.

Back, she thought, to deductive games. On her desk she'd spread out photos of both victims. She knew them intimately now, these women. Perhaps now, after the night she'd spent with Roarke, she understood something of what had driven them.

Sex was a powerful tool to use or have used against you. Both of these women had wanted to wield it, to control it. In the end, it had killed them.

A bullet in the brain had been the official cause of death, but Eve saw sex as the trigger.

It was the only connection between them, and the only link to their murderer.

Thoughtfully, she picked up the .38. It was familiar in her hand now. She knew exactly how it felt when it fired, the way the punch of it sung up the arm. The sound it made when the mechanism and basic physics sent the bullet flying.

Still holding the gun, she cued up the disc she'd requisitioned and watched Sharon DeBlass's murder again.

What did you feel, you bastard? she wondered. What did you feel when you squeezed the trigger and sent that slug of lead into her, when the blood spewed out, when her eyes rolled up dead?

What did you feel?

Eyes narrowed, she reran the disc. She was almost immune to the nastiness of it now. There was, she noted, the slightest waver in the video, as if he'd jostled the camera.

Did your arm jerk? she wondered. Did it shock you, the way her body flew back, how far the blood splattered?

Is that why she could hear the soft sob of breath, the slow exhale before the image changed?

What did you feel? she asked again. Revulsion, pleasure, or just cold satisfaction?

She leaned closer to the monitor. Sharon was carefully arranged now, the scene set as the camera panned her objectively and, yes, Eve thought, coldly.

Then why the jostle? Why the sob?

And the note. She picked up the sealed envelope and read it again. How did you know you'd be satisfied to stop at six? Have you already picked them out? Selected them?

Dissatisfied, she ejected the disc, replaced it and the .38. Loading the Starr disc, taking the second weapon, Eve ran through the process again.

No jostle this time, she noted. No quick, indrawn breath. Everything's smooth, precise, exact. You knew this time, she thought, how it would feel, how she'd look, how the blood would smell.

But you didn't know her. Or she didn't know you. You were just John Smith in her book, marked as a new client.

How did you choose her? And how are you going to pick the next one?

Just before nine, when Feeney knocked on her door, she was studying a map of Manhattan. He stepped behind her, leaned over her shoulder, and breathed candy mints.

"Thinking of relocating?"

"I'm trying geography. Widen view five percent," she ordered the computer. The image adjusted. "First murder, second murder," she said, nodding toward the tiny red pulses on Broadway and in the West Village. "My place." There was a green pulse just off Ninth Avenue.

"Your place?"

"He knows where I live. He's been there twice. These are three places we can put him. I was hoping I'd be able to confine the area, but he spreads himself out. And the security." She indulged in one little sigh, as she eased back in her chair. "Three different systems. Starr's was all but nonexistent. Electronic doorman, inoperable—and it had been, according to other residents, for a couple of weeks. DeBlass had top grade, key code for entry, hand plate, full building security—audio and video. Had to be breached on-site. Our time lag only hits one elevator, and the victim's hallway. Mine's not as fancy. I could breach the entry, any decent B and E man could. But I've got a System Five thousand police lock on the door. You have to be a real pro to pop it without the master code."

Drumming her fingers on the desk, she scowled at the map. "He's a security expert, knows his weapons—old weapons, Feeney. He'd cued in enough to department procedure to tag me for the primary investigator within hours of the first hit. He doesn't leave fingerprints or bodily fluids. Not even a fucking pubic hair. What does that tell you?"

Feeney sucked air through his teeth, rocked back on his heels. "Cop. Military. Maybe paramilitary or government security. Could be a security hobbyist; there are plenty of them. Possible professional criminal, but unlikely."

"Why unlikely?"

"If the guy was making a living off crime, why murder? There's no profit in either of these hits."

"So, he's taking a vacation," Eve said, but it didn't play for her.

"Maybe. I've run known sex offenders, crossed with IRCCA. Nobody pops who fits the MO. You look at this report yet?" he asked, indicating the IRCCA transmission.

"No. Why?"

"I already tagged it this morning. You might be surprised that there were about a hundred gun assaults last year, country wide. About that many accidental, too." He jerked a shoulder. "Bootlegged, homemade, black market, collectors."

"But nobody fits our profile."

"Nope." He chewed contemplatively. "Perverts either, though it's a real education to scan the data. Got a favorite. This guy in Detroit, hit on four before they tagged him. Liked to pick up a lonely heart, go back to her place. He'd tranq her, then he'd strip her down, spray her with glow-in-the-dark red paint, top to toe."

"Weird."

"Lethal. Skin's gotta breathe, so she'd suffocate, and while she was smothering to death, he'd play with her. Wouldn't bang her, no sperm or penetration. He'd just run his eager little hands over her."

"Christ, that's sick."

"Yeah, well, anyway. He gets a little too eager, a little too impatient with one, starts rubbing her before she's dry, you know. Some of the paint rubs off, and she starts to come around. So he panics, runs. Now our girl's naked, covered with paint, wobbly from the tranq, but she's pissed, runs right outside on the street and starts screaming. The unit comes by, catches on quick 'cause she's glowing like a laser show, and starts a standard search. Our boy's only a couple of blocks away. So they catch him . . ."

"Don't say it."

"Red-handed," Feeney said with a wicked grin. "Kiss my ass, that's a good one. Caught him red-handed." When Dallas just rolled her eyes, Feeney decided the guys in his division would appreciate the story more.

"Anyway, we maybe got a pervert. I'll bump up the pervs and the pros. Maybe we'll get lucky. I like the idea of that better than a cop."

"So do I." Lips pursed, she swiveled to look at him. "Feeney, you've got a small collection, know something about antique firearms."

He held out his arms, wrists tight together. "I confess. Book me."

She nearly smiled. "You know any other cops who collect?"

"Sure, a few. It's an expensive hobby, so most of the ones I know collect reproductions. Speaking of expensive," he added, fingering her sleeve. "Nice shirt. You get a raise?"

"It's borrowed," she muttered, and was surprised that she had to control a flush. "Run them for me, Feeney. The ones that have genuine antiques."

"Ah, Dallas." His smile faded away at the thought of focusing in on his own people. "I hate that shit."

"So do I. Run them anyway. Keep it to the city for now."

"Right." He blew out a breath, wondered if she realized his name would be on the list. "Hell of a way to start the day. Now I've got a present for you, kid. There was a memo on my desk when I got in. The chief's on his way in to the commander's office. He wants both of us."

"Fuck that."

Feeney just looked at his watch. "I make it in five minutes. Maybe you want to put on a sweater or something, so Simpson doesn't get a good look at that shirt and decide we're overpaid."

"Fuck that, too."

Chief Edward Simpson was an imposing figure. Well over six feet, fighting trim, he preferred dark suits and vivid ties. His waving brown hair was tipped with gray.

It was well known throughout the department that those distinguished highlights were added by his personal cosmetician. His eyes were a steely blue—a color his polls indicated inspired voter confidence—that rarely showed humor, his mouth a thin comma of command. Looking at him, you thought of power and authority.

It was disillusioning to know how carelessly he used both to do laps in the heady pool of politics.

He sat down, steepling his long, creamy hands that winked with a trio of gold rings. His voice, when he spoke, had an actor's resonance.

"Commander, Captain, Lieutenant, we have a delicate situation."

And an actor's timing. He paused, let those hard blue eyes scan each face in turn.

"You're all aware of how the media enjoys sensationalism," he continued. "Our city has, in the five years of my jurisdiction, lowered its crime rate by five percent. A full percentage a year. However, with recent events, it isn't the progress that will be touted by the press. Already there are headlines of these two killings. Stories that question the investigation and demand answers."

Whitney, detesting Simpson in every pore, answered mildly. "The stories lack details, chief. The Code Five on the DeBlass case makes it impossible to cooperate with the press or feed it."

"By not feeding it," Simpson snapped back. "We allow them to speculate. I'll be making a statement this afternoon." He held up a hand even as Whitney started to protest. "It's necessary to give the public something to assess, and by assessing feel confident that the department has the matter under control. Even if that isn't the case."

His eyes zeroed in on Eve. "As the primary, Lieutenant, you'll attend the press conference as well. My office is preparing a statement for you to give."

"With all respect, Chief Simpson, I can't divulge to the public any details of the case that could undermine the investigation."

Simpson plucked a piece of lint from his sleeve. "Lieutenant, I have thirty years of experience. I believe I know how to handle a press conference. Secondly," he continued, dismissing her by turning back to Commander Whitney, "it's imperative that the link the press has made between the DeBlass and Starr homicides be broken. The department can't be responsible for embarrassing Senator DeBlass personally, or damaging his position, by joining these cases at the hip."

"The murderer did that for us," Eve said between her teeth.

Simpson spared her a glance. "Officially, there is no connection. When asked, deny."

"When asked," Eve corrected. "Lie."

"Save your personal ethics. This is reality. A scandal that starts here and reverberates to East Washington will come back on us like a monsoon. Sharon DeBlass has been dead over a week, and you have nothing."

"We have the weapon," she disagreed. "We have possible motive as blackmail, and a list of suspects."

His color came up as he rose out of the chair. "I'm head of this department, Lieutenant, and the mess you make is left to me to clean. It's time you stop digging at dirt and close the case."

"Sir." Feeney stepped forward. "Lieutenant Dallas and I—"

"Can both be on Traffic Detail in a fucking heartbeat," Simpson finished.

Fists clenched, Whitney lunged to his feet. "Don't threaten my officers, Simpson. You play your games, smile for the cameras, and rub asses with East Washington, but don't you come in on my turf and threaten my people. They're on and they stay on. You want to change that, you try going through me."

Simpson's color deepened further. In fascination, Eve watched a vein throb at his temple. "Your people press the wrong buttons on this, it'll be your ass. I've got Senator DeBlass under control for the moment, but he's not happy having the primary running off to pressure his daughter-in-law, to invade the privacy of her grief and ask her embarrassing, irrelevant questions. Senator DeBlass and his family are victims, not suspects, and are to be accorded respect and dignity during this investigation."

"I accorded Elizabeth Barrister and Richard DeBlass respect and dignity." Very deliberately Eve shut down her temper. "The interview was conducted with their consent and cooperation. I was not aware that I was required to receive permission from you or the senator to proceed as I see warranted on this case."

"And I will not have the press speculating that this department harasses grieving parents, or why the primary resisted required testing after a termination."

"Lieutenant Dallas's testing was postponed at my order," Whitney said with snarling fury. "And with your approval."

"I'm well aware of that." Simpson angled his head. "I'm talking about speculation in the press. We will, all of us, be under a microscope until this man is stopped. Lieutenant Dallas's record and her actions will be up for public dissection."

"My record'll stand it."

"And your actions," Simpson said with a faint smile. "How will you answer the fact that you're jeopardizing the case and your position by indulging in a personal relationship with a suspect? And what do you think my official position will be if and when it comes out that you spent the night with that suspect?"

Control kept her in place, made her eyes flat, had her voice even. "I'm sure you'd hang me to save yourself, Chief Simpson."

"Without hesitation," he agreed. "Be at City Hall. Noon, sharp."

When the door clinked shut behind him, Commander Whitney sat again. "Dickless son of a bitch." Then his eyes, still sharp as razors, cut into Eve. "What the fuck are you doing?"

Eve accepted—was forced to accept—that her privacy was no longer an issue. "I spent the night with Roarke. It was a personal decision, on my personal time. In my professional opinion, as primary investigator, he has been eliminated as a suspect. It doesn't negate the fact that my behavior was inadvisable."

"Inadvisable," Whitney exploded. "Try asinine. Try career suicide. Goddamn it, Dallas, can't you hold your glands in check? I don't expect this from you."

She didn't expect it from herself. "It doesn't affect the investigation, or my ability to continue it. If you think differently, you're wrong. If you pull me off, you'll have to take my badge, too."

Whitney stared at her another moment, swore again. "You make damn sure Roarke is eliminated from the short list, Dallas. Damn sure he's eliminated or booked within thirty-six hours. And you ask yourself a question."

"I've already asked it," she interrupted, with a giddy relief only she knew she experienced when he didn't call for her badge—yet. "How did Simpson know where I spent last night? I'm being monitored. Second question is why. Is it on Simpson's authority, is it DeBlass? Or, did someone leak the information to Simpson in order to damage my credibility and therefore, the investigation."

"I expect you to find out." He jerked a thumb toward the door. "Watch yourself at that press conference, Dallas."

They'd taken no more than three strides down the corridor when Feeney erupted. "What the hell are you thinking of? Jesus Christ, Dallas."

"I didn't plan it, okay?" She jabbed for an elevator, jammed her hands in her pockets. "Back off."

"He's on the short list. He's one of the last people we know of who saw Sharon DeBlass alive. He's got more money than God, and can buy anything, including immunity."

"He doesn't fit type." She stormed into the elevator, barked out her floor. "I know what I'm doing."

"You don't know shit. All the years I've known you, I've never seen you so much as stub your toe on a guy. Now you've fallen fucking over on one."

"It was just sex. Not all of us have a nice comfortable life with a nice comfortable wife. I wanted someone to touch me, and he wanted to be the one. It's none of your goddamn business who I sleep with."

He caught her arm before she could storm out of the elevator. "The hell with that. I care about you."

She fought back the rage at being questioned, at being probed, at having her most private moments invaded. She turned back, lowering her voice so that those who walked the corridor wouldn't overhear.

"Am I a good cop, Feeney?"

"You're the best I ever worked with. That's why—"

She held up a hand. "What makes a good cop?"

He sighed. "Brains, guts, patience, nerve, instinct."

"My brains, my guts, my instincts tell me it's not Roarke. Every time I try to turn it around and point it at him, I hit a wall. It's not him. I've got the patience, Feeney, and the nerve to keep at it until we find out who."

His eyes stayed on hers. "And if you're wrong this time, Dallas?"

"If I'm wrong, they won't have to ask for my badge." She had to take a steadying breath. "Feeney, if I'm wrong about this, about him, I'm finished. All the way finished. Because if I'm not a good cop, I'm nothing."

"Jesus, Dallas, don't—"

She shook her head. "Run the cop list for me, will you? I've got some calls to make."

TWELVE

Press conferences left a bad taste in Eve's mouth. She stood on the steps of City Hall, on a stage set by Simpson with his patriotic tie and his gold I Love New York lapel pin. In his Big Brother of the City mode, his voice rose and fell while he read his statement.

A statement, Eve thought in disgust, that was riddled with lies, half truths, and plenty of self-aggrandizements. According to Simpson he would have no rest until the murderer of young Lola Starr was brought to justice.

When questioned as to whether there was any connection between the Starr homicide and the mysterious death of Senator DeBlass's granddaughter, he flatly denied it.

It wasn't his first mistake and, Eve thought glumly, it would hardly be his last.

The words were barely out of his mouth when he was peppered with shouts from Channel 75's on-air ace, Nadine Furst.

"Chief Simpson, I have information that indicates the Starr homicide is linked with the DeBlass case—not only because both women were engaged in the same profession."

"Now, Nadine." Simpson flashed his patient, avuncular smile. "We all know that information is often passed to you and your associates, and it's often inaccurate. That's why I set up the Data Verification Center in the first year of my term as chief of police. You have only to check with the DVC for accuracy."

Eve managed to hold back a snort, but Nadine, with her sharp cat's eyes and lightning brain didn't bother. "My source claims that Sharon DeBlass's death was not an accident—as the DVC claims—but murder. That both DeBlass and Starr were killed by the same method and the same man."

This caused an uproar in the huddle of news teams, a scatter shot of demands and questions that had Simpson sweating under his monogrammed shirt.

"The department stands behind its position that there is no connection between these unfortunate incidents," Simpson shouted out, but Eve saw little lights of panic flickering in his eyes. "And my office stands behind the investigators."

Those jittery eyes shot to Eve, and she knew, in that instant, what it was to be picked up bodily and thrown to the wolves.

"Lieutenant Dallas, a veteran officer with more than ten years of experience on the force, is in charge of the Starr homicide. She'll be happy to answer your questions."

Trapped, Eve stepped forward while Simpson bent down so that his weasley aide could whisper rapid-fire advice in his ear.

Questions rained down on her, and she waited, filtering them until she found one she could deal with.

"How was Lola Starr murdered?"

"In order to protect the credibility of the investigation, I'm not at liberty to divulge the method." She suffered through the shouts, cursing Simpson. "I will state that Lola Starr, an eighteen-year-old licensed companion, was murdered, with violence and premeditation. Evidence indicates that she was murdered by a client."

That fed them for a while, Eve noted. Several reporters checked their 'links with base.

"Was it a sexual crime?" someone shouted out, and Eve lifted a brow.

"I've just stated that the victim was a prostitute and that she was killed by a client. Put it together."

"Was Sharon DeBlass also killed by a client?" Nadine demanded.

Eve met those cagey feline eyes levelly. "The department has not issued any official statement that Sharon DeBlass was murdered."

"My source names you as primary in both cases. Will you confirm?"

Boggy ground. Eve stepped onto it. "Yes. I'm the primary on several ongoing investigations."

"Why would a ten-year vet be assigned to an accidental death?"

Eve smiled. "Want me to define bureaucracy?"

That drew some chuckles, but it didn't pull Nadine off the scent. "Is the DeBlass case still ongoing?"

Any answer would stir a hornet's nest. Eve opted for the truth. "Yes. And it will remain ongoing until I, as primary, am satisfied with its disposition. However," she continued, rolling over the shouts. "No more emphasis will be given to Sharon DeBlass's death than any other. Including Lola Starr. Any case that comes across my desk is treated equally, regardless of family or social background. Lola Starr was a young woman from a simple family. She had no social status, no influential background, no important friends. Now, after a few short months in New York, she's dead. Murdered. She deserves the best I can give her, and that's what she's going to get."

Eve scanned the crowd, zeroed in on Nadine. "You want a story, Ms. Furst. I want a killer. I figure my wants are more important than yours, so that's all I have to say."

She turned on her heel, shot Simpson one fulminating look, then strode away. She could hear him fighting off questions as she headed for her car.

"Dallas." Nadine, in low-heeled shoes built for style and movement, raced after her.

"I said I'm finished. Talk to Simpson."

"Hey, if I want to wade through bullshit, I can call the DVC. That was a pretty impassioned statement. Didn't sound like Simpson's speech writer."

"I like to talk for myself." Eve reached her car and started to open the door when Nadine touched her shoulder.

"You like to play it straight. So do I. Look, Dallas, we've got different methods, but similar goals." Satisfied that she had Eve's attention, she smiled. When her lips curved, her face turned into a tidy triangle, dominated by those upslanted green eyes. "I'm not going to pull out the old public's right to know."

"You'd be wasting your time."

"What I am going to say is we've got two women dead in a week. My information, and my gut tells me they were both murdered. I don't figure you're going to confirm that."

"You figure right."

"What I want's a deal. You let me know if I'm on the right track, and I hold off going out with anything that undermines your investigation. When you've got something solid and you're ready to move on it, you call me. I get an exclusive on the arrest—live."

Almost amused, Dallas leaned against her car. "What are you going to give me for that, Nadine? A handshake and a smile?"

"For that I'm going to give you everything my source has passed to me. Everything."

Now she was interested. "Including the source?"

"I couldn't do that if I had to. Point is, I don't. What I do have, Dallas, is a disc, delivered to me at the studio. On the disc are copies of police reports, including autopsies on both victims, and a couple of nasty little videos of two dead women."

"Fuck that. If you had half of what you're telling me, you'd have been on air in a heartbeat."

"I thought about it," Nadine admitted. "But this is bigger than ratings. Hell of a lot bigger. I want a story, Dallas, one that's going to cop me the Pulitzer, the International News Award, and a few other major prizes."

Her eyes changed, darkened. She wasn't smiling anymore. "But I saw what someone did to those woman. Maybe the story comes first with me, but it's not all. I pushed Simpson today, and I pushed you, I liked the way you pushed back. You can deal with me, or I can go out on my own. Your choice."

Eve waited. A fleet of taxis cruised by, and a maxibus with its humming electric motor. "We deal." Before Furst's eyes could light in triumph, Eve turned on her. "You cross me on this, Nadine, you cross me by so much as an inch, and I'll bury you."

"Fair enough."

"The Blue Squirrel, twenty minutes."

The afternoon crowd at the club was too bored to do much more than huddle over their drinks. Eve found a corner table, ordered a Pepsi Classic and the veggie pasta. Nadine slid in across from her. She chose the chicken plate with no-oil fries. An indication, Eve thought glumly, of the wide difference between a cop's salary and a reporter's.

"What have you got?" Eve demanded.

"A picture's worth several hundred thousand words." Nadine took a personal palm computer out of her bag—her red leather bag, Eve noted with envy. She had a weakness for leather and bold colors that she could rarely indulge.

Nadine popped in the disc, handed Eve the PPC. There was little use in swearing, Eve decided as she watched her own reports flick on-screen. Brooding, she let the disc run over Code Five data, through official medical reports, the ME's findings. She stopped it when the videos began. There was no need to check out death over a meal.

"Is it accurate?" Nadine asked when Eve passed back the computer.

"It's accurate."

"So the guy's some sort of gun freak, a security expert who patronizes companions."

"The evidence indicates that profile."

"How far have you narrowed it down?"

"Obviously, not far enough."

Nadine waited while their food was served. "There's got to be a lot of political pressure on you—the DeBlass end."

"I don't play politics."

"Your chief does." Nadine took a bite of her chicken. Eve smirked as she winced. "Christ, this is terrible." Philosophically, she shifted to the fries. "It's no secret DeBlass is front runner for the Conservative Party's nomination this summer. Or that the asshole Simpson is shooting for governor. Given the show this afternoon, it looks like cover-up."

"At this point, publicly, there is no connection between the cases. But I meant what I said about equality, Nadine. I don't care who Sharon DeBlass's granddaddy is. I'm going to find the guy who did her."

"And when you do, is he going to be charged with both murders, or only with Starr's?"

"That's up to the prosecuting attorney. Personally, I don't give a shit, as long as I hang him."

"That's the difference between you and me, Dallas." Nadine waved a fry, then bit in. "I want it all. When you get him, and I break the story, the PA's not going to have a choice. The fallout's going to keep DeBlass busy for months."

"Now who's playing politics?"

Nadine lifted a shoulder. "Hey, I just report the story, I don't make it. And this one's got it all. Sex, violence, money. Having a name like Roarke's involved is going to shoot the ratings through the roof."

Very slowly, Eve swallowed pasta. "There's no evidence linking Roarke to the crimes."

"He knew DeBlass—he's a friend of the family. Christ, he owns the building where Sharon was killed. He's got one of the top weapon collections in the world, and rumor is he's an expert shot."

Eve picked up her drink. "Neither murder weapon can be traced to him. He has no connection with Lola Starr."

"Maybe not. But even as a periphery character, Roarke sells news. And it's no state secret that he and the senator have bumped heads in the past. The man's got ice in his veins," she added with a shrug. "I don't imagine he'd have any problem with a couple of cold-blooded killings. But . . ." She paused to lift her own drink. "He's also a fanatic about privacy. It's hard to picture him bragging about the murders by sending discs to reporters. Somebody does that, they want publicity as much as they want to get away with the crime."

"An interesting theory." Eve had had enough. A headache was beginning to brew behind her eyes, and the pasta wasn't going to sit well. She rose, then leaned over the table close to Nadine. "I'll give you another one, formulated by a cop. Do you want to know who your source is, Nadine?"

Her eyes glittered. "Damn right."

"Your source is the killer." Eve paused, watching the light go out of Nadine's eyes. "I'd watch my step if I were you, friend."

Eve strode off, heading around behind the stage. She hoped Mavis was in the narrow cubicle that served as a dressing room. Just then, she needed a pal.

Eve found her, huddled under a blanket and sneezing into a tattered tissue.

"Got a fucking cold." Mavis glared out of puffy eyes and blew like a bullhorn. "I had to be crazy, wearing nothing but goddamn paint for twelve hours in goddamn lousy February."

Warily, Eve kept her distance. "Are you taking anything?"

"I'm taking everything." She gestured to a tabletop littered with over-the-counter drugs and touch-up cosmetics. "It's a fucking pharmaceutical conspiracy, Eve. We've wiped out just about every known plague, disease, and infection. Oh, we come up with a new one every now and again, to give the researchers something to do. But none of these bright-eyed medical types, none of the medi-computers can figure out how to cure the common fucking cold. You know why?"

Even couldn't stop the smile. She waited patiently until Mavis finished another bout of explosive sneezing. "Why?"

"Because the pharmaceutical companies need to sell drugs. You know what a damn sinus tab costs? You can get anticancer injections cheaper. I swear it."

"You can go to the doctor, get a prescription to eradicate the symptoms."

"I got that, too. Damn stuff's only good for eight hours, and I've got a performance tonight. I have to wait until seven o'clock to take it."

"You should be home in bed."

"They're exterminating the building. Some wise guy said he saw a cockroach." She sneezed again, then peered owlishly at Eve from under unpainted lashes. "What are you doing here?"

"I had some business. Look, get some rest. I'll see you later."

"No, stick around. I'm boring myself." She reached for a bottle of some nasty-looking pink liquid and glugged it down. "Hey, nice shirt. You get a bonus or something?"

"Or something."

"So, sit down. I was going to call you, but I've been too busy hacking up my lungs. That was Roarke who came in our fine establishment last night, wasn't it?"

"Yeah, it was Roarke."

"I almost passed out when he walked up to your table. What's the story? You helping him with some security or something?"

"I slept with him," Eve blurted out, and Mavis responded with a fit of helpless choking.

"You—Roarke." Eyes watering, she reached for more tissue. "Jesus, Eve. Jesus Christ, you never sleep with anybody. And you're telling me you slept with Roarke?"

"That's not precisely accurate. We didn't sleep."

Mavis let out a moan. "You didn't sleep. How long?"

Eve jerked a shoulder. "I don't know. I stayed the night. Eight, nine hours, I guess."

"Hours." Mavis shuddered delicately. "And you just kept going."

"Pretty much."

"Is he good? Stupid question," she said quickly. "You wouldn't have stayed otherwise. Wow, Eve, what got into you? Besides his incredibly energetic cock?"

"I don't know. It was stupid." She dragged her hands through her hair. "It's never been like that for me before. I didn't think it could—that I could. It's just never been important then all of a sudden—shit."

"Honey." Mavis snaked a hand from under her blanket and took Eve's tensed fingers. "You've been blocking off normal needs all your life because of things you barely remember. Somebody just found a way to get through. You should be happy."

"It puts him in the pilot's seat, doesn't it?"

"Oh, that's bullshit," Mavis interrupted before Eve could go on. "Sex doesn't have to be a power trip. It sure as hell doesn't have to be a punishment. It's supposed to be fun. And now and again, if you're lucky, it gets to be special."

"Maybe." She closed her eyes. "Oh God, Mavis, my career's on the line."

"What are you talking about?"

"Roarke's involved in a case I'm working on."

"Oh shit." She had to break off and blow again. "You're not going to have to bust him for something, are you?"

"No." Then more emphatically. "No. But if I don't tie it all up fast, with a nice, tidy bow, I'll be out. I'll be finished. Somebody's using me, Mavis." Her eyes sharpened again. "They're clearing the path in one direction, tossing roadblocks in the other. I don't know why. If I don't find out, it's going to cost me everything I have."

"Then you're going to have to find out, aren't you?" Mavis squeezed Eve's fingers.

She would find out, Eve promised herself. It was after ten P.M. when she let herself into the lobby of her building. If she didn't want to think just then, it wasn't a crime. She'd had to swallow a reprimand from the chief's office for veering from the official statement during the press conference.

The commander's unofficial support didn't quite ease the sting.

Once she was inside her apartment she checked her e-mail. She knew it was foolish, this nagging hope that she'd find a message from Roarke.

There wasn't one. But what she found had her flesh crawling with ice.

The video message was unnamed, sent from a public access. The little girl. Her dead father. The blood.

Eve recognized the angles of the official department record, the one taken to document the site of murder and justified termination.

The audio came over it. A playback of her auto-record of the child's screams. Her beating on the door. The warning, and all the horror that followed.

"You bastard," she whispered. "You're not going to get to me with this. You're not going to use that baby to get to me."

But her fingers shook as she ejected the disc. And she jolted when her intercom rang.

"Who is it?"

"Hennessy from apartment two-D." The pale, earnest face of her downstairs neighbor flicked on screen. "I'm sorry, Lieutenant Dallas. I didn't know what to do exactly. We've got trouble down here in the Finestein apartment."

Eve sighed and let the image of the elderly couple flip into her mind. Quiet, friendly, television addicts. "What's the problem?"

"Mr. Finestein's dead, Lieutenant. Keeled over in the kitchen while his wife was out playing mah-jongg with friends. I thought maybe you could come down."

"Yeah." She sighed again. "I'll be there. Don't touch anything, Mr. Hennessy, and try to keep people out of the way." Out of habit she called Dispatch, reported an unattended death and her presence on the scene.

She found the apartment quiet, with Mrs. Finestein sitting on the living room sofa with her tiny white hands folded in her lap. Her hair was white as well, a snowfall around a face that was beginning to line despite antiaging creams and treatments.

The old woman smiled gently at Eve.

"I'm so sorry to trouble you, dear."

"It's okay. Are you all right?"

"Yes, I'm fine." Her soft blue eyes stayed on Eve's. "It was our weekly game, the girls and mine. When I got home, I found him in the kitchen. He'd been eating a custard pie. Joe was overly fond of sweets."

She looked over at Hennessy, who stood, shifting uncomfortably from foot to foot. "I didn't know quite what to do, and went knocking on Mr. Hennessy's door."

"That's fine. If you'd stay with her for a minute please," she said to Mr. Hennessy.

The apartment was set up similarly to her own. It was meticulously neat, despite the abundance of knickknacks and memorabilia.

At the kitchen table with its centerpiece of china flowers, Joe Finestein had lost his life, and considerable dignity.

His head was slumped, half in, half out of a fluffy custard pie. Eve checked for a pulse, found none. His skin had cooled considerably. At a guess, she put his death at one-fifteen, give or take a couple of hours.

"Joseph Finestein," she recited dutifully. "Male, approximately one hundred and fifteen years of age. No signs of forced entry, no signs of violence. There are no marks on the body."

She leaned closer, looked into Joe's surprised and staring eyes, sniffed the pie. After finishing her prelim notes, she went back to relieve Hennessy and interview the deceased's widow.

It was midnight before she was able to crawl into bed. Exhaustion snatched at her like a cross and greedy child. Oblivion was what she wanted, what she prayed for.

No dreams, she ordered her subconscious. Take the night off.

Even as she closed her eyes, her bedside 'link blipped.

"Fry in hell, whoever you are," she muttered, then dutifully wrapped the sheet around her naked shoulders and switched it on.

"Lieutenant." Roarke's image smiled at her. "Did I wake you?"

"You would have in another five minutes." She shifted as the audio hissed with a bit of space interference. "I guess you got where you were going all right."

"I did. There was only a slight delay in transport. I thought I might catch you before you turned in."

"Any particular reason?"

"Because I like looking at you." His smile faded as he stared at her. "What's wrong, Eve?"

Where do you want me to start? she thought, but shrugged. "Long day—ending with one of your other tenants here croaking in his late night snack. He went facedown in a custard pie."

"There are worse ways to go, I suppose." He turned his head, murmured to someone nearby. Eve saw a woman move briskly behind Roarke and out of view. "I've just dismissed my assistant," he explained. "I wanted to be alone when I asked if you're wearing anything under that sheet."

She glanced down, lifted a brow. "Doesn't look like it."

"Why don't you take it off?"

"No way I'm going to satisfy your prurient urges by interspace transmission, Roarke. Use your imagination."

"I am. I'm imagining what I'm going to do to you the next time I get my hands on you. I advise you to rest up, Lieutenant."

She wanted to smile and couldn't. "Roarke, we're going to have to talk when you get back."

"We can do that as well. I've always found conversations with you stimulating, Eve. Get some sleep."

"Yeah, I will. See you, Roarke."

"Think of me, Eve."

He ended the transmission, then sat alone, brooding at the blank monitor. There'd been something in her eyes, he thought. He knew the moods of them now, could see beyond the training into the emotion.

The something had been worry.

Turning his chair, he looked out at his view of star splattered space. She was too far away for him to do any more than wonder about her.

And to ask himself, again, why she mattered so much.

CHAPTER

THIRTEEN

Eve studied the report of the bank search for Sharon DeBlass's deposit box with frustration. No record, no record, no record.

Nothing in New York, New Jersey, Connecticut. Nothing in East Washington or Virginia.

She had rented one somewhere, Eve thought. She'd had diaries, and had kept them tucked away someplace where she could get to them safely and quickly.

In those diaries, Eve was convinced, was a motive for murder.

Unwilling to tag Fenney for another, broader search, she began one herself, starting with Pennsylvania, working west and north toward the borders of Canada and Quebec. In slightly less than twice the time it would have taken Feeney, she came up blank again.

Then, working south, she struck out with Maryland, and down to Florida. Her machine began to chug noisily at the work. Eve issued a warning snarl and a sharp bump to the console. She swore she'd risk the morass of requisition for a new unit if this one just held out for one more case.

More from stubbornness than hope, she did a scan of the Midwest, heading toward the Rockies.

You were too smart, Sharon, Eve thought, as the negative results flickered by. Too smart for your own good. You wouldn't have gone out of the country, or off planet where you'd have to go through a customs scan every trip. Why go far away, someplace where you'd need transport or travel docs? You might want immediate access.

If your mother knew you kept diaries, maybe other people knew it, too. You bragged about it because you liked to make people uncomfortable. And you knew they were safely tucked away.

But close, damn it, Eve thought, closing her eyes to bring the woman she was coming to know so well into full focus. Close enough so that you could feel the power, use it, toy with people.

But not so simple that just anyone could track it down, gain access, spoil the game. You used an alias. Rented your safe box under another name—just in case. And if you were smart enough to use an alias, you'd have used one that was basic, that was familiar. One you wouldn't have to hassle over.

It was so simple, Eve realized as she keyed in Sharon Barrister. So simple both she and Feeney had overlooked it.

She hit pay dirt at the Brinkstone International Bank and Finance, Newark, New Jersey.

Sharon Barrister not only had a safe-deposit box, she had a brokerage account in the amount of $326,000.85.

Grinning at the screen, she hit her tie-in with the PA. "I need a warrant," she announced.

Three hours later, she was back in Commander Whitney's office, try-ing not to gnash her teeth. "She's got another one somewhere," Eve insisted. "And the diaries are in it."

"Nobody's stopping you from looking for it, Dallas."

"Fine, that's fine." She whirled around the office as she spoke. Energy was pumping now, and she wanted action. "What are we going to do about this?"

She jerked a hand at the file on his desk.

"You've got the disc I took from the safe-deposit box and the print out I ran. It's right there, commander. A blackmail list: names and amounts. And Simpson's name is there, in tidy alphabetical order."

"I can read, Dallas." He resisted the urge to rub at the tension gathering at the base of his skull. "The chief isn't the only person named Simpson in the city, much less the country."

"It's him." She was fuming and there was no place to put the steam. "We both know it. There are a number of other interesting names there, too. A governor, a Catholic bishop, a respected leader of the International Organization of Women, two high-ranking cops, an ex–vice president—"

"I'm aware of the names," Whitney interrupted. "Are you aware of your position, Dallas, and the consequences?" He held up a hand to silence her. "A few neat columns of names and numbers don't mean squat. This data gets out of this office, and it's over. You're finished and so's the investigation. Is that what you want?"

"No, sir."

"You get the diaries, Dallas, find the connection between Sharon DeBlass and Lola Starr, and we'll see where we go from there."

"Simpson's dirty." She leaned over the desk. "He knew Sharon De-Blass; he was being blackmailed. And he's doing everything he can to undermine the investigation."

"Then we'll have to work around him, won't we?" Whitney put the file in his lock box. "No one knows what we have in here, Dallas. Not even Feeney. Is that clear?

"Yes, sir." Knowing she had to be satisfied with that, she started for the door. "Commander, I'd like to point out that there's a name absent from that list. Roarke's not on it."

Whitney met her eyes, nodded. "As I said, Dallas. I can read."

Her message light was blinking when she got back to her office. A check of her e-mail turned up two calls from the medical examiner. Impatiently, Eve put the hot lead aside and returned the call.

"Finished running the tests on your neighbor, Dallas. You hit the bull's-eye."

"Oh, hell." She ran her hands over her face. "Send through the results. I'll take it from here."

Hetta Finestein opened her door with a puff of lavender sachet and the yeasty smell of homemade bread.

"Lieutenant Dallas."

She smiled her quiet smile and stepped back in invitation. Inside, the viewing screen was tuned to a chatty talk show where interested members of the home audience could plug in and shoot their holographic images to the studio for fuller interaction. The topic seemed to be higher state salaries for professional mothers. Just now the screen was crowded with women and children of varying sizes and vocal opinions.

"How nice of you to come by. I've had so many visitors today. It's a comfort. Would you like some cookies?"

"Sure," Eve agreed, and felt like slime. "Thanks." She sat on the couch, let her eyes scan the tidy little apartment. "You and Mr. Finestein used to run a bakery?"

"Oh, yes." Hetta's voice carried from the kitchen, along with her bustling movements. "Until just a few years ago. We did very well. People love real cooking, you know. And if I do say so myself, I have quite a hand with pies and cakes."

"You do a lot of baking here, at home."

Hetta came in with a tray of golden cookies. "One of my pleasures. Too many people never know the joy of a home-baked cookie. So many children never experience real sugar. It's hideously expensive, of course, but worth it."

Eve sampled a cookie and had to agree. "I guess you must have baked the pie your husband was eating when he died."

"You won't find store-bought or simulations in my house," Hetta said proudly. "Of course, Joe would gobble everything up almost as soon as I took it out of the oven. There's not an AutoChef on the market as reliable as a good baker's instincts and creativity."

"You did bake the pie, Mrs. Finestein."

The woman blinked, lowered her lashes. "Yes, I did."

"Mrs. Finestein, you know what killed your husband?"

"Yes, I do." She smiled softly. "Gluttony. I told him not to eat it. I specifically told him not to eat it. I said it was for Mrs. Hennessy across the hall."

"Mrs. Hennessy." That jolted Eve back several mental paces. "You—"

"Of course, I knew he'd eat it, anyway. He was very selfish that way."

Eve cleared her throat. "Could we, ah, turn the program off?"

"Hmm? Oh, I'm sorry." The flustered hostess tapped her cheeks with her hands. "That's so rude. I'm so used to letting it play all day I don't even notice it. Um, program—no, screen off."

"And the audio," Eve said patiently.

"Of course." Shaking her head as the sound continued to run, Hetta looked sheepish. "I've just never gotten the hang of the thing since we switched from remote to voice. Sound off, please. There, that's better, isn't it."

The woman could bake a poisoned pie, but couldn't control her own television, Eve thought. It took all kinds. "Mrs. Finestein, I don't want you to say any more until I've read you your rights. Until you're sure you understand them. You're under no obligation to make any statement," Eve began, while Hetta continued to smile gently.

Hetta waited until the recitation was over. "I didn't expect to get away with it. Not really."

"Get away with what, Mrs. Finestein?"

"Poisoning Joe. Although . . ." She pursed her lips like a child. "My grandson's a lawyer—a very clever boy. I think he'd say that since I did tell Joe, very specifically told him not to eat that pie, it was more Joe's doing than mine. In any case," she said and waited patiently.

"Mrs. Finestein, are you telling me that you added synthetic cyanide compound to a custard pie with the intention of killing your husband?"

"No, dear. I'm telling you I added cyanide compound, with a nice dose of extra sugar to a pie, and told my husband not to touch it. 'Joe,' I said, 'Don't you so much as sniff this custard pie. I baked it special, and it's not for you. You hear me, Joe?'"

Hetta smiled again. "He said he heard me all right, and then just before I left for my evening with the girls, I told him again, just to be sure. 'I mean it, Joe. You let that pie be.' I expected he would eat it, though, but that was up to him, wasn't it? Let me tell you about Joe," she continued conversationally, and picked up the cookie tray to urge another on Eve. When Eve hesitated, she laughed gaily. "Oh, dear, these are quite safe, I promise you. I just gave a dozen to the nice little boy upstairs."

To prove her point she chose one herself and bit in.

"Now, where was I? Oh, yes, about Joe. He's my second husband, you know. We've been married fifty years come April. He was a good partner, and quite a fine baker himself. Some men should never retire. The last few years he's been very hard to live with. Cross and complaining all the time, forever finding fault. And never would get flour on his fingers. Not that he'd pass by an almond tart without gobbling it down."

Because it sounded almost reasonable, Eve waited a moment. "Mrs. Feinstein, you poisoned him because he ate too much?"

Hetta's rosy cheeks rounded. "It does seem that way. But it goes deeper. You're so young, dear, and you don't have family, do you?"

"No."

"Families are a source of comfort, and a source of irritation. No one outside can ever understand what goes on in the privacy of a home. Joe wasn't an easy man to live with, and I'm afraid, though I'm sorry to speak ill of the dead, that he had developed bad habits. He'd find a real glee in upsetting me, in ruining my small pleasures. Why just last month he deliberately ate half the Tower of Pleasure Cake I'd baked for the International Betty Crocker cook-off. Then he told me it was dry." Her voice huffed out in obvious insult. "Can you imagine?"

"No," Eve said weakly. "I can't."

"Well, he did it just to make me mad. It was the way he wielded power, you see. So I baked the pie, told him not to touch it, and went out to play mah-jongg with the girls. I wasn't at all surprised when I got back and found he hadn't listened. He was a glutton, you see." She gestured with the cookie before delicately finishing the last bite.

"That's one of the seven deadly sins, gluttony, it just seemed right that he would die by sin. Are you sure you won't have another cookie?"

The world was certainly a mad place, Eve decided, when old women poisoned custard pies. And, she thought, with Hetta's quiet, old-fashioned, grandmotherly demeanor, the woman would probably get off.

If they sent her up, she'd get kitchen duty and happily bake pastries for the other inmates.

Eve filed her report, caught a quick dinner in the eatery, then went back to work on the still simmering lead.

She'd no more than cleared half the New York banks when the call came through. "Yeah, Dallas."

Her answer was the image that flowed onto her screen. A dead woman, arranged all too familiarly on blood-soaked sheets.

THREE OF SIX

She stared at the message imposed over the body and snarled at her computer.

"Trace address. Now, goddamn it."

After the computer obliged, she tagged Dispatch.

"Dallas, Lieutenant Eve, ID 5347BQ. Priority A. Any available units to 156 West Eighty-ninth, apartment twenty-one nineteen. Do not enter premises. Repeat, do not enter premises. Detain any and all persons exiting building. Nobody goes in that apartment, uniform or civilian. My ETA, ten minutes."

"Copy, Dallas, Lieutenant, Eve." The droid on duty spoke coolly and without rush. "Units five-oh and three-six available to respond. Will await your arrival. Priority A. Dispatch, out."

She grabbed her bag and her field kit and was gone.

Eve entered the apartment alone, weapon out and ready. The living room was tidy, even homey with its thick cushions and fringed area rugs. There was a book on the sofa and a slight dip in the cushion, indicating someone had spent some time curled up and reading. Frowning over the image, she moved to a door beyond.

The small room was set up as an office, the workstation tidy as a pin, with little hints of personality in the basket of perfumed silk flowers, the bowl of colorful gumdrops, the shiny white mug decorated with a glossy red heart.

The workstation faced the window, the window faced the sheer side of another building, but no one had bothered with a privacy screen. Lining one wall was a clear shelf holding several more books, a large drop box for discs, another for e-memos, a small treasure trove of pricey graphite pencils and recycled legal pads. Cuddled between was a lopsided baked clay blob that might have been a horse, and had certainly been made by a child.

Eve turned out of the room and opened the opposing door.

She knew what to expect. Her system didn't revolt. The blood was still very fresh. With only a small sigh, she bolstered her weapon, knowing she was alone with the dead.

Through the thin protective spray on her hands, she felt the body. It hadn't had time to cool.

She'd been positioned on the bed, and the weapon had been placed neatly between her legs.

Eve pegged it as a Ruger P-90, a sleek combat weapon popular as home defense during the Urban Revolt. Light, compact, and fully automatic.

No silencer this time. But she'd be willing to bet the bedroom was soundproofed—and that the killer had known it.

She moved over to the fussily female circular dresser, opened a small burlap bag that was currently a fashion rage. Inside she found the dead woman's companion's license.

Pretty woman, she mused. Nice smile, direct eyes, really stunning coffee-and-cream complexion.

"Georgie Castle," Eve recited for the record. "Female. Age fifty-three. Licensed companion. Death probably occurred between seven and seven-forty-five P.M., cause of death gunshot wounds. ME to confirm. Three visible points of violence: forehead, mid-chest, genitalia.

Most likely induced with antique combat style handgun left at scene. No signs of struggle, no appearance of forced entry or robbery."

A whisper of a sound behind her had Eve whipping out her weapon. Crouched, eyes hard and cold, she stared at a fat gray cat who slid into the room.

"Jesus, where'd you come from?" She let out a long, cleansing breath as she replaced her weapon. "There's a cat," she added for the record, and when it blinked at her, flashing one gold and one green eye, she bent down to scoop it up.

The purring sounded like a small, well-oiled engine.

Shifting him, she took out her communicator and called for a homicide team.

A short time later, Eve was in the kitchen, watching the cat sniff with delicate disdain at a bowl of food she'd unearthed when she heard the raised voices outside the apartment door.

When she went to investigate, she found the uniform she'd posted trying to restrain a frantic and very determined woman.

"What's the problem here, Officer?"

"Lieutenant." With obvious relief, the uniform deferred to her superior. "The civilian demands entry. I was—"

"Of course I demand entry." The woman's dark red hair, cut in a perfect wedge, moved and settled around her face with each jerky movement. "This is my mother's home. I want to know what you're doing here."

"And your mother is?" Eve prompted.

"Mrs. Castle. Mrs. Georgie Castle. Was there a break-in?" Anger turned to worry as she tried to squeeze past Eve. "Is she all right? Mom?"

"Come with me." Eve took a firm hold of her arm and steered her inside and into the kitchen. "What's your name?"

"Samantha Bennett."

The cat left his bowl and walked over to curl around and through Samantha's legs. In a gesture Eve recognized as habitual and automatic, Samantha bent to give the cat one quick scratch between the ears.

"Where's my mother?" Now that the worry was heading toward fear, Samantha's voice cracked.

There was no part of the job Eve dreaded more than this, no aspect of police work that scraped at her heart with such dull blades.

"I'm sorry, Ms. Bennett. I'm very sorry. Your mother's dead."

Samantha said nothing. Her eyes, the same warm honey tone as her mother's, unfocused. Before she could fold, Eve eased her into a chair. "There's a mistake," she managed. "There has to be a mistake. We're going to the movies. The nine o'clock show. We always go to the movies on Tuesdays." She stared up at Eve with desperately hopeful eyes. "She can't be dead. She's barely fifty, and she's healthy. She's strong."

"There's no mistake. I'm sorry."

"There was an accident?" Those eyes filled now, flowed over. "She had an accident?"

"It wasn't an accident." There was no way but one to get it down. "Your mother was murdered."

"No, that's impossible." The tears kept flowing. Her voice hitched over them as she continued to shake her head in denial. "Everyone liked her. Everyone. No one would hurt her. I want to see her. I want to see her now."

"I can't let you do that."

"She's my mother." Tears plopped on her lap even as her voice rose. "I have the right I want to see my mother."

Eve clamped both hands on Samantha's shoulders, forcing her back into the chair she'd sprung from. "You're not going to see her. It wouldn't help her. It wouldn't help you. What you're going to do is answer my questions, and that's going to help me find who did this to her. Now, do you want me to get you something? Call anyone for you?"

"No. No." Samantha fumbled in her purse for a tissue. "My husband, my children. I'll have to tell them. My father. How can I tell them?"

"Where is your father, Samantha?"

"He lives—he lives in Westchester. They divorced about two years ago. He kept the house because she wanted to move into the city. She wanted to write books. She wanted to be a writer."

Eve turned to the filtered water unit on the counter, glugged out a glass, pressed it on Samantha. "Do you know how your mother made her living?"

"Yes." Samantha pressed her lips together, crushed the damp tissue in her chilled fingers. "No one could talk her out of it. She used to laugh and say it was time she did something shocking, and what wonderful research it was for her books. My mother—" Samantha broke off to drink. "She got married very young. A few years ago, she said she needed to move on, see what else there was. We couldn't talk her out of that, either. You could never talk her out of anything."

She began to weep again, covering her face and sobbing silently. Eve took the barely touched glass, waited, let the first wave of grief and shock roll. "Was it a difficult divorce? Was your father angry?"

"Baffled. Confused. Sad. He wanted her back, and always said this was just one of her phases. He—" The question behind the question abruptly struck her. She lowered her hands. "He would never hurt her. Never, never, never. He loved her. Everyone did. You couldn't help it."

"Okay." Eve would deal with that later. "You and your mother were close?"

"Yes, very close."

"Did she ever talk to you about her clients?"

"Sometimes. It embarrassed me, but she'd find a way to make it all so outrageously funny. She could do that. Called herself Granny Sex, and you had to laugh."

"Did she ever mention anyone who made her uneasy?"

"No. She could handle people. It was part of her charm. She was only going to do this until she was published."

"Did she ever mention the names Sharon DeBlass or Lola Starr?"

"No." Samantha started to drag her hair back, then her hand froze in midair. "Starr, Lola Starr. I heard, on the news, I heard about her. She was murdered. Oh God. Oh God." She lowered her head and her hair fell in wings to shield her face.

"I'm going to have an officer take you home, Samantha."

"I can't leave. I can't leave her."

"Yes, you can. I'm going to take care of her." Eve laid her hands over Samantha's. "I promise you, I'll take care of her for you. Come on now." Gently, she helped Samantha to her feet. She wrapped an arm around the distraught woman's waist as she led her to the door. She wanted her out before the team had finished in the bedroom. "Is your husband home?"

"Yes. He's home with the children. We have two children. Two years, and six months. Tony's home with the children."

"Good. What's your address?"

The shock was settling in. Eve hoped the numbness she could read on Samantha's face would help as the woman recited an upscale address in Westchester.

"Officer Banks."

"Yes, Lieutenant."

"Take Mrs. Bennett home. I'll call for another officer for the door. Stay with the family as long as you're needed."

"Yes, sir." With compassion, Banks guided Samantha toward the elevators. "This way, Mrs. Bennett," she murmured.

Samantha leaned drunkenly on Banks. "You'll take care of her?"

Eve met Samantha's ravaged eyes. "I promise."

An hour later, Eve walked into the station house with a cat under her arm.

"Hey there, Lieutenant, caught yourself a cat burglar." The desk sergeant snorted at his own humor.

"You're a laugh riot, Riley. Commander still here?"

"He's waiting for you. You're to go up as soon as you show." He leaned forward to scratch the purring cat. "Hooked yourself another homicide?"

"Yeah."

A kissing sound had her glancing over at a leering hunk in a spandex jumpsuit. The jumpsuit, and the blood trickling at the side of his mouth were approximately the same color. His accessories were a set of thin, black restraints that secured one arm to a nearby bench. He rubbed his crotch with his free hand and winked at her.

"Hey, baby. Got something here for you."

"Tell Commander Whitney I'm on my way," she told Riley as the desk sergeant rolled his eyes.

Unable to resist, she swung by the bench, leaned close enough to smell sour vomit. "That was a charming invitation," she murmured, then arched a brow when the man peeled open his fly patch and wagged his personality at her. "Oh, look, kitty. A teeny-tiny little penis." She smiled, leaned just a bit closer. "Better take care of it, asshole, or my pussy here might mistake it for a teeny-tiny little mouse and bite it off."

It made her feel better to see what there was of his pride and joy shrivel before he closed his flaps. The good humor lasted almost until she stepped into the elevator and ordered Commander Whitney's floor.

He was waiting, with Feeney, and the report she'd transmitted directly from the crime scene. In the nature of the repetition required in police work, she went over the same ground verbally.

"So that's the cat," Feeney said.

"I didn't have the heart to dump him on the daughter in the state she was in." Eve shrugged. "And I couldn't very well just leave him there." With her free hand, she reached into her bag. "Her discs. Everything's labeled. I scanned through her appointments. The last one of the day was at six-thirty. John Smith. The weapon." She laid the bagged weapon on Commander Whitney's desk. "Looks like Ruger P-ninety."

Feeney took a look, nodded. "You're learning, kid."

"I've been boning up."

"Early twenty-first, probably oh eight, oh nine." Feeney stated as he turned the sealed weapon in his hands. "Prime condition. Serial number's intact. Won't take long to run it," he added, but moved his shoulders. "But he's too smart to use a registered."

"Run it," Whitney ordered, and gestured to the auxiliary unit across the room. "I've got surveillance on your building, Dallas. If he tries to slip you another disc, we'll spot him."

"If he stays true to form, it'll be within twenty-four hours. He's holding to the pattern so far, though each of his victims has been a distinctly different type: with DeBlass you've got the glitz, the sophistication; with Starr you've got fresh, childlike; and with this one, we've got comfort, still young but mature.

"We're still interviewing neighbors, and I'm going to hit the family again, look into the divorce. It looks to me like she took this guy spur of the moment. She had a standing date with her daughter for Tuesdays. I'd like Feeney to run her 'link, see if he called her direct. We're not going to be able to keep this from the media, commander. And they're going to hit us hard."

"I'm already working on media control."

"It may be hotter than we think." Feeney looked up from the terminal. His eyes lingered on Eve's, made her blood chill.

"The murder weapon's registered. Purchased through silent auction at Sotheby's last fall. Roarke."

Eve didn't speak for a moment. Didn't care. "It breaks pattern," she managed. "And it's stupid. Roarke's not a stupid man."

"Lieutenant—"

"It's a plant, Commander. An obvious one. A silent auction. Any second-rate hacker can use someone's ID and bid. How was it paid for?" she snapped at Feeney.

"I'll need to access Sotheby's records after they open tomorrow."

"My bet's cash, electronic transfer. The auction house gets the money, why should they question it?" Her voice might have been calm, but her mind was racing. "And the delivery. Odds are electronic pick-up station. You don't need ID for an EPS; all you do is key in the delivery code."

"Dallas." Whitney spoke patiently. "Pick him up for questioning."

"I can't."

His eyes remained level, cool. "That's a direct order. If you have a personal problem, save it for personal time."

"I can't pick him up," she repeated. "He's on the FreeStar space station, a fair distance from the murder scene."

"If he put out that he'd be on FreeStar—"

"He didn't," she interrupted. "And that's where the killer made a mistake. Roarke's trip is confidential, with only a few key people apprised. As far as it's generally known, he's right here in New York."

Commander Whitney inclined his head. "Then we'd better check his whereabouts. Now."

Her stomach churned as she engaged Whitney's 'link. Within seconds she was listening to Summerset's prune voice. "Summerset, Lieutenant Dallas. I have to contact Roarke."

"Roarke is in meetings, Lieutenant. He can't be disturbed."

"He told you to put me through, goddamn it. This is police business. Give me his access number or I'm coming over there and hauling your bony ass in for obstructing justice."

Summerset's face puckered up. "I am not authorized to give out that data. I will, however, transfer you. Please stand by."

Eve's palms began to sweat as the screen went to holding blue. She wondered whose idea it was to pipe in the sugary music. Certainly not Roarke's. He had too much class.

Oh God, what was she going to do if he wasn't where he said he'd be?

The blue screen contracted into a pinpoint, then opened up. There was Roarke, a trace of impatience in his eyes, a half smile on his mouth.

"Lieutenant. You've caught me at a bad time. Can I get back to you?"

"No." She could see from the corner of her eye that Feeney was already tracing the transmission. "I need to verify your whereabouts."

"My whereabouts?" His brow cocked. He must have seen something in her face, though Eve would have sworn she kept it as smooth and unreadable as stone. "What's wrong, Eve? What's happened?"

"Your whereabouts, Roarke. Please verify."

He remained silent, studying her. Eve heard someone speak to him. He flicked away the interruption with a dismissing gesture. "I'm in the middle of a meeting in the presidential chamber of Station FreeStar, the location of which is Quadrant Six, Sup Alpha. Scan," he ordered, and the intergalactic 'link circled the room. A dozen men and women sat at a wide, circular table.

The long, bowed port showed a scatter of stars and the perfect blue-green globe of Earth.

"Location of transmission confirmed," Feeney said in an under-tone. "He's just where he says he is."

"Roarke, please switch to privacy mode."

Without a flicker of expression, he lifted a headset. "Yes, Lieutenant?"

"A weapon registered to you was confiscated at a homicide. I have to ask you to come in for questioning at the first possible opportunity. You're free to bring your attorney. I'm advising you to bring your attorney," she added, hoping he understood the emphasis. "If you don't comply within forty-eight hours, the Station Guard will escort you back on-planet. Do you understand your rights and obligations in this matter?"

"Certainly. I'll make arrangements. Good-bye, Lieutenant."

The screen went blank.

CHAPTER

FOURTEEN

More shaken than she cared to admit, Eve entered Dr. Mira's office the following morning. At Mira's invitation, she took a seat, folded her hands to keep them from any telltale restless movements.

"Have you had time to profile?"

"You requested urgent status." Indeed, Mira had been up most of the night, reading reports, using her training and her psych diagnostics to compose a profile. "I'd like more time to work on this, but I can give you an overall view."

"Okay." Eve leaned forward. "What is he?"

"*He* is almost certainly correct. Traditionally, crimes of this nature are not committed within the same sex. He's a man, above average intelligence, with sociopathic and voyeuristic tendencies. He's bold, but not a risk taker, though he probably sees himself as such."

In her graceful way, she linked her fingers together, crossed her legs. "His crimes are well thought out. Whether or not he has sex with his victims is incidental. His pleasure and satisfaction comes from the selection, the preparation, and the execution."

"Why prostitutes?"

"Control. Sex is control. Death is control. And he needs to control people, situations. The first murder was probably impulse."

"Why?"

"He was caught off guard by the violence, his own capability of violence. He had a reaction, a jerk of a movement, the indrawn breath, the shaky exhale. He recovered, systematically protected himself. He doesn't want to be caught, but he wants—needs to be admired, feared. Hence the recordings.

"He uses collector's weapons," she continued in that same moderate voice, "a status symbol of money. Again, power and control. He leaves them behind so that they can show he's unique among men. He appreciates the overt violence of guns and the impersonal aspect of them. The kill from a comfortable distance, the aloofness of that. He's decided on the number he'll kill to show that he's organized, precise. Ambitious."

"Could he have had the six women in mind from the beginning? Six targets?"

"The only verified connection between the three victims is their profession," Mira began, and saw that Eve had already reached the same conclusion, but wanted it confirmed. "He had the profession in mind. It would be my opinion the women are incidental. It's likely he holds a high-level position, certainly a responsible one. If he has a sexual or marriage partner, he or she is subservient. His opinion of women is low. He debases and humiliates them after death to show his disgust and his superiority. He doesn't perceive these as crimes but as moments of personal power, personal statement.

"The prostitute, male or female, remains a profession of low esteem in many minds. Women are not his equals; a prostitute is beneath his contempt, even when he uses her for his own release. He enjoys his work, Lieutenant. He enjoys it very much."

"Is it work, Doctor, or a mission?"

"He has no mission. Only ambitions. It isn't religion, not a moral statement, not a societal stance."

"No, the statement's personal, the stance is control."

"I would agree," Mira said, pleased with the straightforward workings of Eve's mind. "It is, to him, an interest, a new and somewhat fascinating hobby that he has discovered himself adept at. He's dangerous, Lieutenant, not simply because he has no conscience, but because he's good at what he does. And his success feeds him."

"He'll stop at six," Eve murmured. "With this method. But he'll find another creative way to kill. He's too vain to go back on his word to the authorities, but he's enjoying his hobby too much to give it up."

Mira angled her head. "One would think, Lieutenant, that you've already read my report. I believe you're coming to understand him very well."

Eve nodded. "Yeah, piece by piece." There was a question she had to ask, one she had suffered over through a long, sleepless night. "To protect himself, to make the game more difficult, would he hire someone, pay someone to kill a victim he'd chosen while he was alibied?"

"No." Mira's eyes softened with compassion as she watched Eve's close in relief. "In my opinion, he needs to be there. To watch, to record, most of all to experience. He doesn't want vicarious satisfaction. Nor does he believe you'll outsmart him. He enjoys watching you sweat, Lieutenant. He's an observer of people, and I believe he focused on you the moment he learned you were primary. He studies you, and knows you care. He sees that as a weakness to exploit, and does so by presenting you with the murders—not at your place of work, but where you live."

"He sent the last disc. It was in my morning mail drop, posted from a midtown slot about an hour after the murder. We had my building under surveillance. He'd have figured that and found a way to get around it."

"He's a born button pusher." Mira handed Eve a disc and a hard copy of the initial profile. "He is an intelligent and a mature man. Mature enough to restrain his impulses, a man of means and imagination. He would rarely show his emotions, rarely have them to show. It's an intellect with him—and, as you said, vanity."

"I appreciate you getting this for me so quickly."

"Eve," Mira said before Eve could rise. 'There's an addendum. The weapon that was left at the last murder. The man who committed these crimes would not make so foolish a mistake to leave a traceable weapon behind. The diagnostic rejected it at a probability of ninety-three point four percent."

"It was there," Eve said flatly. "I bagged it myself."

"As I'm sure he wanted you to. It's likely he enjoyed implicating someone else to further bog the system, twist the investigation process. And it's likely he chose this particular person to upset you, to distract you, even to hurt you. I've included that in the profile. Personally, I want to tell you that I'm concerned about his interest in you."

"I'm going to see to it that he's a hell of a lot more concerned with my interest in him. Thank you, Doctor."

Eve went directly to Whitney's office to deliver the psychiatric pro-file. With any luck at all, Feeney would have verified her suspicions about the purchase and delivery of the murder weapon.

If she was right, and she had to believe she was, that and the weight of Mira's profile would clear Roarke.

She already knew, by the way Roarke had looked at her—through her—during their last transmission, that her professional duties had destroyed whatever personal bridge they'd been building.

She was only more sure of it when she was cleared into the office, and found Roarke there.

He must have used a private transport, she decided. It would have been impossible for him to have arrived so quickly through normal channels. He only inclined his head, said nothing as she crossed to give Commander Whitney the disc and file.

"Dr. Mira's profile."

"Thank you, Lieutenant." His eyes shifted to Roarke's. "Lieutenant Dallas will show you to an interview area. We appreciate your cooperation."

Still, he said nothing, only rose and waited for Eve to go to the door. "You're entitled to have your attorney present," she began as she called for an elevator.

"I'm aware of that. Am I being charged with any crime, Lieutenant?"

"No." Cursing him, she stepped inside, requested Area B. "This is just standard procedure." His silence continued until she wanted to scream. "Damn it, I don't have a choice here."

"Don't you?" he murmured and preceded her out of the car when the doors opened.

"This is my job." The doors of the interview area whisked open, then snapped closed behind them. The surveillance cameras any petty thief would know were hidden in every wall engaged automatically. Eve took a seat at a small table and waited for him to sit across from her.

"These proceedings are being recorded. Do you understand?"

"Yes."

"Lieutenant Dallas, ID 5347BQ, interviewer. Subject, Roarke. Initial date and time. Subject has waived the presence of an attorney. Is that correct?"

"Yes, the subject has waived the presence of an attorney."

"Are you acquainted with a licensed companion, Georgie Castle?"

"No."

"Have you been to 156 West Eighty-ninth Street?"

"No, I don't believe I have."

"Do you own a Ruger P-ninety, automatic combat weapon, circa 2005?"

"It's likely that I own a weapon of that make and era, I'd have to check to be certain. But for argument's sake, we'll say I do."

"When did you purchase said weapon?"

"Again, I'd have to check." He never blinked, never took his eyes from hers. "I have an extensive collection, and don't carry all the details of it in my head or in my pocket log."

"Did you purchase said weapon at Sotheby's?"

"It's possible. I often add to my collection through auctions."

"Silent auctions?"

"Occasionally."

Her stomach, already knotted, began to roll. "Did you add to your collection with the aforesaid weapon at a silent auction at Sotheby's on October second of last year?"

Roarke slipped his log out of his pocket, skimmed back to the date. "No. I don't have a record of that. It seems I was in Tokyo on that date, engaged in meetings. You can verify that easily."

Damn you, damn you, she thought. You know that's no answer. "Representatives are often used in auctions."

"They are." Watching her dispassionately, he tucked the log away again. "If you check with Sotheby's, you'll be told that I don't use representatives. When I decide to acquire something, it's because I've seen it—with my own eyes. Gauged its worth to me. If and when I decide to bid, I do so personally. In a silent auction, I would either attend, or participate by 'link."

"Isn't it traditional to use a sealed electronic bid, or a representative authorized to go to a certain ceiling?"

"I don't worry about traditions overmuch. The fact is, I could change my mind as to whether I want something. For one reason or another, it could lose its appeal."

She understood the underlying meaning of his statement, tried to accept that he was done with her. "The aforesaid weapon, registered in your name and purchased through silent auction at Sotheby's in October of last year was used to murder Georgie Castle at approximately seven-thirty last evening."

"You and I both know I wasn't in New York at seven-thirty last evening." His gaze skimmed over her face. "You traced the transmission, didn't you?"

She didn't answer. Couldn't. "Your weapon was found at the scene."

"Have we established it was mine?"

"Who has access to your collection?"

"I do. Only I do."

"Your staff?"

"No. If you recall, Lieutenant, my display cases are locked. Only I have the code."

"Codes can be broken."

"Unlikely, but possible," he agreed. "However, unless my palm print is used for entry, any case that is opened by any means triggers an alarm."

Goddamn it, give me an opening. Couldn't he see she was pleading with him, trying to save him? "Alarm's can be bypassed."

"True. When any case is opened without my authorization, all entry to the room is sealed off. There's no way to get out, and security is notified simultaneously. I can assure you, Lieutenant, it's quite foolproof. I believe in protecting what's mine."

She glanced up as Feeney came in. He jerked his head, and she rose.

"Excuse me."

When the doors shut behind them, he dipped his hands into his pockets. "You called it, Dallas. Electronic bid, cash deal, delivered to an EPS. The head snoot at Sotheby's claims this was an unusual procedure for Roarke. He always attends in person, or by direct 'link. Never used this line before in the fifteen years or so he's dealt with them."

She allowed herself one satisfied breath. "That checks with Roarke's statement. What else?"

"Ran an undercheck on the registration. The Ruger only appeared on the books in Roarke's name a week ago. No way in hell we can pin it on him. The commander says to spring him."

She couldn't afford to be relieved, not yet, and only nodded. "Thanks, Feeney."

She slipped back inside. "You're free to go."

He stood as she stepped backward through the open door. "Just like that?"

"We have no reason, at this time, to detain or inconvenience you any further."

"Inconvenience?" He walked toward her until the doors snicked shut at his back. "Is that what you call this? An inconvenience?"

He was, she told herself, entitled to his anger, to his bitterness. She was obliged to do her job. "Three women are dead. Every possibility has to be explored."

"And I'm just one of your possibilities?" He reached out, the sudden violent movement of his hands closing over her shirt, surprising her. "Is that what it comes down to between us?"

"I'm a cop. I can't afford to overlook anything, to assume anything."

"To trust," he interrupted. "Anything. Or anyone. If it had leaned a little the other way, would you have locked me up? Would you have put me in a cage, Eve?"

"Back off." Eyes blazing, Feeney strode down the corridor. "Back fucking off."

"Leave us alone, Feeney."

"Hell I will." Ignoring Eve, he shoved against Roarke. "Don't you come down on her, big shot. She went to bat for you. And the way things stand, it could have cost her the job. Simpson's already prepping her as sacrificial lamb because she was dumb enough to sleep with you."

"Shut up, Feeney."

"Goddamn it, Dallas."

"I said shut up." Calm again, detached, she looked at Roarke. "The department appreciates your cooperation," she said to Roarke and, prying his hand from her shirt, turned and hurried off.

"What the hell did you mean by that?" Roarke demanded.

Feeney only snorted. "I got better things to do than waste my time on you."

Roarke backed him into a wall. "You're going to be free to book me for assaulting an officer in about two breaths, Feeney. Tell me what you meant about Simpson?"

"You want to know, big shot?" Feeney looked around for a place of comparative privacy, jerked a head toward the door of a men's room. "Come into my office, and I'll tell you."

She had the cat for company. Eve was already regretting the fact that she'd have to turn the useless, overweight feline over to Georgie's family. She should have done so already, but found solace in even a pitiful furball's worth of companionship.

Nonetheless, she was nothing but irritated by the beep of her intercom. Human company was not welcomed. Particularly, as she checked her viewing screen, Roarke.

She was raw enough to take the coward's way. Leaving the summons unanswered, she walked back to the couch, curled up with the cat. If she'd had a blanket handy, she'd have pulled it over her head.

The sound of her locks disengaging moments later had her springing to her feet. "You son of a bitch," she said when Roarke walked in. "You cross too many lines."

He simply tucked his master code back in his pocket. "Why didn't you tell me?"

"I don't want to see you." She hated that her voice sounded desperate rather than angry. "Take a hint."

"I don't like being used to hurt you."

"You do fine on your own."

"You expect me to have no reaction when you accuse me of murder? When you believe it?"

"I never believed it." It came out in a hiss, a passionate whisper. "I never believed it," she repeated. "But I put my personal feelings aside and did my job. Now get out."

She headed for the door. When he grabbed her, she swung out, fast and hard. He didn't even attempt to block the blow. Calmly he wiped the blood from his mouth with the back of his hand while she stood rigid, her breathing fast and audible.

"Go ahead," he invited. 'Take another shot. You needn't worry. I don't hit women—or murder them."

"Just leave me alone." She turned away, gripped the back of the sofa where the cat sat eyeing her coolly. The emotions were welling up, threatening to fill her chest to bursting. "You're not going to make me feel guilty for doing what I had to do."

"You sliced me in two, Eve." It infuriated him anew to admit it, to know she could so easily devastate him. "Couldn't you have told me you believe in me?"

"No." She squeezed her eyes tight. "God, don't you realize it would have been worse if I had? If Whitney couldn't believe I'd be objective, if Simpson even got a whiff that I showed you any degree of preferential treatment, it would have been worse. I couldn't have moved on the psych profile so fast. Couldn't have put Feeney on a priority basis to check the trail of the weapon to eliminate probable cause."

"I hadn't thought of that," he said quietly. "I hadn't thought." When he laid a hand on her shoulder, she shrugged it off, turned on him with blazing eyes.

"Goddamn it, I told you to bring an attorney. I told you. If Feeney hadn't hit the right buttons, they could have held you. You're only out because he did, and the profile didn't fit."

He touched her again; she jerked back again. "It appears I didn't need an attorney. All I needed was you."

"It doesn't matter." She battled control back into place. "It's done. The fact that you have an unassailable alibi for the time of the murder, and that the gun was an obvious plant shifts the focus away from you." She felt sick, unbearably tired. "It may not eliminate you completely, but Dr. Mira's profiles are gold. Nobody overturns her diagnostics. She's eliminated you, and that carries a lot of weight with the department and the PA."

"I wasn't worried about the department or the PA."

"You should have been."

"It seems you've worried enough for me. I'm very sorry."

"Forget it."

"I've seen shadows under your eyes too often since I've known you." He traced a thumb along them. "I don't like being responsible for the ones I see now."

"I'm responsible for myself."

"And I had nothing to do with putting your job in jeopardy?"

Damn Feeney, she thought viciously. "I make my own decisions. I pay my own consequences."

Not this time, he thought. Not alone. "The night after we'd been together, I called. I could see you were worried, but you brushed it off. Feeney told me exactly why you were worried that night. Your angry friend wanted to pay me back for making you unhappy. He did."

"Feeney had no right—"

"Perhaps not. He wouldn't have had to if you'd confided in me." He took both her arms to stop her quick movement. "Don't turn away from me," he warned, his voice low. "You're good at shutting people out, Eve. But it won't work with me."

"What did you expect, that I'd come crying to you? 'Roarke, you seduced me, and now I'm in trouble. Help.' The hell with that, you didn't seduce me. I went to bed with you because I wanted to. Wanted to enough that I didn't think about ethics. I got slammed for it, and I'm handling it. I don't need help."

"Don't want it, certainly."

"Don't need it." She wouldn't humiliate herself by struggling away now, but stood passive. "The commander's satisfied that you're not involved in the murders. You're clear, so other than what the department will officially term an error in judgment on my part, so am I. If I'd been wrong about you, it'd be different."

"If you'd been wrong about me, it would have cost you your badge."

"Yes. I'd have lost my badge. I'd have lost everything. I'd have deserved to. But it didn't happen, so it's over. Move on."

"Do you really think I'm going to walk away?"

It weakened her, that soft, gentle lilt that came into his voice. "I can't afford you, Roarke. I can't afford to get involved."

He stepped forward, laid his hands on the back of the couch, caged her in. "I can't afford you, either. It doesn't seem to matter."

"Look—"

"I'm sorry I hurt you," he murmured. "Very sorry that I didn't trust you, then accused you of not trusting me."

"I didn't expect you to think any differently. To act any differently."

That stung more than the blow to the face. "No. I'm sorry for that, too. You risked a great deal for me. Why?"

There were no easy answers. "I believed you."

He pressed his lips to her brow. "Thank you."

"It was a judgment call," she began, letting out a shaky breath when he touched his mouth to her cheek.

"I'm going to stay with you tonight." Then to her temple. "I'm going to see that you sleep."

"Sex as a sedative?"

He frowned, but brushed his lips lightly over hers. "If you like." He lifted her off her feet, flustering her. "Let's see if we can find the right dosage."

Later, with the lights still on low, he watched her. She slept face-down, a limp sprawl of exhaustion. To please himself, he stroked a hand down her back—smooth skin, slim bones, lean muscle. She didn't stir.

Experimentally, he let his fingers comb through her hair. Thick as mink pelt, shades of aged brandy and old gold, poorly cut. It made him smile as he traced those fingers over her lips. Full, firm, fiercely responsive.

However surprised he was that he'd been able to take her beyond what she'd experienced before, he was overwhelmed by the knowledge that had, unknowingly, taken him.

How much farther, he wondered, would they go?

He knew it had ripped him when he'd believed she'd thought him guilty. The sense of betrayal, disillusionment was huge, weakening, and something he hadn't felt in too many years to count.

She'd taken him back to a point of vulnerability he'd escaped from. She could hurt him. They could hurt each other. That was something he would have to consider carefully.

But at the moment, the pressing question was who wanted to hurt them both. And why.

He was still gnawing at the problem when he took her hand, linked fingers, and let himself slide into sleep with her.

CHAPTER
FIFTEEN

He was gone when she woke. It was better that way. Mornings after carried a casual intimacy that made her nervous. She was already more involved with him than she had ever been with anyone. That click between them had the potential, she knew, to reverberate through the rest of her life.

She took a quick shower, bundled into a robe, then headed into the kitchen. There was Roarke, in trousers and a shirt he'd yet to button, scanning the morning paper on her monitor.

Looking, she realized with a quick tug-of-war of delight and dismay, very much at home.

"What are you doing?"

"Hmmm?" He glanced up, reached behind him to open the Auto-Chef. "Making you coffee."

"Making me coffee?"

"I heard you moving around." He took the cups out, carried them to where she was still hovering in the doorway. "You don't do that often enough."

"Move around?"

"No." He chuckled and touched her lips to hers. "Smile at me. Just smile at me."

Was she smiling? She hadn't realized. "I thought you'd left." She walked around the small table, glanced at the monitor. The stock reports. Naturally. "You must have gotten up early."

"I had some calls to make." He watched her, enjoying the way she raked her ringers through her damp hair. A nervous habit he was certain she was unaware of. He picked up the portalink he'd left on the table, slipped it back into his pocket. "I had a conference call scheduled with the station—five A.M. our time."

"Oh." She sipped her coffee, wondering how she had ever lived without the zip of the real thing in the morning. "I know those meetings were important. I'm sorry."

"We'd managed to hammer down most of the details. I can handle the rest from here."

"You're not going back?"

"No."

She turned to the AutoChef, fiddled with her rather limited menu. "I'm out of most everything. Want a bagel or something?"

"Eve." Roarke set his coffee down, laid his hands on her shoulders. "Why don't you want me to know you're pleased I'm staying?"

"Your alibi holds. It's none of my business if you—" She broke off when he turned her to face him. He was angry. She could see it in his eyes and prepared for the argument to come. She hadn't prepared for the kiss, the way his mouth closed firmly over hers, the way her heart rolled over slow and dreamy in her chest.

So she let herself be held, let her head nestle in the curve of his shoulder. "I don't know how to handle this," she murmured. "I don't have any precedent here. I need rules, Roarke. Solid rules."

"I'm not a case you need to solve."

"I don't know what you are. But I know this is going too fast. It shouldn't have even started. I shouldn't have been able to get started with you."

He drew her back so that he could study her face. "Why?"

"It's complicated. I have to get dressed. I have to get to work."

"Give me something." His fingers tightened on her shoulders. "I don't know what you are, either."

"I'm a cop," she blurted out. "That's all I am. I'm thirty years old and I've only been close to two people in my entire life. And even with them, it's easy to hold back."

"Hold back what?"

"Letting it matter too much. If it matters too much, it can grind you down until you're nothing. I've been nothing. I can't be nothing ever again."

"Who hurt you?"

"I don't know." But she did. She did. "I don't remember, and I don't want to remember. I've been a victim, and once you have, you need to do whatever it takes not to be one again. That's all I was before I got into the academy. A victim, with other people pushing the buttons, making the decisions, pushing me one way, pulling me another."

"Is that what you think I'm doing?"

"That's what's happening."

There were questions he needed to ask. Questions, he could see by her face, that needed to wait. Perhaps it was time he took a risk. He dipped a hand into his pocket, drew out what he carried there.

Baffled, Eve stared down at the simple gray button in his palm. "That's off my suit."

"Yes. Not a particularly flattering suit—you need stronger colors. I found it in my limo. I meant to give it back to you."

"Oh." But when she reached out, he closed his fingers over the button.

"A very smooth lie." Amused, he laughed at himself. "I had no intention of giving it back to you."

"You got a button fetish, Roarke?"

"I've been carrying this around like a schoolboy carries a lock of his sweetheart's hair."

Her eyes came back to his, and something sweet moved through her. Sweeter yet as she could see he was embarrassed. "That's weird."

"I thought so, myself." But he slipped the button back in his pocket. "Do you know what else I think, Eve?"

"I don't have a clue."

"I think I'm in love with you."

She felt the color drain out of her cheeks, felt her muscles go lax, even as her heart shot like a missile to her throat. "That's . . ."

"Yes, difficult to come up with the proper word, isn't it?" He slid his hands down her back, up again, but brought her no closer. "I've been giving it a lot of thought and haven't hit on one myself. But I should circle back to my point."

She moistened her lips. "There's a point?"

"A very interesting and important point. I'm every bit as much in your hands as you are in mine. Every bit as uncomfortable, though perhaps not as resistant, to finding myself in that position. I'm not going to let you walk away until we've figured out what to do about it."

"It, ah, complicates things."

"Outrageously," he agreed.

"Roarke, we don't even know each other. Outside of the bedroom."

"Yes, we do. Two lost souls. We've both turned away from something and made ourselves something else. It's hardly a wonder that fate decided to throw a curve into what had been, for both of us, a straight path. We have to decide how far we want to follow the curve."

"I have to concentrate on the investigation. It has to be my priority."

"I understand. But you're entitled to a personal life."

"My personal life, this part of it, grew out of the investigation. And the killer's making it more personal. Planting that gun so that suspicion would swing toward you was a direct response to my involvement with you. He's focused on me."

Roarke's hand jerked up to the lapels of her robe. "What do you mean?"

Rules, she reminded herself. There were rules. And she was about to break them. "I'll tell you what I can while I'm getting dressed."

Eve went to the bedroom with the cat sliding and weaving in front of her. "Do you remember that night you were here when I got home? The package that you'd found on the floor?"

"Yes, it upset you."

With a half laugh she peeled out of her robe. "I've got a rep for having the best poker face in the station."

"I made my first million gambling."

"Really?" She tugged a sweater over her head, reminded herself not to be distracted. "It was a recording of Lola Starr's murder. He sent me Sharon DeBlass's as well."

A cold lance of fear stabbed. "He was in your apartment."

She was busy discovering she had no clean underwear and didn't notice the iced edge of his voice. "Maybe, maybe not. I think not. No signs of forced entry. He could have shoved it under the door. That's what he did the first time. He mailed Georgie's disc. We had the building under surveillance."

Resigned, she pulled slacks over bare skin. "He either knew it or smelled it. But he saw I got the discs, all three of them. He knew I was primary almost before I did."

She searched for socks, got lucky, and found a pair that matched. "He called me, transmitted the video of Georgie Castle's murder scene minutes after he'd whacked her." She sat on the edge of the bed, pulled on the socks. "He planted a weapon, made sure it was traceable. To you. Not to knock how inconvenient a murder charge would have made your life, Roarke, if I hadn't had the commander behind me on this, I'd have been off the case, and out of the department in a blink. He knows what goes on inside Cop Central. He knows what's going on in my life."

"Fortunately, he didn't know that I wasn't even on the planet."

"That was a break for both of us." She located her boots, tugged them on. "But it's not going to stop him." She rose, picked up her holster. "He's still going to try to get to me, and you're his best bet."

Roarke watched her automatically check her laser before strapping it on. "Why you?"

"He doesn't have a high opinion of women. I'd have to say it burns his ass to have a female heading the investigation. It lowers his status." She shrugged, raked her fingers through her hair to whip it into place. "At least that's the shrink's opinion."

Philosophically, she pried the cat free when he started to climb up her leg, gave him a light toss to the bed where he turned his butt in her direction and began to wash.

"And is it the shrink's opinion that he could try to eliminate you by more direct means?"

"I don't fit the pattern."

Fighting back the slippery edge of fear, Roarke fisted his hands in his pockets. "And if he breaks the pattern?"

"I can handle myself."

"It's worth risking your life for three women who are already dead?"

"Yes." She heard the fury pulsing in his voice and faced it. "It's worth risking my life to find justice for three women who are already dead, and to try to prevent three more from dying. He's only half through. He's left a note under each body. He's wanted us to know, right from the start that he had a plan. And he's daring us to stop him. One of six, two of six, three of six. I'll do whatever it takes to keep him from having the fourth."

"Full-out guts. That's what I first admired about you. Now it terrifies me."

For the first time she moved to him, laid a hand on his cheek. Almost as soon as she had, she dropped her hand and stepped back again, embarrassed. "I've been a cop for ten years, Roarke, never had more than some bumps and bruises. Don't worry about it."

"I think you're going to have to get used to having someone worry about you, Eve."

That hadn't been the plan. She walked out of the bedroom to get her jacket and bag. "I'm telling you this so that you'll understand what I'm up against. Why I can't split my energies and start analyzing what's between us."

"There'll always be cases."

"I hope to God there won't always be cases like this one. This isn't murder for gain, or out of passion. It isn't desperate or frenzied. It's cold and calculated. It's . . ."

"Evil?"

"Yes." It relieved her that he'd said it first. It didn't sound so foolish. "Whatever we've done in genetic engineering, in vitro, with social programs, we still can't control basic human failings: violence, lust, envy."

"The seven deadly sins."

She thought of the old woman and her poisoned pie. "Yeah. I've got to go."

"Will you come to me when you're off duty tonight?"

"I don't know when I'll log out. It could be—"

"Will you come?"

"Yeah."

Then he smiled, and she knew he was waiting for her to make the move. She was sure he knew just how hard it was for her to cross to him, to bring her lips up, to press them, however casually, to his.

"See you."

"Eve. You should have gloves."

She decoded the door, tossed a quick smile over her shoulder. "I know—but I just keep losing them."

Her up mood lasted until she walked into her office and found De-Blass and his aide waiting for her.

Deliberately, DeBlass stared at his gold watch. "More banker's hours than police hours, Lieutenant Dallas."

She knew damn well it was only minutes past eight, but shrugged out of her jacket. "Yeah, it's a pretty lush life around here. Is there something I can do for you, Senator?"

"I'm aware there's been yet another murder. I'm obviously dissatisfied with your progress. However, I'm here for damage control. I do not want my granddaughter's name linked with the two other victims."

"You want Simpson for that, or his press secretary."

"Don't smirk at me, young woman." DeBlass leaned forward. "My granddaughter is dead. Nothing can change that. But I will not have the DeBlass name sullied, muddied by the death of two common whores."

"You seem to have a low opinion of women, Senator." She was careful not to smirk this time, but watched him, and considered.

"On the contrary; I revere them. Which is why those who sell themselves, those who disregard morality and common decency, revolt me."

"Including your granddaughter?"

He lurched out of his chair, his face purpling, eyes bulging. Eve was quite certain he would have struck her if Rockman hadn't stepped between them.

"Senator, the lieutenant is only baiting you. Don't give her the satisfaction."

"You will not besmirch my family." DeBlass was breathing fast, and Eve wondered if he had any history of heart trouble. "My granddaughter paid dearly for her sins, and I will not see the rest of my loved ones dragged down into public ridicule. And I will not tolerate your vile insinuations."

"Just trying to get my facts straight." It was fascinating watching him battle for composure. He was having a rough time of it, she noted, hands shaking, chest heaving. "I'm trying to find the man who killed Sharon, Senator. I assume that's also high on your agenda."

"Finding him won't get her back." He sat again, obviously exhausted by the outburst. "What's important now is to protect what's left. To do that, Sharon must be segregated from the other women."

She didn't like his opinion, but neither did she care for his color. It was still alarmingly high. "Can I get you some water, Senator DeBlass?"

He nodded, waved at her. Eve slipped into the corridor and dispensed a cup of bottled water. When she came back, his breathing was more regular, his hands a bit steadier.

"The senator has been overtaxing himself," Rockman put in. "His Morals Bill goes before the House tomorrow. The pressure of this family tragedy is a great weight."

"I appreciate that. I'm doing everything I can to close the case." She tilted her head. "Political pressure is also a great weight on an investigation. I don't care to be monitored on my personal time."

Rockman gave her a mild smile. "I'm sorry. Could you qualify that."

"I was monitored, and my personal relationship with a civilian reported to Chief Simpson. It's no secret that Simpson and the senator are tight."

"The senator and Chief Simpson have a personal and a political allegiance," Rockman agreed. "However, it would hardly be ethical, or in the senator's best interest, to monitor a member of the police force. I assure you, Lieutenant, Senator DeBlass has been much too involved with his own grief and his responsibilities to the country to worry about your . . . personal relationships. It has come to our attention, however, through Chief Simpson, that you've had a number of liaisons with Roarke."

"An amoral opportunist." The senator set his cup aside with a snap. "A man who would stop at nothing to add to his own power."

"A man," Eve added, "who has been cleared of any connection with this investigation."

"Money buys immunity," DeBlass said in disgust.

"Not in this office. I'm sure you'll request the report from the commander. In the meantime, whether or not it assuages your grief, I intend to find the man who killed your granddaughter."

"I suppose I should commend your dedication." DeBlass rose. "See that your dedication doesn't jeopardize my family's reputation."

"What changed your mind, Senator?" Eve wondered. "The first time we spoke, you threatened to have my job if I didn't bring Sharon's murderer to justice, and quickly."

"She's buried," was all he said, and strode out.

"Lieutenant." Rockman kept his voice low. "I will repeat that the pressure on Senator DeBlass is enormous, enough to crush a lesser man." He let out a slow breath. "The fact is, it's destroyed his wife. She's had a breakdown."

"I'm sorry."

"The doctors don't know if she'll recover. This additional tragedy has his son crazed with grief; his daughter has closed herself off from her family and gone into retreat. The senator's only hope of restoring his family is to let Sharon's death, the horror of it, pass."

"Then it might be wise for the senator to take a step back and leave due process to the department."

"Lieutenant—Eve," he said with that rare and quick flash of charm.

"I wish I could convince him of that. But I believe that would be as fruitless an endeavor as convincing you to let Sharon rest in peace."

"You'd be right."

"Well then." He laid a hand on her arm briefly. "We must all do what we can to set things right. It was good to see you again."

Eve closed the door behind him and considered. DeBlass certainly had the kind of hair-trigger temper that could lead to violence. She was almost sorry he didn't also have the control, the calculation, to have meticulously planned three murders.

In any case, she'd have a hard time connecting a rabidly right-wing senator to a couple of New York prostitutes.

Maybe he was protecting his family, she mused. Or maybe he was protecting Simpson, a political ally.

That was crap, Eve decided. He might work on Simpson's behalf if the chief was involved in the Starr and Castle homicides. But a man didn't protect the killer of his grandchild.

Too bad she wasn't looking for two men, Eve mused. Regardless, she was going to do some pecking away at Simpson's underpinnings.

Objectively, she warned herself. And it wouldn't do to forget that there was a strong possibility that DeBlass didn't know one of his favorite political cronies had been blackmailed by his only granddaughter.

She'd have to find out.

But for now, she had another hunch to follow. She located Charles Monroe's number and put through a call.

His voice was smeared with sleep, his eyes heavy. "You spend all your time in bed, Charles?"

"All I can, Lieutenant Sugar." He rubbed a hand over his face and grinned at her. "That's how I think of you."

"Well, don't. Couple of questions."

"Ah, can't you come on over and ask in person? I'm warm and naked and all alone."

"Pal, don't you know there's a law against soliciting a police officer?"

"I'm talking freebie here. I told you—we'd keep it strictly personal."

"We're keeping it strictly impersonal. You had an associate. Georgie Castle. Did you know her?"

The seductive smile faded from his face. "Yeah, actually, I did. Not well, but I met her at a party about a year ago. She was new in the business. Fun, attractive. Game, you know. We hit it off."

"In what way?"

"In a friendly way. We had a drink now and again. Once when Sharon had an overbooking, I had her send a couple of clients Georgie's way."

"They knew each other." Eva pounced on it. "Sharon and Georgie?"

"I don't think so. As far as I remember, Sharon contacted Georgie, asked her if she was interested in a couple of fresh tricks. Georgie gave it the green light, and that was that. Oh, yeah, Sharon said something about Georgie sending her a dozen roses. Real ones, like a thank-you gift. Sharon got a real kick out of the old-fashioned etiquette."

"Just an old-fashioned girl," Eve said under her breath.

"When I heard Georgie was dead, it hit hard. I gotta tell you. With Sharon it was a jolt, but not that much of a surprise. She lived on the edge. But Georgie, she was centered, you know?"

"I may need to follow up on this, Charles. Stay available."

"For you—"

"Knock it off," she ordered, before he could get cute. "What do you know about Sharon's diaries?"

"She never let me read one," he said easily. "I used to tease her about them. Seems to me she said she'd kept them since she was a kid. You got one? Hey, am I in it?"

"Where'd she keep them?"

"In her apartment, I guess. Where else?"

That was the question, Eve mused. "If you think of anything else about Georgie or about the diaries, contact me."

"Day or night, Lieutenant Sugar. Count on me."

"Right." But she was laughing when she broke transmission.

The sun was just setting when she arrived at Roarke's. She didn't consider herself off duty. The favor she was going to ask had been simmering in her mind all day. She'd decided on it, rejected it, and generally vacillated until she'd disgusted herself.

In the end, she'd left the station for the first time in months right on the dot of the end of her shift. With what limited progress she'd made, she'd hardly needed to be there at all.

Feeney had hit nothing but a dead end in his search for a second lock box. He had, with obvious reluctance, given her the list of cops she'd requested. Eve intended to run a make on each of them—on her own time and in her own way.

With some regret, she realized she was going to use Roarke.

Summerset opened the door with his usual disdain. "You're earlier than expected, Lieutenant."

"If he isn't in, I can wait."

"He's in the library."

"Which is where, exactly?"

Summerset permitted himself the tiniest huff. If Roarke hadn't ordered him to show the woman in immediately he would have shuffled her off to some small, poorly lit room. "This way, please."

"What exactly is it about me that rubs you wrong, Summerset?"

With his back poker straight, he led her up a flight and down the wide corridor. "I have no idea what you mean, Lieutenant. The library," he announced in reverent terms, and opened the door for her.

She'd never in her life seen so many books. She never would have believed so many existed outside of museums. The walls were lined with them so that the two-level room positively reeked with books.

On the lower level, on what was surely a leather sofa, Roarke lounged, a book in his hand, the cat on his lap.

"Eve. You're early." He set the book aside, picked up the cat as he rose.

"Jesus, Roarke, where did you get all these?"

"The books?" He let his gaze roam the room. Firelight danced and shifted over colorful spines. "Another of my interests. Don't you like to read?"

"Sure, now and again. But discs are so much more convenient."

"And so much less aesthetic." He stroked the cat's neck and sent him into ecstasy. "You're welcome to borrow any you like."

"I don't think so."

"How about a drink?"

"I could handle that."

His 'link beeped. "This is the call I've been waiting for. Why don't you get us both a glass of wine I've had breathing over on the table?"

"Sure." She took the cat from him and walked over to oblige. Because she wanted to eavesdrop, she forced herself to stay the length of the room away from where he sat murmuring.

It gave her a chance to browse the books, to puzzle over the titles. Some she had heard of. Even with a state education, she'd been required to read Steinbeck and Chaucer, Shakespeare and Dickens. The curriculum had taken her through King and Grisham, Morrison and Grafton.

But there were dozens, perhaps hundreds of names here she'd never heard of. She wondered if anyone could handle so many books, much less read them.

"I'm sorry," he said when the call was complete. "That couldn't wait."

"No problem."

He took the wine she'd poured him. "The cat's becoming quite attached to you."

"I don't think he has any particular loyalties." But Eve had to admit, she enjoyed the way he curled under her stroking hand. "I don't know what I'm going to do about him. I called Georgie's daughter and she said she just couldn't face taking him. Pressing the matter only made her cry."

"You could keep him."

"I don't know. You have to take care of pets."

"Cats are remarkably self-sufficient." He sat on the sofa and waited for her to join him. "Want to tell me about your day?"

"Not very productive. Yours?"

"Very productive."

"A lot of books," Eve said lamely, knowing she was stalling.

"I have an affection for them. I could barely read my name when I was six. Then I came across a battered copy of Yeats. An Irish writer of some note," he said when Eve looked blank. "I badly wanted to figure it out, so I taught myself."

"Didn't you go to school?"

"Not if I could help it. You've got trouble in your eyes, Eve," he murmured.

She blew out a breath. What was the use of stalling when he could see right through her? "I've got a problem. I want to do a run on Simpson. Obviously, I can't go through channels or use either my home or office units. The minute I tried to dig on the chief of police, I'd be flagged."

"And you're wondering if I have a secured, unregistered system. Of course I do."

"Of course," she muttered. "A nonregistered system is in violation of Code four fifty-three-B, section thirty-five."

"I can't tell you how aroused it makes me when you quote codes, Lieutenant."

"It's not funny. And what I'm going to ask you to do is illegal. It's a serious offense to electronically breach the privacy of a state official."

"You could arrest both of us afterward."

"This is serious, Roarke. I go by the book, and now I'm asking you to help me break the law."

He rose, drew her to her feet. "Darling Eve, you have no idea how many I've already broken." He fetched the wine bottle, letting it dangle from two fingers of the hand he slipped around her waist. "I ran an underground dice game when I was ten," he began, leading her from the room. "A legacy from my dear old father who'd earned himself a knife through the gullet in a Dublin alley."

"I'm sorry."

"We weren't close. He was a bastard and no one loved him, least of all me. Summerset, we'll have dinner at seven-thirty," Roarke added as he turned toward the stairs. "But he taught me, by means of a fist to the face, to read the dice, the cards, the odds. He was a thief, not a good one, as his end proved. I was better. I stole, I cheated, I spent some time learning the smuggling trade. So you see, you're hardly corrupting me with such a nominal request."

She didn't look at him as he decoded a locked door on the second floor. "Do you . . ."

"Do I steal, cheat, and smuggle now?" He turned and touched a hand to her face. "Oh, you'd hate that, wouldn't you? I almost wish I could say yes, then give it all up for you. I learned a long time ago that there are gambles more exciting for their legitimacy. And winning is so much more satisfying when you've dealt from the top of the deck."

He pressed a kiss to her brow, then stepped into the room. "But, we have to keep our hand in."

CHAPTER

SIXTEEN

Compared to the rest of the house she'd seen, this room was spartan, designed rigidly for work. No fancy statues, dripping chandeliers. The wide, U-shaped console, the base for communication, research, and information retrieving devices, was unrelieved black, studded with controls, sliced with slots and screens.

Eve had heard that IRCCA had the swankiest base system in the country. She suspected Roarke's matched it.

Eve was no compu-jock, but she knew at a glance that the equipment here was vastly superior to any the New York Police and Security Department used—or could afford—even in the lofty Electronic Detection Division.

The long wall facing the console was taken up by six large monitor screens. A second, auxiliary station held a sleek little tele-link, a second laser fax, a hologram send-receive unit, and several other pieces of hardware she didn't recognize.

The trio of comp stations boasted personal monitors with attached 'links.

The floor was glazed tile, the diamond patterns in muted colors that bled together like liquid. The single window looked over the city and pulsed with the last lights of the setting sun.

It seemed even here, Roarke demanded ambiance.

"Quite a setup," Eve commented.

"Not quite as comfortable as my office, but it has the basics." He moved behind the main console, placed his palm on the identiscreen. "Roarke. Open operations."

After a discreet hum, the lights on the console glowed on. "New palm and voiceprint clearance," he continued and gestured to Eve. "Cleared for yellow status."

At his nod, Eve pressed her hand to the screen, felt the faint warmth of the reading. "Dallas."

"There you are." Roarke took his seat. "The system will accept your voice and hand commands."

"What's yellow status?"

He smiled. "Enough to give you everything you need to know—not quite enough to override my commands."

"Hmmm." She scanned the controls, the patiently blinking lights, the myriad screens and gauges. She wished for Feeney and his computer-minded brain. "Search on Edward T. Simpson, Chief of Police and Security, New York City. All financial data."

"Going right to the heart," Roarke murmured.

"I don't have time to waste. This can't be traced?"

"Not only can't it be traced, but there'll be no record of the search."

"Simpson, Edward T.," the computer announced in a warm, female tone. "Financial records. Searching."

At Eve's lifted brow, Roarke grinned. "I prefer to work with melodious voices."

"I was going to ask," she returned, "how you can access data without alerting the Compuguard."

"No system's foolproof, or completely breach resistant—even the ubiquitous Compuguard. The system is an excellent deterrent to your average hacker or electronic thief. But with the right equipment, it can be compromised. I have the right equipment. Here comes the data. On viewing screen one," he ordered.

Eve glanced up and saw Simpson's credit report flash onto the large monitor. It was the standard business: vehicle loans, mortgages, credit card balances. All the automatic E-transactions.

"That's a hefty AmEx bill," she mused. "And I don't think it's common knowledge he owns a place on Long Island."

"Hardly murderous motives. He maintains a Class A rating, which means he pays what he owes. Ah, here's a bank account. Screen two."

Eve studied the numbers, dissatisfied. "Nothing out of line, pretty average deposits and withdrawals—mostly automatic bill paying transfers that jibe with the credit report. What's Jeremy's?"

"Men's clothier," Roarke told her with the smallest sneer of disdain. "Somewhat second rate."

She wrinkled her nose. "Hell of a lot to spend on clothes."

"Darling, I'm going to have to corrupt you. It's only too much if they're inferior clothes."

She sniffed, stuck her thumbs in the front pockets of her baggy brown trousers.

"Here's his brokerage account. Screen three. Spineless," Roarke added after a quick scan.

"What do you mean?"

"His investments, such as they are. All no risk. Government issue, a few mutual funds, a smattering of blue chip. Everything on-planet."

"What's wrong with that?"

"Nothing if you're content to let your money gather dust." He slanted her a look. "Do you invest, Lieutenant?"

"Yeah, right." She was still trying to make sense of the abbreviations and percentage points. "I watch the stock reports twice a day."

"Not a standard credit account." He nearly shuddered.

"So what?"

"Give me what you have, I'll double it within six months."

She only frowned, struggling to read the brokerage report. "I'm not here to get rich."

"Darling," he corrected in that flowing Irish lilt. "We all are."

"How about contributions, political, charities, that kind of thing?"

"Access tax saving outlay," Roarke ordered. "Viewing screen two."

She waited, impatiently tapping a hand on her thigh. Data scrolled on. "He puts his money where his heart is," she muttered, scanning his payments to the Conservative Party, DeBlass's campaign fund.

"Not particularly generous otherwise. Hmm." Roarke's brow lifted. "Interesting, a very hefty gift to Moral Values."

"That's an extremist group, isn't it?"

"I'd call it that, the faithful prefer to think of it as an organization dedicated to saving all of us sinners from ourselves. DeBlass is a strong proponent."

But she was flipping through her own mental files. "They're suspected of sabotaging the main data banks at several large contraception control clinics."

Roarke clucked his tongue. "All those women deciding for themselves if and when they want to conceive, how many children they want. What's the world coming to? Obviously, someone has to bring them back to their senses."

"Right." Dissatisfied, Eve stuck her hands in her pockets. "It's a dangerous connection for someone like Simpson. He likes to play middle of the road. He ran on a Moderate ticket."

"Cloaking his Conservative ties and leanings. In the last few years he's been cautiously removing the layers. He wants to be governor, perhaps believes DeBlass can put him there. Politics is a bartering game."

"Politics. Sharon DeBlass's blackmail disc was heavy on politicians. Sex, murder, politics," Eve murmured. "The more things change . . ."

"Yes, the more they remain the same. Couples still indulge in courting rituals, humans still kill humans, and politicians still kiss babies and lie."

Something wasn't quite right, and she wished for Feeney again. Twentieth-century murders, she thought, twentieth-century motives. There was one other thing that hadn't changed over the last millennium. Taxes.

"Can we get his IRS data? The past three years?"

"That's a little trickier." His mouth had already quirked up at the challenge.

"It's also a federal offense. Listen, Roarke—"

"Just hold on a minute." He pressed a button and a manual key-board slipped out of the console. With some surprise, Eve watched his fingers fly over the keys. "Where'd you learn to do that?" Even with required department training, she was barely competent on manual.

"Here and there," he said absently, "in my misspent youth. I have to get around the security. It's going to take some time. Why don't you pour us some more wine?"

"Roarke, I shouldn't have asked." An attack of conscience had her walking to him. "I can't let this come back on you—'

"Ssh." His brows drew together in concentration as he maneu-vered his way through the security labyrinth.

"But—"

He head snapped up, impatience vivid in his eyes. "We've already opened the door, Eve. Now we go through, or we turn away from it."

Eve thought of three women, dead because she hadn't been able to stop it. Hadn't known enough to stop it. With a nod, she turned away again. The clatter of the keyboard resumed.

She poured the wine, then moved to stand in front of the screens. Tidy as they came, she mused. Top credit rating, prompt payment of debts, conservative and, she assumed, relatively small investments. Surely that was more money than average spent on clothes, wine shops, and jewelry. But it wasn't a crime to have expensive taste. Not when you paid for it. Even the second home wasn't a criminal offense.

Some of the contributions were dicey for a registered Moderate, but still, not criminal.

She heard Roarke curse softly and looked back. But he was hun-kered over the keyboard. She might not have been there. Odd, she wouldn't have guessed he had the technical skills to access manually. According to Feeney, it was almost a lost art except in tech-clerks and hackers.

Yet here he was, the rich, the privileged, the elegant, clattering over a problem usually delegated to a low-paid, overworked office drone.

For a moment, she let herself forget about the business at hand and smiled at him.

"You know, Roarke, you're kind of cute."

She realized it was the first time she'd really surprised him. His head came up, and his eyes were startled—for perhaps two heartbeats. Then that sly smile came into them. The one that made her own pulse jitter.

"You're going to have to do better than that, Lieutenant. I've got you in."

"No shit?" Excitement flooded through her as she whirled back to the screens. "Put it up."

"Screens four, five, six."

"There's his bottom line." She frowned over gross income. "It's about right, wouldn't you say—salarywise."

"A bit of interest and dividends from investments." Roarke scrolled pages. "A few honorariums for personal appearances and speeches. He lives close, but just within his means, according to all of the data shown."

"Hell." She tossed back wine. "What other data is there?"

"For a sharp woman, that's an incredibly naive question. Underground accounts," he explained. "Two sets of books is a tried and true and very traditional method of hiding illicit income."

"If you had illicit income, why would you be stupid enough to document it?"

"A question for the ages. But people do. Oh yes, they do. Yes," he said, answering her unspoken question as to his own bookkeeping methods. "Of course I do."

She shot him a hard look. "I don't want to know about it."

He only moved his shoulders. "The point being, because I do, I know how it's done. Everything's above board here, wouldn't you say?" With a few commands he had the IRS reports merged on one screen. "Now let's go down a level. Computer, Simpson, Edward T., foreign accounts."

"No known data."

"There's always more data," Roarke murmured, undeterred. He went back to the keyboard, and something began to hum.

"What's that noise?"

"It's just telling me I'm hitting a wall." Like a laborer, he flicked open the buttons at his cuffs, rolled up his sleeves. The gesture made Eve smile. "And if there's a wall, there's something behind it."

He continued to work, one handed, and sipped his wine. When he repeated his command, the response had shifted.

"Data protected."

"Ah, now we've got it."

"How can you—"

"Ssh," he ordered again and had Eve subsiding into impatient silence. "Computer, run numerical and alphabetical combinations for passkey."

Pleased with the progress, he pushed back. "This will take a little time. Why don't you come here?"

"Can you show me how you—" She broke off, shocked, when Roarke pulled her into his lap. "Hey, this is important."

"So's this." He took her mouth, sliding his hand up her hip to just under the curve of her breast. "It could take an hour, maybe more, to find the key." Those quick, clever hands were already moving under her sweater. "You don't like to waste time, as I recall."

"No, I don't." It was the first time in her life she'd ever sat on anyone's lap, and the sensation wasn't at all unpleasant. She was sinking, but the next mechanical hum had her pulling back. Speechless, she stared at the bed gliding out of a panel in the side wall. "The man who has everything," she managed.

"I will have." He hooked an arm under her legs, lifted her. "Very shortly."

"Roarke." She had to admit, maybe just this once, she enjoyed being swept up and carried off.

"Yes."

"I always thought too much emphasis, in society, advertisement, entertainment, was put on sex."

"Did you?"

"I did." Grinning, she shifted her body, quick and agile, and overbalanced him. "I've changed my mind," she said as they tumbled onto the bed.

She'd already learned that lovemaking could be intense, overwhelming, even dangerously exciting. She hadn't known it could be fun. It was a revelation to find that she could laugh and wrestle over the bed like a child.

Quick, nipping kisses, ticklish groping, breathless giggles. She couldn't remember ever giggling before in her life as she pinned Roarke to the mattress.

"Gotcha."

"You do indeed." Delighted with her, he let her hold him down, rain kisses over his face. "Now that you have me, what are you going to do about it?"

"Use you, of course." She bit down, none too gently, on his bottom lip. "Enjoy you." With her brows arched, she unfastened his shirt, spread it open. "You do have a terrific body." To please herself, she ran her hands over his chest. "I used to think that sort of thing was overrated, too. After all, anyone with enough money can have one."

"I didn't buy mine," Roarke said, surprised into defending his physique.

"No, you've got a gym in this place, don't you?" Bending, she let her lips cruise over his shoulder. "You'll have to show it to me some-time. I think I'd like watching you sweat."

He rolled her over, reversing positions. He felt her freeze, then relax under his restraining hands. Progress, he thought. The begin-nings of trust. "I'm ready to work out with you, Lieutenant, anytime." He tugged the sweater over her head. "Anytime at all."

He released her hands. It moved him to have her reach up, draw him down to her to embrace.

So strong, he thought, as the tone of the lovemaking changed from playful to tender. So soft. So troubled. He took her slowly, and very gently over the first rise, watched her crest, listened to the low, hum-ming moan as her system absorbed each velvet shock.

He needed her. It still had the power to shake him to know just how much he needed her. He knelt, lifting her. Her legs wrapped silk-ily around him, her body bowed fluidly back. He could take his mouth over her, tasting warm flesh while he moved inside her, deep, steady, slow.

Each time she shuddered, a fresh stream of pleasure rippled

through him. Her throat was a slim white feast he couldn't resist. He laved it, nipped, nuzzled while the pulse just under that sensitized flesh throbbed like a heart.

And she gasped his name, cupping his head in her hands, pressing him against her as her body rocked, rocked, rocked.

She discovered lovemaking made her loose, and warm. The slow arousal, the long, slow finish energized her. She didn't feel awkward climbing back into her clothes with the scent of him clinging to her. She felt smug.

"I feel good around you." It surprised her to say it aloud, to give him—or anyone—even so slight an advantage.

He understood that such an admission, for her, was tantamount to a shouted declaration of devotion from other women.

"I'm glad." He traced a fingertip down her cheek, dipped it into the faint dent in her chin. "I like the idea of staying around you."

She turned away at that, crossed over to watch the number sequences fly by on the console screen. "Why did you tell me about being a kid in Dublin, about your father, the things you did?"

"You won't stay with someone you don't know." He studied her back as he tucked his shirt into his trousers. "You'd told me a little, so I told you a little. And I think, eventually, you'll tell me who hurt you when you were a child."

"I told you I don't remember." She hated even the whisper of panic in her voice. "I don't need to."

"Don't tighten up." He murmured to her as he walked over to massage her shoulders. "I won't press you. I know exactly what it is to remake yourself, Eve. To distance yourself from what was."

What good would it do to tell her that no matter how far, how fast you ran, the past always stayed two paces behind you?

Instead, he wrapped his arms around her waist, satisfied when she closed her hands over his. He knew she was studying the screens across the room. Knew the instant she saw it.

"Son of a bitch, look at the numbers: income, outgo. They're too damn close. They're practically exact."

"They are exact," Roarke corrected, and released the woman, knowing the cop would want to stand clear. "To the penny."

"But that's impossible." She struggled to do the math in her head. "Nobody spends exactly what they make—not on record. Everyone carries at least a little cash—for the occasional vendor on the sidewalk, the Pepsi machine, the kid who brings the pizza. Sure, it's mostly plastic or electronic, but you've got to have some cash floating around."

She paused, turned around. "You'd already seen it. Why the hell didn't you say something?"

"I thought it would be more interesting to wait until we found his cache." He glanced down as the blinking yellow light for searching switched to green. "And it appears we have. Ah, a traditional man, our Simpson. As I suspected, he relies on the well-respected and discreet Swiss. Display data on screen five."

"Jesus fucking Christ." Eve gaped at the bank listings.

"That's in Swiss francs," Roarke explained. "Translate to USD, screen six. About triple his tax portfolio here, wouldn't you say, Lieutenant?"

Her blood was up. "I knew he was taking. God damn it, I knew it. And look at the withdrawals, Roarke, in the last year. Twenty-five thousand a quarter, every quarter. A hundred thousand." She turned back to Roarke, and her smile was thin. "That matches the figure on Sharon's list. Simpson—one hundred K. She was bleeding him."

"You may be able to prove it."

"I damn well will prove it." She began to pace. "She had something on him. Maybe it was sex, maybe it was graft. Probably a combination of a lot of ugly little sins. So he paid her to keep her quiet."

Eve thrust her hands into her pockets, pulled them out again. "Maybe she upped the ante. Maybe he was just sick and tired of shelling out a hundred a year for insurance. So he offs her. Somebody keeps trying to scuttle the investigation. Somebody with the power and the information to complicate things. It points right at him."

"What about the two other victims?"

She was working on it. Goddamn it, she was working on it. "He used one prostitute. He could have used others. Sharon and the third victim knew each other—or of each other. One of them might have known

Lola, mentioned her, even suggested her as a change of pace. Hell, she could have been a random choice. He got caught up in the thrill of the first murder. It scared him, but it was also a high for him."

She stopped prowling the room long enough to flick a glance at Roarke. He'd taken out a cigarette, lighted it, watching her.

"DeBlass is one of his backers," she continued. "And Simpson's come out strongly in favor of DeBlass's upcoming Morals Bill. They're just prostitutes, he's thinking. Just legal whores, and one of them was threatening him. How much more of a danger to him would she have been once he put in his bid for governor?"

She stopped pacing again, turned back. "And that's just shit."

"I thought it sounded quite reasonable."

"Not when you look at the man." Slowly, she rubbed her fingers between her brows. "He doesn't have the brains for it. Yeah, I think he could kill, Christ knows he's into control, but to pull off a series of murders this slick? He's a desk man—an administrator, an image, not a cop. He can't even remember a penal code without an aide prompting him. Graft's easy, it's just business. And to kill out of panic or passion or fury, yes. But to plan, to execute the plan step by step? No. He isn't even smart enough to juggle his public records well."

"So he had help."

"Possible. Maybe if I could put pressure on him, I'd find out."

"I can help you there." Roarke took a final, thoughtful drag before crushing out his cigarette. "What do you think the media would do if it received an anonymous transmission of Simpson's underground accounts?"

She dropped the hand she'd lifted to rake through her hair. "They'd hang him. If he knows anything, even with a fleet of lawyers around him, we might be able to shake something loose."

"Just so. Your call, Lieutenant."

She thought of rules, of due process, of the system she'd made herself an intregal part of. And she thought of three dead women—three more she might be able to protect.

"There's a reporter. Nadine Furst. Give it to her."

*   *   *

She wouldn't stay with him. Eve knew a call would come, and it was best if she were home and alone when it did. She didn't think she would sleep, but she drifted into dreams.

She dreamed first of murder. Sharon, Lola, Georgie, each of them smiling toward the camera. That instant of fear a lightning bolt in the eyes before they flew back on sex-warmed sheets.

Daddy. Lola had called him Daddy. And Eve stumbled painfully into an older, more terrifying dream.

She was a good girl. She tried to be good, not to cause trouble. If you caused trouble, the cops came and got you, and put you in a deep, dark hole where bugs skittered and spiders crept toward you on silent, slithery legs.

She didn't have friends. If you had friends you had to make up stories about where the bruises came from. How you were clumsy when you weren't clumsy. How you'd fallen when you hadn't fallen. Besides, they never lived in one place very long. If you did, the fucking social workers came nosing around, asking questions. It was the fucking social workers who called the cops that put you away in that dark, bug crawling hole.

Her daddy had warned her.

So she was a good girl, without any friends, who moved from place to place when she was taken.

But it didn't seem to make any difference.

She could hear him coming. She always heard him. Even if she was sound asleep, the creeping shuffle of his bare feet on the floor woke her as quickly as a thunder clap.

Oh, please, oh, please, oh please. She would pray, but she wouldn't cry. If she cried she was beaten, and he did the secret things anyway. The painful and secret thing that she knew, even at five, was somehow bad.

He told her she was good. The whole time he did the secret thing he would tell her she was good. But she knew she was bad, and she would be punished.

Sometimes he tied her up. When she heard her door open, she whimpered softly, praying he wouldn't tie her this time. She wouldn't fight, she wouldn't, if he just didn't tie her up. If he just didn't hold his hand over her mouth, she wouldn't scream or call out.

"Where's my little girl? Where's my good little girl?"

Tears gathered in the corners of her eyes as his hands slipped under the sheets, poking, probing, pinching. She could smell his breath on her face, sweet, like candy.

His fingers rammed inside her, his other hand coming down hard over her mouth as she drew in breath to scream. She couldn't help it.

"Be quiet." His breath was coming in short gasps, in a sickening arousal she didn't understand. His fingers dug into her cheeks where bruises would form by morning. "Be a good girl. There's a good girl."

She couldn't hear his grunts for the screaming inside her head. She screamed it over and over and over.

No, Daddy. No, Daddy.

"*No!*" The scream ripped out of Eve's throat as she reared up in bed. Gooseflesh prickled on her clammy skin, and she shivered and shivered as she tugged the blankets up.

Didn't remember. Wouldn't remember, she comforted herself and drew up her knees, pressed her forehead against them. Just a dream, and it was already fading. She could will it away—had done so before—until there was nothing left but the faint nausea.

Still shaky, she got up, wrapped herself in her robe to combat the chill. In the bath she ran water over her face until she was breathing evenly again. Steadier, she got herself a tube of Pepsi, huddled back into bed, and switched on one of the twenty-four-hour news stations.

And settled down to wait.

It was the lead story at six A.M., the headline read by a cat-eyed Nadine. Eve was already dressed when the call came through summoning her to Cop Central.

CHAPTER

SEVENTEEN

Whatever personal satisfaction Eve felt on finding herself part of the team who questioned Simpson, she hid it well. In deference to his position, they used the office of Security Administration rather than an interrogation area.

The clear wrap of windows and the glossy acrylic table didn't negate the fact that Simpson was in deep trouble. The beading of sweat above his top lip indicated he knew just how deep.

"The media is trying to injure the department," Simpson began, using the statement meticulously prepared by his senior aide. "With the very visible failure of the investigation into the brutal deaths of three women, the media is attempting to incite a witch-hunt. As chief of police, I'm an obvious target."

"Chief Simpson." Not by the flicker of an eyelash did Commander Whitney expose his inner glee. His voice was grave, his eyes somber. His heart was celebrating. "Regardless of the motive, it will be necessary for you to explain the discrepancy in your books."

Simpson sat frozen while one of his attorneys leaned over and murmured in his ear.

"I have not admitted to any discrepancy. If one exists, I'm unaware of it."

"Unaware, Chief Simpson, of more than two million dollars?"

"I've already contacted my accounting firm. Obviously, if there is a mistake of some nature, it was made by them."

"Will you confirm or deny that the account numbered four seventy-eight nine one one two seven, four ninety-nine is yours?"

After another brief consultation, Simpson nodded. "I will confirm that." To lie would only tighten the noose.

Whitney glanced at Eve. They'd agreed the account was an IRS matter. All they'd wanted was for Simpson to confirm.

"Will you explain, Chief Simpson, the withdrawal of one hundred thousand dollars, in twenty-five thousand dollar increments, every three months during the past year?"

Simpson tugged at the knot of his tie. "I see no reason to explain how I spend my money, Lieutenant Dallas."

"Then perhaps you can explain how it is those same amounts were listed by Sharon DeBlass and accredited to you."

"I don't know what you're talking about."

"We have evidence that you paid to Sharon DeBlass one hundred thousand dollars, in twenty-five thousand dollar increments in one year's period." Eve waited a beat. "That's quite a large amount between casual acquaintances."

"I have nothing to say on the matter."

"Was she blackmailing you?"

"I have nothing to say."

"The evidence says it for you," Eve stated. "She was blackmailing you; you were paying her off. I'm sure you're aware there are only two ways to stop extortion, Chief Simpson. One, you cut off the supply. Two . . . you eliminate the blackmailer."

"This is absurd. I didn't kill Sharon. I was paying her like clockwork. I—"

"Chief Simpson." The elder of the team of lawyers put a hand on Simpson's arm, squeezed. He turned his mild gaze to Eve. "My client has no statement to make regarding Sharon DeBlass. Obviously, we will cooperate in any way with the Internal Revenue Service's investigation into my client's records. At this time, however, no charges have been made. We're here only as a courtesy, and to show our goodwill."

"Were you acquainted with a woman known as Lola Starr?" Eve shot out.

"My client has no comment."

"Did you know licensed companion, Georgie Castle?"

"Same response," the lawyer said patiently.

"You've done everything you could to roadblock this murder investigation from the beginning. Why?"

"Is that a statement of fact, Lieutenant Dallas?" the lawyer asked. "Or an opinion?"

"I'll give you facts. You knew Sharon DeBlass, intimately. She was hosing you for a hundred grand a year. She's dead, and someone is leaking confidential information on the investigation. Two more women are dead. All the victims made their living through legal prostitution—something you oppose."

"My opposition of prostitution is a political, moral, and a personal stance," Simpson said tightly. "I will support wholeheartedly any legislation that outlaws it. But I would hardly eliminate the problem by picking off prostitutes one at a time."

"You own a collection of antique weapons," Eve persisted.

"I do," Simpson agreed, ignoring his attorney. "A small, limited collection. All registered, secured, and inventoried. I'll be more than happy to turn them over to Commander Whitney for testing."

"I appreciate that," Whitney said, shocking Simpson by agreeing. "Thank you for your cooperation."

Simpson rose, his face a battleground of emotion. "When this matter is cleared up, I won't forget this meeting." His eyes rested briefly on Eve. "I won't forget who attacked the office of Chief of Police and Security."

Commander Whitney waited until Simpson sailed out, followed by his team of attorneys. "When this is settled, he won't get within a hundred yards of the office of Chief of Police and Security."

"I needed more time to work on him. Why'd you let him walk?"

"His isn't the only name on the DeBlass list," Whitney reminded her. "And there's no tie, as yet, between him and the other two victims.

Whittle the list down, get me a tie, and I'll give you all the time you need." He paused, shuffling through the hard copies of the documents that had been transmitted to his office. "Dallas, you seemed very prepared for this interview. Almost as if you'd been expecting it. I don't suppose I need remind you that tampering with private documents is against the law."

"No, sir."

"I didn't think I did. Dismissed."

As she headed for the door, she thought she heard him murmur "Good job" but she might have been mistaken.

She was taking the elevator to her own section when her communicator blipped. "Dallas."

"Call for you. Charles Monroe."

"I'll get back to him."

She snagged a cup of sludge masquerading as coffee, and what might have been a doughnut as she passed through the bullpen area of the records section. It took nearly twenty minutes for her to requisition copies of the discs for the three homicides.

Closeting herself in her office, she studied them again. She reviewed her notes, made fresh ones.

The victim was on the bed each time. The bed rumpled each time. They were naked each time. Their hair was mussed.

Eyes narrowed, she ordered the image of Lola Starr to freeze, pull into close-up.

"Skin reddened left buttocks," she murmured. "Missed that before. Spanking? Domination thrill? Doesn't appear to be bruising or welting. Have Feeney enhance and determine. Switch to DeBlass tape."

Again, Eve ran it. Sharon laughed at the camera, taunted it, touching herself, shifting. "Freeze image. Quadrant—shit—try sixteen, increase. No marks," she said. "Continue. Come on, Sharon, show me the right side, just in case. Little more. Freeze. Quadrant twelve, increase. No marks on you. Maybe you did the spanking, huh? Run Castle disc. Come on Georgie, let's see."

She watched the woman smile, flirt, lift a hand to smooth down her tousled hair. Eve already knew the dialogue perfectly: *"That was wonderful. You're terrific."*

She was kneeling, sitting back on her haunches, her eyes pleasant and companionable. Silently, Eve began to urge her to move, just a little, shift over. Then Georgie yawned delicately, turned to fluff the pillows.

"Freeze. Oh yeah, paddled you, didn't he? Some guys get off on playing bad girl and Daddy."

She had a flash, like a stab of a knife through the brain. Memories sliced through her, the solid slap of a hand on her bottom, stinging, the heavy breathing. *"You have to be punished, little girl. Then Daddy's going to kiss it better. He's going to kiss it all better."*

"Jesus." She rubbed shaking hands over her face. "Stop. Put it away. Put it away."

She reached for cold coffee and found only dregs. The past was past, she reminded herself, and had nothing to do with her. Nothing to do with the job at hand.

"Victim Two and Three show marks of abuse on buttocks. No marks on Victim One." She let out a long breath, took in a slow one. Steadier. "Break in pattern. Apparent emotional reaction during first murder, absent in subsequent two."

Her 'link buzzed, she ignored it.

"Possible theory: Perpetrator gained confidence, enjoyment in subsequent murders. Note: No security on Victim Two. Time lapse on security cameras, Victim Three, thirty-three minutes less than Victim One. Possible theory: More adept, more confident, less inclined to play with victim. Wants the kick faster."

Possible, possible, she thought, and her computer agreed after a jittery wheeze, with a ninety-six-three probability factor. But something else was clicking as she ran the three discs so closely together, interchanging sections.

"Split screen," she ordered. "Victims One and Two, from beginning."

Sharon's cat smile, Lola's pout. Both women looked toward the camera, toward the man behind it. Spoke to him.

"Freeze images," Eve said so softly only the sharp ears of the computer could have heard her. "Oh God, what have we here?"

It was a small thing, a slight thing, and with the eyes focused on the brutality of the murders, easily missed. But she saw it now, through Sharon's eyes. Through Lola's.

Lola's gaze was angled higher.

The height of the beds could account for it. Eve told herself as she added Georgie's image to the screen. Each woman had their head tilted. After all, they were sitting, he very likely standing. But the angle of the eyes, the point at which they stared . . . Only Sharon's was different.

Still watching the screen, Eve called Dr. Mira.

"I don't care what she's doing," Eve spat out at the drone working reception. "It's urgent."

She snarled as she was put on hold and her ears assaulted with mindless, sugary music.

"Question," she said the moment Mira was on the line.

"Yes, Lieutenant."

"Is it possible we have two killers?"

"A copycat? Unlikely, Lieutenant, given as much of the method and style of the murders has been kept under wraps."

"Shit leaks. I've got breaks in pattern. Small ones, but definite breaks." Impatient, she outlined them. "Theory, Doctor. The first murder committed by someone who knew Sharon well, who killed on impulse, then had enough control to clean up behind himself well. The second two are reflections of the first crime, fined down, thought through, committed by someone cold, calculating, with no connection to his victims. And goddamn it, he's taller."

"It's a theory, Lieutenant. I'm sorry, but it's just as likely, even more so, that all three murders were committed by one man who grows more calculating with each success. In my professional opinion, no one who wasn't privy to the first crime, to the stages of it, could have so perfectly mirrored the events in the second two."

Her computer had ditched her theory as well, with a forty-eight-five. "Okay, thanks." Deflated, Eve disconnected. Stupid to be disappointed, she told herself. How much worse could it be if she were after two men instead of one?

Her 'link buzzed again. Teeth bared in annoyance, she flipped on. "Dallas. What?"

"Hey, Lieutenant Sugar, a guy might think you didn't care."

"I don't have time to play, Charles."

"Hey, don't cut me off. I got something for you."

"Or for lame innuendos—"

"No, really. Boy, flirt with a woman once or twice and she never takes you seriously." His perfect face registered hurt. "You asked me to call if I remembered anything, right?"

"Right." Patience, she warned herself. "So, did you?"

"It was the diaries that got me thinking. You know how I said she was always recording everything. Since you're looking for them, I figure they weren't over at her place."

"You should be a detective."

"I like my line of work. Anyhow, I started wondering where she might put them for safekeeping. And I remembered the safe-deposit box."

"We've already checked it. Thanks, anyway."

"Oh. Well, how'd you get into it without me? She's dead."

Eve paused on the point of cutting him off. "Without you?"

"Yeah. A couple, three years ago, she asked me to sign for one for her. Said she didn't want her name on the record."

Eve's heart began to thump. "Then what good would it do her?"

Charles's smile was sheepish and charming. "Well, technically, I signed her on as my sister. I've got one in Kansas City. So we listed Sharon as Annie Monroe. She paid the rent, and I just forgot about it. I can't even say for sure if she kept it, but I thought you might want to know."

"Where's the bank?"

"First Manhattan, on Madison."

"Listen to me, Charles. You're home, right?"

"That's right."

"You stay there. Right there. I'll be over in fifteen minutes. We're going to go banking, you and me."

"If that's the best I can do. Hey, did I give you a hot lead, Lieutenant Sugar?"

"Just stay put."

She was up and shrugging into her jacket when her 'link buzzed again. "Dallas."

"Dispatch, Dallas. We have a transmission on hold for you. Video blocked. Refuses to identify."

"Tracing?"

"Tracing now."

"Then put it through." She swung up her bag as the audio clicked. "This is Dallas."

"Are you alone?" It was a female voice, tremulous.

"Yes. Do you want me to help you?"

"It wasn't my fault. You have to know it wasn't my fault."

"No one's blaming you." Training had Eve picking up on both fear and grief. "Just tell me what happened."

"He raped me. I couldn't stop him. He raped me. He raped her, too. Then he killed her. He could kill me."

"Tell me where you are." She studied her screen, waiting for the trace to come through. "I want to help, but I have to know where you are."

Breath hitching, a whimper. "He said it was supposed to be a secret. I couldn't tell. He killed her so she couldn't tell. Now there's me. No one will believe me."

"I believe you. I'll help you. Tell me—" She swore as the transmission broke. "Where?" she demanded after switching to Dispatch.

"Front Royal, Virginia. Number seven oh three, five five five, thirty-nine oh eight. Address—"

"I don't need it. Get me Captain Ryan Feeney in EDD. Fast."

Two minutes wasn't fast enough. Eve nearly drilled a hole in her temple rubbing it while she waited. "Feeney, I've got something, and it's big."

"What?"

"I can't go into it yet, but I need you to go pick up Charles Monroe."

"Christ, Eve, have we got him?"

"Not yet. Monroe's going to take you to Sharon's other safe box. You take good care of him, Feeney. We're going to need him. And you take damn good care of whatever you find in the box."

"What are you going to be doing?"

"I've got to catch a plane." She broke transmission, then called

Roarke. It took another three minutes of very precious time before he came on-line.

"I was about to call you, Eve. It looks like I have to fly to Dublin. Care to join me?"

"Roarke, I need your plane. Now. I have to get to Virginia fast. If I go through channels or take public transport—"

"The plane will be ready for you. Terminal C, Gate 22."

She closed her eyes. "Thanks. I owe you."

Her gratitude lasted until she arrived at the gate and found Roarke waiting for her.

"I don't have time to talk." Her voice was a snap, her long legs eating up the distance from gate to lift.

"We'll talk on the plane."

"You're not going with me. This is official—"

"This is my plane, Lieutenant," he interrupted smoothly as the lift closed them in together, gliding silently up.

"Can't you do anything without strings?"

"Yes. This isn't one of them." The hatch opened. The flight attendant waited efficiently.

"Welcome aboard, sir, Lieutenant. Can I offer you refreshments?"

"No, thank you. Have the pilot take off as soon as we're cleared." Roarke took his seat while Eve stood fuming. "We can't take off until you're seated and secured."

"I thought you were going to Ireland." She could argue with him just as easily sitting down.

"It's not a priority. This is. Eve, before you state your case, I'll outline mine. You're going to Virginia in quite a rush. That points to the DeBlass case and some new information. Beth and Richard are friends, close friends. I don't have many close friends, nor do you. Reverse situations. What would you do?"

She drummed her fingers on the arm of her chair as the plane began to taxi. "This can't be personal."

"Not for you. For me, it's very personal. Beth contacted me even as I was arranging for the plane to be readied. She asked me to come."

"Why?"

"She wouldn't say. She didn't have to—she only had to ask."

Loyalty was a trait Eve had a difficult time arguing against. "I can't stop you from going, but I'm warning you, this is department business."

"And the department is in upheaval this morning," he said evenly, "because of certain information leaked to the media—by an unnamed source."

She hissed out a breath. Nothing like backing yourself into a corner. "I'm grateful for your help."

"Enough to tell me the outcome?"

"I imagine the cap will be off by the end of the day." She moved her shoulders restlessly, staring out the window, willing the miles away. "Simpson's going to try to ditch the whole business on his accounting firm. I can't see him pulling it off. The IRS'll get him for tax fraud. I imagine the internal investigation will uncover where he got the money. Considering Simpson's imagination, I'd bet on the standard kickbacks, bribes, and graft."

"And the blackmail?"

"Oh, he was paying her. He admitted as much before his lawyer shut him up. And he'll cop to it, once he realizes paying blackmail's a lot less dicey than accessory to murder."

She took out her communicator, requested Feeney's access.

"Yo, Dallas."

"Did you get them?"

Feeney held a small box up so that she could see it in the tiny viewing screen. "All labeled and dated. About twenty years' worth."

"Start with the last entry, work back. I should hit destination in about twenty minutes. I'll contact you as soon as I can for a status report."

"Hey, Lieutenant Sugar." Charles edged his way on-screen and beamed at her. "How'd I do?"

"You did good. Thanks. Now, until I say different, forget about the safe box, the diaries, everything."

"What diaries?" he said with a wink. He blew her a kiss before Feeney elbowed him aside.

"I'm heading back to Cop Central now. Stay in touch."

"Out." Eve switched off, slipped the communicator back in her pocket.

Roarke waited a beat. "Lieutenant Sugar?"

"Shut up, Roarke." She closed her eyes to ignore him, but couldn't quite wipe the smirk off her face.

When they landed, she was forced to admit that Roarke's name worked even faster than a badge. In minutes they were in a powerful rental car and eating up the miles to Front Royal. She might have objected about being delegated to the passenger seat, but she couldn't fault his driving.

"Ever done the Indy?"

"No." He spared her a brief glance as they bulleted up Route 95 at just under a hundred. "But I've driven in a few Grand Prix."

"Figures." She tapped her fingers against the chicken stick when he shot the car into a vertical rise, skimmed daringly—and illegally— over the top of a small jam of cars. "You say Richard is a good friend. How would you describe him?"

"Intelligent, dedicated, quiet. He rarely speaks unless he has something to say. Overshadowed by his father, often at odds with him."

"How would you describe his relationship with his father?"

He brought the vehicle down again, wheels barely skidding on the road surface. "From the little he might have said, and the things Beth let drop, I'd have to say combative, frustrated."

"And his relationship with his daughter?"

"The choices she made were in direct opposition to his lifestyle, his, well, morals, if you wish. He's a staunch believer in freedom of choice and expression. Still, I can't imagine any father wanting his daughter to become a woman who sells herself for a living."

"Wasn't he involved in designing his father's security for the last senatorial campaign?"

He took the vehicle up again, maneuvered it off the road, muttering something about a shortcut. In the time he took to skim through a glade of trees, over a few residential buildings, and down again onto a quiet suburban street, he was silent.

She stopped counting the traffic violations.

"Family loyalty transcends politics. A man with DeBlass's views is either well loved or well hated. Richard may disagree with his father, but he'd hardly want him assassinated. And as he specializes in security law, it follows he'd assist his father in the matter."

A son protects his father, Eve thought. "And how far would DeBlass go to protect his son?"

"From what? Richard is a moderate's moderate. He maintains a low profile, supports his causes quietly. He—" The import of the question struck. "You're off target," Roarke said between his teeth. "Way off target."

"We'll see."

The house on the hill looked peaceful. Under the cold blue sky, it sat serenely, warmly, with a few brave crocuses beginning to peep out of the winter stung grass.

Appearances, Eve thought, were deceiving more often than not. She knew this wasn't a home of easy wealth, quiet happiness, and tidy lives. She was certain now that she knew what had gone on behind those rosy walls and gleaming glass.

Elizabeth opened the door herself. If anything, she was paler and more drawn than when Eve had last seen her. Her eyes were puffy from weeping, and the mannishly tailored suit she wore bagged at the hips from recent weight loss.

"Oh, Roarke." As Elizabeth went into his arms, Eve could all but hear the fragile bones knocking together. "I'm sorry I dragged you out here. I shouldn't have bothered you."

"Don't be silly." He tilted her face up with a gentleness that tugged at the heart Eve was struggling to hold distant. "Beth, you're not taking care of yourself."

"I can't seem to function, to think, or to do. Everything's crumbling away at my feet, and I—" She broke off, remembering abruptly that they weren't alone. "Lieutenant Dallas."

Eve caught the quick accusation in Elizabeth's eyes when she looked at Roarke. "He didn't bring me, Ms. Barrister. I brought him. I received a call this morning from this location. Did you make it?"

"No." Elizabeth stepped back. Her hands reached for each other, twisted. "No, I didn't. It must have been Catherine. She arrived here last night, suddenly. Hysterical, overwrought. Her mother has been hospitalized, and the prognosis is poor. I can only think the stress of the last few weeks has been too much for her. That's why I called you, Roarke. Richard's at his wit's end. I don't seem to be any help. We needed someone."

"Why don't we go in and sit down?"

"They're in the parlor." In a jittery move, Elizabeth turned to look down the hall. "She won't take a sedative, she won't explain. She refused to let us do more than call her husband and son and tell them she was here, and not to come. She's frantic at the idea they might be in some sort of danger. I suppose what happened to Sharon has made her worry more about her own child. She's obsessed with saving him from God knows what."

"If she called me," Eve put in. "Then maybe she'll talk to me."

"Yes. Yes, all right."

She led the way down the hall, and into the tidy, sunwashed parlor. Catherine DeBlass sat on a sofa, leaning into her brother's arms. Eve couldn't be sure if he was comforting, or restraining.

Richard raised stricken eyes to Roarke's. "It's good of you to come. We're a mess, Roarke." His voice shook, nearly broke. "We're a mess."

"Elizabeth." Roarke crouched in front of Catherine. "Why don't you ring for coffee?"

"Oh, of course. I'm sorry."

"Catherine." His voice was gentle, as was the hand he laid on her arm. But the touch had Catherine jerking up, her eyes going wide.

"Don't. What—what are you doing here?"

"I came to see Beth and Richard. I'm sorry you're not well."

"Well?" She gave what might have been a laugh as she curled into herself. "None of us will ever be well again. How can we? We're all tainted. We're all to blame."

"For what?"

She shook her head, pushed herself into the far corner of the sofa. "I can't talk to you."

"Congresswoman DeBlass, I'm Lieutenant Dallas. You called me a little while ago."

"No, no I didn't." Panicked, Catherine wrapped her arms tightly around her chest. "I didn't call. I didn't say anything."

As Richard leaned over to touch her, Eve shot him a warning glance. Deliberately, she put herself between them, sat and took Catherine's frigid hand. "You wanted me to help. And I will help you."

"You can't. No one can. I was wrong to call. We have to keep it in the family. I have a husband, I have a little boy." Tears began to swim in her eyes. "I have to protect them. I have to go away, far away, so I can protect them."

"We'll protect them," Eve said quietly. "We'll protect you. It was too late to protect Sharon. You can't blame yourself."

"I didn't try to stop it," Catherine said in a whisper. "Maybe I was even glad, because it wasn't me anymore. It wasn't me."

"Ms. DeBlass, I can help you. I can protect you and your family. Tell me who raped you."

Richard let out a hiss of shock. "My God, what are you saying? What—"

Eve turned on him, eyes fierce. "Be quiet. There's no more secrets here."

"Secrets," Catherine said between trembling lips. "It has to be a secret."

"No, it doesn't. This kind of secret hurts. It crawls inside you and eats at you. It makes you scared, and it makes you guilty. The ones who want it to be secret use that—the guilt, the fear, the shame. The only way you can fight back is to tell. Tell me who raped you."

Catherine's breath shuddered out. She looked at her brother, terror bright in her eyes. Eve turned her face back, held it.

"Look at me. Just me. And tell me who raped you. Who raped Sharon?"

"My father." The words burst from her in a howl of pain. "My father. My father. My father." She buried her face in her hands and sobbed.

"Oh God." Across the room, Elizabeth stumbled back into the server droid. China shattered. Coffee seeped dark into the lovely rug. "Oh my God. My baby."

Richard shot off the couch, reaching her as she swayed. He caught her hard against him. "I'll kill him for this. I'll kill him." Then he pressed his face into her hair. "Beth. Oh, Beth."

"Do what you can for them," Eve murmured to Roarke as she gathered Catherine to her.

"You thought it was Richard," Roarke said in an undertone.

"Yes." Her eyes were dull and flat when she lifted them to his. "I thought it was Sharon's father. Maybe I didn't want to think that something so foul could flourish in two generations."

Roarke leaned forward. His face was hard as rock. "One way or the other, DeBlass is a dead man."

"Help your friends," Eve said evenly. "I have work to do here."

CHAPTER

EIGHTEEN

She let Catherine cry it out, though she knew, too well, that the tears wouldn't wash the wound clean. She knew, too, that she wouldn't have been able to handle the situation alone. It was Roarke who calmed Elizabeth and Richard, who ordered in the domestic droid to gather up the broken crockery, who held their hands, and when he gauged the time was right, it was he who gently suggested bringing Catherine some tea.

Elizabeth fetched it herself, carefully closing the parlor doors behind her before she carried the cup to her sister-in-law. "Here, darling, drink a little."

"I'm sorry." Catherine put both shaky hands around the cup to warm them. "I'm sorry. I thought it had stopped. I made myself believe it had stopped. I couldn't live otherwise."

"It's all right." Her face blank, Elizabeth went back to her husband.

"Ms. DeBlass, I need you to tell me everything. Congresswoman DeBlass?" Eve waited until Catherine focused on her again. "Do you understand this is being recorded?"

"He'll stop you."

"No, he won't. That's why you called me, because you know I'll stop him."

"He's afraid of you," Catherine whispered. "He's afraid of you. I could tell. He's afraid of women. That's why he hurts them. I think he may have given something to my mother. Broke her mind. She knew."

"Your mother knew your father was abusing you?"

"She knew. She pretended she didn't, but I could see it in her eyes. She didn't want to know—she just wanted everything quiet and perfect, so she could give her parties and be the senator's wife." She lifted a hand, shielding her eyes. "When he would come into my room at night, I could see it on her face the next morning. But when I tried to talk to her, to tell her to make him stop, she pretended she didn't know what I meant. She told me to stop imagining things. To be good, to respect the family."

She lowered her hand again, cupped her tea with both hands, but didn't drink. "When I was little, seven or eight, he would come in at night and touch me. He said it was all right, because he was Daddy, and I was going to pretend to be Mommy. It was a game, he said, a secret game. He told me I had to do things—to touch him. To—"

"It's all right," Eve soothed as Catherine began to tremble violently. "You don't have to say. Tell me what you can."

"You had to obey him. You had to. He was a force in our house. Richard?"

"Yes." Richard caught his wife's hand in his and squeezed, squeezed. "I know."

"I couldn't tell you because I was ashamed, and I was afraid, and Mom just looked away, so I thought I had to do it." She swallowed hard. "On my twelfth birthday, we had a party. Lots of friends, and a big cake, and the ponies. You remember the ponies, Richard?"

"I remember." Tears tracked silently down his cheeks. "I remember."

"And that night, the night of my birthday, he came. He said I was old enough now. He said he had a present for me, a special present because I was growing up. And he raped me." She buried her face in her hands and rocked. "He said it was a present. Oh God. And I begged him to stop, because it hurt. And because I was old enough to know it was wrong, it was evil. I was evil. But he didn't stop. And he kept coming back. All those years until I could get away. I went to college, far away, where he couldn't touch me. And I told myself it never happened. It never, never happened.

"I tried to be strong, to make a life. I got married because I thought I would be safe. Justin was so kind, so gentle. He never hurt me. And I never told him. I thought if he knew, he'd despise me. So I kept telling myself it never happened."

She lowered her hands and looked at Eve. "I believed it, sometimes. Most of the time. I could lose myself in my work, in my family. But then I could see, I knew he was doing the same thing to Sharon. I wanted to help, but I didn't know how. So I pushed it away, just like my mother did. He killed her. Now he'll kill me."

"Why do you think he killed Sharon?"

"She wasn't weak like me. She turned it on him, used it against him. I heard them arguing. Christmas Day. When we all went to his house to pretend we were a family. I saw them go into his office, and I followed them. I opened the door, and I watched and I listened through the crack. He was so furious with her because she was making a public mockery of everything he stood for. And she said, 'You made me what I am, you bastard.' It warmed me to hear that. It made me want to cheer. She stood up to him. She threatened to expose him unless he paid her. She had it all documented, she said, every dirty detail. So he'd have to play the game her way. They fought, hurling words at each other. And then . . ."

Catherine glanced over at Elizabeth, at her brother, then looked away. "She took off her blouse." Elizabeth's moan had Catherine trembling again. "She told him he could have her, just like any client. But he'd pay more. A lot more. He was looking at her. I knew the way he was looking at her, his eyes glazed over, his mouth slack. He grabbed her breasts. She looked at me. Right at me. She'd known I was there, and she looked at me with such disgust. Maybe even with hate, because she knew I'd do nothing. I closed the door, closed it and ran. I was sick. Oh, Elizabeth."

"It's not your fault. She must have tried to tell me. I never saw, I never heard. I never thought. I was her mother, and I didn't protect her."

"I tried to talk to her." Catherine gripped her hands together. "When I went to New York for the fund-raiser. She said I'd chosen my way, and she'd chosen hers. And hers was better. I played politics, kept my head buried, and she played with power and kept her eyes opened.

"When I heard she was dead, I knew. At the funeral I watched him, and he watched me watching him. He came up to me, put his arms around me, held me close as if in comfort. And he whispered to me to pay attention. To remember, and to see what happened when families don't keep secrets. And he said what a fine boy Franklin was. What big plans he had for him. He said how proud I should be. And how careful." She closed her eyes. "What could I do? He's my child."

"No one's going to hurt your son." Eve closed a hand over Catherine's rigid ones. "I promise you."

"I'll never know if I could have saved her. Your child, Richard."

"You can know you're doing everything possible now." Hardly aware she'd taken Catherine's hand, Eve tightened her grip in reassurance. "It's going to be difficult for you, Ms. DeBlass, to go over all of this again, as you'll have to. To face the publicity. To testify, should it come to trial."

"He'll never let it go to trial," Catherine said wearily.

"I'm not going to give him a choice." Maybe not on murder, she thought. Not yet. But she had him cold on sexual abuse. "Ms. Barrister, I think your sister-in-law should rest now. Could you help her upstairs?"

"Yes, of course." Elizabeth rose, walked over to help Catherine to her feet. "Let's go lie down for a bit, darling."

"I'm sorry." Catherine leaned heavily against Elizabeth as she was led from the room. "God forgive me, I'm so sorry."

"There's a psychiatric counselor attached to the department, Mr. DeBlass. I think your sister should see her."

"Yes." He said it absently, staring at the closed door. "She'll need someone. Something."

You all will, Eve thought. "Are you up to a few questions?"

"I don't know. He's a tyrant, difficult. But this makes him a monster. How am I to accept that my own father is a monster?"

"He has an alibi for the night of your daughter's death," Eve pointed out. "I can't charge him without more."

"An alibi?"

"The record shows that Rockman was with your father, working with him in his East Washington office until nearly two on the night of your daughter's death."

"Rockman would say whatever my father told him to say."

"Including covering up murder?"

"It's simply a matter of the easiest way out. Why should anyone believe my father is connected?" He shuddered once, as if blasted with a sudden chill. "Rockman's statement merely detaches his employer from any suspicion."

"How would your father travel back and forth to New York from East Washington if he wanted no record of the trip?"

"I don't know. If his shuttle went out, there would be a log."

"Logs can be altered," Roarke said.

"Yes." Richard looked up as if remembering all at once that his friend was there. "You'd know more about that than I."

"A reference to my smuggling days," Roarke explained to Eve. "Long behind me. It can be done, but it would require some payoffs. The pilot, perhaps the mechanic, certainly the air engineer."

"So I know where to put the pressure on." And if Eve could prove his shuttle had taken the trip on that night, she'd have probable cause. Enough to break him. "How much do you know about your father's weapon collection?"

"More than I care to." Richard rose on unsteady legs. He went to a cabinet, splashed liquor into a glass. He drank it fast, like medicine. "He enjoys his guns, often shows them off. When I was younger, he tried to interest me in them. Roarke can tell you, it didn't work."

"Richard believes guns are a dangerous symbol of power abuse. And I can tell you that yes, DeBlass occasionally used the black market."

"Why didn't you mention that before?"

"You didn't ask."

She let it drop, for now. "Does your father have a knowledge of security—the technical aspects?"

"Certainly. He takes pride in knowing how to protect himself. It's one of the few things we can discuss without disagreeing."

"Would you consider him an expert?"

"No," Richard said slowly. "A talented amateur."

"His relationship with Chief Simpson? How would you describe it?"

"Self-serving. He considered Simpson a fool. My father enjoys utilizing fools." Abruptly, he sank into a chair. "I'm sorry. I can't do this. I need some time. I need my wife."

"All right. Mr. DeBlass, I'm going to order surveillance on your father. You won't be able to reach him without being monitored. Please don't try."

"You think I'll try to kill him?" Richard gave a mirthless laugh and stared down at his own hands. "I want to. For what he did to my daughter, to my sister, to my life. I wouldn't have the courage."

When they were outside again, Eve headed straight for the car without looking at Roarke. "You suspected this?" she asked.

"That DeBlass was involved? Yes, I did."

"But you didn't tell me."

"No." Roarke stopped her before she could wrench open the door. "It was a feeling, Eve. I had no idea about Catherine. Absolutely none. I suspected that Sharon and DeBlass were having an affair."

"That's too clean a word for it."

"I suspected it," he continued, "because of the way she spoke of him during our single dinner together. But again, it was a feeling, not a fact. That feeling would have done nothing to enhance your case. And," he added, turning her to face him, "once I got to know you, I kept that feeling to myself, because I didn't want to hurt you." She jerked her head away. He brought it patiently back with his fingertips. "You had no one to help you?"

"It isn't about me." But she let out a shuddering breath. "I can't think about it, Roarke. I can't. I'll mess up if I do, and if I mess up, he could get away with it. With rape and murder, with abusing the children he should have been protecting. I won't let him."

"Didn't you say to Catherine that the only way to fight back was to tell?"

"I have work to do."

He fought back frustration. "I assume you'll want to go to the Washington Airport where DeBlass keeps his shuttle."

"Yes." She climbed in the car when Roarke walked around to get in the driver's side. "You can drop me at the nearest transport station."

"I'm sticking, Eve."

"All right, fine. I need to check in."

As he drove down the winding lane, she put in a call to Feeney. "I've got something hot here," she said before he could speak. "I'm on my way to East Washington."

"You've got something hot?" Feeney's voice was almost a song. "Didn't have to look farther than her final entry, Dallas, logged the morning of her murder. God knows why she took it to the bank. Blind luck. She had a date at midnight. You'll never guess who."

"Her grandfather."

Feeney goggled, sputtered. "Fuck it, Dallas, how'd you get it?"

Eve closed her eyes briefly. "Tell me it's documented, Feeney. Tell me she names him."

"Calls him the senator—calls him her old fart of a granddaddy. And she writes pretty cheerfully about the five thousand she charges him for each boink. Quote: 'It's almost worth letting him slobber all over me—and there's a lot of energy left in dear old Granddad. The bastard. Five thousand every couple of weeks isn't such a bad deal. I sure as hell give him his money's worth. Not like when I was a kid and he used me. Table's turned. I won't turn into a dried up prune like poor Aunt Catherine. I'm thriving on it now. And one day, when it bores me enough, I'm sending my diaries to the media. Multiple copies. It drives the bastard crazy when I threaten to do that. Maybe I'll twist the knife a little tonight. Give the senator a good scare. Christ, it's wonderful to have the power to make him squirm after all he's done to me.'"

Feeney shook his head. "It was a long-time deal, Dallas. I've run through several entries. She earned a nice income from blackmail, and names names and deeds. But this puts the senator at her place on the night of her death. And that puts his balls in the old nutcracker."

"Can you get me a warrant?"

"Commander's orders are to patch it through the minute you called in. He says to pick him up. Murder One, three counts."

She let out a slow breath. "Where do I find him?"

"He's at the Senate building, hawking his Morals Bill."

"Fucking perfect. I'm on my way." She switched off, turned to Roarke. "How much faster can this thing go?"

"We'll find out."

If Whitney's orders hadn't come through with the warrant, instruct-ing her to be discreet, Eve would have marched onto the Senate floor and cuffed him in front of his associates. Still, there was considerable satisfaction in the way it went down.

She waited while he completed his impassioned speech on the moral decline of the country, the insidious corruption that stemmed from promiscuity, conception control, genetic engineering. He expounded on the lack of morality in the young, the dearth of organized religion in the home, the school, the workplace. Our one nation under God had become godless. Our constitutional right to bear arms sundered by the liberal left. He touted figures on violent crime, on urban decay, on bootlegged drugs, all a result, the senator claimed, of our increasing moral decline, our softness on criminals, our indulgence in sexual freedom without responsibility.

It made Eve sick to listen.

"In the year 2016," she said softly, "at the end of the Urban Revolt, before the gun ban, there were over ten thousand deaths and injuries from guns in the borough of Manhattan alone."

She continued to watch DeBlass sell his snake oil while Roarke laid a hand at the base of her spine.

"Before we legalized prostitution, there was a rape or attempted rape every three seconds. Of course, we still have rape, because it has much less to do with sex than with power, but the figures have dropped. Licensed prostitutes don't have pimps, so they aren't beaten, battered, killed. And they can't use drugs. There was a time when women went to butchers to deal with an unwanted pregnancy. When they had to risk their lives or ruin them. Babies were born blind, deaf, deformed before genetic engineering and the research it made possible to repair in vitro. It's not a perfect world, but you listen to him and you realize it could be a lot worse."

"Do you know what the media is going to do to him when this hits?"

"Crucify him," Eve murmured. "I hope to God it doesn't make him a martyr."

"The voice of the moral right suspected of incest, trucking with prostitutes, committing murder. I don't think so. He's finished." Roarke nodded. "In more ways than one."

Eve heard the thunderous applause from the gallery. From the sound of it, DeBlass's team had been careful to pepper the spectators with their own.

Discretion be damned, she thought as the gavel was struck and an hour's recess was called. She moved through the milling aides, assistants, and pages until she came to DeBlass. He was being congratulated on his eloquence, slapped on the back by his senatorial supporters.

She waited until he saw her, until his gaze skimmed over her, then Roarke, until his mouth tightened. "Lieutenant. If you need to speak with me, we can adjourn briefly to my office. Alone. I can spare ten minutes."

"You're going to have plenty of time, Senator. Senator DeBlass, you're under arrest for the murders of Sharon DeBlass, Lola Starr, and Georgie Castle." As he blustered in protest and the murmurs began, she lifted her voice. "Additional charges include the incestuous rapes of Catherine DeBlass, your daughter, and Sharon DeBlass, your granddaughter."

He was still standing, frozen in shock when she linked the restraints over his wrist, turned him, and secured his hands behind his back. "You are under no obligation to make a statement."

"This is an outrage." He exploded over the standard recitation of revised Miranda. "I'm a senator of the United States. This is federal property."

"And these two federal agents will escort you," she added. "You are entitled to an attorney or representative." As she continued to recite his rights, a flash from her eyes had the federal deputies and onlookers backing off. "Do you understand these rights?"

"I'll have your badge, you bitch." He began to wheeze as she muscled him through the crowd.

"I'll take that as a yes. Catch your breath, Senator. We can't have you popping off with a cardiac." She leaned closer to his ear. "And you won't have my badge, you bastard. I'm going to have your ass." She turned him over to the federal agents. "They're waiting for him in New York," she said briefly.

She could hardly be heard now. DeBlass was screaming, demanding immediate release. The Senate had erupted with voices and bodies. Through it, she spotted Rockman. He came toward her, his face a cold mask of fury.

"You're making a mistake, Lieutenant."

"No, I'm not. But you made one in your statement. The way I see it, that's going to make you accessory after the fact. I'm going to start working on that when I get back to New York."

"Senator DeBlass is a great man. You're nothing but a pawn for the Liberal Party and their plans to destroy him."

"Senator DeBlass is an incestuous child molester. A rapist and a murderer. And what I am, pal, is the cop who's taking him down. You'd better call a lawyer unless you want to sink with him."

Roarke had to force himself not to snatch her up as she swept through the hallowed Senate halls. Members of the media were already leaping toward her, but she cut through them as if they weren't there.

"I like your style, Lieutenant Dallas," he said when they'd fought their way to the car. "I like it a lot. And by the way, I don't think I'm in love with you anymore. I know I am."

She swallowed hard on the nausea rising in her throat. "Let's get out of here. Let's get the hell out of here."

Sheer force of will kept her steady until she got to the plane. It kept her voice flat and expressionless as she reported in to her superior. Then she stumbled, and shoving away from Roarke's supporting arms, rushed into the head to be wretchedly and violently ill.

On the other side of the door, Roarke stood helplessly. If he understood her at all, it was to know that comforting would make it worse. He murmured instructions to the flight attendant and took his seat. While he waited, he stared out at the tarmac.

He looked up when the door opened. She was ice pale, her eyes too big, too dark. Her usually smooth gait was coltish and stiff.

"Sorry. I guess it got to me."

When she sat, he offered a mug. "Drink this. It'll help."

"What is it?"

"It's tea, a whiff of whiskey."

"I'm on duty," she began, but his quick, vicious eruption cut her off.

"Drink, goddamn it, or I'll pour it into you." He flipped a switch and ordered the pilot to take off.

Telling herself it was easier than arguing, she lifted the mug, but her hands weren't steady. She barely managed to get a sip through her chattering teeth before she set it aside.

She couldn't stop shaking. When Roarke reached for her, she drew herself back. The sickness was still there, sliding slyly through her stomach, making her head pound evilly.

"My father raped me." She heard herself say it. The shock of it, hearing her own voice say the words, mirrored in her eyes. "Repeatedly. And he beat me, repeatedly. If I fought or I didn't fight, it didn't matter. He still raped me. He still beat me. And there was nothing I could do. There's nothing you can do when the people who are supposed to take care of you abuse you that way. Use you. Hurt you."

"Eve." He took her hand then, holding firm when she tried to yank free. "I'm sorry. Terribly sorry."

"They said I was eight when they found me, in some alley in Dallas. I was bleeding, and my arm was broken. He must have dumped me there. I don't know. Maybe I ran away. I don't remember. But he never came for me. No one ever came for me."

"Your mother?"

"I don't know. I don't remember her. Maybe she was dead. Maybe she was like Catherine's mother and pretended not to know. I only get flashes, nightmares of the worst of it. I don't even know my name. They weren't able to identify me."

"You were safe then."

"You've never been shuffled through the system. There's no feeling of safety. Only impotence. They strip you bare with good intentions." She sighed, let her head fall back, her eyes close. "I didn't want to arrest DeBlass, Roarke. I wanted to kill him. I wanted to kill him with my own hands because of what happened to me. I let it get personal."

"You did your job."

"Yeah. I did my job. And I'll keep doing it." But it wasn't the job she was thinking of now. It was life. Hers, and his. "Roarke, you've got to know I've got some bad stuff inside. It's like a virus that sneaks around the system, pops out when your resistance is low. I'm not a good bet."

"I like long odds." He lifted her hand, kissed it. "Why don't we see it through? Find out if we can both win."

"I've never told anybody before."

"Did it help?"

"I don't know. Maybe. Christ, I'm so tired."

"You could lean on me." He slipped an arm around her, nestled her head in the curve of his shoulder.

"For a little while," she murmured. "Until we get to New York."

"For a little while then." He pressed his lips to her hair and hoped she would sleep.

CHAPTER

NINETEEN

DeBlass wouldn't talk. His lawyers put the muzzle on him early, and they put in on tight. The interrogation process was slow, and it was tedious. There were times Eve thought he would burst, when the temper that reddened his face would tip the scales in her favor.

She'd stopped denying it was personal. She didn't want a tricky, media blitzed trial. She wanted a confession.

"You were engaged in an incestuous affair with your granddaughter, Sharon DeBlass."

"My client has not confirmed those allegations."

Eve ignored the lawyer, watched DeBlass's face. "I have here a transcript of a portion of Sharon DeBlass's diary, dated on the night of her murder."

She shoved the paper across the table. DeBlass's lawyer, a trim, tidy man with a neat sandy beard and mild blue eyes picked it up, studied it. Whatever his reaction was, he hid it behind cool indifference.

"This proves nothing, Lieutenant, as I'm sure you know. The destructive fantasies of a dead woman. A woman of dubious reputation who has long been estranged from her family."

"There's a pattern here, Senator DeBlass." Eve stubbornly continued to address the accused rather than his knight at arms. "You sexually abused your daughter, Catherine."

"Preposterous," DeBlass blurted out before his attorney lifted a hand to silence him.

"I have a statement, signed and verified before witnesses from Congresswoman Catherine DeBlass." Eve offered it, and the lawyer nipped it out of her fingers before the senator could move.

He scanned it, then folded his carefully manicured hands over it. "You may not be aware, Lieutenant, that there is an unfortunate history of mental disorder here. Senator DeBlass's wife is even now under observation for a breakdown."

"We are aware." She spared the lawyer a glance. "And we will be investigating her condition, and the cause of it."

"Congresswoman DeBlass has also been treated for symptoms of depression, paranoia, and stress," the lawyer continued in the same neutral tone.

"If she has, Senator DeBlass, we'll find that the roots of it are due to your systematic and continued abuse of her as a child. You were in New York on the night of Sharon DeBlass's murder," she said, switching gears smoothly. "Not, as you previously claimed, in East Washington."

Before the lawyer could block her, she leaned forward, her eyes steady on DeBlass's face. "Let me tell you how it went down. You took your private shuttle, paying the pilot and the flight engineer to doctor the log. You went to Sharon's apartment, had sex with her, recorded it for your own purposes. You took a weapon with you, a thirty-eight caliber Smith & Wesson antique. And because she taunted you, because she threatened you, because you couldn't take the pressure of possible exposure any longer, you shot her. You shot her three times, in the head, in the heart and in the genitalia."

She kept the words coming fast, kept her face close to his. It pleased her that she could smell his sweat. "The last shot was pretty clever. Messed up any chance for us to verify sexual activity. You ripped her open at the crotch. Maybe it was symbolic, maybe it was self-preservation. Why'd you take the gun with you? Had you planned it? Had you decided to end it once and for all?"

DeBlass's eyes darted left and right. His breathing grew hard and fast.

"My client does not acknowledge ownership of the weapon in question."

"Your client's scum."

The lawyer puffed up. "Lieutenant Dallas, you're speaking of a United States senator."

"That makes him elected scum. It shocked you, didn't it, Senator? All the blood, the noise, the way the gun jerked in your hand. Maybe you hadn't really believed you could go through with it. Not when push came to shove and you had to pull the trigger. But once you had, there was no going back. You had to cover it up. She would have ruined you, she never would have let you have peace. She wasn't like Catherine. Sharon wouldn't fade into the background and suffer all the shame and the guilt and the fear. She used it against you, so you had to kill her. Then you had to cover your tracks."

"Lieutenant Dallas—"

She never took her eyes from DeBlass, and ignoring the lawyer's warning, kept beating at him. "That was exciting, wasn't it? You could get away with it. You're a United States senator, the victim's grandfather. Who would believe it of you? So you arranged her on the bed, indulged yourself, your ego. You could do it again, and why not? The killing had stirred something in you. What better way to hide than to make it seem as if there was some maniac at large?"

She waited while DeBlass reached for a glass of water and drank thirstily. "There was a maniac at large. You printed out the note, slipped it under her. And you dressed, calmer now, but excited. You set the 'link to call the cops at two fifty-five. You needed enough time to go down and fix the security tapes. Then you got back on your shuttle, flew back to East Washington, and waited to play the outraged grandfather."

Through it all, DeBlass said nothing. But a muscle jerked in his cheek and his eyes couldn't find a place to land.

"That's a fascinating story, Lieutenant," the lawyer said. "But it remains that—a story. A supposition. A desperate attempt by the police department to fight their way out of a difficult situation with the media and the people of New York. And, of course, it's perfect timing that such ridiculous and damaging accusation should be levied against the senator just as his Morals Bill is coming up for debate."

"How did you pick the other two? How did you select Lola Starr and Georgie Castle? Have you already picked the fourth, the fifth, the sixth? Do you think you could have stopped there? Could you have stopped when it made you feel so powerful, so invincible, so righteous?"

DeBlass wasn't red now. He was gray, and his breathing was harsh and choppy. When he reached for a glass again, his hand jerked and sent it rolling to the floor.

"This interview is over." The lawyer stood, helped DeBlass to his feet. "My client's health is precarious. He requires medical attention immediately."

"Your client's a murderer. He'll get plenty of medical attention in a penal colony, for the rest of his life." She pressed a button. When the doors of the interrogation room opened, a uniform stepped in. "Call the MTs," she ordered. "The senator's feeling a little stressed. It's going to get worse," she warned, turning back to DeBlass. "I haven't even gotten started."

Two hours later, after filing reports and meeting with the prosecuting attorney, Eve fought her way through traffic. She had read a good portion of Sharon DeBlass's diaries. It was something she needed to set aside for now, the pictures of a twisted man and how he had turned a young girl into a woman almost as unbalanced as he.

Because she knew it could have been, all too easily, her story. Choices were there to be taken, she thought, brooding. Sharon's had killed her.

She wanted to blow off some steam, go over the events step by step with someone who would listen, appreciate, support. Someone who, for a little while, would stand between her and the ghosts of what was. And what could have been.

She headed for Roarke's.

When the call came through on her car 'link, she prayed it wasn't a summons back to duty. "Dallas."

"Hey, kid." It was Feeney's tired face on-screen. "I just watched the interrogation discs. Good job."

"Didn't get as far as I'd like, fencing with the damn lawyer. I'm going to break him, Feeney. I swear it."

"Yeah, my money's on you. But, ah, I got to tell you something that's not going to go down well. DeBlass had a little heart blip."

"Christ, he's not going to code out on us?"

"No. No, they medicated him. Some talk about getting him a new one next week."

"Good." She blew out a stream of breath. "I want him to live a long time—behind bars."

"We've got a strong case. The prosecutor's ready to canonize you, but in the meantime, he's sprung."

She hit the brakes. A volley of testy horn blasts behind her had her whipping over to the edge of Tenth and blocking the turning lane. "What the hell do you mean, he's sprang?"

Feeney winced, as much in empathy as reaction. "Released on his own recognizance. U.S. senator, lifetime of patriotic duty, salt of the earth, dinky heart—and a judge in his pocket."

"Fuck that." She pulled her hair until the pain equaled her frustration. "We got him on murder, three counts. Prosecutor said she was going for no bail."

"She got shot down. DeBlass's lawyer made a speech that would have wrung tears from a stone and had a corpse saluting the flag. DeBlass is back in East Washington by now, under doctor's orders to rest. He got a thirty-six-hour hold on further interrogation."

"Shit." She punched the wheel with the heel of her hand. "It's not going to make any difference," she said grimly. "He can play the ill elder statesman, he can do a tap dance at the fucking Lincoln Memorial, I've got him."

"Commander's worried that the time lag will give DeBlass an opportunity to pool his resources. He wants you back working with the prosecutor, going over everything we've got by oh eight hundred tomorrow."

"I'll be there. Feeney, he's not going to slip out of this noose."

"Just make sure you've got the knot nice and tight, kid. See you at eight."

"Yeah." Steaming, she swung back into traffic. She considered going home, burying herself in the chain of evidence. But she was five minutes from Roarke's. Eve opted to use him as a sounding board.

She could count on him to play devil's advocate if she needed it, to point out flaws. And, she admitted, to calm her down so that she could think without all these violent emotions getting in the way. She couldn't afford those emotions, couldn't afford to let Catherine's face pop into her head, as it had time and time again. The shame and the fear and the guilt.

It was impossibly hard to separate it. She knew she wanted DeBlass to pay every bit as much for Catherine as for the three dead women.

She was cleared through Roarke's gate, drove quickly up the sloped driveway. Her pulse began to thud as she raced up the steps. Idiot, she told herself. Like some hormonal plagued teenager. But she was smiling when Summerset opened the door.

"I need to see Roarke," she said, brushing by him.

"I'm sorry, Lieutenant. Roarke isn't at home."

"Oh." The sense of deflation made her feel ridiculous. "Where is he?"

Summerset's face pokered up. "I believe he's in a meeting. He was forced to cancel an important trip to Europe, and was therefore compelled to work late."

"Right." The cat pranced down the steps and immediately began twining himself through Eve's legs. She picked him up, stroked his underbelly. "When do you expect him?"

"Roarke's time is his business, Lieutenant. I don't presume to expect him."

"Look, pal, I haven't been twisting Roarke's arm to get him to spend his valuable time with me. So why don't you pull the stick out of your ass and tell me why you act like I'm some sort of embarrassing rodent whenever I show up."

Shock turned Summerset's face paper white. "I am not comfortable with crude manners, Lieutenant Dallas. Obviously, you are."

"They fit me like old slippers."

"Indeed." Summerset drew himself up. "Roarke is a man of taste, of style, of influence. He has the ear of presidents and kings. He has escorted women of unimpeachable breeding and pedigree."

"And I've got lousy breeding and no pedigree." She would have laughed if the barb hadn't stuck so close to the heart. "It seems even a man like Roarke can find the occasional mongrel appealing. Tell him I took the cat," she added and walked out.

It helped to tell herself Summerset was an insufferable snob. And the cat's silent interest as she vented on the drive home was curiously smoothing. She didn't need some tight-assed butler's approval. As if in agreement, the cat walked over onto her lap and began to knead her thighs.

She winced a little as his claws nipped through her trousers, but didn't move him aside. "I guess we've got to come up with a name for you. Never had a pet before," she murmured. "I don't know what Georgie called you, but we'll start fresh. Don't worry, we won't go for anything wimpy like Fluffy."

She pulled into her garage, parked, saw the yellow light blipping on the wall of her spot. A warning that her payment on the space was over-due. If it went red, the barricade would engage and she'd be screwed.

She swore a little, more from habit than heat. She hadn't had time to pay bills, damn it, and now realized she could face an evening of catching up playing the credit juggle with her bank account.

Hauling the cat under her arm, she walked to the elevator. "Fred, maybe." She tilted her head, stared into his unreadable two-toned eyes. "No, you don't look like Fred. Jesus, you must weigh twenty pounds." Shifting her bag, she stepped into the car. "We'll give the name some thought, Tubbo."

The minute she set him down inside the apartment, he darted for the kitchen. Taking her responsibilities as pet owner seriously, and deciding it was one way to postpone crunching figures, Eve followed and came up with a saucer of milk and some leftover Chinese that smelled slightly off.

The cat apparently had no delicacies when it came to food, and attacked the meal with gusto.

She watched him a moment, letting her mind drift. She'd wanted Roarke. Needed him. That was something else she'd have to give some thought to.

She didn't know how seriously to take the fact that he claimed to be in love with her. Love meant different things to different people. It had never been a part of her life.

She poured herself a half glass of wine, then merely frowned into it.

She felt something for him, certainly. Something new, and uncomfortably strong. Still, it was best to let things coast as they were. Decisions made quickly were almost always regretted quickly.

Why the hell hadn't he been home?

She set the untouched wine aside, dragged a hand through her hair. That was the biggest problem with getting used to someone, she thought. You were lonely when they weren't there.

She had work to do, she reminded herself. A case to close, a little Russian roulette with her credit status. Maybe she'd indulge in a long, hot bath, letting some of the stress steam away before prepping for her morning meeting with the prosecutor.

She left the cat gulping sweet and sour and went to the bedroom. Instincts, sluggish after a long day and personal questions, kicked in a moment too late.

Her hand was on her weapon before she fully registered the move. But it dropped away slowly as she stared into the long barrel of the revolver.

Colt, she thought. Forty-five. The kind that tamed the American west, six bullets at a time.

"This isn't going to help your boss's case, Rockman."

"I disagree." He stepped from behind the door, kept the gun pointed at her heart. "Take your weapon out slowly, Lieutenant, and drop it."

She kept her eyes on his. The laser was fast, but it wouldn't be faster than a cocked .45. At this range, the hole it would put in her would make a nasty impression. She dropped her weapon.

"Kick it toward me. Ah!" He smiled pleasantly as her hand slid toward her pocket. "And the communicator. I prefer keeping this between you and me. Good," he said when her unit hit the floor.

"Some people might find your loyalty to the senator admirable, Rockman. I find it stupid. Lying to give him an alibi is one thing. Threatening a police officer is another."

"You're a remarkably bright woman, Lieutenant. Still, you make remarkably foolish mistakes. Loyalty isn't an issue here. I'd like you to remove your jacket."

She kept her moves slow, her eyes on his. When the jacket was off one shoulder, she engaged the recorder in its pocket. "If holding me at gunpoint isn't due to loyalty to Senator DeBlass, Rockman, what is it?"

"It's a matter of self-preservation and great pleasure. I'd hoped for the opportunity to kill you, Lieutenant, but didn't see clearly how to work it into the plan."

"What plan is that?"

"Why don't you sit down? The side of the bed. Take off your shoes and we'll chat."

"My shoes?"

"Yes, please. This gives me my first, and I'm sure only opportunity to discuss what I've managed to accomplish. Your shoes?"

She sat, choosing the side of the bed nearest her 'link. "You've been working with DeBlass through it all, haven't you?"

"You want to ruin him. He could have been president, and eventually the Chair of the World Federation of Nations. The tide's swinging, and he could have swept it along and sat in the Oval Office. Beyond."

"With you at his side."

"Of course. And with me at his side, we would have taken the country, then the world, in a new direction. The right direction. One of strong morals, strong defense."

She took her time, letting one shoe drop before unstrapping the other. "Defense—like your old pals in SafeNet?"

His smile was hard, his eyes bright. "This country has been run by diplomats for too long. Our generals discuss and negotiate rather than command. With my help, DeBlass would have changed that. But you were determined to bring him down, and me with him. There's no chance for the presidency now."

"He's a murderer, a child abuser—"

"A statesman," Rockman interrupted. "You'll never bring him to trial."

"He'll be brought to trial, and he'll be convicted. Killing me won't stop it."

"No, but it will destroy your case against him—posthumously on both parts. You see, when I left him less than two hours ago, Senator DeBlass was in his office in East Washington. I stood by him as he chose a four fifty-seven Magnum, a very powerful gun. And I watched as he put the barrel into his mouth, and died like a patriot."

"Christ." It jolted her, the image of it. "Suicide."

"The warrior falling on his sword." Admiration shone in Rockman's voice. "I told him it was the only way, and he agreed. He would never have been able to tolerate the humiliation. When his body is found, when yours is found, the senator's reputation will be intact once again. It will be proven that he was dead hours before you. He couldn't have killed you, and as the method will be exactly as the other murders, and as there will be two more, as promised, the evidence against him will cease to matter. He'll be mourned. I'll lead the charge of fury and insult—and step into his bloody shoes."

"This isn't about politics. Goddamn you." She rose then, braced for the blow. She was grateful he didn't use the gun, but the back of his hand to knock her back. She turned with it, fell heavily onto the night table. The glass she'd left there shattered to the floor.

"Get up."

She moaned a little. Indeed, the flash of pain had her cheek singing and her vision blurred. She pushed herself up, turned, careful to keep her body in front of the 'link she'd switched on manually.

"What good is it going to do to kill me, Rockman?"

"It will do me a great deal of good. You were the spearhead of the investigation. You're sexually involved with a man who was an early suspect. Your reputation, and your motives will come under close scrutiny after your death. It's always a mistake to give a woman authority."

She wiped the blood from her mouth. "Don't like women, Rockman?"

"They have their uses, but under it all, they're whores. Perhaps you didn't sell your body to Roarke, but he bought you. Your murder won't really break the pattern I've established."

"You've established?"

"Did you really believe DeBlass was capable of planning out and executing such a meticulous series of murders?" He waited until he saw that she understood. "Yes, he killed Sharon. An impulse. I wasn't even aware he was considering it. He panicked afterward."

"You were there. You were with him the night he killed Sharon."

"I was waiting for him in the car. I always accompanied him on his trysts with her. Driving him so that only I, who he trusted, would be involved."

"His own granddaughter." Eve didn't dare turn to be certain she was transmitting. "Didn't it disgust you?"

"She disgusted me, Lieutenant. She used his weakness. Every man's entitled to one, but she used it, exploited it, then threatened him. After she was dead, I realized it was for the best. She would have waited until he was president, then twisted the knife."

"So you helped him cover it up."

"Of course." Rockman lifted his shoulders. "I'm glad we have this opportunity. It was frustrating for me not to be able to take credit. I'm delighted to share it with you."

Ego, she remembered. Not just intelligence, but ego and vanity. "You had to think fast," she commented. "And you did. Fast and brilliantly."

"Yes." His smile spread. "He called me on the car 'link, told me to come up quickly. He was half mad with fear. If I hadn't calmed him, she might have succeeded in ruining him."

"You can blame her?"

"She was a whore. A dead whore." He shrugged it off, but held the gun steady. "I gave the senator a sedative, and I cleaned up the mess. As I explained to him, it was necessary to make Sharon only part of the whole. To use her failings, her pathetic choice of profession. It was a simple matter to doctor the security discs. The senator's penchant

for recording his sexual activities gave me the idea to use that as part
of the pattern."

"Yes," she said through numbed lips. "That was clever."

"I wiped the place down, wiped the gun. Since he'd been sensible
enough not to use one that was registered, I left it behind. Again, es-
tablishing pattern."

"So you used it," Eve said quietly. "Used him, used Sharon."

"Only fools waste opportunities. He was more himself once we
were away," Rockman mused. "I was able to outline the rest of my
plan. Using Simpson to apply pressure, leak information. It was unfortunate that the senator didn't remember until later to tell me about
Sharon's diaries. I had to risk going back. But, as we know now, she
was clever enough to hide them well."

"You killed Lola Starr and Georgie Castle. You killed them to
cover up the first murder."

"Yes. But unlike the senator, I enjoyed it. From beginning to end.
It was a simple matter to select them, choose names, locations."

It was a little difficult at the moment to enjoy the fact that she'd
been right, and her computer wrong. Two killers after all. "You didn't
know them? You didn't even know them?"

"Did you think I should?" He laughed at that. "Who they were
hardly mattered. Only what. Whores offend me. Women who spread
their legs to weaken a man offend me. You offend me, Lieutenant."

"Why the discs?" Where the hell was Feeney? Why wasn't a rov-
ing unit breaking down her door right now? "Why did you send me
the discs?"

"I liked watching you scramble around like a mouse after cheese—
a woman who believed she could think like a man. I pointed you at
Roarke, but you let him talk you onto your back. All too typical. You
disappointed me. You were emotional, Lieutenant: over the deaths,
over that little girl you didn't save. But you got lucky. Which is why
you're about to become very unlucky."

He sidestepped over to the dresser where he had a camera waiting.
He switched it on. "Take off your clothes."

"You can kill me," she said as her stomach began to churn. "But
you're not going to rape me."

"You'll do exactly what I want you to do. They always do." He lowered the gun until it pointed at her midsection. "With the others, it was a shot to the head first. Instant death, probably painless. Do you have any idea what sort of pain you'll experience with a forty-five slug in your gut? You'll be begging me to kill you."

His eyes lit brilliantly. "Strip."

Eve's hands fell to her sides. She'd face the pain, but not the nightmare. Neither of them saw the cat slink into the room.

"Your choice, Lieutenant," Rockman said, then jerked when the cat brushed between his legs.

Eve sprang forward, head low, and used the force of her body to drive him against the wall.

CHAPTER

TWENTY

Feeney stopped on his way back from the eatery, a half a soy burger in his hand. He loitered by the coffee dispenser, gossiping with a couple of cops on robbery detail. They swapped stories, and Feeney decided he could use one more cup of coffee before calling it a night.

He nearly bypassed his office altogether, with visions of an evening in front of the TV screen and a nice cold beer swimming in his head. His wife might even be up for a little cuddle if he was lucky.

But he was a creature of habit. He breezed in to make certain his precious computer was secured for the night. And heard Eve's voice.

"Hey, Dallas, what brings you—" He stopped, scanning his empty office. "Working too hard," he muttered, then heard her again.

"You were with him. You were with him the night he killed Sharon."

"Oh my Jesus."

He could see little on the screen: Eve's back, the side of the bed. Rockman was blocked from view, but the audio was clear. Feeney was already praying when he called Dispatch.

*   *   *

Eve heard the cat's annoyed screech when her foot stomped his tail, heard too, the clatter as the gun hit the floor. Rockman had her in height, he had her in weight. And he'd recovered from her full body slam too quickly. He proved graphically that he was military trained.

She fought viciously, unable to restrain herself to the cool, efficient moves of hand to hand. She used nails and teeth.

The shortened blow to the ribs stole her breath. She knew she was going down, and she made sure she took him with her. They hit the floor hard, and though she rolled, he came down on top of her.

Lights starred behind her eyes when her head rapped hard against the floor.

His hand was around her throat, bruising her windpipe. She went for the eyes, missed, and raked furrows down his cheek that had him howling like an animal. If he'd used his other hand for a blow to the face, he might have stunned her, but he was too focused on reaching the gun. Her stiff-handed chop to his elbow had his hand shaking from her throat. Painfully gasping in air, she scrambled with him for the gun.

His hand closed over it first.

Roarke tucked a package under his arm as he walked into the lobby of Eve's building. He enjoyed the fact that she'd come to him. It was a habit he didn't intend to see her break. He thought now that she'd closed her case, he could talk her into taking a couple of days off. He had an island in the West Indies he thought she'd enjoy.

He pressed her intercom, and was smiling over the image of swimming naked with her in clear blue water, making love under a hot, white sun when all hell broke loose behind him.

"Get the hell out of the way." Feeney came in like a steamroller, a dozen uniforms in his wake. "Police business."

"Eve!" Roarke's blood drained even as he muscled his way onto the elevator.

Feeney ignored him and barked into his communicator. "Secure all exits. Get those fucking sharpshooters in position."

Roarke fisted his hand uselessly at his sides. "DeBlass?"

"Rockman," Feeney corrected, counting every beat of his own heart. "He's got her. Stay out of the way, Roarke."

"The fuck I will."

Feeney flicked his eyes over, measured. No way he was going to spare a couple of cops to restrain a civilian, and he had a hunch this civilian would go to the wall, as he would, for Eve.

"Then do what I tell you."

They heard the gunshot as the elevator doors opened.

Roarke was two steps ahead of Feeney when he rammed Eve's apartment door. He swore, reared back. They hit it together.

The pain was like being stabbed with ice. Then it was gone, numbed with fury. Eve clamped her hand over the wrist of his gun hand, dug her short nails into his flesh. Rockman's face was close to hers, his body pinning her in an obscene parody of love. His wrist was slippery with his own blood where she clawed at it.

She swore as she lost her grip, as he began to smile.

"You fight like a woman." He shook his hair back from his eyes, and the blood from his torn cheek welled red. "I'm going to rape you. The last thing you'll know before I kill you is that you're no better than a whore."

She sagged, and aroused with victory, he ripped at her blouse.

His smile shattered when she pumped her fist into his mouth. Blood splattered over her like warm rain. She hit him again, heard the crunch of cartilage as his nose fountained more blood. Quick as a snake, she scissored up.

And again, she jabbed at him, an elbow to the jaw, torn knuckles to the face, screaming and cursing as if her words would pummel him as well as her fists.

She didn't hear the battering of the door, the crash of it falling in. With rage behind her, she shoved Rockman to his back, straddled him, and continued to plunge her fists into his face.

"Eve. Sweet God."

It took Roarke and Feeney together to haul her off. She fought, snarling, until Roarke pressed her face into his shoulder.

"Stop. It's done. It's over."

"He was going to kill me. He killed Lola and Georgie. He was going to kill me, but he was going to rape me first." She pulled back, wiped at the blood and sweat on her face. "That's where he made a mistake."

"Sit down." His hands were trembling and slicked with blood when he eased her onto the bed. "You're hurt."

"Not yet. It'll start in a minute." She gathered in a breath, let it out. She was a cop, damn it, she reminded herself. She was a cop, and she'd act like one. "You got the transmission," she said to Feeney.

"Yeah." He took out a handkerchief to wipe his clammy face.

"Then what the hell took you so long?" She managed a ghost of a smile. "You look a little upset, Feeney."

"Shit. All in a day's work." He flipped on his communicator. "Situation under control. We need an ambulance."

"I'm not going to any health center."

"Not for you, champ. For him." He glanced down at Rockman, who managed a weak groan.

"Once you clean him up, book him for the murders of Lola Starr and Georgie Castle."

"You sure about that?"

Her legs were a bit wobbly, but she rose and picked up her jacket. "Got it all." She held out the recorder. "DeBlass did Sharon, but our boy here is accessory after the fact. And I want him charged with the attempted rape and murder of a police officer. Toss in B and E for the hell of it."

"You got it." Feeney tucked the recorder into his pocket. "Christ, Dallas, you're a mess."

"I guess I am. Get him out of here, will you, Feeney?"

"Sure thing."

"Let me help you." Roarke bent down, lifted Rockman by the lapels. He jerked the man up, steadied him. "Look at me, Rockman. Vision clear?"

Rockman blinked blood out of his eyes. "I can see you."

"Good." Roarke's arm shot up, quick as a bullet, and his fist connected with Rockman's already battered face.

"Oops," Feeney said mildly, when Rockman crumbled to the floor again. "Guess he's not too steady on his feet." He bent over himself, slipped on the cuffs. "Maybe a couple of you boys ought to carry him out. Hold the ambulance for me. I'll ride with him."

He took out an evidence bag, slipped the gun into it. "Nice piece—ivory handle. Bet it packs a wallop."

"Tell me about it." Her hand went automatically to her arm.

Feeney stopped admiring the gun and gaped at her. "Shit, Dallas, you shot?"

"I don't know." She said it almost dreamily, surprised when Roarke ripped off the sleeve of her already tattered shirt. "Hey."

"Grazed her." His voice was hollow. He ripped the sleeve again, used it to stanch the wound. "She needs to be looked at."

"I figure I can leave that to you," Feeney remarked. "You might want to stay somewhere else tonight, Dallas. Let a team come in and clean this up for you."

"Yeah." She smiled as the cat leaped onto the bed. "Maybe."

He whistled through his teeth. "Busy day."

"It comes and goes," she murmured, stroking the cat. Galahad, she thought, her white knight.

"See you around, kid."

"Yeah. Thanks, Feeney."

Determined to get through, Roarke crouched in front of her. He waited until Feeney's whistling faded away. "Eve, you're in shock."

"Sort of. I'm starting to hurt though."

"You need a doctor."

She moved her shoulders. "I could use a pain pill, and I need to clean up."

She looked down at herself, took inventory calmly. Her blouse was torn, spotted with blood. Her hands were a mess, ripped and swollen knuckles—she couldn't quite make a fist. A hundred bruises were making themselves known and the wound on her arm where the bullet had nicked it was turning to fire.

"I don't think it's as bad as it looks," she decided, "but I'd better check."

When she started to rise, he picked her up. "I kind of like when you carry me. Makes me all wobbly inside. Then I feel stupid about it after. There's stuff in the bathroom."

Since he wanted to see the damage for himself, he carried her in, set her on the toilet. He found strong, police issue pain pills in a nearly empty medicine cabinet. He offered one, and water, before dampening a cloth.

She pushed at her hair with her good arm. "I forgot to tell Feeney. DeBlass is dead. Suicide. What they used to call eating your gun. Hell of a phrase."

"Don't worry about it now." Roarke worked on the bullet wound first. It was a nasty gash, but the bleeding had already slowed. Any competent MT could close it in a matter of minutes. It didn't make his hands any steadier.

"There were two killers." She frowned at the far wall. "That was the problem. I clicked onto it, but then I let it go. Data indicated low probability percentage. Stupid."

Roarke rinsed out the cloth and started on her face. He was deliriously relieved that most of the blood on it wasn't hers. Her mouth was cut, her left eye already beginning to swell. There was raw color along her cheekbone.

He managed to take a full, almost easy breath. "You're going to have a hell of a bruise."

"I've had them before." The medication was seeping in, turning pain into a mist. She only smiled when he stripped her to the waist and began checking for other injuries. "You've got great hands. I love when you touch me. Nobody ever touched me like that. Did I tell you?"

"No." And he doubted she'd remember she was telling him now. He'd make sure to remind her.

"And you're so pretty. So pretty," she repeated, lifting a bleeding hand to his face. "I keep wondering what you're doing here."

He took her hand, wrapped a cloth gently around it. "I've asked myself the same question."

She grinned foolishly, let herself float. Need to file my report, she thought hazily. Soon. "You don't really think we're going to make anything out of this, do you? Roarke and the cop?"

"I guess we'll have to find out." There were plenty of bruises, but the bluing along her ribs worried him most.

"Okay. Maybe I could lie down now? Can we go to your place, 'cause Feeney's going to send a team in to record the scene and all that. If I could just take a little nap before I go in to make my report."

"You're going to the closest health center."

"No, uh-uh. Can't stand them. Hospitals, health centers, doctors." She gave him a glassy-eyed smile and lifted her arms. "Let me sleep in your bed, Roarke. Okay? The great big one, up on the platform, under the sky."

For lack of anything closer to hand, he took off his jacket and slipped it around her. When he picked her up again, her head lolled on his shoulder.

"Don't forget Galahad. The cat saved my life. Who'd have thought?"

"Then he gets caviar for the whole of his nine lives." Roarke snapped his fingers and the cat fell happily into step.

"Door's broken." Eve chuckled as Roarke stepped around it and into the hall. "Landlord's going to be pissed. But I know how to get around him." She pressed a kiss to Roarke's throat. "I'm glad it's over," she said, sighing. "I'm glad you're here. Be nice if you stuck around."

"Count on it." Shifting her, he bent down and retrieved the package he'd dropped in the hallway in his race to her door. There was a fresh pound of coffee inside. He figured he'd need it as a bribe when she woke up and found herself in a hospital bed.

"Don't wanna dream tonight," she murmured as she drifted off.

He stepped into the elevator, the cat at his feet. "No." He brushed his lips over Eve's hair. "No dreams tonight."

GLORY IN DEATH

Fame then was cheap...
And they have kept it since, by being dead.
— DRYDEN

Chok'd with ambition of the meaner sort.
— SHAKESPEARE

CHAPTER
ONE

The dead were her business. She lived with them, worked with them, studied them. She dreamed of them. And because that didn't seem to be enough, in some deep, secret chamber of her heart, she mourned for them.

A decade as a cop had toughened her, given her a cold, clinical, and often cynical eye toward death and its many causes. It made scenes such as the one she viewed now, on a rainy night on a dark street nasty with litter, almost too usual. But still, she felt.

Murder no longer shocked, but it continued to repel.

The woman had been lovely once. Long trails of her golden hair spread out like rays on the dirty sidewalk. Her eyes, wide and still with that distressed expression death often left in them, were a deep purple against cheeks bloodlessly white and wet with rain.

She'd worn an expensive suit, the same rich color as her eyes. The jacket was neatly buttoned in contrast to the jerked-up skirt that exposed her trim thighs. Jewels glittered on her fingers, at her ears, against the sleek lapel of the jacket. A leather bag with a gold clasp lay near her outstretched fingers.

Her throat had been viciously slashed.

Lieutenant Eve Dallas crouched down beside death and studied it carefully. The sights and scents were familiar, but each time, every time, there was something new. Both victim and killer left their own imprint, their own style, and made murder personal.

The scene had already been recorded. Police sensors and the more intimate touch of the privacy screen were in place to keep the curious barricaded and to preserve the murder site. Street traffic, such as it was in this area, had been diverted. Air traffic was light at this hour of the night and caused little distraction. The backbeat from the music of the sex club across the street thrummed busily in the air, punctuated by the occasional howl from the celebrants. The colored lights from its revolving sign pulsed against the screen, splashing garish colors over the victim's body.

Eve could have ordered it shut down for the night, but it seemed an unnecessary hassle. Even in 2058 with the gun ban, even though genetic testing often weeded out the more violent hereditary traits before they could bloom, murder happened. And it happened with enough regularity that the fun seekers across the street would be miffed at the idea of being moved along for such a minor inconvenience as death.

A uniform stood by continuing video and audio. Beside the screen a couple of forensics sweepers huddled against the driving rain and talked shop and sports. They hadn't bothered to look at the body yet, hadn't recognized her.

Was it worse, Eve wondered, and her eyes hardened as she watched the rain wash through blood, when you knew the victim?

She'd had only a professional relationship with Prosecuting Attorney Cicely Towers, but enough of one to have formed a strong opinion of a strong woman. A successful woman, Eve thought, a fighter, one who had pursued justice doggedly.

Had she been pursuing it here, in this miserable neighborhood?

With a sigh, Eve reached over and opened the elegant and expensive bag to corroborate her visual ID. "Cicely Towers," she said for the recorder. "Female, age forty-five, divorced. Resides twenty-one thirty-two East Eighty-third, number Sixty-one B. No robbery. Victim still wearing jewelry. Approximately . . ." She flipped through the wallet. "Twenty in hard bills, fifty credit tokens, six credit cards left at scene. No overt signs of struggle or sexual assault."

She looked back at the woman sprawled on the sidewalk. What the hell were you doing out here, Towers? she wondered. Here, away from the power center, away from your classy home address?

And dressed for business, she thought. Eve knew Cicely Towers's authoritative wardrobe well, had admired it in court and at City Hall. Strong colors—always camera ready—coordinated accessories, always with a feminine touch.

Eve rose, rubbed absently at the wet knees of her jeans.

"Homicide," she said briefly. "Bag her."

It was no surprise to Eve that the media had caught the scent of murder and were already hunting it down before she'd reached the glossy building where Cicely Towers had lived. Several remotes and eager reporters were camped on the pristine sidewalk. The fact that it was three A.M. and raining buckets didn't deter them. In their eyes, Eve saw the wolf gleam. The story was the prey, ratings the trophy.

She could ignore the cameras that swung in her direction, the questions shot out like stinging darts. She was almost used to the loss of her anonymity. The case she had investigated and closed during the past winter had catapulted her into the public eye. The case, she thought now as she aimed a steely glance at a reporter who had the nerve to block her path, and her relationship with Roarke.

The case had been murder. And violent death, however exciting, soon passed out of the public interest.

But Roarke was always news.

"What do you have, Lieutenant? Do you have a suspect? Is there a motive? Can you confirm that Prosecuting Attorney Towers was decapitated?"

Eve slowed her ground-eating stride briefly and swept her gaze over the huddle of soggy, feral-eyed reporters. She was wet, tired, and revolted, but she was careful. She'd learned that if you gave the media any part of yourself, it squeezed it, twisted it, and wrung it dry.

"The department has no comment at this time other than that the investigation into Prosecuting Attorney Towers's death is proceeding."

"Are you in charge of the case?"

"I'm primary," she said shortly, then swung between the two uniforms guarding the entrance to the building.

The lobby was full of flowers: long banks and flows of fragrant, colorful blooms that made her think of spring in some exotic place—the island where she had spent three dazzling days with Roarke while she'd recovered from a bullet wound and exhaustion.

She didn't take time to smile over the memory, as she would have under other circumstances, but flashed her badge and moved across the terra-cotta tiles to the first elevator.

There were more uniforms inside. Two were behind the lobby desk handling the computerized security, others watched the entrance, still others stood by the elevator tubes. It was more manpower than necessary, but as PA, Towers had been one of their own.

"Her apartment's secured?" Eve asked the closest cop.

"Yes, sir. No one's been in or out since your call at oh two ten."

"I'll want copies of the security discs." She stepped into the elevator. "For the last twenty-four hours, to start." She glanced down at the name on his uniform. "I want a detail of six, for door-to-doors beginning at seven hundred, Biggs. Floor sixty-one," she ordered, and the elevator's clear doors closed silently.

She stepped out into the sixty-first's lush carpet and museum quiet. The halls were narrow, as they were in most multihabitation buildings erected within the last half century. The walls were a flawless creamy white with mirrors at rigid intervals to lend the illusion of space.

Space was no problem within the units, Eve mused. There were only three on the entire floor. She decoded the lock on 61-B using her Police and Security master card and stepped into quiet elegance.

Cicely Towers had done well for herself, Eve decided. And she liked to live well. As Eve took the pocket video from her field kit and clipped it onto her jacket, she scanned the living area. She recognized two paintings by a prominent twenty-first century artist hanging on the pale rose-toned wall above a wide U-shaped conversation area done in muted stripes of pinks and greens. It was her association with

Roarke that had her identifying the paintings and the easy wealth in the simplicity of decor and selected pieces.

How much does a PA pull in per year? she wondered as the camera recorded the scene.

Everything was tidy, meticulously so. But then, Eve reflected, from what she knew of Towers, the woman had been meticulous. In her dress, in her work, in maintaining her privacy.

So, what had an elegant, smart, and meticulous woman been doing in a nasty neighborhood in the middle of a nasty night?

Eve walked through the room. The floor was white wood and shone like a mirror beneath lovely rugs that echoed the dominant colors of the room. On a table were framed holograms of children in varying stages of growth, from babyhood on through to the college years. A boy and girl, both pretty, both beaming.

Odd, Eve thought. She'd worked with Towers on countless cases over the years. Had she known the woman had children? With a shake of her head, she walked over to the small computer built into a stylish workstation in the corner of the room. Again she used her master card to engage it.

"List appointments for Cicely Towers, May two." Eve's lips pursed as she read the data. An hour at an upscale private health club prior to a full day in court followed by a six o'clock with a prominent defense attorney, then a dinner engagement. Eve's brow lifted. Dinner with George Hammett.

Roarke had dealings with Hammett, Eve remembered. She'd met him now twice and knew him to be a charming and canny man who made his rather exorbitant living with transportation.

And Hammett was Cicely Towers's final appointment of the day.

"Print," she murmured and tucked the hard copy in her bag.

She tried the tele-link next, requesting all incoming and outgoing calls for the past forty-eight hours. It was likely she would have to dig deeper, but for now she ordered a recording of the calls, tucked the disc away, and began a long, careful search of the apartment.

By five a.m., her eyes were gritty and her head ached. The single hour's sleep she had managed to tuck in between sex and murder was beginning to wear on her.

"According to known information," she said wearily for the recorder, "the victim lived alone. No indication from initial investigation to the contrary. No indication that the victim left her apartment other than voluntarily, and no record of an appointment that would explain why the victim traveled to the location of the murder. Primary has secured data from her computer and tele-link for further investigation. Door-to-doors will begin at oh seven hundred and building security discs will be confiscated. Primary is leaving victim's residence and will be en route to victim's offices in City Hall. Lieutenant Dallas, Eve. Oh five oh eight."

Eve switched off the audio and video, secured her field kit, and headed out.

It was past ten when she made it back to Cop Central. In concession to her hollow stomach, she zipped through the eatery, disappointed but not surprised to find most of the good stuff long gone by that hour. She settled for a soy muffin and what the eatery liked to pretend was coffee. As bad as it was, she downed everything before she settled in her office.

It was just as well, as her 'link beeped instantly.

"Lieutenant."

She bit back a sigh as she stared into Whitney's wide, grim-eyed face. "Commander."

"My office, now."

There wasn't time to close her mouth before the screen went blank.

The hell with it, she thought. She scrubbed her hands over her face, then through her short, choppy brown hair. There went any chance of checking her messages, of calling Roarke to let him know what she was into, or of the ten-minute catnap she'd been fantasizing about.

She rose again, worked out the kinks in her shoulders. She did take the time to remove her jacket. The leather had protected her shirt, but her jeans were still damp. Philosophically, she ignored the discomfort and gathered up what little data she had. If she was lucky, she might get another cup of cop coffee in the commander's office.

It only took Eve about ten seconds to realize the coffee would have to wait.

Whitney wasn't sitting behind his desk, as was his habit. He was standing, facing the single-wall window that gave him his personal view of the city he'd served and protected for more than thirty years. His hands were clasped behind his back, but the relaxed pose was negated by the white knuckles.

Eve briefly studied the broad shoulders, the grizzled dark hair, and the wide back of the man who had only months before refused the office of chief to remain in command here.

"Commander."

"It's stopped raining."

Her eyes narrowed in puzzlement before she carefully made them blank. "Yes, sir."

"It's a good city all in all, Dallas. It's easy to forget that from up here, but it's a good city all in all. I'm working to remember that right now."

She said nothing, had nothing to say. She waited.

"I made you primary on this. Technically, Deblinsky was up, so I want to know if she gives you any flak."

"Deblinsky's a good cop."

"Yes, she is. You're better."

Because her brows flew up, she was grateful he still had his back to her. "I appreciate your confidence, Commander."

"You've earned it. I overrode procedure to put you in control for personal reasons. I need the best, someone who'll go to the wall and over it."

"Most of us knew PA Towers, Commander. There isn't a cop in New York who wouldn't go to the wall and over it to find who killed her."

He sighed, and the deep inhalation of air rippled through his thick body before he turned. For a moment longer he said nothing, only studied the woman he'd put in charge. She was slim, deceptively so, for he had reason to know she had more stamina than was apparent in that long, slender body.

She was showing some fatigue now, in the shadows under her

whiskey colored eyes, in the pallor of her bony face. He couldn't let that worry him, not now.

"Cicely Towers was a personal friend—a close personal friend."

"I see." Eve wondered if she did. "I'm sorry, Commander."

"I knew her for years. We started out together, a hotdogging cop and an eager-beaver criminal lawyer. My wife and I are godparents to her son." He paused a moment and seemed to fight for control. "I've notified her children. My wife is meeting them. They'll stay with us until after the memorial."

He cleared his throat, pressed his lips together. "Cicely was one of my oldest friends, and above and beyond my professional respect and admiration for her, I loved her very much. My wife is devastated by this; Cicely's children are shattered. All I could tell them was that I would do everything, anything in my power to find the person who did this to her, to give her what she worked for most of her life: justice."

Now he did sit, not with authority but with weariness. "I'm telling you this, Dallas, so that you know up front I have no objectivity on this case. None. Because I don't, I'm depending on you."

"I appreciate you being frank, Commander." She hesitated only an instant. "As a personal friend of the victim's, it'll be necessary to interview you as soon as possible." She watched his eyes flicker and harden. "Your wife as well, Commander. If it's more comfortable, I can conduct the interviews at your home rather than here."

"I see." He drew another breath. "That's why you're primary, Dallas. There aren't many cops who'd have the nerve to zero in so directly. I'd appreciate it if you'd wait until tomorrow, perhaps even a day or two longer, to see my wife, and if you'd see her at home. I'll set it up."

"Yes, sir."

"What have you got so far?"

"I did a recon on the victim's residence and her office. I have files of the cases she had pending and those that she closed over the last five years. I need to cross-check names to see if anyone she sent up has been released recently, their families and associates. Particularly the violent offenders. Her batting average was very high."

"Cicely was a tiger in the courtroom, and I never knew her to miss a detail. Until now."

"Why was she there, Commander, in the middle of the night? Prelim autopsy puts time of death at one sixteen. It's a rough neighborhood—shakedowns, muggings, sex joints. There's a known chemical trading center a couple of blocks from where she was found."

"I don't know. She was a careful woman, but she was also . . . arrogant." He smiled a little. "Admirably so. She'd go head to head with the worst this city's got to offer. But to put herself in deliberate jeopardy . . . I don't know."

"She was trying a case, Fluentes, murder two. Strangulation of a lady friend. His lawyer's using the passion defense, but word is Towers was going to send him away. I'm checking it out."

"Is he on the street or in a cage?"

"On the street. First violent offense, bail was dead low. Being it was murder, he was required to wear a homing bracelet, but that doesn't mean diddly if he knew anything about electronics. Would she have met with him?"

"Absolutely not. It would corrupt her case to meet a defendant out of the courtroom." Thinking of Cicely, remembering Cicely, Whitney shook his head. "That she'd never risk. But he could have used other means to lure her there."

"Like I said, I'm checking it out. She had a dinner appointment last night with George Hammett. Do you know him?"

"Socially. They saw each other occasionally. Nothing serious, according to my wife. She was always trying to find the perfect man for Cicely."

"Commander, it's best if I ask now, off the record. Were you sexually involved with the victim?"

A muscle in his cheek jerked, but his eyes stayed level. "No, I wasn't. We had a friendship, and that friendship was very valuable. In essence, she was family. You wouldn't understand family, Dallas."

"No." Her voice was flat. "I suppose not."

"I'm sorry for that." Squeezing his eyes shut, Whitney rubbed his hands over his face. "That was uncalled for, and unfair. And your question was relevant." He dropped his hands. "You've never lost anyone close to you, have you, Dallas?"

"Not that I remember."

"It shreds you to pieces," he murmured.

She supposed it would. In the decade she had known Whitney, she had seen him furious, impatient, even coldly cruel. But she had never seen him devastated.

If that was what being close, and losing, did to a strong man, Eve supposed she was better off as she was. She had no family to lose, and only vague, ugly flashes of her childhood. Her life as it was now had begun when she was eight years old and had been found, battered and abandoned, in Texas. What had happened before that day didn't matter. She told herself constantly that it didn't matter. She had made herself into what she was, who she was. For friendship she had precious few she cared enough for, trusted enough in. As for more than friendship, there was Roarke. He had whittled away at her until she'd given him more. Enough more to frighten her at odd moments—frighten her because she knew he wouldn't be satisfied until he had all.

If she gave him all, then lost him, would she be in shreds?

Rather than dwell on it, Eve dosed herself with coffee and the remains of a candy bar she unearthed in her desk. The prospect of lunch was a fantasy right up there with spending a week in the tropics. She sipped and munched while she scanned the final autopsy report on her monitor.

The time of death remained as issued in the prelim. The cause, a severed jugular and the resulting loss of blood and oxygen. The victim had enjoyed a meal of sea scallops and wild greens, wine, real coffee, and fresh fruit with whipped cream. Ingestion estimated at five hours before death.

The call had come in quickly. Cicely Towers had been dead only ten minutes before a cab driver, brave or desperate enough to work the neighborhood, had spotted the body and reported it. The first cruiser had arrived three minutes later.

Her killer had moved fast, Eve mused. Then again, it was easy to fade in a neighborhood like that, to slip into a car, a doorway, a club. There would have been blood; the jugular gushed and sprayed. But the rain would have been an asset, washing it from the murderer's hands.

She would have to comb the neighborhood, ask questions that were unlikely to receive any sort of viable answers. Still, bribes often worked where procedure or threats wouldn't.

She was studying the police photo of Cicely Towers with her necklace of blood when her 'link beeped.

"Dallas, Homicide."

A face flashed on her screen, young, beaming, and sly. "Lieutenant, what's the word?"

Eve didn't swear, though she wanted to. Her opinion of reporters wasn't terribly high, but C. J. Morse was on the lowest end of her scale. "You don't want to hear the word I've got for you, Morse."

His round face split with a smile. "Come on, Dallas, the public's right to know. Remember?"

"I've got nothing for you."

"Nothing? You want me to go on air saying that Lieutenant Eve Dallas, the finest of New York's finest, has come up empty in the investigation of the murder of one of the city's most respected, most prominent, and most visible public figures? I could do that, Dallas," he said, clicking his tongue. "I could, but it wouldn't look good for you."

"And you figure that matters to me." Her smile was thin and laser sharp, and her finger hovered over the disconnect. "You figure wrong."

"Maybe not to you personally, but it would reflect on the department." His girlishly long lashes fluttered. "On Commander Whitney for pulling strings to put you on as primary. And there's the backwash on Roarke."

Her finger twitched, then curled into her palm. "Cicely Towers's murder is a priority with the department, with Commander Whitney, and with me."

"I'll quote you."

Fucking little bastard. "And my work with the department has nothing to do with Roarke."

"Hey, brown-eyes, anything that touches you, touches Roarke now, and vice versa. And you know, the fact that your man had business dealings with the recently deceased, her ex-husband, and her current escort ties it up real pretty."

Her hands balled into fists of frustration. "Roarke has a lot of business dealings with a lot of people. I didn't know you were back on the gossip beat, C. J."

That wiped the smarmy little smile off his face. There was nothing C. J. Morse hated more than being reminded of his roots in gossip and society news. Especially now that he'd wormed his way onto the police beat. "I've got contacts, Dallas."

"Yeah, you've also got a pimple in the middle of your forehead. I'd have that taken care of." With that cheap but satisfying shot, Eve cut him off.

Springing up, she paced the small square of her office, jamming her hands into her pockets, pulling them out again. Goddamn it, why did Roarke's name have to come up in connection with the case? Just how closely was he involved with Towers's business dealings and her associates?

Eve dropped into her chair again and scowled at the reports on her desk. She'd have to find out, and quickly.

At least this time, with this murder, she knew he had an alibi. At the time Cicely Towers was having her throat slashed, Roarke had been fucking the hell out of the investigating officer.

CHAPTER

TWO

Eve would have preferred to go back to the apartment she continued to keep despite the fact that she spent most nights at Roarke's. There, she could have brooded, thought, slept, and walked herself back through the last day of Cicely Towers's life. Instead, she headed for Roarke's.

She was tired enough to give up the controls and let the auto program maneuver the car through late-evening traffic. Food was the first thing she needed, Eve decided. And if she could steal ten minutes to clear her mind, so much the better.

Spring had decided to come out and play, prettily. It tempted her to open the windows, ignore the sounds of bustling traffic, the hum of maxibuses, the griping of pedestrians, the overhead swish of air traffic.

To avoid the echoing bellow of the guides from the tourist blimps, she veered over toward Tenth. A shot through midtown and a quick zip up Park would have been quicker, but she would have been treated to the droning recitation of New York's attractions, the history and tradition of Broadway, the brilliance of museums, the variety of shops—and the plug for the blimp's own gift emporium.

As the blimp route skimmed over her apartment, she'd heard the spiel countless times. She didn't care to hear about the convenience of the people glides that connected the sparkling fashion shops from Fifth to Madison or the Empire State Building's newest sky walk.

A minor traffic snag at Fifty-second had her pondering a billboard where a stunning man and a stunning woman exchanged a passionate kiss, sweetened, they claimed each time they came up for air, by Mountain Stream Breath Freshener.

Their vehicles jammed flank to flank, a couple of cabbies shouted inventive insults at each other. A maxibus overflowing with passengers laid on its horn, adding an ear-stinging screech that had pedestrians on rampways and sidewalks shaking their heads or their fists.

A traffic hovercraft dipped low, blasted out the standard order to proceed or be cited. Traffic inched uptown, full of noise and temper.

The city changed as she moved from its core to its edges, where the wealthy and the privileged made their homes. Wider, cleaner streets, the sweep of trees from the islands of parks. Here the vehicles quieted to a whoosh of movement, and those who walked did so in tailored outfits and fine shoes.

She passed a dog walker who handled a brace of elegant gold hounds with the steady aplomb of a seasoned droid.

When she came to the gates of Roarke's estate, her car idled until the program cleared her through. His trees were blooming. White blossoms flowed along with pink, accented by deep, rich reds and blues, all carpeted by a long sweep of emerald grass.

The house itself towered up into the deepening sky, glass sparkling in the late sun, the stone grand and gray. It had been months since she had first seen it, yet she had never grown used to the grandeur, the sumptuousness, the simple, unadulterated wealth. She had yet to stop asking herself what she was doing here—here, with him.

She left her car at the base of the granite steps and climbed them. She wouldn't knock. That was pride, and it was ornery. Roarke's butler despised her and didn't trouble to hide it.

As expected, Summerset appeared in the hall like a puff of black smoke, his silver hair gleaming, a frown of disapproval ready on his long face.

"Lieutenant." His eyes scraped her, making her aware that she was wearing the same clothes she'd left in, and they were considerably rumpled. "We were unaware of the time of your return, or indeed, if you intended to return."

"Were we?" She shrugged, and because she knew it offended him, peeled off her scarred leather jacket and held it out to his elegant hands. "Is Roarke here?"

"He is engaged on an interspace transmission."

"The Olympus Resort?"

Summerset's mouth puckered like a prune. "I don't inquire as to Roarke's business."

You know exactly what he's doing and when, she thought, but turned out of the wide, glittery hall toward the curve of the stairs. "I'm going up. I need a bath." She tossed a glance over her shoulder. "You can let him know where I am when he's finished his transmission."

She climbed up to the master suite. Like Roarke, she rarely used the elevators. The moment she'd slammed the bedroom door behind her, she began to strip, leaving a trail of boots, jeans, shirt, and underwear in her wake on the way to the bath.

She ordered the water at 102 degrees Fahrenheit, and as an afterthought tossed in some of the salts Roarke had brought her back from Silas Three. They foamed into sea green froth that smelled of fairy-tale woods.

She all but rolled into the oversized marble tub, all but wept when the heat seeped into her aching bones. Drawing one deep breath, she submerged, held herself down for a count of thirty seconds, and surfaced with a sigh of sheer sensual pleasure. She kept her eyes closed and drifted.

So he found her.

Most people would have said she was relaxed. But then, Roarke thought, most people didn't really know and certainly didn't understand Eve Dallas. He was more intimate with her, closer to her mind and heart than he had ever been with another. Yet there were still pockets of her he had yet to plumb.

She was, always, a fascinating learning experience.

She was naked, dipped to her chin in steamy water and perfumed bubbles. Her face was flushed from the heat, her eyes closed, but she wasn't relaxed. He could see the tension in the hand that was fisted on the wide ledge of the tub, in the faint frown between her eyes.

No, Eve was thinking, he mused. And worrying. And planning. He moved quietly, as he had grown up doing in the alleyways of Dublin, along wharves and the stinking streets of cities everywhere. When he sat on the ledge to watch her, she didn't stir for several minutes. He knew the instant she sensed him beside her.

Her eyes opened, the golden brown clear and alert as they latched onto his amused blue. As always, just the sight of him gave her a quick inner jolt. His face was like a painting, a depiction in perfect oils of some fallen angel. The sheer beauty of it, framed by all that rich black hair, was forever a surprise to her.

She cocked a brow, tilted her head. "Pervert."

"It's my tub." Watching her still, he slid an elegant hand through the bubbles into the water and along the side of her breast. "You'll boil in there."

"I like it hot. I needed it hot."

"You've had a difficult day."

He would know, she thought, struggling not to resent it. He knew everything. She only moved her shoulder as he rose and went to the automated bar built into the tiles. It hummed briefly as it served up two glasses of wine in faceted crystal.

He came back, sat on the ledge again, and handed her a glass. "You haven't slept; you haven't eaten."

"It goes with the territory." The wine tasted like liquid gold.

"Nonetheless, you worry me, Lieutenant."

"You worry too easily."

"I love you."

It flustered her to hear him say it in that lovely voice that hinted of Irish mists, to know that somehow, incredibly, it was true. Since she had no answer to give him, she frowned into her wine.

He said nothing until he'd managed to tuck away irritation at her lack of response. "Can you tell me what happened to Cicely Towers?"

"You knew her," Eve countered.

"Not well. A light social acquaintance, some business dealings, mostly through her former husband." He sipped his wine, watched the steam rise from her bath. "I found her admirable, wise, and dangerous."

Eve scooted up until the water lapped at the tops of her breasts. "Dangerous? To you?"

"Not directly." His lips curved slightly before he brought the wine to them. "To nefarious practices, to illegalities, small and large, to the criminal mind. She was very like you in that respect. It's fortunate I've mended my ways."

Eve wasn't entirely sure of that, but she let it slide. "Through your business dealings and your light social acquaintance, are you aware of anyone who would have wanted her dead?"

He sipped again, more deeply. "Is this an interrogation, Lieutenant?"

It was the smile in his voice that rubbed her wrong. "It can be," she said shortly.

"As you like." He rose, set his glass aside, and began to unbutton his shirt.

"What are you doing?"

"Getting into the swim, so to speak." He tossed the shirt aside, unhooked his trousers. "If I'm going to be questioned by a naked cop, in my own tub, the least I can do is join her."

"Damn it, Roarke, this is murder."

He winced as the hot water all but scalded him. "You're telling me." He faced her across the sea of froth. "What is it in me that is so perverse it thrives on ruffling you? And," he continued before she could give him her short, pithy opinion, "what is it about you that pulls at me, even when you're sitting there with an invisible badge pinned to your lovely breast?"

He skimmed a hand under, along her ankle, her calf, and to the spot on the back of her knee he knew weakened her. "I want you," he murmured. "Right now."

Her hand had gone limp on the stem of her glass before she managed to shift away. "Talk to me about Cicely Towers."

Philosophically, Roarke settled back. He had no intention of letting her out of the tub until he was finished, so he could afford patience. "She, her former husband, and George Hammett, were on the board of one of my divisions. Mercury, named after the god of speed. Import-export for the most part. Shipping, deliveries, rapid transports."

"I know what Mercury is," she said testily, dealing with the annoyance of not knowing that, too, was one of his companies.

"It was a poorly organized and failing business when I acquired it about ten years ago. Marco Angelini, Cicely's ex, invested, as did she. They were still married at the time, I believe, or just divorced. The termination of their marriage, apparently, was as amicable as such things can be. Hammett was also an investor. I don't believe he became personally involved with Cicely until some years later."

"And this triangle, Angelini, Towers, Hammett, was that amicable, too?"

"It seemed so." Idly he tapped a tile. When it flipped open to reveal the hidden panel, he programmed in music. Something low and weepy. "If you're worried about my end of it, it was business, and successful business at that."

"How much smuggling does Mercury do?"

His grin flashed. "Really, Lieutenant."

Water lapped as she sat forward. "Don't play games with me, Roarke."

"Eve, it's my fondest wish to do just that."

She gritted her teeth, kicked at the hand that was sneaking up her leg. "Cicely Towers had a rep for being a no-nonsense prosecutor, dedicated, clean as they come. If she'd discovered any of Mercury's dealings skirted the law, she'd have gone after you with a vengeance."

"So, she discovered my perfidy, and I had her lured to a dangerous neighborhood and ordered her throat cut." His eyes were level and entirely too bland. "Is that what you think, Lieutenant?"

"No, damn it, you know it's not, but—"

"Others might," he finished. "Which would put you in a delicate position."

"I'm not worried about that." At the moment, she was worried only about him. "Roarke, I need to know. I need you to tell me if there's anything, anything at all, that might involve you in the investigation."

"And if there is?"

She went cold inside. "I'll have to turn it over to someone else."

"Haven't we been through this before?"

"It's not like the DeBlass case. Not anything like that. You're not a suspect." When he cocked a brow, she struggled to put reason rather than irritation in her voice. Why was everything so complicated when it touched on Roarke? "I don't think you had anything to do with Cicely Towers's murder. Is that simple enough?"

"You haven't finished the thought."

"All right. I'm a cop. There are questions I have to ask. I have to ask them of you, of anyone who's even remotely connected to the victim. I can't change that."

"How much do you trust me?"

"It has nothing to do with trusting you."

"That doesn't answer the question." His eyes went cool, remote, and she knew she'd taken the wrong step. "If you don't trust me by now, believe in me, then we have nothing but some rather intriguing sex."

"You're twisting this around." She was fighting to stay calm because he was scaring her. "I'm not accusing you of anything. If I had come into this case without knowing you or caring about you, I would have put you on the list on principle. But I do know you, and that's not what this is about. Hell."

She closed her eyes and rubbed wet hands over her face. It was miserable for her to try to explain her feelings. "I'm trying to get answers that will help to keep you as far out of it as I can because I do care. And I can't stop trying to think of ways I can use you because of your connection with Towers. And your connections, period. It's hard for me to do both."

"It shouldn't have been so hard to simply say it," he murmured, then shook his head. "Mercury is completely legitimate—now— because there's no need for it to be otherwise. It runs well, makes an acceptable profit. And though you might think I'm arrogant enough to engage in criminal acts with a prosecuting attorney on my board of directors, you should know I'm not stupid enough to do so."

Because she believed him, the tightness that she'd carried in her chest for hours broke apart. "All right. There'll still be questions," she told him. "And the media has already made the connection."

"I know. I'm sorry for it. How difficult are they making it for you?"

"They haven't even started." In one of her rare shows of easy affection, she reached for his hand, squeezed it. 'I'm sorry, too. Looks like we're in another one."

"I can help." He slid forward so that he could bring their joined hands to his lips. When she smiled, he knew she was, finally, ready to relax. "It isn't necessary for you to keep me out of anything. I can handle that myself. And there's no need to feel guilty or uncomfortable for considering that I could be useful to you in the investigation."

"I'll let you know when I figure out how you might be." This time she only arched her brows when his free hand snaked up her thigh. "If you try to pull that off in here, we're going to need diving equipment."

He levered himself to her, over her, so that water sloshed dangerously at the lip of the ledge. "Oh, I think we can manage just fine on our own."

And he covered her grinning mouth with his to prove it.

Late in the night when she slept beside him, Roarke lay awake watching the stars whirl through the sky window over the bed. Worry he hadn't let her see was in his eyes now. Their fates had intertwined, personally, professionally. It was murder that had brought them together, and murder that would continue to poke fingers into their lives. The woman beside him defended the dead.

As Cicely Towers had often done, he thought, and wondered if that representation is what had cost her her own life.

He made it a point not to worry too much or too often about how Eve made her living. Her career defined her. He was very much aware of that.

Both of them had made themselves—remade themselves—from the little or nothing they had been. He was a man who bought and sold, who controlled, and who enjoyed the power of it. And the profit.

But it occurred to him that there were pockets of his business that would cause her trouble, if the shadows came to light. It was perfectly true that Mercury was clean, but it hadn't always been true. He had other holdings, other interests that dealt in the gray areas. He had grown up in the darker portions of those gray areas, after all. He had a knack for them.

Smuggling, both terrestrial and interstellar, was a profitable and entertaining business. The truly excellent wines of Taurus Five, the stunning blue diamonds mined in the caves of Refini, the precious transparent porcelain manufactured in the Arts Colony of Mars.

True, he no longer had to bypass the law to live, and live well. But old habits die hard.

The problem remained: What if he hadn't yet converted Mercury into a legitimate operation? What he saw as a harmless business diversion would have weighed on Eve like a stone.

Added to that was the humbling fact that despite what they had begun to build together, she was far from sure of him.

She murmured something, shifted. Even in sleep, he mused, she hesitated before turning to him. He was having a very difficult time with that. Changes were going to be necessary, soon, for both of them.

For the moment, he would deal with what he could control. It would be very simple for him to make a few calls and ask a few questions relating to Cicely Towers. It would be less simple and take a bit more time to convert all of those gray areas of his concerns into the light.

He looked down to study her. She was sleeping well, her hand open and relaxed on the pillow. He knew sometimes she dreamed, badly. But tonight her mind was quiet. Trusting it would remain so, he slipped out of bed to begin.

Eve woke to the fragrance of coffee. Genuine, rich coffee ground from beans cultivated on Roarke's plantation in South America. The luxury of that was, Eve could admit, one of the first things she'd grown accustomed to, indeed come to depend on, when it came to staying at Roarke's.

Her lips were curved before her eyes opened.

"Christ, heaven couldn't be better than this."

"I'm glad you think so."

Her eyes might have still been bleary, but she managed to focus on him. He was fully dressed in one of the dark suits that made him look both capable and dangerous. In the sitting area below the raised platform where the bed stood, he seemed to be enjoying breakfast and his quick daily scan of the day's news on his monitor.

The gray cat she'd named Galahad lay like a fat slug on the arm of the chair and studied Roarke's plate with bicolored, avaricious eyes.

"What time is it?" she demanded, and the bedside clock murmured the answer: oh six hundred. "Jesus, how long have you been up?"

"Awhile. You didn't say when you had to be in."

She ran her hands over her face, up through her hair. "I've got a couple hours." A slow starter, she crawled out of bed and looked groggily around for something to wear.

Roarke watched her a moment. It was always a pleasure to watch Eve in the morning, when she was naked and glassy-eyed. He gestured toward the robe the bedroom droid had picked up from the floor and hung neatly over the foot of the bed. Eve groped into it, too sleepy yet to be baffled by the feel of silk against her skin.

Roarke poured her a cup of coffee and waited while she settled into the chair across from him and savored it. The cat, thinking his luck might change, thudded onto her lap with enough weight to make her grunt.

"You slept well."

"Yeah." She drew the coffee in like breath, winced only a little as Galahad circled her lap and kneaded her thighs with his needle claws. "I feel close to human again."

"Hungry?"

She grunted again. Eve already knew his kitchen was staffed with artists. She took a swan-shaped pastry from the silver tray and downed it in three enthusiastic bites. When she reached for the coffeepot herself, her eyes were fully open and clear. Feeling generous, she broke off a swan's head and gave it to Galahad.

"It's always a pleasure watching you wake up," he commented. "But sometimes I wonder if you want me only for my coffee."

"Well . . ." She grinned at him and sipped again. "I really like the food, too. And the sex isn't bad."

"You seemed to tolerate it fairly well last night. I have to be in Australia today. I may not make it back until tomorrow or the day after."

"Oh."

"I'd like you to stay here while I'm gone."

"We've been through that. I don't feel comfortable."

"Perhaps you would if you'd consider it your home as well as mine. Eve . . ." He laid a hand on hers before she could speak. "When are you going to accept what I feel for you?"

"Look, I'm just more comfortable in my own place when you're away. And I've got a lot of work right now."

"You didn't answer the question," he murmured. "Never mind. I'll let you know when I'll be back." His voice was clipped now, cool, and he turned the monitor toward her. "Speaking of your work, you might like to see what the media is saying."

Eve read the first headline with a kind of weary resignation. Mouth grim, she scanned from paper to paper. The banners were all similar enough. Renowned New York prosecutor murdered. Police baffled. There were images, of course, of Towers. Inside courtrooms, outside courthouses. Images of her children, comments and quotes.

Eve snarled a bit at her own image and the caption that labeled her the top homicide investigator in the city.

"I'm going to get grief on that," she muttered.

There was more, naturally. Several papers had printed a brief rundown of the case she'd closed the previous winter, involving a prominent U.S. senator and three dead whores. As expected, her relationship with Roarke was mentioned in every edition.

"What the hell does it matter who I am or who I'm with?"

"You've leaped into the public arena, Lieutenant. Your name now sells media chips."

"I'm a cop, not a socialite." Fuming, she swiveled to the elaborate grillwork along the far wall. "Open viewing screen," she ordered. "Channel 75."

The grill slid open, revealing the screen. The sound of the early broadcast filled the room. Eve's eyes narrowed, her teeth clenched.

"There's that fang-toothed, dickless weasel."

Amused, Roarke sipped his coffee and watched C. J. Morse give his six o'clock report. He was well aware that Eve's disdain for the media had grown into a full-fledged disgust over the last couple of months. A disgust that stemmed from the simple fact that she now had to deal with them at every turn of her professional and personal life. Even without that, he didn't think he could blame her for despising Morse.

"And so, a great career has been cut off cruelly, violently. A woman of conviction, dedication, and integrity has been murdered on the streets of this great city, left there to bleed in the rain. Cicely Towers will not be forgotten, but will be remembered as a woman who fought for justice in a world where we struggle for it. Even death can't dim her legacy.

"But will her killer be brought to the justice she lived her entire life upholding? The Police and Security Department of New York as yet offers no hope. Primary investigating officer, Lieutenant Eve Dallas, a jewel of the department, is unable to answer that question."

Eve all but growled when her image filled the screen. Morse's voice continued.

"When reached by 'link, Lieutenant Dallas refused to comment on the murder and the progress of the investigation. No denial was issued as to the speculation that a cover-up is in process . . ."

"Why that smarmy-faced bastard. He never asked about a cover-up. What cover-up?" The slap of her hand on the arm of the chair made Galahad leap away to safer ground. "I've barely had the case for thirty hours."

"Ssh," Roarke said mildly and left her to spring up and stalk the room.

". . . the long list of prominent names that are linked with Prosecutor Towers, among them Commander Whitney, Dallas's superior. The commander recently refused the offer of the position as Chief of Police and Security. A long-standing, intimate friend of the victim—"

"That's it!" Furious, Eve slapped the screen off manually. "I'm going to slice that worm into pieces. Where the hell is Nadine Furst? If we've got to have a reporter sniffing up our ass, at least she's got a mind."

"I believe she's on Penal Station Omega, a story on prison reform. You might consider a press conference, Eve. The simplest way to deal with this kind of heat is to toss a well-chosen log on the fire."

"Fuck that. What was that broadcast anyway, a report or an editorial?"

"There's little difference since the revised media bill passed thirty years ago. A reporter has the right to flavor a story with his opinion, as long as it's expressed as such."

"I know the damn law." The robe, brilliant with color, swirled around her legs as she turned. "He's not going to get away with insinuating a cover-up. Whitney runs a clean department. I run a clean investigation. And he's not going to get away with using your name to cloud it, either," she continued. "That's what he was leading up to with that excuse for news. That was next."

"He doesn't worry me, Eve. He shouldn't worry you."

"He doesn't worry me. He pisses me off." She closed her eyes and drew a deep breath to settle herself. Slowly, very slowly and very wickedly, she began to smile. "I've got the perfect payback." She opened her eyes again. "How do you think that little bastard would like it if I contacted Furst, gave her an exclusive?"

Roarke set aside his cup. "Come here."

"Why?"

"Never mind." He rose and went to her instead. Cupping her face in his hands, he kissed her hard. "I'm crazy about you."

"I take that to mean you think it's a pretty good idea."

"My late unlamented father taught me one valuable lesson. 'Boy,' he would say to me in the thick brogue of a champion drunk, 'the only way to fight is to fight dirty. The only place to hit is below the belt.' I have a feeling you'll have Morse nursing his balls before the day's out."

"No, he won't be nursing them." Delighted with herself, Eve kissed him back. "Because I'll have sliced them right off."

Roarke gave a mock shudder. "Vicious women are so attractive. Did you say you had a couple of hours?"

"Not anymore."

"I was afraid of that." He stepped back, took a disc from his pocket. "You might find this useful."

"What is it?"

"Some data I put together, on Towers's ex, on Hammett. Files on Mercury."

Her fingers chilled as they closed over the disc. "I didn't ask you to do this."

"No, you didn't. You'd have gotten access to it, but it would have taken you longer. You know if you require my equipment, it's available to you."

She understood he was talking about the room he had, the unregistered equipment that the sensors of Compuguard couldn't detect. "I prefer going through proper channels for the moment."

"As you like. If you change your mind while I'm gone, Summerset's aware you have access."

"Summerset wishes I had access to hell," she muttered.

"Excuse me?"

"Nothing. I've got to get dressed." She turned away, then stopped. "Roarke, I'm working on it."

"On what?"

"On accepting what you seem to feel for me."

He lifted a brow. "Work harder," he suggested.

CHAPTER

THREE

Eve didn't waste time. Her first order of business when she hit her office was to contact Nadine Furst. The 'link buzzed and crackled over the galactic channel. Sunspots, a satellite dink, or simply the aging equipment held up the transmission for several minutes. Finally, a picture wavered onto the screen, then popped into clear focus.

Eve had the pleasure of seeing Nadine's pale, groggy face. She hadn't considered the time difference.

"Dallas." Nadine's normally fluid voice was scratchy and weak. "Jesus, it's the middle of the night here."

"Sorry. You awake, Nadine?"

"Awake enough to hate you."

"Have you been getting Earth news up there?"

"I've been a little busy." Nadine pushed back her tumbled hair and reached for a cigarette.

"When did you start that?"

With a wince, Nadine drew in the first drag. "If you terrestrial cops ever came up here, you'd give tobacco a shot. Even this dog shit you can buy in this rat hole. And anything else you could get your hands on. It's a fucking disgrace." She hitched in more smoke. "Three people to a cage, most of them zoned on smuggled chemicals. The medical facilities are like something out of the twentieth century. They're still sewing people up with string."

"And limited video privileges," Eve finished. "Imagine, treating murderers like criminals. My heart's breaking."

"You can't get a decent meal anywhere in the entire colony," Nadine griped. "What the hell do you want?"

"To make you smile, Nadine. How soon will you be finished up there and back on planet?"

"Depends." As she began to waken fully, Nadine's senses sharpened. "You have something for me."

"Prosecuting Attorney Cicely Towers was murdered about thirty hours ago." Ignoring Nadine's yelp, Eve continued briskly, "Her throat was slashed, and her body was discovered on the sidewalk of Hundred and forty-fourth between Ninth and Tenth."

"Towers. Jesus wept. I had a one-on-one with her two months ago after the DeBlass case. Hundred and forty-fourth?" The wheels were already turning. "Mugging?"

"No. She still had her jewelry and credit tokens. A mugging in that neighborhood wouldn't have left her shoes behind."

"No." Nadine closed her eyes a moment. "Damn. She was a hell of a woman. You're primary?"

"Right the first time."

"Okay." Nadine let out a long breath. "So, why is the primary on what has to be the top case in the country contacting me?"

"The devil you know, Nadine. Your illustrious associate Morse is drooling down my neck."

"Asshole," Nadine muttered, tamping out the cigarette in quick, jerky bumps. "That's why I didn't get word of it. He'd have blocked me out."

"You play square with me, Nadine, I play square with you."

Nadine's eyes sharpened, her nostrils all but quivered. "Exclusive?"

"We'll discuss terms when you get back. Make it fast."

"I'm practically on planet."

Eve smiled at the blank screen. That ought to stick in your greedy craw, C. J., she mused. She was humming as she pushed away from her desk. She had people to see.

By nine A.M., Eve was cooling her heels in the plush living area of George Hammett's uptown apartment. His taste ran to the dramatic, she noted. Huge squares of crimson and white tiles were cool under her boots. The tinkling music of water striking rock sang from the audio of the hologram sweeping an entire wall with an image of the tropics. The silver cushions of the long, low sofa glittered, and when she pushed a finger into one, it gave like silken flesh.

She decided she'd continue to stand.

Objets d'art were placed selectively around the room. A carved tower that resembled the ruins of some ancient castle, the mask of a woman's face embedded in translucent rose-colored glass, what appeared to be a bottle that flashed with vivid, changing colors with the heat of her hand.

When Hammett entered from an adjoining room, Eve concluded that he was every bit as dramatic as his surroundings.

He looked pale, heavy eyed, but it only increased his stunning looks. He was tall and elegantly slim. His face was poetically hollowed at the cheeks. Unlike many of his contemporaries—Eve knew him to be in his sixties—he had opted to let his hair gray naturally. An excellent choice for him, she thought, as his thick lion's mane was as gleaming a silver as one of Roarke's Georgian candlesticks.

His eyes were the same striking color, though they were dulled now with what might have been grief or weariness.

He crossed to her, cupped her hand in both of his. "Eve." When his lips brushed her cheek, she winced. He was making the connection personal. She thought they both knew it.

"George," she began, subtly drawing back. "I appreciate your time."

"Nonsense. I'm sorry I had to keep you waiting. A call I had to complete." He gestured toward the sofa, the sleeves of his casual shirt billowing with the movement. Eve resigned herself to sitting on it. "What can I offer you?"

"Nothing, really."

"Coffee." He smiled a little. "I recall you're very fond of it. I have some of Roarke's blend." He pressed a button on the arm of the sofa. A small screen popped up. "A pot of Argentine Gold," he ordered, "two cups." Then, with that faint and sober smile still on his lips, he turned back to her. "It'll help me relax," he explained. "I'm not surprised to find you here this morning, Eve. Or perhaps I should be calling you Lieutenant Dallas, under the circumstances."

"Then you understand why I'm here."

"Of course. Cicely. I can't get used to it." His cream-over-cream voice shook a little. "I've heard it countless times on the news. I've spoken with her children and with Marco. But I can't seem to take in the fact that she's gone."

"You saw her the night she was killed."

A muscle in his cheek jerked. "Yes. We had dinner. We often did when our schedules allowed. Once a week at least. More, if we could manage it. We were close."

He paused as a small server droid glided in with the coffee. Hammett poured it himself, concentrating on the small task almost fiercely. "How close?" he murmured, and Eve saw his hand wasn't quite steady as he lifted his cup. "Intimate. We'd been lovers, exclusive lovers, for several years. I loved her very much."

"You maintained separate residences."

"Yes, she—we both preferred it that way. Our tastes, aesthetically speaking, were very different, and the simple truth was we both liked our independence and personal space. We enjoyed each other more, I think, by keeping a certain distance." He took a long breath. "But it was no secret that we had a relationship, at least not among our families and friends." He let the breath out. "Publicly, we both preferred to keep our private lives private. I don't expect that will be possible now."

"I doubt it."

He shook his head. "It doesn't matter. What should matter is finding out who did this to her. I just can't seem to work myself up about it. Nothing can change the fact that she's gone. Cicely was," he said slowly, "the most admirable woman I've ever known."

Every instinct, human and cop, told her this was a man in deep mourning, but she knew that even killers mourned their dead. "I need you to tell me what time you last saw her. George, I'm recording this."

"Yes, of course. It was about ten o'clock. We had dinner at Robert's on East Twelfth. We shared a cab after. I dropped her off first. About ten," he repeated. "I know I got in about quarter after because I had several messages waiting."

"Was that your usual routine?"

"What? Oh." He snapped himself back from some inner world. "We really didn't have one. Often we'd come back here, or go to her apartment. Now and again, when we felt adventurous, we'd take a suite at the Palace for a night." He broke off, and his eyes were suddenly blank and devastated as he shoved off the soft, silver sofa. "Oh God. My God."

"I'm sorry." Useless, she knew, against grief. "I'm so sorry."

"I'm starting to believe it," he said in a voice thick and low. "It's worse, I realize, when you begin to believe it. She laughed when she got out of the cab, and she blew me a kiss from her fingertips. She had such beautiful hands. And I went home, and forgot about her because I had messages waiting. I was in bed by midnight, took a mild tranq because I had an early meeting. While I was in bed, safe, she was lying dead in the rain. I don't know if I can bear that." He turned back, his already pale face bloodless now. "I don't know if I can bear it."

She couldn't help him. Even though his pain was so tangible she could feel it herself, she couldn't help him. "I wish I could do this later, give you time, but I just can't. As far as we know, you're the last person who saw her alive."

"Except her killer." He drew himself up. "Unless, of course, I killed her."

"It would be best for everyone if I ruled that out quickly."

"Yes, naturally, it would—Lieutenant."

She accepted the bitterness in his voice and did her job. "If you could give me the name of the cab company so that I can verify your movements."

"The restaurant called for one. I believe it was a Rapid."

"Did you see or speak with anyone between the hours of midnight and two A.M.?"

"I told you, I took a pill and was in bed by midnight. Alone."

She could verify that with the building security discs, though she had reason to know such things could be doctored. "Can you tell me her mood when you left her?"

"She was a bit distracted, the case she was prosecuting. Optimistic about it. We talked a bit about her children, her daughter in particular. Mirina's planning on getting married next fall. Cicely was pleased with the idea, and excited because Mirina wanted a big wedding with all the old-fashioned trimmings."

"Did she mention anything that was worrying her? Anything or anyone she was concerned about?"

"Nothing that would apply to this. The right wedding gown, flowers. Her hopes that she could swing the maximum sentence in the case."

"Did she mention any threats, any unusual transmissions, messages, contacts?"

"No." He put a hand over his eyes briefly, let it drop to his side. "Don't you think I'd have told you if I had the slightest inkling of why this happened?"

"Why would she have gone to the Upper West Side at that time of night?"

"I have no idea."

"Was she in the habit of meeting snitches, sources?"

He opened his mouth then closed it again. "I don't know," he murmured, struck by it. "I wouldn't have thought . . . but she was so stubborn, so sure of herself."

"Her relationship with her former husband. How would you describe it?"

"Friendly. A bit reserved, but amiable. They were both devoted to the children and that united them. He was a little annoyed when we became intimate, but . . ." Hammett broke off, stared at Eve. "You can't possibly think . . ." With what might have been a laugh, he covered his face. "Marco Angelini skulking around that neighborhood with a knife, plotting to kill his ex? No, Lieutenant." He dropped his hands again. "Marco has his flaws, but he'd never hurt Cicely. And the sight of blood would offend his sense of propriety. He's much too cold, much too conservative to resort to violence. And he'd have no reason, no possible motive for wishing her harm."

That, Eve thought, was for her to decide.

She tripped from one world to another by leaving Hammett's apartment and going to the West End. Here she would find no silvery cushions, no tinkling waterfalls. Instead there were cracked sidewalks, ignored by the latest spruce-up-the-city campaign, graffiti-laced buildings that invited the onlookers to fuck all manner of man and beast. Storefronts were covered by security grills, which were so much cheaper and less effective than the force fields employed in the posher areas.

She wouldn't have been surprised to see a few rodents overlooked by the feline droids that roamed the alleyways.

Of the two-legged rodents, she saw plenty. One chemi-head grinned at her toothily and rubbed his crotch proudly. A street hawker sized her up quickly and accurately as cop, ducked his head under the wreath of feathers he sported around his magenta hair, and scurried off to safer pastures.

A selected list of drugs were still illegal. Some cops actually bothered to pay attention.

At the moment, Eve wasn't one of them. Unless a little arm twisting helped her get answers.

The rain had washed most of the blood away. The sweepers from the department would have sucked up anything in the immediate area that could be sifted through for evidence. But she stood for a moment over the spot where Towers had died, and she had no trouble envisioning the scene.

Now, she needed to work backward. Had she stood here, Eve wondered, facing her killer? Most likely. Did she see the knife before it sliced across her throat? Possibly. But not quickly enough to react with anything more than a jerk, a gasp.

Lifting her gaze, Eve scanned the street. Her skin prickled, but she ignored the stares of those leaning against the buildings or loitering around rusting cars.

Cicely Towers had come uptown. Not by cab. There was, to date, no record of a pickup or drop-off from any of the official companies. Eve doubted she would have been foolish enough to try a gypsy.

The subway, she deduced. It was fast and, with the scanners and droid cops, safe as a church, at least until you hit the street. Eve spotted the signal for the underground less than half a block away.

The subway, she decided. Maybe she was in a hurry? Annoyed to be dragged out on a wet night. Sure of herself, as Hammett had said. She wouldn't have been afraid.

She marched up the stairs to the street in her power suit, her expensive shoes. She—

Stopping, Eve narrowed her eyes. No umbrella? Where was her damn umbrella? A meticulous woman, a practical organized woman didn't go out in the rain without protection. Briskly, Eve pulled out her recorder and muttered a note to herself to check on it.

Was the killer waiting for her on the street? In a room? She studied the disintegrating brick of the unrehabbed buildings. A bar? One of the flesh clubs?

"Hey, white girl."

Brows knit, Eve turned at the interruption. The man was tall as a house and from the deepness of his complexion, a full black. He sported, as many did in this part of town, feathers in his hair. His cheek tattoo was vivid green and in the shape of a grinning human skull. He wore an open red vest and matching pants snug enough to show the bulge of his cock.

"Hey, black boy," she said in the same casually insulting tone.

He flashed a wide, dazzling grin at her from an unbelievably ugly face. "You looking for action?" He jerked his head toward the garish sign of the all-nude club across the street. "You a little skinny, but they be hiring. Don't get many white as you. Mostly mixed." He chucked her under the chin with fingers the width of soy wieners. "I be the bouncer, put in a word for you."

"Now why would you do that?"

"Out of the goodness of my heart, and five percent of your tips, honeypot. A long white girl like you make plenty jiggling her stuff."

"I appreciate the thought, but I've got a job." Almost with regret, she pulled out her badge.

He whistled through his teeth. "Now how come I don't be seeing that? White girl, you just don't smell like cop."

"Must be the new soap I'm using. Got a name?"

"They just call me Crack. That's the sound it makes when I bust heads." He grinned again, and illustrated by bringing his two huge hands together. "Crack! Get it?"

"I'm catching on. Were you on the door night before last, Crack?"

"Now, I'm sorry to say I was otherwise engaged, and missed all the excitement. That be my night off, and I spent it catching up on cultural events."

"And those events were?"

"Vampire flick festival down to Grammercy, with my current young nibble. I sure do enjoy watching them bloodsuckers. But I hear we had ourselves a show right here. Got ourselves a dead lawyer. Big, important, fancy one, too. White girl, wasn't she? Just like you, honeypot."

"That's right. What else do you hear?"

"Me?" He trailed a finger down the front of his vest. The nail on his index finger was sharpened to a lethal point and painted black. "I'm too dignified to listen to street talk."

"I bet you are." Understanding the rules, Eve slipped a hundred-credit token from her pocket. "How about I buy a little of that dignity?"

"Well, the price, she looks right." His big hand enveloped the tokens and made them disappear. "I hear she was hanging around in the Five Moons 'long about midnight, give or take. Like she was hanging for somebody, somebody who don't show. Then she ditched."

He glanced down at the sidewalk. "Didn't go far though, did she?"

"No, she didn't. Did she ask for anyone?"

"Not so's I heard."

"Anyone see her with anyone?"

"Bad night. People stay off the street mostly. Some chemi-heads maybe wander, but business going to be slow."

"You know anyone around here who likes to cut?"

"Plenty carry blades and stickers, white girl." His eyes rolled in amusement. "Why you going to carry if you ain't going to use?"

"Anybody just likes to cut," she repeated. "Somebody who doesn't care about making a score."

His grin spread again. The skull on his cheek seemed to nod with the movement. "Everybody cares about making a score. Ain't you trying to?"

She accepted that. "Who do you know around here who's out of a cage recently?"

His laugh was like mortar fire. "Better if you ask don't I know anybody who ain't. And your money's done."

"All right." To his disappointment, she took a card rather than more tokens out of her pocket. "There may be more if you hear anything I can use."

"Keep it in mind. You decide you want to earn a little extra shaking those little white tits, you let Crack know." With this, he loped across the street with the surprising grace of an enormous black gazelle.

Eve turned and went in to try her luck at the Five Moons.

The dive might have seen better days, but she doubted it. It was strictly a drinking establishment: no dancers, no screens, no videos booths. The clientele who patronized the Five Moons weren't there to socialize. From the smell that slapped Eve the moment she stepped through the door, burning off stomach lining was the order of the day.

Even at this hour, the small, square room was well populated. Silent drinkers stood at stingy pedestals knocking back their poison of choice. Others huddled by the bar, closer to the bottles. Eve rated a few glances as she crossed the sticky floor, then people got back to the business of serious drinking.

The bartender was a droid, as most were, but she doubted this one had been programmed to listen cheerfully to the customers' hard luck stories. More likely an arm breaker, she mused, sizing it up as she sidled up to the bar. The manufacturers had given him the tilted eye, golden-skinned appearance of a mixed race. Unlike most of the drinkers, the droid didn't sport feathers or beads, but a plain white smock over a wrestler's body.

Droids couldn't be bribed, she thought with some regret. And threats had to be both clever and logical.

"Drink?" the droid demanded. His voice had a ping to it, a slight echo that indicated overdue maintenance problems.

"No." Eve wanted to keep her health. She showed her badge and had several customers shifting toward corners. "There was a murder two nights ago."

"Not in here."

"But the victim was."

"She was alive then." At some signal Eve didn't catch, the droid took a smudged glass from a drinker midbar, poured some noxious looking liquid into it, and slid it back.

"You were on duty."

"I'm a twenty-four/seven," he told her, indicating he was programmed for full operation without required rest or recharge periods.

"Did you ever see the victim before, in here, around the area?"

"No."

"Who did she meet here?"

"No one."

Eve drummed her fingers on the cloudy surface of the bar. "Okay, let's just make this simple. You tell me what time she came in, what she did, when she left, and how she left."

"I am not required to maintain surveillance on the customers."

"Right." Slowly, Eve rubbed a finger on the bar. When she lifted it, she pursed her lips at the smear of gunk staining the tip. "I'm Homicide, but I'm not required to overlook health violations. You know, I think if I called the Sensor Bugs in here, and they did a sweep, why they'd be shocked. So shocked they'd delete the liquor license."

As threats went, she didn't think it was particularly clever, but it was logical.

The droid took a moment to access the probabilities. "The

woman came in at oh sixteen. She didn't drink. She left at one twelve. Alone."

"Did she speak to anyone?"

"She said nothing."

"Was she looking for someone?"

"I didn't ask."

Eve lifted a brow. "You observed her. Did it appear she was looking for someone?"

"It appeared, but she found no one."

"But she stayed nearly an hour. What did she do?"

"Stood, looked, frowned. Checked her watch often. Left."

"Did anyone follow her outside?"

"No."

Absently, Eve scrubbed her soiled finger on her jeans. "Did she have an umbrella?"

The droid looked as surprised by the question as droids were capable of looking. "Yes, a purple one, the same color as her suit."

"Did she leave with it?"

"Yes; it was raining."

Eve nodded, then worked her way through the bar, questioning unhappy customers.

All she really wanted when she returned to Cop Central was a long shower. An hour in the Five Moons had left what felt like a thin layer of muck on her skin. Even her teeth, she thought, running her tongue over them.

But the report came first. She swung into her office, then stopped, studying the wiry-haired man sitting at her desk plucking candied almonds from a bag.

"Nice work if you can get it."

Feeney crossed the feet he'd propped on the edge of her desk. "Good to see you, Dallas. You're a busy lady."

"Some of us cops actually work for a living. Others just play computer games all day."

"You should've taken my advice and worked on your comp skills."

With more affection than annoyance, she knocked his feet from the desk and plopped her butt down in the vacated space. "You just passing by?"

"I've come to offer my services, old pal." Generously, he held out the bag of nuts.

She munched and watched him. He had a hangdog face, one he had never bothered to have enhanced. Baggy eyes, the beginning of jowls, ears that were slightly too big for his head. She liked it just the way it was.

"Why?"

"Well, I got three reasons. First, the commander made an unofficial request; second, I had a lot of admiration for the prosecutor."

"Whitney called you?"

"Unofficially," Feeney explained again. "He thought that if you had someone with my outstanding skills working the data route with you, we'd tie this thing up faster. Never hurts to have a direct line to the Electronic Detection Division."

She considered it, and because she knew Feeney's skills were indeed outstanding, she approved. "Are you going to sign on the case officially or unofficially?"

"That's up to you."

"Then let's make it officially, Feeney."

He grinned and winked. "I figured you'd say that."

"The first thing I need you to do is run the victim's 'link. There's no record either on the log or on the security tapes that she had a visitor the night she was killed. So somebody called her, arranged a meet."

"Good as done."

"And I need a run on everybody she put away—"

"Everybody?" he interrupted, only slightly appalled.

"Everybody." Her face broke into sunny smiles. "I figure you can do it in about half the time I could. I need relatives, loved ones, associates, too. Also cases in progress and pending."

"Jesus, Dallas." But he rolled his shoulders, flexed his fingers like a pianist about to play a concert. "My wife's going to miss me."

"Being married to a cop sucks," she said, patting his shoulder.

"Is that what Roarke says?"

She dropped her hand. "We're not married."

Feeney merely hummed in his throat. He enjoyed seeing Eve's quick frown, quick nerves. "So how's he doing?"

"He's fine. He's in Australia." Her hands found their way into her pockets. "He's fine."

"Uh-huh. Caught the two of you on the news a few weeks ago. At some fancy do at the Palace. You look real sharp in a dress, Dallas."

She shifted uncomfortably, caught herself, and shrugged. "I didn't know you took in the gossip channels."

"Love them," he said unrepentantly. "Must be interesting, leading that high life."

"It has its moments," she muttered. "Are we going to discuss my social life, Feeney, or investigate a murder?"

"We'll have to make time to do both." He rose and stretched. "I'll go run the check on the victim's 'link before I get started on the years of perps she put away. I'll be in touch."

"Feeney." When he turned at her door, she cocked her head. "You said there were three reasons you wanted in. You only gave me two."

"Number three, I missed you, Dallas." He grinned. "Damn if I haven't missed you."

She was smiling when she sat down to work. Damn if she hadn't missed him, too.

CHAPTER

FOUR

The Blue Squirrel was one teetering step up from the Five Moons. Eve had a cautious affection for it. There were times she even enjoyed the noise, the press of bodies, and the ever-changing costumes of the clientele. Most of the time she enjoyed the stage show.

The featured singer was one of the rare people Eve considered a genuine friend. The friendship might have had its roots in Eve's arrest of Mavis Freestone several years earlier, but it had flowered, nonetheless. Mavis might have gone straight, but she would never go ordinary.

Tonight, the slim, exuberant woman was screeching out her lyrics against the scream of trumpets, the brass waved by a three-piece female band on the holoscreen backdrop. That, and the quality of the single wine Eve had risked were enough to make her eyes water.

For tonight's show, Mavis's hair was a stunning emerald green. Eve knew Mavis preferred jewel colors. She continued the theme with the single swatch of glistening sapphire material she had somehow draped over herself to cover one generous breast and her crotch. Her other breast was decorated with shimmering stones, with a strategically placed silver star over the nipple.

One misplaced stud or swatch, and the Blue Squirrel could be fined for exceeding its license. The proprietors weren't willing to pay the hefty fee for nude class.

When Mavis whirled, Eve saw that the singer's heart-shaped butt was similarly decorated on each slim cheek. Just, she mused, within the limits of the law.

The crowd loved her. When she stepped from the stage after her set, it was to thunderous applause and drunken cheers. Patrons in the private smoking booths thumped fists enthusiastically on their tiny tables.

"How do you sit down in that?" Eve asked when Mavis arrived at her booth.

"Slowly, carefully, and with great discomfort." Mavis demonstrated, then let out a sigh. "What'd you think of the last number?"

"A real crowd pleaser."

"I wrote it."

"No shit?" Eve hadn't understood a single word, but pride swelled, nonetheless. "That's great, Mavis. I'm awed."

"I might have a shot at a recording contract." Beneath the glitter on her face, Mavis's cheeks flushed. "And I got a raise."

"Well, here's to it." In toast, Eve lifted her glass.

"I didn't know you were coming in tonight." Mavis punched her code into the menu and ordered bubble water. She had to baby her throat for the next set.

"I'm meeting someone."

"Roarke?" Mavis's eyes, currently green, shone. "Is he coming? I'll have to do that last number again."

"He's in Australia. I'm meeting Nadine Furst."

Mavis's disappointment at the opportunity to impress Roarke shifted quickly to surprise. "You're meeting a reporter? On purpose?"

"I can trust her." Eve lifted a shoulder. "I can use her."

"If you say so. Hey, you think maybe she'd do a piece on me?"

Not for worlds would Eve have extinguished the light in Mavis's eyes. "I'll mention it."

"Decent. Listen, tomorrow's my night off. Want to catch some dinner or hang someplace?"

"If I can manage it. But I thought you were seeing that performance artist—the one with the pet monkey."

"Flicked him off." Mavis illustrated by brushing a finger over her bare shoulder. "He was just too static. Gotta go." She slid out of the booth, her butt decor making little scraping sounds. Her emerald hair gleamed in the swirling lights as she edged through the crowd.

Eve decided she didn't want to know what Mavis considered too static.

When her communicator hummed, Eve pulled it out and punched in her code. Roarke's face filled the miniscreen. Her first reaction, unbidden, was a huge, delighted smile.

"Lieutenant, I've tracked you down."

"Apparently so." She worked on dimming the smile. "This is an official channel, Roarke."

"Is it?" His brow lifted. "It doesn't sound like official surroundings. The Blue Squirrel."

"I'm meeting someone. How's Australia?"

"Crowded. With luck I'll be back within thirty-six hours. I'll find you."

"I'm not hard to find." She smiled again. "Obviously. Listen." To amuse them both, she tilted the unit as Mavis roared into her next set.

"She's unique," Roarke managed after several bars. "Give her my best."

"I will. I'll—ah—see you when you get back."

"Count on it. You'll think of me."

"Sure. Safe trip, Roarke."

"Eve, I love you."

She let out a baffled breath when his image dissolved.

"Well, well." Nadine Furst moved from her position behind Eve's shoulder and slid into the booth opposite. "Wasn't that sweet?"

Torn between annoyance and embarrassment, Eve jammed her communicator back in her pocket. "I thought you had more class than to eavesdrop."

"Any reporter worth her salary eavesdrops, Lieutenant. Just like a good cop." Nadine stretched back in the booth. "So, what does it feel like to have a man like Roarke in love with you?"

Even if she could have explained it, Eve wouldn't have. "Thinking of switching from hard news to the romance channel, Nadine?"

Nadine merely held up a hand, then let out a sigh when she scanned the club. "I can't believe you wanted to meet here again. The food's terrible."

"But the atmosphere, Nadine, the atmosphere."

Mavis hit a piercing note and Nadine shuddered. "Fine, it's your deal."

"You got back on planet quickly."

"I managed to catch a flash transport. One of your boyfriend's."

"Roarke's not a boy."

"You're telling me. Anyway . . ." Nadine waved that away. She was obviously tired and a little lagged. "I've got to eat, even if it kills me." She scanned the menu and settled dubiously on the stuffed shells supreme. "What are you drinking?"

"Number fifty-four; it's supposed to be a chardonnay." Experimentally, Eve sipped again. "It's at least three steps up from horse piss. I recommend it."

"Fine." Nadine programmed her order and sat back again. "I was able to access all the data available on the Towers's homicide on the trip back. Everything the media has broadcast so far."

"Morse know you're back?"

Nadine's smile was thin and feral. "Oh, he knows. I've got seniority on the crime beat. I'm in, he's out. And is he pissed!"

"Then my mission is a success."

"But it's not complete. You promised an exclusive."

"And I'll deliver." Eve studied the noodle dish that slid through the serving slot. It didn't look half bad. "Under my terms, Nadine. What I feed you, you broadcast when I give you the light."

"What else is new?" Nadine sampled the first shell, decided it was nearly palatable.

"I'll see that you get more data, and that you get it ahead of the pack."

"And when you've got a suspect."

"You'll get the name first."

Trusting Eve's word, Nadine nodded as she forked up another shell. "Plus a one-on-one with the suspect and another with you."

"I can't guarantee the suspect. You know I can't," Eve continued before Nadine could interrupt. "The perp has rights to choose his own media, or to refuse it all. The best I can do is suggest, maybe even encourage."

"I want pictures. Don't tell me you can't guarantee. You can find a way to see that I get video of the arrest. I want to be on the scene."

"I'll weigh that in when the time comes. In exchange, I want everything you have, every tip that comes in, every rumor, every story lead. No broadcast surprises."

Nadine slipped pasta between her lips. "I can't guarantee," she said sweetly. "My associates have their own agenda."

"What you know, when you know it," Eve said flatly. "And anything that comes out of intramedia espionage." At Nadine's innocent expression, Eve snorted. "Stations spy on stations, reporters spy on reporters. Getting the story on air first is the name of the game. You've got a good batting average, Nadine, or I wouldn't be bothering with you."

"I'll say the same." Nadine sipped her wine. "And for the most part, I trust you, even if you have no taste in wine. This is barely one step up from horse piss."

Eve sat back and laughed. It felt good, it felt easy, and when Nadine grinned in return, they had a deal.

"Let me see yours," Nadine requested. "And I'll let you see mine."

"The biggest thing I've got," Eve began, "is a missing umbrella."

Eve met Feeney at Cicely Towers's apartment at ten the following morning. One look at his hangdog expression and she knew the news wasn't going to be sunny.

"What wall did you hit?"

"On the 'link." He waited while Eve disarmed the police security on the door, then followed her inside. "She had plenty of transmissions, kept the unit on auto record. Your tag was on the disc."

"That's right, I took it into evidence. Are you trying to tell me no one contacted her to arrange a meet at the Five Moons?"

"I'm trying to tell you I can't tell you." In disgust, Feeney ran a hand through his wiry hair. "Her last call came in at eleven thirty, the transmission ended at eleven forty-three."

"And?"

"She erased the recording. I can get the times, but that's it. The communication, audio, video, are zapped. She zapped them," he continued. "From this unit."

"She erased the call," Eve murmured and began to pace. "Why would she do that? She had the unit on auto; that's standard for law enforcers, even for personal calls. But she erased this one. Because she didn't want any record of who called and why."

She turned back. "You're sure nobody tampered with the disc after it was in evidence?"

Feeney looked pained, then insulted. "Dallas," was all he said.

"Okay, okay, so she zapped it before she went out. That tells me she wasn't afraid, personally, but was protecting herself—or somebody else. If it had to do with a case, she'd have wanted it on record. She'd have made damn sure it was on record."

"I'd say so. If it was a snitch, she could have put a lock on it under her private code, but it doesn't make sense to zap it."

"We'll check her cases anyway, all the way back." She didn't have to see his face to know Feeney was rolling his eyes. "Let me think," she muttered. "She left City Hall at nineteen twenty-six. That's on her log. And several witnesses saw her. Her last stop was the women's lounge where she freshened up for the evening and chatted with an associate. The associate tells me her mood was calm but upbeat. She'd had a good day in court."

"Fluentes is going up. She laid the groundwork. Taking her out won't change that."

"He might have thought different. We'll see about that. She didn't come back here." Frowning, Eve scanned the room. "She didn't have time, so she went straight to the restaurant and met Hammett. I've been by there. His story and his time frame check out with the staff."

"You've been busy."

"Time's passing. The maître d' called them a cab, a Rapid. They were picked up at a twenty-one forty-eight. It was starting to rain."

In her mind, Eve pictured it. The handsome couple in the back of the cab, chatting, maybe brushing fingertips while the cab zipped uptown with raindrops pattering on the roof. She'd been wearing a red dress and matching jacket, according to their server. Power colors for court that she'd dressed up with good pearls and silver heels for the evening.

"The cab dropped her off first," Eve continued. "She told Hammett not to get out, why get wet? She was laughing when she ran for the building, then turned and blew him a kiss."

"Your report said they were tight."

"He loved her." More from habit than hunger, she dipped a hand into the bag Feeney held out. "Doesn't mean he didn't kill her, but he loved her. According to him, they were both happy with their arrangement, but . . ." She lifted her shoulders. "If he wasn't, and was looking to set up a good alibi, he set a nice romantic, cozy stage. It doesn't work for me, but it's early yet. So, she came up," Eve continued, moving to the door. "Her dress is a little damp, so she goes to the bedroom to hang it up."

As she spoke, Eve followed the projected route, walking over the lovely rugs into the spacious bedroom with its quiet colors and lovely antique bed.

She ordered lights to brighten the area. The police shields on the windows not only frustrated the fly-bys, but blocked most of the sunlight.

"To the closet," she said and pressed the button that opened the long, mirrored sliding doors. "She hangs up the suit." Eve pointed to the red dress and jacket, neatly arranged in a wardrobe ordered in sweeps of color. "Puts away her shoes, puts on a robe."

Eve turned to the bed. A long flow of ivory was spread there. Not folded, not neatly arranged as was the rest of the room, but rumpled, as though it had been impatiently tossed.

"She puts her jewelry in the safe in the side wall of the closet, but she doesn't go to bed. Maybe she goes out to catch the news, to have a nightcap."

With Feeney following, Eve went back to the living area. A brief-case, neatly closed, sat on the table in front of the sofa with a single empty glass beside it.

"She's relaxing, maybe thinking over the evening, rehearsing her court strategy for the next day or her planning her daughter's wedding. Her 'link beeps. Whoever it was, whatever they tell her, gets her moving. She's settled in for the night, but she goes back to the bedroom, after she's zapped the record. She dresses again. Another power suit. She's going to the West End. She doesn't want to blend, she wants to exude authority, confidence. She doesn't call a cab. That's another record. She decides she'll take the subway. It's raining."

Eve moved to a closet tucked into the wall near the front door and pressed it to open. Inside were jackets, wraps, a man's overcoat she suspected was Hammett's, and a fleet of umbrellas in varying colors.

"She takes out the umbrella she bought to match the suit. It's automatic, her mind is on her meet. She doesn't take a lot of money, so it's not a payoff. She doesn't call anyone, because she wants to handle it herself. But when she gets to the Five Moons, nobody meets her. She waits nearly an hour, impatient, checking her watch. She leaves a few minutes after one, back into the rain. She's got her umbrella and starts to walk back to the subway. I figure she's steamed."

"Classy woman, kicking in a dive for an hour for a no show." Feeney popped another nut. "Yeah, steamed would be my take."

"So, she heads out. It's raining pretty hard. Her umbrella's up. She only gets a few feet. Someone's there, probably been close by all along, waiting for her to come out."

"Doesn't want to see her inside," Feeney put in. "Doesn't want to be seen."

"Right. They have to talk a couple of minutes according to the time frame. Maybe they argue—not much of an argument, there isn't time. Nobody's on the street—nobody who'd pay attention, anyway. A couple of minutes later, her throat's slashed, she's bleeding on the sidewalk. Did he plan to do her all along?"

"Lotsa people carry stickers in that area." Thoughtful, Feeney rubbed his chin. "Couldn't get premeditated on that by itself. But the timing, the setup. Yeah, that's how it shakes down to me."

"Me, too. One slice. No defensive wounds, so she didn't have time to feel threatened. The killer doesn't take her jewelry, the leather bag, her shoes, or her credits. He just takes her umbrella, and he walks away."

"Why the umbrella?" Feeney wondered.

"Hell, it's raining. I don't know, an impulse, a souvenir. As far as I can see, it's the only mistake he made. I've got grunts out checking a ten-block area to see if he ditched it."

"If he ditched it in that area, some chemi-head's walking around with a purple parasol."

"Yeah." A visual of that almost made her smile. "How could he be sure she'd zap the recording, Feeney? He had to be sure."

"Threat?"

"A PA lives with threats. One like Towers would shake them off like lint."

"If they were aimed at her," he agreed. "She's got kids." He nodded toward the framed holograms. "She wasn't just a lawyer. She was a mother."

With a frown, Eve walked over to the holograms. Curious, she picked up one of the boy and girl together as young teenagers. A flick of her finger over the back had the audio bubbling out.

Hey, big shot. Happy Mother's Day. This will last longer than the flowers. We love you.

Oddly disturbed, Eve set the frame down again. "They're adults now. They're not kids anymore."

"Dallas, once a parent, always a parent. You never finish the job."

Hers had, she thought. A long time finished.

"Then I guess my next stop is Marco Angelini."

Angelini had offices in Roarke's building on Fifth. Eve stepped into the now familiar lobby with its huge tiles and pricey boutiques. The cooing voices of computer guides offered assistance to various locations. She scanned one of the moving maps and ignoring the glides, hiked her way to the elevators along the south end.

The glass tube shot her to the fifty-eighth floor, then opened onto solemn gray carpet and blinding white walls.

Angelini Exports claimed a suite of five offices in this location. After one quick scan, Eve noted that the company was small potatoes in relation to Roarke Industries.

Then again, she thought with a tight smile, what isn't?

The receptionist in the greeting area showed great respect and not a little nerves at the sight of Eve's badge. She fumbled and swallowed so much Eve wondered if the woman had a cache of illegal substances in her desk drawer.

But the fear of cop had her all but shoving Eve into Angelini's office after less than ninety seconds of lag time.

"Mr. Angelini, I appreciate your time. My sympathies for your loss."

"Thank you, Lieutenant Dallas, please sit."

He wasn't elegant, as Hammett was, but he was powerful. A small man, solidly built with jet hair combed slickly back from a prominent widow's peak. His skin was a pale, dusky gold, his eyes bright, hard marbles of azure under thick brows. He had a long nose, thin lips, and the glitter of a diamond on his hand.

If he was grieving, the former husband of the victim hid it better than her lover had.

He sat behind a console-style desk that was smooth as satin. It was absolutely clear but for his still and folded hands. Behind him was a tinted window that blocked the UV rays while letting in the view of New York.

"You've come about Cicely."

"Yes, I was hoping you could spare some time now to answer some questions."

"You have my full cooperation, Lieutenant. Cicely and I were divorced, but we remained partners, in business and in parenthood. I admired and respected her."

There was a hint of his native country in his voice. Just a whisper of it. It reminded her that, according to his dossier, Marco Angelini spent a large part of his time in Italy.

"Mr. Angelini, can you tell me the last time you saw or spoke with Prosecutor Towers?"

"I saw her on March eighteenth, at my home on Long Island."

"She came to your home."

"Yes, for my son's twenty-fifth birthday. We gave him a party together, using my estate there, as it was most convenient. David, our son, often stays there when he is on the East Coast."

"You hadn't seen her since that date."

"No, we were both busy, but we had planned to meet in the next week or two to discuss plans for Mirina's wedding. Our daughter." He cleared his throat gently. "I was in Europe for most of April."

"You called Prosecutor Towers on the night of her death."

"Yes, I left a message to see if we could meet for lunch or drinks at her convenience."

"About the wedding," Eve prompted.

"Yes, about Mirina's wedding."

"Had you spoken with Prosecutor Towers since the day of March eighteenth and the night of her death?"

"Several times." He pulled his fingers apart, linked them again. "As I said, we considered ourselves partners. We had the children, and there were a few business interests."

"Including Mercury."

"Yes." His lips curved ever so slightly. "You are an . . . acquaintance of Roarke's."

"That's right. Did you and your former wife disagree on any of your partnerships, personally or professionally?"

"Naturally we did, on both. But we'd learned, as we had been unable to learn during our marriage, the value of compromise."

"Mr. Angelini, who inherits Prosecutor Towers's interest in Mercury after her death?"

His brow lifted. "I do, Lieutenant, according to the terms of our business contract. There are also a few holdings in some real estate that will revert to me. This was an arrangement of our divorce settlement. I would guide the interests, advise her on investments. Upon the death of one of us, the interests and profits or losses would revert to the other. We both agreed, you see, and trusted that in the end, all either of us had of value would go to our children."

"And the rest of her estate. Her apartment, her jewelry, whatever possessions that weren't part of your agreement?"

"Would, I assume, be left to our children. I imagine there would be a few bequests to personal friends or charities."

Eve was going to dig quickly to learn just how much Towers had tucked away. "Mr. Angelini, you were aware that your ex-wife was intimately involved with George Hammett."

"Naturally."

"And this was . . . not a problem?"

"A problem? Do you mean, Lieutenant, did I, after nearly twelve years of divorce, harbor homicidal jealousy for my ex-wife? And did I slice the throat of the mother of my children and leave her dead on the street?"

"In words to that effect, Mr. Angelini."

He said something in Italian under his breath. Something, Eve suspected, uncomplimentary. "No, I did not kill Cicely."

"Can you tell me your whereabouts on the night of her death?"

She could see his jaw tense and noticed the control it took for him to relax it again, but his eyes never flickered. She imagined he could stare a hole through steel.

"I was at home in my townhouse from eight o'clock on."

"Alone?"

"Yes."

"Did you see or speak with anyone who can verify that?"

"No. I have two domestics, and both were out on their night off, which was why I was home. I wanted quiet and privacy for an evening."

"You made no calls, received none during the evening?"

"I received a call at about three A.M. from Commander Whitney informing me of my wife's death. I was in bed, alone, when the call came in."

"Mr. Angelini, your ex-wife was in a West End dive at one o'clock in the morning. Why?"

"I haven't any idea. No idea at all."

Later, when Eve stepped into the glass tube to descend, she beeped Feeney. "I want to know if Marco Angelini was in any kind of financial squeeze, and how much that squeeze would have loosened at his ex-wife's sudden death."

"You smell something, Dallas?"

"Something," she muttered. "I just don't know what."

CHAPTER
FIVE

Eve stumbled into her apartment at nearly one A.M. Her head was ringing. Mavis's idea of dinner on her night off had been to take in a rival club. Already aware she would pay for the evening's entertainment in the morning, Eve stripped on the way to the bedroom.

At least the evening out with Mavis had pushed the Towers case out of her mind. Eve might have worried she had no mind left, but she was too exhausted to think about it.

She fell naked and facedown on the bed and was asleep in seconds.

Eve woke, violently aroused.

It was Roarke's hands on her. She knew their texture, their rhythm. Her heart tripped against her ribs, then bounded into her throat as his mouth covered hers. His was greedy, hot, giving her no choice, really no choice at all but to respond in kind. Even as she fumbled for him, those long, clever fingers pierced her, diving into her so that she bowed up into the frenzy of orgasm.

His mouth on her breast, sucking, teeth scraping. His elegant hands relentless so that her cries came out in whimpers of shock and gratitude. Another staggering climax to layer thick over the first.

Her hands sought purchase in the tangled sheets, but nothing could anchor her. As she flew up again, she gripped him, nails scraping down his back, up to grab handfuls of his hair.

"God!" It was the single coherent word she managed as he plunged into her, so hard, so deep she was amazed she didn't die from the pleasure of it. Her body bucked helplessly, frantically, continued to shudder even after he'd collapsed on her.

He let out a long, satisfied sigh and lazily nuzzled her ear. "Sorry to wake you."

"Roarke? Oh, was that you?"

He bit her.

She smiled quietly in the dark. "I didn't think you'd be back until tomorrow."

"I got lucky. Then I followed your trail into the bedroom."

"I was out with Mavis. We went to a place called Armageddon. My hearing's starting to come back." She stroked his back, yawned hugely. "It's not morning, is it?"

"No." Recognizing the weariness in her voice, he shifted, gathered her close against him, and kissed her temple. "Go to sleep, Eve."

"Okay." She obliged him in less than ten seconds.

He woke at first light and left her curled in the middle of the bed. In the kitchen, he programmed the AutoChef for coffee and a toasted bagel. The bagel was stale, but that was to be expected. Making himself at home, he sat by the kitchen monitor and skimmed through the paper to the financial section.

He couldn't concentrate.

He was trying not to resent the fact that she'd chosen her bed over their bed. Or what he wanted her to think of as their bed. He didn't begrudge her the need for personal space; he understood well the need for privacy. But his house was large enough that she could have appropriated an entire wing for herself if she wanted it.

Pushing away from the monitor, he paced to the window. He wasn't used to this struggle, this war to balance his needs with someone else's. He'd grown up thinking of himself first and last. He'd had to, in order to survive and then to succeed. One was every bit as important to him as the other.

The habit was difficult to break—or had been, until Eve.

It was humiliating to admit, even to himself, that every time he went away to see to business, a seed of fear rooted in his heart that she would have shaken herself loose of him by the time he returned.

The simple fact was, he needed the one thing she had refused him. A commitment.

Turning from the window, he went back to the monitor and forced himself to read.

"Good morning," Eve said from the doorway. Her smile was quick and bright, as much from the pleasure of seeing him as from the fact that her trip to Armageddon didn't have the consequences she'd feared. She felt terrific.

"Your bagels are stale."

"Mmm." She tested by trying a bite of the one on the table. "You're right." Coffee was always a better bet. "Anything in the news I should worry about?"

"Are you concerned with the Treegro takeover?"

Eve knuckled one eye as she sipped her first cup of coffee. "What's Treegro and who's taking it over?"

"Treegro's a reforestry company, hence the overly adorable name. I'm taking it over."

She grunted. "Figures. I was thinking more of the Towers case."

"Cicely's memorial service is scheduled for tomorrow. She was important enough, and Catholic enough, to warrant St. Patrick's Cathedral."

"Will you go?"

"If I can reschedule a few appointments. Will you?"

"Yeah." Thinking, Eve leaned back on the counter. "Maybe her killer will be there."

She studied him as he scanned the monitor. He should have looked out of place in her kitchen, she mused, in his expensive, meticulously tailored linen shirt and with the luxurious mane of hair swept back from that remarkable face.

She kept waiting for him to look out of place there, with her.

"Problem?" he murmured, well aware that she was staring at him.

"No. Things on my mind. How well do you know Angelini?"

"Marco?" Roarke frowned over something he saw on the monitor, took out his notebook, entered a memo. "Our paths cross often enough. Normally a careful businessman, always a devoted father. Prefers spending his time in Italy, but his power base is here in New York. Contributes generously to the Catholic Church."

"He stands to gain financially from Towers's death. Maybe it's just a drop in the bucket, but Feeney's checking it out."

"You could have asked me," Roarke murmured. "I would have told you Marco's in trouble. Not desperate trouble," he amended when Eve's eyes sharpened. "He's made some ill-advised acquisitions over the past year or so."

"You said he was careful."

"I said he was normally careful. He bought several religious artifacts without having them thoroughly authenticated. His zeal got in the way of his business sense. They were forgeries, and he's taken a hard loss."

"How hard?"

"In excess of three million. I can get you exact figures, if necessary. He'll recover," Roarke added with a shrug for three million dollars Eve knew she would never get used to. "He needs to focus and downsize a bit here and there. I'd say his pride was hurt more than his portfolio."

"How much was Towers's share of Mercury worth?"

"On today's market?" He took out his pocket diary, jiggled some numbers. "Somewhere between five and seven."

"Million?"

"Yes," Roarke said with the faintest hint of a smile. "Of course."

"Good Christ. No wonder she could live like a queen."

"Marco made very good investments for her. He would have wanted the mother of his children to live comfortably."

"You and I have dramatically different ideas about comfort."

"Apparently." Roarke tucked the diary away and rose to refill his coffee and hers. An airbus rumbled by the window, chased by a fleet of private shuttles. "You suspect that Marco killed her to recoup his losses?"

"Money's a motive that never goes out of style. I interviewed him yesterday. I knew something didn't quite fit. Now it's beginning to."

She took the fresh coffee he offered, paced to the window where the noise level was rising, then away again. Her robe was slipping off her shoulder. Casually, Roarke tucked it back into place. Bored commuters often carried long-range viewers for just such an opportunity.

"Then there's the friendly divorce," she went on, "but whose idea was it? Divorce is complicated for Catholics when there are children involved. Don't they have to get some sort of clearance?"

"Dispensation," Roarke corrected. "A complex business, but both Cicely and Marco had connections with the hierarchy."

"He's never remarried," Eve pointed out, setting her coffee aside. "I haven't been able to find even a whiff of a steady or serious companion. But Towers was having a long-term intimate relationship with Hammett. Just how did Angelini feel about the mother of his children snuggling with a business partner?"

"If it were me, I'd kill the business partner."

"That's you," Eve said with a quick glance. "And I imagine you'd kill both of them."

"You know me so well." He stepped toward her, put his hands on her shoulders. "On the financial end, you may want to consider that whatever Cicely's share of Mercury was, Angelini's matches it. They held equal shares."

"Fuck." She struggled with it. "Still, money's money. I have to follow that scent until I get a new one." He continued to stand there, his hands cupping her shoulders, his eyes on hers. "What are you looking at?"

"The gleam in your eye." He touched his lips to hers once, then again. "I have some sympathy for Marco, you see, because I remember what it's like to be on the receiving end of that look, and that tenacity."

"You hadn't killed anyone," she reminded him. "Lately."

"Ah, but you weren't sure of that for a time, and still you were . . . drawn. Now we're—" The beeper on his watch pinged. "Hell." He kissed her again, quick and distracted. "We'll have to reminisce later. I have a meeting."

Just as well, Eve thought. Hot blood interfered with a clear head. "I'll see you later then."

"At home?"

She fiddled with her coffee cup. "At your place, sure."

Impatience flickered in his eyes as he shrugged into his jacket. The slight bulge in the pocket reminded him. "I'd nearly forgotten. I bought you a present in Australia."

With some reluctance, Eve took the slim gold box. When she opened it, reluctance scattered. There was no room for it in shocked panic. "Jesus bleeding Christ, Roarke. Are you insane?"

It was a diamond. She knew enough to be sure of that. The stone graced a twisted gold chain and glinted fire. Shaped like a tear, it was as long and wide as the first joint of a man's thumb.

"They call it the Giant's Tear," he said as he casually took it from the box and draped the chain over her head. "It was mined about a hundred and fifty years ago. It happened to come up for auction while I was in Sydney." He stepped back and studied its shooting sparks against the plain blue robe she wore. "Yes, it suits you. I thought it would." Then he looked at her face and smiled. "Oh, I see you were counting on kiwi. Well, perhaps next time." When he leaned in to kiss her good-bye, he was brought up short by the slap of her hand against his chest. "Problem?"

"This is crazy. You can't expect me to take something like this."

"You do occasionally wear jewelry." To prove his point, he flicked a finger at the gold dangling from her ear.

"Yeah, and I buy it from the street stall on Lex."

"I don't," he said easily.

"You take this back."

She started to pull at the chain, but he closed his hands over hers. "It doesn't go with my suit. Eve, a gift is not supposed to make the blood drain out of your cheeks." Suddenly exasperated, he gave her a quick shake. "It caught my eye, and I was thinking of you. Damn you, I always am. I bought it because I love you. Christ Jesus, when are you going to swallow that?"

"You're not going to do this to me." She told herself she was calm, very calm. Because she was right, very right. His temper didn't worry her, she'd seen it flare before. But the stone weighed around her neck, and what she feared it represented worried her very much.

"Do what to you, Eve? Exactly what?"

"You're not going to give me diamonds." Terrified and furious, she shoved away from him. "You're not going to pressure me into taking what I don't want, or being what I can't be. You think I don't know what you've been doing these past few months. Do you think I'm stupid?"

His eyes flashed, hard as the stone between her breasts. "No, I don't think you're stupid. I think you're a coward."

Her fist came up automatically. Oh, how she would have loved to have used it to wipe that self-righteous sneer from his face. If he hadn't been right, she could have. So she used other weapons.

"You think you can make me depend on you, get used to living in that glorified fortress of yours and wearing silk. Well, I don't give a damn about any of that."

"I'm well aware of that."

"I don't need your fancy food or your fancy gifts or your fancy words. I see the pattern, Roarke. Say I love you at regular intervals until she learns to respond. Like a well-trained pet."

"Like a pet," he repeated as his fury froze into ice. "I see I'm wrong. You are stupid. You really think this is about power and control? Have it your way. I'm tired of having you toss my feelings back in my face. My mistake for allowing it, but that can be rectified."

"I never—"

"No, you never," he interrupted coolly. "Never once risked your pride by saying those words back to me. You keep this place as your escape hatch rather than commit to staying with me. I let you draw the line, Eve, and now I'm moving it." It wasn't just temper pushing him now, nor was it just pain. It was the truth. "I want all," he said flatly. "Or I want nothing."

She wouldn't panic. He wouldn't make her panic like a first-time rookie on a night run. "What exactly does that mean?"

"It means sex isn't enough."

"It's not just sex. You know—"

"No, I don't. The choice is yours now—it always was. But now you'll have to come to me."

"Ultimatums just piss me off."

"That's a pity." He gave her one long last look. "Good-bye, Eve."

"You can't just walk—"

"Oh yes." And he didn't look back. "I can."

Her mouth dropped open when she heard the door slam. For a moment she simply stood, rigid, the sun glinting off the jewel around her neck. Then she began to vibrate. With fury, of course, she told herself and ripped the precious diamond off to toss it on the counter.

He thought she would go crawling after him, begging him to stay. Well, he could go on thinking that into the next millennium. Eve Dallas didn't crawl, and she didn't beg.

She closed her eyes against a pain more shocking than a laser strike. Who the hell is Eve Dallas? she wondered. And isn't that the core of it all?

She blocked it out. What choice did she have? The job came first. Had to come first. If she wasn't a good cop, she was nothing. She was as empty and as helpless as the child she had been, lying broken and traumatized in a dark alley in Dallas.

She could bury herself in work. The demands and pressures of it. When she was standing in Commander Whitney's office, she was only a cop with murder on her hands.

"She had plenty of enemies, Commander."

"Don't we all." His eyes were clear again, sharp. Grief could never outweigh responsibility.

"Feeney's run a list of her convictions. We're breaking them down, concentrating on the lifers first—family and known associates. Someone she put in a cage for the duration would have the strongest revenge ratio. Next down the line are the uncorrected deviants. UDs sometimes slip through the cracks. She put plenty away on mental, and some of them are bound to have crawled their way out."

"That's a lot of computer time, Dallas."

It was a subtle warning about budgets, which she chose to ignore. "I appreciate you putting Feeney on this with me. I couldn't get through it without him. Commander, these checks are SOP, but I don't think this was an attack on the prosecutor."

He sat back, inclined his head, waiting.

"I think it was personal. She was covering something. For herself, for somebody else. She zapped the 'link recording."

"I read your report, Lieutenant. Are you telling me you believe Prosecuting Attorney Towers was involved in something illegal?"

"Are you asking me as my friend or as my commander?"

He bared his teeth before he could control himself. After a short internal struggle, he nodded. "Well put, Lieutenant. As your commander."

"I don't know if it was illegal. It's my opinion at this stage of the investigation that there was something on that recording the victim wanted kept private. It was important enough to have her get dressed and go out again into the rain to meet someone. Whoever that was, was certain she would come alone and that she would leave no record of the contact. Commander, I need to speak with the rest of the victim's family, her close friends, your wife."

He'd accepted that, or tried to. Throughout his career he had worked hard to keep his loved ones out of the often nasty air of his job. Now he had to expose them.

"You have my address, Lieutenant. I'll contact my wife now and tell her to expect you."

"Yes, sir. Thank you."

Anna Whitney had made a fine home from the two-level house in the quiet street in the suburbs of White Plains. She had raised her children there, and raised them well, choosing the profession of mother over a teaching career. It wasn't the state salary for full-time parents that had swayed her. It had been the thrill of being in on each and every stage of childhood development.

She'd earned her salary. Now, with her children grown, she earned her retirement stipend by putting the same dedication into nurturing her home, her husband, and her reputation as a hostess. Whenever she could, she filled the house with her grandchildren. In the evenings, she filled it with dinner parties.

Anna Whitney hated solitude.

But she was alone when Eve arrived. As always, she was perfectly groomed: her cosmetics were carefully and expertly applied, and her pale blond hair was coiffed in a swept-back style that suited her attractive face.

She wore a one-piece suit of good American cotton, and held out a hand adorned only with a wedding ring to welcome Eve.

"Lieutenant Dallas, my husband said you would come."

"I'm sorry to intrude, Mrs. Whitney."

"Don't apologize. I'm a cop's wife. Come in. I've made some lemonade. It's tablet, I'm afraid. Fresh or frozen is so monstrously hard to come by. It's a little early for lemonade, but I had a yen for it today."

Eve let Anna chatter as they walked into the formal living area with its stiff-backed chairs and straight-edged sofa.

The lemonade was fine, and Eve said so after the first sip.

"You know the memorial service is at ten tomorrow."

"Yes, ma'am. I'll be there."

"There are so many flowers already. We've made arrangements to have them distributed after . . . but that's not why you're here."

"Prosecutor Towers was a good friend to you."

"She was a very good friend to me and my husband."

"Her children are staying with you?"

"Yes, they're . . . they've gone with Marco just now to speak with the archbishop about the service."

"They're close to their father."

"Yes."

"Mrs. Whitney, why are they staying here, rather than with their father?"

"We all thought it best. The house—Marco's house—holds so many memories. Cicely lived there when the children were young. Then there's the media. They don't have our address, and we wanted to keep the children from dealing with reporters. They've swamped poor Marco. It'll be different tomorrow, of course."

Her pretty hands plucked at the knee of her suit, then calmed and lay still again. "They'll have to face it. They're still in shock. Even Randall. Randall Slade, Mirina's fiancé. He'd gotten very close to Cicely."

"He's here as well."

"He'd never leave Mirina alone at such a time. She's a strong young woman, Lieutenant, but even strong women need an arm to lean on now and then."

Eve blocked out the quick image of Roarke that popped into her brain. As a result of the effort, her voice was a bit more formal than usual as she led Anna through the routine questions.

"I've asked myself over and over what could have possessed her to go to that neighborhood," Anna concluded. "Cicely could be stubborn, and certainly strong willed, but she was rarely impulsive and never foolish."

"She talked to you, confided in you."

"We were like sisters."

"Would she have told you if she was in trouble of some kind? If someone close to her was in trouble?"

"I would have thought so. She would have handled it herself, or tried to first." Her eyes swam, but the tears didn't fall. "But sooner or later she would have blown off steam with me."

If she'd had time, Eve thought. "You can think of nothing she was concerned about before her death?"

"Nothing major. Her daughter's wedding—getting older. We joked about her becoming a grandmother. No," Anna said with a laugh as she recognized Eve's look. "Mirina isn't pregnant, though that would have only pleased her mother. She was always concerned for David as well: Would he settle down? Was he happy?"

"And is he?"

Another cloud came into her eyes before she lowered them. "David is a great deal like his father. He likes to wheel and deal. He does a great deal of traveling for the business, always looking for new arenas, new opportunities. There's no doubt he'll take the helm if and when Marco decided to turn it over."

She hesitated, as if about to add something, then smoothly switched gears. "Mirina, on the other hand, prefers to live in one spot. She manages a boutique in Rome. That's where she met Randall. He's a designer. Her shop handles his line exclusively now. He's quite talented. This is his," she said, indicating the slim suit she wore.

"It's lovely. So as far as you know, Prosecutor Towers had no reason to be concerned for her children. Nothing she would have felt obliged to smooth out or cover over?"

"Cover over? No, of course not. They're both bright, successful people."

"And her ex-husband. He's having some business difficulties?"

"Marco? Is he?" Anna shrugged that off. "I'm sure he'll straighten them out. I never shared Cicely's interest in business."

"She was involved then, in business. Directly?"

"Of course. Cicely insisted on knowing exactly what was going on and having a say in it. I never knew how she could keep so many things in her head. If Marco was having difficulties, she'd have known, and probably have suggested a half dozen ways to right things. She was quite brilliant." When her voice broke, Anna pressed a hand to her lips.

"I'm sorry, Mrs. Whitney."

"No, it's all right. I'm better. Having her children with me helped so much. I feel I can stand for her with them. I can't do what you do, and look for her killer. But I can stand for her with her children."

"They're very lucky to have you," Eve murmured, surprised to hear herself say it and mean it. Odd, she'd always considered Anna Whitney a mild pain in the ass. "Mrs. Whitney, can you tell me about Prosecutor Towers's relationship with George Hammett?"

Anna pokered up. "They were dear, good friends."

"Mr. Hammett has told me they were lovers."

Anna huffed out a breath. She was a traditionalist, and unashamed of it. "Very well, that's true. But he wasn't the right man for her."

"Why?"

"Set in his ways. I'm very fond of George, and he made an excellent escort for Cicely. But a woman can hardly be completely happy when she goes home to an empty apartment most nights, to an empty bed. She needed a mate. George wanted it both ways, and Cicely deluded herself into thinking she wanted that, too."

"And she didn't."

"She shouldn't have," Anna snapped, obviously going over an old argument. "Work isn't enough, as I pointed out to her many times. She simply wasn't serious enough about George to risk."

"Risk?"

"I'm speaking of emotional risk," Anna said impatiently. "You cops are so literal-minded. She wanted her life tidy more than she wanted the mess of a full-time relationship."

"I had the impression that Mr. Hammett regretted that, that he loved her very much."

"If he did, why didn't he push?" Anna demanded, and tears threatened. "She wouldn't have died alone then, would she? She wouldn't have been alone."

Eve drove out of the quiet suburbs, and on impulse she pulled her car over to the curb and slumped down in the seat. She needed to think. Not about Roarke, she assured herself. There was nothing to think about there. That was settled.

On a hunch, she called up her computer at her office and had it get to work on David Angelini. If he was like his father, maybe he had also made a few poor investments. While she was at it, she ordered a run on Randall Slade and the boutique in Rome.

If anything popped up, she would have a scan on the flights from Europe to New York.

Damn it, a woman who had nothing to worry about didn't leave her warm, dry apartment in the middle of the night.

Stubbornly, Eve retraced all the steps in her head. As she thought it through, she studied the neighborhood. Nice old trees spreading shade, neat postcard-sized yards with one- and two-story fully detached houses.

What would it have been like to have been raised in a pretty, settled community? Would it make you secure, confident, the way being dragged from filthy room to filthy room, from stinking street to stinking street made her jittery, moody?

Maybe there were fathers here who snuck into their little girls' bedrooms, too. But it was hard to believe it. The fathers here couldn't smell of bad liquor and sour sweat and have thick fingers that pushed themselves into innocent flesh.

Eve caught herself rocking in the seat and choked back a sob.

She wouldn't do it. She wouldn't remember. She wouldn't let herself conjure up that face looming over her in the dark, or the taste of that hand clamping over her mouth to smother her screams.

She wouldn't do it. It had all happened to someone else, some little girl whose name she couldn't even remember. If she tried to, if she let herself remember it all, she would become that helpless child again and lose Eve.

She laid her head back on the seat and concentrated on calming herself. If she hadn't been wallowing in self-pity, she would have seen the woman breaking the window at the side of the modified rancher across the street before the first shard fell.

As it was, Eve scowled, asked herself why she'd had to pull over at just this spot. And did she really want the hassle of dealing with intra-jurisdiction paperwork?

Then she thought about the nice family who would come home that night and find their valuables gone.

With a long-suffering sigh, she got out of the car.

The woman was half in and half out of the window when Eve reached her. The security shield had been deactivated by a cheap jammer, available at any electronic outlet. With a shake of her head for the naïveté of suburbanites, Eve tapped the thief smartly on the butt that was struggling to wiggle through the opening.

"Forget your code, ma'am?"

Her answer was a hard donkey-style kick to the left shoulder. Eve considered herself lucky it had missed her face. Still, she went down, crushing some early tulips. The perp popped out of the window like a cork and bolted across the lawn.

If her shoulder hadn't been aching, Eve might have let her go. She caught her quarry in a flying tackle that sent them both sprawling into a bed of sunny-faced pansies.

"Get your fucking hands off me, or I'll kill you."

Eve thought briefly that it was a possibility. The woman outweighed her by a good twenty pounds. To ensure it didn't happen, she jammed an elbow against the woman's windpipe and dug for her badge.

"You're busted."

The woman's dark eyes rolled in disgust. "What the hell's a city cop doing here? Don't you know where Manhattan is, asshole?"

"Looks like I'm lost." Eve kept her elbow in place, adding just a little more pressure for her own satisfaction while she pulled out her communicator and requested the closest 'burb cruiser.

By the next morning, her shoulder was singing as fiercely as Mavis on a final set. Eve admitted the extra hours she'd put in with Feeney and a night tossing alone in bed hadn't helped it any. She was leery of anything but the mildest painkillers, and took a single stingy dose before she dressed for the memorial service.

She and Feeney had come across one tasty little tidbit. David Angelini had withdrawn three large payments from his accounts over the last six months, to a grand total of one million six hundred and thirty-two dollars, American.

That was more than three-quarters of his personal savings, and he'd drawn it in anonymous credit tokens and cash.

They were still digging on Randall Slade and Mirina, but so far, they were both clean. Just a happy young couple on the brink of matrimony.

God knew how anybody could be happy on the brink, Eve thought as she located her gray suit.

The damn button on the jacket was still missing, she realized as she started to fasten it. And she remembered Roarke had it, carried it like some sort of superstitious talisman. She'd been wearing the suit the first time she'd seen him—at a memorial for the dead.

She ran a hasty comb through her hair and escaped the apartment and the memories.

St. Patrick's was bulging by the time she arrived. Uniforms in the best dress blues flanked the perimeter for a full three blocks on Fifth. A kind of honor guard, Eve mused, for a lawyer who cops had respected. Both street and air traffic had been diverted from the usually choked avenue, and the media was thronged like a busy parade across the wide street.

After the third uniform stopped her, Eve attached her badge to her jacket and moved unhampered into the ancient cathedral and the sounds of the dirge.

She didn't care for churches much. They made her feel guilty for reasons she didn't care to explore. The scent of candle wax and incense was ripe. Some rituals, she thought as she slipped into a side pew, were as timeless as the moon. She gave up any hope of speaking directly with Cicely Towers's family that morning and settled down to watch the show.

Catholic rites had gone back to Latin some time in the last decade. Eve supposed it added a kind of mysticism and a unity. The ancient language certainly seemed appropriate to her in the Mass for the Dead.

The priest's voice boomed out, reaching to the lofty ceilings, and the congregation's responses echoed after. Silent and watchful, Eve scanned the crowd. Dignitaries and politicians sat with bowed heads. She'd positioned herself just close enough to catch glimpses of the family. When Feeney slipped in beside her, she inclined her head.

"Angelini," she murmured. "That would be the daughter beside him."

"With her fiancé on her right."

"Um-hmm." Eve studied the couple: young, attractive. The woman was of slight build with golden hair, like her mother. The unrelieved black she wore swept down from a high neck, covered her arms to the wrists, and skimmed her ankles. She wore no veil or shaded glasses to shield her red-rimmed, puffy eyes. Grief, simple, basic, and undiluted, seemed to shimmer around her.

Beside her, Randall Slade stood tall, one long arm supporting her shoulders. He had a striking, almost brutally handsome face, which Eve remembered well from the image she'd generated on her computer screen: large jaw, long nose, hooded eyes. He looked big and tough, but the arm around the woman lay gently.

Flanking Angelini's other side was his son. David stood just a space apart. That sort of body language hinted at friction. He stared straight ahead, his face a blank. He stood slightly shorter than his father, as dark as his sister was fair. And he was alone, Eve thought. Very much alone.

The family pew was completed by George Hammett.

Directly behind were the commander, his wife, and his family.

She knew Roarke was there. She had already glimpsed him once at the end of an aisle beside a teary-eyed blonde. Now, when Eve skimmed a glance his way, she saw him lean down to the woman and murmur something that had her turning her face into his shoulder.

Furious at the quick pang of jealousy, Eve scanned the crowd again. Her eyes met C. J. Morse's.

"How'd that little bastard manage to get in?"

Feeney, a good Catholic, winced at the use of profanity in church. "Who?"

"Morse—at eight o'clock."

Shifting his eyes, Feeney spotted the reporter. "A crowd like this, I guess some of the slippery ones could slide through security."

Eve debated hauling him out just for the satisfaction of it, then decided the scuffle would give him just the kind of attention he craved.

"Fuck him."

Feeney made a sound like a man who'd been pinched. "Christ Jesus, Dallas, you're in St. Pat's."

"If God's going to make little weasels like him, she's going to have to listen to complaints."

"Have some respect."

Eve looked back to Mirina, who lifted a hand to her face. "I've got plenty of respect," she murmured. "Plenty." With this she stepped around Feeney and strode down the side to the exit.

By the time he caught up with her, she was just finishing issuing instructions to one of the uniforms.

"What's the problem?"

"I needed some air." Churches always smelled like the dying or the dead to her. "And I wanted to get a jump on the weasel." Smiling now, she turned to Feeney. "I've got the uniforms looking out for him. They'll confiscate any communication or recording devices he's got on him. Privacy law."

"You're just going to steam him."

"Good. He steams me." She let out a long breath, studying the media horde across the avenue. "I'll be damned if the public has a right to know everything. But at least those reporters are playing by the rules and showing some of that respect you were talking about for the family."

"I take it you're done in there."

"There's nothing I can do in there."

"I figured you'd be sitting with Roarke."

"No."

Feeney nodded slowly and nearly dug into his pocket for his bag of nuts before he remembered the occasion. "Is that the burr up your butt, kid?"

"I don't know what you're talking about." She started to walk without any destination in mind, stopped, and turned around. "Who the hell was that blonde he was wrapped around?"

"I couldn't say." He sucked air through his teeth. "She was a looker though. Want me to rough him up for you?"

"Just shut up." She jammed her hands in her pockets. "The commander's wife said they were having a small, private memorial at their home. How long do you figure this sideshow will take?"

"Another hour, minimum."

"I'm heading back to Cop Central. I'll meet you at the commander's in two hours."

"You're the boss."

*   *   *

Small and private meant there were more than a hundred people packed into the commander's suburban home. There was food to comfort the living, liquor to dull the grieving. The perfect hostess, Anna Whitney hurried over the moment she spotted Eve. She kept her voice down and a carefully pleasant expression on her face.

"Lieutenant, must you do this now, here and now?"

"Mrs. Whitney, I'll be as discreet as I possibly can. The sooner I complete the interview stage, the sooner we'll find Prosecutor Towers's killer."

"Her children are devastated. Poor Mirina can barely function. It would be more appropriate if you'd—"

"Anna." Commander Whitney laid a hand on his wife's shoulder. "Let Lieutenant Dallas do her job."

Anna said nothing, merely turned and walked stiffly away.

"We said good-bye to a very dear friend today."

"I understand, Commander. I'll finish here as quickly as I can."

"Be careful with Mirina, Dallas. She's very fragile at the moment."

"Yes, sir. Perhaps I could speak to her first, privately."

"I'll see to it."

When he left her alone, Eve backed up toward the foyer and turned directly into Roarke.

"Lieutenant."

"Roarke." She glanced at the glass of wine in his hand. "I'm on duty."

"So I see. This wasn't for you."

Eve followed his gaze to the blonde sitting in the corner. "Right." She could all but feel the marrow of her bones turn green. "You move fast."

Before she could step aside, he put a hand on her arm. His voice, like his eyes, was carefully neutral. "Suzanna is a mutual friend of mine and Cicely's. The widow of a cop, killed in the line of duty. Cicely put his murderer away."

"Suzanna Kimball," Eve said, battling back shame. "Her husband was a good cop."

"So I'm told." With the faintest trace of amusement shadowing his mouth, he skimmed a glance down her suit. "I'd hoped you'd burned that thing. Gray's not your color, Lieutenant."

"I'm not making a fashion statement. Now, if you'll excuse me—"

The fingers on her arm tightened. "You might look into Randall Slade's gambling problem. He owes considerable sums to several people. As does David Angelini."

"Is that right?"

"That's quite right. I'm one of the several."

Her eyes hardened. "And you've just decided I might be interested."

"I've just discovered my own interest. He's worked up a rather impressive debt at one of my casinos on Vegas II. Then there's a matter of a little scandal some years back involving roulette, a redhead, and a fatality on an obscure gaming satellite in Sector 38."

"What scandal?"

"You're the cop," he said and smiled. "Find out."

He left Eve to go to the cop's widow and hold her hand.

"I have Mirina in my office," Whitney murmured at Eve's ear. "I promised you wouldn't keep her long."

"I won't." Struggling to smooth the feathers Roarke had ruffled, she followed the commander's broad back down the hall.

Though his home office wasn't quite as spartan as the one at Cop Central, it was obvious that Whitney kept his wife's lush feminine taste at bay here. The walls were a plain beige, the carpet a deeper tone, and the chairs were wide and a practical brown.

His work counter and console were in the center of the room. In the corner by the window, Mirina Angelini waited in her long sweep of mourning black. Whitney went to her first, spoke quietly, and squeezed her hand. With one warning glance at Eve, he left them alone.

"Ms. Angelini," Eve began. "I knew your mother, worked with her, admired her. I'm very sorry for your loss."

"Everyone is," Mirina responded in a voice as fragile and pale as her white cheeks. Her eyes were dark, nearly black, and glassy. "Except the person who killed her, I suppose. I'll apologize ahead of time if I'm of little help to you, Lieutenant Dallas. I bowed to pressure and let myself be tranq'ed. I am, as anyone will tell you, taking this rather hard."

"You and your mother were close."

"She was the most wonderful woman I've ever known. Why should I have to be calm and composed when I've lost her like this?"

Eve came closer, sat in one of the wide brown chairs. "I can't think of any reason why you should be."

"My father wants a public show of strength." Mirina turned her face to the window. "I'm letting him down. Appearances are important to my father."

"Was your mother important to him?"

"Yes. Their personal and professional lives were twined together. The divorce didn't change that. He's hurting." She drew in a shaky breath. "He won't show it because he's too proud, but he's hurting. He loved her. We all loved her."

"Ms. Angelini, tell me about your mother's mood, what you spoke of, who you spoke of, the last time you had contact."

"The day before she died we were on the 'link for an hour, maybe more. Wedding plans." Tears dripped out and spilled over the pale cheeks. "We were both so full of wedding plans. I'd send her trans- missions of dresses: wedding dresses, mother-of-the-bride ensembles. Randall was designing them. We talked about clothes. Doesn't that seem shallow, Lieutenant, that the last time I'll ever speak with my mother, I spoke of fashion?"

"No, it doesn't seem shallow. It seems friendly. Loving."

Mirina pressed a hand to her lips. "Do you think?"

"Yes, I do."

"What do you talk to your mother about?"

"I don't have a mother. I never did."

Mirina blinked, focused again. "How odd. What does it feel like?"

"I . . ." There was no way to describe what simply was. "It wouldn't be the same for you, Ms. Angelini," Eve said gently. "When you were speaking to your mother, did she mention anything, anyone who was concerning her?"

"No. If you're thinking about her work, we rarely talked of it. I wasn't very interested in the law. She was happy, excited that I was coming over for a few days. We laughed a lot. I know she had this image, her professional image, but with me, with the family she was . . . softer, looser. I teased her about George, saying that Randy could design her wedding dress while he was doing mine."

"Her reaction?"

"We just laughed. Mama liked to laugh," she said, a little dreamy now as the tranq began to work. "She said she was having too much fun being mother of the bride to spoil it with the headaches of being a bride herself. She was very fond of George, and I think they were good together. But I don't suppose she loved him."

"Don't you?"

"Why, no." There was a faint smile on her lips, a glassy gleam to her eyes. "When you love someone, you have to be with them, don't you? To be part of their life, to have them be part of yours. She wasn't looking for that with George. With anyone."

"Was Mr. Hammett looking for that with her?"

"I don't know. If he was, he was happy enough to let their relationship drift. I'm drifting now," she murmured. "I don't feel as though I'm here at all."

Because she needed Mirina to hold off on the float a bit longer, Eve rose to request water from the console. Carrying the glass back, she pushed it into Mirina's hands.

"Did that relationship cause problems between him and your father? Between your mother and father?"

"It . . . was awkward, but not uncomfortable." Mirina smiled again. She was sleepy now, so relaxed she could have folded her arms on the window ledge and slipped away. "That sounds contradictory. You'd have to know my father. He would refuse to let it bother him, or at least to let it affect him. He's still friendly with George."

She blinked down at the glass in her hand as if she'd just realized it was there, and took a delicate sip. "I don't know how he might have felt if they had decided to marry, but well, that isn't an issue now."

"Are you involved in your father's business, Ms. Angelini?"

"In the fashion arm. I do all the buying for the shops in Rome and Milan, have the final say as to what's exported to our shops in Paris and New York and so forth. Travel a bit to attend shows, though I don't care much for traveling. I hate going off planet, don't you?"

Eve realized she was losing her. "I haven't done it."

"Oh, it's horrid. Randy likes it. Says it's an adventure. What was I saying?" She pushed a hand through her lovely golden hair, and Eve rescued the glass before it could tumble to the floor. "About the buying. I like to buy clothes. Other aspects of the business never interested me."

"Your parents and Mr. Hammett were all stockholders in a company called Mercury."

"Of course. We use Mercury exclusively for our shipping needs." Her eyelids drooped. "It's fast, dependable."

"There were no problems that you know of, in that or any other of your family holdings?"

"No, none at all."

It was time to try a different tack. "Was your mother aware of Randall Slade's gambling debts?"

For the first time Mirina showed a spark of life, and the life was anger, flashing in the pale eyes. She seemed to snap awake. "Randall's debts were not my mother's concern, but his, and mine. We're dealing with them."

"You didn't tell her?"

"There was no reason to worry her about something that was being handled. Randall has a problem with gambling, but he's gotten help. He doesn't wager anymore."

"The debts are considerable?"

"They're being paid," Mirina said hollowly. "Arrangements have been made."

"Your mother was a wealthy woman in her own right. You'll inherit a large portion of her estate."

Either the tranqs or grief dulled Mirina's wits. She seemed oblivious to the implication. "Yes, but I won't have my mother, will I? I won't have Mama. When I marry Randall, she won't be there. She won't be there," she repeated, and began to weep quietly.

*   *   *

David Angelini wasn't fragile. His emotions showed themselves in stiff impatience with undercurrents of chained rage. For all appearances, this was a man insulted at the very idea that he would be expected to speak to a cop.

When Eve sat across from him in Whitney's office, he answered her questions briefly in a clipped, cultured voice.

"Obviously it was some maniac she'd prosecuted who did this to her," he stated. "Her work brought her entirely too close to violence."

"Did you object to her work?"

"I didn't understand why she loved it. Why she needed it." He lifted the glass he'd brought with him and drank. "But she did, and in the end, it killed her."

"When did you see her last?"

"On March eighteenth. My birthday."

"Did you have contact with her since then?"

"I spoke with her about a week before she died. Just a family call. We never went more than a week without speaking."

"How would you describe her mood?"

"Obsessed—with Mirina's wedding. My mother never did things by halves. She was planning the wedding as meticulously as she did any of her criminal cases. She was hoping it would rub off on me."

"What would?"

"The wedding fever. My mother was a romantic woman under the prosecutor's armor. She hoped I would find the right mate and make a family. I told her I'd leave that to Mirina and Randy and stay married to business awhile."

"You're actively involved in Angelini Exports. You'd be aware of the financial difficulties."

His face tightened. "They're blips, Lieutenant. Bumps. Nothing more."

"My information indicates there are more serious difficulties than blips and bumps."

"Angelini is solid. There's simply a need for some reorganization, some diversification, which is being done." He flicked a hand, elegant fingers, a sparkle of gold. "A few key people have made unfortunate mistakes that can and will be rectified. And that has nothing to do with my mother's case."

"It's my job to explore all angles, Mr. Angelini. Your mother's estate is substantial. Your father will come into a number of holdings, as will you."

David got to his feet. "You're speaking of my mother. If you suspect that anyone in the family would cause her harm, then Commander Whitney has made a monstrous error in judgment putting you in charge of the investigation."

"You're entitled to your opinion. Do you gamble, Mr. Angelini?"

"What business is that of yours?"

Since he was going to stand, Eve rose to face him. "It's a simple question."

"Yes, I gamble on occasion, as do countless others. I find it relaxing."

"How much do you owe?"

His fingers tightened on the glass. "I believe at this point, my mother would have advised me to consult counsel."

"That's certainly your right. I'm not accusing you of anything, Mr. Angelini. I'm fully aware that you were in Paris on the night of your mother's death." Just as she was fully aware that shuttles skimmed across the Atlantic hourly. "It's my job to get a clear picture, a full and clear picture. You're under no obligation to answer my question. But I can, with very little trouble, access that information."

The muscles in his jaw worked a moment. "Eight hundred thousand, give or take a few dollars."

"Are you unable to settle the debt?"

"I am neither a welsher nor a pauper, Lieutenant Dallas," he said stiffly. "It can and will be settled shortly."

"Was your mother aware of it?"

"Neither am I a child, Lieutenant, who needs to run to his mother for help whenever he skins a knuckle."

"You and Randall Slade gambled together?"

"We did. My sister disapproves, so Randy has given up the hobby."

"Not before he incurred debts of his own."

His eyes, very like his father's, chilled. "I wouldn't know about that, nor would I discuss his business with you."

Oh yes, you would, Eve thought, but let it slide for the moment. "And the trouble in Sector 38 a few years ago? You were there?"

"Sector 38?" He looked convincingly blank.

"A gambling satellite."

"I often go to Vegas II for a quick weekend, but I don't recall patronizing a casino in that sector. I don't know what trouble you're referring to."

"Do you play roulette?"

"No, it's a fool's game. Randy's fond of it. I prefer blackjack."

Randall Slade didn't look like a fool. He looked to Eve like a man who could knock anything out of his path without breaking stride. Nor was he her image of a fashion designer. He dressed simply, his black suit unadorned by any of the studs or braids currently in fashion. And his wide hands had the look of a laborer rather than an artist.

"I hope you'll be brief," he said in the tone of a man used to giving orders. "Mirina is upstairs lying down. I don't want to leave her for long."

"Then I'll be brief." Eve didn't object when he took out a gold case containing ten slim black cigarettes. Technically, she could have, but she waited until he'd lighted one. "What was your relationship with Prosecutor Towers?"

"We were friendly. She was soon to become my mother-in-law. We shared a deep love for Mirina."

"She approved of you."

"I have no reason to believe otherwise."

"Your career has benefited quite a lot through your association with Angelini Exports."

"True." He blew out smoke that smelled lightly of lemon mint. "I like to think Angelini has also benefited quite a lot through their association with me." He surveyed Eve's gray suit. "That cut and color are both incredibly unflattering. You might want to take a look at my on-the-rack line here in New York."

"I'll keep it in mind, thanks."

"I dislike seeing attractive women in unattractive clothes." He smiled and surprised Eve with a flare of charm. "You should wear bolder colors, sleeker lines. A woman with your build would carry them well."

"So I'm told," she muttered, thinking of Roarke. "You're about to marry a very wealthy woman."

"I'm about to marry the woman I love."

"It's a happy coincidence that she's wealthy."

"It is."

"And money is something you have a need for."

"Don't we all?" Smooth, unoffended, again amused.

"You have debts, Mr. Slade. Large, outstanding debts in an area that can cause considerable pain in the collecting process."

"That's accurate." He drew smoke in again. "I'm a gambling addict, Lieutenant. Recovering. With Mirina's help and support, I've undergone treatment. I haven't made a wager in two months, five days."

"Roulette, wasn't it?"

"I'm afraid so."

"And the amount you owe, in round figures?"

"Five hundred thousand."

"And the amount of your fiancée's inheritance?"

"Probably triple that, in round figures. More, considering the stocks and holdings that wouldn't be converted into credit or cash. Killing my fiancée's mother would certainly have been one way to solve my financial difficulties." He stubbed his cigarette out thoughtfully. "Then again, so would the contract I've just signed for my fall line. Money isn't important enough to me to kill for it."

"But gambling was important enough?"

"Gambling was like a beautiful woman. Desirable, exciting, capricious. I had a choice between her and Mirina. There was nothing I wouldn't do to keep Mirina."

"Nothing?"

He understood, and inclined his head. "Nothing at all."

"Does she know about the scandal in Sector 38?"

His amused, faintly smug expression froze, and he paled. "That was nearly ten years ago. That has nothing to do with Mirina. Nothing to do with anything."

"You haven't told her."

"I didn't know her. I was young, foolish, and I paid for my mistake."

"Why don't you explain to me, Mr. Slade, how you came to make that mistake?"

"It has nothing to do with this."

"Indulge me."

"Damn it, it was one night out of my life. One night. I'd had too much to drink, was stupid enough to mix the liquor with chemicals. The woman killed herself. It was proven the overdose was self-inflicted."

Interesting, Eve thought. "But you were there," she hazarded.

"I was zoned. I'd lost more heavily than I could afford at roulette, and between us we made a scene. I told you I was young. I blamed my bad luck on her. Maybe I did threaten her. I just don't remember. Yes, we argued publicly, she struck me, and I struck her back. I'm not proud of it. Then I just don't remember."

"Don't remember, Mr. Slade?"

"As I testified, the next thing I remember is waking up in some filthy little room. We were in bed, naked. And she was dead. I was still groggy. Security came in. I must have called them. They took pictures. I was assured the pictures were destroyed after the case was closed and I was exonerated. I barely knew the woman," he continued, heating up. "I'd picked her up in the bar—or thought I had. My attorney discovered she was a professional companion, unlicensed, working the casinos."

He closed his eyes. "Do you think I want Mirina to know that I was, however briefly, accused of murdering an unlicensed whore?"

"No," Eve said quietly. "I don't imagine you do. And as you said, Mr. Slade, you'd do anything to keep her. Anything at all."

*   *   *

Hammett was waiting for her the moment she stepped out of the commander's office. The hollows in his cheeks seemed deeper, his skin grayer.

"I'd hoped to have a moment, Lieutenant—Eve."

She gestured behind her, let him slip into the room first, then closed the door on the murmurs of conversation.

"This is a difficult day for you, George."

"Yes, very difficult. I wanted to ask, needed to know . . . Is there anything more? Anything at all?"

"The investigation's proceeding. There's nothing I can tell you that you wouldn't have heard through the media."

"There must be more." His voice rose before he could control it. "Something."

She could feel pity, even when there was suspicion. "Everything that can be done is being done."

"You've interviewed Marco, her children, even Randy. If there is anything they knew, anything they told you that might help, I have a right to be told."

Nerves? she wondered. Or grief? "No," she said quietly, "you don't. I can't give you any information acquired during an interview or through investigative procedure."

"We're talking about the murder of the woman I loved!" He exploded with it, his pale face flushing dark. "We might have been married."

"Were you planning to be married, George?"

"We'd discussed it." He passed a hand over his face, a hand that shook slightly. "We'd discussed it," he repeated, and the flush washed away from his skin. "There was always another case, another summation to prepare. There was supposed to be plenty of time."

With his hands balled into fists, he turned away from her. "I apologize for shouting at you. I'm not myself."

"It's all right, George. I'm very sorry."

"She's gone." He said it quietly, brokenly. "She's gone."

There was nothing left for her to do but give him privacy. She closed the door behind her, then rubbed a hand at the back of her neck where tension was lodged.

On her way out, Eve signaled to Feeney. "Need you to do some digging," she told him as they headed outside. "Old case, about ten years past, on one of the gambling hells in Sector 38."

"What you got, Dallas?"

"Sex, scandal, and probable suicide. Accidental."

"Hot damn," Feeney said mournfully. "And I was hoping to catch a ball game on the screen tonight."

"This should be just as entertaining." She spied Roarke helping the blonde into his car, hesitated, then detoured past him. "Thanks for the tip, Roarke."

"Any time, Lieutenant. Feeney," he added with a brief nod before he slipped into the car.

"Hey," Feeney said when the car glided away. "He's really pissed at you."

"He seemed fine to me," Eve muttered and wrenched open her car door.

Feeney snorted. "Some detective you are, pal."

"Just dig up the case, Feeney. Randall Slade's the accused." She slammed her door and sulked.

CHAPTER
SEVEN

Feeney knew Eve wasn't going to like the data he'd unearthed. Anticipating her reaction, and being a wise man, he sent it through computer rather than delivering it in person.

"I've got the goods on the Slade incident," he said when his droopy face blipped onto her monitor. "I'm going to send it through. I'm—ah—going to be stuck here for a while. I've got about twenty percent of Tower's conviction list eliminated. It's slow going."

"Try to speed it up, Feeney. We've got to narrow the field."

"Right. Ready for transmission." His face blinked off. In its place was the police report from Sector 38.

Eve frowned over it as the data scrolled. There was little more information above what Randal Slade had already told her. Suspicious death, overdose. The victim's name was Carolle Lee, age 24, birthplace New Chicago Colony, unemployed. The image showed a young, black-haired woman of mixed heritage with exotic eyes and coffee-toned skin. Randall looked pale, his eyes glazed, in his mug shot.

She skimmed through, searching for any detail Randall might have left out. It was bad enough as it was, Eve mused. The murder charges had been dropped, but he'd copped to soliciting an unlicensed companion, possession of illegal chemicals, and contributing to a fatality.

He'd been lucky, she decided, very lucky that the incident had occurred on such an obscure sector, in a hellhole that didn't garner much attention. But if someone—anyone—had come across the details, had threatened to take them to his pretty, fragile fiancée, it would have been a real mess.

Had Towers known? Eve wondered. That was the big question. And if she had, how would she have handled it? The attorney might have looked at the facts, weighed them, and dismissed the case as resolved.

But the mother? Would the loving mother who chatted about fashion for an hour with her daughter, the devoted parent who carved out time to help plan the perfect wedding, have accepted the scandal as the wild oats of a young, foolish man? Or would she have stood like a barricade between the older, less foolish man and what he wanted most?

Eve narrowed her eyes and continued to scan the documents. Then she stopped cold when Roarke's name jumped out at her.

"Son of a bitch," she muttered, slamming a fist on the desk. "Son of a bitch."

Within fifteen minutes, she was striding across the glossy tiles of the lobby of Roarke's building in midtown. Her jaw was set as she accessed the code, then slapped her palm onto the handplate of his private elevator. She hadn't bothered to call, but let righteous fury zip her up to the top floor.

The receptionist in his elegant outer office started to smile in greeting. One look at Eve's face had her blinking. "Lieutenant Dallas."

"Tell him I'm here, and that I see him now, or down at Cop Central."

"He's—he's in a meeting."

"Now."

"I'll call through." She swiveled and punched a button for private communication. She murmured the message and apologies while Eve stood fuming.

"If you would wait in his office for a moment, Lieutenant—" the receptionist began and rose.

"I know the way," Eve snapped, striding across the plush carpet through the towering double doors and into Roarke's New York sanctum.

There had been a time when she would have helped herself to a cup of coffee or wandered over to admire his view from a hundred fifty stories up. Today she stood, every nerve quivering with temper. And beneath that was fear.

The panel on the east wall slid open silently, and he walked through. He still wore the dark suit he'd chosen for the memorial service. As the panel closed behind him, he fingered the button in his pocket that belonged on Eve's gray jacket.

"You were quick," he said easily. "I thought I would finish my board meeting before you came by."

"You think you're clever," she shot back. "Giving me just enough to start digging with. Damn it, Roarke, you're right in the middle of this."

"Am I?" Unconcerned, he walked to a chair, sat, stretched out his legs. "And how is that, Lieutenant?"

"You owned the damn casino where Slade was gambling. You owned the fucking fleabag hotel where the woman died. You had an unlicensed hooker working your hellhole."

"Unlicensed companions in Sector 38?" He smiled a little. "Why, I'm shocked."

"Don't get cute with me. It connects you. Mercury was bad enough, but this is deeper. Your statement's on record."

"Naturally."

"Why are you making it so hard for me to keep your name out of this?"

"I'm not interested in making it hard or easy for you, Lieutenant."

"Fine, then. Just fine." If he could be cold, so could she. "Then we'll just get the questions and answers out of the way and move on. You knew Slade."

"Actually, I didn't. Not personally. Actually, I'd forgotten all about it, and him, until I did some research of my own. Wouldn't you like some coffee?"

"You forgot you were involved in a murder investigation?"

"Yes." Idly, he steepled his hands. "It wasn't the first brush I'd had with the police, nor apparently, is it the last. In the grand scheme of things, Lieutenant, it really didn't concern me."

"Didn't concern you," she repeated. "You had Slade tossed out of your casino."

"I believe the manager of the casino handled that."

"You were there."

"Yes, I was there, somewhere on the premises, in any case. Dissatisfied clients often become rowdy. I didn't pay much attention at that time."

She took a deep breath. "If it meant so little, and the entire matter slipped your mind, why did you sell the casino, the hotel, everything you owned in Sector 38 within forty-eight hours of Cicely Towers's murder?"

He said nothing for a moment, his eyes on hers. "For personal reasons."

"Roarke, just tell me so I can put this whole connection to bed. I know the sale didn't have anything to do with Towers's murder, but it looks dicey. 'For personal reasons' isn't good enough."

"It was for me. At the time. Tell me, Lieutenant Dallas, are you thinking I decided to blackmail Cicely over her future son-in-law's youthful indiscretion, had some henchman in my employ lure her to the West End, and when she didn't cooperate, slit her throat?"

She wanted to hate him for putting her in the position of having to answer. "I told you I didn't believe you had anything to do with her death, and I meant it. You've put me in a position where it's a scenario we'll have to work with. One that will take time and manpower away from finding the killer."

"Damn you, Eve." He said it quietly; so quietly, so calmly, her throat burned in reaction.

"What do you want from me, Roarke? You said you'd help, that I could use your connections. Now, because you're pissed about something else, you're blocking me."

"I changed my mind." His tone was dismissive as he rose and

walked behind his desk. "About several things," he added, watching her with eyes that sliced at her heart.

"If you would just tell me why you sold. The coincidence of that can't be ignored."

He considered for a moment his decision to reorganize some of his less-than-legal enterprises and shake loose of what couldn't be changed. "No," he murmured. "I don't believe I will."

"Why are you putting me in this position?" she demanded. "Is this some sort of punishment?"

He sat, leaned back, steepled his fingers. "If you like."

"You're going to be pulled into this, just like the last time. There's just no need for it." Driven by frustration, she slapped her hands on his desk. "Can't you see that?"

He looked at her face, the dark, worried eyes, the ridiculously chopped hair. "I know what I'm doing." He hoped he did.

"Roarke, don't you understand, it's not enough for me to know you had nothing to do with it. Now I have to prove it."

He wanted to touch her, so much that his fingers ached from it. More than anything at that moment, he wished he could hate her for it. "Do you know, Eve?"

She straightened, dropped her hands to her sides. "It doesn't matter," she said and turned and left him.

But it did matter, he thought. At the moment, it was all that really mattered. Shaken, he shifted forward. He could curse her now, now that those big, whiskey-colored eyes were no longer staring into him. He could curse her for bringing him so low he was nearly ready to beg for whatever scraps of her life she was willing to share with him.

And if he begged, if he settled, he would probably grow to hate her almost as much as he would hate himself.

He knew how to outwait a rival, how to outmanuever an opponent. He certainly knew how to fight for what he wanted or intended to have. But he was no longer sure he could outwait, outmanuever, or fight Eve.

Taking the button out of his pocket, he toyed with it, studied it as though it were some intriguing puzzle to be solved.

He was an idiot, Roarke realized. It was humiliating to admit what an incredible fool love could make of a man. He stood, slipped the button back in his pocket. He had a board meeting to complete, business to take care of.

And, he thought, some research to do on whether any details of the Slade arrest had left Sector 38. And if they had, how and why.

Eve couldn't put off her appointment with Nadine. The necessity of it irritated, as did the fact she had to schedule the time between Nadine's evening and late live broadcasts.

She plopped down at a table at a small café near Channel 75 called Images. It was, with its quiet corners and leafy trees, several large steps away from the Blue Squirrel. Eve winced at the prices on the menu—broadcasters were paid a great deal more than cops—and settled on a Classic Pepsi.

"You ought to try the muffins," Nadine told her. "The place is famous for them."

"I bet it is." At about five bucks a rehydrated blueberry, Eve thought. "I don't have a lot of time."

"Neither do I." Nadine's on-camera makeup was still perfectly in place. Eve could only wonder how anyone could stand having their pores gunked for hours at a time.

"You go first."

"Fine." Nadine broke open her muffin and it steamed fragrantly. "Obviously the memorial is the big news of the day. Who came, who said what. Lots of side stories about the family, focus is tight on the grieving daughter and her fiancé."

"Why?"

"Human interest, Dallas. Big splashy wedding plans interrupted by violent murder. Word's leaked that the ceremony will be postponed until the first part of next year."

Nadine took a bite of muffin. Eve ignored the envious reaction of her stomach juices. "Gossip isn't what I'm after, Nadine."

"But it adds color. Look, it was more like a plant than a leak. Somebody wanted the media to know the wedding's been postponed. So I wonder if this means there'll be a wedding after all. What I smell is the scent of trouble in paradise. Why would Mirina turn away from Slade at a time like this? Seems to me they'd have a nice quiet private ceremony so he'd be there to comfort her."

"Maybe that's the plan exactly, and they're throwing you off the scent."

"It's possible. Anyway, without Towers as buffer, speculation's running that Angelini and Hammett will dissolve their business associations. They were very cool to each other, never spoke during the service—before or after it, either."

"How do you know?"

Nadine smiled, feline and pleased. "I have my sources. Angelini needs income, and fast. Roarke's made him an offer for his shares, which now include Towers's interest, in Mercury."

"Has he?"

"You didn't know. Interesting." Sly as a cat, Nadine licked crumbs from her fingertips. "I thought it was interesting, too, that you didn't attend the service with Roarke."

"I was there in an official capacity," Eve said shortly. "Let's stick to the point."

"More trouble in paradise," Nadine murmured, then her eyes sobered. "Look, Dallas, I like you. I don't know why, but I do. If you and Roarke are having problems, I'm sorry for it."

Buddy-to-buddy confidences were something Eve was never comfortable with. She shifted, surprised that she was tempted, even for an instant, to share. Then she set it down to Nadine's skill as a reporter. "The point," she repeated.

"Okay." Nadine moved a shoulder and took another bite of muffin. "Nobody knows dick," she said briefly. "We've got speculation. Angelini's financial difficulties, the son's gambling habits, the Fluentes case."

"You can forget the Fluentes case," Eve interrupted. "He's going down. Both he and his lawyer know it. The evidence is clean. Taking Towers out won't change a thing."

"He might have been pissed."

"Maybe. But he's small time. He doesn't have the contacts or the money to buy a hit the size of Towers. It doesn't check out. We're running everybody she ever put away. So far we've got zip."

"You've cooled off on the revenge theory, haven't you?"

"Yeah. I think it was closer to home."

"Anyone in particular?"

"No." Eve shook her head when Nadine studied her. "No," she repeated. "I don't have anything solid yet. Here's what I want you to look into, and I need you to hold it off the air until I clear it."

"That was the deal."

Briefly, Eve told her of the incident in Sector 38.

"Holy shit, that's hot. And it's public record, Dallas."

"That may be, but you wouldn't know where to look unless I'd tipped you. Stick with the deal, Nadine. You hold it off air, and you poke around. See if you can find out if anyone knows, or cares. If there's a connection to the murder, I'll hand it to you. If not, I guess it'll be up to your conscience whether you want to broadcast something that could ruin the reputation of a man and his relationship with his fiancée."

"Low blow, Dallas."

"Depends on where you're standing. Keep the cover on it, Nadine."

"Um-hmm." Her mind was humming. "Slade was in San Francisco the night of the murder." She waited a beat. "Wasn't he?"

"So the record shows."

"And there are dozens of coast-to-coast shuttles, public and private, running every hour, back and forth."

"That's right. You keep in touch, Nadine," Eve said as she rose. "And you keep the cover on."

Eve made it an early night. When her 'link beeped at one, she was screaming her way out of a nightmare. Sweating, shaking, she tore off the covers that wrapped around her, fought off the hands that were groping over her body.

She choked back another scream, pressed her fingers against her eyes, and ordered herself not to be sick. She answered the call without turning the lights on, and blocked video.

"Dallas."

"Dispatch. Voiceprint verified. Probable homicide, female. Report Five thirty-two Central Park South, rear of building. Code Yellow."

"Acknowledged." Eve ended the transmission and, still trembling from the aftershocks of the dream, crawled out of bed.

It took her twenty minutes. She'd needed the comfort of a hot shower, even if it had only been for thirty seconds.

It was a trendy neighborhood, peopled by residents who patronized fashionable shops and private clubs, and who aspired to move just another notch up the social and economic ladder.

The streets were quiet here, though it wasn't quite out of the realm of public taxis and into private transpo-cars. Upper middle class all the way, she mused as she made her way around to the back of a sleek steel building with its pleasant view of the park.

Then again, murder happened everywhere.

It had certainly happened here.

The rear of the building couldn't boast a view of the park, but the developers had made up for it with a nice plot of green. Beyond the trim trees was a security wall that separated one building from the next.

On the narrow stone path through a border of gold petunias, the body sprawled, facedown.

Female, Eve noted, flashing her badge at the waiting uniforms. Dark hair, dark skin, well dressed. She studied the stylish red-and-white-striped heel that lay point up on the path.

Death had knocked her out of her shoes.

"Pictures?"

"Yes, sir, Lieutenant. ME on the way."

"Who reported it?"

"Neighbor. Came out to let his dog use the facilities. We've got him inside."

"Do we have a name on her?"

"Yvonne Metcalf, Lieutenant. She lives in eleven twenty-six."

"Actress," Eve murmured as the name struck a cord. "Up and coming."

"Yes, sir." One of the uniforms looked down at the body. "She won an Emmy last year. Been doing the talk show rounds. She's pretty famous."

"Now she's pretty dead. Keep the camera running. I need to turn her over."

Even before she used the protective spray to seal her hands, before she crouched down to turn the body, Eve knew. Blood was everywhere. Someone hissed sharply as the body rolled faceup, but it wasn't Eve. She'd been braced for it.

The throat was cut, and the cut was deep. Yvonne's lovely green eyes stared up at Eve: two blank questions.

"What the hell did you have to do with Cicely Towers?" she murmured. "Same MO: one wound to the throat, severed jugular. No robbery, no signs of sexual assault or struggle." Gently, Eve lifted one of Yvonne's limp hands, shone her light at the nails, under them. They were painted a sparkling scarlet with tiny white stripes. And they were perfect. No chips, no snags, no scrapes of flesh or stains of blood under them.

"All dressed up and no place to go," Eve commented, studying the victim's flashy red-and-white-striped bodysuit. "Let's find out where she'd been or where she was going," Eve began. Her head came around as she heard the sound of approaching feet.

But it wasn't the medical examiner and his team, nor was it the sweepers. It was, she saw with disgust, C. J. Morse and a crew from Channel 75.

"Get that camera out of here." Temper vibrating, she sprang to her feet, instinctively shielding the body. "This is a crime scene."

"You haven't posted it," Morse said, smiling sweetly. "Until you do, it's public access. Sherry, get a shot of that shoe."

"Post the goddamn scene," Eve ordered a uniform. "Confiscate that camera, the recorders."

"You can't confiscate media equipment until the scene's posted," C. J. reminded her, as he tried to rubberneck around her to get a good look. "Sherry, get me a nice pan, then focus on the lieutenant's pretty face."

"I'm going to kick your ass, Morse."

"Oh, I wish you'd try, Dallas." Some of his bubbling resentment simmered into his eyes. "I'd love to bring you up on charges, and broadcast it, after that stunt you pulled on me."

"If you're still on this scene when it's posted, you'll be the one facing charges."

He only smiled again, backing off. He calculated he had another fifteen seconds of video time before he ran into trouble. "Channel 75 has a fine team of lawyers."

"Detain him and his crew." Eve flashed a snarl at a uniform. "Off scene, until I'm through."

"Interfering with media—"

"Kiss ass, Morse."

"I bet yours is tasty." He continued to grin as he was escorted away.

When Eve came around the building, he was doing a sober stand-up report on the recent homicide. Without missing a beat, he angled himself toward her. "Lieutenant Dallas, will you confirm that Yvonne Metcalf, the star of *Tune In* has been murdered?"

"The department has no comment to make at this time."

"Isn't it true that Ms. Metcalf was a resident of this building, and that her body was discovered this morning on the rear patio? Hadn't her throat been cut?"

"No comment."

"Our viewing audience is waiting, Lieutenant. Two prominent women have been violently murdered by the same method, and in all likelihood by the same person, barely a week apart. And you have no comment?"

"Unlike certain irresponsible reporters, the police are more careful, and more concerned with facts than speculation."

"Or is it that the police are simply unable to solve these crimes?" Quick on his feet, he sidestepped, came up in her face again. "Aren't you concerned about your reputation, Lieutenant, and the connection between the two victims and your close friend Roarke?"

"My reputation isn't at issue here. The investigation is."

Morse turned back to the camera. "At this hour, the investigation, headed by Lieutenant Eve Dallas, is at an apparent deadlock. Another murder has taken place less than a hundred yards from where I stand.

A young woman, talented, beautiful, and full of promise has had her life sliced off by a violent sweep of a knife. Just as only one week ago, the respected and dedicated defender of justice, Cicely Towers had her life brought to an end. Perhaps the question is not when will the killer be caught, but what prominent woman will be next? This is C. J. Morse for Channel 75, reporting live from Central Park South."

He nodded to the camera operator before turning to beam at Eve. "See, if you'd cooperate, Dallas, I might be able to help you out with public opinion."

"Fuck you, Morse."

"Oh, well, maybe if you asked nice." His grin never wavered when she grabbed him by the shirtfront. "Now, now, don't touch unless you mean it."

She was a full head taller than he, and gave serious thought to pounding him into the sidewalk. "Here's what I want to know, Morse. I want to know how a third-rate reporter ends up on a crime scene, with a crew, ten minutes after the primary."

He smoothed down the front of his shirt. "Sources, Lieutenant, which, as you know I'm under no obligation to share with you." His smile dimmed into a sneer. "And at this stage, I'd say we're talking third-rate primary. You'd have been better off hooking up with me instead of Nadine. That was a nasty turn you served, helping her bump me off the Towers story."

"Was it? Well, I'm glad to hear that, C. J., because I just plain hate your guts. It didn't bother you at all, did it, to go back there, camera running, and broadcast pictures of that woman? You didn't think about her right to a little dignity or the fact that someone who cared about her might not have been notified. Her family, for instance."

"Hey, you do your job, I do mine. You didn't look too bothered poking at her."

"What time did you get the tip?" Eve asked briefly.

He hesitated, stringing it out. "I guess it wouldn't hurt to tell you that. It came in on my private line at twelve thirty."

"From?"

"Nope. I protect my sources. I called the station, drummed up a crew. Right, Sherry?"

"Right." The camera operator moved a shoulder. "The night desk sent us out to meet C. J. here. That's show biz."

"I'm going to do whatever I can to confiscate your logs, Morse, to bring you in for questioning, to make your life hell."

"Oh, I hope you do." His round face gleamed. "You'll give me double my usual airtime and put my popularity quotient through the roof. And you know what's going to be fun? The side story I'm going to work up on Roarke and his cozy relationship with Yvonne Metcalf."

Her stomach shuddered, but she kept her voice bland. "Watch your step there, C. J., Roarke's not nearly as nice as I am. Keep your crew off scene," she warned. "Put one toe on, and I confiscate your equipment."

She turned, and when she was far enough away, pulled out her communicator. She was going outside of procedure, risking a reprimand or worse. But it had to be done.

She could tell when Roarke answered that he hadn't yet been to bed.

"Well, Lieutenant, this is a surprise."

"I've only got a minute. Tell me what your relationship was with Yvonne Metcalf."

He lifted a brow. "We're friends, were close at one time."

"You were lovers."

"Yes, briefly. Why?"

"Because she's dead, Roarke."

His faint smile faded. "Oh Christ, how?"

"She had her throat cut. Stay available."

"Is that an official request, Lieutenant?" he asked, and his voice was hard as rock.

"It has to be. Roarke . . ." She hesitated. "I'm sorry."

"So am I." He ended the transmission.

CHAPTER

EIGHT

Eve had no problem listing several connections between Cicely Towers and Yvonne Metcalf. Number one was murder. The method and the perpetrator. They had both been women in the public eye, well respected, and held in great affection. They were successful in their chosen fields and were dedicated to that field. They both had families who loved and who mourned.

Yet they had worked and played in dramatically different social and professional circles. Yvonne's friends had been artists, actors, and musicians, while Cicely had socialized with law enforcers, business-people, and politicians.

Cicely had been an organized career woman of impeccable taste who had guarded her privacy fiercely.

Yvonne had been a cheerfully disorganized, borderline messy actor who courted the public eye.

But someone had known them both well enough and felt strongly enough about both to kill them.

The only name Eve found in Cicely's tidy address book and Yvonne's disordered one that matched was Roarke.

For the third time in an hour, Eve ran the lists through her computer, pushing for a connection. A name that clicked with another name, an address, a profession, a personal interest. The few connections that came through were so loosely linked she could barely justify taking the next step toward the interview.

But she would do it, because the alternative was Roarke.

While the computer handled the short list, she took another pass through Yvonne's electronic diary.

"Why the hell didn't the woman put in names?" Eve muttered. There were times, dates, occasionally initials, often little side notes or symbols of Yvonne's mood.

1:00—lunch at the Crown Room with B. C. Yippee! Don't be late, Yvonne, and wear the green number with the short skirt. He likes prompt women with legs.

Beauty day at Paradise. Thank God. 10:00. Should try to hit Fitness Palace at 8 for workout. Ugh.

Fancy lunches, Eve mused. Pampering in the top salon in the city. Sweating a little in a luxury gym. Not a bad life, all in all. Who had wanted to end it?

She flipped through to the day of the murder.

8:00—Power breakfast—little blue suit with matching shoes. LOOK PROFESSIONAL FOR CHRIST'S SAKE, YVONNE!!

11:00—P. P.'s office to discuss contract negotiations. Maybe sneak in some shopping first. SHOE SALE AT SAKS. Hot damn.

Lunch—skip dessert. Maybe. Tell cutie he was wonderful in show. No penalty for lying to pals about their acting. God, wasn't he awful?

Call home.

Hit Saks if you missed it earlier.

*5ish. Drinks. Stick with spring water, babe. You talk too much when you're loose. Be bright, sparkle. Push Tune In. $$$***. Don't forget photo layout in morning and stay away from that wine. Go home, take a nap.*

Midnight meeting. Could be hot stuff. Wear the red-and-white-striped number, and smile, smile, smile. Bygones are bygones, right? Never close that door. Small world, and so on. What a dumb ass.

So she'd documented the meeting at midnight. Not who, not

where, not what, but she'd wanted to be well dressed for it. Someone she'd known, had a history with. Bygones. A past problem with?

Lover? Eve mused. She didn't think so. Yvonne hadn't put little hearts around the notation or told herself to be sexy, sexy, sexy. Eve thought she was beginning to understand the woman. Yvonne had been amused at herself, ready for fun, enjoying her lifestyle. And she'd been ambitious.

Wouldn't she have told herself to smile, smile, smile, for a career opportunity? A part, good press, a new script, an influential fan.

What would she have said about Roarke? Eve wondered. Most likely she'd have noted him down with a big, bold-faced capital R. She would have put hearts around the date, or dollar signs, or smiles. As she had eighteen months before she died.

Eve didn't have to look at Yvonne's previous diaries. She remembered perfectly the woman's last notation on Roarke.

Dinner with R—8:30. YUM-YUM. Wear the white satin—matching teddy. Be prepared, might get lucky. The man's body is awesome—wish I could figure out his head. Oh well, just think sexy and see what happens.

Eve didn't particularly want to know if Yvonne had gotten lucky. Obviously they'd been lovers—Roarke had said so himself. So why hadn't she put down any more dates with him after the white satin?

It was something, she supposed, she'd have to find out—for investigative purposes only.

Meanwhile, she would make another trip to Yvonne's apartment, try again to reconstruct the last day of her life. She had interviews to schedule. And, as Yvonne's parents called her at least once a day, Eve knew she would have to talk with them again, steel herself against their horrible grief and disbelief.

She didn't mind the fourteen- and sixteen-hour days. In fact, at this stage of her life she welcomed them.

Four days after Yvonne Metcalf's murder, Eve was running on empty. She had questioned over three dozen people extensively, exhaustively. Not only had she been unable to discover a single viable motive, she'd found no one who hadn't adored the victim.

There wasn't a hint of an obsessed fan. Yvonne's mail had been mountainous, and Feeney and his computer were still scanning the correspondence. But among the first section, there had been no threats, veiled or overt, no weird or unsavory offers or suggestions.

There had been a hefty percentage of marriage proposals and other propositions. Eve culled them out with little hope or enthusiasm. There was still a chance that someone who had written to Yvonne had written or contacted Cicely. As time passed, the chance became a long shot.

Eve did what was expected in unsolved multiple homicides, what departmental procedure called for at this stage of an investigation. She made an appointment with the shrink.

While she waited, Eve struggled with her mixed feelings for Dr. Mira. The woman was brilliant, insightful, quietly efficient, and compassionate.

Those were the precise reasons Eve dragged her feet. She had to remind herself again that she hadn't come to Mira for personal reasons or because the department was sending her for therapy. She wasn't going through Testing, they weren't going to discuss her thoughts, her feelings—or her memory.

They were going to dissect the mind of a killer.

Still, she had to concentrate on keeping her heart rate level, her hands still and dry. When she was gestured into Mira's office, Eve told herself her legs were shaky because she was tired, nothing more.

"Lieutenant Dallas." Mira's pale blue eyes skimmed over Eve's face, noted the fatigue. "I'm sorry you had to wait."

"No problem." Though she would have preferred standing, Eve took the blue scoop chair beside Mira's. "I appreciate you getting to the case so quickly."

"We all do our jobs as best we can," Mira said in her soothing voice. "And I had a great deal of respect and affection for Cicely Towers."

"You knew her?"

"We were contemporaries, and she consulted me on many cases. I often testified for the prosecution—as well as the defense," she added, smiling a little. "But you knew that."

"Just making conversation."

"I also admired Yvonne Metcalf's talent. She brought a lot of happiness to the world. She'll be missed."

"Someone isn't going to miss either of them."

"True enough." In her smooth, graceful way, Mira programmed her AutoChef for tea. "I realize you might be a bit pressed for time, but I work better with a little stimulation. And you look as though you could use some."

"I'm fine."

Recognizing the tightly controlled hostility in the tone, Mira only lifted a brow. "Overworked, as usual. It happens to those who are particularly good at their jobs." She handed Eve a cup of tea in one of the pretty china cups. "Now, I've read over your reports, the evidence you've gathered, and your theories. My psychiatric profile," she said, tapping a sealed disc on the table between them.

"You've completed it." Eve didn't trouble to mask the irritation. "You could have transmitted the data and saved me a trip."

"I could have, but I preferred to discuss this with you, face to face. Eve, you're dealing with something, someone, very dangerous."

"I think I picked up on that, Doctor. Two women have had their throats slashed."

"Two women, thus far," Mira said quietly and sat back. "I'm very much afraid there will be more. And soon."

Because she believed the same, Eve ignored the quick chill that sprinted up her spine. "Why?"

"It was so easy, you see. And so simple. A job well done. There's a satisfaction in that. There's also the attention factor. Whoever accomplished the murders can now sit back in his or her home and watch the show. The reports, the editorials, the grieving, the services, the public arena of the investigation."

She paused to savor her tea. "You have your theory, Eve. You're here so that I can corroborate it or argue against it."

"I have several theories."

"Only one you believe in." Mira smiled her wise smile, aware that it made Eve bristle. "Fame. What else did these two women have in common but their public prominence? They didn't share the same social circle or professional one. Knew few of the same people, even on a casual level. They didn't patronize the same shops, health centers, or cosmetic experts. What they did share was fame, public interest, and a kind of power."

"Which the killer envied."

"I would say exactly that. Resented as well and wished, by killing them, to bask in the reflected attention. The murders themselves were both vicious and uncommonly clean. Their faces weren't marred, nor their bodies. One quick slice across the throat, according to the ME, from the front. Face to face. A blade is a personal weapon, an extension of the hand. It isn't distant like a laser, or aloof like poison. Your murderer wanted the feel of killing, the sight of blood, the smell of it. The full experience that makes him or her one who appreciates having control, following through on a plan."

"You don't believe it was a hired hit."

"There's always that possibility, Eve, but I'm more inclined to see the killer as an active participant rather than a hireling. Then there are the souvenirs."

"Towers's umbrella."

"And Metcalf's right shoe. You've managed to keep that out of the press."

"Barely." Eve scowled over the memory of Morse and his crew invading the murder scene. "A pro wouldn't have taken a souvenir, and the killings were too well thought out to have been planned by a street hit."

"I agree. You have an organized mind, an ambitious one. Your murderer is enjoying his work, which is why there'll be another."

"Or hers," Eve put in. "The envy factor can be leaned toward a female. These two women were what she wanted to be. Beautiful, successful, admired, famous, strong. It's often the weak who kill."

"Yes, quite often. No, it isn't possible to determine gender from the data we have at this point, only to access the probability factor that the killer targets females who have reached a high level of public attention."

"What am I supposed to do about that, Dr. Mira? Put a security beeper on every prominent, well-known, or successful woman in the city? Including yourself?"

"Odd, I was thinking more about you."

"Me?" Eve jiggled the tea she hadn't touched, then set it on the table with a snap. "That's ridiculous."

"I don't think so. You've become a familiar face, Eve. For your work, certainly, and most particularly since the case last winter. You're very respected in your field. And," she continued before Eve could interrupt, "you also have one more important connection to both victims. All of you have had a relationship with Roarke."

Eve knew her blood drained from her face. That wasn't something she could control. But she could keep her voice level and hard. "Roarke had a business partnership, a relatively minor one, with Towers. With Metcalf, the intimate side of their relationship has been over for quite some time."

"Yet you feel the need to defend him to me."

"I'm not defending him," Eve snapped. "I'm stating facts. Roarke's more than capable of defending himself."

"Undoubtedly. He's a strong, vital, and clever man. Still, you worry for him."

"In your professional opinion, is Roarke the killer?"

"Absolutely not. I have no doubt that were I to analyze him, I would find his killer instinct well developed." The fact was, Mira would have loved the opportunity to study Roarke's mind. "But his motive would have to be very defined. Great love or great hate. I doubt there is much else that would push him over the line. Relax, Eve," Mira said quietly. "You're not in love with a murderer."

"I'm not in love with anyone. And my personal feelings aren't at issue here."

"On the contrary, the investigator's state of mind is always an issue. And, if I'm required to give my opinion on yours, I'll have to say I found you near exhaustion, emotionally torn, and deeply troubled."

Eve picked up the profile disc and rose. "Then it's fortunate you're not going to be required to give your opinion. I'm perfectly capable of doing my job."

"I don't doubt it for a moment. But at what cost to yourself?"

"The cost would be higher if I didn't do it. I'm going to find who killed these women. Then it'll be up to someone like Cicely Towers to put them away." Eve tucked the disk in her bag. "There's a connection you left out, Dr. Mira. Something these two women had in common." Eve's eyes were hard and cold. "Family. Both of them had close family that was a large and important part of their lives. I'd say that lets me out as a possible target. Wouldn't you?"

"Perhaps. Have you been thinking of your family, Eve?"

"Don't play with me."

"You mentioned it," Mira pointed out. "You're always careful in what you say to me, so I must assume family is on your mind."

"I don't have family," Eve shot back. "And I've got murder on my mind. If you want to report to the commander that I'm unfit for duty, that's just fine."

"When are you going to trust me?" There was impatience, for the first time in Eve's memory, in the careful voice. "Is it so impossible for you to believe that I care about you? Yes, I care," Mira said when Eve blinked in surprise. "And I understand you better than you wish to admit."

"I don't need for you to understand me." But there were nerves in Eve's voice now. She heard them herself. "I'm not in Testing or here for a therapy session."

"There are no recorders on here." Mira set her tea down with a snap that had Eve jamming her hands in her pockets. "Do you think you're the only child who lived with horror and abuse? The only woman who's struggled to overcome it?"

"I don't have to overcome anything. I don't remember—"

"My stepfather raped me repeatedly from the time I was twelve until I was fifteen," Mira said calmly, and stopped Eve's protest cold. "For those three years I lived never knowing when it would happen, only that it would. And no one would listen to me."

Shaken, sick, Eve wrapped her arms around her body. "I don't want to know this. Why are you telling me this?"

"Because I look in your eyes and see myself. But you have someone who'll listen to you, Eve."

Eve stood where she was, moistened her dry lips. "Why did it stop?"

"Because I finally found the courage to go to an abuse center, tell the counselor everything, to submit to the examinations, both physical and psychiatric. The terror of that, the humiliation of that, was no longer as huge as the alternative."

"Why should I have to remember it?" Eve demanded. "It's over."

"Why aren't you sleeping?"

"The investigation—"

"Eve."

The gentle tone had Eve closing her eyes. It was so hard, so trying, to fight that quiet compassion. "Flashbacks," she murmured, hating herself for the weakness. "Nightmares."

"Of before you were found in Texas?"

"Just blips, just pieces."

"I can help you put them together."

"Why should I want to put them together?"

"Haven't you already started to?" Now Mira rose. "You can work with this haunting your subconscious. I've watched you do so for years. But happiness eludes you, and will continue to do so until you've convinced yourself you deserve it."

"It wasn't my fault."

"No." Mira touched a gentle hand to Eve's arm. "No, it wasn't your fault."

Tears were threatening, and that was a shock and an embarrassment. "I can't talk about this."

"My dear, you've already begun to. I'll be here when you're ready to do so again." She waited until Eve had reached the door. "Can I ask you a question?"

"You always ask questions."

"Why stop now?" Mira said and smiled. "Does Roarke make you happy?"

"Sometimes." Eve squeezed her eyes shut and swore. "Yes, yes, he makes me happy. Unless he's making me miserable."

"That's lovely. I'm very pleased for both of you. Try to get some sleep, Eve. If you won't take chemicals, you might use simple visualization."

"I'll keep it in mind." Eve opened the door, kept her back to the room. "Thank you."

"You're welcome."

*   *   *

Visualization wouldn't be much help, Eve decided. Not after a re-scan of autopsy reports.

The apartment was too quiet, too empty. She was sorry she'd left the cat with Roarke. At least Galahad would have been company.

Because her eyes burned from studying data, she pushed away from her desk. She didn't have the energy to seek out Mavis, and she was bored senseless with the video offerings on her screen.

She ordered music, listened for thirty seconds, then switched it off.

Food usually worked, but when she poked into the kitchen, she was reminded she hadn't restocked her AutoChef in weeks. The pick-ings were slim, and she didn't have enough of an appetite to order in.

Determined to relax, she tried out the virtual reality goggles Mavis had given her for Christmas. Because Mavis had used them last, they were set for Nightclub, at full volume. After a hurried adjustment and a great deal of swearing, Eve programmed Tropics, Beach.

She could feel the grit of hot, white sand under her bare feet, the punch of the sun on her skin, the soft, ocean breeze. It was lovely to stand in the gentle surf, watch the swoop of gulls, and sip from an icy drink that carried the zing of rum and fruit.

There were hands on her bare shoulders, rubbing. Sighing, she leaned back into them, felt the firm length of male against her back. Far out on the blue sea a white ship sailed toward the horizon.

It was easy to turn into the arms that waited for her, to lift her mouth to the mouth she wanted. And to lie on the hot sand with the body that fit so perfectly with hers.

The excitement was as sweet as the peace. The rhythm as old as the waves that lapped over her skin. She let herself be taken, shivered as the needs built toward fulfillment. His breath was on her face, his body linked with her when she groaned out his name.

Roarke.

Furious with herself, Eve tore off the goggles and heaved them aside. He had no right to intrude, even here, inside her head. No right to bring her pain and pleasure when all she wanted was privacy.

Oh, he knew what he was doing, she thought as she sprang up to pace. He knew exactly what he was doing. And they were going to settle it, once and for all.

She slammed the apartment door behind her. It didn't occur to her until she was speeding through his gates that he might not be alone.

The idea of that was so infuriating, so devastating, that she took the stone steps two at a time, hit the door with a fresh burst of violent energy.

Summerset was waiting for her. "Lieutenant, it's one twenty in the morning."

"I know what time it is." She bared her teeth when he stepped in front of her to block the staircase. "Let's understand each other, pal. I hate you, you hate me. The difference is I've got a badge. Now get the hell out of my way or I'll haul your bony ass in for obstructing an officer."

Dignity coated him like silk. "Do I take that to mean you're here, at this hour, in an official capacity, Lieutenant?"

"Take it any way you want. Where is he?"

"If you'll state your business, I'll be happy to determine Roarke's current whereabouts and see if he's available to you."

Out of patience, Eve jammed an elbow in his gut and skirted his wheezing form. "I'll find him myself," she stated as she bounded up the stairs.

He wasn't in bed, alone or otherwise. She wasn't entirely sure how she felt about that, or what she would have done if she'd found him twined around some blonde. Refusing to think about it, she turned on her heel and marched away toward his office, with Summerset hot on her trail.

"I intend to file a complaint."

"File away," she shot back over her shoulder.

"You have no right to intrude on private property, in the middle of the night. You will not disturb Roarke." He slapped a hand on the door as she reached it. "I will not allow it."

To Eve's surprise, he was out of breath and red-faced. His eyes were all but jittering in their sockets. It was, she decided, more emotion than she'd believed him capable of.

"This really puts your jocks in a twist, doesn't it?" Before he could prevent it, she hit the mechanism and the door slid open.

He made a grab for her, and Roarke, who turned from his study of the city, had the curious surprise of watching them grapple.

"Put a hand on me again, you tight-assed son of a bitch, and I'll deck you." She lifted a fist to demonstrate. "The satisfaction would be worth my badge."

"Summerset," Roarke said mildly. "I believe she means it. Leave us alone."

"She's exceeded her authority—"

"Leave us alone," Roarke repeated. "I'll deal with this."

"As you wish." Summerset jerked his starched jacket back into place and strode out—with only the slightest of limps.

"If you want to keep me out," Eve snapped on her march toward the desk, "you're going to have to do better than that flat-assed guard dog."

Roarke merely folded his hands on the desktop. "If I'd wanted to keep you out, you would no longer be cleared through gate security." Deliberately, he flicked a glance at his watch. "It's a bit late for official interviews."

"I'm tired of people telling me what time it is."

"Well then." He leaned back in the chair. "What can I do for you?"

CHAPTER

NINE

Attack was the emotional choice. Eve could justify it as the logical one as well.

"You were involved with Yvonne Metcalf."

"As I told you, we were friends." He opened an antique silver box on the desk and took out a cigarette. "At one time, intimate friends."

"Who changed the aspect of your relationship, and when?"

"Who? Hmmm." Roarke thought it over as he lighted the cigarette, blew out a thin haze of smoke. "I believe it was a mutual decision. Her career was rising quickly, causing numerous demands on her time and energy. You could say we drifted apart."

"You quarreled?"

"I don't believe we did. Yvonne was rarely quarrelsome. She found life too . . . amusing. Would you like a brandy?"

"I'm on duty."

"Yes, of course you are. I'm not."

When he rose, Eve saw the cat spring from his lap. Galahad examined her with his bicolored eyes before plunking down to wash. She was too busy scowling at the cat to note that Roarke's hands weren't quite steady as he stood at the carved liquor cabinet pouring brandy from decanter to snifter.

"Well," he said, swirling the glass with half the width of the room between them. "Is that all?"

No, she thought, that was far from all. If he wouldn't help her voluntarily, she would poke and prod and use his canny brain without mercy and without a qualm. "The last time you're noted in her diary was a year and a half ago."

"So long," Roarke murmured. He had regret, a great deal of it, for Yvonne. But he had his own problems at the moment, the biggest of which was standing across the room, watching him with turbulent eyes. "I didn't realize."

"Was that the last time you saw her?"

"No, I'm sure it wasn't." He stared into his brandy, remembering her. "I recall dancing with her at a party, last New Year's Eve. She came back here with me."

"You slept with her," Eve said evenly.

"Technically, no." His voice took on a clip of annoyance. "I had sex with her, conversation, brunch."

"You resumed your former relationship?"

"No." He chose a chair and ordered himself to enjoy his brandy and cigarette. Casually, he crossed his feet at the ankles. "We might have, but we were both quite busy with our own projects. I didn't hear from her again for six weeks, maybe seven."

"And?"

He'd brushed her off, he recalled. Casually, easily. Perhaps thoughtlessly. "I told her I was . . . involved." He examined the bright tip of his cigarette. "At that time I was falling in love with someone else."

Her heartbeat hitched. She stared at him, jammed her hands in her pockets. "I can't eliminate you from the list unless you help me."

"Can't you? Well, then."

"Damn it, Roarke, you're the only one who was involved with both victims."

"And what's my motive, Lieutenant?"

"Don't use that tone with me. I hate it when you do that. Cold, controlled, superior." Giving up, she began to pace. "I know you didn't have anything to do with the murders, and there's no evidence to support your involvement. But that doesn't break the link."

"And that makes it difficult for you, because your name is, in turn, linked with mine. Or was."

"I can handle that."

"Then why have you lost weight?" he demanded. "Why are there shadows under your eyes? Why do you look so unhappy?"

She yanked out her recorder, slapped it on his desk. A barrier between them. "I need you to tell me everything you know about these women. Every small, insignificant detail. Damn it, damn it, damn it, I need help. I have to know why Towers would go to the West End in the middle of the night. Why Metcalf would dress herself up and go out to the patio at midnight."

He tapped out his cigarette, then rose slowly. "You're giving me more credit than I deserve, Eve. I didn't know Cicely that well. We did business, socialized in the most distant of fashions. Remember my background and her position. As to Yvonne, we were lovers. I enjoyed her, her energy, her zest. I know she had ambition. She wanted stardom and she earned it, deserved it. But I can't tell you the minds of either of these women."

"You know people," she argued. "You have a way of getting inside their heads. Nothing ever surprises you."

"You do," he murmured. "Continually."

She only shook her head. "Tell me why you think Yvonne Metcalf went out to meet someone on the patio."

He sipped brandy, shrugged. "For advancement, glory, excitement, love. Probably in that order. She would have dressed carefully because she was vain, admirably so. The time of the meeting wouldn't have meant anything to her. She was impulsive, entertainingly so."

She let out a little breath. This was what she needed. He could help her see the victims. "Were there other men?"

He was brooding, he realized, and forced himself to stop. "She was lovely, entertaining, bright, excellent in bed. I imagine there were a great many men in her life."

"Jealous men, angry men?"

He lifted a brow. "Do you mean someone might have killed her because she wouldn't give him what he wanted? Needed?" His eyes stayed steady on hers. "It's a thought. A man could do a great deal of damage to a woman for that, if he wanted or needed badly enough. Then again, I haven't killed you. Yet."

"This is a murder investigation, Roarke. Don't get cute with me."

"Cute?" He stunned them both by flinging the half-empty snifter across the room. Glass shattered on the wall, liquor sprayed. "You come bursting in here, without warning, without invitation, and expect me to sit cooperatively, like a trained dog, while you interrogate me? You ask me questions about Yvonne, a woman I cared for, and expect me to cheerfully answer them while you imagine me in bed with her."

She'd seen his temper spurt and flash before. She usually preferred it to his icy control. But at the moment her nerves had shattered along with the glass. "It's not personal, and it's not an interrogation. It's a consultation with a useful source. I'm doing my job."

"This has nothing to do with your job, and we both know it. If there's even a germ of belief in you that I had anything to do with slitting the throats of those two women, then I've made even a bigger mistake than I'd imagined. If you want to poke holes in me, Lieutenant, do it on your own time, not mine." He scooped her recorder off the desk and tossed it to her. "Next time, bring a warrant."

"I'm trying to eliminate you completely."

"Haven't you done that already?" He moved back behind his desk and sat wearily. "Get out. I'm done with this."

She was surprised she didn't stumble on her way to the door, the way her heart was pounding and her knees were shaking. She fought for breath as she reached for it. At the desk, Roarke cursed himself for a fool and hit the button to engage the locks. Damn her, and damn himself, but she wasn't walking out on him.

He was opening his mouth to speak when she turned, inches from the door. There was fury on her face now. "All right. Goddamn it, all right, you win. I'm miserable. Isn't that what you want? I can't sleep, I can't eat. It's like something's broken inside me, and I can barely do my job. Happy now?"

He felt the first tingle of relief loosen the fist around his heart. "Should I be?"

"I'm here, aren't I? I'm here because I couldn't stay away anymore." Dragging at the chain under her shirt, she strode to him. "I'm wearing the damn thing."

He glanced at the diamond she thrust in his face. It flashed at him, full of fire and secrets. "As I said, it suits you."

"A lot you know," she muttered and swung around. "It makes me feel like an idiot. This whole thing makes me feel like an idiot. So fine; I'll be an idiot. I'll move in here. I'll tolerate that insulting robot you call a butler. I'll wear diamonds. Just don't—" She broke, covering her face as the sobs took over. "I can't take this anymore."

"Don't. For Christ's sake, don't cry."

"I'm just tired." She rocked herself for comfort. "I'm just tired, that's all."

"Call me names." He rose, shaken and more than a little terrified by the storm of weeping. "Throw something. Take a swing at me."

She jerked back when he reached for her. "Don't. I need a minute when I'm making a fool of myself."

Ignoring her, he gathered her close. She pulled back twice, was brought back firmly against him. Then, in a desperate move, her arms came around him, clutched. "Don't go away." She pressed her face to his shoulder. "Don't go away."

"I'm not going anywhere." Gently, he stroked her back, cradled her head. Was there anything more astounding or more frightening to a man, he wondered, than a strong woman in tears? "I've been right here all along. I love you, Eve, almost more than I can stand."

"I need you. I can't help it. I don't want to."

"I know." He eased back, tucking a hand under her chin to lift her face to his. "We're going to have to deal with it." He kissed one wet cheek, then the other. "I really can't do without you."

"You told me to go."

"I locked the door." His lips curved a little before they brushed over hers. "If you'd waited a few more hours, I would have come to you. I was sitting here tonight, trying to talk myself out of it and not having any luck. Then you stalked in. I was perilously close to getting on my knees."

"Why?" She touched his face. "You could have anyone. You probably have."

"Why?" He tilted his head. "That's a tricky one. Could it be your serenity, your quiet manner, your flawless fashion sense?" It did his heart good to see her quick, amused grin. "No, I must be thinking of someone else. It must be your courage, your absolute dedication to balancing scales, that restless mind, and that sweet corner of your heart that pushes you to care so much about so many."

"That's not me."

"Oh, but it is you, darling Eve." He touched his lips to hers. "Just as that taste is you, the smell, the look, the sound. You've undone me. We'll talk," he murmured, brushing his thumbs over drying tears. "We'll figure out a way to make this work for both of us."

She drew in a shuddering breath. "I love you." And let it out. "God."

The emotion that swept through him was like a summer storm, quick, violent, then clean. Swamped with it, he rested his brow on hers. "You didn't choke on it."

"I guess not. Maybe I'll get used to it." And maybe her stomach wouldn't jump like a pond of frogs next time. Angling her face up, she found his mouth.

In an instant the kiss was hot, greedy, and full of edgy need. The blood was roaring in her head, so loud and fierce she didn't hear herself say the words again, but she felt them, in the way her heart stuttered and swelled.

Breathless and already wet, she tugged at his slacks. "Now. Right now."

"Absolutely now." He'd dragged her shirt over her head before they hit the floor.

They rolled, groping for each other. Limbs tangled. Giddy with hunger, she sank her teeth into his shoulder as he yanked down her jeans. He had a moment to register the feel of her skin under his hands, the shape of her, the heat of her, then it was a morass of the senses, a clash of scents and textures abrading against the urgent need to mate.

Finesse would have to wait, as would tenderness. The beast clawed at them both, devouring even when he was deep inside her, pumping wildly. He could feel her body clutch and tense, heard her long, low moan of staggering release. And let himself empty, heart, soul, and seed.

She awoke in his bed with soft sunlight creeping through the win-dow filters. With her eyes closed, she reached out and found the space beside her warm but empty.

"How the hell did I get here?" she wondered.

"I carried you."

Her eyes sprang open and focused on Roarke. He sat naked, cross-legged at her knees, watching her. "Carried me?"

"You fell asleep on the floor." He leaned over to rub a thumb over her cheek. "You shouldn't work yourself into exhaustion, Eve."

"You carried me," she said again, too groggy to decide if she was embarrassed or not. "I guess I'm sorry I missed it."

"We have plenty of time for repeat performances. You worry me."

"I'm fine. I'm just—" She caught the time on the bedside clock. "Holy Christ, ten. Ten A.M.?"

He used one hand to shove her back when she started to scramble out of bed. "It's Sunday."

"Sunday?" Completely disoriented now, she rubbed her eyes clear. "I lost track." She wasn't on duty, she remembered, but regardless—

"You needed sleep," he said, reading her mind. "And you need fuel, something other than caffeine." He reached for the glass on the night-stand and held it out.

Eve studied the pale pink liquid dubiously. "What is it?"

"Good for you. Drink it." To make sure she did, he held the glass to her lips. He could have given her the energy booster in pill form, but he knew well her dislike for anything resembling drugs. "It's a little something one of my labs has been working on. We should have it on the market in about six months."

Her eyes narrowed. "Experimental?"

"It's quite safe." He smiled and set the empty glass aside. "Hardly anyone's died."

"Ha-ha." She sat back again, feeling amazingly relaxed, amazingly alert. "I have to go in to Cop Central, do some work on the other cases on my desk."

"You need some time off." He held up a hand before she could argue. "A day. Even an afternoon. I'd like you to spend it with me, but even if you spend it alone, you need it."

"I guess I could take a couple of hours." She sat up, linked her arms around his neck. "What did you have in mind?"

Grinning, he rolled her back onto the bed. This time there was finesse, and there was tenderness.

Eve wasn't surprised to find a pile of messages waiting. Sunday had stopped being a day of rest decades before. Her message disc beeped along, recounting transmissions from Nadine Furst, the arrogant weasel Morse, another from Yvonne Metcalf's parents that had her rubbing her temples, and a short message from Mirina Angelini.

"You can't take on their grief, Eve," Roarke said from behind her.

"What?"

"The Metcalfs. I can see it in your face."

"I'm all they've got to hold on to." She initialed the messages to document her receipt. "They have to know someone's looking after her."

"I'd like to say something."

Eve rolled her eyes, prepared for him to lecture her about rest, objectivity, or professional distance. "Spit it out then so I can get to work."

"I've dealt with a lot of cops in my time. Evaded them, bribed them, outmaneuvered them, or simply outran them."

Amused, she nudged a hip onto the corner of her desk. "I'm not sure you should be telling me that. Your record's suspiciously clean."

"Of course it is." On impulse he kissed the tip of her nose. "I paid for it."

She winced. "Really, Roarke, what I don't know can't hurt you."

"The point is," he continued blandly, "I've dealt with a lot of cops over the years. You're the best."

Caught completely off guard, she blinked. "Well."

"You'll stand, Eve, for the dead and the grieving. I'm staggered by you."

"Cut it out." Miserably embarrassed, she shifted. "I mean it."

"You can use that when you call Morse back and run up against his irritating whine."

"I'm not calling him back."

"You initialed the transmissions."

"I zapped his first." She smiled. "Oops."

With a laugh he picked her up off the desk. "I like your style."

She indulged herself by combing her fingers through his hair before she tried to wriggle free. "Right now you're cramping it. So back off while I see what Mirina Angelini wants." Brushing him off, she engaged the number, waited.

It was Mirina herself who answered, her pale, tense face on-screen. "Yes, oh, Lieutenant Dallas. Thank you for getting back to me so quickly. I was afraid I wouldn't hear from you until tomorrow."

"What can I do for you, Ms. Angelini?"

"I need to speak with you as soon as possible. I don't want to go through the commander, Lieutenant. He's done enough for me and my family."

"Is this regarding the investigation?"

"Yes, at least, I suppose it is."

Eve signaled to Roarke to leave the office. He merely leaned against the wall. She snarled at him, then looked back at the screen. "I'll be happy to meet with you at your convenience."

"That's just it, Lieutenant, it's going to have to be at my convenience. My doctors don't want me to travel again just now. I need you to come to me."

"You want me to come to Rome? Ms. Angelini, even if the department would clear the trip, I need something concrete to justify the time and expense."

"I'll take you," Roarke said easily.

"Keep quiet."

"Who else is there? Is someone else there?" Mirina's voice trembled.

"Roarke is with me," Eve said between her teeth. "Ms. Angelini—"

"Oh, that's fine. I've been trying to reach him. Could you come together? I realize this is an imposition, Lieutenant. I hesitate to pull strings, but I will, if necessary. The commander will clear it."

"I'm sure he will," Eve muttered. "I'll leave as soon as he does. I'll be in touch." She broke transmission. "The spoiled rich irritate the hell out of me."

"Grief and worry don't have economic boundaries," Roarke said.

"Oh shut up." She huffed, kicked bad-temperedly at the desk.

"You'll like Rome, darling," Roarke said and smiled.

Eve did like Rome. At least she thought she did from the brief blur she caught of it on the zooming trip from the airport to Angelini's flat overlooking the Spanish Steps: fountains and traffic and ruins too ancient to be believed.

From the rear of the private limo, Eve watched the fashionable pedestrians with a kind of baffled awe. Sweeping robes were in this season, apparently. Clingy, sheer, voluminous, in colors from the palest white to the deepest bronze. Jeweled belts hung from waists, coordinating with crusted gems on flat-soled shoes and little jeweled bags carried by men and women alike. Everyone looked like royalty.

Roarke hadn't known she could gawk. It pleased him enormously to see that she could forget her mission long enough to stare and wonder. It was a shame, he thought, that they couldn't take a day or two so that he could show her the city, the grandeur of it, and its impossible continuity.

He was sorry when the car pulled jerkily to the curb and yanked her back to reality.

"This better be good." Without waiting for the driver, she slammed out of the car. When Roarke took her elbow to lead her inside the apartment building, she turned her head and frowned at him. "Aren't you even the least bit annoyed at being summoned across a damn ocean for a conversation?"

"Darling, I often go a great deal farther for less. And without such charming company."

She snorted and had nearly taken out her badge to flash at the security droid before she remembered herself. "Eve Dallas and Roarke for Mirina Angelini."

"You're expected, Eve Dallas and Roarke." The droid glided to a gilt-barred elevator and keyed in a code.

"You could get one of those," Eve nodded toward the droid before the elevator's doors closed, "and ditch Summerset."

"Summerset has his own charm."

She snorted again, louder. "Yeah. You bet."

The doors slid open into a gold and ivory foyer with a small, tinkling fountain in the shape of a mermaid.

"Jesus," Eve whispered, scanning the palm trees and paintings. "I didn't think anybody but you really lived like this."

"Welcome to Rome." Randall Slade stepped forward. "Thank you for coming. Please come in. Mirina's in the sitting room."

"She didn't mention you'd be here, Mr. Slade."

"We made the decision to call you together."

Biding her time for questions, Eve walked passed him. The sitting room was sided on the front wall in sheer glass. One-way glass, Eve assumed, as the building was only six stories high. Despite the relatively short height, it afforded an eye-popping view of the city.

Mirina sat daintily on a curved chair, sipping tea from a hand that shook slightly.

She seemed paler, if possible, and even more fragile in her trendy robe of ice blue. Her feet were bare, the nails painted to match her robe. She'd dressed her hair up in a severe knot, secured with a jeweled comb. Eve thought she looked like one of the ancient Roman goddesses, but her mythology was too sketchy to choose which one.

Mirina didn't rise, nor did she smile, but set her cup aside to pick up a slim white pot and pour two more.

"I hope you'll join me for tea."

"I didn't come for a party, Ms. Angelini."

"No, but you've come, and I'm grateful."

"Here, let me do that." With a smooth grace that almost masked the way the cups rattled in Mirina's hands, Slade took them from her. "Please sit down," he invited. "We won't keep you any longer than necessary, but you might as well be comfortable."

"I don't have any jurisdiction here," Eve began as she took a cushioned chair with a low back, "but I'd like to record this meeting, with your permission."

Mirina looked at Slade, bit her lip. "Yes, of course." She cleared her throat when Eve took out her recorder and set it on the table between them. "You know about the . . . difficulties Randy had several years ago in Sector 38."

"I know," Eve confirmed. "I was told you didn't."

"Randy told me yesterday." Mirina reached up blindly, and his hand was there. "You're a strong, confident woman, Lieutenant. It may be difficult for you to understand those of us who aren't so strong. Randy didn't tell me before because he was afraid I wouldn't handle it well. My nerves." She moved her thin shoulders. "Business crises energize me. Personal crises devastate me. The doctors call it an avoidance tendency. I'd rather not face trouble."

"You're delicate," Slade stated, squeezing her hand. "It's nothing to be ashamed of."

"In any case, this is something I have to face. You were there," she said to Roarke, "during the incident."

"I was on the station, probably in the casino."

"And the security at the hotel, the security Randy called, they were yours."

"That's right. Everyone has private security. Criminal cases are transferred to the magistrate—unless they can be dealt with privately."

"You mean through bribes."

"Naturally."

"Randy could have bribed security. He didn't."

"Mirina." He hushed her with another squeeze of his hand. "I didn't bribe them because I wasn't thinking clearly enough to bribe them. If I had, there wouldn't have been a record, and we wouldn't be discussing it now."

"The heavy charges were dropped," Eve pointed out. "You were given the minimum penalty for the ones that stood."

"And I was assured that the entire matter would remain buried. It didn't. I prefer something stronger than tea. Roarke?"

"Whiskey if you have it, two fingers."

"Tell them, Randy," Mirina whispered while he programmed two whiskeys from the recessed bar.

He nodded, brought Roarke his glass, then knocked back the contents of his own. "Cicely called me on the night she was murdered."

Eve's head jerked up like a hound scenting blood. "There was no record of that on her 'link. No record of an outgoing call."

"She called from a public phone. I don't know where. It was just after midnight, your time. She was agitated, angry."

"Mr. Slade, you told me in our official interview that you had not had contact with Prosecutor Towers on that night."

"I lied. I was afraid."

"You now choose to recant your earlier statement."

"I wish to revise it. Without benefit of counsel, Lieutenant, and fully aware of the penalty for giving a false statement during a police investigation. I'm telling you now that she contacted me shortly before she was killed. That, of course, gives me an alibi, if you like. It would have been very close to impossible for me to have traveled cross-country and killed her in the amount of time I had. You can, of course, check my transmission records."

"Be sure that I will. What did she want?"

"She asked me if it was true. Just that, at first. I was distracted, working. It took me a moment to realize how upset she was, and then when she was more definite, to understand she was referring to Sector 38. I panicked, made some excuses. But you couldn't lie to Cicely. She pinned me to the wall. I was angry, too, and we argued."

He paused, his eyes going to Mirina. He watched her, Eve thought, as if he waited for her to shatter like glass.

"You argued, Mr. Slade?" Eve prompted.

"Yes. About what had happened, why. I wanted to know how she had found out about it, but she cut me off. Lieutenant, she was furious. She told me she was going to deal with it for her daughter's sake. Then she would deal with me. She ended transmission abruptly, and I settled down to brood and to drink."

He walked back to Mirina, laid a hand on her shoulder, stroked. "It was early in the morning, just before dawn, when I heard the news report and knew she was dead."

"She had never spoken to you about the incident before."

"No. We had an excellent relationship. She knew about the gambling, disapproved, but in a mild way. She was used to David. I don't think she understood how deeply we were both involved."

"She did," Roarke corrected. "She asked me to cut you both off."

"Ah." Slade smiled into his empty glass. "That's why I couldn't get through the door of your place in Vegas II."

"That's why."

"Why now?" Eve asked. "Why have you decided to revise your previous statement?"

"I felt it was closing in on me. I knew how hurt Mirina would be if she heard it from someone else. I needed to tell her. It was her decision to contact you."

"Our decision." Mirina reached for his hand again. "I can't bring my mother back, and I know how it will affect my father when we tell him Randy was used to hurt her. Those are things I have to learn to live with. I can do that, if I know that whoever used Randy, and me, will pay for it. She would never have gone out there, she would never have gone, but to protect me."

When they were flying west, Eve paced the comfortable cabin. "Families." She tucked her thumbs into her back pockets. "Do you ever think about them, Roarke?"

"Occasionally." Since she was going to talk, he switched the business news off his personal monitor.

"If we follow one theory, Cicely Towers went out on that rainy night as a mother. Someone was threatening her child's happiness. She was going to fix it. Even if she gave Slade the heave-ho, she was going to fix it first."

"That's what we assume is the natural instinct of a parent."

She slanted him a glance. "We both know better."

"I wouldn't claim that either of our experiences are the norm, Eve."

"Okay." Thoughtful, she sat on the arm of his chair. "So, if it's normal for a mother to jump to shield her child against any trouble,

Towers did exactly as her killer expected. He understood her, judged her character well."

"Perfectly, I'd say."

"She was also a servant of the court. It was her duty, and certainly should have been her instinct, to call the authorities, report any threats or blackmail attempts."

"A mother's love is stronger than the law."

"Hers was, and whoever killed her knew it. Who knew her? Her lover, her ex-husband, her son, her daughter, Slade."

"And others, Eve. She was a strong, vocal supporter of professional motherhood, of family rights. There have been dozens of stories about her over the years highlighting her personal commitment to her family."

"That's risking a lot, going by press. Media can be—and is—biased, or it slants a story to suit its own ends. I say her killer knew, not assumed, but knew. There'd been personal contact or extensive research."

"That hardly narrows the field."

Eve brushed that aside with a flick of the hand. "And the same goes for Metcalf. A meeting's set, but it isn't going to be specifically documented in her diary. How does the killer know that? Because he knows her habits. My job is to figure out his or hers. Because there'll be another one."

"You're so sure?"

"I'm sure, and Mira confirmed it."

"You've spoken to her then."

Restless, she rose again. "He—it's just easier to say he—envies, resents, is fascinated by powerful women. Women in the public eye, women who make a mark. Mira thinks the killings may be motivated by control, but I wonder. Maybe that's giving him too much credit. Maybe it's just the thrill. The stalking, the luring, the planning. Who is he stalking now?"

"Have you looked in the mirror?"

"Hmm?"

"Do you realize how often your face is on the screen, in the papers?" Fighting back fear, he rose and put his hands on her shoulders, and read her face. "You've thought of it already?"

"I've wished for it," she corrected, "because I'd be ready."

"You terrify me," he managed.

"You said I was the best." She grinned, patted his cheek. "Relax, Roarke, I'm not going to do anything stupid."

"Oh, I'll sleep easy now."

"How much longer before we land?" Impatient, she turned to walk to the viewscreen.

"Thirty minutes or so, I imagine."

"I need Nadine."

"What are you planning, Eve?"

"Me? Oh, I'm planning on getting lots of press." She shoveled her fingers through her untidy hair. "Haven't you got some ritzy affairs, the kind the media just love to cover, that we can go to?"

He let out a sigh. "I suppose I could come up with a few."

"Great. Let's set some up." She plopped down in a seat and tapped her fingers on her knee. "I guess I can even push it to getting a couple of new outfits."

"Above and beyond." He scooped her up and sat her on his lap. "But I'm sticking close, Lieutenant."

"I don't work with civilians."

"I was talking about the shopping."

Her eyes narrowed as his hand snaked under her shirt. "Is that a dig?"

"Yes."

"Okay." She swiveled around to straddle him. "Just checking."

CHAPTER
TEN

"I'm going to do my lead-in first." Nadine looked around Eve's office and cocked a brow. "Not much of a sanctum."

"Excuse me?"

Casually, Nadine adjusted the angle of Eve's monitor. It squeaked. "Up till now, you've guarded this room like holy ground. I expected something more than a closet with a desk and a couple of ratty chairs."

"Home's where the heart is," Eve said mildly, and leaned back in one of those ratty chairs.

Nadine had never considered herself claustrophobic, but the industrial beige walls were awfully close together, making her rethink the notion. And the single, stingy window, though undoubtedly blast treated, was unshaded and offered a narrow view of an air traffic snarl over a local transport station.

The little room, Nadine mused, was full of crowds.

"I'd have thought after you broke the DeBlass case last winter, you'd have rated a snazzier office. With a real window and maybe a little carpet."

"Are you here to decorate or to do a story?"

"And your equipment's pathetic." Enjoying herself, Nadine clucked her tongue over Eve's work units. "At the station, relics like this would be delegated to some low-level drone, or more likely, kicked to a charity rehab center."

She would not scowl, Eve told herself. She would not scowl. "Remember that, the next time you're tagged for a donation to the Police and Security Fund."

Nadine smiled, leaned back on the desk. "At Channel 75, even drones have their own AutoChef."

"I'm learning to hate you, Nadine."

"Just trying to get you pumped for the interview. You know what I'd like, Dallas, since you're in the mood for exposure? A one-on-one, an in-depth interview with the woman behind the badge. The life and loves of Eve Dallas, NYPSD. The personal side of the public servant."

Eve couldn't stop it. She scowled. "Don't push your luck, Nadine."

"Pushing my luck's what I do best." Nadine dropped down into a chair, shifted it. "How's the angle, Pete?"

The operator held his palm-sized remote up to his face. "Yo."

"Pete's a man of few words," Nadine commented. "Just how I like them. Want to fix your hair?"

Eve caught herself before she tunneled her fingers through it. She hated being on camera, hated it a lot. "No."

"Suit yourself." Nadine took a small, mirrored compact out of her oversized bag, patted something under her eyes, checked her teeth for lipstick smears. "Okay." She dropped the compact back in her bag, crossed her legs smoothly with the faintest whisper of silk against silk, and turned toward camera. "Roll."

"Rolling."

Her face changed. Eve found it interesting to watch. The minute the red light glowed, her features became glossier, more intense. Her voice, which had been brisk and light, slowed and deepened, demanding attention.

"This is Nadine Furst, reporting direct from Lieutenant Eve Dallas's office in the Homicide Division of Cop Central. This exclusive interview centers on the violent and as yet unsolved murders of Prosecutor Cicely Towers and award-winning actor Yvonne Metcalf. Lieutenant, are these murders linked?"

"The evidence indicates that probability. We can confirm from the medical examiner's report that both victims were killed by the same weapon, and by the same hand."

"There's no doubt of that?"

"None. Both women were killed by a thin, smooth-edged blade, nine inches in length, tapered from point to hilt. The point was honed to a V. In both cases, the victims were frontally attacked with one swipe of the weapon across the throat from right to left, and at a slight angle."

Eve picked up a signature pen from her desk, causing Nadine to jerk and blink when she slashed it a fraction of an inch from Nadine's throat. "Like that."

"I see."

"This would have severed the jugular, causing instant and dramatic blood loss, disabling the victim immediately, preventing her from calling for help or defending herself in any way. Death would have occurred within seconds."

"In other words, the killer needed very little time. A frontal attack, Lieutenant. Doesn't that indicate that the victims knew their attacker?"

"Not necessarily, but there is other evidence that leads to the conclusion that the victims knew their attacker, or were expecting to meet someone. The absence of any defense wounds for example. If I came at you . . ." Eve thrust out with the pen again, and Nadine threw a hand in front of her throat. "You see, it's automatic defense."

"That's interesting," Nadine said and had to school her face before it scowled. "We have the details on the murders themselves, but not on the motive behind them, or the killer. What is it that connects Prosecutor Towers to Yvonne Metcalf?"

"We're investigating several lines of inquiry."

"Prosecutor Towers was killed three weeks ago, Lieutenant, yet you have no suspects?"

"We have no evidence to support an arrest at this time."

"Then you do have suspects?"

"The investigation is proceeding with all possible speed."

"And motive?"

"People kill people, Ms. Furst, for all manner of reasons. They've done so since we crawled out of the muck."

"Biblically speaking," Nadine put in, "murder is the oldest crime."

"You could say it has a long tradition. We may be able to filter out certain undesirable tendencies through genetics, chemical treatments, beta scans, we deter with penal colonies and the absence of freedom. But human nature remains human nature."

"Those basic motives for violence that science is unable to filter: love, hate, greed, envy, anger."

"They separate us from the droids, don't they?"

"And make us susceptible to joy, sorrow, and passion. That's a debate for the scientists and the intellectuals. But which of those motives killed Cicely Towers and Yvonne Metcalf?"

"A person killed them, Ms. Furst. His or her purpose remains unknown."

"You have a psychiatric profile, of course."

"We do," Eve confirmed. "And we will use it and all of the tools at our disposal to find the murderer. I'll find him," Eve said deliberately flicking her eyes toward the camera. "And once the cage door is closed, motive won't matter. Only justice."

"That sounds like a promise, Lieutenant. A personal promise."

"It is."

"The people of New York will depend on you keeping that promise. This is Nadine Furst, reporting for Channel 75." She waited a beat, then nodded. "Not bad, Dallas. Not bad at all. We'll run it again at six and eleven, with the recap at midnight."

"Good. Take a walk, Pete."

The operator shrugged and wandered out of the room.

"Off the record," Eve began. "How much airtime can you give me?"

"For?"

"Exposure. I want plenty of it."

"I figured there was something behind this little gift." Nadine let out a little breath that was nearly a sigh. "I have to say I'm disappointed, Dallas. I never figured you for a camera hound."

"I've got to testify on the Mondell case in a couple of hours. Can you get a camera there?"

"Sure. The Mondell case is small ratings, but it's worth a couple zips." She pulled her diary out and noted it.

"I've got this thing tonight, too, at the New Astoria. One of those gold plate dinners."

"The Astoria dinner ball, sure." Her smile turned derisive. "I don't work the social beat, Dallas, but I can tell the assignment desk to cue on you. You and Roarke are always good for the gossip eaters. It is you and Roarke, isn't it?"

"I'll let you know where you can catch me over the next couple of days," Eve continued, ignoring the insult. "I'll feed you regular updates to air."

"Fine." Nadine rose. "Maybe you'll trip over the killer on your way to fame and fortune. Got an agent yet?"

For a moment, Eve said nothing, just tapped her fingertips together. "I thought it was your job to fill airtime and guard the public's right to know, not to moralize."

"And I thought it was yours to serve and protect, not to cash in." Nadine snagged up her bag by the strap. "Catch you on the screen, Lieutenant."

"Nadine." Pleased, Eve tipped back in her chair. "You left out one of those basic human motives for violence before. Thrill."

"I'll make a note of it." Nadine wrenched at the door, then let it slip out of her hands. When she turned back, her face was white and shocked under its sheen of camera makeup. "Are you out of your mind? You're bait? You're fucking bait?"

"Pissed you off, didn't it?" Smiling, Eve allowed herself the luxury of propping her feet on the desk. Nadine's reaction had brought the reporter up several notches on Eve's opinion scale. "Thinking about me wanting all that airtime, and getting it, really steamed you. It's going to steam him, too. Can't you hear him, Nadine? 'Look at that lousy cop getting all my press.'"

Nadine came back in and sat down carefully. "You had me. Dallas, I'm not about to tell you how to do your job—"

"Then don't."

"Let me see if I'm figuring this right. You deduce the motive was, at least partially, for the thrill, for the attention in the media. Kill a couple of ordinary citizens, you get press, sure, but not so intense, not so complete."

"Kill two prominent citizens, familiar faces, and the sky's the limit."

"So you make yourself a target."

"It's just a hunch." Thoughtfully, Eve scratched a vague itch on her knee. "It could be that all I'll end up with is a lot of idiotic blips of me on screen."

"Or a knife at your throat."

"Gee, Nadine, I'm going to start to think you care."

"I think I do." She spent a moment studying Eve's face. "I've worked with, around, and through cops for a long time now. You get instincts on who's putting in time and who gives a damn. You know what worries me, Dallas? You give too much of a damn."

"I carry a badge," Eve said soberly and made Nadine laugh.

"Obviously you've been watching too many old videos, too. Well, it's your neck—literally. I'll see to it that you get it exposed."

"Thanks. One more thing," she added when Nadine stood again. "If this theory has weight, then future targets would fall into the well-known, media-hyped female variety. Keep an eye on your own neck, Nadine."

"Jesus." Shuddering, Nadine rubbed fingers over her throat. "Thanks for sharing that, Dallas."

"My pleasure—literally." Eve had time to chuckle between the time the door closed and the call came through from the commander's office.

Obviously, he'd heard about the broadcast.

She was still stinging a bit when she bolted up the steps of the courthouse. The cameras were there, as Nadine had promised. They were there in the evening at the New Astoria when she stepped out of Roarke's limo and tried to pretend she was enjoying herself.

After two days of tripping over a camera every time she took three steps, she was surprised she didn't find one zooming over her in bed, and she said as much to Roarke.

"You asked for it, darling."

She was straddling him, in what was left of the three-piece cocktail suit he'd chosen for her to wear to the governor's mansion. The glittering black and gold vest skimmed her hips and was already unbuttoned to her navel.

"I don't have to like it. How do you stand it? You live with this stuff all the time. Isn't it creepy?"

"You just ignore it." He flipped open another button. "And go on. I liked the way you looked tonight." Idly he toyed with the diamond that hung between her breasts. "Of course, I'm enjoying the way you look right now more."

"I'm never going to get used to it. All the fancy work. Small talk, big hair. And I don't fit the clothes, either."

"They might not suit the lieutenant, but they suit Eve. You can be both." He watched her pupils dilate when he spread his hands over her breasts, cupped them. "You liked the food."

"Well, sure, but . . ." She shivered into a moan as he scraped his thumbs over her nipples. "I think I was trying to make a point. I should never talk to you in bed."

"Excellent deduction." He reared up and replaced his thumbs with his teeth.

She was sleeping deeply, dreamlessly, when he woke her. The cop surfaced first, alert and braced.

"What?" Despite being naked, she reached for her weapon. "What is it?"

"I'm sorry." When he leaned over the bed to kiss her, she could tell from the vibrations of his body that he was laughing.

"It's not funny. If I'd been armed, you'd have been on your ass."

"Lucky me."

Absently, she shoved at Galahad who'd decided to sit on her head. "Why are you dressed? What's going on?"

"I've had a call. I'm needed on FreeStar One."

"The Olympus Resort. Lights, dim," she ordered and blinked to focus as they highlighted his face. God, she thought, he looked like an angel. A fallen one. A dangerous one. "Is there a problem?"

"Apparently. Nothing that can't be handled." Roarke picked up the cat himself, stroked it, then set Galahad on the floor. "But I have to handle it personally. It may take a couple of days."

"Oh." It was because she was groggy, she told herself, that this awful sense of deflation snuck in. "Well, I'll see you when you get back."

He skimmed a finger over the dent in her chin. "You'll miss me."

"Maybe. Some." It was his quick smile that defeated her. "Yes."

"Here, put this on." He shoved a robe in her hands. "There's something I want to show you before I go."

"You're going now?"

"The transport's waiting. It can wait."

"I guess I'm supposed to come down and kiss you good-bye," she muttered as she fumbled into the robe.

"That would be nice, but first things first." He took her hand and pulled her from the platform to the elevator. "There isn't any need for you to be uncomfortable here while I'm gone."

"Right."

He put his hands on her shoulders as the car began to glide. "Eve, it's your home now."

"I'm going to be busy, anyway." She felt the slight shift as the car veered to horizontal mode. "Aren't we going all the way down?"

"Not just yet." He slipped an arm around her shoulders when the doors opened.

It was a room she hadn't seen. Then again, she mused, there were probably dozens of rooms she'd yet to tour in the labyrinth of the building. But it took only one quick glimpse for her to realize it was hers.

The few things she considered of any value from her apartment were here, with new pieces added to fill it out into a pleasant, workable space. Stepping away from Roarke, she wandered in.

The floors were wood and smooth, and there was a carpet woven in slate blue and mossy green, probably from one of his factories in the East. Her desk, battered as it was, stood on the priceless wool and held her equipment.

A frosted-glass wall separated a small kitchen area, fully equipped, that led to a terrace.

There was more, of course. With Roarke there was always more. A communications board would allow her to call up any room in the house. The entertainment center offered music, video, a hologram screen with dozens of visualization options. A small indoor garden bloomed riotously below an arching window where dawn was breaking.

"You can replace what you don't like," he said as she ran her hand over the soft back of a sleep chair. "Everything's been programmed for your voice and your palm print."

"Very efficient," she said and cleared her throat. "Very nice."

Surprised to find himself riddled with nerves, he tucked his hands in his pockets. "Your work requires your own space. I understand that. You require your own space and privacy. My office is through there, the west panel. But it locks on either side."

"I see."

Now he felt temper snapping at the nerves. "If you can't be comfortable in the house while I'm not here, you can barricade yourself in this apartment. You can damn well barricade yourself in it while I am here. It's up to you."

"Yes, it is." She took a deep breath and turned to him. "You did this for me."

Annoyed, he inclined his head. "There doesn't seem to be much I wouldn't do for you."

"I think that's starting to sink in." No one had ever given her anything quite so perfect. No one, she realized, understood her quite so well. "That makes me a lucky woman, doesn't it?"

He opened his mouth, bit back something particularly nasty. "The hell with it," he decided. "I have to go."

"Roarke, one thing." She walked to him, well aware he was all but snarling with temper. "I haven't kissed you good-bye," she murmured and did so with a thoroughness that rocked him back on his heels. "Thank you." Before he could speak, she kissed him again. "For always knowing what matters to me."

"You're welcome." Possessively, he ran a hand over her tousled hair. "Miss me."

"I already am."

"Don't take any unnecessary chances." His hands gripped in her hair hard, briefly. "There's no use asking you not to take the necessary ones."

"Then don't." Her heart stuttered when he kissed her hand. "Safe trip," she told him when he stepped into the elevator. She was new at it, so waited until the doors were almost shut. "I love you."

The last thing she saw was the flash of his grin.

"What have you got, Feeney?"

"Maybe something, maybe nothing."

It was early, just eight o'clock on the morning after Roarke left for FreeStar One, but Feeney already looked haggard. Eve punched two coffees, double strength, from her AutoChef.

"You're in here at this hour, looking like you've been up all night, and in that suit, I have to deduce it's something. And I'm a gold-star detective."

"Yeah. I've been noodling the computer, going down another level on the families and personal relations of the victims like you wanted."

"And?"

Stalling, he drank his coffee, dug out his bag of candied nuts, scratched his ear. "Saw you on the news last night. The wife did, actually. Said you looked flash. That's one of the kid's expressions. We try to keep up."

"In that case, you're rocking me, Feeney. That's one of the kid's expressions, too. Translation, you're not coming clear."

"I know what it means. Shit. This one cuts close to home, Dallas. Too close."

"Which is why you're here instead of transmitting what you've got over a channel. So let's have it."

"Okay." He puffed out a breath. "I was dicking around with David Angelini's records. Financial stuff mostly. We knew he was into some spine twisters for gambling debts. He's been holding them off, giving them a little trickle here and there. Could be he's dipped into the company till, but I can't get a lock on that. He's covered his ass."

"So, we'll uncover it. I can get the name of the spine twisters," she mused, thinking of Roarke. "Let's see if he made them any promises—like he'd be coming into an inheritance." Her brows knit. "If it wasn't for Metcalf, I'd think hard about somebody he owed hurrying up on the IOUs by taking out Towers."

"Might be that simple, even with Metcalf. She had a nice nest egg set aside. I haven't found anybody among the beneficiaries who needed quick money, but that doesn't mean I won't."

"Okay, you keep working that angle. But that isn't why you're here playing with your nuts."

He nearly managed a laugh. "Cute. Okay, here it is. I turned up the commander's wife."

"Run that by slow, Feeney. Real slow."

He couldn't sit, so he sprang up to pace the small space. "David Angelini made some healthy deposits into his personal credit account. Four deposits of fifty K over the last four months. The final one was keyed in two weeks before his mother got terminated."

"All right, he got his hands on two hundred K in four months, and banked it like a good boy. Where'd he get it? Fuck." She already knew.

"Yeah. I accessed the E-transactions. Backtracked. She transferred it to his New York bank, and he flipped it over into his personal account in Milan. Then he withdraws it, in cash, hard bills, at an Auto-Tell on Vegas II."

"Jesus Christ, why didn't she tell me?" Eve pressed her balled fists to her temples. "Why the hell did she make us look for it?"

"It wasn't like she tried to hide it," Feeney said quickly. "When I clicked over to her records, it was all out front. She has an account of her own, just like the commander." He cleared his throat at Eve's level stare. "I had to look, Dallas. He hasn't made any unusual transactions

out of his, or out of their joint. But she's cut her principal in half dol-
ing out to Angelini. Christ, he was bleeding her."

"Blackmail," Eve speculated, struggling to think coolly. "Maybe
they had an affair. Maybe she was stuck on the bastard."

"Oh man, oh Jesus." Feeney's stomach did a long sickening roll.
"The commander."

"I know. We have to go to him with this."

"I knew you were going to say that." Mournfully, Feeney took a
disc out of his pocket. "I got it all. How do you want to play it?"

"What I want to do is go out to White Plains and knock Mrs.
Whitney on her perfect ass. Barring that, we go to the commander's
office and lay it out for him."

"They've still got some of that old body armor down in storage,"
Feeney suggested as Eve rose.

"Good thinking."

They could have used it. Whitney didn't climb over his desk and
body slam them, nor did he pull out his stunner. He did all the damage
necessary with the lethal glare of his eyes.

"You accessed my wife's personal accounts, Feeney."

"Yes, sir, I did."

"And took this information to Lieutenant Dallas."

"As per procedure."

"As per procedure," Whitney repeated. "Now you're bringing it
to me."

"To the commanding officer," Feeney began, then drooped. "Oh
hell, Jack, was I supposed to bury it?"

"You could have come to me first. But then . . ." Whitney trailed
off, shifted his hard eyes to Eve's. "Your stand on this, Lieutenant?"

"Mrs. Whitney paid David Angelini a sum of two hundred thousand dollars over a four-month period. This fact was not volunteered
during either primary or follow-up interviews. It's necessary to the
investigation that—" She broke off. "We have to know why, Commander." The apology was in her eyes, lurking just behind the cop.
"We have to know why the money was paid, why there have been no

more payments since the death of Cicely Towers. And I have to ask, Commander, as primary, if you were aware of the transactions and the reason behind them."

There was a clutching in his stomach, a burning that warned of untreated stress. "I'll answer that after I've spoken with my wife."

"Sir." Eve's voice was a quiet plea. "You know we can't allow you to consult with Mrs. Whitney before we question her. This meeting has already risked contaminating the investigation. I'm sorry, Commander."

"You're not bringing my wife in to interview."

"Jack—"

"Fuck this, Feeney, she's not going to be dragged down here like a criminal." He clutched his hands into fists under the desk and struggled to remain in control. "Question her at home, with our attorney present. That doesn't violate procedure, does it, Lieutenant Dallas?"

"No, sir. With respect, Commander, will you come with us?"

"With respect, Lieutenant," he said bitterly. "You couldn't stop me."

Anna Whitney met them at the door. Her hands fluttered, then gripped together at her waist. "Jack, what's happening? Linda's here. She said you called her and told her I needed counsel." Her gaze darted from Eve to Feeney, then back to her husband. "Why would I need counsel?"

"It's all right." He put a tense but protective hand on her shoulder. "Let's go inside, Anna."

"But I haven't done anything." She managed one nervous laugh. "I haven't even gotten a traffic ticket lately."

"Just sit down, honey. Linda, thanks for coming so quickly."

"No problem."

The Whiteys' attorney was young, sharp-eyed, and polished to a gleam. It took Eve several moments to remember she was also their daughter.

"Lieutenant Dallas, isn't it?" Linda scanned and summed up quickly. "I recognize you." She gestured to a chair before either of her parents thought of it. "Please sit."

"Captain Feeney, EDD."

"Yes, my father's mentioned you many times, Captain Feeney. Now." She laid a hand over her mother's. "What's this all about?"

"Information has just come to light that needs clarification." Eve took out her recorder, offered it to Linda for examination. She tried not to think that Linda favored her father, the caramel-colored skin, the cool eyes. Genes and family traits both fascinated and frightened her.

"I take it this is going to be a formal interview." With careful calm, Linda set the recorder on the table and took out her own.

"That's right." Eve recited the date and time. "Interviewing officer Dallas, Lieutenant Eve. Also present, Whitney, Commander Jack, and Feeney, Captain Ryan. Interviewee Whitney, Anna, represented by counsel."

"Whitney, Linda. My client is aware of all rights and agrees to this time and place of interview. Counsel reserves the right to terminate at her discretion. Proceed, Lieutenant."

"Mrs. Whitney," Eve began. "You were acquainted with Cicely Towers, deceased."

"Yes, of course. Is this about Cicely? Jack—"

He only shook his head and kept his hand on her shoulder.

"You are also acquainted with the deceased's family. Her former husband Marco Angelini, her son, David Angelini, and her daughter, Mirina."

"I'm more than acquainted. Her children are like family. Why, Linda even dated—"

"Mom." With a bolstering smile, Linda interrupted. "Just answer the question. Don't elaborate."

"But this is ridiculous." Some of Anna's puzzlement edged over into irritation. It was her home, after all, her family. "Lieutenant Dallas already knows the answers."

"I'm sorry to go over the same ground, Mrs. Whitney. Would you describe your relationship with David Angelini?"

"David? Why I'm his godmother. I watched him grow up."

"You're aware that David Angelini was in financial distress prior to the death of his mother."

"Yes, he was . . ." Her eyes went huge. "You don't seriously believe that David . . . That's hideous." She snapped it out before her mouth compressed into a thin red line. "I'm not going to dignify this with an answer."

"I understand you feel protective toward your godson, Mrs. Whitney. I understand you would go to some lengths to protect him—and to some expense. Two hundred thousand dollars."

Anna's face whitened under her careful cosmetics. "I don't know what you mean."

"Mrs. Whitney, do you deny paying to David Angelini the sum of two hundred thousand dollars, in installments of fifty thousand dollars over a four-month period, beginning in February of this year and ending in May?"

"I . . ." She clutched at her daughter's hand, avoided her husband's. "Do I have to answer that, Linda?"

"A moment please, to confer with my client." Briskly, Linda scooped an arm around her mother and led her into the next room.

"You're very good, Lieutenant," Whitney said tightly. "It's been some time since I observed one of your interviews."

"Jack." Feeney sighed, hurting for everyone. "She's doing her job."

"Yes, she is. It's what she's best at." He looked over as his wife came back into the room.

She was pale, trembling a little. The burning in his gut flared.

"We'll continue," Linda said. There was a warrior glint in her eye when she focused on Eve. "My client wishes to make a statement. Go ahead, Mom, it's all right."

"I'm sorry." Tears starred on her lashes. "Jack, I'm sorry. I couldn't help it. He was in trouble. I know what you said, but I couldn't help it."

"It's all right." Resigned, he took the hand that reached out for his and stood beside her. "Tell the lieutenant the truth, and we'll deal with it."

"I gave him the money."

"Did he threaten you, Mrs. Whitney?"

"What?" Shock seemed to dry up the tears swimming in her eyes. "Oh my goodness. Of course he didn't threaten me. He was in trouble," she repeated, as if that should be enough for anyone. "He owed a very great deal of money to the wrong kind of people. His business—that portion of his father's business that he oversaw—was in some temporary upheaval. And he had a new project he was trying to get off the ground. He explained it," she added with a wave of her free hand. "I don't remember precisely. I don't bother overmuch with business."

"Mrs. Whitney, you gave him four payments of fifty thousand. You didn't relay this information to me in our other interviews."

"What business of yours was it?" Her spine was back, snapped hard and cold so that she sat like a statue. "It was my money, and a personal loan to my godchild."

"A godchild," Eve said with straining patience, "who was being questioned in a murder investigation."

"His mother's murder. You might as well accuse me of killing her as David."

"You didn't inherit a sizable portion of her estate."

"Now, you listen to me." Anger suited her. Anna's face glowed as she leaned forward. "That boy adored his mother, and she him. He was devastated by her death. I know. I sat with him, I comforted him."

"You gave him two hundred thousand dollars."

"It was my money to do with as I chose." She bit her lip. "No one would help him. His parents refused. They'd agreed to refuse this time. I spoke with Cicely about it months ago. She was a wonderful mother, and she loved her children, but she was a very strong believer in discipline. She was determined that he had to handle his problem on his own, without her help. Without mine. But when he came to me, desperate, what was I to do? What was I to do?" she demanded, turning to her husband. "Jack, I know you told me to stay out of it, but he was terrified, afraid they would cripple him, even kill him. What if it had been Linda, or Steven? Wouldn't you have wanted someone to help?"

"Anna, feeding his problem isn't help."

"He was going to pay me back," she insisted. "He wasn't going to gamble with it. He promised. He only needed to buy some time. I couldn't turn him away."

"Lieutenant Dallas," Linda began. "My client lent her own money to a family member in good faith. There is no crime in that."

"Your client hasn't been charged with a crime, counselor."

"Did you, in any of your previous interviews, ask my client directly about disposition of funds? Did you ask my client if she had any financial dealings with David Angelini?"

"No, I did not."

"Then she is not required to volunteer such information, which would appear to be personal and unconnected to your investigation. To the best of her knowledge."

"She's a cop's wife," Eve said wearily. "Her knowledge ought to be better than most. Mrs. Whitney, did Cicely Towers argue with her son over money, over his gambling, over his debts and the settlement thereof?"

"She was upset. Naturally they argued. Families argue. They don't hurt each other."

Maybe not in your cozy little world, Eve thought. "Your last contact with Angelini?"

"A week ago. He called to make sure I was all right, that Jack was all right. We discussed plans for setting up a memorial scholarship fund in his mother's name. His idea, Lieutenant," she said with swimming eyes. "He wanted her to be remembered."

"What can you tell me about his relationship with Yvonne Metcalf?"

"The actress." Anna's eyes went blank before she dabbed at them. "Did he know her? He never mentioned it."

It had been a shot in the dark, and hadn't found a target. "Thank you." Eve picked up her recorder, logged in the end of the interview. "Counselor, you should advise your client that it would be in her best interest not to mention this interview or any portion of it to anyone outside this room."

"I'm a cop's wife." Anna neatly tossed Eve's words back in her face. "I understand the drill."

The last glimpse Eve had of the commander as she stepped outside, he was holding his wife and daughter.

*   *   *

Eve wanted a drink. By the time she'd logged out for the day, she had spent the better part of the afternoon chasing after David Angelini's tail. He was in a meeting, he was out of contact, he was anywhere but where she looked. Without any other choice, she'd left messages at every possible point on the planet and figured she'd be lucky to hear from him before the following day.

Meanwhile, she was faced with an enormous, empty house and a butler who hated the air she breathed. The impulse struck as she zipped through the gates. She grabbed her car 'link and ordered Mavis's number.

"Your night off, right?" she asked the instant Mavis's face blipped on screen.

"You bet. Gotta rest those vocal chords."

"Plans?"

"Nothing that can't be tossed out for better. What do you have in mind?"

"Roarke's off planet. You want to come over here and hang, stay over, get drunk?"

"Hang at Roarke's, stay over at Roarke's, get drunk at Roarke's? I'm on my way."

"Wait, wait. Let's do it up big. I'll send a car for you."

"A limo?" Mavis forgot her vocal chords and squealed. "Jesus, Dallas, make sure the driver wears, like, a uniform. The people in my building will be hanging out the windows with their eyes popped out."

"Fifteen minutes." Eve broke transmission and all but danced up the steps to the door. Summerset was there, just as expected, and she sent him a haughty nod. She'd been practicing. "I'm having a friend over for the evening. Send a car and driver to 28 Avenue C."

"A friend." His voice was ripe with suspicion.

"That's right, Summerset." She glided up the stairs. "A very good, very close friend. Be sure and tell the cook there'll be two for dinner."

She managed to get out of earshot before doubling over with

laughter. Summerset was expecting a tryst, she was sure. But it was going to be even more of a scandal when he got a load of Mavis.

Mavis didn't disappoint her. Though for Mavis, she was conserva- tively dressed. Her hair de jour was rather tame, a glittery gold fashioned in what was called a half-swing. One glistening side curved to her ear while the other half skimmed her shoulder.

She'd only worn perhaps a half dozen varied earrings—and all in her ears. A distinguished look for Mavis Freestone.

She stepped out of a torrential spring downpour, handing a speechless Summerset her transparent cloak strung with tiny lights, and turned three circles. More, Eve thought, in awe of the hallway than to show off her skin-hugging red bodysuit.

"Wow."

"My thoughts exactly," Eve said. She'd hovered near the hallway waiting, not wanting Mavis to face Summerset alone. The strategy was obviously unnecessary, as the usually disdainful butler was struck dumb.

"It's just mag," Mavis said in reverent tones. "Really mag. And you've got the whole digs to yourself."

Eve sent Summerset a cool, sidelong glance. "Just about."

"Decent." With a flutter of inch-long lashes, Mavis held out a hand with interlinking hearts tattooed on the back. "And you must be Summerset. I've heard so much about you."

Summerset took the hand, so staggered he nearly lifted it to his lips before he remembered himself. "Madam," he said stiffly.

"Oh, you just call me Mavis. Great place to work, huh? You must get a hard charge out of it."

Unsure if he was appalled or enchanted, Summerset stepped back, managed a half bow, and disappeared down the hall with her dripping cloak.

"A man of few words." Mavis winked, giggled, then clattered down the hall on six-inch inflatable platforms. And let out a sensual groan at the first doorway. "You've got a real fireplace."

"A couple dozen of them, I think."

"Jesus, do you do it in front of the fire? Like in the old flicks?"

"I'll leave that up to your imagination."

"I can imagine good. Christ, Dallas, that car you sent. A real limo, a classic. It just had to be raining." She whirled back, sending her earrings dancing. "Only about half the people I wanted to impress saw me. What are we going to do first?"

"We can eat."

"I'm starving, but I've got to see the place first. Show me something."

Eve pondered. The roof terrace was incredible, but it was raining furiously. The weapon room was out, as was the target range. Eve considered those areas off limits to guests without Roarke's presence. There was plenty more, of course. Dubiously Eve studied Mavis's shoes.

"Can you really walk in those?"

"They're air glided. I hardly know I've got them on."

"All right then, we'll take the stairs. You'll see more that way."

She took Mavis to the solarium first, amused by her friend's dropped-jaw reaction to the exotic plants and trees, the sparkling waterfalls, and chattering birds. The curved glass wall was battered with rain, but through it the lights of New York gleamed.

In the music room, Eve programmed a trash band and let Mavis entertain her with a glass-shattering short set of current favorites.

They spent an hour in the game room, competing with the computer, each other, and hologram opponents at Free Zone and Apocalypse.

Mavis did a lot of oohing and ahing over the bedrooms, and finally chose the suite for her overnight stay.

"I can have a fire if I want?" Mavis ran a possessive hand over the rich lapis lazuli of the hearth.

"Sure, but it is nearly June."

"I don't care if I roast." Arms out, she took long swinging steps over the floor, gazed up through the sky dome, and plopped down on the lake-sized bed with its thick silver cushions. "I feel like a queen. No, no, an empress." She rolled over and over while the floating mattress undulated beneath her. "How do you stay normal in a place like this?"

"I don't know. I haven't lived here very long."

Still rolling lavishly from one side of the air cushions to the other, Mavis laughed. "It would only take me one night. I'm never going to be the same." Scooting up to the padded headboard, she punched buttons. Lights flickered on and off, revolved, sparkled. Music throbbed, pulsed. Water began to run in the next room.

"What's that?"

"You programmed your bath," Eve informed her.

"Oops. Not yet." Mavis flicked it off, tried another, and had the panel on the far wall sliding open to reveal a ten-foot video screen. "Definitely decent. Wanna eat?"

While Eve settled in the dining room with Mavis, enjoying her first full evening off in weeks, Nadine Furst scowled over the editing of her next broadcast.

"I want to enhance that, freeze on Dallas," she ordered the tech. "Yeah, yeah, bring her up. She looks damn good on camera."

Sitting back, she studied the five screens while the tech worked the panel. Editing Room One was quiet, but for the murmuring clash of voices from the screen. For Nadine, putting images together seamlessly was as exciting as sex. The majority of broadcasters left the process to their techs, but Nadine wanted her hand in here. Everywhere.

In the newsroom one level down, it would be bedlam. She enjoyed that, too. The scurry to beat the competition to the latest sound bite, the latest picture, the most immediate angle. Reporters manning their 'links for one more quote, bumping their computers for that last bit of data.

The competition wasn't all outside on Broadcast Avenue. There was plenty of it right in the Channel 75 newsroom.

Everybody wanted the big story, the big picture, the big ratings. Right now, she had it all. And Nadine didn't intend to lose it.

"There, hold it there, when I'm standing on Metcalf's patio. Yeah, now try a split screen, use the shot of me on the sidewalk where Towers bought it. Um-hmm." Eyes narrowed, she studied the image. She looked good, she decided. Dignified, sober-eyed. Our intrepid, clear-sighted reporter, revisiting the scenes of the crimes.

"Okay." She folded her hands and rested her chin on them. "Cue in the voice-over."

Two women, talented, dedicated, innocent. Two lives brutally ended. The city reels, looks over its shoulder, and asks why. Loving families mourn, bury their dead, and ask for justice. There is one person working to answer that question, to meet that demand.

"Freeze," Nadine ordered. "Bleed to Dallas, exterior courtroom shot. Bring up audio."

Eve's image filled the screens, full length, with Nadine beside her. That was good, Nadine thought. The visual lent the impression they were a team, working together. Couldn't hurt. There had been the faintest of breezes, ruffling their hair. Behind them, the courthouse speared up, a monument to justice, its elevators busily gliding up and down, its glass walkway crowded with people.

My job is to find a killer, and I take my job seriously. When I finish mine, the courts begin theirs.

"Perfect." Nadine fisted her hand. "Oh yes, just perfect. Fade it there, and I'll pick it up on live. Time?"

"Three forty-five."

"Louise, I'm a genius, and you're not so bad yourself. Print it."

"Printed." Louise swiveled away from the console and stretched. They'd worked together for three years and were friends. "It's a good piece, Nadine."

"Damn right it is." Nadine angled her head. "But."

"Okay." Louise released her stubby ponytail and ran a hand through her thick, dark curls. "We're getting close to retreading here. We've had nothing new in a couple of days."

"Neither has anybody else. And I've got Dallas."

"And that's a big one." Louise was a pretty woman, soft-featured, bright-eyed. She'd come to Channel 75 direct from college. After less than a month on the job, Nadine had scooped her up as her main tech. The arrangement suited them both. "She's got a solid visual and an excellent throat. The Roarke factor adds a gold edge. That's not including the fact she's got a rep as a good cop."

"So?"

"So, I'm thinking," continued Louise, "until you get some new bites on this, you might want to splice in some of the business from the DeBlass case. Remind people our lieutenant broke one of the big ones, took a hit in the line of duty. Build up confidence."

"I don't want to take the focus off the current investigation."

"Maybe you do," Louise disagreed. "At least until there's a new lead. Or a new victim."

Nadine grinned. "A little more blood would heat things up. Another couple of days, we'll be out of the sweeps and into the June doldrums. Okay, I'll keep it in mind. You might want to put something together."

Louise cocked a brow. "I might?"

"And if I use it, you get full on-air credit, you greedy bitch."

"Deal." Louise tapped the pocket of her editing vest, winced. "Out of smokes."

"You've got to stop that. You know how the brass feel about employees taking health risks."

"I'm sticking with the herb shit."

"Shit's right. Get me a couple while you're at it." Nadine had the grace to look sheepish. "And keep it to yourself. They're tougher on the on-air talent than you techs."

"You've got some time before the midnight recap. Aren't you going to take your break?"

"No, I've got a couple of calls to make. Besides, it's pouring out." Nadine patted her perfectly coiffed hair. "You go." She reached into her bag. "I'll pay."

"Good deal—since I have to go all the way to Second to find a store that's licensed to sell smokes." Resigned, she rose. "I'm using your raincoat."

"Go ahead." Nadine passed her a handful of credits. "Just put my share in the pocket, okay? I'll be in the newsroom."

They walked out together, with Louise bundling into the stylish blue coat. "Nice material."

"Sheds water like a duck."

They crossed the rampway, passed a series of editing and production rooms, and walked toward a descending people glide. Noise began to filter through, so Nadine pitched her voice over it.

"Are you and Bongo still thinking of taking the big step?"

"Thinking hard enough that we've started looking at apartments. We're going the traditional route. We'll give living together a try for a year. If it works, we'll make it legal."

"Better you than me," Nadine said with feeling. "I can't think of a single reason why a rational person would lock themselves to another rational person."

"Love." Louise put a dramatic hand to her heart. "It makes reason and rationality fly out the old window."

"You're young and free, Louise."

"And if I'm lucky, I'm going to be old and chained to Bongo."

"Who the hell wants to be chained to anybody named Bongo?" Nadine muttered.

"Me. Catch you later." With a quick salute, Louise continued on the descent while Nadine stepped off toward the newsroom.

And thinking of Bongo, Louise wondered if she'd be able to get home before one A.M. It was their night at her place. That was a little inconvenience that would end once they found one suitable apartment rather than shifting back and forth between his rooms and hers.

Idly, she glanced over at one of the many monitors lining the walls, playing Channel 75's current broadcast. Right now it was a popular sitcom, a dead medium that had been revived over the past couple years by talent such as Yvonne Metcalf's.

Louise shook her head over that thought, then chuckled a little as the life-sized actor on screen mugged outrageously for the viewing audience.

Nadine might have been married to the news, but Louise liked sheer entertainment. She looked forward to those rare evenings when she and Bongo could cuddle up in front of the screen.

In Channel 75's wide lobby there were more monitors, security stations, and a pleasant sitting area ringed with holograms of the station's stars. And, of course, a gift shop stocked with souvenir T-shirts, hats, signed mugs, and holograms of the station's biggest stars.

Twice a day, between the hours of ten and four, tours were guided through the station. Louise had taken one herself as a child, had gawked with the best of them, and had, she remembered with a smug smile, decided then and there on her career.

She waved to the guard at the front entrance, detoured to the east end, which was the shortest route to Second. At the side door for employees, she passed her palm over the handplate to deactivate the lock. As the door swung open, she winced at the heavy sound of drumming rain. She almost changed her mind.

Was one sneaky smoke worth a two-block sprint through the cold and damp? Damn right, she thought and flipped up the hood. The good, expensive raincoat would keep her dry enough, and she'd been stuck in Editing with Nadine for more than an hour.

Hunching her shoulders, she bolted outside.

The wind kicked so that she broke her stride just long enough to secure the coat at the waist. Her shoes were soaked before she reached the bottom of the steps, and looking down at them, she swore under her breath.

"Well, shit."

They were the last words she spoke.

A movement caught her attention and she looked up, blinking once to clear the rain from her eyes. She never saw the knife, already in an arching slash, glint wetly in the rain then slice viciously across her throat.

The killer studied her for only a moment, watched the blood fountain, the body collapse like a puppet cut from its strings. There was shock, then anger, then a quick, jittering fear. The gored knife hurried back into a deep pocket before the darkly clad figure ran off into the shadows.

"I think I could live like this." After a meal of rare Montana beef accented with lobsters harvested from Icelandic waters, washed down with French champagne, Mavis lounged in the lush indoor lagoon off the solarium. She yawned, blissfully naked and just a little drunk. "You are living like this."

"Sort of." Not quite as free-spirited as Mavis, Eve wore a snug one-piece tank suit. She'd cozied herself on a smooth seat made of stone, and was still drinking. She hadn't allowed herself to relax to this extent in too long to remember. "I don't really have a lot of time for this part of it."

"Make time, babe." Mavis submerged, popped up again, perfect round breasts gleaming in the showy blue lights she'd programmed. Lazily, she paddled over to a water lily, gave a sniff. "Christ, this is the real thing. Do you know what you've got here, Dallas?"

"Indoor swimming?"

"What you've got," Mavis began as she frog kicked her way over to the float that held her glass, "is a grade one fantasy. The kind you can't get from the top-line VR goggles." She took a long sip of icy champagne. "You're not going to get all weirded out and blow it, are you?"

"What are you talking about?"

"I know you. You'll pick it apart, question everything, analyze." Noting Eve's glass was empty, Mavis did the honors. "Well, I'm telling you, pal. Don't."

"I don't pick things apart."

"You're the champion picked—pick it part—damn it, pick it aparter. Whew. Try saying that five times fast when your tongue's numb." She used a bare hip to nudge Eve over and squeezed in next to her. "He's crazy about you, isn't he?"

Eve jerked her shoulders and drank.

"He's rich, I mean mag rich, gorgeous as a god, and that body—"

"What d'you know about his body?"

"I got eyes. I use 'em. I've got a pretty good idea of what he looks like naked." Amused by the glint in Eve's eyes, Mavis licked her lips. "Of course, any time you want to fill in the missing details, I'm here for you."

"What a pal."

"That's me. Anyway, he's all that stuff. Then there's that power trip. He's got all that power, sort of shoots out from him." She highlighted the statement by splashing up water. "And he looks at you like he could eat you alive. In big . . . greedy . . . bites. Shit, I'm getting hot."

"Keep your hands off me."

Mavis snorted. "Maybe I'll go seduce Summerset."

"I don't think he has a dick."

"Bet I could find out." But she was just too lazy at the moment. "You're in love with him, aren't you?"

"Summerset? I've had a hell of a time controlling myself around him."

"Look me dead in the eye. Come on." To ensure obedience, Mavis snagged Eve's chin, swiveled until they were face to face, glassy eye to glassy eye. "You're in love with Roarke."

"It looks that way. I don't want to think about it."

"Good. Don't. Always said you thought too damn much." Holding the glass over her head, Mavis pushed off into the lagoon. "Can we use the jets?"

"Sure." Impaired with wine, Eve fumbled a bit for the correct control. Once the water started to bubble and spew, Mavis let out a laughing moan.

"Christ Jesus, who needs a man when you've got one of these? Come on, Eve, bump up the music. Let's party."

Obliging, Eve doubled the volume on the controls so that the music screamed off the walls and water. The Rolling Stones, Mavis's favorite classic artists, wailed. Lounged back, Eve laughed as Mavis improvised dance steps and started to send the server droid after another bottle.

"I beg your pardon."

"Huh?" Bleary-eyed, Eve studied the glossy black shoes at the lip of the lagoon. Slowly, and with mild curiosity, she let her gaze travel up the smoke-colored, pipe-stemmed pants, the short, stiff jacket, and into Summerset's stony face. "Hey, you wanna take a little dip?"

"Come on in, Summerset." Water lapped around Mavis's waist and dripped cheerfully from her classy breasts as she waved. "The more the merrier."

He sniffed, his lips curled. Sheer habit had the words dropping out of his mouth like knife-edged ice cubes, but his gaze kept wandering back to Mavis's swirling body.

"There's a transmission for you, Lieutenant. Apparently you were unable to hear my attempts to inform you."

"What? Okay, okay." She sniggered, paddled toward the 'link set in the side of the lagoon. "Is it Roarke?"

"It is not." It affronted his dignity to shout, but it would have offended his pride to order the music lower. "It is Dispatch from Cop Central."

Even as Eve reached for the 'link, she stopped, swore. Then slicked the hair back from her face. "Music off," she snapped, and had Mick and his pals echoing into silence. "Mavis, stay out of video range, please." Eve sucked in a deep breath, then opened the 'link. "Dallas."

"Dispatch, Dallas, Lieutenant Eve. Voiceprint verified. Report immediately to Broadcast Avenue, Channel 75. Confirmed Homicide. Code Yellow."

Eve's blood ran cold. Her fingers gripped on the edge of the pool. "Victim's name?"

"That information is not cleared for transmission at this time. Confirm receipt of orders, Dallas, Lieutenant Eve."

"Confirmed. ETA twenty minutes. Request Feeney, Captain, EDD on scene."

"Request verified. Dispatch out."

"Oh God. Oh God." Weak with guilt and liquor, Eve laid her head on the edge of the pool. "I fucking killed her."

"Stop it." Mavis swam over, laid a hand on Eve's shoulder. "Cut it out, Eve," she said briskly.

"He took the wrong bait, the wrong bait, Mavis, and she's dead. It was supposed to be me."

"I said stop it." Confused by the words, but not by the sentiment, Mavis pulled her back and gave Eve a quick shake. "Snap out of it, Dallas."

Helpless, Eve pressed a hand to her spinning head. "Oh my Christ, I'm drunk. That's perfect."

"I can fix that. I've got some Sober Up in my bag." At Eve's moan, Mavis gave her another shake. "I know you hate pills, but they'll clean the alcohol out of your bloodstream in ten minutes flat. Come on, we'll get some into you."

"Fine. Dandy. I'll be sober when I have to look at her."

She started up the steps, slipped, was surprised to find her arm taken firmly. "Lieutenant." Summerset's voice was still cool, but he held out a towel and helped her up onto the stone skirt of the pool. "I'll see that your car's ready."

"Yeah, thanks."

TWELVE

Mavis's handy antidote worked like a charm. Eve had a foul taste in the back of her throat, but she was stone-cold sober when she reached Channel 75's sleek silver building.

It had been constructed in the mid-twenties when the media boom had hit such astronomical proportions as to generate more profits than a small country. One of the loftier buildings on Broadcast Avenue, it towered up from a wide, flat hilt, housed several thousand employees, five elaborate studios, including the most lavish new set on the East Coast, and enough power to beam transmissions to every pocket of the planet and its orbiting stations.

The east wing, where Eve was directed, faced Third with its tony mutiplexes and apartment buildings designed for the convenience of the broadcast industry.

Due to the thick air traffic, Eve realized word had already hit. Control was going to be a problem. Even as she rounded the building, she called Dispatch and requested air barricades as well as ground security. A homicide right in the lap of the media was going to be hard enough to deal with, without the vultures flying.

Steady now, she locked away guilt and stepped from her car to approach the scene. The uniforms had been busy, she saw with some relief. They'd cleared the area and had the outside door sealed off. Reporters and their teams were there, naturally. There would be no keeping them away. But she'd have room to breathe.

She'd already attached her badge to her jacket and moved through the rain to the porta-tarp some wise soul had tossed over the crime scene. Raindrops pinged musically against the strong, clear plastic.

She recognized the raincoat, dealt viciously with the quick, instinctive lurch of her stomach. She asked if the immediate scene had been scanned and recorded, and receiving the affirmative, crouched down.

Her hands were rock steady as they reached for the hood that had fallen forward over the victim's face. She ignored the blood that pooled in a sticky puddle at the toes of her boots and managed to smother the gasp and the shudder as she tossed the hood away from a stranger's face.

"Who the hell is this?" she demanded.

"Victim's been preliminarily identified as Louise Kirski, editorial tech for Channel 75." The uniform pulled a log out of the pocket of her slick black raincoat. "She was found at approximately eleven fifteen by C. J. Morse. He tossed his cookies just over there," she went on with light disdain for civilian delicacy. "Went inside through this door, screaming his head off. Building security verified his story, such as it was, called it in. Dispatch logged the call at eleven twenty-two. I arrived on scene at eleven twenty-seven."

"You made good time, Officer . . . ?"

"Peabody, Lieutenant. I was on a swing of First Avenue. I verified homicide, secured the outer door, called for additional uniforms and a primary."

Eve nodded toward the building. "They get any of this on camera?"

"Sir." Peabody's mouth thinned. "I ordered a news team off scene when I arrived. I'd say they got plenty before we secured."

"Okay." With fingertips encased in clear seal, Eve did a search of the body. A few credits, a little jingling change, a pricey mini 'link attached to the belt. No defense wounds, no signs of struggle or assault.

She recorded it all dutifully, her mind working fast. Yes, she recognized the raincoat, she thought, and her initial exam complete, she straightened.

"I'm going in. I'm expecting Captain Feeney. Pass him through. She can go with the ME."

"Yes, sir."

"You stand, Peabody," Eve decided. The cop had a good, firm style. "Keep those reporters in line." Eve glanced over her shoulder, ignoring the shouted questions, the glint of lenses. "Give no comment, no statement."

"I've got nothing to say to them."

"Good. Keep it that way."

Eve unsealed the door, passed through, resealed it. The lobby was nearly empty. Peabody, or someone like her, had cleared it of all but essential personnel. Eve shot a look at the security behind the main console. "C. J. Morse. Where?"

"His station's on level six, section eight. Some of your people took him up that way."

"I'm expecting another cop. Send him after me." Eve turned and stepped onto the ascent.

There were people here and there, some huddled together, others standing against video backdrops talking furiously to cameras. She caught the scent of coffee, the stale just-burned fragrance so similar to a cop's bull pen. Another time, it might have made her smile.

The noise level was climbing, even as she did. She stepped off on level six into the frantic buzz of the newsroom.

Consoles were set back to back, with traffic areas snaking through. Like police work, broadcasting was a twenty-four-hour business. Even at this hour, there were more than a dozen stations manned.

The difference, Eve noted, was that cops looked overworked, rumpled, even sweaty. This crew was video perfect. Clothes were streamlined, jewelry camera friendly, faces carefully polished.

Everyone seemed to have a job to do. Some were talking quickly to their 'link screens—feeding their satellites updates, Eve imagined. Others barked at their computers or were barked at by them as data was requested, accessed, and transmitted to the desired source.

It all looked perfectly normal, except mixed with the stale scent of bad coffee was the sticky odor of fear.

One or two noticed her, started to rise, questions in their eyes. Her brutally cold stare was as effective as a steel shield.

She turned to the wall where screens hugged against each other. Roarke had a similar setup, and she knew each screen could be used for a separate image, or in any combination. Now the wall was filled with a huge picture of Nadine Furst on the news set. The familiar three-dimensional view of New York's skyline rose behind her.

She, too, looked polished, perfect. Her eyes seemed to meet and hold on Eve's as Eve stepped closer to listen to the audio.

"And again tonight, a senseless killing. Louise Kirski, an employee of this station, was murdered only a few steps away from the building where I am now broadcasting this report."

Eve didn't bother to curse as Nadine added a few more details and segued to Morse. She'd expected this.

"An ordinary evening," Morse said in a clear reporter's voice. "A rainy night in the city. But once again, despite the best offered by our police force, murder happens. This reporter is now able to give you a first-hand view of the horror, the shock, and the waste."

He paused, timing perfect, as the camera zoomed in on his face. "I found Louise Kirski's body, crumpled, bleeding, at the bottom of the steps of this building where both she and I have worked many nights. Her throat had been slashed, her blood pouring out on the wet pavement. I'm not ashamed to say that I froze, that I was revolted, that the smell of death clogged in my lungs. I stood, looking down at her, unable to believe what I saw with my own eyes. How could this be? A woman I knew, a woman who I had often shared a friendly word with, a woman I had occasionally had the privilege of working with. How could she be lying there, lifeless?"

The screen dissolved from his pale, serious face, to a gruesomely graphic shot of the body.

They hadn't missed a beat, Eve thought in disgust, and whirled on the closest manned console. "Where's the studio?"

"Excuse me?"

"I said, where's the goddamn studio?" She jerked a thumb toward the screen.

"Well, ah . . ."

Furious, she leaned over, caged him between her stiffened arms. "You want to see how fast I can shut this place down?"

"Level twelve, Studio A."

She whirled away just as Feeney stepped off the ascent. "Took your sweet time."

"Hey, I was in New Jersey visiting my folks." He didn't bother to ask, but fell into step with her.

"I need a gag on the broadcast."

"Well." He scratched his head as they headed up. "We can probably finagle an order to confiscate the pictures of the scene." He moved his shoulders at Eve's glance. "I caught some of it on the screen in the car on the way here. They'll get it back, but we can hang them up for a few hours, anyway."

"Get to work on it. I need all the data available on the victim. They should have records here."

"That's simple enough."

"Feed them to my office, will you, Feeney? I'll be on my way there shortly."

"No problem. Anything else?"

Eve stepped off, scowled at the thick white doors of Studio A. "I might need some backup in here."

"That'd be my pleasure."

The doors were locked, the On Air sign glowing. Eve struggled with a desperate urge to draw her weapon and blow the security panel apart. Instead, she jabbed the emergency button and waited for response.

"Channel 75 News now in progress, live," came the soothing electronic voice. "What is the nature of your problem?"

"Police emergency." She held her ID up to the small scanner.

"One moment, Lieutenant Dallas, while your request is accessed."

"It's not a request," Eve said evenly. "I want these doors open now, or I'll be forced to break in under Code 83B, subsection J."

There was a quiet hum, an electronic hiss, as if the computer were considering, then expressing annoyance. "Clearing doors. Please remain quiet and do not pass the white line. Thank you."

Inside the studio, the temperature dropped ten degrees. Eve stalked directly toward a glass partition facing the set and rapped hard enough to have the news director go white with worry. He held a desperate finger to his lips. Eve held up her badge.

With obvious reluctance, he clicked open the door and gestured them in. "We're live," he snapped and turned back to his view of the set. "Camera Three on Nadine. Back image of Louise. Mark."

The robotics on set obeyed smoothly. Eve watched the small suspended camera shift. On the control monitor, Louise Kirski smiled cheerily.

"Slow down, Nadine. Don't rush it. C. J., ready in ten."

"Go to commercial," Eve told him.

"We're running without ads on this broadcast."

"Go to commercial," she repeated, "or you're going to go to black."

He screwed up his forehead, puffed out his chest. "Now listen here—"

"You listen." She poked him none too gently in that expanded chest. "You've got my eyewitness out there. You do what you're told, or your competitors are going to have ratings through the roof with the story I'm going to give them on how Channel 75 interfered with a police investigation on the murder of one of its own people." She lifted a brow while he considered. "And maybe I'm going to start to think you look like a suspect. He strike you as the cold-blooded killer type, Feeney?"

"I was just thinking that. Maybe we need to take him in, have a nice long chat. After a strip search."

"Just hold on. Hold on." He wiped a hand across his mouth. What could a quick ninety-second commercial break hurt? "Go to Zippy spot in ten. C. J., wind it up. Cue music. Camera One pan back. Mark."

He let out a long breath. "I'm calling legal on this."

"You do that." Eve stepped out of the booth and stalked to the long black console Morse and Nadine shared.

"We've got a right to—"

"I'm going to tell you all about your rights," Eve interrupted Morse. "You've got a right to call your lawyer and have him meet you at Cop Central."

He went dead white. "You're arresting me. Jesus Christ, are you nuts?"

"You're a witness, asshole. And you're not going to make any further statements until you've made one to me. Officially." She flicked a scathing gaze in Nadine's direction. "You'll just have to muddle through the rest on your own."

"I want to go with you." On shaky legs, Nadine rose. To dispense with the frantic shouts from the control booth, she tugged her earpiece free and tossed it down. "I was probably the last person to speak to her."

"Fine. We'll talk about that." Eve led them out, pausing only to grin nastily toward control. "You could fill in with some old reruns of *NYPD Blue*. It's a classic."

"Well, well, C. J." However miserable she was, Eve could appreciate the moment. "I've finally got you where I want you. Comfy?"

He looked a little green around the gills, but managed to sneer as he took a long scan of the interview room. "You guys could use a decorator."

"We're trying to work that into the budget." She settled back at the single table in the room. "Record," she requested. "June 1—Jeez, where did May go?—Subject C. J. Morse, position Interview Room C, Interview conducted by Dallas, Lieutenant Eve, re Homicide, victim Louise Kirsky. Time oh oh forty-five. Mr. Morse, you've been advised of your rights. Do you want your attorney present during this interview?"

He reached for his glass of water and took a sip. "Am I being charged with anything?"

"Not at this time."

"Then get on with it."

"Take me back, C. J. Tell me exactly what happened."

"Fine." He drank again, as if his throat was parched. "I was coming into the station. I had the coanchor on the midnight report."

"What time did you arrive?"

"About quarter after eleven. I went to the east side entrance, most of us use that end because it's more direct to the newsroom. It was raining, so I made a quick dash from the car. I saw something at the base of the steps. I couldn't tell what it was, at first."

He stopped speaking, covered his face with his hands, and rubbed hard. "I couldn't tell," he continued, "until I was practically on top of her. I thought—I don't know what I thought, really. Somebody took a hell of a spill."

"You didn't recognize the victim?"

"The—the hood." he gestured vaguely, helplessly with his hands. "It was over her face. I reached down, and I started to move it away from her face." He gave one violent shudder. "Then I saw the blood— her throat. The blood," he repeated, and covered his eyes.

"Did you touch the body?"

"No, I don't think—no. She was just lying there, and her throat was wide open. Her eyes. No, I didn't touch her." He dropped his hand again, made what appeared to be a herculean effort for control. "I got sick. You probably don't understand that, Dallas. Some people have basic human reactions. All that blood, her eyes. God. I got sick, and I got scared and I ran inside. The guard on the desk. I told him."

"You knew the victim?"

"Sure, I knew her. Louise had edited a few pieces for me. Mostly she worked with Nadine, but she did some pieces for me and for some others. She was good, real good. Quick, a sharp eye. One of the best. Christ." He reached for the pitcher on the table. Water sloshed as he poured it. "There was no reason to kill her. No reason at all."

"Was it her habit to go out that exit at that time?"

"I don't know. I don't think—she should have been in Editing," he said fiercely.

"Were you close, personally?"

His head came up, and his eyes narrowed. "You're trying to pin this on me, aren't you? You'd really like that."

"Just answer the questions, C. J. Were you involved with her?"

"She had a relationship, talked about some guy named Bongo. We worked together, Dallas. That's all."

"You arrived at Channel 75 at eleven fifteen. Before that?"

"Before that I was at home. When I have the midnight shift, I catch a couple hours' sleep. I didn't have a feature running, so I didn't have much prep. It was supposed to be just a read, a recap of the day. I had dinner with some friends about seven, headed home around eight, and took a nap."

He propped his elbows on the table and lowered his head into his hands. "I had my wake-up at ten, then headed out just before eleven. Gave myself a little extra travel time because of the weather. Jesus, Jesus, Jesus."

If Eve hadn't watched him report on camera minutes after his discovery of the body, she might have felt sorry for him. "Did you see anyone at or near the scene?"

"Just Louise. There's not a lot of people going in and out that time of night. I didn't see anybody. Just Louise. Just Louise."

"Okay, C. J., that's about it this time around."

He set down the glass he'd guzzled from again. "I can go?"

"Keep in mind you're a witness. If you're holding back, or if you remember anything not revealed in this interview, I'll charge you with withholding evidence and impeding an investigation." She smiled pleasantly. "Oh, and give me the names of your friends, C. J. I didn't think you had any."

She let him go and brooded while she waited for Nadine to be brought in. The scenario was all too clear. And the guilt came with it. To keep both fresh, she flipped open the file and studied the hard copy photos of Louise Kirski's body. She turned them facedown when the door opened.

Nadine didn't look polished now. The professional gloss of the on-air personality had given way to a pale, shaken woman with swollen eyes and a trembling mouth. Saying nothing, Eve gestured to the chair and poured water in a fresh glass.

"You were quick," she said coolly, "getting your report on the air."

"That's my job." Nadine didn't touch the glass, but gripped her hands in her lap. "You do yours, I do mine."

"Right. Just serving the public, aren't we?"

"I'm not very interested in what you think of me right now, Dallas."

"Just as well, because I don't think very much of you right now."
For the second time, she started the recorder, fed in the necessary
information. "When did you last see Louise Kirski alive?"

"We were working in Editing, refining and timing a piece for the
midnight spot. It didn't take as much time as we'd scheduled to finish.
Louise was good, really good." Nadine drew a deep breath and continued to stare at a spot an inch above Eve's left shoulder. "We talked for
a few minutes. She and the man she'd been seeing for the last several
months were looking for an apartment together. She was happy. Louise was a happy person, easy to get along with, bright."

She had to stop again, had to. Her breath was backing up. Carefully, firmly, she ordered herself to inhale, exhale. Twice. "Anyway, she
was out of cigarettes. She liked to catch a quick smoke between assign-
ments. Everybody looked the other way, even though she'd sneak off
into a closet somewhere and light up. I told her to pick me up a couple
while she was at it, gave her some credits. We went down together,
and I got off at the newsroom. I had some calls to make. Otherwise,
I'd have gone with her. I'd have been with her."

"Did you usually go out together before the broadcast?"

"No. Normally, I take a short break, head out, have a quiet cup of
coffee in this little café on Third. I like to—get away from the station,
especially before the midnight. We've got a restaurant, lounges, a coffee shop in house, but I like to break off and take ten on my own."

"Habitually?"

"Yeah." Nadine met Eve's eyes, veered away. "Habitually. But I
wanted to make those calls, and it was raining, so . . . so I didn't go. I
lent her my raincoat, and she went out." Her eyes shifted back, straight
to Eve's. And were devastated. "She's dead instead of me. You know
that, and I know that. Don't we, Dallas?"

"I recognized your coat," Eve said briefly. "I thought it was you."

"She didn't do anything but run out for a few cigarettes. Wrong
place, wrong time. Wrong coat."

Wrong bait, Eve thought, but didn't say it. "Let's take this a step at
a time, Nadine. An editor has a certain amount of power, of control."

"No." Slowly, methodically, Nadine shook her head. The sickness in her stomach had snuck into her throat, and tasted foul. "It's the story, Dallas, and the on-air personality. Nobody appreciates, or even thinks of an editor but the reporter. She wasn't the target, Dallas. Let's not pretend otherwise."

"What I think and what I know are handled in different ways, Nadine. But let's go with what I think for now. I think you were the target, and I think the killer mistook Louise for you. You've got different builds, but it was raining, she was wearing your coat, had the hood on. There either wasn't time, or there wasn't a choice once the mistake was realized."

"What?" Dazed at having it all said so flatly, Nadine struggled to focus. "What did you say?"

"It was over quickly. I've got the time she left from the security desk. She waved to the guard. We've got Morse stumbling over her ten minutes later. Either it was timed extremely well, or our killer was cocky. And you can bet your ass he wanted to see it on the news before she'd gotten cold."

"We accommodated him, didn't we?"

"Yeah." Eve nodded. "You did."

"You think it was easy for me?" Nadine's voice, raspy and thick, burst out. "You think it was easy to sit there and give a report knowing she was still lying outside?"

"I don't know," Eve said mildly. "Was it?"

"She was my friend." Nadine began to weep, tears rushing out, pouring down her cheeks and leaving trails in her camera makeup. "I cared about her. Damn it, she mattered to me, not just a story. She isn't just a fucking story."

Struggling to carry her own guilt, Eve nudged the glass toward Nadine. "Drink," she ordered. "Take a minute."

Nadine had to use both hands to keep the glass even partially steady. She would, she realized, have preferred brandy, but that would have to wait. "I see this kind of thing all the time, not so different from you."

"You saw the body," Eve snapped. "You went out on the scene."

"I had to see." With eyes still swimming, she looked back at Eve.

"That was personal, Dallas. I had to see. I didn't want to believe it when word came up."

"How did word come up?"

"Somebody heard Morse yelling to the guard that somebody was dead, that somebody had been murdered right outside. That drew a lot of attention," she said, rubbing her temples. "Word travels. I hadn't finished my second call before I caught the buzz. I hung up on my source and went down. And I saw her." Her smile was grim and humorless. "I beat the cameras—and the cops."

"And you and your pals risked contaminating a crime scene." Eve swiped a hand through the air. "That's done. Did anybody touch her? Did you see anybody touch her?"

"No, nobody was that stupid. It was obvious she was dead. You could see—you could see the wound, the blood. We sent for an ambulance anyway. The first police unit was there within minutes, ordered us back inside, sealed the door. I talked to somebody. Peabody." She rubbed fingers over her temples. Not because they hurt; because they were numb. "I told her it was Louise, then I went up to prep for broadcast. And the whole time I was thinking, *It was supposed to be me.* I was alive, facing the camera, and she was dead. It was supposed to be me."

"It wasn't supposed to be anyone."

"We killed her, Dallas." Nadine's voice was steady again. "You and me."

"I guess we'll have to live with that." Eve drew a breath and leaned forward. "Let's go over the timing again, Nadine. Step by step."

THIRTEEN

Sometimes, Eve thought, the drudge of routine police work payed off. Like a slot machine, fed habitually, mindlessly, monotonously, so that you're almost shocked when the jackpot falls in your lap.

That's just the way it was when David Angelini fell into hers.

She'd had several questions on small details of the Kirski case. The timing was one of them.

Nadine skips her usual break. Kirksi goes out instead, passing the lobby desk at approximately 23:04. She steps out into the rain, and into a knife. Minutes later, running late, Morse arrives at the station lot, stumbles over the body, vomits, and runs inside to report a murder.

All of it, she mused, quick, fast, and in a hurry.

As a matter of course, she ran the discs from the security gate at Channel 75. It wasn't possible to know if the killer had driven through them, parked a car on the station's lot, strolled over to wait for Nadine, sliced Louise by mistake, then driven off again.

An assailant could just as easily have cut across the property from Third on foot, just as Louise had intended to do. Gate security was to make sure that there were parking facilities for station employees and that guests weren't infringed upon by every frustrated driver looking for a place to stick his car or minishuttle off the street.

Eve reviewed the discs because it was a matter of routine, and because, she admitted to herself, she hoped Morse's story wouldn't gel. He'd have recognized Nadine's raincoat, and he'd have known her habit of cutting out for some solo time before the midnight broadcast.

There was nothing she'd have enjoyed more, on a basic, even primal personal level, than nailing his skinny butt to the wall.

And that's when she saw the sleek little two-passenger Italian model cruise like a shiny cat to the gate. She'd seen that car before, parked outside of the commander's home after the memorial service.

"Stop," she ordered, and the image on screen froze. "Enhance sector twenty-three through thirty, full screen." The machine clicked, then clunked, wobbling the image. With an impatient snarl, Eve smacked the screen with the heel of her hand, jarring it back on course. "Goddamn budget cuts," she muttered, and then her smile began, slow and savoring. "Well, well, Mr. Angelini."

She took a deep breath as David's face filled her screen. He looked impatient, she thought. Distracted. Nervous.

"What were you doing there?" she murmured, flicking her glance down to the digital time frozen at the bottom left corner. "At twenty-three oh two and five seconds?"

She leaned back in her chair, rifling through a drawer with one hand as she continued to study the screen. Absently, she bit into a candy bar that was going to pass for breakfast. She'd yet to go home.

"Hard copy," she ordered. "Then go back to original view and hard copy." She waited patiently while her machine wheezed its way through the process. "Continue disc run, normal speed."

Nibbling on her breakfast, she watched the pricey sports car whiz past camera range. The image blinked. Channel 75 could afford the latest in motion-activated security cameras. Eleven minutes had passed on the counter when Morse's car approached.

"Interesting," she murmured. "Copy disc, transfer copy to file 47833-K, Kirski, Louise. Homicide. Cross reference to case file 47801-T, Towers, Cicely and 47815-M, Metcalf, Yvonne. Homicides."

Turning from the screen, she engaged her 'link. "Feeney."

"Dallas." He stuffed the last of a danish into his mouth. "I'm working on it. Christ, it's barely seven A.M."

"I know what time it is. I've got a sensitive matter here, Feeney."

"Hell." His already rumpled face grew more wrinkles. "I hate when you say that."

"I've got David Angelini on the gate security disc at Channel 75, coming in about ten minutes before Louise Kirski's body was discovered."

"Shit, shit, shit. Who's going to tell the commander?"

"I am—after I've had a talk with Angelini. I need you to cover for me, Feeney. I'm going to transmit what I've got, excluding Angelini. You take it in to the commander. Tell him I'm hooking a couple hours of personal time."

"Yeah, like he'll buy that one."

"Feeney, tell me I need some sleep. Tell me you'll report to the commander, and to go home and catch a couple hours of sleep."

Feeney heaved a long sigh. "Dallas, you need some sleep. I'll report to the commander. Go home and catch a couple hours."

"Now you can tell him you told me," she said, and flicked off.

Like routine police work, a cop's gut often paid off. Eve's told her that David Angelini would close himself in with family. Her first stop was the Angelini pied-à-terre, cozied in an affluent East Side neighborhood.

Here the brownstones had been constructed barely thirty years before, reproductions of those designed during the nineteenth, and destroyed during the dawn of the twenty-first when most of New York's infrastructure had failed. A large portion of New York's posher homes in this area had been condemned and razed. After much debate, this area had been rebuilt in the old tradition—a tradition only the very wealthy had been able to afford.

After a ten-minute search, Eve managed to find a spot among the expensive European and American cars. Overhead, a trio of private minishuttles jockeyed for air space, circling as they looked for a clear landing.

Apparently, public transportation wasn't high on the list in the neighborhood, and property was too dear to waste on garage facilities.

Still, New York was New York, and she locked the doors on her battered police issue before heading up the sidewalk. She watched a teenager skim by on an airboard. He took the opportunity to impress his small audience with a few complicated maneuvers, ending with a long, looping flip. Rather than disappoint him, Eve flashed him an appreciative grin.

"Nice moves."

"I got the groove," he claimed in a voice that was hovering between puberty and manhood with less security than he hovered over the sidewalk. "You board?"

"No. Too risky for me." When she continued to walk, he circled around her, pivoting on the board with quick footwork.

"I could show you some of the easy scoots in five minutes."

"I'll keep it in mind. You know who lives there, in twenty-one?"

"Twenty-one? Sure, Mr. Angelini. You're not one of his nibbles." She stopped. "I'm not?"

"Come on." The boy cocked a grin, showing perfect teeth. "He goes for the dignified type. Older, too." He did a quick vertical rock, side to side. "You don't look like a domestic, either. Anyway, he mostly does the droid thing for that."

"Does he have a lot of nibbles?"

"Only seen a few around here. Always come up in a private car. Sometimes they'll stay till morning, but mostly not."

"And how would you know?"

He grinned, unabashed. "I live right over there." He pointed to a townhouse across the street. "I like to keep my eye on what's doing."

"Okay, why don't you tell me if anybody came around last night?" He swiveled his board, spun. "How come?"

"Cause I'm a cop."

His eyes widened as he studied her badge. "Wow. Decent. Hey, you think he popped his old lady? Gotta keep up with current events and shit for school."

"This isn't a quiz. Were you keeping your eye out last night? What's your name?"

"It's Barry. I was kind of hanging loose last night, watching some screen, listening to some tune. Supposed to be studying for this monster final in Comp Tech."

"Why aren't you in school today?"

"Hey, you're not with the Truant Division?" His grin turned a little nervous. "It's too early for class. Anyway, I got the three-day thing, E-school at home."

"Okay. Last night?"

"While I was hanging, I saw Mr. Angelini go out. About eight, I guess. Then, late, probably closing on midnight, this other dude, flash car pulls up. He didn't get out for awhile, just kinda sat there like he couldn't make up his mind."

Barry did a quick whirl-a-loop, dancing up the length of the board. "Then he went in. Walking funny. I figured he'd been dousing a few. Went right on in, so he knew the code. Didn't see Mr. Angelini come back. I was probably zeeing by then. You know, catching winks."

"Sleeping, yeah. I get it. Did you see anybody leave this morning?"

"Nope, but the flash car's still there."

"I see. Thanks."

"Hey." He scooted behind her. "Is being a cop a rocking thing?"

"Sometimes it rocks, sometimes it doesn't." She climbed the short steps to the Angelini home and identified herself to the cool tones of the greeting scanner.

"I'm sorry, Lieutenant, there is no one at home. If you would like to leave a message, it will be returned at the first opportunity."

Eve looked directly at the scanner. "Process this. If there's no one at home, I'm going to walk back to my car, request an entry and search warrant. That should take about ten minutes."

She stood her ground and waited less than two before David Angelini opened the door.

"Lieutenant."

"Mr. Angelini. Here or Cop Central? Your choice."

"Come in." He stepped back. "I just arrived in New York last night. I'm still a bit disorganized this morning."

He led her into a dark-toned, high-ceilinged sitting room and offered her coffee politely, which she declined with equal politeness. He wore the slim, narrow cuffed slacks she'd seen on the streets of Rome with a wide-sleeved silk shirt of the same neutral cream color. His shoes matched the tone and looked soft enough to dent with a fingertip.

But his eyes were restless, and his hands tapped rhythmically on the arms of his chair when he sat.

"You have more information about my mother's case."

"You know why I'm here."

He flicked his tongue over his lips, shifted. Eve thought she understood why he did so poorly at gaming. "Excuse me?"

She set her recorder on the table in full view. "David Angelini, your rights are as follows. You are under no obligation to make a statement. If you do make a statement, it will be logged into record and can and will be used against you in court or any legal proceeding. You have a right to the presence and advice of an attorney or representative."

She continued the brisk recitation of his rights while his breathing quickened and grew more audible. "The charges?"

"You are not yet charged. Do you understand your rights?"

"Of course I understand them."

"Do you wish to call your attorney?"

His mouth opened, a breath shuddered out. "Not yet. I assume you're going to make the purpose of this interrogation clear, Lieutenant."

"I think it's going to be crystal. Mr. Angelini, where were you between the hours of eleven P.M., May 31 and twelve A.M., June 1?"

"I told you I'd just gotten into the city. I drove in from the airport and came here."

"You came here, directly from the airport?"

"That's right. I had a late meeting, but I—I canceled it." He flicked open the top hook of his shirt, as if he needed air. "Rescheduled it."

"What time did you arrive at the airport?"

"My flight got in around ten-thirty, I believe."

"You came here."

"I've said so."

"Yes, you did." Eve angled her head. "And you're a liar. A bad liar. You sweat when you bluff."

Aware of the damp line running down his back, he rose. His voice tried for outrage but ended on fear. "I believe I'll contact my attorney after all, Lieutenant. And your superior. Is it standard police procedure to harass innocent people in their own homes?"

"Whatever works," she murmured. "Then again, you're not innocent. Go ahead and call your attorney, and we'll all go down to Cop Central."

But he didn't move toward his 'link. "I haven't done anything."

"For starters, you've lied on record to an investigating officer. Call your attorney."

"Wait, wait." Rubbing a hand over his mouth, David paced the room. "It isn't necessary. It isn't necessary to take this that far."

"That's your choice. Would you care to revise your previous statement?"

"This is a delicate matter, Lieutenant."

"Funny, I've always thought of murder as a crude matter, myself."

He continued to pace, working his hands together. "You have to understand the business is in a tenuous position at the moment. The wrong kind of publicity will influence certain transactions. In a week, two at the most, it will all be resolved."

"And you think I should hold off on all this until you get your financial ducks in a row?"

"I'd be willing to compensate you for your time and your discretion."

"Would you?" Eve widened her eyes. "What sort of compensation are you suggesting, Mr. Angelini?"

"I can swing ten thousand." He struggled for a smile. "Double that if you simply bury all of this for good."

Eve crossed her arms. "Let the record show that David Angelini offered a monetary bribe to investigating primary Lieutenant Eve Dallas, and the aforesaid bribe was refused."

"Bitch," he said softly.

"You bet. Why were you at Channel 75 last night?"

"I've never said I was."

"Let's cut the dreck. You were recorded by gate security entering the property." To emphasize, she opened her bag, took out the hard copy of his face, tossed it on the table.

"Gate security." His legs seemed to fold from under him and he groped into a chair. "I never thought—never considered. I panicked."

"Slicing someone's jugular can do that to you."

"I never touched her. I never went near her. Good God, do I look like a murderer?"

"They come in all styles. You were there. I have documentation. Hands!" she said sharply as her own jumped to her shoulder harness. "Keep your hands out of your pockets."

"Name of God, do you think I'm carrying a knife?" Slowly he drew out a handkerchief, wiped his brow. "I didn't even know Louise Kirski."

"But you know her name."

"I saw it on the news." He closed his eyes. "I saw it on the news. And I saw him kill her."

The muscles in Eve's shoulders bunched, but unlike David she was good at the game. Both her face and voice were bland. "Well then, why don't you tell me all about it?"

He worked his hands together again, linking fingers, twisting. He wore two rings, one diamond, one ruby, both set in heavy gold. They clinked together musically.

"You have to keep my name out of this."

"No," she said evenly, "I don't. I don't make deals. Your mother was a PA, Mr. Angelini. You should know if there are going to be any deals, they're going to come through that office, not me. You've already lied on the record." She kept her tone flat, easy. It was best when working with a nervous suspect to ease them in. "I'm giving you a chance to revise your previous statement, and again reminding you that you have the right to contact your attorney at any time during this interview. But if you want to talk to me, talk now. And I'll start, to make it easy for you. What were you doing at Channel 75 last night?"

"I had a late meeting. I told you that I had one and canceled. That's the truth. We've been—I've been working on an expansion deal. Angelini has some interest in the entertainment industry. We've been developing projects, programs, features for in-home viewing. Carlson Young, the head of the entertainment division of the channel, had done quite a bit to bring these projects to fruition. I was to meet him in his office there."

"A little after business hours, wasn't it?"

"The entertainment field doesn't have what you might call normal business hours. Both of our schedules were tight, and this was a time that suited us both."

"Why not handle it over the 'link?"

"A great deal of our business was done that way. But we both felt it was time for a personal meeting. We'd hoped—still hope—to have the first project on air by fall. We have the script," he continued, almost talking to himself now. "The production team's in place. We've already signed some of the cast."

"So, you had a late night meeting with Carlson Young of Channel 75."

"Yes. The weather held me up a bit. I was running late." His head came up. "I called him from my car. You can check that, too. You can check. I called him a few minutes before eleven when I realized I would be late."

"We'll check everything, Mr. Angelini. Count on it."

"I arrived at the main gate. I was distracted, thinking of . . . of some casting problems. I turned. I should have gone straight to the main entrance, but I was thinking of something else. I stopped the car, realized I'd have to backtrack. Then I saw—" He used his handkerchief, rubbed at his mouth. "I saw someone come out of a door. Then there was someone else, he must have been standing there watching, waiting. He moved so fast. It all moved so fast. She turned, and I saw her face. Just for a second, I saw her face in the light. His hand jerked up. Fast, very fast. And . . . dear God. The blood. It gushed, like a fountain. I didn't understand. I couldn't believe—it just spurted out of her. She fell, and he was running, running away."

"What did you do?"

"I—I just sat there. I don't know how long. I was driving away. I don't even remember. I was driving and everything was like a dream. The rain, and the lights from other cars. Then I was here. I can't even remember how I got here. But I was outside in the car. I called Young, and told him I'd been delayed again, that we needed to reschedule. I came inside, there was no one here. I took a sedative and went to bed."

Eve let the silence hum a moment. "Let's see if I've got this. You were on your way to a meeting, took a wrong turn, and saw a woman brutally murdered. Then you drove away, canceled your meeting, and went to bed. Is that accurate?"

"Yes. Yes, I suppose it is."

"It didn't occur to you to get out of your car, to see if she could be helped? Or perhaps to use your 'link to notify the authorities, the MTs?"

"I wasn't thinking. I was shaken."

"You were shaken. So you came here, took a pill, and went to bed."

"That's what I said," he snapped out. "I need a drink." With sweaty fingers, he fumbled for a control. "Vodka," he ordered. "Bring the bottle."

Eve let him stew until the server droid arrived with a bottle of Stoli and a short thick glass on its tray. She let him drink.

"There was nothing I could do," he mumbled, goaded, as she'd intended, by her silence. "I wasn't involved."

"Your mother was murdered a few weeks ago by the method you've just described to me. And this didn't involve you?"

"That was part of the problem." He poured again, drank again. Shuddered. "I was shocked, and—and afraid. Violence isn't part of my life, Lieutenant. It was part of my mother's, a part I could never understand. She understood violence," he said quietly. "She understood it."

"And did you resent that, Mr. Angelini? That she understood violence, was strong enough to face it? Fight against it?"

His breathing was shallow. "I loved my mother. When I saw this other woman murdered, as my mother had been murdered, all I could think of to do was run."

He paused, took a last quick swallow of vodka. "Do you think I don't know you've been checking on me, asking questions, digging into my personal and professional lives? I'm a suspect already. How much worse would it have been for me to be there, right there, at the scene of another murder?"

Eve rose. "You're about to find out."

CHAPTER

FOURTEEN

Eve questioned him again, in the less comforting surroundings of Interview Room C. He'd finally taken up his right for counsel, and three pin-striped, cold-eyed lawyers ranged beside their client at the conference table.

Eve had privately dubbed them Moe, Larry, and Curly.

Moe apparently was in charge. She was a tough-voiced woman with a severe bowl-cut hairstyle that had inspired Eve to christen her. Her associates said little but looked sober and occasionally made important-looking notations on the yellow legal pads that lawyers never seemed to tire of.

Now and again Curly, his wide forehead creased, would tap a few buttons on his log book and murmur conspiratorially in Larry's ear.

"Lieutenant Dallas." Moe folded her hands, which were tipped with wicked looking inch-long scarlet nails, on the table. "My client is eager to cooperate."

"He wasn't," Eve stated, "as you've seen for yourself from the first interview. After recanting his original story, your client admitted to leaving the scene of a crime and failing to report said crime to the proper authorities."

Moe sighed. It was a windy, disappointed sound. "You can, of course, charge Mr. Angelini with those lapses. We will, in turn, claim diminished capacity, shock, and the emotional trauma of his mother's recent murder. This would all be a waste of the court's time, and the taxpayer's dollar."

"I haven't charged your client with those . . . lapses as yet. We're dealing with a larger theme here."

Curly scribbled something, tilted his pad for Larry to read. The two of them murmured together and looked grave.

"You have confirmed my client's appointment at Channel 75."

"Yeah, he had an appointment, which he canceled at eleven thirty-five. Odd that his diminished capacity and his emotional trauma eased off enough for him to take care of business." Before Moe could speak again, Eve turned and pinned Angelini with one hard stare. "You know Nadine Furst?"

"I know who she is. I've seen her on the news." He hesitated, leaned over to consult Moe. After a moment, he nodded. "I'd met her a few times socially, and spoke with her briefly after my mother's death."

Eve already knew all of that, and circled her quarry. "I'm sure you've seen her reports. You'd have a vested interest, as she's been covering the recent murders. Your mother's murder."

"Lieutenant, what does my client's interest in the news coverage of his mother's death have to do with the murder of Ms. Kirski?"

"I'm wondering. You have seen Nadine Furst's reports over the last couple weeks, Mr. Angelini."

"Of course." He'd recovered enough to sneer. "You've gotten a lot of airtime out of it, Lieutenant."

"Does that bother you?"

"I think it's appalling that a public servant, paid by the city, would seek notoriety through tragedy."

"Sounds like it pissed you off," Eve said with an easy shrug. "Ms. Furst has been getting plenty of notoriety out of it, too."

"One learns to expect someone like her to use someone else's pain for her own advancement."

"You didn't like the coverage?"

"Lieutenant," Moe said with her patience obviously straining. "Where's the point in this?"

"This isn't a trial, yet. I don't need a point. Were you annoyed by the coverage, Mr. Angelini? Angry?"

"I—" He broke off at a sharp look from Moe. "I come from a prominent family," he said more carefully. "We're accustomed to such things."

"If we could get back to the business at hand," Moe requested.

"This is the business at hand. Louise Kirski was wearing Nadine Furst's raincoat when she was killed. You know what I think, Mr. Angelini? I think the killer hit the wrong target. I think he was waiting for Nadine and Louise just happened to choose the wrong time to go out in the rain for cigarettes."

"It doesn't have anything to do with me." His eyes darted toward his attorneys. "It still doesn't have anything to do with me. I saw it. That's all."

"You said it was a man. What did he look like?"

"I don't know. I didn't see him clearly, his back was to me. It happened so fast."

"But you saw enough to know it was a man."

"I assumed." He broke off, struggling to control his breathing while Moe whispered in his ear. "It was raining," he began. "I was several meters away, in my car."

"You said you saw the victim's face."

"The light, she turned her head toward the light when he—or when the killer—went toward her."

"And this killer, who might have been a man, and who came out of nowhere. Was he tall, short, old, young?"

"I don't know. It was dark."

"You said there was light."

"Just that circle of light. He'd been in the shadows. He was wearing black," David said on a burst of inspiration. "A long black coat—and a hat, a hat that drooped down low."

"That's convenient. He was wearing black. It's so original."

"Lieutenant, I can't advise my client to continue to cooperate if you persist in sarcasm."

"Your client's in hip deep. My sarcasm's the least of his worries. We've got the three big ones. Means, motive, opportunity."

"You have nothing but my client's admission that he witnessed a crime. Further," Moe went on, tapping those dangerous nails on the conference table, "you have absolutely nothing to link him with the other murders. What you've got, Lieutenant, is a maniac on the loose, and a desperate need to appease your superiors and the public with an arrest. It's not going to be my client."

"We'll have to see about that. Now—" Her communicator beeped, twice, a signal from Feeney. Her adrenaline surged, and she masked it with a bland smile. "Excuse me, I'll only be a moment."

She stepped out of the room into the hallway. Behind her through the one-way glass, a huddle was in progress. "Give me good news, Feeney. I want to nail this son of a bitch."

"Good news?" Feeney rubbed his chin. "Well, you might like this. Yvonne Metcalf was in negotiations with our pal in there. Covert negotiations."

"For?"

"The lead in some flick. It was all on the Q.T. because her contract for *Tune In* was coming up. I finally pinned her agent down. If she snagged the part, she was willing to ditch the sitcom. But they were going to have to up the ante, guarantee a three-feature deal, international distribution, and twenty hours' straight promo."

"Sounds like she wanted a lot."

"She was squeezing him some. My take from what the agent said is he needed Metcalf to guarantee some of the financial backing, but they wanted a chunk on the front end. He was scrambling to come up with it and save his project."

"He knew her. And she had the controls."

"According to the agent, he came in to meet Metcalf personally, several times. They had a couple of tête-à-têtes at her apartment. He got a little hot, but Metcalf laughed it off. She was banking that he'd come around."

"I love when it falls into place, don't you?" She turned, studying Angelini through the glass. "We've got a connection, Feeney. He knew them all."

"He was supposed to be on the coast when Metcalf got whacked."

"How much do you want to bet he's got a private plane? You know something I've learned since Roarke, Feeney? Flight plans don't mean squat if you've got money, and your own transpo. No, unless he comes up with ten witnesses who were kissing his ass when Metcalf went down, I've got him. Watch him sweat," she muttered as she swung back into the interview room.

She sat, crossed her arms on the table, and met Angelini's eyes. "You knew Yvonne Metcalf."

"I—" Off balance, David reached up, tugged at the collar of his shirt. "Certainly, I . . . everyone did."

"You had business with her, met her personally, you'd been to her apartment."

This was obviously news to Moe, who bared her teeth, tossed up a hand. "One moment, Lieutenant. I'd like to speak to my client privately."

"All right." Obliging, Eve rose. Outside, she watched the show through the glass, and thought it a pity that the law prevented her from turning on the audio.

Still, she could see Moe fire questions at David and could gauge his stuttering responses while Larry and Curly looked grim and scribbled furiously on their pads.

Moe shook her head at one of David's answers, stabbed him with one of her lethal red nails. Eve was smiling when Moe lifted a hand and signaled her back into the room.

"My client is prepared to state that he was acquainted with Yvonne Metcalf, on a professional level."

"Uh-huh." This time Eve leaned a hip on the table. "Yvonne Metcalf was giving you some grief, wasn't she, Mr. Angelini?"

"We were in negotiations." His hands linked together again, twisted. "It's standard for the talent side of a project to demand the moon. We were . . . coming to terms."

"You met her in her apartment. Argued?"

"We—I—we had meetings at several locations. Her home was one of them. We discussed terms and options."

"Where were you, Mr. Angelini, on the night Yvonne Metcalf was murdered?"

"I'd have to check my diary," he said with surprising control. "But I believe I was in New Los Angeles, the Planet Hollywood complex. I stay there whenever I'm in town."

"And where might you have been between oh, seven and midnight, West Coast time?"

"I couldn't say."

"You're going to want to say, Mr. Angelini."

"Most likely in my room. I had a great deal of business to see to. The script needed reworking."

"The script you were tailoring for Ms. Metcalf."

"Yes, actually."

"And you were working alone?"

"I prefer to be alone when I write. I wrote the script, you see." He flushed a little, the color rising from the collar of his shirt. "I put a great deal of time and effort into preparing it."

"You keep a plane?"

"A plane. Naturally, the way I travel, I—"

"Was your plane in New Los Angeles?"

"Yes, I—" His eyes went wide and blank as he realized the implication. "You can't seriously believe this!"

"David, sit down," Moe said firmly when he lurched to his feet. "You have nothing more to say at this time."

"She thinks I killed them. That's insane. My own mother, for God's sake. What reason? What possible reason could there be for that?"

"Oh, I've got a few ideas on that. We'll see if the shrink agrees with me."

"My client is under no obligation to submit to psychiatric testing."

"I think you're going to advise him to do just that."

"This interview," Moe said in snippy tones, "is terminated."

"Fine." Eve straightened, enjoyed the moment when her eyes met David's. "David Angelini, you're under arrest. You are charged with leaving the scene of a crime, obstruction of justice, and attempted bribery of a police officer."

He lunged at her, going ironically, Eve thought, for the throat. She waited until his hands had closed over it, his eyes bulging with fury, before she knocked him down.

Ignoring the snapping orders of his attorney, Eve leaned over him. "We won't bother with adding assaulting an officer and resisting arrest. I don't think we're going to need it. Book him," she snapped at the uniforms who had charged the door.

"Nice work, Dallas," Feeney congratulated as they watched David being led away.

"Let's hope the PA's office thinks so, enough to block bail. We have to hold him and sweat him. I want him on murder one, Feeney. I want him bad."

"We're close to it, kid."

"We need the physical evidence. We need the damn weapon, blood, the souvenirs. Mira's psychiatric will help, but I can't bump up the charges without some physical." Impatient, she consulted her watch. "Shouldn't take too long to get a search warrant, even with the lawyers trying to block.'"

"How long you been up?" he wondered. "I can count the circles under your eyes."

"Long enough that another couple of hours won't matter. How about I buy you a drink while we wait for the warrant?"

He put a paternal hand on her shoulder. "I think we're both going to need one. The commander got wind of it. He wants us, Dallas. Now."

She dug a finger along the center of her brow. "Let's get it together then. And make it two drinks after we're done."

Whitney didn't waste time. The moment Eve and Feeney stepped into his office, he scalded them both with one long look. "You brought David in to Interview."

"I did, yes, sir." Eve took an extra step forward to take the heat. "We have video of him on the gate security at Channel 75 at the time of Louise Kirski's murder." She didn't pause, but streamed through her report, her voice brisk, her eyes level.

"David says he saw the murder."

"He claims he saw someone, possibly male, in a long black coat and a hat, attack Kirski, then run toward Third."

"And he panicked," Whitney added, still in control. His hands were quiet on his desk. "Left the scene without reporting the incident." Whitney may have been cursing inwardly, his stomach might have been in greasy knots of tension, but his eyes were cool, hard, and steady. "It's not an atypical reaction from a witness to a violent crime."

"He denied he was on scene," Eve said calmly. "Tried to cover, offered a bribe. He had the opportunity, Commander. And he's linked to all three victims. He knew Metcalf, was working with her on a project, had been to her apartment."

Whitney's only reaction was to curl his fingers, then uncurl them. "Motive, Lieutenant?"

"Money first," she said. "He's having financial difficulties that will be eased after his mother's will is probated. The victims, or in the third case, the intended victim, were all strong women in the public eye. Were all, in some manner, causing him distress. Unless his lawyers try to block it, Dr. Mira will test him, determine his emotional and mental state, the probability factor of his aptitude toward violence."

She thought of the press of his hands around her throat and figured the probability was going to be nice and high.

"He wasn't in New York for the first two murders."

"Sir." She felt a bolt of pity, but suppressed it. "He has a private plane. He can shuttle anywhere he likes. It's pathetically simple to doctor flight plans. I can't book him for the murders yet, but I want him held until we gather more evidence."

"You're holding him on leaving the scene and the bribery charge?"

"It's a good arrest, Commander. I'm requesting search warrants. When we find any physical evidence—"

"If," Whitney interrupted. He rose now, no longer able to sit behind his desk. "That's a very big difference, Dallas. Without physical evidence, your murder case can't hold."

"Which is why he has yet to be charged for murder." She laid a hard copy on his desk. She and Feeney had taken the time to swing past her office and use her computer for the probability ratio. "He knew the first two victims and Nadine Furst, had contact with them, was on the scene of the last murder. We suspect that Towers was covering for someone when she zapped the last call on her 'link. She would have covered for her son. And their relationship was strained due to his gambling problem and her refusal to bail him out. With known data, the probability factor of guilt is eighty-three point one percent."

"You haven't taken into account that he's incapable of that kind of violence." Whitney laid his hands on the edge of his desk and leaned forward. "You didn't factor that in to the mix, did you, Lieutenant? I know David Angelini, Dallas. I know him as well as I know my own children. He isn't a killer. He's a fool, perhaps. He's weak, perhaps. But he isn't a cold-blooded killer."

"Sometimes the weak and the foolish strike out. Commander, I'm sorry. I can't kick him loose."

"Do you have any idea what it would do to a man like him to be penned? To know he's suspected of killing his own mother?" There was no choice left for him, in Whitney's mind, but a plea. "I can't deny that he was spoiled. His father wanted the best for him and for Mirina, and saw that they got it. From childhood he was accustomed to asking for something and having it fall into his lap. Yes, his life has been easy, privileged, even indulgent. He's made mistakes, errors in judgment, and they've been fixed for him. But there's no malice in him, Dallas. No violence. I know him."

Whitney's voice didn't rise, but it reverberated with emotion. "You'll never convince me that David took a knife and ripped it across his mother's throat. I'm asking you to consider that, and to delay the paperwork on the yellow sheet and recommend his release on his own recognizance."

Feeney started to speak, but Eve shook her head. He may have outranked her, but she was primary. She was in charge. "Three women are dead, Commander. We have a suspect in custody. I can't do what you're asking. You put me on as primary because you knew I wouldn't."

He turned and stared hard out of the window. "Compassion's not your strong suit, is it, Dallas?"

She winced, but said nothing.

"That's a wrong swing, Jack," Feeney said, with heat. "And if you're going to take one at her, then you'll have to take one at me, 'cause I'm with Dallas on this. We've got enough to book him on the small shit, to take him off the street, and that's what we're doing."

"You'll ruin him." Whitney turned back. "But that's not your problem. You get your warrants, and you do your search. But as your commanding officer, I'm ordering you to keep the case open. You keep looking. Have your reports on my desk by fourteen hundred." He flicked a last glance at Dallas. "You're dismissed."

She walked out, surprised that her legs felt like glass: the thin, fragile kind that could be shattered with a careless brush of the hand.

"He was out of line, Dallas," Feeney said, catching at her arm. "He's hurting, and he took a bad shot at you."

"Not so bad." Her voice was rough and raw. "Compassion's not my strong suit, is it? I don't know shit about family ties and loyalties, do I?"

Uncomfortable, Feeney shifted his feet. "Come on, Dallas, you don't want to take it personal."

"Don't I? He's stood behind me plenty of times. Now he's asking me to stand behind him, and I have to say sorry, no chance. That's pretty fucking personal, Feeney." She shook off his hand. "Let's take a rain check on the drinks. I'm not feeling sociable."

At a loss, Feeney dumped his hands in his pockets. Eve strode off in one direction, the commander remained behind closed doors in the other. Feeney stood unhappily between them.

Eve supervised the search of Marco Angelini's brownstone personally. She wasn't needed there. The sweepers knew their job, and their equipment was as good as the budget allowed. Still, she sprayed her hands, coated her boots, and moved through the three-story home looking for anything that would tie up the case, or, thinking of Whitney's face, break it.

Marco Angelini remained on the premises. That was his right as owner of the property, and as the father of the prime suspect. Eve blocked out his presence, the cold azure eyes that followed her moves, the haggard look to his face, the quick muscle twitch in his jaw.

One of the sweepers did a thorough check of David's wardrobe with a porta-sensor, looking for bloodstains. While he worked, Eve meticulously searched the rest of the room.

"Coulda ditched the weapon," the sweeper commented. He was an old, buck-toothed vet nicknamed Beaver. He traced the sensor, the arm of it wrapped over his left shoulder, down a thousand-dollar sport coat.

"He used the same one on all three women," Eve answered, speaking more to herself than Beaver. "The lab confirms it. Why would he ditch it now?"

"Maybe he was done." The sensor switched from its muted hum to a quick beep. "Just a little salad oil," Beaver announced. "Extra virgin olive. Spotted his pretty tie. Maybe he was done," Beaver said again.

He admired detectives, had once had ambitions to become one. The closest he'd managed to get was as a field tech. But he read every detective story available on disc.

"See, three's like a magic number. An important number." His eyes sharpened behind his tinted glasses as the treated lenses picked up a minute spot of talc on a cuff. He moved on, warming to the theme. "So this guy, see, he fixes on three women, women he knows, sees all the time on the screen. Maybe he's hot for them."

"The first victim was his mother."

"Hey." Beaver paused long enough to swivel a look toward Eve. "You never heard of Oedipus? That Greek guy, you know, had the hots for his mama. Anyhow, he does the three, then ditches the weapon and the clothes he was wearing when he did them. This guy's got enough clothes for six people, anyway."

Frowning, Eve walked over to the spacious closet, scanned the automatic racks, the motorized shelves. "He doesn't even live here."

"Dude's rich, right?" To Beaver that explained everything. "He's got a couple suits in here ain't never been worn. Shoes, too." He reached down, picked up one of a pair of leather half boots, turned them over.

"Nothing, see?" He skimmed the sensor over the unscuffed bottom. "No dirt, no dust, no sidewalk scrapes, no fibers."

"That only makes him guilty of self-indulgence. Goddamn it, Beaver, get me some blood."

"I'm working on it. Probably tossed what he was wearing, though."

"You're a real optimist, Beaver."

In disgust, she turned toward a U-shaped lacquered desk and began to rifle through the drawers. The discs she would bag and run through her own computer. They could get lucky and find some correspondence between David Angelini and his mother or Metcalf. Or luckier yet, she mused, and find some rambling confessional diary that described the murders.

Where the hell had he put the umbrella? she wondered. The shoe? She wondered if the sweepers in N.L.A. or the ones in Europe were having any better luck. The thought of backtracking and searching all the cozy little homes and luxury hideaways of David Angelini was giving her a bad case of indigestion.

Then she found the knife.

It was so simple. Open the middle drawer of the work console, and there it was. Long, slim, and lethal. It had a fancy handle, carved out of what might have been genuine ivory, which would have made it an antique—or an international crime. Harvesting ivory, or purchasing it in any form had been outlawed planetwide for more than half a century after the near extinction of African elephants.

Eve wasn't an antique buff, nor was she an expert on environmental crime, but she'd studied forensics enough to know that the shape and length of the blade were right.

"Well, well." Her indigestion was gone, like a bad guest. In its place was the clear, clean high of success. "Maybe three wasn't his magic number after all."

"He kept it? Son of a bitch." Disappointed in the foolishness of a murderer, Beaver shook his head. "Guy's an idiot."

"Scan it," she ordered, crossing to him.

Beaver shifted the bulk of the scanner, changed the program from clothing. After a quick adjustment of his lenses, he ran the funnel of the arm up the knife. The scanner beeped helpfully.

"Got some shit on it," Beaver muttered, his thick fingertips playing over controls like a concert pianist's over keys. "Fiber—maybe paper. Some kind of adhesive. Prints on the handle. Want a hard copy of 'em?"

"Yeah."

"Kay." The scanner spit out a square of paper dotted with fingerprints. "Turn her over. And bingo. There's your blood. Not much of it." He frowned, skimming the funnel along the edge of the blade. "Going to be lucky if it's enough for typing, much less DNA."

"You keep that positive outlook, Beaver. How old's the blood?"

"Come on, Lieutenant." Behind the sensor lenses, his eyes were huge and cynical. "You know I can't give you that from one of the portables. Gotta take it in. All this little girl does is identify. No skin," he announced. "Be better if you had some skin."

"I'll take the blood." As she sealed the knife into evidence, a movement caught her eyes. She looked up and into the dark, damning eyes of Marco Angelini.

He glanced down at the knife, then back into her face. Something moved across his, something wrenching that had the muscle jerking in his jaw.

"I'd like a moment of your time, Lieutenant Dallas."

"I can't give you much more than that."

"It won't take long." His eyes flicked to Beaver, then back to the knife as Dallas slipped it into her bag. "In private, please."

"All right." She nodded to the uniform who stood at Angelini's shoulder. "Tell one of the team to come up and finish the hands-on search in here," she ordered Beaver, then followed Angelini out of the room.

He turned toward a set of narrow, carpeted steps, his hand trailing along a glossy banister as he climbed. At the top, he shifted right and stepped into a room.

An office, Eve discovered. Sunwashed now in the brilliant afternoon. Light beamed and glinted off the surfaces of communication equipment, struck and bounced from the smooth semi-circular console of sober black, flashed and pooled on the surface of the gleaming floor.

As if annoyed with the strength of the sunlight, Angelini hit a switch that had the windows tinted to a soft amber. Now the room had shadows around pale gold edges.

Angelini walked directly to a wall unit and ordered a bourbon on the rocks. He held the square glass in his hand, took one careful sip.

"You believe my son murdered his mother and two other women."

"Your son has been questioned on those charges, Mr. Angelini. He is a suspect. If you have any questions about the procedure, you should speak with his counsel."

"I've spoken with them." He took another sip. "They believe there's a good chance you will charge him, but that he won't be indicted."

"That's up to the grand jury."

"But you think he will."

"Mr. Angelini, if and when I have arrested your son and charged him with three counts of first-degree murder, it will be because I believe he will be indicted, tried, and convicted on those charges, and that I have the evidence to ensure that conviction."

He looked at her field bag where she'd put some of that evidence. "I've done some research on you, Lieutenant Dallas."

"Have you?"

"I like to know the odds," he said with a humorless smile that came and went in a blink. "Commander Whitney respects you. And I respect him. My former wife admired your tenacity and your thoroughness, and she was not a fool. She spoke of you, did you know that?"

"No, I didn't."

"She was impressed by your mind. A clean cop's mind she called it. You're good at your job, aren't you, Lieutenant?"

"Yeah, I'm good at it."

"But you make mistakes."

"I try to keep them to a minimum."

"A mistake in your profession, however minimal, can cause incredible pain to the innocent." His eyes stayed on hers, relentlessly. "You found a knife in my son's room."

"I can't discuss that with you."

"He rarely uses this house," Angelini said carefully. "Three or four times a year perhaps. He prefers the Long Island estate when he's in the area."

"That may be, Mr. Angelini, but he used this house on the night Louise Kirski was killed." Impatient now, eager to get the evidence to the lab, Eve moved a shoulder. "Mr. Angelini, I can't debate the state's case with you—"

"But you're very confident that the state has a good case," he interrupted. When she didn't answer, he took another long study of her face. Then he finished the drink in one swallow, set the glass aside. "But you're wrong, Lieutenant. You've got the wrong man."

"You believe in your son's innocence, Mr. Angelini. I understand that."

"Not believe, Lieutenant, know. My son didn't kill those women." He took a breath, like a diver about to plunge under the surface. "I did."

FIFTEEN

Eve had no choice. She took him in and grilled him. After a full hour, she had a vicious headache and the calm, unshakable statement from Marco Angelini that he had killed three women.

He refused counsel, and refused to or was unable to elaborate.

Each time Eve asked him why he had killed, he stared straight into her eyes and claimed it had been impulse. He'd been annoyed with his wife, he stated. Personally embarrassed by her continued intimacy with a business partner. He'd killed her because he couldn't have her back. Then he'd gotten a taste for it.

It was all very simple, and to Eve's mind, very rehearsed. She could picture him repeating and refining the lines in his head before he spoke them.

"This is bullshit," she said abruptly and pushed back from the conference table. "You didn't kill anybody."

"I say I did." His voice was eerily calm. "You have my confession on record."

"Then tell me again." Leaning forward, she slapped her hands on the table. "Why did you ask your wife to meet you at the Five Moons?"

"I wanted it to happen somewhere out of our milieu. I thought I could get away with it, you see. I told her there was trouble with Randy. She didn't know the full problem of his gambling. I did. So, of course, she came."

"And you slit her throat."

"Yes." His skin whitened slightly. "It was very quick."

"What did you do then?"

"I went home."

"How?"

He blinked. "I drove. I'd parked my car a couple of blocks away."

"What about the blood?" She peered into his eyes, watching his pupils. "There'd have been a lot of it. She'd have gushed all over you."

The pupils dilated, but his voice remained steady. "I was wearing a top coat, rain resistant. I discarded it along the way." He smiled a little. "I imagine some itinerant found it and made use of it."

"What did you take from the scene?"

"The knife, of course."

"Nothing of hers?" She waited a beat. "Nothing to make it look like a robbery, a mugging?"

He hesitated. She could almost see his mind working behind his eyes. "I was shaken. I hadn't expected it to be so unpleasant. I had planned to take her bag, the jewelry, but I forgot, and just ran."

"You ran, taking nothing, but were smart enough to ditch your blood-splattered coat."

"That's right."

"Then you went after Metcalf."

"She was an impulse. I kept dreaming about what it had been like, and I wanted to do it again. She was easy." His breathing leveled and his hands lay still on the table. "She was ambitious and rather naive. I knew David had written a screenplay with her in mind. He was determined to complete this entertainment project—it was something we disagreed over. It annoyed me, and it would have cost the company resources that are, at the moment, a bit strained. I decided to kill her, and I contacted her. Of course she agreed to meet me."

"What was she wearing?"

"Wearing?" He fumbled for a moment. "I didn't pay attention. It wasn't important. She smiled, held out both of her hands as I walked toward her. And I did it."

"Why are you coming forward now?"

"As I said, I thought I could get away with it. Perhaps I could have. I never expected my son to be arrested in my place."

"So, you're protecting him?"

"I killed them, Lieutenant. What more do you want?"

"Why did you leave the knife in his drawer, in his room?"

His eyes slid away, slid back. "As I said, he rarely stays there. I thought it was safe. Then I was contacted about the search warrant. I didn't have time to remove it."

"You expect me to buy this? You think you're helping him by clouding the case, by coming forward with this lame confession. You think he's guilty." She lowered her voice, bit off each word. "You're so terrified that your son is a murderer that you're willing to take the rap rather than see him face the consequences. Are you going to let another woman die, Angelini? Or two, or three before you swallow reality?"

His lips trembled once, then firmed. "I've given you my statement."

"You've given me bullshit." Turning on her heel, Eve left the room. Struggling to calm herself, she stood outside, watched with a jaundiced eye as Angelini pressed his face into his hands.

She could break him, eventually. But there was always a chance that word would leak and the media would scream that there was a confession from someone other than the prime.

She looked over at the sound of footsteps, and her body stiffened like steel. "Commander."

"Lieutenant. Progress?"

"He's sticking to his story. It's got holes you could drive a shuttle through. I've given him the opening to bring up the souvenirs from the first two hits. He didn't bite."

"I'd like to talk to him. Privately, Lieutenant, and off the record." Before she could speak, he held up a hand. "I realize it's not procedure. I'm asking you for a favor."

"And if he incriminates himself or his son?"

Whitney's jaw tightened. "I'm still a cop, Dallas. Goddamn it."

"Yes, sir." She unlocked the door, then after only a faint hesitation, darkened the two-way glass and shut off audio. "I'll be in my office."

"Thank you." He stepped inside. He gave her one last look before shutting the door and turning to the man slumped at the table. "Marco," Whitney said on a long sigh. "What the fuck do you think you're doing?"

"Jack." Marco offered a thin smile. "I wondered if you'd be along. We never did make that golf date."

"Talk to me." Whitney sat down heavily.

"Hasn't your efficient and dogged lieutenant filled you in?"

"The recorder's off," Whitney said sharply. "We're alone. Talk to me, Marco. We both know you didn't kill Cicely or anyone else."

For a moment, Marco stared up at the ceiling, as if pondering. "People never know each other as well as they believe. Not even the people they care for. I loved her, Jack. I never stopped loving her. But she stopped loving me. Part of me was always waiting for her to start loving me again. But she never would have."

"Damn it, Marco, do you expect me to believe that you slit her throat because she divorced you twelve years ago?"

"Maybe I thought she might have married Hammett. He wanted that," Marco said quietly. "I could see that he wanted that. Cicely was reluctant." His voice remained calm, quiet, faintly nostalgic. "She enjoyed her independence, but she was sorry to disappoint Hammett. Sorry enough that she might have given in eventually. Married him. It would have really been over then, wouldn't it?"

"You killed Cicely because she might have married another man?"

"She was my wife, Jack. Whatever the courts and the Church said."

Whitney sat a moment, silent. "I've played poker with you too many times over the years, Marco. You've got tells." Folding his arms on the table, he leaned forward. "When you bluff, you tap your finger on your knee."

The finger stopped tapping. "This is a long way from poker, Jack."

"You can't help David this way. You've got to let the system work."

"David and I . . . there's been a lot of friction between us in the last several months. Business disagreements and personal ones." For the first time he sighed, deep and long and wearily. "There shouldn't be distance between father and son over such foolishness."

"This is hardly the way to mend fences, Marco."

The steel came back into Angelini's eyes. There would be no more sighs. "Let me ask you something, Jack, just between us. If it was one of yours, and there was the slightest chance—just the slightest—that they'd be convicted of murder, would anything stop you from protecting them?"

"You can't protect David by stepping in with some bullshit confession."

"Who said it was bullshit?" The word sounded like cream in Angelini's cultured voice. "I did it, and I'm confessing because I can't live with myself if my own child pays for my crime. Now tell me, Jack, would you stand behind your son, or in front of him?"

"Ah, hell, Marco," was all Whitney could say.

He stayed for twenty minutes, but got nothing more. For a time he guided the conversation into casual lines, golf scores, the standings of the baseball team Marco had a piece of. Then, quick and sleek as a snake, he'd toss out a hard, leading question on the murders.

But Marco Angelini was an expert negotiator, and had already given his bottom line. He wouldn't budge.

Guilt, grief, and the beginnings of real fear made an unsettling stew in Whitney's stomach as he stepped into Eve's office. She was hunched over her computer, scanning data, calling up more.

For the first time in days, his eyes cleared of their own fatigue and saw hers. She was pale, her eyes shadowed, her mouth grim. Her hair stood up in spikes as if she'd dragged her hands through it countless times. Even as he watched, she did so again, then pressed her fingers to her eyes as if they burned.

He remembered the morning in his office, the morning after Cicely had been murdered. And the responsibility he'd hung around Eve's neck.

"Lieutenant."

Her shoulders straightened as if she'd slammed steel poles into them. Her head came up, her eyes carefully blank.

"Commander." She got to her feet. Got to attention, Whitney thought, annoyed by the stiff and impersonal formality.

"Marco's in holding. We can keep him for forty-eight hours without charging him. I thought it best to let him think behind bars for a while. He still refuses counsel."

Whitney stepped in while she stood there, and he looked around. He wasn't often in this sector of the complex. His officers came to him. Another weight of command.

She could have had a bigger office. She'd earned one. But she seemed to prefer to work in a room so small that if three people crowded into it, they'd be in sin.

"Good thing you're not claustrophobic," he commented. She gave no response, didn't so much as twitch an eyebrow. Whitney muttered an oath. "Listen, Dallas—"

"Sir." Her interruption was fast and brittle. "Forensics has the weapon retrieved from David Angelini's room. I'm informed that there will be some delay on the results as the blood traces detected by the sweeper are of an amount borderline for typing and DNA."

"So noted, Lieutenant."

"The fingerprints on the weapon in evidence have been matched to those of David Angelini. My report—"

"We'll get to your report momentarily."

Her chin jutted up. "Yes, sir."

"Goddamn it, Dallas, yank that stick out of your butt and sit down."

"Is that an order, Commander?"

"Ah, hell," he began.

Mirina Angelini burst through the doorway in a clatter of high heels and a crackle of silk. "Why are you trying to destroy my family?" she demanded, shaking off the restraining hand of Slade who had come in behind her.

"Mirina, this isn't going to help."

She jerked away and crowded into Eve. "Isn't it enough that my mother was murdered on the street? Murdered because American cops are too busy chasing shadows and filling out useless reports to protect the innocent?"

"Mirina," Whitney said, "come on to my office. We'll talk."

"Talk?" She turned on him like a cat, gold and sleek, teeth bared for blood. "How can I talk to you? I trusted you. I thought you cared about me, about David, about all of us. You've let her lock David in a cell. And now my father."

"Mirina, Marco came in voluntarily. We'll talk about this. I'll explain it all to you."

"There's nothing to explain." She turned her back on him and aimed her scorching fury at Eve. "I went to my father's house. He wanted me to stay in Rome, but I couldn't. Not when every report in the media is smearing my brother's name. When we arrived, a neighbor was more than happy, even gleeful, to tell me that my father had been taken away by the police."

"I can arrange for you to speak with your father, Ms. Angelini," Eve said coolly. "And your brother."

"You're damn right you'll arrange it. And now. Where is my father?" She used both hands to shove Eve back a pace before Whitney or Slade could stop her. "What have you done with him, you bitch!"

"You want to keep your hands off me," Eve warned. "I've just about had my fill of Angelinis. Your father's in holding, here. Your brother's in the tower at Riker's. You can see your father now. If you want to see your brother, you'll be shuttled over." Her gaze flicked to Whitney, and stung. "Or since you've got some pull around here, you can probably have him transported to Visitation for an hour."

"I know what you're doing." This was no fragile flower now. Mirina fairly vibrated with power. "You need a scapegoat. You need an arrest so that the media will get out of your face. You're playing politics, using my brother, even my murdered mother, so that you won't lose your job."

"Yeah, some cushy job." She smiled sourly. "I toss innocent people in a cage every day so I can keep all the benefits."

"It keeps your face on the screen, doesn't it?" Mirina tossed her glorious hair. "How much publicity have you traded over my mother's dead body?"

"That's enough, Mirina." Whitney's voice lashed like a whip, in one vicious snap. "Go to my office and wait." He looked over her shoulder at Slade. "Take her out of here."

"Mirina, this is useless," Slade murmured, trying to tuck her under his arm. "Let's go now."

"Don't hold me." She bit off each word as if they were stringy meat, then shrugged away from him. "I'll go. But you're going to pay for the grief you've brought my family, Lieutenant. You're going to pay for every bit of it."

She stalked out, giving Slade time for only a muttered apology before he followed after her.

Whitney stepped quietly into the silence. "You okay?"

"I've dealt with worse." Eve jerked a shoulder. Inside she was sick with anger and guilt. Sick enough that she wanted badly to be alone behind closed doors. "If you'll excuse me, Commander, I want to finish going over this report."

"Dallas—Eve." It was the weariness in his tone that had her gaze lifting warily to his. "Mirina's upset, understandably so. But she was out of line, way out of line."

"She was entitled to a couple of shots at me." Because she wanted to press her hands to her throbbing head, she tucked them negligently into her pockets. "I've just put what's left of her family in a cage. Who else is she going to be pissed at? I can take it." Her gaze remained cool, steely. "Feelings aren't my strong suit."

He nodded slowly. "I had that coming. I put you on this case, Dallas, because you're the best I've got. Your mind's good, your gut's good. And you care. You care about the victim." Letting out a long breath, he dragged a hand over his hair. "I was off base this morning, Dallas, in my office. I've been off base a number of times with you since this whole mess began. I apologize for it."

"It doesn't matter."

"I wish it didn't." He searched her face, saw the stiff restraint. "But I see it does. I'll take care of Mirina, arrange the visitations."

"Yes, sir. I'd like to continue my interview with Marco Angelini."

"Tomorrow," Whitney said and set his teeth when she didn't quite mask the sneer. "You're tired, Lieutenant, and tired cops make mistakes and miss details. You'll pick it up tomorrow." He headed for the door, swore again, and stopped without looking back at her. "Get some sleep, and for Christ's sake, take a painkiller for that headache. You look like hell."

She resisted slamming the door after him. Resisted because it would be petty and unprofessional. But she sat down, stared at the screen, and pretended her head wasn't shuddering with pain.

When a shadow fell over her desk moments later, she looked up, eyes fired for battle.

"Well," Roarke said mildly and leaned over to kiss her snarling mouth. "That's quite a welcome." He patted his chest. "Am I bleeding?"

"Ha-ha."

"There's that sparkling wit I missed." He sat on the edge of the desk where he could look at her and catch a glimpse of the data on the screen to see if that was what had put the miserable anger in her eyes. "Well, Lieutenant, and how was your day?"

"Let's see. I booked my superior's favorite godson on obstruction and other assorted charges, found what may be the murder weapon in his console drawer in the family townhouse, took a confession from the prime suspect's father, who claims he did it, and just took a couple of shots between the eyes from the sister, who thinks I'm a media grabbing bitch." She tried on a small smile. "Other than that, it's been pretty quiet. How about you?"

"Fortunes won, fortunes lost," he said mildly, worried about her. "Nothing nearly as exciting as police work."

"I wasn't sure you were coming back tonight."

"Neither was I. The construction on the resort's moving ahead well enough. I should be able to handle things from here for a time."

She tried not to be so relieved. It irritated her that in a few short months she'd gotten so used to his being there. Even dependent upon it. "That's good, I guess."

"Mmm." He read her well. "What can you tell me about the case?"

"It's all over the media. Pick a channel."

"I'd rather hear it from you."

She brought him up to date in much the way she would file a report: in quick, efficient terms, heavy on facts, light on personal comments. And, she discovered, she felt better for it afterward. Roarke had a way of listening that made her hear herself more clearly.

"You believe it's the younger Angelini."

"We've got means and opportunity, and a good handle on motive. If the knife matches . . . Anyway, I'll be meeting with Dr. Mira tomorrow to discuss his psych testing."

"And Marco," Roarke continued. "What do you think of his confession?"

"It's a handy way to confuse things, tie up the investigation. He's a clever man, and he'll find a way to leak it to the media." She scowled over Roarke's shoulder. "It'll jerk everything around for a while, cost us some time and trouble. But we'll smooth it out."

"You think he confessed to the murders to complicate the investigation?"

"That's right." She shifted her gaze to his, lifted a brow. "You've got another theory."

"The drowning child," Roarke murmured. "The father believes his son is about to go under for the third time, jumps into the torrent. His life for his child's. Love, Eve." He cupped her chin in his hand. "Love stops at nothing. Marco believes his son is guilty, and would rather sacrifice himself than see his child pay the price."

"If he knows, or even believes, that David killed those women, it would be insane to protect him."

"No, it would be love. There's probably none stronger than a parent's for a child. You and I don't have any experience with that, but it exists."

She shook her head. "Even when the child's defective?"

"Perhaps especially then. When I was a boy in Dublin, there was a woman whose daughter had lost an arm in an accident. There was no money for a replacement. She had five children, and loved them all. But four were whole, and one was damaged. She built a shield around that girl, to protect her from the stares and the whispers and the pity.

It was the damaged child she pushed to excel, who they all devoted themselves to. The others didn't need her as much, you see, as the one who was flawed."

"There's a difference between a physical defect and a mental one," Eve insisted.

"I wonder if there is, to a parent."

"Whatever Marco Angelini's motive, we'll cut through to the truth in the end."

"No doubt you will. When's your shift over?"

"What?"

"Your shift," he repeated. "When is it over?"

She glanced at the screen, noted the time in the bottom corner. "About an hour ago."

"Good." He rose and held out a hand. "Come with me."

"Roarke, there are some things I should tie up here. I want to review the interview with Marco Angelini. I may find a hole."

He was patient because he had no doubt he'd have his own way. "Eve, you're so tired you wouldn't see a hundred-meter hole until you'd fallen into it." Determined, he took her hand and pulled her to her feet. "Come with me."

"All right, maybe I could use a break." Grumbling a bit, she ordered her computer off and locked. "I'm going to have to goose the techs at the lab. They're taking forever on the knife." Her hand felt good in his. She didn't even worry about the ribbing she'd take from the other cops who might see them in the hall or elevator. "Where are we going?"

He brought their linked hands to his lips and smiled at her over them. "I haven't decided."

He opted for Mexico, it was a quick, easy flight, and his villa there on the turbulent west coast was always prepared. Unlike his home in New York, he kept it fully automated, calling in domestics only for lengthy stays.

In Roarke's mind, droids and computers were convenient but impersonal. For the purposes of this visit, however, he was content to rely on them. He wanted Eve alone, he wanted her relaxed, and he wanted her happy.

"Jesus, Roarke."

She took one look at the towering, multilayered building on the brink of a cliff and goggled. It looked like a extension of the rock, as if the sheer glass walls had been polished from it. Gardens tumbled over terraces in vivid colors, shapes, and fragrances.

Above, the deepening sky was devoid of any traffic. Just blue, the swirl of white clouds, the flashing wings of birds. It looked like another world.

She'd slept like a stone on the plane, barely surfacing when the pilot had executed a snazzy drop landing that had placed them neatly at the foot of zigzagging stone steps that climbed the towering cliff. She was groggy enough to reach up to be certain he hadn't slipped VR goggles on her while she'd slept.

"Where are we?"

"Mexico," he said simply.

"Mexico?" Stunned, she tried to rub the sleep and the shock from her eyes. Roarke thought, with affection, that she looked like a cranky child awakened from a nap. "But I can't be in Mexico. I have to—"

"Ride or walk?" he asked, pulling her along like a stubborn puppy.

"I have to—"

"Ride," he decided. "You're still groggy."

She could enjoy the climb later, he thought, and its many views of sea and cliffs. Instead, he nudged her into a sleek little air cart, taking the controls himself and shooting them up to vertical with a speed that knocked the rest of sleep out of her system.

"Christ, not so fast." Her instinct for survival had her clutching the side, wincing as rocks, flowers, and water whizzed by. He was roaring with laughter when he slipped the little cart into place at the front patio.

"Awake now, darling?"

She had her breath back, barely. "I'm going to kill you as soon as I make sure all my internal organs are in place. What the hell are we doing in Mexico?"

"Taking a break. I need one." He stepped out of the cart and came around to her side. "There's no doubt you do." Since she was still holding on to the side, knuckles white, he reached in, plucked her up, and carried her over the irregularly shaped stones toward the door.

"Cut it out. I can walk."

"Stop complaining." He turned his head, expertly finding her mouth, deepening the kiss until her hand stopped pushing at his shoulder and began to knead it.

"Damn it," she murmured. "How come you can always do that to me?"

"Just lucky, I guess. Roarke, disengage," he said, and the decorative bars across the entrance slid apart. Behind them, doors ornate with carving and etched glass clicked open and swung back in welcome. He stepped inside. "Secure," he ordered, and the doors efficiently closed while Eve stared.

One wall of the entrance level was glass, and through it she could see the ocean. She'd never seen the Pacific, and she wondered now how it had earned its serene name when it looked so alive, so ready to boil.

They were in time for sunset, and as she watched, speechless, the sky exploded and shimmered with bolts and streams of wild color. And the fat red globe of the sun sank slowly, inevitably, toward the blue line of water.

"You'll like it here," he murmured.

She was staggered by the beauty of an ending day. It seemed that nature had waited for her, held the show. "It's wonderful. I can't stay."

"A few hours." He pressed a kiss to her temple. "Just overnight for now. We'll come back and spend a few days when we have more time."

Still carrying her, he walked closer to the glass wall until it seemed to Eve that the entire world was made of frantic color and shifting shapes.

"I love you, Eve."

She looked away from the sun, the ocean, and into his eyes. And it was wonderful, and for the moment, it was simple. "I missed you."

She pressed her cheek to his and held him tightly. "I really missed you. I wore one of your shirts." She could laugh at herself now because he was here. She could smell him, touch him. "I actually went into your closet and stole one of your shirts—one of the black silk ones you have dozens of. I put it on, then snuck out of the house like a thief so Summerset wouldn't catch me."

Absurdly touched, he nuzzled her neck. "At night, I'd play your transmissions over, just so I could look at you, hear your voice."

"Really?" She giggled, a rare sound from her. "God, Roarke, we've gotten so sappy."

"We'll keep it our little secret."

"Deal." She leaned back to look at his face. "I have to ask you something. It's so lame, but I have to."

"What?"

"Was it ever . . . " She winced, wished she could muffle the need to ask. "Before, with anyone else—"

"No." He touched his lips to her brow, her nose, the dip in her chin. "It was never, with no one else."

"Not for me, either." She simply breathed him in. "Put your hands on me. I want your hands on me."

"I can do that."

He did, tumbling with her to a spread of floor cushions while the sun died brilliantly in the ocean.

CHAPTER
SIXTEEN

Taking a break with Roarke wasn't quite like stopping off at the deli for a quick veggie hash salad and soy coffee. She wasn't sure how he managed it all, but then, great quantities of money talk, and talk big.

They dined on succulent grilled lobster, drenched in real, creamy, rich butter. They sipped champagne so cold it frosted Eve's throat. A symphony of fruit was there for the sampling, exotic hybrids that sprinkled harmonized flavors on the tongue.

Long before she could admit that she loved him, Eve had accepted the fact that she was addicted to the food he could summon up with the flick of a wrist.

She soaked naked in a small whirling lagoon cupped under palm trees and moonlight, her muscles slack from the heated water and thorough sex. She listened to the song of night birds—no simulation, but the real thing—that hung on the fragrant air like tears.

For now, for one night, the pressures of the job were light-years away.

He could do that to her, and for her, she realized. He could open little pockets of peace.

Roarke watched her, pleased at the way the tension had melted from her face with a bit of pampering. He loved seeing her this way, unwound, limp with pleasuring her senses, too lax to remember to be guilty for indulging herself. Just as he loved seeing her revved, her mind racing, her body braced for action.

No, it had never been like this for him before, with anyone. Of all the women he'd known, she was the only one he was compelled to be with, driven to touch. Beyond the physical, the basic and apparently unsatiable lust she inspired in him, was a constant fascination. Her mind, her heart, her secrets, her scars.

He had told her once they were two lost souls. He thought now he'd spoken no more than the truth. But with each other, they'd found something that rooted them.

For a man who had been wary of cops all of his life, it was staggering to know his happiness now depended on one.

Amused at himself, he slipped into the water with her. Eve managed to drum up enough energy to open her eyes to slits.

"I don't think I can move."

"Then don't." He handed her another flute of champagne, wrapping her fingers around the stem.

"I'm too relaxed to be drunk." But she managed to find her mouth with the glass. "It's such a weird life. Yours," she elaborated. "I mean you can have anything you want, go anywhere, do anything. You want to take a night off, you zip over to Mexico and nibble on lobster and—what was that stuff again, the stuff you spread on crackers?"

"Goose liver."

She winced and shuddered. "That's not what you called it when you shoved it in my mouth. It sounded nicer."

"Foie gras. Same thing."

"That's better." She shifted her legs, tangled them with his. "Anyway, most people program a video or take a quick trip with their VR goggles, maybe plug a few credits into a simulation booth down at Times Square. But you do the real thing."

"I prefer the real thing."

"I know. That's another odd piece of you. You like old stuff. You'd rather read a book than scan a disc, rather go to the trouble to come out here when you could have programmed a simulation in your holo-room." Her lips curved a little, dreamily. "I like that about you."

"That's handy."

"When you were a kid, and things were bad for you, is this what you dreamed about?"

"I dreamed about surviving, getting out. Having control. Didn't you?"

"I guess I did." Too many of her dreams were jumbled and dark. "After I was in the system, anyway. Then what I wanted most was to be a cop. A good cop. A smart cop. What did you want?"

"To be rich. Not to be hungry."

"We both got what we wanted, more or less."

"You had nightmares while I was gone."

She didn't have to open her eyes to see the concern in his. She could hear it in his voice. "They aren't too bad. They're just more regular."

"Eve, if you'd work with Dr. Mira—"

"I'm not ready to remember it. Not all of it. Do you ever feel the scars, from what your father did to you?"

Restless with the memories, he shifted and sank deeper in the hot, frothy water. "A few beatings, careless cruelty. Why should it matter now?"

"You shrug it off." Now she opened her eyes, looked at him, saw he was brooding. "But it made you, didn't it? What happened then made you."

"I suppose it did, roughly."

She nodded, tried to speak casually. "Roarke, do you think if some people lack something, and that lack lets them brutalize their kids— the way we were—do you think it passes on? Do you think—"

"No."

"But—"

"No." He cupped a hand over her calf and squeezed. "We make ourselves, in the long run. You and I did. If that wasn't true, I'd be drunk in some Dublin slum, looking for something weaker to pummel. And you, Eve, would be cold and brittle and without pity."

She closed her eyes again. "Sometimes I am."

"No, that you never are. You're strong, and you're moral, and sometimes you make yourself ill with compassion for the innocent."

Her eyes stung behind her closed lids. "Someone I admire and respect asked me for help, asked me for a favor. I turned him down flat. What does that make me?"

"A woman who had a choice to make."

"Roarke, the last woman who was killed. Louise Kirski. That's on my head. She was twenty-four, talented, eager, in love with a second-rate musician. She had a cluttered one-room apartment on West Twenty-sixth and liked Chinese food. She had a family in Texas that will never be the same. She was innocent, Roarke, and she's haunting me."

Relieved, Eve let out a long breath. "I haven't been able to tell anyone that. I wasn't sure I could say it out loud."

"I'm glad you could say it to me. Now, listen." He set his glass down, scooted forward to take her face in his hands. Her skin was soft, her eyes a narrow slant of dark amber. "Fate rules, Eve. You follow the steps, and you plan and you work, then fate slips in laughing and makes fools of us. Sometimes we can trick it or outguess it, but most often it's already written. For some, it's written in blood. That doesn't mean we stop, but it does mean we can't always comfort ourselves with blame."

"Is that what you think I'm doing? Comforting myself?"

"It's easier to take the blame than it is to admit there was nothing you could do to stop what happened. You're an arrogant woman, Eve. Just one more aspect of you that I find attractive. It's arrogant to assume responsibility for events beyond our control."

"I should have controlled it."

"Ah, yes." He smiled. "Of course."

"It's not arrogance," she insisted, miffed. "It's my job."

"You taunted him, assuming he'd come after you." Because the thought of that still twisted in his gut like hissing snakes, Roarke tightened his grip on her face. "Now you're insulted, annoyed that he didn't follow your rules."

"That's a hideous thing to say. Goddamn you, I don't—" She broke off, sucked in her breath. "You're pissing me off so I'll stop feeling sorry for myself."

"It seems to have worked."

"All right." She let her eyes close again. "All right. I'm not going to think about it anymore right now. Maybe by tomorrow I'll have a better shot at sorting it out. You're pretty good, Roarke," she said with a ghost of a smile.

"Thousands concur," he murmured and caught her nipple lightly between his thumb and forefinger.

The ripple effect made it all the way down to her toes. "That's not what I meant."

"It's what I meant." He tugged gently, listened to her breath catch.

"Maybe if I can manage to crawl out of here, I can take you up on your interesting offer."

"Just relax." Watching her face, he slid his hand between her legs, cupped her. "Let me." He managed to catch her glass as it slipped from her hand, and he set it aside. "Let me have you, Eve."

Before she could answer, he shot her to a fast, wracking orgasm. Her hips arched up, pumped against his busy hand, then went lax.

She wouldn't think now, he knew. She would be wrapped in layered sensations. She never seemed to expect it. And her surprise, her sweet and naive response was, as always, murderously arousing. He could have pleasured her endlessly, for the simple delight of watching her absorb every touch, every jolt.

So he indulged himself, exploring that long, lean body, suckling the small, hot breasts, wet with perfumed water, gulping in the rapid breath that gasped from her lips.

She felt drugged, helpless, her mind and body burdened with pleasure. Part of her was shocked, or tried to be. Not so much at what she let him do, but at the fact that she allowed him complete and total control of her. She couldn't have stopped him, wouldn't have, even when he held her near to screaming on the edge before shoving her over into another shuddering climax.

"Again." Greedy, he dragged her head back by the hair and stabbed his fingers inside her, worked her ruthlessly until her hands splashed bonelessly in the water. "I'm all there is tonight. We're all there is." He savaged her throat on the way to her mouth, and his eyes were like fierce blue suns. "Tell me you love me. Say it."

"I do. I do love you." A moan ripped from her throat when he plunged himself into her, jerked her hips high, and plunged deeper.

"Tell me again." He felt her muscles squeeze him like a fist and gritted his teeth to keep from exploding. "Tell me again."

"I love you." Trembling from it, she wrapped her legs around him and let him batter her past delirium.

She did have to crawl out of the pool. Her head was spinning, her body limp. "I don't have any bones left."

Roarke chuckled and gave her a friendly slap on the butt. "I'm not carrying you this time, darling. We'd both end up on our faces."

"Maybe I'll just lie down right here." It was a struggle to remain on her hands and knees on the smooth tiles.

"You'll get cold." With an effort, he summoned the strength to drag her to her feet where they rocked together like drunks.

She began to snicker, teetering. "What the hell did you do to me? I feel like I've downed a couple of Freebirds."

He managed to grip her waist. "Since when did you play with illegals?"

"Standard police training." She bit experimentally at her bottom lip and found that it was, indeed, numb. "We have to take a course in illegals at the academy. I palmed most of mine and flushed them. Is your head spinning?"

"I'll let you know when I regain feeling above the waist." He tipped her head back and kissed her lightly. "Why don't we see if we can make it inside. We can . . ." He trailed off, eyes narrowing over her shoulder.

She might have been impaired, but she was still a cop. Instinctively, she whirled and braced, unconsciously shielding his body with hers. "What? What is it?"

"Nothing." He cleared his throat, patted her shoulder. "Nothing," he repeated. "Go on in, I'll be right along."

"What?" She stood her ground, scanning for trouble.

"It's nothing, really. I just . . . I neglected to disengage the security camera. It's, ah, activated by motion or voice." Naked, he strode over toward a low stone wall, flicked a switch and palmed a disc.

"Camera." Eve held up a finger. "There was a recording on the entire time we've been out here?" She flicked a narrow-eyed stare at the lagoon. "The entire time."

"Which is why I generally prefer people to automations."

"We're on there? All on there?"

"I'll take care of it."

She started to speak again, then got a good look at his face. The devil took over. "I'll be damned, Roarke. You're embarrassed."

"Certainly not." If he'd been wearing anything but skin, he would have pushed his hands into his pockets. "It was simply an oversight. I said I'd take care of it."

"Let's play it back."

He stopped short, and gave Eve the rare pleasure of seeing him goggle. "I beg your pardon?"

"You are embarrassed." She leaned over to kiss him, and while he was distracted, snatched the disc. "That's cute. Really cute."

"Shut up. Give me that."

"I don't think so." Delighted, she danced back a step and held the disc out of reach. "I bet this is very hot. Aren't you curious?"

"No." He made a grab, but she was very quick. "Eve, give me the damn thing."

"This is fascinating." She edged back toward the open patio doors. "The sophisticated, seen-it-all Roarke is blushing."

"I am not." He hoped to Christ he wasn't. That would top it. "I simply see no reason to document lovemaking. It's private."

"I'm not going to pass it on to Nadine Furst for broadcast. I'm just going to review it. Right now." She dashed inside while he swore and ran after her.

She walked into her office at nine A.M. sharp with a spring to her step. Her eyes were clear and unshadowed, her system toned and her shoulders free of tension. She was all but humming.

"Somebody got lucky," Feeney said mournfully and kept his feet planted on her desk. "Roarke's back on planet, I take it."

"I got a good night's sleep," she retorted and shoved his feet aside.

He grunted. "Be grateful, 'cause you're not going to find much peace today. Lab report's in. The fucking knife doesn't match."

Her sunny mood vanished. "What do you mean, the knife doesn't match?"

"The blade's too thick. A centimeter. Might as well be a meter, goddamn it."

"That could be the angle of the wounds, the thrust of the blow." Mexico vanished like a bubble of air. Thinking fast, she began to pace. "What about the blood?"

"They managed to scrape off enough to get type, DNA." His already gloomy face sagged. "It matches our boy. It's David Angelini's blood, Dallas. Lab says it's old, six months minimum. From the fibers they got, it looks like he used it to open packages, probably nicked himself somewhere along the line. It's not our weapon."

"Screw it." She heaved a breath, refused to be discouraged. "If he had one knife, he could have had two. We'll wait to hear from the other sweepers." Taking a moment, she scrubbed her face with her hands. "Listen to me, Feeney, if we go with Marco's confession as bogus, we have to ask why. He's not a crank or a loony calling in trying to take credit. He's saving his son's ass is what he's doing. So we work on him, and we work hard. I'll bring him in to interview, try to crack him."

"I'm with you there."

"I've got a session with Mira in a couple hours. We'll just let our main boy stew for awhile."

"While we pray one of the teams turns up something."

"Praying can't hurt. Here's the big one, Feeney, our boy's lawyers get a hold of Marco's confession, it's going to corrupt the hearing on the minor charges. We'll whistle for an indictment."

"With that, and without physical evidence, he's going back out, Dallas."

"Yeah. Son of a bitch."

*   *   *

Marco Angelini was like a boulder cemented to concrete. He wasn't going to budge. Two hours of intense interrogation didn't shake his story. Though, Eve consoled herself, he hadn't shored up any of the holes in it, either. At the moment, she had little choice but to pin her hopes on Mira's report.

"I can tell you," Mira said in her usual unruffled fashion, "that David Angelini is a troubled young man with a highly developed sense of self-indulgence and protection."

"Tell me he's capable of slicing his mother's throat."

"Ah." Mira sat back and folded her neat hands. "What I can tell you is, in my opinion, he is more capable of running from trouble than confronting it, on any level. When combining and averaging his placements on the Murdock-Lowell and the Synergy Evaluations—"

"Can we skip over the psych buzz, Doctor? I can read that in the report."

"All right." Mira shifted away from the screen where she had been about to bring up the evaluations. "We'll keep this in simple terms for the time being. Your man is a liar, one who convinces himself with little effort that his lies are truth in order to maintain his self-esteem. He requires good opinion, even praise, and is accustomed to having it. And having his own way."

"And if he doesn't get his own way?"

"He casts blame elsewhere. It is not his fault, nor his responsibility. His world is insular, Lieutenant, comprised for the most part of himself alone. He considers himself successful and talented, and when he fails, it's because someone else made a mistake. He gambles because he doesn't believe he can lose, and he enjoys the thrill of risk. He loses because he believes himself above the game."

"How would he react at the risk of having his bones snapped over gambling debts?"

"He would run and he would hide, and being abnormally dependent on his parents, he would expect them to clean up the mess."

"And if they refused?"

Mira was silent for a moment. "You want me to tell you that he would strike out, react violently, even murderously. I can't do that. It is, of course, a possibility that can't be ruled out in any of us. No test, no evaluation can absolutely conclude the reaction of an individual under certain circumstances. But in those tests and those evaluations, the subject reacted consistently by covering, by running, by shifting blame rather than by attacking the source of his problem."

"And he could be covering his reaction, to skew the evaluation."

"It's possible, but unlikely. I'm sorry."

Eve stopped pacing and sank into a chair. "You're saying that in your opinion, the murderer may still be out there."

"I'm afraid so. It makes your job more difficult."

"If I'm looking in the wrong place," Eve said to herself, "where's the right place? And who's next?"

"Unfortunately, neither science nor technology is yet able to forecast the future. You can program possibilities, even probabilities, but they can't take into account impulse or emotion. Do you have Nadine Furst under protection?"

"As much as possible." Eve tapped a finger on her knee. "She's difficult, and she's torn up about Louise Kirski."

"And so are you."

Eve slid her gaze over, nodded stiffly. "Yeah, you could say that."

"Yet you look uncommonly rested this morning."

"I got a good night's sleep."

"Untroubled?"

Eve moved a shoulder, tucked Angelini and the case into a corner of her mind where she hoped it would simmer into something fresh. "What would you say about a woman who can't seem to sleep well unless this man's in bed with her?"

"I'd say she may be in love with him, is certainly growing used to him."

"You wouldn't say she's overly dependent?"

"Can you function without him? Do you feel able to make a decision without asking his advice, opinion, or direction?"

"Well, sure, but . . ." She trailed off, feeling foolish. Well, if one was to feel foolish, what better place than a shrink's office? "The other day, when he was off planet, I wore one of his shirts to work. That's—"

"Lovely," Mira said with a slow, easy smile. "Romantic. Why does romance worry you?"

"It doesn't. I— Okay, it scares the shit out of me, and I don't know why. I'm not used to having someone there, having someone look at me like—the way he does. Sometimes it's unnerving."

"Why is that?"

"Because I haven't done anything to make him care about me as much as he does. I know he does."

"Eve, your self-worth has always been focused on your job. Now a relationship has forced you to begin evaluating yourself as a woman. Are you afraid of what you'll find?"

"I haven't figured that out. It's always been the job. The highs and lows, the rush, the monotony. Everything I needed to be was there. I busted my ass to make lieutenant, and I figure I can sweat my way up to captain, maybe more. Doing the job was it, all of it. It was important to be the best, to make a mark. It's still important, but it's not all anymore."

"I would say, Eve, that you'll be a better cop, and a better woman because of it. Single focus limits us, and can too often obsess us. A healthy life needs more than one goal, one passion."

"Then I guess my life's getting healthier."

Eve's communicator beeped, reminding her that she was on the clock, a cop first. "Dallas."

"You're going to want to switch over to public broadcast, Channel 75," Feeney announced. "Then get your butt back here to the Tower. The new chief wants to fry our asses."

Eve cut him off, and Mira had already opened her viewing screen. They came in on C. J. Morse's noon update.

". . . continuing problems with the investigation of the murders. A Cop Central source has confirmed that while David Angelini has been charged with obstruction of justice, and remains prime suspect for the three murders, Marco Angelini, the accused's father, has confessed to those murders. The senior Angelini, president of Angelini Exports and former husband of the first victim, Prosecuting Attorney Cicely Towers, surrendered to the police yesterday. Though he has confessed to all three murders, he has not been charged, and the police continue to hold David Angelini."

Morse paused, shifted slightly to face a new camera angle. His pleasant, youthful face radiated concern. "In other developments, a knife taken from the Angelini home during a police search has proven through testing not to be the murder weapon. Mirina Angelini, daughter of the late Cicely Towers, spoke to this reporter in an exclusive interview this morning."

The screen snapped to a new video and filled with Mirina's lovely, outraged face. "The police are persecuting my family. It isn't enough that my mother is dead, murdered on the street. Now, in a desperate attempt to cover their own ineptitude, they've arrested my brother and they're holding my father. It wouldn't surprise me to find myself taken away in restraints at any moment."

Eve ground her teeth while Morse led Mirina through questions, prodded her to make accusations, tears gleaming in her eyes. When the broadcast switched back to the news desk, he was frowning seriously.

"A family under siege? There are rumors of cover-ups clouding the investigation. Primary investigating officer, Lieutenant Eve Dallas could not be reached for comment."

"Little bastard. Little bastard," Eve muttered and swung away from the screen. "He never tried to reach me for comment. I'd give him a comment." Furious, she snatched up her bag and shot Mira one last look. "You ought to analyze that one," she said jerking her head toward the screen. "That little prick has delusions of grandeur."

SEVENTEEN

Harrison Tibble was a thirty-five-year vet on the police force. He'd plodded his way up from beat cop, working the West Side barrios when cops and their quarries still carried guns. He'd even taken a hit once: three nasty rounds in the abdomen that might have killed a lesser man and would certainly have given most ordinary cops cause to consider their career choices. Tibble had been back on full duty within six weeks.

He was an enormous man, a full six foot six and two hundred sixty pounds of solid muscle. After the gun ban, he'd used his bulk and cold, terrifying grin to intimidate his quarries. He still had the mind of a street cop, and his record was clean enough to serve tea on.

He had a large, square face, skin the color of polished onyx, hands the size of steamship rounds, and no patience for bullshit.

Eve liked him and could privately admit she was a little afraid of him.

"What is this pile of shit we've got ourselves into, Lieutenant?"

"Sir." Eve faced him, flanked by Feeney and Whitney. But at the moment, she knew she was very much alone. "David Angelini was on scene the night Louise Kirski was killed. We have that locked. He has no solid alibi for the times of the other two murders. He's in debt big time to the spine twisters, and with his mother's death, he comes into a nice, healthy inheritance. It's been confirmed that she had refused to bail him out this time."

"Look for the money's a tried and true investigative tool, Lieutenant. But what about the other two?"

He knew all of this, Eve thought and struggled not to squirm. Every word of every report had passed by him. "He knew Metcalf, had been to her apartment, was working with her on a project. He needed her to commit, but she was playing coy, covering her bases. The third victim was a mistake. We believe strongly that the intended victim was Nadine Furst, who at my suggestion and with my cooperation was putting a great deal of pressure on the story. He also knew her personally."

"That's real good so far." His chair creaked under his weight as he shifted back. "Real good. You've placed him at one of the scenes, established motives, dug up the links. Now we run into the hard place. You don't have a weapon, you don't have any blood. You don't have diddly as far as physical evidence."

"Not at this time."

"You've also got a confession, but not from the accused."

"That confession's nothing more than a smoke screen," Whitney put in. "An attempt by a father to protect his son."

"So you believe," Tibble said mildly. "But the fact is, it's now on record and is public knowledge. The psych profile doesn't fit, the weapon doesn't fit, and in my opinion, the PA's office was too eager to put the spotlight on. It happens when it's one of your own."

He held up a plate-sized hand before Eve could speak. "I'll tell you what we've got, what it looks like to all those fine people watching their screens. A grieving family hammered by cops, circumstantial evidence, and three women with their throats cut open."

"No one's throat's been cut open since David Angelinas been locked up. And the charges filed against him are clean."

"True enough, but that handy fact won't get an indictment on the lessers—not when the jury's going to feel sorry for him, and the counsel starts hawking diminished capacity."

He waited, scanning faces, tapped his fingers when no one disagreed with him. "You're the number whiz, Feeney, the electronic genius. What are the odds on the grand jury if we send our boy over tomorrow on the obstruction and bribery charges?"

Feeney hunched his shoulders. "Fifty-fifty," he said mournfully. "At the outside, considering that idiot Morse's latest news flash."

"That's not good enough. Spring him."

"Spring him? Chief Tibble—"

"All we're going to get if we push those charges is bad press and public sympathy for the son of a martyred public servant. Cut him loose, Lieutenant, and dig deeper. Put someone on him," he ordered Whitney. "And on his daddy. I don't want them to fart without hearing about it. And find the fucking leak," he added, his eyes going hard. "I want to know what asshole fed that idiot Morse data." His grin spread suddenly, terrifyingly. "Then I want to talk to him, personally. Keep your distance from the Angelinis, Jack. This isn't any time for friendship."

"I'd hoped to talk to Mirina. I might be able to persuade her not to give any more interviews."

"It's a little late for damage control there," Tibble considered. "Hold off on that. I've worked hard to get the stink of the word *cover-up* out of this office. I want to keep it that way. Get me a weapon. Get me some blood. And for Christ's sake do it before somebody else gets sliced."

His voice boomed out, fingers jabbing, as he snapped orders. "Feeney, work some of your magic. Go over the names from the victims' diaries again, cross them with Furst's. Find me somebody else who had an interest in those ladies. That'll be all, gentlemen." He got to his feet. "Lieutenant Dallas, another moment of your time."

"Chief Tibble," Whitney began formally. "I want it on record that as Lieutenant Dallas's commanding officer, I consider her pursuit of this investigation to be exemplary. Her work has been top rate despite difficult circumstances, both professional and personal, some of which I have caused."

Tibble cocked a bushy brow. "I'm sure the lieutenant appreciates your review, Jack." He said nothing more, waiting until the men left.

"Me and Jack, we go back a ways," he began conversationally. "Now he thinks since I'm sitting here where that corrupt pie-faced fucker Simpson used to rest his sorry ass, I'm going to use you as a handy scapegoat and feed you to the media dogs." He held Eve's eyes steadily. "Is that what you think, Dallas?"

"No, sir. But you could."

"Yeah." He scratched the side of his neck. "I could. Have you bumbled this investigation, Lieutenant?"

"Maybe I have." It was a hard one to swallow. "If David Angelini is innocent—"

"The courts decide innocence or guilt," he interrupted. "You gather evidence. You gathered some nice evidence, and the jerk was there for Kirski. If he didn't kill her, the bastard watched some woman get slaughtered and walked away. He don't win any prizes in my book."

Tibble steepled his fingers and peered over them. "You know what would make me take you off this case, Dallas? If I thought you were carrying around too much baggage about Kirski." When she opened her mouth, then shut it again, he gave her a thin-lipped smile. "Yeah, best to keep it shut. You laid out some bait, took a chance. There was a pretty good shot he'd come after you. I'd have done the same thing in my glory days," he added with some wistful regret that they were over. "Problem is, he didn't, and some poor woman with a tobacco habit gets hit instead. You figure you're responsible for that?"

She struggled with the lie, gave up to the truth. "Yes."

"Get over it," he said with a snap. "The trouble with this case is, there's too much emotion. Jack can't get past his grief, you can't get past your guilt. That makes the two of you useless. You want to be guilty, you want to be pissed, wait till you nail him. Clear?"

"Yes, sir."

Satisfied, he leaned back again. "You walk out of here, the media's going to be all over you like lice."

"I can handle the media."

"I'm sure you can." He blew out a breath. "So can I. I've got a fucking press conference. Clear out."

*   *   *

There was only one place to go, and that was back to the begin-
ning. Eve stood on the sidewalk outside the Five Moons and stared
down. Playing the route back in her mind, she strode to the subway
entrance.

It was raining, she remembered. *I'd have a hand on my umbrella, my
purse over my shoulder with a good grip on that, too. Bad neighborhood. I'm
pissed. I walk fast, but I keep an eye shifting for anybody who wants my purse
as much as I do.*

She walked into the Five Moons, ignoring the quick glances and
the bland face of the droid behind the bar as she tried to read Cicely
Towers's thoughts.

*Disgusting place. Dirty. I'm not going to drink, not even going to sit
down. God knows what I'd pick up on my suit. Check the watch. Where the
hell is he? Let's get this over with. Why the hell did I meet him here? Stupid,
stupid. Should have used my office, my turf.*

Why didn't I?

Because it's private, Eve thought, closing her eyes. It's personal.
Too many people there, too many questions. Not city business. Her
business.

Why not her apartment?

Didn't want him there. Too angry—upset—eager—to argue when
he named the time and place.

No, it's just angry, impatient, Eve decided, remembering the droid's
statement. She'd checked her watch again and again, she'd frowned,
she'd given up, and walked out.

Eve followed the route, remembering the umbrella, the purse.
Quick steps, heels clicking. Someone there. She stops. Does she see
him, recognize him? Has to, it's face to face. Maybe she speaks to him:
"You're late."

He does it quick. It's a bad neighborhood. Not much cruising traffic, but you can never tell. Security lights are dinky, always are around
here. Nobody complains much because it's safer to score in the dark.

But someone might come out of the bar, or the club across the
street. One swipe and she's down. Her blood's all over him. The fucking blood's got to be all over him.

He takes her umbrella. An impulse, or maybe for a shield. Walks away, fast. Not to the subway. He's covered with blood. Even around here, somebody would notice.

She covered two blocks in either direction, then covered them again, questioning anyone who was loitering on the street. Most of the responses were shrugs, angry eyes. Cops weren't popular on the West End.

She watched a street hawker, who she suspected was pushing more than fashion beads and feathers, skim around the corner on motor skates. She scowled after him.

"You been round here before."

Eve glanced over. The woman was so white she was next to invisible. Her face was like bleached putty, her hair cropped so close it showed her bone-white scalp, and her eyes were colorless down to the pinprick pupil.

Funky junkie, Eve thought. They popped the white tablet that kept the mind misted and pigments bleached.

"Yeah, I've been around."

"Cop." The junkie jerked forward, stiff jointed, like a droid coming up on maintenance. A sign she was low on a fix. "Seen you talking with Crack a while ago. He's some dude."

"Yeah, he's some dude. Were you around the night that woman got whacked down the street?"

"Fancy lady, rich, fancy lady. Caught it on the screen in detox."

Eve bit back an oath, stopped, and backtracked. "If you were in detox, how'd you see me talking to Crack?"

"Went in that day. Maybe the next day. Time's relative, right?"

"Maybe you saw the rich, fancy lady before you caught her on the screen."

"Nope." The albino sucked her finger. "Didn't."

Eve scanned the building behind the junkie, gauged the view. "Is this where you live?"

"I live here, I live there. Got me a crash flop upstairs."

"You were there the night the lady got slashed?"

"Probably. Got a credit problem." She flashed tiny, round teeth in a smile. And her breath was awesome. "Not much fun on the street when you ain't got a credit."

"It was raining," Eve prompted.

"Oh yeah. I like the rain." Her muscles continued to jerk, but her eyes went dreamy. "I watch it out the window."

"Did you see anything else out the window?"

"People come, people go," she said in a singsong voice. "Sometimes you can hear the music from down the street. But not that night. Rain's too loud. People running to get out of it. Like they'd melt or something."

"You saw someone running in the rain."

The colorless eyes sharpened. "Maybe. What's it worth?"

Eve dug into her pocket. She had enough loose credit tokens for a quick, small score. The junkie's eyes rolled and her hand jerked out.

"What did you see?" Eve said slowly, snatching the credits out of reach.

"A guy pissing in the alley over there." She shrugged, her eyes focused on the credits. "Maybe jerking off. Hard to tell."

"Did he have anything with him? Was he carrying anything?"

"Just his dick." She laughed uproariously at that and nearly tumbled. Her eyes were beginning to water heavily. "He just walked away in the rain. Hardly anybody out that night. Guy got in a car."

"Same guy?"

"Nah, another guy, had it parked over there." She gestured vaguely. "Not from 'round here."

"Why?"

"Car had a shine to it. Nobody got a car with a shine to it 'round here. If they got a car. Now Crack, he's got one, and that pissant Reeve down the hall from me. But they don't shine."

"Tell me about the guy who got in the car."

"Got in the car, drove away."

"What time was it?"

"Hey, I look like a clock. Ticktock." She snorted another laugh. "It was nighttime. Nighttime's the best. My eyes hurt in daytime," she whined. "Lost my sunshields."

Eve dragged a pair of eye protectors out of her pocket. She never remembered to wear the damn things, anyway. She shoved them at the albino, who hooked them on.

"Cheap. Cop issue. Shit."

"What was he wearing? The guy who got in the car."

"Hell, I don't know." The junkie toyed with the sunglasses. Her eyes didn't burn quite so much behind the treated lenses. "A coat maybe. Dark coat, flapped around. Yeah, it flapped around when he was closing the umbrella."

Eve felt a jolt, like a punch in the stomach. "He had an umbrella?"

"Hey, it was raining. Some people don't like getting wet. Pretty," she said, dreaming again. "Bright."

"What color was it?"

"Bright," she repeated. "You going to give me those credits?"

"Yeah, you're going to get them." But Eve took her arm, led her to the broken steps of the building, and sat her down. "But let's talk about this a little more first."

"The uniforms missed her." Eve paced her office while Feeney lolled in her chair. "She went into detox the day after the first murder. I checked it. She got out a week ago."

"You got an albino addict," Feeney put in.

"She saw him, Feeney. She saw him get in a car, she saw the umbrella."

"You know what a funky junkie's vision's like, Dallas. In the dark, in the rain, from across the street?"

"She gave me the umbrella. Goddamn it, nobody knew about the umbrella."

"And the color was, I quote, *bright*." He held up both hands before Eve could snap at him. "I'm just trying to save you some grief. You got an idea of putting the Angelinis in a lineup for a funky junkie, their lawyers are going to whip your little ass, kid."

She had thought of it. And she, too, had rejected it. "She wouldn't hold up on direct ID. I'm not stupid. But it was a man, she's damn sure of that. He drove away. He had the umbrella. He was wearing a long coat, dark."

"Which jibes with David Angelini's statement."

"It was a new car. I juggled that out of her. Shiny, bright."

"Back with bright."

"So, they don't see colors well," she snarled. "The guy was alone, and the car was a small, personal vehicle. The driver's side door opened up, not to the side, and he had to swivel down to get in."

"Could be a Rocket, a Midas, or a Spur. Maybe a Midget, if it's a late model."

"She said new, and she's got a thing for cars. Likes to watch them."

"Okay, I'll run it." He gave a sour smile. "Any idea how many of those models been sold in the last two years in the five boroughs alone? Now, if she'd come up with an ID plate, even a partial—"

"Quit bitching. I've been back over Metcalf's. There's a couple dozen bright new cars in the garage there."

"Oh joy."

"Possibility he's a neighbor," Eve said with a shrug. It was a very low possibility. "Wherever he lives, he has to be able to get in and out without being noticed. Or where people don't notice. Maybe he leaves the coat in the car, or he puts it in something to get it inside and clean it up. There's going to be blood in that car, Feeney, and on that coat, no matter how much he's scrubbed and sprayed. I've got to get over to Channel 75."

"Are you crazy?"

"I need to talk to Nadine. She's dodging me."

"Jesus, talk about the lion's den."

"Oh, I'll be fine." She smiled viciously. "I'm taking Roarke with me. They're scared of him."

"It's so sweet of you to ask for my company." Roarke pulled his car into the visitors' lot at Channel 75 and beamed at her. "I'm touched."

"All right, I owe you." The man never let her get away with anything, Eve thought in disgust as she climbed out of the car.

"I'll collect." He caught her arm. "You can start paying off by telling me why you want me along."

"I told you, it'll save time, since you want to go to this opera thing."

Very slowly, very thoroughly, he scanned over her dusty trousers and battered boots. "Darling Eve, though you always look perfect to me, you're not going to the opera dressed like that. So we're going to have to go home to change, anyway. Come clean."

"Maybe I don't want to go to the opera."

"So you've already said. Several times, I believe. But we had a deal."

She lowered her brows, toyed with one of the buttons of his shirt. "It's just singing."

"I've agreed to sit through two sets at the Blue Squirrel, with the idea of helping Mavis into a recording contract. And no one—no one with ears—would consider that singing of any kind."

She huffed out a breath. A deal was, after all, a deal. "Okay, fine. I said I'm going."

"Now that you've managed to avoid the question, I'll repeat it. Why am I here?"

She looked up from his button, into his face. It was always hell for her to admit she could use help. "Feeney's got to dig into the E-work. He can't be spared right now. I want another pair of eyes, ears, another impression."

His lips curved. "So, I'm your second choice."

"You're my first civilian choice. You read people well."

"I'm flattered. And perhaps, while I'm here, I could break Morse's face for you."

Her grin came quickly. "I like you, Roarke. I really like you."

"I like you, too. Is that a yes? I'd enjoy it very much."

She laughed, but there was a part of her that warmed foolishly over the idea of having an avenger. "It's a happy thought, Roarke, but I'd really rather break his face myself. At the right time and in the right place."

"Can I watch?"

"Sure. But for the moment, can you just be the rich and powerful Roarke, my personal trophy?"

"Ah, how sexist. I'm excited."

"Good. Hold that thought. Maybe we'll skip the opera after all."

They walked together through the main entrance, and Roarke had the pleasure of watching her shrug on the cop. She flashed her badge at security, gave him a pithy suggestion that he keep out of her face, then strode toward the ascent.

"I love to watch you work," he murmured in her ear. "You're so . . . forceful," he decided as his hand slid down her back toward her butt.

"Cut it out."

"See what I mean?" He rubbed his gut where her elbow had jabbed. "Hit me again. I could learn to love it."

She managed, barely, to turn a chuckle into a snort. "Civilians," was all she said.

The newsroom was busy, noisy. At least half of the on-desk reporters were plugged into 'links, headsets, or computers. Screens flashed current broadcasts. A number of conversations stopped dead when Eve and Roarke stepped from the ascent. Then, like a horde of dogs with the same scent in their nostrils, reporters scrambled forward.

"Back off," Eve ordered with enough force to have one eager beaver stumbling backward and stomping on the foot of a cohort. "Nobody gets a comment. Nobody gets squat until I'm ready."

"If I do buy this place," Roarke said to Eve in a voice just loud enough to carry, "I'll have to make several staff cuts."

That created a swath wide enough to stride through. Eve zeroed in on a face she recognized. "Rigley, where's Furst?"

"Hey, Lieutenant." He was all teeth and hair and ambition. "If you'd like to step into my office," he invited, gesturing toward his console.

"Furst," she repeated, in a voice like a bullet. "Where?"

"I haven't seen her all day. I covered her morning report myself."

"She called in." Beaming smiles, Morse sauntered over. "Taking some time off," he explained, and his mobile face shifted to sober lines. "She's pretty ripped up about Louise. We all are."

"Is she at home?"

"Said she needed some time, is all I know. Management cut her a break. She's got a couple of weeks coming. I'm taking over her beat." His smile flashed again. "So, if you'd like a little airtime, Dallas. I'm your man."

"I've had plenty of your airtime, Morse."

"Well then." He dismissed her and shifted toward Roarke. His smile bumped up in wattage. "It's a pleasure to meet you. You're a difficult man to contact."

Deliberately insulting, Roarke ignored Morse's offered hand. "I only give time to people I consider interesting."

Morse lowered his hand, but kept his smile in place. "I'm sure if you spared me a few minutes, I'd find several areas of interest for you."

Roarke's smile flashed, quick and lethal. "You really are an idiot, aren't you."

"Down, boy," Eve murmured, patting Roarke's arm. "Who leaked confidential data?"

Morse was obviously struggling to recover his dignity. He veered his gaze to hers and nearly managed an arrogant sneer. "Now, now, sources are protected. Let's not forget the Constitution." Patriotically, he laid his palm over his heart. "Now, if you wish to comment on, contradict, or add to any of my information, I'd be more than happy to listen."

"Why don't we try this?" she said, shifting gears. "You found Louise Kirski's body—while it was still warm."

"That's right." He folded his mouth into grim lines. "I've given my statement."

"You were pretty upset, weren't you? Jittery. Shot your dinner in the bushes. Feeling better now?"

"It's something I'll never forget, but yes, I'm feeling better. Thanks for asking."

She stepped forward, backing him up. "You felt good enough to go on air within minutes, to make sure there was a camera out there getting a nice close-up of your dead associate."

"Immediacy is part of the business. I did what I was trained to do. That doesn't mean I didn't feel." His voice trembled and was manfully controlled. "That doesn't mean I don't see her face, her eyes, every time I try to sleep at night."

"Did you ever wonder what would have happened if you'd gotten there five minutes sooner?"

That jarred him, and though she knew it was nasty, and personal, it pleased her.

"Yes, I have," he said with dignity. "I might have seen him or stopped him. Louise might be alive if I hadn't been caught in traffic. But that doesn't change the facts. She's dead, and so are two others. And you don't have anyone in custody."

"Maybe it hasn't occurred to you that you're feeding him. That you've given him just what he wants." She took her gaze from Morse long enough to scan the room and all the people who were listening eagerly. "He must love watching all the reports, hearing all the details, the speculation. You've made him the biggest star on the screen."

"It's our responsibility to report—" Morse began.

"Morse, you don't know shit about responsibility. All you know is how to count the minutes you're on air, front and center. The more people die, the bigger your ratings. You can quote me on that one." She turned on her heel.

"Feel better?" Roarke asked her when they were outside again.

"Not a hell of a lot. Impressions?"

"The newsroom's in turmoil, too many people doing too many things. They're all jumpy. The one you talked to initially about Nadine?"

"Rigley. He's a little fish. I think they hired him for his teeth."

"He's been biting his nails. There were several others who looked ashamed when you made your little speech. They turned away, got very busy, but they weren't doing anything. Several more looked quietly pleased when you took a couple layers off Morse. I don't believe he's well liked."

"Big surprise."

"He's better than I'd thought," Roarke mused.

"Morse? At what? Slinging shit?"

"Image," Roarke corrected. "Which is often the same thing. He pulls out all those emotions. He doesn't feel any of them, but he knows how to make them play over his face, in his voice. He's in the right field and will definitely move up."

"God help us." She leaned against Roarke's car. "Do you think he knows more than he's put on air?"

"I think it's possible. Highly possible. He's enjoying stringing this out, particularly now that he's in charge of the story. And he hates your guts."

"Oh, now I'm hurt." She started to open the door, then turned back. "Hates me?"

"He'll ruin you if he can. Watch yourself."

"He can make me look foolish, but he can't ruin me." She wrenched the door open. "Where the hell is Nadine? It's not like her, Roarke. I understand how she feels about Louise, but it's not like her to take off, not to tell me, to hand a story this size to that bastard."

"People react in different ways to shock and grief."

"It's stupid. She was a target. She could still be a target. We have to find her."

"Is that your way of squirming out of the opera?"

Eve got in the car, stretched out her legs. "No, that's just a little side benefit. Let's run by her place, okay? She's on Eightieth between Second and Third."

"All right. But you have no excuse to squirm out of the cocktail party tomorrow night."

"Cocktail party? What cocktail party?"

"The one I arranged fully a month ago," he reminded her as he slipped in beside her. "To kick off the fund-raiser for the Art Institute on Station Grimaldi. Which you agreed to attend and to help host."

She remembered, all right. He'd brought home some fancy dress she was supposed to wear. "Wasn't I drunk when I agreed? The word of a drunk is worthless."

"No, you weren't." He smiled as he skimmed from the visitors' lot. "You were, however, naked, panting, and I believe very close to begging."

"Bull." Actually, she thought, folding her arms, he may have been right. The details were hazy. "Okay, okay, I'll be there, I'll be there with a stupid smile in some fancy dress that cost you too much money for too little material. Unless . . . something comes up."

"Something?"

She sighed. He only asked her to do one of his silly gigs when it was important to him. "Police business. Only if it's urgent police business. Barring that, I'll stick for the whole fussy mess."

"I don't suppose you could try to enjoy it?"

"Maybe I could." She turned her head and on impulse lifted a hand to his cheek. "A little."

EIGHTEEN

No one answered the buzzer at Nadine's door. The recording requested simply that the caller leave a message, which would be returned at the earliest possible time.

"She could be in there brooding," Eve mused, rocking on her heels as she considered. "Or she could be at some tony resort. She slipped her guard plenty over the past few days. She's a slick one, our Nadine."

"And you'll feel better if you know."

"Yeah." Brow furrowed, Eve considered using her police emergency code to bypass security. She didn't have enough cause, and she balled her hands in her pockets.

"Ethics," Roarke said. "It's always an education to watch you struggle with them. Let me help you out." He took out a small pocket knife and pried open the handplate.

"Jesus, Roarke, tampering with security will get you six months house arrest."

"Um-hmm." Calmly, he studied the circuits. "I'm a bit out of practice. We make this model, you know."

"Put that damn thing back together, and don't—"

But he was already bypassing the main board, working with a speed and efficiency that made her wince.

"Out of practice, my butt," she mumbled when the lock light went from red to green.

"I always had a knack." The door slid open, and he tugged her inside.

"Security tampering, breaking and entering, private property trespass. Oh, it's just mounting up."

"But you'll wait for me, won't you?" With one hand still on Eve's arm, he studied the living area. It was clean, cool, spare in furnishings, but with an expensive minimalistic style.

"She lives well," he commented, noting the gleam on the tile floor, the few objects d'art on spearing clear pedestals. "But she doesn't come here often."

Eve knew he had a good eye, and nodded. "No, she doesn't really live here, just sleeps here sometimes. There's nothing out of place, no dents in the cushions." She walked past him toward the adjoining kitchen, punched the available menu on the AutoChef. "Doesn't keep a lot of food on hand, either. Mostly cheese and fruit."

Eve thought about her empty stomach, was tempted, but resisted. She headed out across the wide living space toward a bedroom. "Office," she stated, studying the equipment, the console, the wide screen it faced. "She lives here some. Shoes under the console, single earring by the 'link, empty cup, probably coffee."

The second bedroom was larger, the sheets on the unmade bed twisted as if someone had wrapped and unwrapped themselves through a particularly long night.

Eve spotted the suit Nadine had been wearing on the night of Louise's murder on the floor, kicked under a table where a vase of daisies wilted.

They were signs of pain, and they made her sorry. She walked to the closet and hit the button to open it. "Christ, how could you tell if she packed anything? She's got enough clothes for a ten-woman model troupe."

Still, she looked through them while Roarke moved to the bedside 'link and ran the record disc back to the beginning. Eve glanced over her shoulder, saw what he was up to. She only moved her shoulders.

"Might as well completely invade her privacy."

Eve continued to search for some sign that Nadine had gone off on a trip while the calls and messages played back.

She listened with some amusement to some frank sexual byplay between Nadine and some man named Ralph. There were a lot of innuendos, overt suggestions, and laughter before the transmission ended with a promise to get together when he got into town.

Other calls breezed by: work-oriented, a call to a nearby restaurant for delivery. Ordinary, everyday calls. Then it changed.

Nadine was speaking to the Kirskis the day after the last murder. All of them were weeping. Maybe there was comfort in it, Eve thought as she walked toward the viewer. Maybe sharing tears and shock helped.

I don't know if it matters right now, but the primary investigator, Dallas—Lieutenant Dallas—she won't stop until she finds out who did this to Louise. She won't stop.

"Oh, man." Eve closed her eyes as the transmission ended. There was nothing more, just blank disc, and she opened her eyes again. "Where's the call to the station?" she demanded. "Where's the call? Morse said she called in and requested time off."

"Could have done it from her car, from a portable. In person."

"Let's find out." She whipped out her communicator. "Feeney. I need make, model, and ID number on Nadine Furst's vehicle."

It didn't take long to access the data or to read the garage inventory and discover her car had been logged out the day before and hadn't been returned.

"I don't like it." Eve fretted as she sat back in Roarke's car. "She'd have left me a message. She'd have left word. I need to talk to some brass at the station, find out who took her call." She started to key it into Roarke's car 'link, then stopped. "One other thing." Taking out her log, she requested a different number. "Kirski, Deborah and James, Portland, Maine." The number beeped on, and she transferred it to the 'link. It was answered quickly by a pale-haired woman with exhausted eyes.

"Mrs. Kirski, this is Lieutenant Dallas, NYPSD."

"Yes, Lieutenant, I remember you. Is there any news?"

"There's nothing I can tell you right now. I'm sorry." Damn it, she had to give the woman something. "We're pursuing some new information. We're hopeful, Mrs. Kirski."

"We said good-bye to Louise today." She struggled to smile. "It was a comfort to see how many people cared for her. So many of her friends from school, and there were flowers, messages from everyone she worked with in New York."

"She won't be forgotten, Mrs. Kirski. Could you tell me if Nadine Furst attended the memorial today?"

"We expected her." The swollen eyes looked lost a moment. "I'd spoken with her at her office only a few days ago to give her the date and time of the services. She said she would be here, but something must have come up."

"She didn't make it." A sour feeling spread in Eve's stomach. "You haven't heard from her?"

"No, not for a few days. She's a very busy woman, I know. She has to get on with her life, of course. What else can she do?"

Eve could offer no comfort without adding worry. "I'm sorry for your loss, Mrs. Kirski. If you have any questions or need to speak with me, please call. Anytime."

"You're very kind. Nadine said you wouldn't stop until you'd found the man who did this to my girl. You won't stop, will you, Lieutenant Dallas?"

"No, ma'am, I won't." She broke transmission, let her head fall back, closed her eyes. "I'm not kind. I didn't call her to say I was sorry, but because she might have given me an answer."

"But you were sorry." Roarke closed his hand gently over hers. "And you were kind."

"I can count the people who mean something to me without coming close to double digits. The same with the people I mean something to. If he'd have come after me, like the bastard was supposed to, I would have dealt with him. And if I hadn't—"

"Shut up." His hand vised over hers with a force that had her muffling a yelp, and his eyes were fierce and angry. "Just shut up."

Absently, she nursed her hand as he raced along the street. "You're right, I'm doing it wrong. I'm taking it in, and that doesn't help anything. Too much emotion on the case," she murmured, remembering the chiefs warning. "I started out today thinking clean, and that's what I've got to keep doing. Next step is to find Nadine."

She called Dispatch and ordered an all points on the woman and her vehicle.

Calmer, with the twist of her earlier words unraveling in his gut, he slowed, glanced at her. "How many homicide victims have you stood for in your illustrious career, Lieutenant?"

"Stood for? That's an odd way of putting it." She moved her shoulders, trying to focus her mind on a man in a long, dark coat with a shiny new car. "I don't know. Hundreds. Murder never goes out of style."

"Then I'd say you're well past the double digits, on both sides. You need to eat."

She was too hungry to argue with him.

"The trouble with the cross-check is Metcalf's diary," Feeney explained. "It's full of cutesy little codes and symbols. And she changes them, so we can't work a pattern. We've got names like Sweet Face, Hot Buns, Dumb Ass. We got initials, we got stars, hearts, little smiley faces or scowly faces. It'll take time, and lots of it, to cross it with the copy of Nadine's or the prosecutor's."

"So what you're telling me is you can't do it."

"I didn't say can't." He looked insulted.

"Okay, sorry. I know you're busting your computer chips on this, but I don't know how much time we've got. He's got to go for somebody else. Until we find Nadine . . ."

"You think he snatched her." Feeney scratched his nose, his chin, reached for his bag of little candied nuts. "That breaks pattern, Dallas. And all three bodies he hit he left where someone was going to stumble over them pretty quick."

"So he's got a new pattern." She sat on the edge of the desk and immediately shifted off, too edgy for stillness. "Listen, he's pissed. He missed his target. It was all going his way, then he fucks up, downloads the wrong woman. If we go with Mira, he got plenty of attention, hours of air-time, but he failed. It's a power thing."

She wandered to her stingy window, stared out, watched as an air-bus rumbled past at eye level like an awkward, overweight bird. Below, people were scattered like ants, rushing on the sidewalks, the ramps, the handy-glides to wherever their pressing business took them.

There were so many of them, Eve thought. So many targets.

"It's a power thing," Eve repeated, frowning down at the pedestrian traffic. "This woman's been getting all the attention, all the glory. His attention, his glory. When he takes them out, he gets the kick of the kill, all the publicity. The woman's gone, and that's good. She was trying to run everything her way. Now the public is focused on him. Who is he, what is he, where is he?"

"You're sounding like Mira," Feeney commented. "Without the thousand-credit words."

"Maybe she's nailed him. The what is he, anyway. She thinks male, she thinks unattached. Because women are a problem for him. Can't let them get the upper hand, like his mother did. Or the prominent female figure in his life. He's had some success, but not enough. He can't quite get to the top. Maybe because a woman's in the way. Or women."

She narrowed her eyes, closed them. "Women who speak," she murmured. "Women who use words to wield power."

"That's a new one."

"That's mine," she said, turning back. "He cuts their throats. He doesn't rough them up, doesn't sexually assault or mutilate. It's not about sexual power, though it's about sex. If you term it as gender. There's all sorts of ways to kill, Feeney."

"Tell me about it. Somebody's always finding some new, inventive way to ditch somebody else."

"He uses a knife, and that's an extension of the body. A personal weapon. He could stab them in the heart, rip them in the gut, disembowel—"

"Okay, okay." He swallowed a nut manfully and waved a hand. "You don't have to draw a picture."

"Towers made her mark in court, her voice a powerful tool. Metcalf, the actress, dialogue. Furst, talking to viewers. Maybe that's why he didn't go after me," she murmured. "Talking isn't my source of power."

"You're doing all right now, kid."

"It doesn't really matter," she said with a shake of the head. "What we've got is an unattached male, in a career where he's unable to make a deep mark, one who had a strong, successful female influence."

"Fits David Angelini."

"Yeah, and his father if we add in the fact that his business is in trouble. Slade, too. Mirina Angelini isn't the fragile flower I thought she was. There's Hammett. He was in love with Towers but she wasn't taking him quite as seriously. That's a squeeze on the balls."

Feeney grunted, shifted.

"Or there's a couple thousand men out there, frustrated, angry, with violent tendencies." Eve hissed a breath through her teeth. "Where the hell is Nadine?"

"Look, they haven't located her vehicle. She hasn't been gone that long."

"Any record of her using credits in the last twenty-four hours?"

"No." Feeney sighed. "Still, if she decided to go off planet, it takes longer to access."

"She didn't go off planet. She'd want to stay close. Damn it, I should have known she'd do something stupid. I could see how ripped she was. I could see it in her eyes."

Frustrated, Eve dragged her hands through her hair. Then her fingers curled in, went tense. "I could see it in her eyes," she repeated slowly. "Oh my Jesus. The eyes."

"What? What?"

"The eyes. He saw her eyes." She leaped toward her 'link. "Get me Peabody," she ordered, "Field officer at the—shit, shit—what is it? The four oh two."

"What have you got, Dallas?"

"Let's wait." She rubbed her fingers over her mouth. "Let's just wait."

"Peabody." The officer's face flipped on screen, irritation showing around the mouth. There was a riot of noise on audio, voices, music.

"Christ, Peabody, where are you?"

"Crowd control." Irritation edged toward a sneer. "Parade on Lex. It's some Irish thing."

"Freedom of the Six Counties Day," Feeney said with a hint of pride. "Don't knock it."

"Can you get away from the noise?" Eve shouted.

"Sure. If I leave my post and walk three blocks crosstown." She remembered herself. "Sir."

"Hell," Eve muttered and made do. "The Kirski homicide, Peabody. I'm going to transmit a picture of the body. You take a look."

Eve called up the file, flipped through, sent the shot of Kirski sprawled in the rain.

"Is that how you found her? Exactly how you found her?" Eve demanded over audio.

"Yes, sir. Exactly."

Eve pulled the image back, left it in the bottom corner of her screen. "The hood over her face. Nobody messed with the hood?"

"No, sir. As I stated in my report, the TV crew was taking pictures. I moved them back, sealed the door. Her face was covered to just above the mouth. She had not been officially identified when I arrived on scene. The statement from the witness who found the body was fairly useless. He was hysterical. You have the record."

"Yeah, I've got the record. Thanks, Peabody."

"So," Feeney began when she ended the transmission. "What does that tell you?"

"Let's look at the record again. Morse's initial statement." Eve eased back so that Feeney could bring it up. Together they studied Morse. His face was wet with what looked like a combination of rain and sweat, possibly tears. He was white around the lips, and his eyes jittered.

"Guy's shook," Feeney commented. "Dead bodies do that to some people. Peabody's good," he added, listening. "Slow, thorough."

"Yeah, she'll move up," Eve said absently.

Then I saw it was a person. A body. God, all the blood. There was so much blood. Everywhere. And her throat . . . I got sick. You could smell—I got sick. Couldn't help it. Then I ran inside for help.

"That's the gist of it." Eve steepled her hands, tapped them against her jaw. "Okay, run through to where I talked to him after we shut down the broadcast that night."

He still looked pale, she noted, but he had that little superior smirk around his mouth. She'd run him through the details much the same as Peabody had and received basically the same responses. Calmer now. That was expected, that was usual.

Did you touch the body?

No, I don't think—no. She was just lying there, and her throat was wide open. Her eyes. No, I didn't touch her. I got sick. You probably don't understand that, Dallas. Some people have basic human reactions. All that blood, her eyes. God.

"He said almost the same thing to me yesterday," Eve murmured. "He'd never forget her face. Her eyes."

"Dead eyes are spooky. They can stay with you."

"Yeah, hers have stayed with me." She shifted her gaze to Feeney's. "But nobody saw her face until I got there that night, Feeney. The hood had fallen over it. Nobody saw her face before I did. Except the murderer."

"Jesus, Dallas. You don't seriously think some little media creep like Morse is slicing throats in his off time. He probably added it for impact, to make himself more important."

Now her lips curved, just a little, in a smile more feral than amused. "Yeah, he likes being important, doesn't he? He likes being the focus. What do you do when you're an ambitious, unethical, second-string reporter, Feeney, and you can't find a hot story?"

He let out a low whistle. "You make one."

"Let's run his background. See where our pal comes from."

It didn't take Feeney long to pull up a basic sheet.

C. J. Morse had been born in Stamford, Connecticut, thirty-three years before. That was the first surprise. Eve would have pegged him as several years younger. His mother, deceased, had been head of computer science at Carnegie Mellon, where her son had graduated with double majors in broadcasting and compuscience.

"Smart little fucker," Feeney commented. "Twentieth in his class."

"I wonder if it was good enough."

His employment record was varied. He'd bumped from station to station. One year at a small affiliate near his hometown. Six months with a satellite in Pennsylvania. Nearly two years at a top-rated channel in New Los Angeles, then a stretch in a half-baked independent in Arizona before heading back East. Another gig in Detroit before hitting New York. He'd worked on All News 60, then made the lateral transfer to Channel 75, first in the social data unit, then into hard news.

"Our boy doesn't hold down a job long. Channel 75's his record with three years. And there's no mention of his father in family data."

"Just mama," Feeney agreed. "A successful, highly positioned mama." A dead mama, she thought. They'd have to take time to check on how she died.

"Let's check criminal."

"No record," Feeney said, frowning at the screen. "A clean-living boy."

"Go into juvie. Well, well," she said, reading the data. "We've got ourselves a sealed record here, Feeney. What do you suppose our clean-living boy did in his misspent youth bad enough that somebody used an arm to have it sealed up?"

"Won't take me long to find out." He was cheering up, fingers ready to dance. "I'll want my own equipment, and a green light from the commander."

"Do it. And dig into each of those job positions. Let's see if there was any trouble. I think I'll take a swing by Channel 75, have a nice, fresh chat with our boy."

"We're going to need more to take him down than a possible match with the psych profile."

"Then we'll get it." She shrugged into her shoulder harness. "You know, if I hadn't had such a personal beef with him, I might have seen it before. Who benefited from the murders? The media." She locked in her weapon. "And the first murder took place when Nadine was conveniently off planet on assignment. Morse could step right in."

"And Metcalf?"

"The fucker was on scene almost before I was. It pissed me off, but it never clicked. He was so damn cool. And then who finds Kirski's body? Who's on air in minutes giving his personal report?"

"It doesn't make him a killer. That's what the PA's office is going to say."

"They want a connection. Ratings," she said as she headed for the door. "There's the goddamn connection."

CHAPTER
NINETEEN

Eve did a quick pass through the newsroom, studied the viewing screens. There was no sign of Morse, but that didn't worry her. It was a big complex. And he had no reason to hide, no reason to worry.

She wasn't going to give him one.

The plan she'd formulated on the trip over was simple. Not as satisfying as hauling him out by his camera-friendly hair and into lockup, but simpler.

She'd talk to him about Nadine, let it leak that she was worried. From there, it would be natural to steer things to Kirski. She could play good cop, for a good cause. She could sympathize with his trauma, add a war story from her first encounter with the dead to nudge him along. She could even ask him for help in broadcasting Nadine's picture, her vehicle, agree to work with him.

Not too friendly, she decided. It should be grudging, with underlying urgency. If she was right about him, he'd love the fact that she needed him, and that he could use her to pump up his own airtime.

Then again, if she was right about him, Nadine could already be dead.

Eve blocked that out. It couldn't be changed, and regrets could come later.

"Looking for something?"

Eve glanced down. The woman was so perfect, Eve might have been tempted to check for a pulse. Her face could have been carved from alabaster, her eyes painted with liquid emerald, her lips with crushed ruby. On-air talents were often known to leverage their first three years' salaries against cosmetic enhancement.

Eve figured unless this one had been born very lucky, she'd bet the first five. Her hair was gold-tipped bronze swept up and away from that staggering face. Her voice was trained to a throaty purr that transmitted competent sex.

"Gossip line, right?"

"Social information. Larinda Mars." She offered a perfect, long-fingered hand with tapered scarlet tips. "And you're Lieutenant Dallas."

"Mars. That's familiar."

"It should be." If Larinda was irked that Eve didn't place her instantly, she hid it well behind a dazzling white-toothed smile and a voice that held the faintest whiff of upper-class Brit. "I've been trying for weeks to nail down an interview with you and your fascinating companion. You haven't returned my messages."

"Bad habit of mine. Just like thinking my personal life is personal."

"When you're involved with a man like Roarke, personal life becomes public domain." Her gaze skittered down, latched like a hook on a point between Eve's breasts. "My, my, that's quite a little bauble. A gift from Roarke?"

Eve bit off an oath, closed her hand over the diamond. She'd taken to playing with it while she was thinking and had forgotten to shove it back under her shirt.

"I'm looking for Morse."

"Hmmm." Larinda had already calculated the size and value of the stone. It would make a nice side piece to her broadcast. Cop wears billionaire's ice. "I might be able to help you with that. And you'll return the favor. There's a little soiree at Roarke's tonight." She fluttered her incredible two-layer, two-toned lashes. "My invitation must have been lost."

"That's Roarke's deal. Talk to him."

"Oh." An expert on button pushing, Larinda leaned back. "So, he runs the show, does he? I suppose when a man's so used to making decisions, he wouldn't consult the little woman."

"I'm nobody's little woman," Eve shot back before she could stop herself. She took a breath for control, reevaluated the eerily beautiful face. "Nice one, Larinda."

"Yes, it was. So, how about a pass for tonight? I can save you a lot of time looking for Morse," she added, when Eve sent a new narrow-eyed stare around the room.

"Prove it, and we'll see."

"He left five minutes before you walked in." Without looking, Larinda punched the call coming in on her 'link to hold. Practically, she used a slim pointer rather than her expensive manicure. "In a hurry, I'd say, as he nearly knocked me off the ascent. He looked quite ill. Poor baby."

The venom there had Eve feeling more in tune with Larinda. "You don't like him."

"He's a puss ball," Larinda said in her melodious voice. "This is a competitive business, darling, and I'm not against stepping on some-one's back now and then to get ahead. Morse is the kind who'd step on you, then sneak in a nice kick to the crotch and never break a sweat. He tried it with me when we were on the social beat together."

"And how did you handle that?"

She rolled a gorgeous shoulder. "Darling, I eat little weenies like him for breakfast. Still, he wasn't altogether bad, a whiz with research, and a good camera presence. Just thought he was too manly to scoop up gossip."

"Social information," Eve corrected with a thin smile.

"Right. Anyway, I wasn't sorry to see him shift over to hard news. You won't find that he's made many friends there, either. He's cut Nadine."

"What?" Bells rang in Eve's head.

"He wants to anchor, and he wants it solo. Every time he's on the news desk with her, he pulls little shit. Steps on her lines, adds a few seconds to his own time. Cuts her copy. Once or twice the Tele-PrompTer's been screwed up on her copy, too. Nobody could prove it, but Morse is the boy genius with electronics."

"Is he?"

"We all hate him," she said cheerfully. "Except upstairs. The brass think he's good ratings and appreciate his killer instinct."

"I wonder if they do," Eve murmured. "Where did he go?"

"We didn't stop to chat, but the way he looked, I'd say home and bed. He really looked sagged." She moved her curvy shoulders, sent some classy fragrance wafting up. "Maybe he's still shaking about finding Louise, and I should have more sympathy, but it's tough when it's Morse. Now, about that invitation?"

"Where's his station?"

Larinda sighed, flipped her call onto message mode and rose. "Over here." She glided through the aisles, proving that her body was every bit as impressive as her face. "Whatever you're looking for, you won't find it." She sent a wicked smile over her shoulder. "Did he do something? Did they finally pass a law making puss ball tendencies a crime?"

"I just need to talk to him. Why won't I find anything?"

Larinda paused at a corner cubicle, the console facing out so that anyone sitting behind it had his back to the wall and his eyes on the room. Nice little sign of paranoia, Eve thought.

"He never leaves anything out, not the tiniest memo, the bitsiest note. He locks down his computer if he stands up to scratch his butt. Claims somebody stole some of his research on one of his other gigs. He even uses an audio enhance, so he can whisper on calls and nobody can hear. As if we all strain to catch those golden words from his throat."

"So, how do you know he uses audio enhance?"

Larinda smiled. "Good one, Lieutenant. His console's locked, too," she added. "Discs secured." She flicked up a glance from under gold-tipped lashes. "Being a detective, you can probably figure out how I know that. Now, the invite?"

The cubicle was perfect, Eve thought. Awfully perfect for someone who had been hard at work, then had dashed out, ill. "Does he have a source at Cop Central?"

"I guess he may, though I can't imagine an actual human playing ball with Morse."

"Does he talk about it, brag about it?"

"Hey, in the gospel according to Morse, he's got top-level sources in the four corners of the universe." Her voice lost a bit of its sophistication on the dig, and whispered unmistakably of Queens. "But he never scooped Nadine. Well, until the Towers's murder, but he didn't last long on that."

Eve's heart was pounding now, strong and steady. She nodded, turned on her heel.

"Hey," Larinda called after her. "How about tonight? Tit for tat, Dallas."

"No cameras, or you're out before you're in," Eve warned and kept walking.

Because she remembered her days in uniform, and her ambition, Eve requested Peabody as her backup.

"He's going to remember your face." Eve waited impatiently as the elevator climbed to the thirty-third floor of Morse's building. "He's good with faces. I don't want you to say anything unless I give you an opening, then keep it brief, official. And look stern."

"I was born looking stern."

"Maybe toy with the hilt of your stunner now and again. You could look a little . . . anxious."

The corner of Peabody's mouth twitched. "Like I'd like to use it, but can't in the presence of a superior officer."

"You got it." She stepped off the elevator, turned left. "Feeney's still working on data, so I don't have as much as I'd like to pressure him with. The fact is, I could be wrong."

"But you don't think so."

"No, I don't think so. But I was wrong about David Angelini."

"You built a good circumstantial case, and he looked guilty as hell in interview." At Eve's casual glance, Peabody flushed. "Officers involved in a case are entitled to review all data pertaining to said case."

"I know the drill, Peabody." Very cool, very official, Eve announced herself through the entrance intercom. "You looking for a detective badge, Officer?"

Peabody squared her shoulders. "Yes, sir."

Eve merely nodded, announced herself again, and waited. "Walk down the hall, Peabody, see if the emergency exit is secure."

"Sir?"

"Walk down the hall," Eve repeated, holding Peabody's baffled gaze. "That's an order."

"Yes, sir."

The minute Peabody's back was turned, Eve took out her master code and disengaged the locks. She slid the door open a fraction and had the code back in her bag before Peabody came back.

"Secured, sir."

"Good. Doesn't look like he's home, unless . . . Well, look here, Peabody, the door isn't fully secured."

Peabody looked at the door, then back at Eve, and pursed her lips. "I would consider that unusual. We could have a break-in here, Lieutenant. Mr. Morse may be in trouble."

"You've got a point, Peabody. Let's put this on record." While Peabody engaged her recorder, Eve slid the door open, drew her weapon. "Morse? This is Lieutenant Dallas, NYPSD. The entrance is unsecured. We suspect a break-in and are entering the premises." She stepped in, signaled for Peabody to stand tight.

She slipped into the bedroom, checked closets, and skimmed a glance over the communications center that took up more room than the bed.

"No sign of an intruder," she said to Peabody, then ducked into the kitchen. "Where has our little bird flown?" she wondered. Pulling out her communicator, she contacted Feeney. "Give me everything you've got so far. I'm in his apartment, and he's not."

"I'm only about halfway there, but I think you're going to like it. First, the sealed juvie record—and I had to sweat for this one, kid.

Little C. J. had a problem with his social science instructor when he was ten. She didn't give him an A on an assignment."

"Well, that bitch."

"That's what he figured, apparently. He broke into her house, wrecked the place. And killed her little doggie."

"Jesus, killed her dog?"

"Sliced its throat, Dallas. Ear to floppy ear. Ended up with mandatory therapy, probation, and community service."

"That's good." Eve felt the pieces shifting into place. "Keep going."

"Okay. I'm here to serve. Our pal drives a brand-new two-passenger Rocket."

"God bless you, Feeney."

"More," he said, preening a bit. "His first adult job was on Dispatch at a little station in his own hometown. He quit when another reporter jogged ahead of him to an on-air assignment. A woman."

"Don't stop now. I think I love you."

"All the gold shields do. It's my pretty face. Got on air on the next gig, weekends only, subbing for the first and second string. Left in a huff, claiming discrimination. Assignment editor, female."

"Better and better."

"But here's the big one. Station he worked at in California. He was making it pretty good there, scrambled up from third string, got a regular spot on the midday, coanchoring."

"With a woman?"

"Yeah, but that's not the big guns, Dallas. Wait for it. Pretty little weather girl that was pulling in all the mail. Brass liked her so much they let her do some of the soft features on the midday. Ratings went up when she was on, and she started to get press of her own. Morse quit, citing he refused to work with a nonprofessional. That was just before the little weather girl got her big break, a recurring bit part in a comedy. Want to guess her name?"

Eve closed her eyes. "Tell me it's Yvonne Metcalf."

"Give the lieutenant a cigar. Metcalf had a notation about meeting the Dumb Ass from the partly sunny days. I'd say it's a good bet our boy looked her up in our fair city. Funny he never mentioned they were old pals in his reports. Would've given them such a nice shine."

"I do love you, desperately. I'm going to kiss your ugly face."

"Hey, it's lived in. That's what my wife tells me."

"Yeah, right. I need a search warrant, Feeney, and I need you here at Morse's to break down his computer."

"I've already requested the warrant. I'll have it transmitted to you as soon as it comes in. Then I'm on my way."

Sometimes the wheels moved smoothly. Eve had the warrant and Feeney within thirty minutes. She did kiss him, enthusiastically enough to have him going red as a hybrid beet.

"Secure the door, Peabody, then take the living area. Don't bother to be neat."

Eve swung into the bedroom, two steps ahead of Feeney. He was already rubbing his hands together.

"That's a beautiful system," he said. "Whatever his faults, the asshole knows his computers. It's going to be a pleasure to play with her." He sat down as Eve started to hunt through drawers.

"Obsessively trendy," she commented. "Nothing that shows too much sign of wear, nothing too expensive."

"He's putting all his money in his toys." Feeney hunched over, brows knit. "This guy respects his equipment, and he's careful. There are code blocks everywhere. Jesus, he's got a fail-safe."

"What?" Eve straightened up. "On a home unit?"

"He's got one, all right." Gingerly, Feeney eased back. "If I don't use the right code, the data's zapped. Odds are it's voiceprinted, too. It's not going to let me in easy, Dallas. I'm going to have to bring in some equipment, and it's going to take time."

"He's on the run. I know he's on the run. He knew we were coming after him."

Rocking back on her heels, she considered the possibilities: leaks— human—or electronic leaks.

"Call in your best man to come over here. You take the computer at the station. That's where he was when he ran."

"It's going to be a long night."

"Lieutenant." Peabody came to the door. Her face was impassive, but for the eyes. And the eyes were on fire. "I think you'd better see this."

In the living room, Peabody gestured to the blocky platform sofa. "I was giving it the once-over. Probably would have missed it, except my dad likes to build stuff. He was always putting in hidden drawers and hidey-holes. We got a kick out of it, used to play hidden treasure. I got curious when I saw the knob on the side. It looks like an ordinary decorative device that simulates old-fashioned turn bolts." She stepped around the front of the couch and gestured.

Eve could almost feel the vibrations rising from her skin.

Peabody's voice rose slightly in octave. "Hidden treasure."

Eve felt her heart kick once, hard. There in a long, wide drawer that slid from under the cushions lay a purple umbrella and a high-heeled red-and-white-striped shoe.

"Got him." Eve turned to Peabody with a fierce and powerful grin. "Officer, you've just taken one giant step toward your detective shield."

"My man says you're harassing him."

Eve scowled at Feeney's face in her communicator. "I'm simply asking him for periodic updates." She paced away from the sweepers who were scanning the living area of Morse's apartment. They had the lights on high. The sun was going down.

"And interrupting his flow. Dallas, I told you this would be slow work. Morse was an expert on compuscience. He knew all the tricks."

"He'd have written it down, Feeney. Like a fucking news report. And if he's got Nadine, that's on one of those damned discs, too."

"I'm with you on that, kid, but breathing down my man's neck isn't going to free up the data any quicker. Give us some space here, for Christ's sake. Don't you have a fancy do tonight?"

"What?" She grimaced. "Oh hell."

"Go put on your party dress and leave us alone."

"I'm not going to dress up like some brainless idiot and eat canapés while he's out there."

"He's going to be out there, whatever you're wearing. Listen up, we've got a citywide net out on him, his car. His apartment's under heavy surveillance, so's the station. You can't help us here. This part's my job."

"I can—"

"Slow up the process by making me talk to you," he snapped. "Go away, Dallas. The minute I get anything, the first byte, I'll call you in."

"We've got him, Feeney. We've got the who, the what."

"Let me try to find the where. If Nadine Furst is still alive, every minute counts."

That was what haunted her. She wanted to argue, but there was no ammunition. "Okay, I'll go, but—"

"Don't call me," Feeney interrupted. "I'll call you." He broke transmission before she could swear at him.

Eve was trying hard to understand relationships, the importance of balancing lives and obligations, the value of compromise. What she had with Roarke was still new enough to fit snugly, like a vaguely uncomfortable shoe, and lovely enough to keep wearing it until it stretched to accommodate.

So she dashed into the bedroom at a full run, saw him standing in the dressing area, and launched into the offense strategy.

"Don't give me any grief about being late. Summerset already handled that." She whipped off her harness, tossed it on a chair. Roarke finished securing a square of gold to his cuff, hands elegant, steady.

"You don't answer to Summerset." He looked at her then, a brief flick of the eyes as she tugged off her shirt. "Nor to me."

"Look, I had work." Naked from the waist up, she dropped into a chair to pull off her boots. "I said I'd be here, and I'm here. I know guests are going to be arriving in ten minutes." She heaved a boot aside as Summerset's abrasive words scraped through her head. "I'll be ready. I don't take hours to put some dress on and trowel a bunch of gunk on my face."

Boots disposed of, she arched her hips and wiggled out of her jeans. Before they hit the floor she was dashing into the adjoining bath. With a smile for the exit, Roarke followed her.

"There's no hurry, Eve. You don't clock in to a cocktail party, or get docked for tardiness."

"I said I'd be ready." She stood in the crisscrossing sprays of his shower, lathering pale green liquid into her hair. Suds dripped into her eyes. "I'll be ready."

"Fine, but no one will be offended if you come down in twenty minutes, or thirty for that matter. Do you expect me to be annoyed with you because you have another life?"

She swiped at her stinging eyes, tried to see him through suds and steam. "Maybe."

"Then you're doomed to disappointment. If you recall, I met you via that other life. And I have a number of other obligations as well." He watched her rinse her hair. It was pleasant to see the way she tilted her face back, the way water and soap sleeked down and away from her skin. "I'm not trying to box you in. I'm just trying to live with you."

She blew her wet hair out of her eyes as he opened the body dryer for her. She stepped toward it, pivoted. Then surprised him by grabbing his face in both of her hands and kissing him with a burst of enthusiasm.

"It can't be easy." She stepped into the tube and hit the power that swirled warm, dry air over her. "I can have a hard time living with myself. Sometimes I wonder why you don't just deck me when I start on you."

"It's occurred to me, but you're so often armed."

Dry and fragrant from the perfumed soap, she stepped out. "I'm not now."

He caught her by the waist, then stroked his hands down over her firm, muscled bottom. "Other things occur to me when you're naked."

"Yeah." She wrapped her arms around his neck, enjoying the fact that by rising slightly on her toes they were eye to eye, mouth to mouth. "Like what?"

With more than a little regret, he eased her back to arm's length. "Why don't you tell me why you're so revved?"

"Maybe it's because I like seeing you in a fancy shirt." She moved away, tugged a short dressing robe off a hanger. "Or maybe it's because I'm stimulated by the idea of wearing shoes that will make my arches scream for the next couple hours."

She peered into the mirror, and supposed she was obliged to put on a little of the paint Mavis was always pushing off on her. Leaning closer, she steadied the lash darkener and lengthener, closed it firmly over the lashes of her left eye, and hit the plunger.

"Just maybe," she continued glancing around, "it's because Officer Peabody found the hidden treasure."

"Good for Officer Peabody. What hidden treasure?"

Eve dealt with her right eyelashes, then blinked them experimentally. "One umbrella and one shoe."

"You've got him." Taking her shoulders, Roarke kissed her on the nape of the neck. "Congratulations."

"We've nearly got him," she corrected. She tried to remember what was next and chose lipstick. Mavis touted the virtues of lip dye, but Eve was wary of a color commitment that could last for three weeks. "We've got the evidence. The sweep confirmed his prints on the souvenirs. His and the victim's only on the umbrella. Got a few others on the shoe, but we expect salespeople or other customers. Brand-new shoes, hardly a scuff on the bottoms, and she picked up several pairs at Saks right before she died."

She went back to the bedroom, remembered the scented cream Roarke had brought back from Paris, and shrugged out of the robe to smear it on.

"The problem is, we don't have him. He got tipped somehow that I was coming and skipped. Feeney's working on his equipment now to see if we can shake loose some data that'll lead us to him. There's a net out, but he may have ditched the city. I wouldn't have made it tonight, but Feeney gave me the boot. Said I was harassing his man."

She opened the closet, pushed for revolve, and spotted the minuscule copper-colored dress. She took it out, held it in front of her. The sleeves were long and snug from a deep scooped neck. The skirt ended somewhere just south of the law.

"Am I supposed to wear anything under this?"

He reached in her top drawer, pulled out a matching colored triangle that might have laughingly been called panties. "These should do it."

She caught them from his underhand toss, wiggled in. "Jesus," she said after a quick look in the mirror. "Why bother?" Since it was too late to debate, she stepped into the dress and began to tug the clingy material up.

"It's always entertaining to watch you dress, but I'm distracted at the moment."

"I know, I know. Go on down. I'll be right there."

"No, Eve. Who?"

"Who?" She snapped the low shoulders into place. "Didn't I say?"

"No," Roarke said with admirable patience. "You didn't."

"Morse." She ducked into the closet for shoes.

"You're joking."

"C. J. Morse." She held the shoes as she might hold a weapon, and her eyes went dark and fixed. "And when I'm finished with the little son of a bitch, he's going to get more airtime than he ever dreamed of."

The in-house 'link beeped. Summerset's disapproving voice floated out. "The first guests are arriving, sir."

"Fine. Morse?" he said to Eve.

"That's right. I'll fill you in between canapés." She scooped a hand through her hair. "Told you I'd be ready. Oh, and Roarke?" She linked fingers with him as they started from the room. "I need you to pass a last-minute guest through for me. Larinda Mars."

CHAPTER

TWENTY

Eve supposed there could have been worse ways to wait through the last stages of an investigation. The atmosphere had it all over her cramped office at Cop Central, and the food was certainly a long leg up from the eatery.

Roarke had opened up his dome-ceilinged reception room with its glossy wood floors, mirrored walls, and sparkling lights. Long, curved tables followed the rounded walls and were artistically crowded with exotic finger foods.

Colorful bite-sized eggs harvested from the dwarf pigeons of the moon's farm colony, delicate pink shrimp from the Sea of Japan, elegant cheese swirls that melted on the tongue, pastries pumped with pâtés or creams in a menagerie of shapes, the gleam of caviar heaped on shaved ice, the richness of fresh fruit with frosty sugar coating.

There was more. The hot table across the room steamed with heat and spices. One entire area was a treasure trove for those of a vegetarian persuasion, with another, at a discreet distance, decked out for carnivores.

Roarke had opted for live music rather than simulation, and the band out on the adjoining terrace played quiet conversation-enhancing tunes. They would heat up as the night went on, to seduce dancers.

Through the swirl of color, of scent, of gleam and gloss, waiters in severe black wandered with silver trays topped with crystal flutes of champagne.

"This is so decent." Mavis popped a black button mushroom in her mouth. She'd dressed conservatively for the occasion, which meant a great deal of her skin was actually covered, and her hair was a tame medium red. Being Mavis, so were her irises. "I can't believe Roarke actually invited me."

"You're my friend."

"Yeah. Hey, you think if later on, after everybody's imbibed freely, could I ask the band to let me do a number?"

Eve scanned the rich, privileged crowd, the glint of real gold and real stones, and smiled. "I think that would be great."

"Superior." Mavis gave Eve's hand a quick squeeze. "I'm going to go talk to the band now, sort of worm my way into their hearts."

"Lieutenant."

Eve shifted her gaze from Mavis's retreating form over and up into Chief Tibble's face. "Sir."

"You're looking . . . unprofessional tonight." When she squirmed, he laughed. "That was a compliment. Roarke puts on quite a show."

"Yes, sir, he does. It's for a worthy cause." But she couldn't quite remember what that worthy cause was.

"I happen to think so. My wife is very involved." He took a flute from a passing tray and sipped. "My only regret is that these monkey suits never go out of style." With his free hand, he tugged at his collar.

It made her smile. "You should try wearing these shoes."

"There's a heavy price for fashion."

"I'd rather be dowdy and comfortable." But she resisted tugging at her butt-molding skirt.

"Well." He took her arm, eased her toward a shielding arborvitae. "Now that we've exchanged the obligatory small talk, I'd like to tell you you've done an excellent job on the investigation."

"I bumped with Angelini."

"No, you pursued a logical line, then you backtracked and found pieces others had missed."

"The albino junkie was a fluke, sir. Just luck."

"Luck counts. So does tenacity—and attention to detail. You cornered him, Dallas."

"He's still at large."

"He won't get far. His own ambition will help us find him. His face is known."

Eve was counting on it. "Sir, Officer Peabody did fine work. She has a sharp eye and good instincts."

"So you noted in your report. I won't forget it." When he glanced at his watch, she realized he was as edgy as she. "I promised Feeney a bottle of Irish whiskey if he broke it by midnight."

"If that doesn't do it, nothing will." She put on a smile. There was no use reminding the chief that they hadn't found the murder weapon in Morse's apartment. He already knew.

When she spotted Marco Angelini step into the room, her shoulders stiffened. "Excuse me, Chief Tibble. There's someone I have to speak to."

He laid a hand on her arm. "It isn't necessary, Dallas."

"Yes, sir, it is."

She knew the moment he became aware of her by the quick upward jut of his chin. He stopped, linked his hands behind his back, and waited.

"Mr. Angelini."

"Lieutenant Dallas."

"I regret the difficulties I caused you and your family during the investigation."

"Do you?" His eyes were cool, unblinking. "Accusing my son of murder, subjecting him to terror and humiliation, bringing more grief upon already impossible grief, putting him behind bars when his only crime was witnessing violence?"

She could have justified her actions. She could have reminded him that his son had not only witnessed violence, but had turned away from it without a thought but to his own survival, and had compounded his crime by attempting to bribe his way out of involvement.

"I regret adding to your family's emotional trauma."

"I doubt if you understand the phrase." He skimmed his eyes down. "And I wonder if, had you not been so busy enjoying your companion's position, you might have caught the real murderer. It's easy enough to see what you are. You're an opportunist, a climber, a media whore."

"Marco." Roarke spoke softly as he laid a hand on Eve's shoulder.

"No." She went stiff under the touch. "Don't defend me. Let him finish."

"I can't do that. I'm willing to take your state of mind into account, Marco, as the reason you would attack Eve in her own home. You don't want to be here," he said in an undertone of steel that indicated he was taking nothing into account. "I'll show you out."

"I know the way." Marco's eyes stabbed at Eve. "We'll put our business association to an end as soon as possible, Roarke. I no longer trust your judgment."

Hands balled into fists at her side, Eve trembled with fury as Marco strode away. "Why did you do that? I could have handled it."

"You could have," Roarke agreed, and turned her to face him. "But that was personal. No one, absolutely no one, comes into our home and speaks to you that way."

She tried to shrug it off. "Summerset does."

Roarke smiled, touched his lips to hers. "The exception, for reasons too complicated to explain." He rubbed away the frown line between her brows with his thumb.

"Okay. I guess I'm not going to be exchanging Christmas cards with the Angelinis."

"We'll learn to live with it. How about some champagne?"

"In a minute. I'm going to go freshen up." She touched his face. It was getting easier to do that, to touch him when they weren't alone. "I guess I ought to tell you that Mars has a recorder in her bag."

Roarke gave the dent in her chin a quick flick. "She did. I have it in mine now, after I let her crowd me at the vegetarian table."

"Very slick. You never mentioned pickpocketing as one of your skills."

"You never asked."

"Remind me to ask, and ask a lot. I'll be back."

She didn't care about freshening up. She wanted a few minutes to simmer down, and maybe a few more to call Feeney, though she imagined he'd bite her head off for interrupting his compusearch.

He still had an hour to go before he lost his bottle of Irish. She didn't think it would hurt to remind him. She was at the door to the library, preparing to code herself in, when Summerset melted out of the shadows behind her.

"Lieutenant, you have a call, termed both personal and urgent."

"Feeney?"

"He did not grant me his name," Summerset said down his nose.

"I'll take it in here." She had the small but worthy satisfaction of letting the door close smartly in his face. "Lights," she ordered and the room brightened.

She'd almost gotten used to the walls of books with leather bindings and paper pages that crackled when you leafed through. For once she didn't give them so much as a glance as she hurried to the 'link on Roarke's library desk.

She engaged, then froze.

"Surprise, surprise." Morse beamed at her. "Bet you weren't expecting me. All dressed up for your party, I see. You look flash."

"I've been looking for you, C. J."

"Oh yeah, I know. You've been looking for a lot of things. I know this is on record, and it doesn't matter. But you listen close. You keep this between you and me, or I'm going to start slicing off little tiny pieces of a friend of yours. Say hi to Dallas, Nadine."

He reached out, and Nadine's face came on screen. Eve, who'd seen terror too many times to count, looked at it now. "Has he hurt you, Nadine?"

"I—" She whimpered when he jerked her head back by the hair, touched a long slim blade to her throat.

"Now, you tell her I've been real nice to you. Tell her." He skimmed the flat of the blade over her throat. "Bitch."

"I'm fine. I'm okay." She closed her eyes and a tear squeezed through. "I'm sorry."

"She's sorry," Morse said between pursed lips and pressed his cheek to Nadine's so both of their faces were in view. "She's sorry she was so hungry to be top bitch that she slipped the guard you put on her and fell right into my waiting arms. Isn't that right, Nadine?"

"Yes."

"And I'm going to kill you, but not quick like the others. I'm going to kill you slowly, and with a lot of pain, unless your pal the lieutenant does everything I say. Isn't that right? You tell her, Nadine."

"He's going to kill me." She pressed her lips together hard, but nothing would stop the trembling. "He's going to kill me, Dallas."

"That's right. You don't want her to die, do you, Dallas? It's your fault Louise died, yours and Nadine's fault. She didn't deserve it. She knew her place. She wasn't trying to be top cunt. It's your fault she's dead. You don't want that to happen again."

He still had the knife at Nadine's throat, and Eve could see his hand shake. "What do you want, Morse?" Calling up Mira's profile, she carefully hit the right buttons. "You're in control. You call the shots."

"That's right." His smile exploded. "Damn right. You've got my position coming up on screen by now. You see I'm at a nice quiet spot in Greenpeace Park, where nobody's going to bother us. All those nice green-lovers planted these pretty trees. It's a wonderful spot. Of course, nobody comes here after dark. Unless they're smart enough to know how to bypass the electronic field that discourages loiterers and chemi-heads. You've got exactly six minutes to get here so we can conduct our negotiations."

"Six minutes. I can barely make that at full speed. If I run into traffic—"

"Then don't," he snapped. "Six minutes from end of transmission, Dallas. Ten seconds over, ten seconds you might use to call this in, to contact anyone, to so much as blink for backup, and I start ripping Nadine. You come alone. If I smell an extra cop, I start on her. You want her to come alone, right, Nadine." As incentive, he turned the point of the blade to prick a narrow slice at the side of her throat.

"Please." She tried to arch back as the blood trickled. "Please."

"Cut her again, and I won't deal."

"You'll deal," Morse said. "Six minutes. Starting now."

The screen went blank. Eve's finger poised over the controls, thought of Dispatch, of the dozens of units that could be around the park in minutes. She thought of leaks, electronic leaks.

And she thought of the blood dribbling down Nadine's throat.

She bolted across the room and hit the elevator panel on the run. She needed her weapon.

C. J. Morse was having the time of his life. He'd begun to see that he'd sold himself short by killing quickly. There was so much more kick in courting fear, seducing it, watching it swell and climax.

He saw it in Nadine Furst's eyes. They were glassy now, the pupils huge, slick and black, with barely a rim of color at the edges. He was, he realized with great relish, literally scaring her to death.

He hadn't cut her again. Oh, he wanted to, and made sure he showed her the knife often so that she would never lose the fear that he could. But a part of him worried about the cunt cop.

Not that he couldn't handle her, Morse mused. He could handle her the only way women understood. By killing her. But he wouldn't make it fast, like the others. She'd tried to outsmart him, and that was an insult he wouldn't tolerate.

Women always tried to run the show, always got in the way, just when you were about to grab that fat brass ring. It had happened to him all of his life. All of his fucking life starting with his pushy bitch of a mother.

You haven't done your best, C. J. Use your brains, for God's sake. You'll never get through life on looks or charm. You haven't got any. I expected more from you. If you can't be the best, you'll be nothing.

He'd taken it, hadn't he? Smiling to himself, he began to stroke Nadine's hair while she shuddered. He'd taken it for years, playing the good, devoted son, while at night he'd dreamed of ways to kill her. Wonderful dreams, sweaty and sweet, where he'd finally silenced that grating, demanding voice.

"So I did," he said conversationally, touching the tip of the knife to the pulse jerking in Nadine's throat. "And it was so easy. She was all alone in that big, important house, busy with her big, important business. And I walked right in. 'C. J.,' she said, 'what are you doing here? Don't tell me you've lost your job again. You'll never succeed in life unless you focus.' And I just smiled at her and I said, 'Shut up, Mother, shut the fuck up.' And I cut her throat."

To demonstrate, he trailed the blade over Nadine's throat, lightly, just enough to scrape the skin. "She gushed and she goggled, and she shut the fuck up. But you know, Nadine, I learned something from the old bitch. It was time I focused. I needed a goal. And I decided that goal would be to rid the world of loudmouthed, pushy women, the ball breakers of the world. Like Towers and Metcalf. Like you, Nadine." He leaned over, kissed her dead center of the forehead. "Just like you."

She was reduced to whimpers. Her mind had frozen. She'd stopped trying to twist her wrists out of the restraints, stopped trying anything. She sat docile as a doll, with the occasional quiver breaking her stillness.

"You kept trying to shove me aside. You even went to management to try to get me off the news desk. You told them I was a . . ." He tapped the blade against her throat for emphasis. "Pain in the ass. You know that bitch Towers wouldn't even give me an interview. She embarrassed me, Nadine. Wouldn't even acknowledge me at press conferences. But I fixed her. A good reporter digs, right Nadine? And I dug, and I got a nice juicy story about her darling daughter's idiot lover. Oh, I sat on it, and sat on it, while the happy mother of the bride to be made all her wedding plans. I could have blackmailed her, but that wasn't the goal, was it? She was so ticked when I called her that night, when I dumped it all in her face."

His eyes narrowed. They gleamed. "She was going to talk to me then, Nadine. Oh, you bet she was going to talk. She'd have tried to ruin me, even though I was only going to report the facts. But Towers was a big fucking deal, and she would have tried to squash me like a bug. That's exactly what she said over the 'link. But she did exactly what she was told. And when I walked toward her on that nasty little street, she sneered at me. The bitch sneered at me and she said, 'You're late. Now, you little bastard, we're going to set things straight.'"

He laughed so hard he had to press a hand to his stomach. "Oh, I set her straight. Gush and goggle, just like my dear old mother."

He gave Nadine a quick slap on the top of the head, rose, and faced the camera he had set up. "This is C. J. Morse reporting. As the clock ticks away the seconds, it appears that the heroic Lieutenant Cunt will not arrive in time to save her fellow bitch from execution. Though it has long been considered a sexist cliché, this experiment has proven that women are always late."

He laughed uproariously and gave Nadine a careless backhanded slap that knocked her back on the bench where he'd put her. After one last, high-pitched giggle, he controlled himself and frowned soberly into the lens.

"The public broadcasting of executions was banned in this country in 2012, five years before the Supreme Court once again ruled that capital punishment was unconstitutional. Of course, the court was forced into that decision by five idiot, bigmouthed women, so this reporter deems that ruling null and void."

He took a small pocket beam out of his jacket before turning to Nadine. "I'm going to key into the station now, Nadine. On air in twenty." Thoughtfully, he tilted his head. "You know, you could use a little makeup. It's a pity there isn't time. I'm sure you'd want to look your best for your final broadcast."

He walked to her, laid the length of the knife at her throat, and faced the camera. "In ten, nine, eight . . ." He glanced over at the sound of rushing feet on the crushed stone path. "Well, well, here she is now. And with seconds to spare."

Eve skidded to a halt on the path and stared. She'd seen a great deal in her decade on the force. Plenty that she often wished could be erased from her memory. But she'd never seen anything to compare with this.

She'd followed the light, the single light that beamed a circle around the tableau. The park bench where Nadine sat passively, blood drying on her skin, a knife at her throat. C. J. Morse behind her, dressed nattily in a round-collared shirt and color-coordinated jacket, facing a camera on a slim tripod. Its red light beamed as steadily as judgment's eye.

"What the hell are you doing, Morse?"

"Live stand-up," he said cheerfully. "Please, step into the light, Lieutenant, so our viewers can see you."

Keeping her eyes on his, Eve stepped into the circle.

She'd been gone too long, Roarke thought and found himself irritated by the party chat. Obviously, she'd been more upset than he'd realized, and he regretted not dealing with Angelini more effectively.

Damn if he'd let her brood or take on blame. The only way to make sure she didn't was to amuse or annoy the mood out of her. He slipped quietly from the room, away from the lights and music and voices. The house was too big to search, but he could pinpoint her location with one question.

"Eve," he said, the moment Summerset stepped from a room to the right.

"She's gone."

"What do you mean gone? Gone where?"

Because discussing the woman always put Summerset's back up, he lifted his shoulders. "I couldn't say, she simply ran out of the house, got into her vehicle, and drove off. She did not deign to inform me of her plans."

The nasty twisting in Roarke's gut sharpened his voice. "Don't fuck with me, Summerset. Why did she leave?"

Insulted, Summerset tightened his jaw. "Perhaps it was due to the call she received a few moments ago. She took it in the library."

Turning on his heel, Roarke strode to the library door, uncoded it. With Summerset at his heels, he stepped up to the table. "Replay, last call."

As he watched, listened, the twisting in his gut turned to a burning that was fear. "Christ Jesus, she's gone for him. She's gone alone."

He was out of the door and moving fast, the order shot over his shoulder like a laser. "Relay that information to Chief Tibble—privately."

*   *   *

"**Though our time is short, Lieutenant, I'm sure our viewers would** be fascinated by the investigative process." Morse kept the pleasant, camera smile on his face, the knife at Nadine's throat. "You did pursue a false lead for a time, and were, I believe, on the point of charging an innocent man."

"Why did you kill them, Morse?"

"Oh, I've documented that extensively, for future broadcast. Let's talk about you."

"You must have felt terrible when you realized you'd killed Louise Kirski instead of Nadine."

"I felt very bad about that, sickened. Louise was a nice, quiet woman with an appropriate attitude. But it wasn't my fault. It was yours and Nadine's for trying to bait me."

"You wanted exposure." She flicked a glance toward the camera. "You're certainly getting it now. But this is putting you in a spot, Morse. You won't get out of this park now."

"Oh, I have a plan, don't worry about me. And we have just a few minutes left before we have to end this. The public has a right to know. I want them to see this execution. But I wanted you to see it in person. To witness what you caused."

She looked at Nadine. No help there, she noted. The woman was in deep shock, possibly drugged. "I won't be as easy to take."

"You'll be more fun."

"How did you take Nadine?" Eve stepped closer, keeping her eyes on his and her hands in sight. "You had to be clever."

"I'm very clever. People—women in particular—don't give me enough credit. I just leaked a tip to her about the murders. A message from a frightened witness who wanted to speak to her, alone. I knew she'd ditch her guard, an ambitious woman after the big story. I got her in the parking garage. Just as simple as that. Gave her a dose of a deep tranq, loaded her in her own trunk, and drove off. Left her and the car in a little rent space zone way downtown."

"You were smart." She stepped closer, stopping when he lifted his brows and pressed the knife more firmly. "Really smart," she said, lifting her hands up. "You knew I was coming for you. How did you know?"

"You think your wrinkled pal Feeney knows everything about computers? Hell, I can run rings around that hacker. I've been keyed in to your system for weeks. Every transmission, every plan, every step you took. I was always ahead of you, Dallas."

"Yeah, you were ahead of me. You don't want to kill her, Morse. You want me. I'm the one who ragged on you, gave you all the grief. Why don't you let her go? She's zoned, anyway. Take me on."

He flashed his quick, boyish smile. "Why don't I kill her first, then you?"

Eve lifted a shoulder. "I thought you liked a challenge. Guess I was wrong. Towers was a challenge. You had to do a lot of fast talking to get her where you wanted her. But Metcalf was nothing."

"Are you serious? She thought I was puss." He bared his teeth, hissed through them. "She'd still be doing weather if she hadn't had tits, and they were giving her my airtime. My fucking airtime! I had to pretend I was a big fan, tell her I was going to do a twenty-minute feature on her. Just her. Told her we had a shot at international satellite, and she bit good."

"So she met you that night on the patio."

"Yeah, she got herself all slicked up, was all smiles and no hard feelings. Tried to tell me she was glad I'd found my niche. My goddamn niche. Well, I shut her up."

"You did. I guess you were pretty smart with her, too. But Nadine, she's not saying anything. She can't even think right now. She won't know you're paying her back."

"I'll know. Time's up. You might want to stand to the side, Dallas, or you're going to get blood all over your party dress."

"Wait." She took a step and, feinting to the side and reaching a hand to the small of her back, she whipped out her weapon. "Blink, you bastard, and I'll fry you."

He did blink, several times. It seemed to him the weapon had come from nowhere. "You use that, my hand's going to jerk. She'll be dead before I am."

"Maybe," Eve said steadily. "Maybe not. You're dead, either way. Drop the knife, Morse, step away from her, or your nervous system's going to go on fast overload."

"Bitch. You think you're going to beat me." He jerked Nadine to her feet, shielding himself from a clean shot, then shoved her forward.

Eve caught Nadine with one arm while she aimed with her weapon hand, but he was already into the trees. Seeing no choice, Eve slapped Nadine hard, front handed, then back. "Snap out of it. Goddamn it."

"He's killing me." Nadine's eyes rolled back, then forward when Eve hit her again.

"Get moving, do you hear me? You get moving, call this in. Now."

"Call it in."

"That way." Eve gave Nadine a shove toward the path, hoped she'd stay on her feet, and dashed toward the trees.

He'd said he had a plan, and she didn't doubt it. Even if he managed to get out of the park, they'd bring him in, eventually. But he was primed to kill now—some woman walking her dog on the sidewalk, or someone coming home from a late date.

He'd use the knife on anyone now because he'd failed again.

She stopped in the shadows, ears straining for sound, breath rigidly controlled. Dimly, she could hear the sounds of street and air traffic, could see the lights of the city beyond the thick border of trees.

A dozen paths spread out before her that would wind through the glade and the gardens so lovingly planted, so carefully designed.

She heard something. Perhaps a footstep, perhaps a bush rustled by some small animal. With her weapon blinking ready, she stepped deeper into the shadows.

There was a fountain, its waters silent in the dark. A small children's playground, with glide swings, twisty slides, the foamy jungle gym that prevented little climbers from bruising shins and elbows.

She scanned the area, cursing herself for not grabbing a search beam out of her car. There was too much dark pouring dangerously out of the trees. Too much silence hanging on the air like a shroud.

Then she heard the scream.

He's circled back, she thought. The bastard has circled back and gone for Nadine after all. Eve spun around, and her instinct to protect saved her life.

The knife caught her on the collarbone, a long, shallow cut that stung ridiculously. She blocked with her elbow, connected with his jaw, spoiled his aim. But the blade flew out, slicing her just above the wrist. Her weapon spun uselessly out of her wounded hand.

"You thought I was going to run." His eyes glowed sickly in the dark as he circled her. "Women always underestimate me, Dallas. I'm going to cut you to pieces. I'm going to rip your throat." He jabbed, sending her back a step. "I'm going to rip your guts." He swung again, and she felt the wind from the blade. "I'm in charge now, aren't I?"

"Like hell." Her kick was well aimed, a woman's ultimate defense. He went down, air bursting through his lips like a popped balloon. The knife clattered on stone. And she was on him.

He fought like what he was—a madman. His fingers tore at her, his teeth snapped as they sought flesh to sink into. Her wounded arm was slick with blood, and slipped off him as she struggled to find the point under his jaw that would immobilize him.

They rolled over the crushed stone and trimmed sod, viciously silent but for grunts and labored breathing. His hand dug along the path for the hilt of the knife, hers clawing after it. Then stars exploded in her head as he pumped his fist into her face.

She was dazed for only an instant, but she knew she was dead. She saw the knife, and her fate, and sucked in her breath to meet it.

Later she would think it had sounded like a wolf, that howl of rage, a blood cry. Morse's weight was off of her, his body spinning away. She rolled to her hands and knees, shaking her head.

The knife, she thought frantically, the goddamn knife. But she couldn't find it, and crawled toward the dull gleam of her weapon.

It was in her hand, poised, when her mind cleared enough to understand. Two men were fighting, grappling like dogs in the pretty playground. And one of them was Roarke.

"Get away from him." She scrambled to her feet, teetered, braced. "Get away from him so I can get a shot."

They rolled again, end over end. Roarke's hand gripped Morse's, but Morse's held the knife. Through the rage, the duty, the instinct, came a titanic, jittering fear.

Weak, still losing blood, she leaned back on the padded bars of the gym, steadied her weapon hand with the other. In the dappled moonlight she could see Roarke's fist plunge, hear the crack of bone on bone. The knife strained, the blade angling.

Then she watched it plunge, watched it quiver as it found its home in Morse's throat.

Someone was praying. When Roarke got to his feet, she realized it was herself. She stared at him, let her weapon lower. His face was fierce, his eyes hot enough to burn. There was blood soaking his elegant dinner jacket.

"You're a goddamn mess," she managed.

"You should look at yourself." His breathing was labored, and he knew from experience that he would feel every miserable bruise and scrape later. "Don't you know it's rude to leave a party without making your excuses?"

Legs trembling with reaction, she took a step toward him, then stopped, swallowing the sob that was bubbled in her throat. "Sorry. I'm sorry. God, are you hurt?"

She launched herself at him, all but burrowing when he caught her close. "Did he cut you? Are you cut?" She yanked back, began to fumble at his clothes.

"Eve." He jerked her chin up, steadied it. "You're bleeding badly."

"He caught me a couple times." She swiped a hand under her nose. "It's not bad." But Roarke was already using a square of Irish linen from his pocket to staunch and wrap the arm wound. "And it's my job." She took a deep breath, felt the black edges around her vision creeping back until she could see clearly. "Where are you cut?"

"It's his blood," Roarke said calmly. "Not mine."

"His blood." She nearly wobbled again, forced her knees to lock. "You're not hurt?"

"Nothing major." Concerned, he angled her head back to examine the shallow slice along her collarbone, the rapidly swelling eye. "You need a medic, Lieutenant."

"In a minute. Let me ask you something."

"Ask away." Having nothing else, he tore part of his ripped sleeve to dab at the blood on her shoulder.

"Do I come charging into one of your board rooms when you're having trouble with a business deal?"

His eyes flicked to hers. Some of the fierceness died out of them into what was almost a smile. "No, Eve, you don't. I don't know what got into me."

"It's okay." Since there was nowhere else to put it, she jabbed her weapon onto her lower back where she'd fixed it with adhesive. "This once," she murmured and caught his face in her hands, "it's okay. It's okay. I was scared when I couldn't get past you for a shot. I thought he would kill you before I could stop him."

"Then you should understand the feeling." Giving her a supporting arm around the waist, they began to limp off. After a moment, Eve realized she was limping primarily because she'd lost a shoe. Hardly breaking stride, she stepped out of the other. Then she spotted lights up ahead.

"Cops?"

"I imagine. I ran into Nadine as she was stumbling along the path toward the main gate. He'd given her a pretty rough time, but she'd pulled it together enough to tell me which direction you'd gone off in."

"I could probably have dealt with the bastard on my own," Eve murmured, recovered enough to worry about it. "But you sure handled yourself, Roarke. You got a real knack for hand to hand."

Neither of them mentioned how the knife had come to be planted in Morse's throat.

She saw Feeney in the circle of light, near the camera, with a dozen other cops. He merely shook his head and signaled for the medteam. Nadine was already on a stretcher, pale as wax.

"Dallas." She lifted a hand, let it fall. "I blew it."

Eve leaned over as one of the medics dispensed with Roarke's first aid on her arm and began his own. "He pumped you full of chemicals."

"I blew it," Nadine repeated, as the stretcher lifted toward a medunit. "Thanks for the rest of my life."

"Yeah." She turned away, sat heavily on the cushioned support in the triage area. "You got something for my eye?" she asked. "It's throbbing bad."

"Going to be black," she was told cheerfully as an ice gel was laid over it.

"There's good news. No hospitals," she said, firm. The medic just clucked his tongue and began work on cleaning and closing her wounds.

"Sorry about the dress." She smiled up at Roarke and fingered a tattered sleeve. "It didn't hold up very well." Getting to her feet, she brushed the fussing medic aside. "I'm going to need to go back and change, then go in to file my report." She looked steadily into his eyes. "It's too bad Morse rolled on his knife. The PA's office would have loved to bring him to trial." She held out a hand, then examined the raw knuckles of Roarke's and shook her head. "Did you howl?"

"I beg your pardon?"

She chuckled, leaned on him as they headed out of the park. "All in all, it was a hell of a party."

"Hmm. We'll have others. But there's one thing."

"Hmm?" She flexed her fingers, relieved that they seemed to be back in full working order. The MTs knew their stuff.

"I want you to marry me."

"Uh-huh. Well, we'll—" She stopped, nearly stumbled, then gaped at him with her good eye. "You want what?"

"I want you to marry me."

He had a bruise on his jaw, blood on his coat, and a gleam in his eye. She wondered if he'd lost his mind. "We're standing here, beat to shit, walking away from a crime scene where either or both of us could have bought it, and you're asking me to marry you?"

He tucked his arm around her waist again, nudged her forward. "Perfect timing."